SANTA FE BONES

VOLUME TWO OF THE NEW MEXICO TRILOGY

GLORIA H. GIROUX

SANTA FE BONES
VOLUME TWO OF THE NEW MEXICO TRILOGY

iUniverse books may be ordered through booksellers or by contacting:

iUniverse
1663 Liberty Drive
Bloomington, IN 47403
www.iuniverse.com
844-349-9409

ISBN: 978-1-6632-1277-1 (sc)
ISBN: 978-1-6632-1278-8 (hc)
ISBN: 978-1-6632-1276-4 (e)

Library of Congress Control Number: 2020922120

Print information available on the last page.

iUniverse rev. date: 12/09/2020

By the author

Fireheart, Volume One of the Chay Trilogy
Whitefire, Volume Two of the Chay Trilogy
Firesoul, Volume Three of the Chay Trilogy
Bloodfire, Prequel to the Chay Trilogy

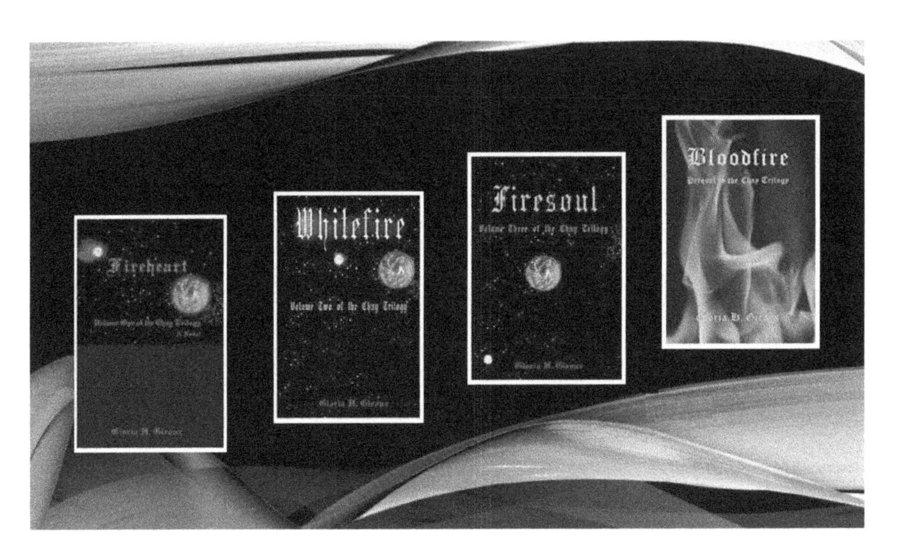

Copper Snake, Volume One of the San Francisco Trilogy
Voices of Angels, Volume Two of the San Francisco Trilogy
Out of the Ash, Volume Three of the San Francisco Trilogy
Bloodline in Chiaroscuro, Prequel to the San Francisco Trilogy

Saguaro, Volume One of the Arizona Trilogy
Crucifixion Thorn, Volume Two of the Arizona Trilogy
Devil Cholla, Volume Three of the Arizona Trilogy
Ironwood, Sequel to the Arizona Trilogy

Santa Fe Blood, Volume One of the New Mexico Trilogy

Santa Fe Bones, Volume Two of the New Mexico Trilogy

MAP OF THE UNITED STATES

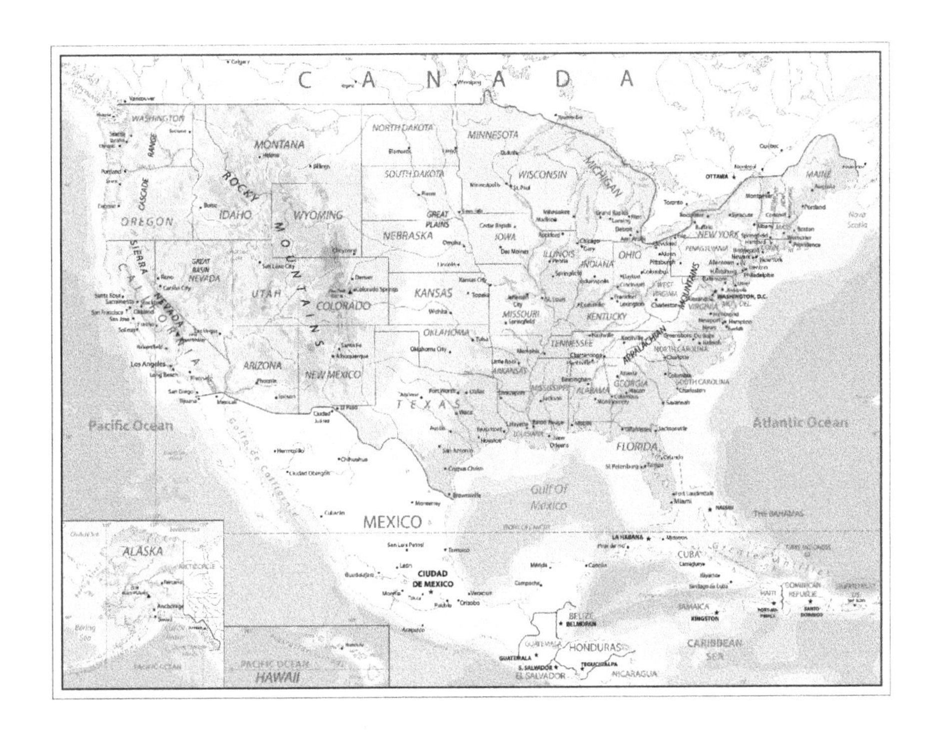

MAP OF EUROPE

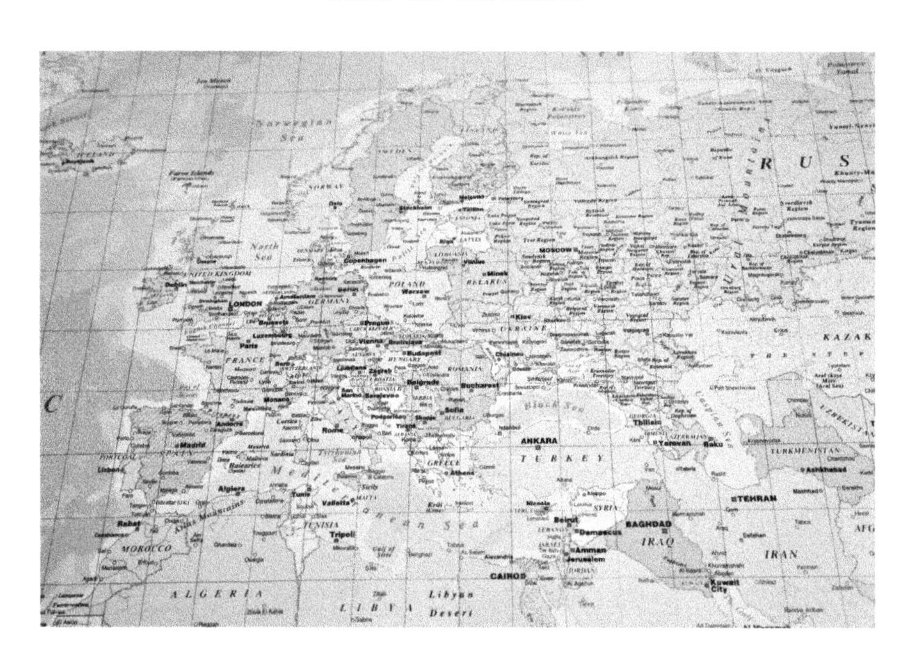

MAP OF NEW MEXICO

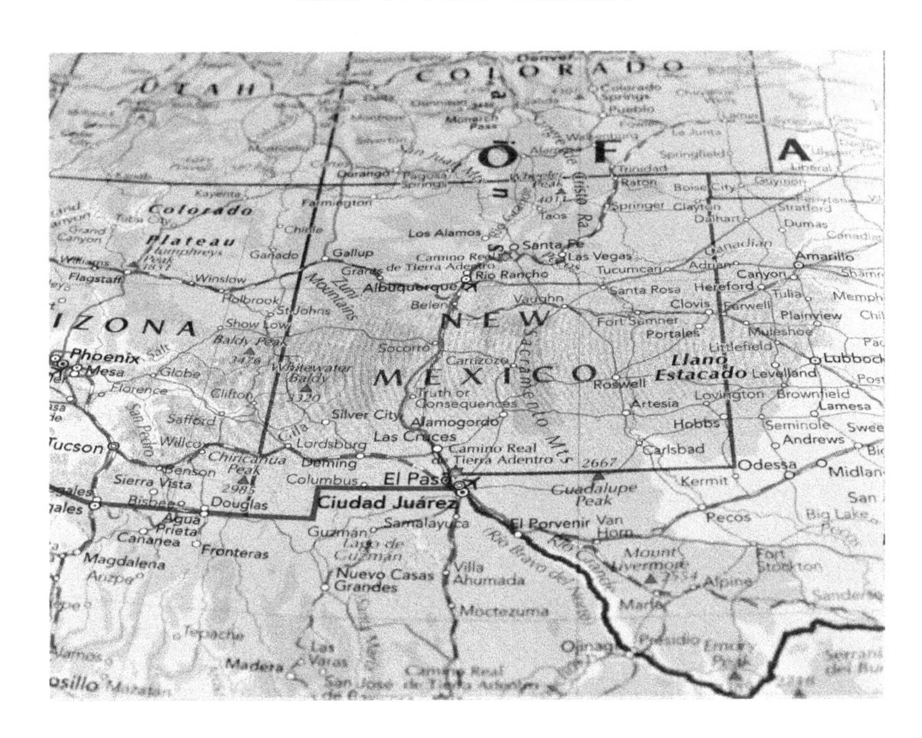

MAP OF SANTA FE

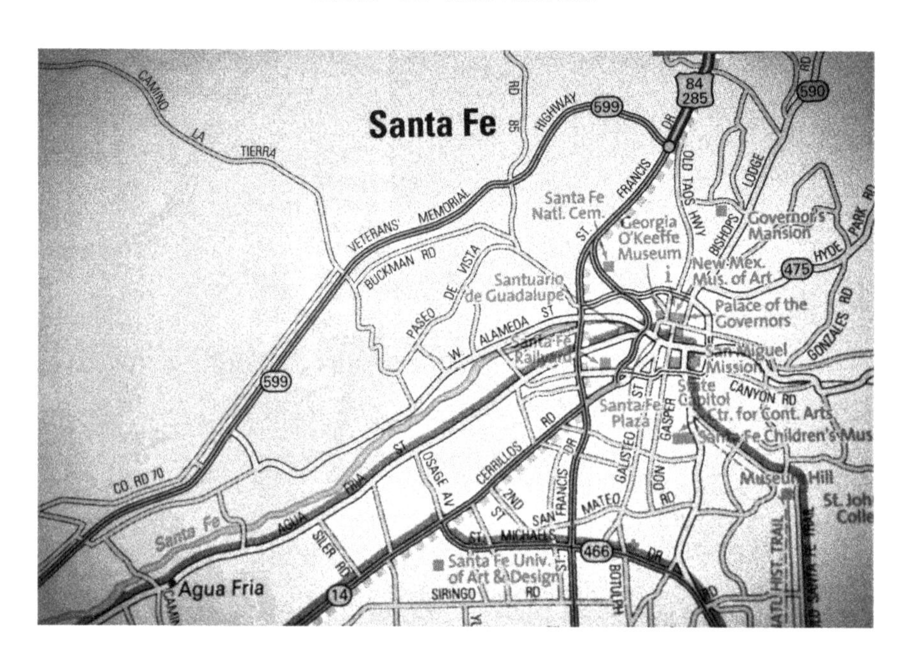

All photographs including cover shot
courtesy of author Gloria H. Giroux
Maps and Special Images by Shutterstock

206.

That is the number of bones in an adult human body. Babies are born with around 300 bones, many of which knit together in the process called ossification from cartilage to a single bone as the infant grows. For example, a baby's skull originates as five soft, cartilaginous plates that eventually fuse into a single hard bone. Babies do not have knee bones, which are formed as the infant grows. The ossification process ceases after the body has stopped growing, generally around the age of twenty.

The human skeleton has specific sections of bones:

- Skull—28 bones, including the jawbone
- Spine—26 bones, including cervical, thoracic and lumbar vertebrae, sacrum and tailbone (coccyx)
- Chest—26 bones, including ribs and breastbone (sternum)
- Arms—64 bones, including shoulder blade (scapula), collar bone (clavicle), humerus, radius and ulna, wrist bones (carpals), metacarpals and phalanges
- Pelvis—2 bones (three regions, the ilium, ischium, and pubis form 2 coxal bones)
- Legs—60 bones, including thigh bone (femur), kneecap (patella), shin bone (tibia) and fibula, tarsals, metatarsals and phalanges.

Within the 206 matured bones there are four different types in the human body:

- Long bone—has a long, thin shape. Examples include the bones of the arms and legs (excluding the wrists, ankles and kneecaps). With the help of muscles, long bones work as levers to permit movement.

- Short bone—has a squat, cubed shape. Examples include the bones that make up the wrists and the ankles.
- Flat bone—has a flattened, broad surface. Examples include ribs, shoulder blades, breastbone and skull bones.
- Irregular bone—has a shape that does not conform to the above three types. Examples include the bones of the spine (vertebrae).

The noun "bone" came into existence in the eleventh century AD. The etymology of the word comes from Middle English through a quite circuitous route according to Merriam-Webster: the Middle English *bon,* going back to Old English *bān,* going back to Germanic *baina-* (whence also Old Frisian and Old Saxon *bēn* "bone," Old High German *bein* "bone, leg," Old Norse *bein* "bone" and probably *beinn* "straight"), perhaps going back to Indo-European *bhoi̯H-n-o-,* a derivative of a verbal base *bhei̯H-* "strike, hew," whence, with varying suffixation, Old Irish *benaid* "(s/he) hews, cuts," *robíth* "(it) has been struck," Middle Breton *benaff* "(I) cut," Latin *perfinēs* (glossed by the Roman grammarian Festus as *perfringās* "you should break") and probably Old Church Slavic *biję, biti* "to hit."

Whew!

Bones have played an integral part of true history as well as cultural mythology. Earliest man had no concept of the components of their bodies, perhaps only believing that some kind of hard "thing" rested beneath their flesh and could cause terrible pain when damaged. Only by trial and error could he have realized that bones could be repaired or not, and that like the flesh grew in volume, weight, and length as a young human grew into an adult. He realized, of course, that animals also had these hard things, certainly clear when one was gnawing on roasted flesh.

Gradually as man progressed into intellectual and emotional thought, he used bones to express a variety of instances, from triumph over a dangerous animal or human foe, to superstitious charms or magical amulets that protected man or were honors to the gods. Gradually as oral and written mythology emerged from the depths of early ignorance, bones were incorporated into tales and beliefs, and often served as the basis for religions.

In Greek mythology the poet Hesiod articulated the Trick at Mekone. Zeus and the gods descended to a meeting with mortals at Mekone, which is believed to be situated in the northern Peloponnesus between Corinth and Achaea on the territory of the present-day regional unit of Corinthia. The god Prometheus slew a large ox, deboning it and placing the disguised meat in one pile and the bones in another. Zeus was asked to choose a pile, and because of the subterfuge that made the bone pile look like the more desired meat pile Zeus chose the pile of bones. Angered at the trick Zeus hid fire from the mortals. Prometheus then stole the hidden fire and gave it to humanity, thus incurring Zeus's wrath and a dire punishment. It could not have been enjoyable to be chained to a rock and have your regenerating liver ripped out each day by a merciless eagle.

The story explains mythologically the practice of sacrificing only the bones to the gods, while humans keep the edible meat and fat. It is also widely considered the first sacrifice to the gods and set the precedent for humans establishing or renewing a covenant with sacrifice.

Catholicism also employs the concept of bones as a special tribute to God and his minions. In religion a bone is considered a relic, a piece of a saint or another venerated person preserved as a tangible memorial. Relic derives from the Latin reliquiae, meaning "remains," and a form of the Latin verb relinquere, to "leave behind, or abandon." A reliquary is a shrine that houses one or more religious relics. In some cases, the relics or bones are thought to contain magical properties. In the Bible, 2 Kings, 13:20-21, this is explicitly stated:

Elisha died and was buried. Now Moabite raiders used to enter the country every spring. Once while some Israelites were burying a man, suddenly they saw a band of raiders; so, they threw the man's body into Elisha's tomb. When the body touched Elisha's bones, the man came to life and stood up on his feet.

In Hinduism, relics are less common than in other religions since the physical remains of most saints are cremated. The veneration of corporeal relics may have originated with the Sramana movement or the appearance of Buddhism, and burial practices became more common after the Muslim invasions. One prominent example is the preserved body of Swami Ramanuja in a separate shrine inside Sri Rangam Temple.

In Buddhism, relics of the Buddha and various sages are venerated. After the Buddha's death, his remains were divided into eight portions. Afterward, these relics were enshrined in stupas wherever Buddhism was spread.

While various relics are preserved by different Muslim communities, the most important are those known as the Sacred Trusts, more than six hundred pieces treasured in the Privy Chamber of the Topkapi Palace Museum in Istanbul, Turkey. One of these is the forearm and hand of Yahya, otherwise known as John the Baptist.

On the other end of the spectrum bones are often used as revenge or dire warnings. The Ottoman empire was known to use the skulls of defeated rebel fighters to build towers of skulls as a declaration of victory as well as a tangible eliciting of terror from its enemies. For example, the Skull Tower is a stone structure embedded with human skulls located in Niš, Serbia. During the first Serbian uprising against the Ottoman empire in May 1809 the Ottomans surrounded the rebels at Čegar Hill. Stevan Sinđelić, the revolutionary leader, knew that defeat would result in his troops being impaled, so he detonated a powder magazine killing himself, his soldiers, and the approaching Ottomans. The governor of the Rumelia Eyalet, Hurshid Pasha, ordered that a tower be made from the skulls of the fallen rebels. The tower is fifteen feet high, and originally contained 952 skulls embedded on four sides in fourteen rows. Over the centuries most of the skulls were removed by family members or ghouls seeking a craven trophy of history. Currently, the tower houses fifty-eight skulls and has been designated a Cultural Monument of Exceptional Importance.

The concepts and words "bone" and "skeleton" appear throughout history in writings, poetry, quotes, and verbalization. They appear as matter-of-facts, vitriol, honors, prayers, curses, and every method of expression that can be imagined.

"As Cuvier could correctly describe a whole animal by the contemplation of a single bone, so the observer who has thoroughly understood one link in a series of incidents should be able to accurately state all the other ones, both before and after."
Arthur Conan Doyle

"A family spirit is not always synonymous with family life. Bone of our bone and flesh of our flesh makes for brothers, sisters and relatives, who may be as distant as strangers in a foreign land."
Mother Angelica

"Oh literature, oh the glorious Art, how it preys upon the marrow in our bones. It scoops the stuffing out of us, and chucks us aside. Alas!"
D. H. Lawrence

"Whoever had designed the skeletons of creatures had even less imagination than whoever had done the outsides. At least the outside-designer had tried a few novelties in the spots, wool and stripes department, but the bone-builder had generally just put a skull on a ribcage, shoved a pelvis in further along, stuck on some arms and legs and had the rest of the day off. Some ribcages were longer, some legs were shorter, some hands became wings, but they all seemed to be based on one design, one size stretched or shrunk to fit all."
Terry Pratchett

"Once we get to know where and why the skeletons of the past are buried, we can start wading across our muddled memories into the open plains of a new horizon."
Erik Pevernagie

"There is something about a closet that
makes a skeleton terribly restless."
Wilson Mizner

"A belief in hell and the knowledge that every ambition is doomed to frustration at the hands of a skeleton have never prevented the majority of human beings from behaving as though death were no more than an unfounded rumor."
Aldous Huxley

"These old bones will tell your story
These old bones will never lie
These old bones will tell you surely
What you can't see with your eye
These old bones I shake and rattle
These old bones I toss and roll
And it's all in where they scatter
Tells you what the future holds"
Dolly Parton

Bones rest in our bodies.
Bones rest under the earth.
Bones rest in coffins housed in mausoleums.
Bones rest in museums.
Bones rest in their ash form in urns.
Bones rest in many places and many things.

Sometimes, however, bones don't rest at all …

Sometimes, bones rumble and whisper and cry out for vengeance …

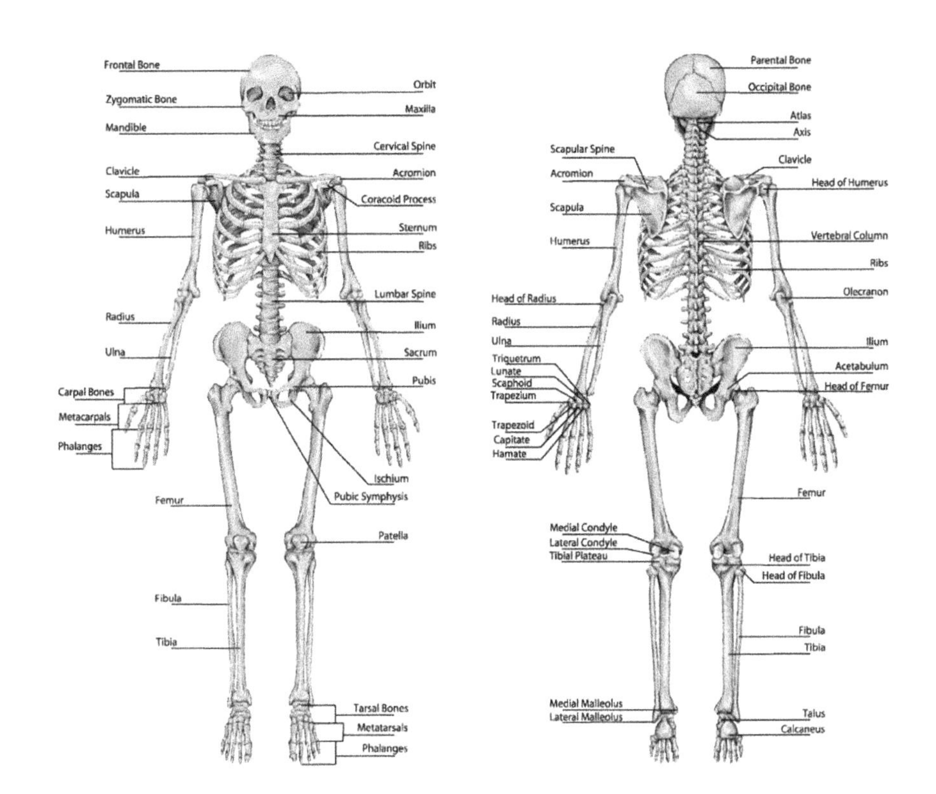

Frontal Bone
Orbit
Zygomatic Bone
Maxilla
Mandible
Cervical Spine
Clavicle
Acromion
Scapula
Coracoid Process
Humerus
Sternum
Ribs
Lumbar Spine
Radius
Ilium
Ulna
Sacrum
Carpal Bones
Pubis
Metacarpals
Phalanges
Ischium
Femur
Pubic Symphysis
Patella
Fibula
Tibia
Tarsal Bones
Metatarsals
Phalanges
Parental Bone
Occipital Bone
Atlas
Axis
Scapular Spine
Clavicle
Acromion
Head of Humerus
Scapula
Vertebral Column
Humerus
Ribs
Olecranon
Head of Radius
Radius
Ulna
Ilium
Triquetrum
Lunate
Acetabulum
Scaphoid
Head of Femur
Trapezium
Trapezoid
Capitate
Hamate
Femur
Medial Condyle
Lateral Condyle
Tibial Plateau
Head of Tibia
Head of Fibula
Fibula
Tibia
Medial Malleolus
Talus
Lateral Malleolus
Calcaneus

Cast of Returning Characters

Memphis Grayhawk:	P.I. and lawyer in Santa Fe, New Mexico; firstborn son of Hehewuti and Jakub; Swan's husband; founder of the Warrior Spirit Investigations firm
Tucson Grayhawk:	Doctor of Psychology in Santa Fe, New Mexico; second son of Hehewuti and Jakub; ex-Navy
Luc Grayhawk:	College student in Santa Fe, New Mexico; fourth son of Hehewuti and Jakub
Raleigh Grayhawk:	High School student in Santa Fe, New Mexico; youngest child and only daughter of Hehewuti and Jakub

Sage Mariah Grayhawk:	Daughter of Memphis and Swan Grayhawk
Hehewuti Maasikiisa:	Native American, Hopi medicine woman; Jakub's wife
Jakub Kosmicki:	Polish-born naturalized American; musician; Hehewuti's husband
Tansee Qöyawayma McBean:	Medical intern at Sangre de Cristo hospital; first cousin to the Grayhawk siblings; Percival's wife
Candelaria Grayhawk:	Troy Grayhawk's wife; daughter of Carmen Castillo
Sand Hazelwood:	P.I. in Santa Fe, New Mexico; Snow's and Swan's brother; Akiro's significant other
Swan Hazelwood:	P.I. in Santa Fe, New Mexico; Sand's sister; Snow's twin; Memphis's wife
Snow Hazelwood:	Social activist, various locations; Sand's sister; Swan's twin
Nick Griffin:	P.I. in Santa Fe, New Mexico; Percival's brother; Yuki's husband
Percival McBean:	Doctor of Psychology in Santa Fe, New Mexico; Nick's brother; Tansee's husband
Carmen Castillo:	Professor of History at Sangre de Cristo College, Santa Fe, New Mexico
London Monroe:	Professor of Anthropology specializing in Indian Studies, Sangre de Cristo College, Santa Fe, New Mexico
Pryce Gallagher:	Professor of Psychology at Sangre de Cristo College, Santa Fe, New Mexico

Caleb Winsted:	Owner and publisher of the *Sangre de Cristo Courant* newspaper in Santa Fe, New Mexico
Cassidy Carr:	Former reporter on the *Sangre de Cristo Courant* newspaper, Santa Fe, New Mexico
Akiro Okuma:	Lawyer; native of Santa Fe, New Mexico; Yuki's brother; Sand's significant other
Yuki Okuma Griffin:	Chemistry professor at Sangre de Cristo College, Santa Fe, New Mexico; Akiro's sister; Nick's wife
Bart Smith (Frick):	Police detective, Homicide Division, Santa Fe, New Mexico
Jesse Morgan (Frack):	Police detective, Homicide Division, Santa Fe, New Mexico
Carlito Cruz:	Forensics technician, Santa Fe, New Mexico police department
Skye Summers:	Executive assistant, Warrior Spirit Investigations, Santa Fe, New Mexico

Cast of New Characters

Sara Marlowe Grayhawk:	Daughter of Memphis and Swan Grayhawk; Shea's twin
Shea Marissa Grayhawk:	Daughter of Memphis and Swan Grayhawk; Sara's twin
Elspeth Kaiah McBean:	Daughter of Percival and Tansee McBean
Francesca Troy Grayhawk:	Daughter of Troy and Candelaria Grayhawk
Mariko Adelind Griffin:	Daughter of Nicholas and Yuki Griffin
Elijah Ryder Jackson:	Son of domestic terrorist Ryder Jackson
Braeden Charleston:	Brianna's twin brother
Brianna Savannah:	Braeden's twin sister
Cameo Adams:	Client of Warrior Spirit Investigations
Hashkeh Naabah:	Indian artist in Taos, New Mexico; signs name as HashNaa
Captain Reed Carraway:	Police captain, Santa Fe, New Mexico
Dennis Dunbar:	Police detective, Homicide Division, Santa Fe, New Mexico
Rockmond Abbott:	Police detective, Homicide Division, Santa Fe, New Mexico
Devon Killian:	P.I. in Warrior Spirit Investigations, Santa Fe, New Mexico

Dante Redwolf:	P.I. in Warrior Spirit Investigations, Santa Fe, New Mexico
DeVere York:	Police officer in Pittsfield, Massachusetts; ReVere's brother
ReVere York:	Police detective in Portsmouth, New Hampshire; DeVere's brother
Damien Savage:	ADA, Boston, Massachusetts
Connor Donnelly:	Mechanic from Bennington, Vermont
Declan O'Malley:	English nanny; owner of a microbrewery in Santa Fe, New Mexico
Eddie Troy:	Photographer from Gloucester, Massachusetts
Shiloh Frost:	FBI agent in Albuquerque, New Mexico
Chelan Chee:	Indian activist, Santa Fe, New Mexico
Chelan's brothers:	Ata'halne', Gaagii, Shilah, and Jack
Aponi Quará Nez:	Indian teacher on the Navajo Nation at Gallup, New Mexico
Lancelot LaPointe:	Carnival performer

Cast of Additional Characters[1]

Adam Manzone:	Private investigator, San Francisco, California
Norah Maguire:	Magazine publisher and writer, San Francisco, California
Richard Ballard:	FBI agent, Albuquerque, New Mexico

[1] Please see the novels *Voices of Angels* and *Out of the Ash* for background on Adam Manzone and Norah Maguire. Please see the novel *Saguaro, Volume One of the Arizona Trilogy* for background on Richard Ballard.

PROLOGUE

1780s, Paris, France

Paris, the heart and soul of France, is also known as "the City of Lights." Although some people believe that the city's name is derived from the Paris of Greek mythology, in reality it is derived from the earliest inhabitants, the Celtic Parisii tribe. Its nickname derives from two separate historical events; one, its leading role in the Age of Enlightenment; and two, more literally because Paris was one of the first large European cities to use gas street lighting on a grand scale on its boulevards and monuments. Gas lights were installed on the Place du Carousel, Rue de Rivoli and Place Vendome in 1829. By 1857, the Grand boulevards were lit. By the 1860s, the boulevards and streets of Paris were illuminated by 56,000 gas lamps.

Paris is a vibrant city, full of residents, full of tourists, and full of life. It is one of the most-visited places in the world for awestruck tourists of every country, for honeymooners, for artists, for musicians, for business, for everything. Besides being the heart of France, it can arguably be said that Paris is the heart of Europe, starting back during its origins in the middle of the third century BC. Occupied by its original tribes, the Romans took over as they were wont to do around 52 BC, and the town became prosperous with business, trade routes, forums, theatres, and temples.

Clovis the Frank, the first king of the Merovingian dynasty, made the city his capital from 508 AD. By the twelfth century AD the city had become the capital of France with all that implies. Invasions, battles, peace, and ethnicities varied over the next centuries, bringing with them a huge influx of people from emigration as well as birth. By 1328 Paris had 200,000 residents and was the largest city in Europe. The city expanded and continued growing, and that inevitably brought with it the need not only for living places but for burial places. Limestone quarries provided the material for many Parisian structures before they were played out. When they were played out, they provided a purpose which no one would have thought possible.

Paris's earliest burial grounds were founded on its Left Bank until the Roman Empire disintegrated in the fifth century AD. With Paris left in ruins after the subsequent Frankish invasions, Parisians moved to the marshier Right Bank. As in all other countries during the time before and during the Middle Ages personal hygiene was miniscule at best. People rarely bathed, and cleanliness was a rarity even in the upper classes. Illnesses abounded, and medicine was in its infancy, and useless procedures such as bloodletting through leeches and covering open wounds with rancid poultices were common. Plague, tuberculosis, famine, warfare, personal violence, sweating sicknesses, and infections produced a very limited life expectancy. Males born into landowning families in England had a life expectancy of a mere thirty-one years. Children born into a peasant culture quite often did not survive childhood; infant mortality was rampant, as was women dying in childbirth. Since Europe had become a mainly Christian civilization, burying the dead was the norm; Jews and Muslims also buried their dead.

Urban expansion saw the evolution of burying the dead in rural cemeteries, and Paris began interring its dead in the confines of the city. By the end of the eighteenth century, Parisian burial grounds were chock full of the remains of the dead over the course of centuries. Matters required change, and the city's rulers decreed that parish cemeteries within the cities would be condemned and three new suburban cemeteries would be established.

The worst of the urban cemeteries was the Holy Innocents' Cemetery, the largest in Paris and the resting place of not only individuals but of mass graves. The need to eliminate this cemetery gained urgency from May 31, 1780, when a basement wall in a property adjoining the cemetery collapsed under the weight of the mass grave behind it. The cemetery was closed to the public and all intra muros (Latin: "within the [city] walls") burials were forbidden after 1780. The problem of what to do with the remains crowding intra muros cemeteries was still unresolved. A few years later its decomposed inhabitants were removed and re-interred in what would become a fascinating location of history and legend.

A vast expanse of Paris's Left Bank rested on Lutetian limestone deposits, which provided the quarry material used to build much of the city; some of the limestone was mined from suburban areas. Post-twelfth-century haphazard mining techniques dug wells down to the deposit and extracted the rock horizontally along the vein until it was depleted. Many of these (often illicit) mines were undocumented, and when depleted they were often abandoned and forgotten. Paris had annexed its suburbs many times over the centuries, and by the eighteenth century many of its arrondissements (administrative districts) were or included previously mined territories.

The state of the Left Bank was generally undermined, and known to architects as early as the early seventeenth-century construction of the Val-de-Grâce hospital. A series of mine cave-ins beginning in 1774 with the collapse of a house along the "rue d'Enfer" (near today's crossing of the Avenue Denfert-Rochereau and the boulevard Saint-Michel) prompted King Louis XVI to establish a commission to investigate the state of the Parisian underground. This resulted in the creation of the inspection Générale des Carrières (Inspection of Mines) service.

Mine consolidations continued to occur. The underground around the site of the 1777 collapse that had initiated the project had already become a series of stone and masonry inspection passageways that reinforced the streets above. Mine renovations and the closure of cemeteries were issues within the jurisdiction of the Police Prefect Police Lieutenant-General Alexandre Lenoir, who had been directly involved in the creation of a mine inspection service. Lenoir endorsed the idea of relocating the dead of Paris to the subterranean passageways that were renovated during 1782. In 1785 after the decision to further renovate the "Tombe-Issoire" passageways for their future role as an underground sepulchre, the law was passed formalizing the relocation to what was now known as "the Catacombs of Paris."

A well was dug within a walled property above one of the principal subterranean passageways to receive Holy Innocents' unearthed remains. The property itself was transformed into a sort of museum for all the headstones, sculptures and other artifacts recuperated from the former cemetery. The route between Holy Innocents and the "clos de la Tombe-Issoire" became a nightly procession of black cloth-covered wagons carrying the millions of Parisian dead. It would take twelve years to empty most Paris's cemeteries and move the bones to their new resting place, known as an ossuary. An ossuary is a chest, box, building, well, or site that serves as the final resting place of human skeletal remains. They are frequently used where burial space is scarce. A body is first buried in a temporary grave, then after some years the skeletal remains are removed and placed in an ossuary.

Cemeteries whose remains were moved to the catacombs include Saints-Innocents (the largest by far with about two million buried over six hundred years of operation), Saint-Étienne-des-Grès (one of the oldest), Madeleine Cemetery, Errancis Cemetery (used for the victims of the French Revolution), and Notre-Dame-des-Blancs-Manteaux. Not truly a religious burial site—unlike the catacombs of Rome—the Paris catacombs were simply a place to deposit the unexpectedly inevitable remains of humanity as a convenience to those still awaiting their fate.

In their first years the catacombs were a disorganized bone repository. Carts simply dumped bones into haphazard piles and went back for more. However, Louis-Étienne Héricart de Thury, the director of the Paris Mine Inspection Service, authorized renovations to transform the caverns into a mausoleum that one could visit. In addition to directing the stacking of skulls and femurs into the patterns seen in the catacombs today, he used the cemetery decorations he could find (formerly stored on the Tombe-Issoire property, many had disappeared after the 1789 Revolution) to complement the walls of bones. Perhaps the most iconic display is known as "the Barrel." It consists of a large, circular pillar surrounded by skulls and tibiae which also acts as a support for the roof of the area in which it's housed, which is referred to as the Crypt of the Passion or the Tibia Rotunda. The Barrel is a little more morbid than a traditional support beam, but it holds firm.

A room was also created and dedicated to the display of the various minerals found under Paris, and another showing various skeletal deformities found during the catacombs' creation and renovation. De Thury also added monumental tablets and archways bearing ominous warning inscriptions and added stone tablets bearing descriptions or other comments about the nature of the ossuary. He ensured the safety of eventual visitors by walling it off from the rest of the Paris's Left Bank's already-extensive tunnel network. The underground tunnels—also nicknamed "the Empire of Death" and encompassing over two hundred miles—eventually held the bones of over six million people, the oldest reaching back to the Merovingian Era of the sixth century AD.

New internments began during the French Revolution, include Jean-Paul Marat, one of the revolution's most virulent voices, and Maximilien de Robespierre, influential in both the revolution and the subsequent Reign of Terror. The moving of bones ceased in 1860.

After the establishment of the catacombs in their eventual form, the underground ossuary was used in many non-burial events.

- Bodies of the dead from the riots in the Place de Grève, the Hôtel de Brienne, and Rue Meslée were put in the catacombs on August 28-29, 1788.
- The tomb of the Val-de-Grâce hospital doorkeeper, Philibert Aspairt, lost in the catacombs during 1793 and found eleven years later, is located in the catacombs on the spot where his body was found.
- During 1871, Communards killed a group of monarchists there.
- During World War II, Parisian members of the French Resistance used the tunnel system.
- The Nazis established an underground bunker below Lycée Montaigne, a high school in the 6th arrondissement.
- During 1954, the film *Father Brown* had pivotal scenes set within the Catacombs of Paris.

- During 1974, the film *The Holes* was set within the Catacombs of Paris.
- During 2004, police discovered a fully equipped movie theater in one of the caverns. It was equipped with a giant cinema screen, seats for the audience, projection equipment, film reels of recent thrillers and film noir classics, a fully stocked bar, and a complete restaurant with tables and chairs. The group *les UX* took responsibility for the installation.
- The film *As Above, So Below*, released in 2014, was the first production that secured permission from the French government to film in the catacombs. They aimed to use no alterations to the environment except for a piano and a car which were hauled into the catacombs and set on fire.
- During 2015, Airbnb paid €350,000 as part of a publicity stunt offering customers the chance to stay overnight in the catacombs.
- In August 2017, thieves broke into a cellar from the catacombs and stole more than €250,000 of wine.
- As historically relevant and unique as the Catacombs of Paris are, they are not the only such burial ossuaries in ancient and modern times. As mentioned, Rome also has catacombs although not as voluminous in size or residency. They are sacred burial grounds constructed by the Catholics (although the ancient Etruscans originally began the excavation process). Visitors to these catacombs are expected to dress and act with the reverence due any of God's late acolytes.

There are fourteen catacombs under the Eternal City, dug into the tofu, or soft volcanic rock beneath the surface just outside of the city.

- Catacombs of Marcellinus and Peter
- Catacombs of Domitilla
- Catacombs of Commodilla
- Catacombs of Generosa
- Catacombs of Praetextatus

- Catacombs of Priscilla
- Catacombs of San Callisto
- Catacombs of San Lorenzo
- Catacombs of San Pancrazio
- Catacombs of San Sebastiano
- Catacombs of San Valentino
- Catacombs of Saint Agnes
- Catacombs of via Anapo
- Jewish catacombs

The Catacombs of Rome are divided into five chapels called the "Capuchin Crypts." Each Crypt is decorated with remains that correspond to the Crypt's title designation. The five Crypts are:

- Crypt of the Resurrection
- Crypt of the Skulls
- Crypt of the Pelvises
- Crypt of the Leg Bones and Thigh Bones
- Crypt of the Three Skeletons

For example, the Crypt of the Pelvises is adorned with mostly pelvises and the Crypt of the Skulls is adorned entirely out of skulls. Although all crypts feature a full skeleton or more, the main display of the Crypts are supposed to match whatever title is specified.

The Catacombs of Rome also include the Domitilla Catacombs, which are an elaborate maze of underground tunnels stretching for miles just fifteen minutes outside of Rome. Like the Paris Catacombs, the Domitilla Catacombs were constructed because there was also a shortage in burial space in Rome. Although, the Domitilla Catacombs only hold about 150,000 remains and bodies.

Galleries and passages abound in the underground tunnels, which are also replete with art and icons. The Crypt of St. Agnes contains a small church. The maintenance of the Catacombs of Rome are under the auspices of the papacy, particularly with the Pontifical Commission of Sacred Archaeology.

Rome and Paris may house the largest and most famous of these bone sanctuaries, but there are many cultures across the globe that enjoy a similar notoriety for their own underground ossuaries.

In Lima, Peru, there exists the Monastery of San Francisco Catacombs. Over 25,000 people are buried there in crypts whose bone contents have been used to create intricate designs on the walls and ceilings.

The subterranean Odessa Catacombs in the Ukraine form an immense maze of tunnels almost two hundred feet below sea level. To date the extent of the catacombs is unknown, and although there are the bones of many deceased the maze was mainly used for mining and smuggling.

The Brno Ossuary in the Czech Republic holds the honor of being the second largest ossuary after the Catacombs of Paris. It holds over 50,000 sets of human bones. Once laid neatly and reverently with human skeletons the remnants of bones were disturbed and often buried due to flooding and mud. This catacomb, too, contains art including an obelisk made entirely out of human skulls.

On a much smaller scale there are ossuaries around the world that for one reason or another house human artifacts that mark unusual customs or beliefs.

The Marville Ossuary in France houses the remains of 40,000 skeletons, stacked in a churchyard shed.

The Wamba Ossuary in Spain is home to bones packed floor to ceiling. The cache of bones developed there from the 12th to the 18th centuries. Over 3,000 skulls peek out from the jumble of other bones. Words of warning and philosophy dot the walls, including, "As you see, I saw myself as you see me, you see all ends here. Think about it and you will not sin …"

In Kudowa-Zdrój, Poland the walls and ceiling of Kaplica Czaszek (the Chapel of Skulls) are decorated with thousands of skulls, and another 21,000 skeletons housed down below.

In Cologne, Germany the Church of Saint Ursula is filled with the bones of hundreds of virgin martyrs.

The crypt under the Saint Peter and Paul's church in Melník, the Czech Republic, was intended to be a holy burial ground for Bohemia's royal ladies; however, in the 1520s a plague epidemic swept through the area and necessitated a huge demand for burial ground. The corpses which had been occupying the cemeteries surrounding the church were promptly dug up, and some 15,000 corpses were cleaned and dumped into the vault.

In Austria the Eggenburg Charnel has meticulously arranged bones of 5,800 friars.

In Cambodia the Phnom Penn Memorial Stupa has 5,000 skulls arranged in memorial to those murdered by the Khmer Rouge under the monstrous dictator Pol Pot.

Even the United States has the distinction of having an ossuary. In Wellfleet Harbor on the bay side of Cape Cod lies the Indian Neck Ossuary, a burial site dating back to 1100 AD. The site was discovered in 1979 when a backhoe digging a trench for a home improvement project unearthed human bones. A salvage operation by the National Park Service uncovered a site packed together tightly in an oval approximately one-point-five-meters by three meters. The bones represented around fifty-six individuals, both male and female, young and old.

Other smaller ossuaries dot the country, but in far less volume or content than those found in Europe.

As fascinating as these sites are, and although some definitive facts and intelligent assumptions can be made as to their origin and contents, there are always questions about these remarkable underground bone burial sites.

Who were the people whose bones rest there?

What were their hopes and dreams?

How did they die?

Would their beliefs and faiths have supported the final resting place of their bones?

Were their souls disturbed as their resting places were?

Is this resting place one of peace, or … are the dead just angrier there?

The Catacombs of Paris

BOOK ONE

"New Mexico was supposedly a place with magical healing properties, a place where a hundred years ago tuberculosis patients traveled in droves, like gold prospectors in covered wagons, thinking the dry mountain air would cure them."
Willa Strayhorn, The Way We Bared Our Souls

CHAPTER ONE

August 8, 1974, Santa Fe, New Mexico

"Have you considered barbed wire and gun turrets?" Sand asked Memphis as they stood inside the door to the first-floor family daycare center. "Tanks, maybe?"

"Those wouldn't stand a chance against these inmates," Memphis replied, sighing. "Finally, after all these years, I'm beginning to realize just how wonderful Luc and Raleigh really were during their formative years."

"Don't tell them that."

The two men watched and couldn't help smiling at the five kinetic little girls that were making a racket and providing a true challenge to the nannies that were hired to care for them during the working day.

Memphis's and Swan's three-year-old twins, Sara and Shea, were clearly the leaders of the pack, the alpha females. Behind them was beta kid Francesca (Chessie), Troy's four-year-old daughter, then Elspeth McBean, Percy's and Tansee's nearly three-year-old daughter. Mariko, Nick's and Yuki's eighteen-month-old child brought up the rear as the youngest. Every one of them was a loud, smart scrapper vying for dominance in their little clique of femininity. No one bemoaned the fact that the new generation included no baby boys, and Luc was smugly self-satisfied that he held the title of last male born.

Like their eight-year-old sister, Sage, the twins had inherited their mother's blonde hair and blue eyes. They were as light as their blonde mother and had no hint of paternal ethnicity in their features. Mariko, half-Japanese, favored her mother in coloring and epicanthic eye shape. Troy's daughter, Chessie, looked like her mother and had clearly Hispanic coloring and features.

Elspeth, Tansee's and Percy's daughter, was a happy surprise to her parents. After two more miscarriages following their wedding, Tansee and Percy were certain that they couldn't conceive and bring a live child to birth. They were wrong. As the pregnancy progressed past the point of where Tansee had miscarried the previous three times, it became wonderfully obvious that this pregnancy might survive the full gestation period. Whether the baby was a dwarf or not was the question that the parents-to-be agonized over. At least, Percy agonized—Tansee was happy to have any child as she patiently explained to her husband over and over.

On November 8, 1971, Tansee went into labor two weeks early during her medical internship at Sangre de Cristo Hospital. Seventeen hours later, with Percy by her side, she gave birth to their daughter, whom the doctor pronounced as "completely normal and damned beautiful." Percy didn't think he could love any human being more than Tansee until he held his seven-pound-two-ounce baby daughter in his arms. They named her after their respective mothers.

With weddings taking place and babies being born right and left, and mindful of the events that preceded their births, the extended clan's parents took extra precautions for their care and safety. Since all the parents worked and none were particularly thrilled about staying home as a mom or a dad, they came to a reasonable consensus to provide a mutual location and environment to allow them access to the children.

When Elspeth was born three weeks after Sara and Shea made their entrance into the world, Memphis had the rear section of the first floor of his office building converted to a nursery/daycare center. Swan brutally interviewed women for a nanny position, finally settling on a woman from Connecticut who had a Bachelor's degree in nursing and a Master's degree in childhood development. Within two months Whitney Oakwood began taking care of three infants in the same building where their parents worked. Year-old Chessie Grayhawk was quickly added to the mix, with Mariko joining the all-female baby crew not too long thereafter. Swan hired a second part-time English nanny, Ansonia Fairfield, to help with the baby crew. There was a rumor that she had once been part of Britain's MI5 security organization, but she neither confirmed nor denied that rumor.

No children could be more protected than the offspring of the extended Grayhawk clan. The building itself was a safe haven for all who worked or played there. Over the past six years Memphis and his family had made distinct and subtle changes to their physical surroundings as well as their professional lives. The three-story building that Memphis had "inherited" from serial killer Joanna Frid housed a complex of private investigators, psychologists, and lawyers, each floor assigned a particular discipline.

Besides housing the daycare center of three rooms and a full kitchen, the first floor held the offices of psychologists Tucson Grayhawk and Percy McBean along with their assistant Candy Grayhawk and the office of Dr. Tansee McBean. Although she was still doing her residency at the hospital Tansee planned on moving forward into genetic practice and research.

Akiro ran the second-floor suite of offices dedicated to his expanding legal practice. Besides being in-house counsel for Warrior Spirit Investigations he had a burgeoning private practice that he addressed with two associates and a secretary that made Carmen Miranda look prim and proper.

The third floor was the bailiwick of the investigators and their support personnel. Skye Summers still reigned with an iron fist over administrative matters. Somewhere around the middle of 1970 she decided to accommodate her professional position and mostly abandoned her hippie garb and was now rarely seen in the office without a pastel polyester pantsuit. She favored peach and pink. Skye was wearing pink when her bosses trudged up the stairs from their visit to the "kid factory" (as she called it). She waved a piece of paper in front of Memphis and scowled.

"You need to have this notarized by tomorrow, big guy," Skye said as she handed the document to Memphis. "Tax stuff waits for no man."

Memphis scanned the data and nodded before he led Sand into the Hazelwood Conference Room where nearly the full complement of the crew was waiting. Tansee was missing since she was making her rounds at the hospital. The noise of talking and laughing and chewing and the rustling of fast-food wrappers was deafening. Memphis loved it. He took a minute to study his friends and colleagues as Sand meandered over to the window table where two Mr. Coffee drip machines had full carafes of premium French roast. The new coffeemakers with their vivid yellow and white gingham decal had only been around for two years, but they were gaining in popularity since they made coffee fast and without the bitterness or burn of a percolator. Everyone had his or her own personal Mr. Coffee in their office.

Akiro patted the seat next to him and once Sand had his mug of caffeine, he parked himself next to his boyfriend and whispered something into Akiro's ear. Memphis thought that of all of them perhaps Akiro had matured in more ways than most. Once a tentative, unsure young lawyer who feared the revelation of his sexuality and lacked full confidence in his abilities, at thirty-two he had blossomed into a crack legal expert. He rarely litigated, but when he did, he never lost. He selected associates with the same life viewpoint as he had, and who were as diverse as he in a world that didn't yet value diversity.

Rodrigo Cortez came to Santa Fe from Miami, to which he and his family had fled from Cuba and the oppressive Castro regime. His father, a physician, got a job as a janitor and his mother worked in a laundry. They managed to put their son through college, and he worked his way through law school, graduating in the middle of his class in 1972. He worked his way west, sending out job applications until one appeared on Akiro's desk. On an impulse he called in the young lawyer and an hour later hired him. He never regretted it.

Jenna Collins was a fifty-year-old ex-Vietnam nurse who left the war after a crippling injury in 1969. She put herself through law school, but in the youth culture of the day no one wanted to hire a physically disabled "old woman." Akiro did. She was smart and on top of things and would have taken a bullet for her younger boss. She also knew how to bake an exemplary peach cobbler. The fact that she was confined to a wheelchair didn't hamper her spirit or efforts.

Akiro and Sand still maintained separate residences since their sexuality was still illegal in New Mexico, but they were more out in the open and the winds of change indicated that someday soon their relationship would be as legal as any heterosexual one was. In 1972 Judge Lewis R. Sutin of the New Mexico Supreme Court dissented in the case of the *State v, Trejo*, stating that the current law was, "unconstitutional and void because it is vague, overbroad, uncertain, and is an unreasonable exercise of the police power of the state." Groups were taking up the banner to repeal the oppressive anti-sodomy law.

Sand had moved out of his sister's house and into a condo he bought in a new development just outside of the city's northern limits. His "studio apartment" section of the house became Memphis's and Swan's new master bedroom, and Sage moved into their room. Sand acquired his private investigator license in 1970, the same year that Memphis and Swan did. Nick followed suit in 1971 and Percy in 1972.

Nick in 1974 was far from the quintessential angry young man that he had been in 1965. His exoneration of his birth family's murders and the part he played in finding the real killer changed him. He was calmer and surer of himself and faced the future with hope instead of despair. The love and support of his hitherto unknown brother, Percy, and the Grayhawk family and friends poured the foundation for a future filled with purpose and promise. He grew to love his job as an investigator and finished college four years later than normal with a degree in history, specializing in true crime. In the firm he specialized in missing persons but worked alongside everyone at one time or another, spreading his talents and interests. He kept his hair long but not hippie-long, and wore neat, stylish clothes that could be found in any 1970s fashion magazine. He was a devoted fan of bell-bottomed jeans.

He had sustained a long-term romance with Yuki Okuma, and they married in a traditional Buddhist ceremony in 1971. She had given up her teaching job at Pueblo High School and worked as a researcher in Chemistry at Sangre de Cristo College as well as teaching two courses per semester. Her parents had long since accepted Nick as a member of the family; that relationship was solidified with the birth of their first grandchild. They were lobbying for a second. Yuki made it clear that wasn't going to happen in the foreseeable future. She was a modern woman with a family and a career.

Nick and Percy became very close as the years passed. After all the dust had settled down from the final flight of the "vampire killer" they spent quality time getting to know one another. It wasn't long before they were as close as any brothers who were raised together could be. They met as men, their youth devoid of each other, but they couldn't change that. They shared common interests and quirks but were also very different men due to their upbringings and Percy's unique physical configuration.

He was born in 1935 in Rhode Island as an achondroplasiac dwarf. His horrified parents surrendered him to an orphanage right after birth and he spent the first five years of his life there before he was adopted by a loving couple. Despite those parents he suffered through his childhood, youth, and adult years from other people's stupidity and ignorance. He tracked down his birth family only to find them murdered with the oldest son missing. Nick Griffin was that son. He'd changed his name and drifted aimlessly to the west where he wound up in Santa Fe as a suspect in a young hippie girl's murder. Percy found him and helped clear him, and they developed a cautious then close relationship. They settled down into brotherhood and found women they wanted to share their lives with and a circle of friends who accepted them, warts and all, as part of an extended family.

Percy couldn't do anything about his height—four-foot-four—but for the last few years went about clean-shaven, his moustache and goatee abandoned when his daughter cringed at the rough bristle. A devotee of education and intellect, he'd acquired a second PhD, this one in Psychology, and opened a practice in conjunction with Tucson Grayhawk. They both worked on occasional private investigation tasks, but their main drive was the exploration of the mind. That's not to say that they eschewed more physical pursuits; both were crack shots with a handgun, and Tucson was a black belt in karate.

Swan Hazelwood could kick her brother-in-law's ass in karate and pretty much any other hand-to-hand combat discipline. The ex-cop, married to the firm's founder, Memphis, was, as inimitable Detective Bart Smith—AKA, Frick—would say, one tough cookie. One of the first women officers in the Santa Fe police department she had her eye on a detective's shield, but her career was sandbagged when she kicked two detectives in the balls after they insulted her fired brother, Sand. Sand was gay and forced to quit the force despite being one of their best detectives. They both wound up in Memphis's firm due to unexpected circumstances. They both made their mark with their first case and went on to be as essential to building the firm as Memphis was.

Both Sand and Swan had a love-hate relationship with the Santa Fe police force because of their past employment and the parts they played in identifying a serial killer that had been murdering young women in the area. They had at least two reasonably solid supporters in detectives Frick (née, Bart Smith) and Frack (née, Jesse Morgan), a pair of cops that had been working together long enough to finish one another's sentences. Frack had nearly died of a gunshot wound seven years earlier when Joanna Frid had returned to Santa Fe for an act of revenge; he had survived, and she had vanished once more only to be a permanent resident on the FBI's Most Wanted list.

Unfortunately, both Frick and Frack were at retirement age and would be leaving the police force in the next couple of months.

That meant that the Warrior Spirit investigators wouldn't have an in with the police that they had. Sand and Swan still had a few former colleagues that might be helpful, but their own personal comedy team would be lost to them. Sand especially had tried to cultivate a few law enforcement resources over the years. They had a couple of FBI contacts down in Albuquerque although they sorely missed their old friend, Tom Ballard, who had relocated to Philly after the Frid case.

So many changes, Memphis thought as he filled his mug. At thirty-four he was no longer that callow, somewhat naïve young man who had once aspired to be a lawyer along the lines of Clarence Darrow. His law studies had been interrupted by unexpected zigzags in his life, including his surprise fatherhood with Snow Hazelwood of his now eight-year-old daughter, Sage. Snow had dumped him and left town, but he found true love with her twin sister, Swan, who was now Sage's legal mother. His education was temporarily derailed but in 1969 he finished his courses and passed the bar. He didn't practice law but understanding its ins and outs gave him a leg up on his daily work. On occasion Akiro would run things by him for an opinion. Memphis liked being a P.I., a surprising niche that appeared under strange circumstances but came to define his life.

He eyed the newbie P.I. that Swan had hired two months earlier. The young woman was a New England transplant with one of those horrible east-coast accents that grated on his nerves. Still, she was smart and driven. In 1972 after J. Edgar Hoover died and F. Patrick Gray took over as Acting Director of the FBI the agency was then opened to women applicants. She applied and was rejected, although two other women were accepted. Joanne Pierce, a former nun and Susan Roley, a Marine, made history as they were admitted to the former boys-only federal club.

Devon Killian didn't make the cut but was determined to make some sort of law enforcement her career. A plucky half-black, half-Irish woman with café-au-lait skin, freckles, green eyes, and kinky red-brown hair in a large afro, she grew up in the rough north end of Hartford, Connecticut. She put herself through Trinity College and graduated near the top of her class. She graduated with a degree in Philosophy in 1970. She was rejected twice in her application to become a Hartford police officer, but on the third try she succeeded and shone in her academy class. Her tenure as a patrol officer lasted six months. She got past the sexism and racism, but not past the gang member bullet that blasted her left shoulder. She had no choice but to leave the force or be confined to a desk job. Her boyfriend, another cop, said to her, fuck it, let's book. He quit his job, they piled their essential items into a couple of battered old suitcases from Goodwill, and they headed west in his rusted Camaro. The car gave out in Albuquerque.

They began rooting around for jobs and he found one with the New Mexico State Police. He found himself stationed up near Taos, so she moved with him but set up house in Santa Fe. After a couple of disastrous attempts at being employed in retail she ran into a guy who knew a guy who knew a P.I. named Nick Griffin. They met for coffee and he introduced her to Memphis. While he did a background check on her he hired her part-time as a research assistant. The background check was clean, and she proved enthusiastic in her minor tasks and showed that she was clever and insightful. Memphis hired her as a probationary associate for a month; a month later she became a full-time employee. She dumped her boyfriend (who had been screwing around with an Indian woman in Taos) and decided to start a new life. So far, so good, although sometimes her rapier-like wit bordered on the sarcastic. She got along well with Swan.

As Memphis sat down at the head of the table Nick asked, "So, does having a meeting today mean we don't have to suffer through one next Monday?" Memphis had instituted a weekly Monday-morning meeting two years earlier much to the grumbling of his associates, who preferred a more free-form method of administration. They didn't like the formal structure, but he was insistent and since he owned fifty-one percent of the firm his word was law. At the office—at home Swan's word was law.

"Nice try, Renegade," Memphis replied, using an old nickname from Nick's hippie days. When they were initially antagonistic Nick would insult him by calling him Geronimo; Memphis was half Polish and half Indian.

"Why don't we take a vote?" Sand asked.

Memphis rolled his eyes and sighed theatrically as he ran his fingers through his shoulder-length black hair. "Okay, fine. Monday's meeting is canceled." A roar of approval and clapping burst forth. "Nice. I'm only trying to keep us on track."

"Lighten up," Nick said. "We'll be celebrating all weekend and most of us will be too hung over to concentrate."

"Which reminds me," Sand said. "Are we all meeting at six-thirty over at the Sweet Revenge Saloon?"

"Yeah, definitely," Swan replied. "I wouldn't miss this for the world."

"Charlie Brewster is setting up a couple of TVs and tables out in the parking lot for the spillover crowd," Nick said. "I slipped him a twenty to save us a table inside near the bar. I want to be up close and personal when I stare at that ugly face."

"No spitting," Swan warned.

"Cheering?" Nick asked, an eyebrow arched.

"Cheering is not only permitted but encouraged," Sand said.

"All right, let's put this evening's festivities off to the side while we give brief—let me repeat that—*brief* updates on our active cases," Memphis said. "Nick—you're up. The Baxter case?"

"Done," Nick replied.

"That's it?" Memphis said.

"You said brief."

Before Memphis could ask for a more detailed explanation Swan broke in. "All of the cases are either done, in progress, or not started. Nobody cares, Memphis. This is an historic day, and no one cares."

Memphis allowed himself a pregnant pause before replying. "So, what you're saying is that no one cares."

"That's what I'm saying."

"Fine," Memphis snapped. "Let's give the nannies a breather. Everyone has the rest of the day off so grab your kids, go home, go to your offices, go anywhere, and we'll see you tonight." Memphis had barely finished the last word before Percy slid off his chair and went through the door followed closely by his brother. The remaining crew ambled out leaving only Memphis and Swan.

Swan hugged her husband and brushed a lock of hair out of his eyes. "Talked to Tucson today?"

"Nope, not since Wednesday."

"Is he having one of his blue periods?"

"I think so. Best just to let him work his way out of it. I think tonight may have exacerbated his emotions."

"Maybe it'll help him put some things to rest."

"Maybe. Come on—let's grab the girls and head over to the park. I feel like some outdoor time with my ladies." They linked hands and headed downstairs where two grateful nannies turned each little girl over to her parent. Candy was holding Chessie who was babbling about kittens as her mother carried her out of the office.

"It's nice owning the firm, isn't it?" Swan said to Memphis.

"Yup."

The firm's associates met up at the Sweet Revenge Saloon at six-thirty. The parking lot was crowded with cars and celebrating people that spilled out from the back door of the bar. A large group was assembled outside the front door, hoping to get inside where the proximity to the booze and comfort was at a premium. It was still light out, but it was hot and there was a sultry humidity about the evening; the air seemed to hang heavy and most people had a light sheen of sweat on their expectant faces.

Memphis couldn't hear himself think as his wife dragged him through the indoor crowd to their reserved table in front of the large TV at the end of the bar. Swan dragged a few extra chairs close by as Sand and Akiro made their appearance, trailed by Nick, Percy, Tansee, and Yuki. The elder Grayhawks were home with all the kids as the younger generation waited for the moment they had all been waiting for. Just before seven Luc and Raleigh shoved their way over to their family and Memphis gave up his seat to his sister. Actually, she pulled him out of his seat and parked her shapely butt as she took a long slug of his beer. He scowled at her; she was only sixteen, not old enough to drink. He was under no illusions that she abstained. He took the beer out of her hand.

Memphis was surprised when Frick and Frack wended their way through the crowd, muttering and flashing their badges to get through the sea of human beings.

"I can't believe you two came," Swan yelled over the crowd even though the two detectives were only three feet away.

"Hey," Frick said, frowning, "just because we're dinosaurs compared to you kids doesn't mean we can't enjoy a well-deserved comeuppance." He yelled towards the bar. "Two beers, pronto." He saw the look on Swan's face and added, "Please."

"Besides," Frack said as he stood behind Sand, "we've only got a few months left to enjoy bullying our cop selves through life. After that we'll be normal human beings."

"We've never thought of you as normal," Swan said.

"Ball kicker," Frack muttered as he took hold of the two frosty beers and handed one to Frick. He glanced over to the right and saw a young guy lighting up a joint. It took all his willpower not to stalk over and pull it out of his mouth. But, perhaps, tonight was a time for letting some things slide.

"Shh, shh, shh," Tansee said. "He's coming on."

All eyes in the bar riveted on the two TVs there; the people outdoors in the parking lot and front had their own small TVs at which to stare.

The pasty, familiar hangdog visage of the thirty-seventh president of the United States, Richard M. Nixon, filled the screens. You could hear a pin drop in the formerly raucous saloon.

Good evening.

This is the 37th time I have spoken to you from this office, where so many decisions have been made that shaped the history of this

Nation. Each time I have done so to discuss with you some matter that I believe affected the national interest.

In all the decisions I have made in my public life, I have always tried to do what was best for the Nation. Throughout the long and difficult period of Watergate, I have felt it was my duty to persevere, to make every possible effort to complete the term of office to which you elected me.

In the past few days, however, it has become evident to me that I no longer have a strong enough political base in the Congress to justify continuing that effort. As long as there was such a base, I felt strongly that it was necessary to see the constitutional process through to its conclusion, that to do otherwise would be unfaithful to the spirit of that deliberately difficult process and a dangerously destabilizing precedent for the future.

But with the disappearance of that base, I now believe that the constitutional purpose has been served, and there is no longer a need for the process to be prolonged.

...

...

Therefore, I shall resign the Presidency effective at noon tomorrow. Vice President Ford will be sworn in as President at that hour in this office.

This, more than anything, is what I hoped to achieve when I sought the Presidency. This, more than anything, is what I hope will be my legacy to you, to our country, as I leave the Presidency.

To have served in this office is to have felt a very personal sense of kinship with each and every American. In leaving it, I do so with this prayer: May God's grace be with you in all the days ahead.

A deafening roar erupted from everyone in the saloon, outside, and in homes and businesses across the country.

CHAPTER TWO

The San Miguel Chapel is a quaint Spanish colonial mission church with roots back to the 1600s; it was built between 1610 and 1626. It has the honor of being the oldest church in the continental United States. Badly damaged during the Pueblo Revolt of 1680 when Native Americans rebelled against their Spanish overseers, the roof was set ablaze as barrio residents took shelter there; the church was destroyed. Don Diego de Vargas reconquered the pueblo in 1692, and one of his first proclamations was to have the church rebuilt. By 1710 that charge was completed, and for a time it served as a chapel only for Spanish soldiers. One of the wooden reredoses—the large altar pieces placed behind the altar and are often niche-shaped to contain religious icons—is an image of Saint Michael dating back to 1709. The inscription on the lower left-hand corner reads, "This altar was erected through the piety of Don Jose Antonio Ortis in the year 1798."

In modern times, due to the decades that passed and encompassed reconstruction, repair, and rebuilding, the original adobe walls are mainly intact but hidden behind more modern façades. The church is one of seven properties resident in the Barrio de Analco Historic District of Santa Fe, located at the junction of East de Vargas Street and Old Santa Fe Trail. The district and its buildings are a United States National Historic Landmark.

The outside of the church is sleek and simple. The double wooden front doors are recessed into a narrow, boxy façade of light desert brown, with a simple, stark cross sitting atop the roof. Below the roof is a large, open viewing space highlighted by a large bell that rings and signals its call to services. The small interior of the chapel has a high ceiling with rough-hewn wooden beams covering it. The whitewashed stucco walls are decorated with religious pictures and icons. Two rows of simple wooden pews cling to the sides of the chapel, facing the minimalist but comforting altar at the front. To sit in the chapel, alone, was perhaps the best expression of peacefulness one could encounter. Masses are held in both English and Latin.

Tucson sat in a middle pew at the right of the church. He wasn't alone; four women and one old man dotted the other pews as they bowed their heads in prayer. He wasn't praying, just sitting there with a blank mind. That happened every so often, when he blanked out and became cognizant again after time had passed, sometimes minutes, sometimes hours. A few times he had lost days. It was worse right after he returned from North Korea, but every so often the blackness came upon him and he was unable to fight it off. It had been six years, and the symptoms of his mental issues had mostly faded, but every so often they roared back at the least expected time. Lately, he had been having night terrors once or twice a week.

He told no one. He wanted his family and friends to believe—and they wanted to believe—that he was "okay" and the consequences of his imprisonment with the other crewmembers of the doomed *USS Pueblo* had faded into the past.

They hadn't.

They hadn't despite throwing himself into every bastion of normalcy that he could find. He spent a year roaming the country after he left San Diego, only returning for the official military hearings at the Navy Court of Inquiry where he and all crewmembers had to testify as to what occurred during the "Pueblo Incident." A court martial was recommended for Commander Lloyd Bucher and the Officer in Charge of the Research Department, Lieutenant Steve Harris, for surrendering without a fight and for failing to destroy classified material. Fortunately, the Secretary of the Navy, John Chafee, rejected the recommendation, stating, "They have suffered enough." Still, the Navy refused to authorize the survivors their Prisoner of War Medals. In 1970 Bucher published an autobiographical account of the incident, entitled *Bucher: My Story*. In 1973 a TV movie was made entitled *Pueblo*; it starred Hal Holbrook as Bucher.

Tucson neither read the book nor watched the movie. He had lived it and couldn't stand the thought of portraying the harrowing real-life incident with purple text and fictionalization that couldn't even come close to what they all suffered.

The humiliation of being captured by Communist forces.

The restraints.

The beatings.

The starvation.

The beatings.

The mental torture.

The physical torture.

The hopelessness.

The fear, 24/7.

The hatred.

The physical filth.

The despair.

The belief that none of them would ever see home or their loved ones again.

Repeat … day after day, month after month.

Tucson had a few permanent physical reminders of that year, the lightning-bolt scar on his left cheek from a North Korean bayonet, and the limp from a badly broken and badly set leg. To this day he couldn't even look at rice let alone eat it after the constant diet of terrible and often spoiled rice fed to the prisoners. He'd tried to get past the revulsion and eat it twice; he threw up both times.

Perhaps Lloyd Bucher had the worst of the mistreatment and was the primary target for much of the North Koreans' brutality. He was psychologically tortured, including being put through a mock firing squad in an effort to make him confess. Eventually the North Koreans threatened to execute his men in front of him, and Bucher relented and agreed to "confess to his and the crew's transgression." Bucher wrote the confession since a "confession" by definition needed to be written by the confessor himself. Everyone knew the confession was false but was simply a propaganda move to embarrass the United States.

Tucson wasn't ignorant of the fact that his family knew that he was still very much haunted by the past. His parents and Memphis had urged him, gently at first and then more aggressively, to seek professional help. He talked informally a few times with Percy, but a year after returning to Santa Fe he decided he was fine and cut off those talks. Percy made it clear that he was open to resuming their dialogue. Tucson traveled to the UNM down in Albuquerque and got his PhD in psychology, and he and Percy were partners in their own practice. He hadn't planned on specializing in any particular type of patient, but he found himself sought out by veterans who were trying to get past their own demons. It was his own private joke that he couldn't get past his.

He was startled out of his drifting reverie by a strong hand on his shoulder. He looked up into Memphis's eyes then scooted over so his brother could sit. He noticed that three of the women had left, and the other one and the man were kneeling in front of the altar, making the sign of the cross before they, too, turned and made their way to the church door.

"I wish I could have been here for your wedding," Tucson said.

"It was nice," Memphis said, nodding. "But you were missing so it wasn't complete. That, and Sand was fired the day before. Kind of a pall over the proceedings, but mostly, yeah, nice. Anyway, better than a drunken Juárez wedding neither of us remembered." He grinned; he and Swan had been investigating in El Paso and went below the border. The next day they woke up with hangovers, wearing mariachi clothes and with a wedding certificate on Spanish on the dresser.

Memphis still had the leather vest and blue mariachi hat. Swan still wore the silver and turquoise wedding ring.

"I would have sold my soul to be at that ceremony," Tucson replied, flashing a genuine, unaffected smile.

"I would have sold my soul to be conscious at that ceremony." They both laughed then looked around guiltily; you just didn't make noise in a Catholic church.

Both men fell silent.

"Are you … okay?" Memphis finally asked quietly.

"At this moment in time," Tucson said in a hesitant, hushed voice.

"I'm always here for you."

"I know."

Memphis patted his brother's leg and stood. "See you at the office?" Tucson nodded, so Memphis wisely refrained from any other comment and left his brother alone to finish whatever he needed to finish before rejoining the world.

Tucson sat for another ten minutes then heard the door open and saw an elderly Hispanic woman draped in black entering. He rose and went over to the candles, and lit one for Duane Hodges, the only casualty on the *USS Pueblo*, the only crewmember who didn't come back alive. He made the sign of the cross and turned to leave, passing the old woman who was sitting in the front pew murmuring words over her rosary while tears rolled down her cheeks.

"Boss, I got a woman out here who wants to see a P.I.," Skye said over the intercom. "She doesn't have an appointment."

Memphis shook his head. He'd planned to have some me-time to focus on a few administrative matters, but all day long he'd been interrupted in one way or another. His firm was bustling and had been for years. In addition to the "vampire killer" case he and his teammates had been involved in several high-profile cases that brought more publicity and new clients. Besides the larger cases the firm had handled dozens of small cases that weren't flashy but filled the coffers. He could afford to turn down a client that hadn't come through the usual channels, but as he stared down at the fine print on a few contracts on his desk he made a snap decision and told Skye to send her in.

He stuck the papers in a folder and put them in his top drawer, then rose just as a sharp rap on the door signaled Skye's presence. She didn't wait for a come-in before she opened the door and filled it with her sky-blue polyester glory and her new pageboy haircut reminiscent of singer Toni Tennille. She entered and waved in the woman without an appointment.

"Here she is, boss. Have fun." With that Skye departed.

Memphis found himself six feet away from a woman about twenty-five, a near six-footer in two-inch heels. She had short, shiny chestnut-brown hair parted on the right side with a wide hank covering most of her left eye, and a distinctive widow's peak. Her clear, wide-set eyes were hazel, her symmetrical, heart-shaped face set in a neutral expression. Her complexion was pure peaches and cream, her lips full and inviting. She was wearing a forest-green linen pantsuit without a wrinkle on it, and a leather purse slung over her shoulder. Half-carat diamond studs in her ears were her only jewelry. There were no rings on her fingers; her nails were short and painted pale pink, a personal effort, not professional.

Memphis extended his hand towards his guest chair. "Please. Have a seat Miss ...?"

"Thank you," she said as she seated herself smoothly and crossed her legs. "And it's Ms."

"Super. Ms.?" Her preferred title made him think of Swan, who used the same designation. His wife also had a subscription to *Ms.* magazine, the radical new feminist homage that Gloria Steinem has started publishing two years earlier. His only subscriptions were to *Field & Stream* and *Guns & Ammo.* Swan read those, too.

"Adams. Cameo Adams."

Memphis arched an eyebrow. "Lovely name. So, what can I do for you Ms. Adams?"

She fixed her eyes directly on his. "I'd like you to find a missing person."

Memphis nodded. "We do that. Who's this missing person?"

"Me," she said evenly without blinking or elaborating.

Memphis stared at her for a few seconds, then hit the intercom and asked Skye to have Tucson and Swan join him. He smiled tightly at Ms. Adams and said he wanted to have his colleagues listen to her story, too. She gave a short nod. He could see that she was suddenly wound as tightly as a Swiss watch.

Tucson came in without knocking followed by Swan. Swan parked herself in the guest chair next to Ms. Adams while Tucson stood beside his brother.

"This is Miss—sorry, Ms.—Cameo Adams. Ms. Adams, my wife, Swan Hazelwood, and my brother, Tucson. Swan is a full-time P.I. and Tucson is a Doctor of Psychology who often assists us in our investigations." He looked at Swan. "Ms. Adams seeks to employ us to find a missing person."

"Who?" Swan asked.

"Me," Cameo said succinctly and without any emotional inflection in her voice.

"One of our easier cases," Swan said coolly.

"I doubt that," Cameo said. "Would you like to hear my story?"

Swan smiled. "The consultation is free."

"Excellent," Cameo murmured, then withdrew a checkbook from her purse. "Would five thousand be a sufficient retainer?"

"That'll do," Memphis said mildly.

Cameo wrote out the check and handed it to Memphis. "Shall we begin?" she asked.

"Your money, your time," Swan said.

Cameo cocked her head. "You don't like me much, do you?"

"I don't know you well enough to like or dislike you," Swan replied. "Right now, I'm just acting on instinct."

"Fair enough." She paused. "Do you have a glass of water?"

Tucson walked over to the mini-fridge and took out a bottle of Schweppe's and handed it to her. She took a long drink.

"The name I've given you is not the name on my birth certificate. I have no idea what that was but I'm hoping your efforts will prove fruitful in determining that. I was given the name at a hospital up in Pittsfield, Massachusetts five years ago."

"You don't seem to have a Massachusetts accent," Memphis said.

"Apparently not. The doctors seem to think my accent is east coast, but not anywhere near the clearly defined one in, say, New York or New Jersey."

"Why were you in the hospital?" Tucson asked.

"I was found naked and bloody on the banks of the Housatonic River in Pittsfield. I had no memory of who I was, what had happened, or how I had gotten there. At the hospital the doctors examined me and found that I had a severe concussion, a broken wrist, multiple bruises all over my body, and I had been raped. Fortunately, that latter injury didn't result in either a pregnancy or an STD. Small favors."

"Jesus," Tucson said softly.

"I mentioned being naked. However, I was wearing a ratty canvas backpack that had money in it. Cash money, old nonsequential bills, with fingerprints on it that weren't mine."

"How much?" Memphis asked.

"$52,369, mainly in fifties and twenties."

"The police did an investigation, right?" Swan said.

Cameo nodded. "They did but came up empty. I was in the hospital for four days then released—along with my money, minus the hospital bill—and holed up in a small hotel. The main physician gave me my name. Cameo is Greek for 'shadow portrait,' and since Pittsfield wasn't much of a realistic last name, they used the next town over, Adams. They fixed my 'birth date' at the day I was found, May 4, 1969. They thought I was around twenty, so they interpreted my birth year to be 1949."

"What steps did the police take to ascertain your real identity?" Memphis asked.

"They canvased the area, talked to people, knocked on doors, checked other police reports that might be similar, checked the nearby colleges, and put a photo of me and a story in the regional papers. They got a lot of tips but none of them panned out. I spent a lot of time with several detectives that had the habit of treating me like a suspect rather than a victim. I confess that I have a bad taste in my mouth for law enforcement."

"I used to be a cop," Swan said mildly.

"But apparently you've left the dark side and moved on to a more tasteful profession," Cameo said tartly. "I applaud you."

Swan smiled brightly. "I'm beginning to understand my initial instinct about you."

Cameo looked at Memphis. "Are you willing to take on this case and, if so, can I request that your wife not be assigned to it?"

Memphis flicked the check back at her, a slight Cheshire Cat smile on his face. "It was nice speaking with you, Ms. Adams. Tucson will see you out."

Cameo stood slowly and picked up the check, locking eyes with Memphis and ignoring Swan. Wordlessly she turned. Tucson brushed past her and opened the door, and she preceded him out of the office.

"Bitch," Swan muttered.

"She reminds me a little of you," Memphis said, grinning.

"That remark's going to get you a week's stay on the couch."

"And if I apologize?"

"Then you'll only have to spend tonight on the couch."

"I apologize."

"The pillow and blanket are in the coat closet."

Tucson walked Cameo out to Skye's receptionist area, then gently touched her arm to stop her from leaving. She looked at him curiously.

"My office is downstairs. If you have the time, I'd like to talk to you a little more about your situation. I'd also like my partner to attend. No charge," Tucson said.

"Why?" Cameo asked.

"Perhaps because I'm fascinated with your case, psychologically speaking. That, and I think you really do need help." He smiled. "If you need another more visceral reason, I take pride in making the best cup of espresso you'll find in Santa Fe."

"I love espresso. It's a deal."

Skye watched them enter the elevator and shook her head. *Men and their dicks*, she thought.

Cameo watched Tucson prepare the espresso in what looked to be a state-of-the-art machine. His office projected an aura of professional tradition with only glimpses as to its occupant in the Indian prints on the walls and the family photos on a mahogany sideboard under the picture window that overlooked a side street. The desk was wide and long, a burnished walnut that matched the two tall bookcases standing against the west wall. Except for the espresso machine (sitting next to a Mr. Coffee) there didn't seem to be much modernity imbuing the space with a sense of present rather than past.

The man himself was physically intriguing. Tall, with copper skin and long, layered black hair, the zigzag scar on his cheek gave him a rakish cast that was appealing rather than off-putting. He had a mild limp. She wondered how he had gotten those flaws.

Tucson carried a ceramic mug with a roadrunner on it over to Cameo and put it down in front of her.

"A triple espresso?" she asked, amused.

"I thought it might be apropos." He sat down behind his desk with his own mug and called Candy, asking her to send Percy in.

Cameo sipped her ultra-strong espresso and felt it warm her entire soul. She wondered if she drank coffee in her other life or had developed the passion when she entered her new one. Not that it mattered.

The office door opened, and Cameo turned and coughed as her espresso went down the wrong way. She hadn't expected to see a dwarf dressed in a swanky three-piece suit walk in.

Percy smiled slightly; he was used to getting that reaction upon first meetings. He hated it, but he was used to it. At least this new client didn't gulp or drop her cup. He walked up to her and extended his hand. To her credit, she shook it immediately.

"Dr. Percival McBean," Percy said. "And you are?"

"Ms. Cameo Adams," Tucson answered. "A potential client that Memphis turned down because Swan doesn't like her." He fought back a chuckle.

"Ah," Percy said, nodding. "Getting on Swan's bad side is a fairly simple matter but isn't a good idea."

"I learned that the hard way," Cameo said as she took another sip.

"So, Ms. Adams," Tucson began.

"Cameo, please."

"Cameo. Let me give you a quick update on our practice. Percy and I are partners in our psychologist firm. We both have doctorates—Percy has two, one in Sociology as well. We treat all sorts of disorders although those associated with veterans' issues are generally confined to my side of the practice."

"Are you a vet?" she asked.

"I am, so I have a better background to understand and assess their issues although Percy dives in whenever I beg him to."

"How long have you been practicing together?" Cameo asked.

"Around four years although we worked together in Memphis's firm as P.I.s years before that. It's a long story." He looked over at his partner. "Cameo briefed us on her background and needs, but I'll have her do so again so we can bring you up to scratch. Then, we can decide whether our branch of the firm can assist in her search."

"Search?" Percy asked in his deep baritone. "For whom is she searching?"

"I'm searching for me," Cameo said quietly.

Percy's eyebrows crawled up his forehead and he nodded thoughtfully. He looked at Tucson.

"I think I need a double espresso. A shot of Kahlua in it wouldn't be unwelcome."

"Coming right up," Tucson said as he stood and walked over to his beloved new machine.

CHAPTER THREE

Frick made a mental note to stop at the pet shop before heading home. He was just about out of cat food and cat litter, and Bast wouldn't be happy if she weren't inundated with either one. He had had the cat for five years, ever since his beloved Spade passed on. He swore that he wouldn't let another feline into his heart or home; the pain of losing one was just too much. Frack understood all too well since his precious bulldog, John Barleycorn, had ascended to dog heaven six months earlier. Both swore off pets.

That didn't cut it with their friends in the Grayhawk circle. A month after Spade died there was a knock at Frick's front door. Luc and Raleigh Grayhawk stood on his front step; the girl was holding a small cardboard box. "Here," she said, thrusting the box at him. He took it automatically but before he could question them the two youngest Grayhawks whirled around and ran off to their brother's car. Memphis screeched the Mustang away from curb.

Frick opened the box to find a tiny coal-black kitten staring up at him with huge green eyes. Against his better judgment Frick fell in love with the kitten in approximately four seconds. He cursed the Grayhawks loudly, then went indoors, sat down on his threadbare recliner, and cuddled his new pet. He named her Bast after the

Egyptian goddess of cats. He learned later when he called Frack to inform him about the new family addition that the rotten Grayhawk kids had appeared on his doorstep, too, presenting him with a French bulldog puppy before fleeing in Memphis's sky-blue Mustang. Frack named the puppy Pierre. He agreed with Frick that the Grayhawk clan were rotten bastards that fortunately had a few good character aspects.

Frick pulled his car to the side of the road as he approached the two police cars and uniformed officers that were milling about the desert twenty feet away from the asphalt. The patch of land under inspection was just at the foot of the Sangre de Cristo Mountains, well past any residential enclaves. The terrain was sparse, mainly sand dotted with shrubs and cacti, animate only with the skittering of snakes, geckos, and other small desert animals and the screes of hawks soaring low seeking their next meal.

Frack was standing around twenty feet from the road. He looked like a lumbering, pissed-off grizzly bear in a wrinkled suit. Frick was taller, gangly, and walked in a loping fashion. His face always looked sad even when his heart was soaring. Physical opposites, they had spent the last fifteen years as devoted partners. Now, with Frick fifty-nine and Frack sixty-one, they were anticipating their retirement after thirty years of police work. They pretended to look forward to the respite from active law enforcement, but each knew they were lying. The job was as much a part of their flesh and blood as, well, their flesh and blood.

Frack was talking to a uniformed policeman and a sixty-something guy dressed in hiking clothes. He had a hand-carved walking stick, knee-length shorts, decent hiking boots, a baseball cap, and only one quart of water hanging in a holder from his belt. The water bottle was almost empty. The man was sweating profusely, his face a cherry red and what was left of his hair plastered to the back of his neck. There were sweat spots all over his tee-shirt and cap. Frick rolled his eyes as he approached his partner.

Frack nodded at Frick. "This is Bruno Cuches. He was hiking out here and discovered some bones that appeared to be human."

Frick nodded. "Mr. Cuches. How did you get this far out? I don't see any cars."

"My son dropped me off this morning about a mile from here. He's supposed to pick me up at three," Cuches said, a little out of breath. "I was out here maybe a coupla hours hiking and that's when I saw the bones. I hauled ass back to the road and flagged down a car that took me to some house where I called you guys."

Frick cringed inside. That accent. "Where you from, Mr. Cuches?"

"New York City."

To Frick it sounded like "Noo Yawk." He heard the accent all too often at the police station since a new detective, Tom "Shooter" Christensen, had transferred in from the Big Apple. Nice enough guy, but Frick had to resist the urge to go around with earplugs in the precinct and making derogatory comments about the Yankees. For some reason, Shooter was also sensitive about remarks made against the New England Patriots.

Frick said, "You thought it was a good idea to come out here alone in the middle of the day with no clouds and the sun blasting everything in sight?"

Cuches seemed embarrassed. "Um, the newspaper said the average temperature in September is around eighty. That's not too bad. I mean … is it?"

"Depends," Frack said after waving off the uniformed cop. "You used to hiking back east?"

"Well, sure. I walk around Central Park all the time, even in the winter."

"Central Park?"

"Yeah. It's huge."

"Any desert climate or critters in that park?"

"Um, no, but …"

"Do you know what the temperature is right now, Mr. Cuches?"

"Um … hot?"

"It's an unseasonable 91.9°F. According to the weatherman that makes it the hottest day this month, probably this year. People who live around here wouldn't go hiking in this weather. And certainly not without a gallon of water. If they do, they can expect to find their skeletons picked clean by vultures within twenty-four hours. Ever seen a stripped body with a big hungry bird on top pulling off the last of the muscle tendons?"

"N-no."

"It's definitely a closed-casket situation. You're not wearing sunscreen, are you?"

"N-no."

"Carrying any weapons?"

"N-no, of course not."

"Look over there, about fifteen feet to your right. By that large rock."

Cuches glanced around nervously, finally spotting the rock. He frowned.

"Look at the ground," Frack said patiently.

Cuches looked at the ground, scouring the general area with his swollen red eyes. Then he spotted it, a huge rattlesnake curled up next to the rock. Cuches opened and closed his mouth like a fish, then keeled over unconscious. Frick and Frack managed to catch him before he hit the ground.

"Thanks a bunch," Frick grumbled at his partner. "I'll probably throw my back out lugging this tenderfoot to the patrol car."

"Just be glad he's not a relative," Frack said, then whistled loudly, bringing two cops running over. "Get this dude in the back of your car, force some water down his throat, and take him to the hospital. Tell him we'll be in touch." The two cops relieved the detectives of their dead weight and carried Cuches off to cool safety. Before they left Frack grabbed the Canon camera that was strapped to Cuches' belt. He checked the readout; there were only a few pictures left untaken.

"They should make it illegal for New Yorkers to come into this state. Or anywhere west of the Mississippi," Frick said, half seriously.

"Anyone from the east coast. Except our Grayhawk east-coast dudes." He waved the camera at Frick. "We should get this film developed as soon as possible. He might have taken some pics of the area and bones." He stood over the bones resting on the desert floor and snapped off a few pictures, then used the last three shots for the area. "The forensics guys will take more shots but at least we have these." He nodded back towards Santa Fe. "Here comes the bandito now."

Carlito Cruz screeched up to within ten feet of Frick's car, kicking up sand and rocks and eliciting a scowl and muttered curse from the uniformed cop standing nearby. He jumped out, carrying his evidence bag and tools, followed momentarily by a young man who looked like Alfred E. Neuman, red hair, gap-toothed silly grin and all.

"Where's my evidence?" Carlito asked brusquely. The term "bandito" was more than accurate; Carlito had thick, long, dark brown hair, wideset chocolate eyes, and a Fu Manchu moustache over a close-cropped goatee that was an eye-roller for his colleagues but a turn-on to the ladies he solicited at the Sweet Revenge Saloon. He was only five-seven and wiry, but he was known for having a very active social life.

Frick pointed to the bones lying on the sand. "Careful. Big-ass snake at twelve o'clock high."

Carlito glanced over and spied the rattler immediately. It had awakened due to the nearby activity and vibrations and was rattling its tail.

Carlito casually unsnapped his waist holster, withdrew his Colt 45, and said, "Die, sucker." A second later he blasted the snake right in two.

"Nice shot," Frack said.

"Thanks," Carlito said as he walked over to the dead snake and scooped up both pieces, dumping them in a large plastic bag. He held it up and grinned. "Dinner. And another rattle to add to my collection."

"Ghoul," Frack said. "Get going on the bones."

When Carlito focused on his duties and talents, there was no one better in forensics. He focused now, spending a half hour photographing, measuring, making notes, dictating into a small recording device, and even sniffing the bones from an inch away.

When he was finished, he gently collected each of the three bones, putting them in separate bags. He filled another bag with the soil under and around them.

"Done," he said with finality. "I'll start analyzing them back at the lab. Anything else?"

"Are we invited for dinner?" Frick said.

"Sure, just bring the honey barbecue sauce." With that he sauntered off to his van, followed by his adoring puppy dog of an assistant.

"Do you think he's really going to eat that snake?" Frick asked, wiping the sweat off his brow.

"Yup."

"He gets weirder by the year."

"Yup. So, okay, we've got the Noo Yawker's initial statement. Should we head over to the hospital and see if he's conscious enough to give us some more detail?" Frack asked.

"That sounds like a plan. I need to stop at the pet store for food and litter," Frick said.

"I need some chow for Pierre, too, so I'll follow you in," Frack said. As they reached their cars he said, "You know, I really miss those Omaha Steaks."

"Maybe Memphis will need us again and we can strong-arm him into new deliveries."

"One can only hope."

Memphis looked like a judgmental owl, Tucson thought. That stare on his face exuded skepticism and perhaps just a little disbelief that his brother and Percy had taken on Cameo Adams as a client.

"Explain to me again why a woman searching for her identity would settle on a couple of shrinks to assist in that matter," Memphis said.

Tucson fought back the urge to roll his eyes. Memphis pretended to be enlightened about psychological matters, but he was not fully on board with the science and results. Perhaps because Tucson hadn't set all of his demons to rest.

"She went through as many of the non-psychological aspects of searching for her identity which, to date, haven't produced results. She spent some time with psychiatrists at the hospital and then over the last few years, but that, too, proved fruitless," Percy said.

"And with all of that mental help that as you say proved fruitless, you think that you two mind dudes can change that fruitlessness," Memphis said, his tone neutral with just a tad of disbelief saturating through.

"Mind dudes?" Percy said. "We're definitely going to add that to our business cards."

"She has nothing to lose," Tucson said tartly. "The concussion she had may or may not have resulted in her amnesia, but we've read the medical records and it doesn't seem probable that the physical injury caused her identity loss. That leaves a psychological reason."

"And you think you can unlock that reason?"

"If we can't then she's no worse off than she was before we met her."

"Did she explain how she wound up in Santa Fe since this all happened three thousand miles away?" Memphis's tone had evolved into genuine skepticism.

"Yes, but we're not going to tell you," Percy said mildly, a small grin tugging at the corners of his mouth.

"Why?" Memphis said, surprised.

"Because this isn't your case. You turned it down. You are, in effect, an outsider," Tucson said with just enough condemnation to get a rise out of his older sibling.

"Well, maybe I can help, provide a different perspective."

"You turned her down."

"Well, maybe that was …"

"A mistake?"

"No," Memphis exclaimed.

"Because you don't make mistakes."

"I did when you were ten and I pulled you out of that river when you fell in. I should have let you tumble downstream."

"We all make mistakes," Tucson said, laughing. "So, are you and Swan ready to consider taking Cameo as a client for your end of the investigative process?"

"I'll have to talk to my wife."

"Wimp," Tucson said, shaking his head.

"Say that when you have a wife that can shoot like Annie Oakley, has a black belt in karate, can fling a knife dead center at fifty yards, and who recently learned how to use a samurai sword. Oh—and she bites." To highlight that point Memphis pushed up his left sleeve to reveal a red, recent bite mark on his forearm.

"I don't think we want to know the story behind that, thanks," Percy said. "So, will you consider taking her case? Come on, Memphis—you can make this decision on your own."

"Fifty-one percent of the firm," Tucson added.

"Okay, fine," Memphis expelled. "but you'll both be very sorry if I come into work tomorrow all bruised up."

"Not really," Tucson said.

"Nope," Percy said.

"My loving family." Memphis flipped open his appointment book and said, "Can you get her in here tomorrow morning at nine?"

"That's doable," Tucson said, rising.

"We'd like to attend, of course," Percy said as he wriggled off the chair.

"Not gonna happen," Memphis said firmly. "Your sessions with her are confidential and so mine will be. I'll consider powwowing after I've digested the story."

"Fair enough," Percy said. He saluted as he followed Tucson out of the office.

Memphis sighed deeply, dawdled for five minutes, then called his wife.

"Baby? I've been thinking. We need a night out, away from work, away from the kids. What say I make dinner reservations at the La Fonda and then we take in a movie over at the Rialto? All the champagne and popcorn you can eat. *The Longest Yard*'s still playing, and I know you have a soft spot for Burt Reynolds." He paused and listened. "No, nothing's wrong. Can't I treat my wife to a nice night out? I swear—I have no ulterior motives." He listened again as her voice grew louder. Then he sighed. "Yeah, yeah, okay. There is something I want to talk to you about. Yeah, okay, Dom Perignon. Fine, fine, if they have it, lobster."

Memphis hung up the phone and sagged in his chair. Yeah, he was a wimp.

Swan put her receiver down and grinned at Tucson and Percy. "You called it," she said.

"I know my brother," Tucson replied. "Make him work at convincing you to take on Cameo's case. Don't let him off the hook easy."

"Easy? Me? Yeah, right."

"Look, we're glad you changed your mind about the lady," Percy said.

"I still don't like her, but I'm intrigued by your perspectives. I'm willing to take a chance. And, anytime I can get my macho Indian husband under my thumb, it's an effort well spent. I do need to set an example to my daughters as to how they should approach their eventual romantic lives."

"I understand why he's scared of you," Tucson said.

"We are, too," Percy added.

"Smart men. Now, skedaddle. I have real work to do. Shoo."

Swan smiled affectionately after the men left. Her in-laws were special all the way round, and she loved them. She had never seen her life turning out the way it did, but persnickety fate had sent her on a winding, occasionally broken road that was more satisfying than the one she had envisioned.

All Swan had wanted to be during her formative years was a cop, a detective. She had battled to get onto the Santa Fe police force and spent a year there, half the time good, half the time bad. Female cops weren't the norm and she took a lot of shit from her male colleagues. Before she could achieve her dream her husband, Memphis, and his crew were involved in a serial killer case. Joanna Frid, an older lawyer that had been a mentor to Memphis, turned out to be a long-term serial killer that stalked and killed young women so she could use their blood to stave off the ageing process. Joanna sought to derail the investigation by murdering Sand's partner, detective Cole Garrison. Then, Joanna sought to derail Sand by outing him as gay. He was forced to resign from the police force, and a week later, after returning from her honeymoon, Swan had gotten into a fight with colleagues about their treatment of her brother, kicked two in the balls, and was fired by the hateful Captain Steele. She immediately joined Memphis's investigation firm and was instrumental in bringing Joanna down.

But Joanna had escaped—twice. The first time she had fled the country just as her identity was being revealed. Memphis developed a plan to lure her back. It worked, but once again she escaped along with a child she had "borrowed" for her nefarious purpose. Before Joanna absconded once again, she had shot Sand, Memphis, Frack, and a patrol officer as well as the two young men Memphis hired as security; the officer and the guards had died. Swan had been incapacitated with a paralyzing drug. Tansee and Percy were hostages in their own home, and as final evil act Joanna had paralyzed Memphis and made him watch as she extracted three vials of blood from his little daughter, Sage. That Christmas, she had sent a jar of special anti-ageing cream to Memphis, cream that contained his daughter's blood.

Memphis was never the same after that; no one was. He instituted crazy intense security measures that held today. He was overprotective of Sage, and of the twin daughters Swan had borne him a few years later. All the family homes were wired to the max with alarms, and all the adult family members had become experts with guns. She had accelerated her own hand-to-hand training and could kick significant ass. Memphis, Sand, Nick, Tucson, Luc, and Raleigh were almost as good; Raleigh had a real talent for shooting.

Swan managed to build a lucrative and respected reputation as a crack private investigator, just like her husband, brother, and in-laws.

She'd been engaged in several high-profile cases over the past six years, including helping to bust a white-slavery ring down in Las Cruces; a missing persons case of a state senator's daughter; and an industrial espionage case that had repercussions in all of the Four Corners states. She also endured the small, not necessarily critical cases that were the firm's bread and butter.

Swan was happy, content most of the time, and she genuinely loved her life. The boogeymen in the back of her mind, however, were Joanna and her own sister, Snow. Snow was Sage's biological mother, but she'd dumped Memphis and ran off pregnant. Nick had found her and brought the baby back, but Snow was still out there somewhere. Swan hoped she'd never reappear. The one thing Swan would never do was to give up Sage or let Snow have a personal relationship with her. As far as Swan was concerned, Snow was dead.

She shook off her musings and opened the folder on Cameo Adams. No, she didn't particularly like the woman and didn't quite know why, but the case was challenging, and Swan needed a challenge. Maybe just a little she was looking forward to searching for the woman's identity.

Maybe more than just a little.

CHAPTER FOUR

"These bones have been cleaned extremely well of any flesh remnants," Carlito said to Frack. "It's clear that they've been processed to maximize the white color."

"Is there any way to tell how old the bones are?" Frick asked. He studied the three bones laid out next to one another. The largest was a femur, followed by an ulna and a rib. The bones were stark white and had a slight sheen to them. The sheen, Carlito had told them, was not a natural progression of flesh divestiture or ageing; someone had applied the sheen as a thin, clear varnish that would protect the outer layer of the bone as well as making it more vivid.

"That's not an exact science," Carlito replied. "Carbon-14 dating can significantly narrow down the age, but even that isn't explicitly accurate. Without the skull or pelvis, it's also hard to tell if the bones belong to a male or a female. However, since the femur generally makes up one-quarter of a normal person's height, we can ascertain from this bone that the rest of the skeleton was approximately five-foot-seven."

"That could be a man or a woman," Frick said and Carlito nodded. "But no way to tell, huh?"

Carlito shook his head. "If I had the skull, I could make a better determination as to both gender and age. For example, if the skull has wisdom teeth then the person is over eighteen. If there's considerable bone loss the person was much older. I've checked for ossification of these bones but didn't find enough evidence to figure out an age range."

"Ossification?" Frick asked.

"It means the thickening of bone material. There are over eight hundred points on a human skeleton that can ossify as the person ages. Bones also fuse as we age."

"But you're a hundred percent sure that these are human bones," Frack said.

"Well, either that or we found the remains of a short Sasquatch. Yes, I'm sure," Carlito said, shaking his head in disgust.

Frick ignored him and said, "Are there any signs of trauma on the bones, like a knife cut?"

"No, the bones are fine."

"Let's say this person was recently alive," Frack said. "How could the flesh be removed so well as to produce such a clean bone? I mean, if the corpse were buried, it would take a long time for the flesh to decompose. If there aren't any knife or scrape marks on the bones, then isn't it unlikely that someone scraped off the flesh?"

"Or, leaving the body out in the open where animals could strip the flesh?" Frick added. "But there's no teeth marks on the bones for that possibility, are there?"

"Correct. There are a lot of ways to remove flesh from the bones without harming them," Carlito said.

"Like boiling the bones?" Frick said.

"Not the best method," Carlito replied. "When you boil fleshed bone, it thins out the fat in the flesh and that seeps into the bones. When the bones cool that fat is locked into them. Eventually, that fat will rise to the surface of the bone and make it look yellowish. You can use hydrogen peroxide or bleach to whiten the bones and de-flesh portions of them, but the best way of producing clean, undamaged bones is to use dermestid beetles."

"What are those?" Frick asked. "Don't beetles just eat plants and move dung around?"

"Troglodyte," Carlito said under his breath. "There are many types of beetles with many types of talents for existing in this world. For example, you've got the Japanese beetle, the boll weevil, scarabs, the leaf beetle, the ladybug—"

"Okay, okay we get the point," Frack said. "So, tell us about this dermal beetle."

"Dermestid," Carlito corrected.

"Whatever."

Carlito rolled his eyes, then said, "The dermestid beetle group belongs to the order called Coleoptera. Their common characteristics are a pair of wings hardened into wing cases. The Coleoptera order has around 400,000 species."

"How do you know all this shit?" Frick asked.

"I spent a summer at a UCLA course in entomology, the study of insects. I particularly studied beetles because they have a special function in forensics. You see, the dermestid is frequently used in both relation to human beings and animals for stripping flesh and leaving clean, undamaged bones."

"These are flesh-eating beetles?" Frick asked.

"They are indeed. However, they are destructive to a lot of other natural fibers, like silk, wool, cotton, fur, and feathers. Scientists use them to remove flesh from decaying or even non-decaying animals to spare the bones from any injury. Taxidermists often use them to acquire skeletons."

"How do they … do it?" Frack asked.

"Well," Carlito began, "you need a large tank, best if it's glass like a giant aquarium so you can watch the progress. Beforehand the beetles should be kept in a special tank that's warm and dark, and you have to feed them bits and pieces of stuff constantly. They work best with fresh flesh."

"Yum," Frack said.

"They do a great job at stripping flesh, but often with a larger object there's still a bit of flesh left that has to be cleaned by hand."

"How long does this take for, say, a grown man?"

"It depends on the actual size of a body as well as the number of beetles employed to do the task. A large beetle colony can clean the bones of a small animal like a rabbit or owl in twenty-four to forty-eight hours. It might take a full week to clean a deer."

"Where do you get these beetles?"

"Some people make a living selling them. You could ask hunting stores if they know of any tanks or people that use them. Doesn't your buddy Memphis hunt? Ask him."

"We will. What about the varnish on the bones?"

"Nothing special about it, just a common clear coat. It can be bought everywhere."

"Did you get anything from the sand and earth around where the bones were found?"

"Nada. Standard sand, no trace of blood or any flesh." Carlito frowned. "I can't tell you anymore. This'll all be in my official report. The rest is up to you. Beat it."

Frick and Frack grumbled their way out of the lab and headed to their desks. Their desks faced each other in the bullpen and were in the window area, a prime location they conscripted since they were the senior men on the force. There wasn't much of a view save the parking lot, but at least one could see the outdoors, the sky and sun. It was overcast today, but warm. The clouds seemed to promise a glimpse of blue sky later in the day. The weather forecast decreed sunny and warm for the next five days.

"So," Frack said as he plunked his substantial butt into his creaky chair, "do we even know if there's been a crime, or if these bones were from a skeleton that was not nefariously acquired?"

"No idea," Frick said as he opened his top drawer and took out a half-eaten Ding Dong. "There's no sign of foul play. We can't even identify whether the bones belong to a man or woman."

"I had Shooter check out missing persons reports from hereabouts and Albuquerque." Frack swiveled his head and called out, "Shooter. Over here."

Tom "Shooter" Christensen jumped out of his chair across the room and hustled over to Frack. Without waiting to be asked he placed a thin folder in front of Frack and said, "Coupla missing persons, two women and one man."

"How tall were they?" Frick asked.

Shooter frowned. "How tall? Why?"

"Answer the question, apple boy," Frack said coolly.

"Apple boy?"

"Big Apple?"

Shooter rolled his eyes and flipped through the pages. "One woman is five-two. The other one is five-four. The guy was … six-one."

"Bummer," Frick said. "Doesn't match our bones." He glanced up at Shooter. "Carlito estimates the dead guy or gal to be around five-seven. It's not a perfect estimation but it kind of eliminates those missing people."

"Do you want me to expand the search?" Shooter asked.

"Yeah, do that," Frick said. "Put feelers out to the whole state and Arizona."

"Will do," Shooter said and hustled off.

"So, now what?" Frick asked.

"Lunch," Frack said succinctly. "I'm suddenly in the mood for ribs."

"The history of hypnosis is a long one, full of fantasy, excitement, and purpose, but also rife with myths and misconceptions. Practically all ancient cultures used hypnosis in some form for both religious and medical reasons. The exact timeline of the development and use of hypnosis cannot be ascertained, since many instances occurred before the onset of writing. One of the first known documents on the process comes from the Egyptian Ebers papyrus, dated 1550 BC. Another Egyptian record of the use came much later, around the third century AD, mentioning the laying of hands on the patient, and eye fixation.

"The modern concept of hypnotism goes back only two hundred years with Franz Mesmer, a doctor in Germany. The roots of trances go back to time immemorial and were used by shamans, medicine men, and witch doctors. It was generally associated with the occult as well as mythology. It was Mesmer, however, who delved into the physical and psychological explanations of the phenomenon. He developed a hypothesis that some universal fluid was controlled by what he called 'animal magnetism.' In 1784 the French Academy of Medicine disavowed his theory and he and the concept of hypnotism fell into disrepute.

"Hypnosis is the manipulation of a human being's mind and senses involving focused attention, reduced peripheral sight awareness, and an enhanced ability to initiate and succumb to suggestion. The subject of a successful hypnosis is in a trance, or an altered state of reality; i.e., a different mindset than one has normally when awake. In this trance state a person is under the influence of the hypnotist and can accept behavioral suggestions. Hypnosis can be used for losing weight, stopping cigarette smoking, calming anger, and any number of purposes. Most mental health professionals believe that a hypnotized subject cannot, however, be made to do something against their moral fiber," Percy said in conclusion of his explanation of hypnosis to Cameo.

"How does it ... exactly how does it work?" Cameo asked hesitatingly. Her previous hypnotists had barely explained anything of the history or process.

"It's derived from the Greek word hupnos, which means sleep," Tucson replied. "It refers to 'the coming of sleep,' and was only coined in the later nineteenth century. Its meaning changed from that concept revolving around sleep to one denoting artificially induced conditions. Essentially, hypnosis works by altering the subject's conscious state so that the left side of the brain—the analytical side—is shut down, while the right side of the brain—the non-analytical side—is made more alert. The subject's control of the conscious is suspended, and the subconscious mind awoken."

"Let me be clear," Percy said. "At no time are you unconscious or asleep, and you are not under anyone's control. You won't do anything you don't want to do."

Cameo smiled weakly. "So, you won't make me run around clucking like a chicken."

"I didn't say that," Percy said, a smile tugging at his lips.

"He did make a lady strip down and do a pole dance during a dinner party once," Tucson said, deadpan. He quickly backpedaled. "Just kidding."

Cameo stared at Tucson for a few seconds then burst out laughing. She wiped a tear from her eye and said, "This is the first time in all these years that I actually feel that someone can really help me."

"At the very least," Percy said in his booming baritone, "we can make you laugh."

"So, you said that a doctor tried to hypnotize you once before," Tucson said. Cameo nodded. "What was the outcome?"

"He said he couldn't get me to relax enough. I couldn't free up my mind. He thought I was resisting him."

"Were you?" Percy asked.

"Maybe," she admitted. "It was about six months after I got out of the hospital. I was in a state of mental chaos. My body felt like the muscles were twisted. I couldn't get more than two hours sleep each night. He prescribed sleeping pills, but I didn't want any drugs in my system. After a few sessions I just gave up and moved on. He never gave me much of an explanation."

"Is that how you wound up here?" Tucson asked.

Cameo nodded. "I began investigating doctors that might be better talented in hypnosis. I found one in New York City, but he was too full of himself and saw me as a paycheck, not a person in need. I learned of one doctor in Philly that might be able to help, but by the time I got there he'd retired and wouldn't take me on as a client. He recommended a psychology firm in D.C."

"That didn't work out?" Percy said.

"I thought it might, but no luck there, either. I worked my way down the coast, even trying, um, non-traditional methods."

"How non-traditional?" Tucson asked, his curiosity peaked.

"A couple of psychics, and a couple of, well ... voodoo practitioners."

"Cameo ..." Tucson began, a frustrated tone in his voice.

"I know, I know. But I was desperate. When I was in North Carolina I even found an Indian shaman and spent a hellacious night in a sweat lodge trying to force the past out of my pores."

"You can die in one of those things if you don't know what you're doing," Tucson said. "It's not like a sauna."

"You said you hit some voodoo practitioners?" Percy asked. "Where?"

"New Orleans. Baton Rouge. Actually, it was one in New Orleans that suggested I head west and come here."

"Really?" Percy said. He and Tucson looked at one another. Percy got an odd feeling.

"Really. She even suggested the specific investigative firm, which is why I turned up on your brother's doorstep."

"What was her name?" Percy asked.

"I don't think it's her real name, but she called herself Lady Cheval. She had a small shop off Bourbon Street, and I saw her maybe three or four times. She said she wouldn't take my money because she couldn't help me, then recommended Memphis Grayhawk. I asked her how she knew him, but she wouldn't say, and then one day I couldn't find her. So, I bought a plane ticket to Albuquerque and came here."

"What did she look like?" Percy asked.

"An elderly black woman. She wore colorful clothes and a hat that seemed African. She spoke with a French accent. There was an air of cigar smoke about her although I never saw her actually smoke."

"So, she didn't say how she knew about our firm?"

"She said she knew someone who interacted with you a long time ago. I didn't press her. Then one day she seemed to vanish and when I asked around no one knew that name. When I tried to describe her people seemed to be put off and wouldn't give me the time of day. It was odd, but I figured I had nothing to lose and if I didn't find anything in Santa Fe I'd head to L.A. or San Francisco and try my luck there."

"Have you had any contact with the original detectives in the past five years?" Tucson asked.

"Not much. When they hit a dead end, I think they lost interest in me."

Percy tapped his pen on Tucson's desk. "I'm curious—what did the so-called psychics tell you?"

Cameo sighed. "The usual bullshit. That I had a bad childhood. That I had a trauma in my life. That I could benefit from multiple sessions to unlock my soul." She shuddered. "I spent thousands on them before I came to my senses." She paused, then looked both in the eye. "This is my last hurrah."

"What do you mean?" Tucson asked.

"I've spent five years trying to find my past. That means I've really lost five years of my present. I don't think I want to spend my life looking for something I may never find or may find but regret. Maybe it's time to move on."

"Maybe," Tucson said, nodding, "but let's see if this last hurrah is worth the effort."

"You might indeed find something you'd prefer not to know about," Percy said thoughtfully, "but you may find something wonderful. A family. Parents. Siblings. People that love you and may be looking for you, too. I know from personal experience that unlocking the past has both pain and joy, but the joy far outweighed the pain. Isn't that worth a try?"

"I suppose it is," Cameo said quietly. She smiled suddenly. "I think I may have turned your brother and his wife around as far as taking me on. I still don't think Swan likes me much, but she seemed willing to listen, and she asked a lot of questions. I have another meeting with them tomorrow. So, when do you want to start this trance thing? And which of you will be doing it?"

"I will," Percy said. "I knew this discipline would be extremely beneficial to a successful psychology practice, so a few years ago I sought out specialized training."

"The Amazing Kreskin?" Cameo said lightly.

Percy smiled. "No, his class was filled. I spent a few months in classes at the Hypnosis Motivation Institute. It's in Tarzana, north of Los Angeles. It was founded in 1968 by Dr. John Kappas, a prominent psychologist that specialized in subconscious behavior. I've also spent time with other well-respected hypnotists to learn more and delve into the ins and outs of hypnotherapy. I'm by no means an expert, but I've used the technique successfully on several clients with good and bad results."

"Bad results?" Cameo said, her eyebrow arching.

"Sometimes people unearth things they'd rather not, and it changes them. That could be the case with you, just a fair warning."

"Consider me warned. Is there any special preparation you or I need to do?"

"I'd just like you to relax for a few days and try to be as receptive to the whole process as possible. I'd like to perform the session in a quiet, safe place, so I suggest the den at my home. My wife works at the hospital and our daughter is here all day in the family childcare center. Tucson will be present, too."

"I live at Percy's house, by the way," Tucson said.

"You do?" Cameo exclaimed, surprised.

"It's a long story, but I live in the third-floor turret in the front, kind of like the weird family member no one talks about and would prefer to keep hidden."

"We let him out to work and on special holidays," Percy said. "Except the summer solstice."

"The more I know about this clan the more perplexed and curious I am," Cameo said mildly.

"We usually terrify people, so perplexed is good," Percy said. "Let's schedule our session for Thursday at ten o'clock. Tucson will pick you up and drive you over."

Cameo rose and slung her purse over her shoulder. "Will you two be at the meeting with Memphis tomorrow?"

"He forbad us from attending until he makes up his mind," Tucson said.

Cameo frowned. “Well, I’m sorry, but that’s not what I want, and I’m paying the bill. If you can be there, I’d appreciate it. I’ll handle your brother.”

“I’ll bet you can,” Tucson said. “We’ll be there. Do you need a ride back to your motel?”

“No, I’ll take a taxi.”

“Nonsense,” Percy said. “Tucson will drive you.”

“I’d be happy to,” Tucson agreed. Cameo nodded her acquiescence, and he ushered her out of the office.

“Hmm,” Percy said thoughtfully as he looked out the window and watched his partner open the car door for their new client.

CHAPTER FIVE

Around one hundred miles north of Santa Fe and less than twenty miles from the Colorado border lies the small village named Questa. At the western base of the Taos Mountains (part of the Sangre de Cristo range) it is little more than a speck on the map. Originally named San Antonio del Rio Colorado by its Spanish colonists, the village was later changed to Questa by an unknown postmaster. He misspelled the name chosen by the administration—Cuesta, a Spanish word meaning ridge or slope.

To the west and north lies the Rio Grande Gorge where that river follows a tectonic chasm eight hundred feet deep. To the southeast lies Wheeler Peak, the highest peak in New Mexico, just south of the Red River.

Questa is close to the Kiowa Trail, a Native American trade route that linked the Ute, Kiowa, and Comanche tribes to the north. Although long gone by the 1970s the trail is documented through the discovery of artifacts, remnant paths, and petroglyphs along the western slopes of the Sangre de Cristos. It is generally accepted that the first Spaniard to visit the area was Francisco Vásquez de Coronado, a conquistador who was searching for Cibola, the legendary Seven Cities of Gold. Other gold seekers followed, notably

Juan Humana and Francisco Borilla, who were killed by tribes along the Purgatoire River.

The village was alternately occupied or abandoned ever since its initial colonization. There was a never-ending conflict between the indigenous people and the invaders, and time and time again the invaders put down roots, fled, put down roots, and fled again. Eventually the might and numbers of the colonists overrode the native peoples and Questa became a permanent fixture in the new territory. It wasn't only the Spanish that invaded the area; French-Canadian trappers filtered in during their quest for otter and beaver hides. The eventual names of the inhabitants reflected Native American, Spanish, and French nomenclatures. Jews expelled from Spain also migrated to the territory and settled around Questa; the common name Rael appears often.

The danger and deprivation of searching for gold didn't deter the Spanish or any who came after them. The allure of finding that one mine that could provide untold riches and change a man's life forever never dissipated to the reality of harsh life in the new land. Daring and determined men set up camps and dug mines hoping to find that rich vein. Some found gold; some didn't. Rarely did a find meet expectations or truly change lives. As the decades went by mines were founded, excavated, and then abandoned. Most fell to the inevitability of nature and were forever hidden from the world.

Many of the mines were born through the forced labor of Spanish slaves, Native Americans who were deemed inferior and whose only use was as hard labor for the Spanish colonization. The Pueblo Revolt of 1680 had this sad state of affairs as one of its precursors since the Indians had been subjected to harsh treatment in these mines and life in general for nearly one hundred years. Battles between the conquerors and the conquered drastically reduced the gold mining activity, but it continued over the years; gold was an ever-present lure for desperate or greedy men.

In modern times few thought to search for gold in old or new mines. Most of those looking for an old mine were simply searching for Indian artifacts or simply for the thrill of finding one. A few such searchers met their fate falling down mine shafts, never to be seen again. The lucky ones were found before they expired and had quite a tale with which to regale their family and friends. One such old mine was set back into a steep, craggy rock outcropping deep into the mountains east of Moly Mine Road. The road cuts off north from Route 38 halfway between Questa and Red River and parallels the foot of the mountains for about a mile before it swings north towards Cabresto Lake. There aren't any roads—dirt or otherwise—into the mountains, which are accessible only by foot. It's easy to get lost since there are no landmarks to indicate direction and no maps that indicate anything other than a huge swath of mountain and forest. Still, people find their way in and climb the mountain peaks, including Wheeler Peak, if only to punctuate the commonness of their daily lives with exhilaration and accomplishment.

The man who called himself Po'Pay trudged through familiar paths in the forest, heading for his secret place, a heavy backpack straining his left arm and shoulder. He was a sturdy man in his forties, broad-shouldered with legs like tree trunks and a will of iron. His hawk-bill nose was his most prominent facial feature; after that his deep-set eyes under a protruding brow defined his ethnicity. There were callouses on his strong hands from a lifetime of hard manual work. He rarely exhibited anger or menace but even so something about him made people avoid eye contact, leaving him to his desired solitude. Like his people he approached death with calm stoicism. He feared no one's death, not even his own.

He moved nearly soundlessly through the forest, barely registering his internalized landmarks. A creature of the desert he could close his eyes and not take a misstep. He reached the old mine, pushed away the camouflaging branches at the entrance, and went in for twenty feet, checking on a store of supplies that he'd accumulated over the years. Satisfied that no one had invaded his storage place, he picked up a few needed supplies and left the mine, continuing on to his final destination two miles away. When he reached that sacred place he carefully placed his backpack on the ground so as not to disturb the contents. He deftly moved the camouflage away from the cave entrance, which was invisible to the naked eye. He had found this place when he was a teenager and had come here many times. When after many years he realized and accepted his calling he chose this place as his temple.

When the brush was moved away, he turned on his flashlight and illuminated the inside of the cave. He checked the trap he always set; it hadn't been sprung so he knew no one had entered his special place since the last time he was there. He retrieved the backpack and carried it inside, laying it down so he could pull the concealing shrubs and branches so that the cave opening was no longer visible from the outside. He had pounded stakes into the walls of the cave every ten feet and appended torches to them. He lit each one as he made his way deeper into the cave. He was in the process of installing electrical wires run by a gas generator so that the cave interior could be well lit; that task was almost complete. When he arrived at the place on which he was currently working he lay the backpack down and kneeled on the ground in front of the carefully constructed circle. He touched his forehead to the center of the circle and murmured, "Beehaz'aani."

Then he went to work.

Sand expelled a deep, exhausted breath as he pulled into his condo garage. He'd been driving nonstop from Phoenix where his latest case had taken him for the past week. Phoenix was in the middle of a hot spell and the one hundred-plus degrees was just too damn hot. The next person who dared opine, "But it's a dry heat" would wind up digesting a knuckle sandwich. He was glad that he lived in a high elevation that mitigated the summer temperatures. At least his trip was successful, and he got the photos and documents needed to ensure that Mrs. Barker got a fair settlement in her contentious divorce. He hated the occasional divorce work that the firm took on, but this time the outcome was more than satisfactory. She was a sweet, decent woman and needed help with her deceitful soon-to-be-ex spouse.

Sand had spied the bruises on her wrist when she met with him and Memphis even though she tried to pull her blouse cuff over them. She had averted her eyes, but he knew that she knew that he had seen the light yellow and purple skin that bespoke of a brutal grasp. Still, she was tough enough to make the decision to leave her abusive husband and seek a better life for her and for her daughter. The little girl sat by Skye's desk while her mother met with the men who would help her mommy.

After she left Sand nearly exploded and said he'd like to beat the son of a bitch into the ground, but Memphis pointed out that that was illegal, and the best place to hit an abuser like the one they were dealing with would be in the pocket. That necessitated evidence of his infidelity and abuse. Sand tailed the guy around Santa Fe for several days and then to Albuquerque, and when he found out about a "business" trip to Phoenix he jumped into his car and followed the man there.

It was almost too easy, finding his girlfriends and watching him spend money on one-night bimbos and in rough bars. Sand had a mountain of evidence that would produce a decent settlement of alimony and child support. Every night after he'd finished stalking the guy, he'd take a long, hot shower to wash off the stink of the man's disgusting behavior. He also swore to himself that this would be his last divorce case. Memphis could hand any new ones over to the newbie.

He hauled his suitcase out of the trunk of his fire-engine-red Firebird and headed up to his condo. He expected it to be empty, but as soon as he opened the door, he smelled the tantalizing aromas of spicy cooking wafting from the kitchen. That could only mean one thing—Akiro was here and was whipping up a gourmet welcome-home meal. Thank God he didn't stop at KFC.

"I'm home," he called, and a pot clattered in response. Akiro came out of the kitchen wearing a silly apron with "Love the Cook" embroidered on it. He had on oven mitts and a wide smile.

And nothing else.

"Now that's the way to welcome home a loved one," Sand said, laughing.

"I'm just glad it was you," Akiro said. He winked, then turned, wiggled his bare butt, and headed back into the kitchen. "Take a shower," he threw over his shoulder. "I can smell you from here."

Sand dropped his clothes in a pile as he headed into the bathroom and stood under the cool water for ten minutes. He lathered and rinsed then did it again until his skin felt squeaky clean and all the grit of the road had vanished. He threw on a pair of jeans and a tee-shirt and padded into the kitchen barefoot where his now-clothed boyfriend was piling enchiladas onto his dinner plate. He gave Akiro a fast peck on the lips before sitting down and attacking the food.

In between bites he said, "Did you really have to slip on a pair of pants? I kind of liked the other view."

Akiro smiled slyly and poured a margarita into a big tumbler. "Just a glimpse of coming attractions. How was Phoenix?"

"Hot and crowded. But I got what I needed."

"Did you find the guy holed up with his girlfriend?"

"I found that girlfriend and the one he was cheating on her with. Mrs. Barker's going to get more than a fair shake in divorce court." Sand dumped a few tablespoons of tabasco sauce on his enchilada. "How's it going with the Lopez case?"

Akiro sighed. "The state Supreme Court is taking the appeal under advisement, but I don't hold out much hope. He's exhausted all but this appeal."

"Can't say that I'm sorry," Sand said, knowing it would set Akiro's teeth on edge. Akiro was brought in last-minute on a death penalty appeals case for a man who had been on Death Row for fifteen years. Miguel Lopez was convicted of raping and strangling a thirteen-year-old girl to death and throwing her body in a dumpster. Taking on the case was a sore point between the men. Akiro wasn't sure he believed in the death penalty, and his indecision had prompted him to take the case. The convicted man had only been sixteen when he committed the crime. Sand, however, had no qualms about the death penalty, opining only that it should be used faster and more often. They'd argued that point quite a lot.

"Remember our deal?" Akiro said. "Let's not talk about it."

"Works for me," Sand said. "Anything happen at work that I should know about?" He had touched base only briefly with Memphis during his stay in Phoenix. Memphis mentioned a new client but didn't give any details.

"You can catch up tomorrow," Akiro said. "I do know you've got a new client that is using both your side of the street as well as Tucson's and Percy's. I've seen her come and go a couple of times in the lobby and hallway."

"She?"

"Yup. A looker, mid-twenties. I think Tucson's intrigued by her."

"That would be wonderful," Sand said. His friend had been wrapped up in himself and away from real human contact save his family since he came home. To Sand's knowledge Tucson hadn't even had a date in the last six years unless he met a woman during the year he stayed away. He never mentioned Cassidy or why she left, and no one wanted to pry. No one had heard from her in all those years. Sand wondered idly where she had gone. He'd asked Caleb Winsted a couple of times if he'd heard from his former star reporter, but Caleb hadn't.

"I've been thinking," Akiro said as he salted his Spanish rice.

"That always scares me," Sand replied archly.

"I've been thinking that maybe it's time we moved in together. I know the laws are still on the books, but that's going to change, and soon, I think. Anyway, I sincerely doubt that anyone would try to prosecute either of us given our respective reputations and accomplishments. It would be bad publicity."

Sand stared at his longtime lover and put down his fork. "I've been waiting for you to say that."

"Why didn't you say it first?"

"Because I'm a stubborn idiot."

"Well, at least we have our roles accurately defined." Akiro laughed and rushed to Sand and they embraced. When they broke apart Akiro said, "This place is too small for us. So's mine. How about we find an actual house to buy together?"

"I get the distinct impression you have one in mind," Sand said, arching an eyebrow suspiciously.

"As it so happens, I have a client that's selling his house and moving to California. God knows why. The price is right, and we can close in three weeks. Interested in seeing it?"

"Where is it?"

"It's equidistant between the office and my parents' house. A half-acre, fenced, great mountain views. Lemon and grapefruit trees in the back yard. Three bedrooms. Huge den and a two-car garage. We need to upgrade the kitchen appliances and re-panel the living room, but except for a coat of paint it's in move-in condition. We'll go see it tomorrow."

"You've drawn up the papers, haven't you?"

"All I need is your signature and half the down payment."

"What if I said no?"

"I'd strip off the pants and put the apron back on and entice you with wild, wanton sex."

"And if I say yes?"

"I'll just strip off the pants. You'd still get the wild, wanton sex."

"You know how to get to me, don't you?"

"You may be a big, bad ex-cop private eye, but I've got your number."

"Take off the pants."

There were only shadows, really, coming from the second-floor window of the condo, but the watcher knew that Sand Hazelwood and his romantic partner were moving about, having dinner, probably. Sand had been under surveillance off and on for years, just to keep abreast of his life. He was doing well, and apparently happy. His sexuality was out in the open although the outing was unkind and damaging to his career. Now, he had a new career and was making it work. He was stable. He was safe. The watcher needed safe.

The chosen life was getting more dangerous and more problematic.

The innocent needed a safe haven.

Innocent was something the watcher hadn't been for far too long.

It was too late to go back.

But it wasn't too late for him.

Soon, the watcher thought. Soon.

CHAPTER SIX

"Tucson, turn on the camera," Percy said. Tucson turned the camera on and checked the focus through the viewfinder before returning to his seat. He had a tape recorder on the end table next to Cameo and turned that on, too, so he could have the verbalizations transcribed.

Percy said, "Today is Thursday, September 19, 1974. It's ten-fifteen in the morning. Present are psychologists Dr. Percival McBean, myself, psychologist Dr. Tucson Grayhawk, and Ms. Cameo Adams. This session is taking place in my home den. Ms. Adams has consented to a hypnotherapy session in order to retrieve memories lost to her after a trauma five years ago. Ms. Adams—do you consent to this session?"

"I consent," Cameo said.

"There are several ways to hypnotize a subject," Percy said. He was sitting in a wing chair three feet away from Cameo, who was facing him. Tucson sat to the left of Percy. They were in the Victorian's den. The bay window curtains were drawn with just a slit to let in a little bit of daylight. There were two Tiffany lamps providing light; between them a Super 8 video camera was set up to record the session. No one else was in the house; Tansee was at the hospital and Elspeth was in the family daycare. All three were dressed very casually, for comfort rather than style. Cameo wore a washed-out pair of bellbottom jeans and a loose linen blouse. She wore no jewelry and her hair was brushed back from her face so that her eyes were unencumbered. She had slipped off her sandals and her bare feet were tucked under her as she nestled on a plush loveseat beside the fireplace.

"You said you've been hypnotized before?" Tucson asked.

Cameo nodded. "Sort of. It didn't really work."

"What method did the doctor use?" Percy asked.

"He dangled a gold pocket watch in front of me and told me I was getting sleepy." A smile tugged at her full lips.

"Classy," Tucson murmured.

"We won't use a gold watch this time," Percy said. "The best results will come from a subject's comfort with all aspects of the process, including the hypnotist, the surroundings, the sounds, the physical senses, and anything else that a person expects to encounter in a normal world. It also depends upon the commitment of the subject—"

"I would feel more comfortable if you would stop referring to me as 'the subject,' Percy," Cameo said quietly.

"I'm sorry," Percy said immediately. "You're absolutely right. Sometimes in my practice I tend to divorce myself from familiarity to ensure the most professional session. That protects me, too, from getting emotionally involved. If I become too emotionally involved, it hinders my ability to help you. I don't mean to seem cold."

"I understand," Cameo said, softening. Neither psychologist was anything except warm and caring. Rather than diving directly into a hypnosis session they had spent a few days introducing her to the concepts of psychology. Memphis had done the same as he and Swan laid out a plan for delving into her past. They had given her the time to see them as human beings and vice versa. For the first time in a long time she had genuine hope.

"Good," Percy said. "Let me explain in a nutshell what we'll be doing today. This session is not going to be a long or intense one where miracle of miracles we unlock your past. This is a session to ease both of us into a symbiotic relationship which will extend and deepen when we're both comfortable with each other and the process. There are three steps, however, that will define any session we undertake. One, induction. That's the process by which I will entice you into a trance. Two, the analytic and suggestion process. That will be a series of questions, statements, and suggestions meant to tease out the knowledge we are seeking. And three, the exit process whereby I bring you out of the trance and return you to your normal conscious state. Do you understand?"

"I understand."

"What are your questions?"

"You're assuming I have questions," Cameo said.

"An intelligent, determined person such as yourself must have questions. If you didn't, I'd be concerned."

"Don't be concerned. How long will this session take?"

"Perhaps thirty minutes if you're receptive to the induction. If not, longer or, depending on your physical reactions, shorter if I determine it best to end the session." Percy gestured at a stethoscope on the end table. "My wife instructed me how to use this to determine whether you have an elevated heart rate."

"What do you hope to achieve by this first session?"

"A determination of how susceptible you are to the process and how to proceed depending upon your reactions."

"What would you consider a success?"

"A normal heart rate and other typical physical reactions, and hopefully some tidbit extracted from deep down inside you to guide us in further efforts."

"What would you consider a failure?"

"Nothing. There is no failure in this process. Anything we learn is a success."

"Will I come out of this clucking like the proverbial chicken?"

"He actually makes people quack like a duck," Tucson said. "We lost a client up at Spirit Lake last year by a hunter. But I promise to rein him in."

"Thank you," Cameo said. She shrugged her shoulders and took a deep breath. "I'm ready."

"I'm going to start by showing you a series of photographs. I'll speak the image as well to record it and face it towards the camera after I show it to you. For each one I want you to say the first thing that pops into your head whether or not it's a description or just how the picture makes you feel. I want to gauge your reaction to visual stimuli. Ready?" Percy said.

"Ready," Cameo said firmly. She shrugged her shoulders again and relaxed her body.

Percy showed Cameo a photo of a red rose.

"Pretty," Cameo said instantly.

A photo of a rocky ocean coastline.

"Peaceful."

A photo of a campfire.

Cameo paused. "I don't … I don't know."

"That's fine," Percy said, and he revealed a photo of Notre Dame Cathedral.

Cameo said nothing and shook her head.

A photo of the Grand Canyon.

"Red."

A photo of the Housatonic River.

"Confused. Sad."

A photo of a ceramic sugar skull; Cameo began mildly hyperventilating so Percy quickly put the photo down. He flashed a photo of a St. Bernard puppy.

"Soft," Cameo said, her breathing back to normal.

Percy flashed a half dozen pictures of nature and Cameo had an immediate, positive response to all of them. He seemed to be finishing up when he flashed the coastline photo again close to her face.

"Home," Cameo said immediately. She was startled and her body tightened.

"Interesting," Tucson murmured.

"Yes," Percy agreed. "However, let's not rush to judgment." He looked at Cameo. "This could mean nothing more than you enjoy water scenes. Or, it could mean you're from a location close to water or have a spent a lot of time there. There are multiple interpretations."

"But," Tucson interjected, "since you said the word so quickly and instinctively, it most likely means you've unlocked something from your past that we need to explore."

"I'd like to attempt a trance now, a minimal one just to see how suggestible you are," Percy said. "When I'm ready to bring you out I'll snap my fingers twice."

"I'm ready," Cameo replied, her voice strong and determined. She brushed a lock of her hair behind her ear and straightened. She unfolded her legs from under her and sat in a normal seated position, her bare feet flat on the floor. She let her hands rest casually in her lap, her fingers interlocked.

"Good," Percy said. He held up the coastline photo. "Look at this. Focus on it and try to block out anything else visual. Look at every nuance, every rock, every wisp of a wave. Picture the sounds that might be surrounding this scene, from the hiss of the water hitting the rocks to the screeing of nearby seagulls. Think about the salt water, how it would taste on your tongue, how it would feel on your skin. Think about this and nothing else."

Percy stopped speaking and the silence hung heavy in the den, heavy but not oppressive, heavy with a thread of electricity between the hypnotist and the subject. Cameo stared at the photo without blinking, her eyes totally focused on the image as a whole and each of its components. The silence soon became an imagined tapestry of ocean sounds, like the waves hitting the rocks. Without being asked to, she closed her eyes and swayed gently.

"Is the picture in your mind, Cameo?" Percy asked quietly. She nodded slowly. "Keep focusing on that image. Let it take you back, back to where you've experienced the associated sensations before. Can you taste the salt water?"

"Yes," Cameo replied in a distant monotone.

"Do you like the feel of the water on your skin?"

"Yes."

"What else do you feel on your skin?"

"The sun. Hot. My face burns."

"Does it hurt?"

"No. It feels good."

"What do you smell?"

"Salt." Cameo frowned; her eyes still closed. "Roasting … meat … hotdogs. Cinnamon."

"Can you taste them?"

"Yes."

"Does eating them make you happy or merely full?"

Cameo smiled; her eyes still shut tightly. "Happy."

"Are you alone?"

Cameo frowned again. Her lips parted. "No," she whispered.

"Who's with you, Cameo?"

"Mommy."

"What is she doing?"

"Holding my hand."

"Is her hand bigger than yours or the same size?"

"Bigger."

"Are you a little girl?"

"Yes."

"Is your daddy with you?" When there was no response from Cameo, Percy asked the question again.

Percy and Tucson nearly fell off their chairs when Cameo let out a bloodcurdling scream that tore through the still air like an explosion. Her eyes popped open and she began hyperventilating. Tucson jumped up and grabbed her shoulders and shook her until the focus returned to her eyes. He stood behind her chair still holding onto her shoulders. Percy snapped his fingers twice then grabbed the stethoscope and placed the diaphragm on her chest.

"Easy, easy," he said softly as he listened and counted. He finished and pulled the earpieces out. "One-twenty beats. Normal is between sixty and one hundred. Just breathe and relax for a few minutes. Don't speak." Percy held her hand and was surprised at her strength as she grasped his tightly. Percy took her heart rate again. "Ninety. Good."

"That's more than enough for today," Tucson said. He turned off the camera and tape recorder.

"No, no," Cameo said. "Let's keep going. I don't remember what I said but I just feel in my bones that it was important."

"You don't remember?" Percy asked.

Cameo shook her head and said, "Can you tell me? Or can I watch the video?"

"Tucson and I need to have the film processed and analyze every detail so that we can come to a consensus on what precisely happened and how to proceed. Of course, we'll tell you what happened. You need to know, but first we need to understand."

"But as far as today goes," Tucson said, "that's more than enough on your part. You need to rest and relax."

"How long will it take for the film to be developed?"

"I've got a buddy at a camera shop, so we'll put a rush on it. Until we get it back, Percy and I will go over the notes I've made and the tape recording."

"Can we get together tomorrow?" Cameo asked eagerly.

Percy shook his head. "That's too soon for us to analyze the session. Let's just all take a few days and we'll meet at the office Monday morning." He held a hand up when he saw she was about to protest. "Cameo, please. We've made some genuine progress here today and we've just started. We're going to make more progress, so I'm asking you to be patient, and trust us."

"I do," she said softly. "I do trust you, both of you. And your friend, Memphis. You've all given me more hope than I've had for a very long time. I'll be patient. I'll try to relax."

"You like lakes and mountains?" Tucson asked suddenly. Cameo nodded. "How about I take you up to our family cabin for the day Saturday and we can talk, and hike, and you can enjoy the serenity of the forest and the lake. I guarantee you'll be able to relax."

"You know, I'd love that," she said.

"Good," Percy said. "I'm sure you can both use the break. You have to promise us one thing, though."

"What's that?" Cameo asked.

"No badgering Tucson about our analysis or thoughts. Just take the day off from your quest."

Cameo smiled widely. "I promise." She took in a deep breath then let it out. "I feel … relaxed."

"Good. Tucson will drive you back to your motel. He'll—"

Percy's last sentence was interrupted by the slamming of a door and a high-pitched child's voice yelling, "Daddy! Daddy! I'm hoooooooooome!" The words were punctuated with a soft clump-clump-clump of a child running down the hallway just before a tiny fist knocked vigorously on the den's closed door. Elspeth didn't wait for an invitation and barreled into the den followed by her mother.

Percy stood immediately and Elspeth threw herself into her father's arms, nearly knocking him over. At thirty-six inches tall Elspeth was just sixteen inches shorter than her father. At three years old she was sturdy yet slender, with long sable hair done up in a single French braid; her dark chocolate eyes were intelligent and lively, and her infectious giggle was like a tinkling glass windchime.

Tansee was wearing her scrubs. She said, "Antonia said El had a slight cough, so I decided to check her out at the hospital." Before Percy could interrogate her, she continued. "She's fine, just a little throat tickle, but since I have the weekend off, I thought I'd bring her home early." Tansee smiled and stuck her hand out towards Cameo. "Tansee McBean, Percy's wife and mother to the little whirlwind that nearly knocked him over. You must be Cameo Adams. It's a pleasure to meet you."

"Likewise," Cameo said, liking Tansee instantly.

Tansee went on. "I'm sorry we interrupted. I'll take the little monkey upstairs while you finish up."

"We're finished," Percy said. "Tucson was just about to drive Cameo home."

"Really?" Tansee said. She turned to Cameo. "Why don't the two of you stay for lunch?"

"I think Tucson was going to take Cameo out to lunch," Percy said quickly.

"Oh," Tansee replied. She paused for a beat. "Oh. That's great. Maybe next time." She smiled widely at Tucson. "Bye."

Tucson and Cameo said their goodbyes and Percy escorted them to the front door. Tansee followed, carrying Elspeth. The McBeans stood at the open door and waved as Tucson drove away.

As Percy shut the door Tansee laughed and said, "You sly little fellow."

"What?"

"That was so subtle. A masterpiece in subtlety. Why didn't you just shove her into his arms?"

"Too obvious?"

"Uh … *yeah*." She let Elspeth slide down and took her hand as she led her husband and daughter into the kitchen.

"I think he's intrigued by her, perhaps more than just professionally. He's been without companionship for far too long," Percy said as he pulled out the kitchen table chair for Elspeth and helped her climb on. "It wouldn't hurt for him to come out of his shell."

"I agree with that sentiment," Tansee said as she took the pastrami out of the fridge, "but she may not be the right kind of woman. Let's face it—she has an unknown past and a very uncertain future. Tucson's still fighting his demons and I think he needs more stability to help with that."

"That has to be up to him."

"What if she's married? Has kids? A husband that's been looking for her and wants her back?"

"The medical report from the hospital in Pittsfield stated that she had never given birth or had an abortion."

"You know what I mean," Tansee said crossly as she sliced the rye bread. With her swift and sure technique Percy thought she could have been a surgeon.

"I know what you mean. Let's just take it a day at a time. What kind of mustard do you want—yellow or brown?"

"Yellow, of course. Have I taught you nothing in all these years?"

"You've taught me everything."

"Bear that in mind next time you decide to play matchmaker. Get the cheddar cheese out of the crisper."

CHAPTER SEVEN

Po'Pay sanded a sharp edge off the pelvic bone. He had prepared the skeleton as he usually did, stripping the flesh off it with his tiny little helpers. The bones were clean and smooth. Now, he needed to bleach them as white as he could before he shellacked them in preparation for their final disposition. Those processes would take three days. Even then he would have to wait for the remaining bones that would accompany them to their resting place; another week or ten days. He was in no hurry.

He carried the disarticulated bones into the boiling room and gently placed them in the water. He added the bleach. He'd let them soak for a day, then turn on the fire for the last couple of hours. There was nothing else he needed to do with these bones right now. He sighed and debated with himself whether to continue his work or take a break for lunch. He was hungry. He had prepared a Tupperware container full of his favorite dish, squash blossoms stuffed with blue corn mush. He liked cooking his native foods, generally eschewing modern food—especially fast food—for homemade, nutritious, and traditional meals. However, he had strayed today and picked up a huge blueberry muffin at the local bakery. He sprang up the basement stairs.

When he finished the squash blossoms, he washed out the plastic container, then poured himself a glass of milk and went about devouring the muffin. He brushed the crumbs onto a napkin meticulously and tossed it in the trash. Then he descended to the basement. He could hear the mewling even before he got to the bottom of the stairs. He opened the door and the mewling stopped.

The woman's terror-filled eyes riveted on his face from her corner of the basement where she was bound, gagged, and chained. She stank; after a week of voiding her bladder and bowels on herself she stank of both the urine and feces but even more strongly of the sickening fear that saturated every cell of her body. Her long blonde hair was straggly and greasy from the sweat that had flooded out of her pores; there were tear streaks down her grimy face. She began involuntarily yipping behind the tight gag.

Po'Pay set the clean dishes and utensils on the small table where he'd feast. He used the same implements that he'd used for the man. For him, Po'Pay had devoured venison stew and acorn bread, and distilled raspberry liquor that he'd made himself. He had eaten slowly, relishing each bite, knowing how important the ritual was. He was doing it for the doomed one, to give him a clean soul when he met his maker. Perhaps the cleansing would work, perhaps not. Still, he considered the ancient practice a viable attempt at salvation.

Sin-eating.

The practice wasn't Native American but mainly European, specifically for the Welsh. True, the Aztecs honored their goddess of the earth, motherhood, and fertility, Tlazolteotl, who had a redemptive role in Meso-American religious practices. When a person came to the end of his life, he would confess his sins to the deity, and she would "cleanse" his soul by consuming its filth.

In non-Native American cultures the sin-eater would consume a ritual meal to assume the sins of a deceased person. The food was believed to absorb the sins of the dead person, thereby absolving his soul. The downside was that the sin-eater himself now carried all the sins of those for whom he had performed the ritual. The practice was documented in several old writings, which Po'Pay had studied when he began his cleansings.

Diarist John Aubrey, who died in 1697, in the earliest source on the practice wrote that "an old Custome" in Herefordshire had been "*at funerals to hire poor people, who were to take upon them all the sinnes of the party deceased. One of them I remember lived in a Cottage on Rosse-high way. (He was a long, lean, ugly, lamentable Raskel.) The manner was that when the Corps was brought out of the house, and layd on the Biere; a Loafe of bread was brought out, and delivered to the Sinne-eater over the Corps, and also a Mazar-bowl of maple (Gossips bowle) full of beer, which he was to drinke up, and sixpence in money, in consideration whereof he took upon him (ipso facto) all the Sinnes of the Defunct, and freed him (or her) from walking after they were dead.*"

A local legend in Shropshire, England, concerned the grave of Richard Munslow, who died in 1906, and was said to be the last sin-eater of the area: "*By eating bread and drinking ale, and by making a short speech at the graveside, the sin-eater took upon themselves the sins of the deceased. The speech was written as: 'I give easement and rest now to thee, dear man. Come not down the lanes or in our meadows. And for thy peace I pawn my own soul. Amen.'*"

Po'Pay found the history and mythology fascinating and decided to adopt it as part of his own rituals. And, since the doomed ones were descendants of that racial branch, he felt it his honorable duty to perform something akin to absolution.

Po'Pay walked to the east wall and flung open the hinged lid which banged loudly against the back of the coffin. He had cleaned it after removing the first set of bones. He had taken pity on the man and slit his throat before dumping him in and introducing the corpse to the little cleaners. He had no pity for the woman. She had desecrated a sacred site and deserved her punishment. He turned back towards her and saw tears streaming from her red eyes like a waterfall. He grabbed the padlock key and made it to her crumpled form in three strides. He choked from the smell.

Po'Pay unlocked the manacles and chains and dragged the woman to her feet. She couldn't stand; her leg muscles were weak. Surprisingly, she tried to put up a struggle. He backhanded her and knocked her down, then grabbed her greasy long hair and dragged her across the floor. Without a wasted movement he swept her up into his arms and dumped her into the coffin. He padlocked the chains across her legs and chest, then simply stared down at her for a long moment. Her eyes were blank; she knew what was coming.

He turned and walked to the corner where the three ten-gallon steel drums were lined up next to one another. Each was heavy and had to be carried back to the coffin individually. When all three were on the floor beside the coffin, he stared down at the woman one last time. Her eyes had rolled back in her head, and her chest barely rose and fell.

He closed his eyes and murmured a comforting prayer that his mother had taught him when he was a young child.

"Hold on to what is good, even if it's a handful of earth. Hold on to what you believe, even if it's a tree that stands by itself. Hold on to what you must do, even if it's a long way from here. Hold on to your life, even if it's easier to let go. Hold on to my hand, even if someday I'll be gone away from you."

He was immediately comforted by the words and the feelings they evoked. In a world of chaos filled with constant change one must hold on to a set of beliefs, a set of actions. His mother had imbued in him the traditions of their people, how sacred they were, not to be breached or disrespected. Transgressions needed to be addressed. It took him years to fully understand this, and to finally act.

He unscrewed the top of the first steel drum and felt a thrill at the hushed crackling sounds of the movement within. He raised the drum, spent five more seconds staring at the woman, then dumped the first load of thousands of dermestid beetles over her warm body. Her eyes refocused and opened wide as she realized what was happening. She managed a scream behind her gag and tried to wriggle out from the restraints, but she couldn't.

Po'Pay quickly dumped the remaining two drums of beetles onto her then shut and locked the coffin. He listened to the sounds within as the insects began eating their living victim. The dozen air holes poked into the coffin lid prevented asphyxiation but allowed for the sweet emanation of feasting noises and the ambient sounds of the victim meeting her fate.

He walked to the stairs and mounted them. He turned off the basement light. When he checked the coffin feasting later to ensure that the entrée was no longer amongst the living, he would fill his plates and feast.

And the woman's sins would not follow her into eternity.

"So, we drop this, right?" Frack said to Captain Reed Carraway. He and Frick were in their superior's office as he studied the scant folder of information on the discovered bones. Carraway had been installed as their captain after Pierce Steele was inelegantly removed from his position and transferred down to Albuquerque where he was overseeing the evidence department.

Carraway closed the folder and looked up at his most senior detectives. "So, to summarize," he said, "we have three bones found in the desert. They're a little odd because of the lacquering, but there's no sign of foul play, and no possible identification of who the bones might have belonged to. I stress the concept of no foul play."

"Well, yes. Yes, that's true," Frick admitted. "Still, Captain, I just have this feeling."

Carraway glanced over to Frack. "You have this feeling, too?"

"Um, sort of," Frack said. "Maybe not as strong as my partner, but I trust his instincts."

"I trust both your instincts, but there's just no proof of any crime. We have real, in-your-face crimes out there and I can't expend any more time on an instinct. Consider this case still open but dormant." He handed Frick a folder. "Two tourists, missing."

Frick glanced at the first page. "This happened a couple of weeks ago."

"I know. Abbott and Dunbar took the call but came up with nothing. One of the kids' fathers is a minor politician in Frisco and he's making noise. I need to get this case resolved. So, I thought a couple of new old eyes might help."

"Old?"

"Your spring chicken days are over, Frack. Deal with it. This'll keep you busy for a while, that and a couple of other cases, until we pop balloons and drink cheap beer at your retirement party. Get on it."

Frack jerked into a straight position, saluted, and said, "Yes, Sir!" He whirled around and marched out of Carraway's office.

Frick grinned. "You'll miss us when we're gone."

"Ah, no," Carraway said lightly. Yes, he would miss them. "Beat it."

Frick flashed off a casual salute and left. Frack was already at his desk studying the new case. Frick sat opposite him and said, "Well? Where do you want to start?"

"Let's talk to Abbott and Dunbar, see what their take is on this that's not in their notes. Then we recreate their steps and see where that takes us." Frack scanned the bullpen and saw that Dunbar and Abbott weren't at their desks. It was high noon, and they never missed lunch. Frick commented on that indisputable fact and Frack agreed to a lunch of their own before settling down to their non-bones case.

Before they could leave the station, Frick got a phone call. He listened for a minute before nodding and hanging up. "That was Nick Griffin," he said to Frack. "He offered to take us to lunch. I get the impression he wants to pick our brains."

"Not much nutrition there," Frack muttered. "Where?"

"The Pink Adobe. Thirty minutes."

"My kind of restaurant," Frack said.

Frick pulled into the Pink Adobe parking lot, which was full considering that it was a weekday and it wasn't quite tourist season yet. The restaurant was a Santa Fe fixture, established by Rosalea Murphy in 1944 on Old Santa Fe Trail. Nick's car was in the lot already. They entered the establishment where Nick was standing by the hostess chatting. He saw them and nodded to the hostess who took them to a wrought iron table and chairs out back on the patio. The table was shaded by a large red umbrella. She placed menus in front of each man then left. A few moments later she returned with glasses of water and a basket of fresh bread.

"Thanks for coming," Nick said. "I know it was short notice, but I figured the enticement of a free meal would make you more inclined." He glanced down at the menu and immediately fixed on the Enchilada Pink Adobe with the green chili with onions. Served on blue corn tortillas with cheese, beans, rice and posole, he ordered it ninety percent of the time that he dined here.

"We're cops," Frick said in his mournful voice. "Free food always entices us. Is this a cheap invite or can we order anything on the menu?" His eye and caught and held the Tournedos Bordelaise, the most tender, perfectly sized, grass-fed filet atop a puff pastry, topped with a mushroom cap and homemade bordelaise sauce. It was served with spinach almandine and a browned potato.

"Anything on the menu, drinks included."

"We're on duty," Frack grumbled. He smiled to himself as he spied the Rack of Lamb; two grilled Colorado lambs chops topped with a mint compound herb butter and served with garlic mashed potatoes, sautéed Brussel sprouts and a jalapeño jelly.

"It's not like I'm going to report you," Nick countered and waved over the waitress who proceeded to take their drink orders, beers all the way around.

"So, why are we here besides the excitement of our scintillating personalities and conversation?" Frack asked.

"That's the main reason, of course," Nick replied, smiling slightly. "The other reason is a new client whose case you might have insight on."

"Yeah?" Frick said. "What kind of case?"

"Missing persons. Two, to be exact."

"Tourists from San Francisco?" Frick said, an eyebrow arched sardonically.

Nick sat back and stared at them. "This your case?"

"As of about forty minutes ago," Frack said. "Dunbar and Abbott were handling it but Carraway wanted fresh eyes."

"And he picked you two?" Nick said skeptically.

"That remark is so going to cost you in terms of the appetizers, entrée, and dessert," Frick said ominously.

"And beers are the least of your worries," Frack added. Just then the waitress returned with their beers. All three were ready to order and Frack added a pitcher of frozen margaritas. At Frick's semi-disapproving look he said, "What are they going to do—fire us?" To the waitress he added, "Make that strawberry."

"I shudder to think what you two will order for dessert," Nick muttered.

"An entire Rosalea's Legendary French Apple Pie," Frick said placidly. "With a pint of homemade vanilla ice cream."

"I underestimated you," Nick said.

"You always did. Now, how's about you tell us about this new client and what you know about the case."

"Fair enough," Nick replied. "Our client is Ellis Geary, a former member of Frisco's Board of Supervisors. I guess that's San Francisco's version of the City Council. He's a lawyer in private practice now, but he still has juice. His daughter, Taylor, and her boyfriend, Stone Powell, graduated college in May and then hit the road to 'explore America the beautiful,' as she said to him. They flew to Boston, bought a cheap car, and began making their way back home while stopping at various famous sites like Gettysburg. She called her dad seventeen days ago and said they were in San Luis, Colorado and were headed down to Santa Fe for a day or two then they'd drive to Albuquerque and head west through Arizona back to California. She estimated that good old Dad would see her in about five days. She promised to call every day, but that was the last call he got from her."

"Did she or the boyfriend have credit cards?" Frick asked.

"Mr. Geary said she had a card for his American Express account, but there was no activity on it since the day before she last called. The boyfriend was a cash-only kind of guy."

"How did this Geary guy wind up on Warrior Spirit's doorstep?" Frack asked.

Nick grinned. "He hit a couple of Frisco P.I. offices and wound up at Lee Jernigan's P.I. firm."

"Why is that name familiar?"

"Lee Jernigan was the P.I. in Los Angeles that helped us on the Frid case. His partner, Adam Manzone, runs the Frisco branch of the firm. When Adam talked to Lee about the case, he suggested our firm since he knew me and Swan. The three of us have kind of a mutual admiration society going. Anyway, I talked to Adam on the phone this morning and he's going to fly out Monday to confer with us. I'd hoped to get an official police perspective, hence the altogether too expensive meals I'll be paying for post-digestion. Sheer luck that I got the actual coppers that have the case."

"You are lucky," Frack said. "Dunbar can't stand your firm and probably wouldn't be too helpful. Frick and I, on the other hand, are easily bribed and we don't dislike you as much. At least, we don't dislike you as much as we used to."

"Thanks. So, what can you tell me about the case?"

"Not much," Frick said. "We just got it and haven't had a chance to talk to the original detectives. We're going to talk to them after lunch. But we'll be happy to powwow with you and this Manzone guy Monday."

"Ten o'clock, my office. Thanks."

"We'll be expecting coffee and donuts," Frick said.

"Of course. I didn't doubt that for a minute. Bagels and cream cheese, too?"

"You really aren't that bad despite the long hair and ridiculous Elvis sideburns."

"Thanks. Here's our food."

The waitress placed the entrée plates in front of each man and another waiter was on her heels with the pitcher of margaritas. She refilled their water glasses, wished them bon appetit, and left. All three of them were starving and fell on the food like jackals. They kept up a running conversation about anything other than the case.

Nick smiled shyly and told them that Yuki was expecting again, and they were the first to know; she'd only told him this morning. They were both hoping for a boy. Frack waxed enthusiastic about being a boy dad, playing baseball, teaching the kid how to swim and box, and especially how to ride a bicycle. Nick pointedly told Frack that he planned on doing all those things with Mariko.

Damned if Frack didn't order a whole pie and ice cream to go, but Nick anted up the payment cheerfully and drove off to his office while Frick and Frack returned to the precinct.

Dunbar and Abbott were back from lunch, apparently at Burger King based on the fast-food wrappers covering their desks. They seemed to be done so Frick and Frack cornered them and asked about the case. Dunbar was grouchy; he didn't like his case being reassigned. Abbott was a little less perturbed since he hadn't considered the case either interesting or important. Grudgingly, they gave Frick and Frack as much insight as they could, filling in a few details that weren't in their notes.

Frick asked if they'd found the kids' car, but since Mr. Geary didn't even know the make and model, it was impossible. There was no record of a car sale to either young person in Boston, so they might have bought it for cash from a stranger and not even reregistered it. As far as abandoned and stolen cars, well, the area was rife with them, but none showed any evidence of the missing couple or any violence.

Dunbar went over the list of regional people that he had interviewed, from motel clerks to car repair shops to cheap eateries. No one in Santa Fe had seen or heard from the couple. He and Abbott had driven north and hit each town and enclave to the Colorado border, including the Taos Pueblo and San Luis, Colorado, where the missing kids apparently made their last phone call to the girl's father. They even hit towns around San Luis, including San Acacio, Chama, Mesita, Garcia, and Jaroso. A gas station attendant in San Luis thought he might have serviced them, but he couldn't identify their photos or describe their car. Abbott said they touched base with the San Francisco police and the girl's family but got nowhere. No, they didn't know that the father had hired a Frisco P.I.; that was a new development.

Frick and Frack squeezed every bit of information they could get then understood that no more would be forthcoming, so they let Dunbar and Abbott off the hook. Frick knew a couple of cops in San Francisco so he called one and asked him to see what he could find out about this P.I. guy Manzone. He wanted to be prepared for the Monday meeting. He sensed that this might be an interesting case, one into which he could sink his teeth. Maybe he and his partner only had a few months of cop time left but that didn't mean they couldn't do top-notch work and accomplish something meaningful. He felt a sudden sense of sadness that his investigative abilities would soon be in the past. He just couldn't see himself staying at home cuddling Bast for entertainment. He knew that Frack felt the same way although he might enjoy spending more time with Pierre. Ever since his wife Carly had passed away two years earlier Frack was even more attached to his pet and his partner.

The two detectives spent the rest of the afternoon reviewing the case file and statements and made a tentative plan that would be fleshed out after Monday. The Frisco P.I. probably had some detailed information that Abbott and Dunbar were missing since the gumshoe was new to the case.

Frack commented that he wished he knew the guy so he could have him bring a couple of loaves of sourdough bread with him. Frack had been to Frisco several times and every time he hit Fisherman's Wharf for a bread bowl full of clam chowder. They agreed that it would be rude to ask the favor of a stranger.

At six they clocked out for the day and went to Frick's house for some leftover spaghetti and meatballs. They spent a lot of evenings together enjoying their long friendship and staving off the loneliness each widower had in his heart.

The two bottles of Boone's Farm Sangria while watching the Friday night NBC lineup—*Sanford and Son*, *Chico and the Man*, *The Rockford Files*, and *Police Woman*—were quite satisfying. Both men were of the opinion that Angie Dickinson was one hot babe.

CHAPTER EIGHT

"The news is depressing," Cameo said as Tucson drove up to Spirit Lake. She was reading the *Sangre de Cristo Courant* and the *Santa Fe New Mexican* as the car smoothly ran along the paved roads before it got to the bumpy, rutted dirt roads leading to the cabin. Tucson mentioned that his father was going to have a strip of road leading to the cabin paved but he hadn't gotten around to it. He and Hehewuti were out of town for a couple of months on a cruise from L.A. to Sydney, Australia; Jakub was hired to provide musical entertainment and Hehewuti came along to find a good poker game. At nineteen Luc was old enough to stay at home while he commuted to college and took care of his feisty sixteen-year-old sister; besides, they were right next door to Memphis.

Tucson hmm'd as he kept focused on the road and tried to ignore the beautiful woman very close to him. He thought it best to let her read.

Cameo studied the two newspapers. The *Courant* had a front-page story on the Kootenai War. Native American Amelia Cutsack Trice, the chairwoman of the Kootenai Tribal Council in Bonners Ferry, Idaho was a fervent advocate for her people. At her prompting the tribe declared war on the United States of America.

The Kootenai Indians lived in teepees near Bonners Ferry, Idaho. Their lands had been dissipated by the BIA, the Bureau of Indian Affairs, not a surprising situation given the terrible treatment of Indians over the last several hundred years. A compassionate local doctor somehow persuaded the government to build them eighteen houses in the 1930s. The buildings had running water but no bathing facilities other than at a community center. By the 1970s nothing had changed for the small tribe; the people were poor and existing in substandard conditions.

On September 20, 1974 Amy Trice and her people declared war. Tribal members set up informational pickets and asked for ten-cent tolls on U.S. Highway 95 on the north and south sides of Bonners Ferry. This didn't sit well with authorities, and soon enough State Police arrived with mace and sawed-off shotguns.

The standoff was still tense, and Trice was threatening to call on the American Indian Movement (AIM) for assistance in resolving the matter to the tribe's benefit. Only the year before, 1973, the AIM had gotten into an armed standoff at Wounded Knee, South Dakota. AIM leaders Dennis Banks and Russell Means were indicted for their actions, but the case had been dismissed this year. Means was known for his occupation tactics to further his causes. Several of his efforts were well-publicized. He had helped occupy Alcatraz in 1969; he had helped occupy the *Mayflower II* in Boston on Thanksgiving Day, 1970; in 1971 he helped take over Mount Rushmore; and in November 1972 he and others had occupied the Bureau of Indian Affairs in Washington, D.C. causing over two million dollars' worth of damage.

Cameo mentioned the story to Tucson who said he hoped that the government capitulated; not surprising given the fact that he was half-Indian. *And a damned handsome half-breed, too*, she thought before refocusing her attention on the papers.

Three members of the Japanese Red Army, a communist group founded in Lebanon in 1971 and dedicated to overthrowing Japan's monarchy, stormed the French embassy in the Netherlands on September 13, 1974, taking the ambassador and ten others hostage. The reason? The JRA's leader, Fusaku Shigenobu, was being held in a French prison. It had taken five days of tense negotiations for the siege to come to an end, and only after Fusaku was released, a ransom of $300,000 U.S. Dollars was paid, and the terrorists were flown out of the Netherlands on an Air-France Boeing 707 to Yemen. The refueled plane brought them to Damascus, Syria, where they were forced to give up their ransom and their weapons. Today's *Courant* story described the organized effort that the French Secret Service would devise to track down and eliminate the JRA.

The *Courant* also had an update on the Ethiopian Civil War, which had begun on September 12, 1974. Emperor Haile Selassie and his government were violently overthrown by the Derg, a non-ideological committee of low-ranking officers and enlisted men in the Ethiopian Army who had become the ruling military junta. Elimination of remaining government officials was ongoing as the Derg sought to consolidate their power. Their goal was to abolish the monarchy and establish a Marxist-Lenin communist state. Since the United States was still in a state of Cold War with the communist Soviet Union, this was troubling.

The newspaper showcased a small story about the continued hunt for fugitive and former kidnap victim Patty Hearst, who was dragged out of her apartment in February and held prisoner by the SLA (Symbionese Liberation Army) for ridiculous demands and ransom. A great deal of sympathy for her vanished after she helped rob the Hibernia bank in April with SLA members. Next to the frequently reproduced photo of an M1 carbine-toting Patty (now "Tania") at the bank was a gruesome photo of the Los Angeles safehouse where six members of the SLA fought a furious gun battle in May with police before their house was burned to the ground. The photo showed the house in flames.

The *New Mexican* had an editorial critical of new president Gerald Ford, who had succeeded Richard Nixon after the latter resigned the presidency on August 9th. On September 8th Ford had pardoned Richard Nixon—a "full, free, and absolute pardon" that prevented any type of indictment. Nixon accepted the pardon, releasing a statement:

"I was wrong in not acting more decisively and more forthrightly in dealing with Watergate, particularly when it reached the stage

of judicial proceedings and grew from a political scandal into a national tragedy. No words can describe the depth of my regret and pain at the anguish my mistakes over Watergate have caused the nation and the presidency, a nation I so deeply love, and an institution I so greatly respect."

Cameo folded the newspaper and tossed it into the back seat. "I can't read any more bad news," she said.

"We're almost there," Tucson replied as he made a bumpy turn onto the dirt road leading to the cabin. A rumbling ten minutes later he turned into the gravel driveway leading to the cabin; fifty feet later he stopped the car. "Here we are."

Cameo got out of the car slowly and surveyed the place. The log cabin was beautiful, with a front porch complete with two rocking chairs. The front yard was a wide oval, and the brick pathway to the porch was rimmed with perennial flowers. Sculpted bushes dotted both sides of the yard and a huge pine tree loomed to the right; large pinecones had fallen on the ground. A squirrel skittered across the lawn, stopped, stared at the human intruders, then vanished into the woods.

Cameo looked at Tucson and smiled. "It's magnificent here. Did your family build the cabin?"

Tucson nodded. "Twice. Long story. Let's go inside."

Cameo followed Tucson to the porch, and he unlocked the front door. He stepped aside to let her enter first. She brushed past him, just touching him. She shivered and moved quickly to the center of the room. "It's wonderful," she said.

"There's this large family area with the kitchenette over there" —he pointed to the left— "and the two bedrooms and bathroom—complete with shower—are in back. We've got two sets of bunkbeds in one so we can accommodate a half dozen guests."

"Do you have electricity? I didn't see any poles."

"Not yet, but we have a gas generator that powers us up."

"You said your family built the cabin twice."

Tucson nodded. "We did. Worked hard on the first version. I was in the Navy away from home when we lost it."

"What happened?"

"A really evil killer named Joanna Frid had it out for us. She burned it down."

"Oh, my God," Cameo exclaimed. "Did they catch her?"

Tucson shook his head. "Nope. She's still out there somewhere. She's on the FBI's Most Wanted list. No one's seen hide nor hair of her since 1967. She was also known as the Santa Fe Vampire Killer. You've never heard of her?"

"Maybe in my former life," Cameo murmured.

"Several books came out on her crime sprees. I'll lend them to you when we get back if you want to catch up." He remembered that Cassidy had planned on writing a book, but she never did.

"Thank you. I'd like that."

"Come on—I'll show you the rest of the cabin and the back yard, and then we can head off for a hike to a place I think you'll love."

"Sounds like a plan." Cameo followed Tucson through the cabin, admiring the sturdy construction and the clever way the furniture was placed to host a lot of people. The back yard was spacious and about fifty feet long as it reached the forest. There was a clothesline and an oak washtub. A couple of large tree stumps were left from where they had been cut down to open up the area. She felt relaxed.

"All right," Tucson said. "Let's fill the portable cooler with drinks and snacks and head off."

"You lead, I follow."

Tucson slung a nylon cooler over his right shoulder and a large nylon backpack over his left. Ten minutes later they were on the path heading towards the lake. It was cool in the forest since it wasn't even 10 AM. The path was well-worn and wide, stomped to relative smoothness by the hundreds if not thousands of hikers gone before them. Tucson pointed out some species of birds, and they were both startled when a small bobcat crossed in front of them, ignoring the silly humans as he went about searching for small animals for lunch.

"He's more afraid of us than we are of him," Tucson said reassuringly.

"Sure. Let's hold onto that thought."

Tucson laughed and they kept moving until suddenly the view to the lake and the cliffs beyond exploded in front of their eyes. Cameo took a few more steps and stopped and stared.

"Wow," she said softly. "Just, wow."

"Spirit Lake," Tucson said. The clear blue lake glistened under the bright sun. The lake was surrounded by tall pines and other trees and several large rock cliffs. There were only a couple of other people fishing and wading in the lake; unlike the summer season there weren't any couples or families spread out on blankets just enjoying communing with nature. This was nothing like New England, Cameo thought, but it was magnificent.

Tucson pointed to a small bank of rocks jutting out a few feet into the lake. They were large enough to seat two people comfortably but no more, and the tree lines came too close for anyone to put down a blanket for relaxation or fishing. He walked to the biggest flat rock and sat down. She sat beside him, removed her hiking boots, and gingerly dipped her toes into the later.

"Cold," she said, but she kept her feet in the crystal lake. She wriggled her toes and thought the water was invigorating. Something hazy wisped past her mind, unfocused but something that reminded her of the lake.

"This was always one of my favorite spots to go when I was bored or stressed. My family built the cabin in the mid-sixties and it went up in flames in '67. They rebuilt it almost immediately. I was in the Navy then so couldn't help. By the time I came home it was up and ready."

"When did you muster out?" Cameo could swear that his jaw tightened.

"December, '68. I spent the year after that roaming the country, getting my head straight."

"Were you in Vietnam?"

"No," he said more shortly than he'd meant to. "Sorry. Not a happy time."

"You're interested in my past, my history, aren't you?"

"Yes, of course." He added quickly, "In a professional capacity."

"Well, I'm interested in you in a personal capacity. I like you. I trust you. I'd like to know more about you as a man, not as a therapist." She let the challenge hang in the air.

Tucson looked at her hard and was silent for an interminable moment. He blew out a long breath of air and shrugged. "What do you want to know?"

"Are you seeing anyone?" Cameo smiled at him, getting right to the heart of the matter.

"Nope. Not in years."

"Years?" she said skeptically.

He stared out at the glistening lake. "Not since the end of October 1967."

"Come on. Be serious."

"I am serious," he said quietly. "Her name was Carrie Mattson, a Navy WAVE in San Diego where I was stationed."

"Was it serious?"

"No. It was a one-night stand that cost me the woman I loved. I was seeing a wonderful woman in Santa Fe. She was a reporter on the *Courant*, a damn good writer. She promised to wait for me. In a moment of weakness and uncertainty about the future before my boat shipped out, I cheated on her for that one night. Then, I had either the guts or the stupidity to confess my digression to Cassidy in a letter, tell her how sorry I was, and beg her forgiveness. Shortly after that she left town and vanished. I've never heard from her since."

Cameo was silent for a moment. A few fish hit the water surface, sending ripples out in concentric circles. "That was stupid. You learned a really hard lesson."

"For sure."

"Do you ever think about her?"

"Sometimes." He paused. "A lot lately. I just hope she's okay and happy. I hope she's found a man who's worthy of her."

"Have you ever tried to find her?"

"No."

Cameo was quiet for several minutes while they enjoyed the sun and the peacefulness of the lake. "I think a lot about what I might have left behind. You know, if I was married or engaged or in a relationship. And if I was, is he still waiting for me or has he moved on?"

"Percy mentioned that. He warned me not to get too emotionally involved and stay on professional track."

Instead of pursuing that subject Cameo asked, "What made you have a one-night stand? You weren't going to Vietnam, right?"

"No. We were shipping out to Japan to patrol around the Sea of Japan."

"Sounds fairly safe. Were you nervous?"

"No," Tucson said quietly. "I was scared. Hard to believe but I'm a home boy. I love living here. I don't particularly care for travel, but I do it when I have to. Besides, I'm not especially thrilled with boats."

"And yet you joined the Navy. Or were you drafted?"

"I was drafted but my family decided that I should join the Navy since it was the least leg of the Armed Forces that might see action in the war. Turns out I might have been better off in the Army and fighting the war on land."

"Why? You came home."

"A little worse for wear," he said as he absently stroked his cheek scar.

"How'd you get that?" She grinned. "Fall off the ship?"

"North Korean bayonet," he replied flatly.

"W-what?"

Tucson looked her directly in the eyes. "Ever hear of the *USS Pueblo*?"

"I don't think so. Did it happen before 1969?"

"Yes. I imagine it dominated much of the news during 1968, but I don't expect you'd remember those stories if you lost your memory."

"What happened?"

"In a nutshell my ship was patrolling in international waters between Japan and North Korea, which is a communist country supported by the Soviet Union. The North Koreans accosted us, and our commander surrendered. Another long story short, the whole crew were held as prisoners in North Korea for eleven months. We were released just before Christmas 1968."

“Oh, my God,” she whispered. “You were a prisoner of war.”

“Yeah, we were that even though we weren’t being held by the North Vietnamese. Even so our loving government denied giving us any POW medals as they did for those who served directly in Vietnam. They said we weren’t really ‘prisoners’ but detainees.” He stroked his scar again. “And let’s just say that our captors weren’t the most humanitarian or kind human beings.”

“They tortured you?” Cameo asked almost inaudibly.

“Yeah,” Tucson said flatly. “You could say that. Look, I don’t want to get into the details. Maybe someday. Today is a day to relax and enjoy, not to bring back bad memories.”

“What about … ghostly memories?”

Tucson squinted at Cameo. “Did something come back to you?”

“I think so. Sitting here I got a sense of … familiarity when I put my feet in the water, and when I look at the cliffs.”

“Do you think you were someplace similar?”

“Maybe. It wasn’t an image, a feeling, really. It was there for a split second then gone.”

“That’s okay. It might mean something; it might mean nothing. As I said, let’s not drag the therapy into today. Have you ever fished in the past five years?”

“Good God, no.”

“Then I’ll teach you today. Afraid of worms?”

“Yuck.”

“We’ll get past that. This lake has some great trout in it and if we catch a couple, we can build a fire back at the cabin and cook ’em up.”

“I am not going to gut a fish or scrape its scales off. Forget it, mountain man.”

“I’ll do that. All you have to do is catch a fish and eat it once I’ve prepared it with my mom’s special herbs and spices. Or, we can do the civilized thing and eat the sandwiches I brought with us. Ham on rye.”

Cameo cocked her head and smiled at him. “Let’s get me past my fear of worms.”

Tucson scrambled to his feet and grabbed his backpack. He rummaged around and withdrew a small lidded metal can with holes poked in the top. He unscrewed it and showed it to cameo.

"Eew," she exclaimed as she stared at the spaghetti-like mass of nightcrawlers writhing inside the can filled with moist leaves.

Tucson laughed and put down the can then took out two collapsible fishing rods and assembled them. He handed her the smaller red rod after he affixed a bobber to the line.

"And this is how you do it," he said as he stuck his fingers into the can and pulled out a stubborn worm.

"That's so disgusting," Cameo said as she frowned at his deft effort to stab the fishing hook into the worm.

He pulled out another worm from the can. "Your turn." He held out the worm to Cameo. Both were surprised when she immediately took the worm and threaded it onto the hook in three seconds. "I'm impressed," he said.

Without a word Cameo stood at the edge of the flat rock and cast her line far into the lake with ease and grace. Wordlessly Tucson stood beside her and did the same. They stood there silently, watching the bobbers for movement. He thought about engaging her in conversation, but the comfortable silence just felt right.

After ten minutes or so Cameo's bobber was jerked and went underwater for a second. It jerked again and she began to gently reel and pull, reel and pull. It was clear that something was tugging at the other end. Tucson put his rod down and picked up the net. After another minute Cameo gave a final jerk and pulled a huge trout out of the lake. Tucson grabbed the line and captured the fish in the net.

"Slippery critter," he said as he grabbed ahold of the fish and unhooked it. He grinned at Cameo. "A three-pounder if not more. One fine lunch."

"Look, look," she exclaimed, pointing to his line where his own bobber was jerking and pulling the rod into the lake. Tucson grabbed the rod and reeled in another trout, a small one no bigger than a pound and a half. After he got the second fish in the net he said, "You definitely win. Thanks to you we won't starve."

"You have those sandwiches."

"Not remotely comparable. Let's try for a couple more and then we can go back to the cabin."

A half hour later Tucson and Cameo trudged back to the cabin with her two three-pound trout and his one small one. When they arrived, Tucson put the now-headless fish in the sink while he went to start a fire in the cast-iron-topped wood stove. He lit the kindling and blew on it then stuffed three dry logs into the fire and waited until they were burning enough to heat the top griddle. He turned back to Cameo and stopped in his tracks.

She was at the sink with a gutted fish in her hands. She put it down next to another one and picked up the third fish. He didn't say a word, just watched. When she finished gutting his small fish with speed and precision, she picked up another knife and began descaling the fish. It was obvious that this wasn't the first time she had fished and prepared the booty. She was humming a song he didn't recognize, and she was totally focused on the task at hand.

When Cameo was finished, she turned to see Tucson watching her. "All done," she said.

"I see that," Tucson replied. He opened a cabinet and took out a cast iron frying pan and poured a very thin layer of olive oil into it. He shook a small plastic container with a mixture of spices and herbs over the oil. He put the pan on the wood stove and waited for the oil to heat before placing the fish fillets in the oil. He tossed back over his shoulder, "Plates are in the top right cabinet." While Cameo retrieved the plates and utensils Tucson watched the fish, ensuring the fillets were frying without burning.

"Let's eat out on the porch," she said.

"Good idea. Grab the Pepsis out of the cooler."

Cameo cleaned off the porch table and set it with forks, knives, and napkins. She sat in one of the rocking chairs and breathed in deeply of the fresh wilderness air. It wasn't too long before Tucson came out carrying two plates loaded with fried trout fillets. He placed one next to her and sat down on the other rocker. He popped open a Pepsi and took a sip.

"It smells delicious," Cameo murmured, taking in a deep breath.

"Dig in."

They both dug in and mutual eye-rolling gave testament to the quality of her catch and his cooking. When they finished, they just sat there on the porch, rocking.

"How do you feel?" Tucson finally asked.

"So relaxed," she murmured. "Very … peaceful. Thank you for today."

"You're very welcome. You know, the day doesn't have to be over."

"How do you mean?"

"We'll get back to the city by five. We could eat a light dinner and go to the movies. Do you like movies?"

"Yes, but I rarely go to them. It's not that much fun going alone."

"You wouldn't be alone today."

"That's correct." She smiled. "What's playing?"

"We've got a few theaters in Santa Fe as well as a few drive-ins." He picked up the *Courant* from the table where Cameo had left it after reading the rest while she waited for the meal. "Well, the golden age of film it's not. For new flicks we have *Phase IV*, about killer ants, *Big Bad Mama*, about a killer Angie Dickinson, and *Nightmare Honeymoon*, starring people I've never heard of. The Rialto has a comedy double feature, *The Girl from Petrovka* with Goldie Hawn, and *For Pete's Sake*, with Streisand." Tucson shook his head. "Slim pickings." He sighed. "Any preferences?"

"Definitely." A beat. "None of them. Why don't we stay here until it starts getting dark then head home? I'd rather be out in the open than clustered in a crowded theater watching something I'm not interested it."

"Deal. How about the dinner option?"

"Mexican food?"

"Absolutely."

"Good. So, why don't we pass the time with you telling me all about your family and the evil Joanna Frid that burned the cabin down? I'm dying of curiosity."

"It's a long and twisted tale."

"The twistier the better. Start with the unusual sibling names."

Tucson laughed and said okay. He went back to the start where his Indian mother had run off with his immigrant Polish father and started crisscrossing the country and having kids. He weaved a tale of how his parents still had their nomadic ways, which is why they were on a ship in the South Pacific. He told her that their last name was the anglicized version of their mother's Indian surname, and that they'd settled down in Santa Fe when he was ten. Thankfully, he said, the next generation wasn't hampered by conception point names.

"So, you've got three nieces by Memphis?" she asked.

"Uh-huh. I … I have a fourth niece, Francesca. We call her Chessie."

"Surely she's not Luc's daughter?"

Tucson was quiet for a long moment before clearing his throat. "No, she's my brother Troy's daughter. Her mother is Candy, my and Percy's executive assistant."

"Where's your brother?"

Tucson inhaled sharply. This always upset him. "Troy's dead. He was killed during the Vietnam War."

"Oh, my God. I'm so sorry."

"Yeah, me too." Tucson waited a long moment before explaining. "While I was being held in North Korea my idiot brother quit college and joined the army. He wanted to fight the spread of Communism in southeast Asia. I know that part of his motivation was my capture. Anyway, he wound up in boot camp at Fort Jackson, South Carolina, then spent some time at Fort Bragg before he was shipped out." Tucson shook his head. "The day before he left for Columbia, he bought a diamond ring and got engaged to Candy. They were just kids, but I'd have to say they were genuinely in love and devoted to one another.

"In the Army he worked his way up to become a member of the Army's Special Forces. He was able to come home a couple of times and the time he came home in 1969 he and Candy were married. Nine months later in June of 1970 their daughter was born. He'd been shipped out to Laos two months before she was born. He never met her. He never met his own goddamn daughter," Tucson said in a low, angry voice.

Cameo reached out and gently put her hand on his arm. He was staring straight ahead, seemingly unaware of the tactile compassion. He went on.

"The covert war in Laos was floundering. The U.S. was supporting the war although you'd be hard-pressed at the time to get anyone in the government to admit to that. The Laotian Army contacted the MACV-SOG in Saigon. That's the Military Assistance Command, Vietnam Studies and Observations Group. That was a very specialized, classified unit run by Colonel John Sadler. Sadler agreed to help and sent three platoons deeper into Laos than the U.S. had ever gone. Long story short, over fifty of the enemy were killed and all the Americans in the Special Forces were wounded. All but one. Troy was killed. September 13th. He's buried here, of course."

"Your parents must have been devastated," Cameo whispered.

"You could say that. We all were. We're a very tightly knit family. Maybe the worse, though, is Candy and Chessie. She was a widow at nineteen and Chessie will never know her father." Tucson rose suddenly and walked to the end of the porch, leaning against the rail. He shook his head.

"I've spent the last four years trying to understand how I came home, and my kid brother didn't."

"You feel guilty about that." It was a statement, not a question.

"Hell, yeah."

"It wasn't your fault."

"Doesn't make it any easier."

"Have you talked to anyone about that? Percy, maybe?"

"He corralled me for a couple of sessions, but we weren't getting anywhere. I'm dealing with it." He smiled tightly. "Anyway, on to more pleasant topics. Let me tell you about our infamous vampire killer."

Cameo smiled. "I'm all fangs."

CHAPTER NINE

Monday morning was busy on all three floors of the office building. Akiro had a waiting room full of existing and prospective clients, as well as a half dozen people that had answered his newspaper ad for a new secretary. His previous secretary had worked for the firm for only ten months. She wasn't a good fit, and Jenna Collins had once described her as a "toxic bitch." She was on the verge of being fired when she quit, leaving a nasty letter and cleaning out the office coffee and sugar supplies. Akiro decided not to press charges, relieved that she hadn't screwed with the client files.

Jenna and Rodrigo were handling the clients while Akiro interviewed the job applicants. He was surprised that amongst the six applicants there was one young man, who was sitting in the waiting room, straight as a ramrod, and by the movement of his lips, talking to himself. Akiro decided to save him for last.

On the first floor Percy and Tucson were cloistered with Cameo, reviewing their evaluation of the hypnosis session from the previous Thursday. Tucson had set up a projector so that they could all watch the entire session. At Cameo's agreement Percy had invited Swan to join since she would be heading the non-therapist part of the investigation into Cameo's past and trauma.

In the Graceland Conference Room on the third floor Memphis, Nick, Sand, Frick and Frack were enjoying an easy conversation while noshing on coffee and donuts. Frick updated Memphis and Nick on what they'd learned about the missing persons case. They were halfway through the box of donuts when Skye called to say that "An awesome-looking guy from Frisco just turned up." Memphis sighed and told her to bring him in. A half minute later Skye appeared at the door with a tall, good-looking man around thirty-five towering over her. Memphis shooed her out, she scowled, then left.

Memphis walked over and extended his hand. "Memphis Grayhawk," he said.

"Adam Manzone," the man replied. He was tall, with dark brown hair and eyes, and an athletic body. Ethnically, he was either Italian or Greek.

"Let me introduce everyone," Memphis said. "That's Nick Griffin. You spoke to him on the phone."

"Glad to meet you," Nick said, shaking Adam's hand.

"Sand Hazelwood," Sand said, introducing himself.

"And these are detectives Bart Smith and Jesse Morgan, or, as we know them affectionately, Frick and Frack. They were assigned to the case a few days ago."

"I'm Frick," Frick said, giving Adam's hand a strong, sharp tug.

"Then you must be Frack," Adam said, a smile tugging at the corners of his mouth.

"That's me," Frack said, shaking Adam's hand.

"Have a seat," Memphis said. "Coffee?"

"Love some." Adam sat down and put his briefcase on the floor.

Memphis poured a cup and handed it to Adam, who took a sip.

"How was your trip?" Memphis asked.

"Good. Short. Two hours in a flying tin can at thirty thousand feet that can hurtle to the earth and vaporize you on contact is about all I can handle."

"I hear you," Memphis said. "Before we start, can you give us some brief background on you, then we'll reciprocate?"

"Glad to. I work with Lee Jernigan, whom Nick is familiar with."

"Great guy," Nick said, grinning. "Are the kids still stealing his building numbers?"

Adam laughed. "Sadly, yes. He's doing well. He took me on in '69 and trained me as an investigator. A few years ago, I moved north to Frisco—excuse me, San Francisco—citizens get pissed when you bastardize the name—and began working there. I opened an office and right now it's just me and my young cohort, Bandit, who do the investigative work."

"Why'd you move?" Frick asked.

"My girlfriend and son live there. She's a writer and owns a magazine. Maybe you've heard of it—*Seraphim*?"

"No shit?" Memphis said. "My wife has a subscription. She's been reading it since the Manson thing."

Adam nodded. "That was Norah's first story, her big break."

"You're not married?" Memphis asked.

Adam sighed deeply. "I've been trying. She's an independent and stubborn woman."

Sand laughed. "Memphis might be able to relate."

Memphis nodded at Adam. "She could be my wife's doppelganger."

"That's scary," Adam said. "Anyway, that's what I do for a living. Ellis Geary contacted several P.I. firms when his daughter went missing. I guess he wasn't too pleased with their lack of results. One of his colleagues was a client of mine for a minor background check job and he suggested me. Geary and I had a conference call with Lee, and we decided to take the case. I've spent the last week grilling Geary and his daughter's friends and classmates, ditto the boyfriend. Since she was last heard from close to New Mexico Lee suggested that I contact your firm." He grinned widely. "He adores Nick and Swan, couldn't say enough nice things about them."

"That's only because we paid for an expensive dinner for two at the Brown Derby for him and his wife," Nick said. "And after we got back from L.A. I sent him a case of Pabst."

Adam nodded. "That would be one of the reasons. Lee enjoys his food, loves his beer, and worships his wife."

"What did you find out about the kids?" Frack asked.

Adam leaned down and put his briefcase on the table. He snapped open the lock and withdrew two thick folders before putting the briefcase back on the floor. He opened one and handed Memphis and Frick copies of his report summary.

"Taylor Tiffany Geary, age twenty-two. An average student in high school and an average student in college studying Business Administration. She had started college with an eye to pre-law since her old man was a lawyer and had visions of her joining his firm. She's an only child and he saw her as his legacy. From what her friends told me she chafed for years under her father's expectations and by the time she graduated San Francisco State University she was ready to abandon his upper-middle-class expectations and fly off on her own path."

"What's the father like?" Frack asked. "Tight ass?"

"On the surface, but underneath I just saw a grieving dad scared to death about the fate of his child. It humanized him."

"What about the mother?"

"Tight ass. Cold. You could splash her face with alcohol and it'd freeze."

"What about the boyfriend?" Frick asked.

"Stonewall Jackson Powell, age twenty-three. Dropped out of the City College of San Francisco in his junior year and devoted himself to his art. He's a painter."

"Good painter?" Nick asked.

"Let's just say you'd have to imbibe a few shots of LSD with a marijuana chaser to appreciate the depth and meaning of his work."

"Lousy painter," Nick said, nodding.

"I was being kind," Adam said. "Andy Warhol he's not. My kid does a better job with Paint by Numbers. However, from what I've gathered he's a nice guy and worships Taylor. He follows her around like a puppy dog and treats her like a queen. That was from her best friend."

"Which one wanted to see the USA in a Chevrolet?" Frick asked.

"She did," Adam said. "She fancied herself a budding Richard Avedon and wanted to travel the world to snap pictures that would make her famous."

"Who's Richard Avedon?" Frick asked.

"Really?" Frack said to his partner. "Philistine. He's a photographer that's done a lot of *Vogue* covers."

"*Vogue*? You read *Vogue*?" Frick exclaimed in disbelief.

"I read a lot of things." Frack looked around and everyone was staring at him with amusement or skepticism. "I have a lot of time on my hands."

"Anyway," Adam said, "as you probably know Taylor and Stone flew to Boston, bought a car, and started driving west across country in their 1964 grey Pontiac LeMans."

"Whoa, whoa," Frick exclaimed. "How the hell do you know that? Her old man didn't know what kind of car they bought. Neither did the Boston cops."

"I'm an investigator. It's what I do," Adam said solemnly, then laughed. "When I got the case, I had Lee contact an old friend on the *Boston Globe*—Lee's from Boston—and had a personal ad put in the paper describing the couple and timeframe and offering a hundred-dollar reward for information. Got a dozen nibbles and one panned out. The kids bought the car from a Ted Kerry in Brookline. He even mailed us an old photo of it and the VIN." He handed Frick a note with the car information, seller, and the contacts at the *Globe* and the police department. He pulled out a photo of the car. "Here it is, a few years ago. Kerry said it was in pretty good shape when he sold it."

"That's awesome," Nick said. "Great work." He was beginning to admire Adam almost as much as he admired Lee.

"Thanks. I notified the FBI contact in Albuquerque as well as the State Police here and in Colorado and Arizona."

"We have an FBI contact?" Memphis said. He had worked closely with the FBI for the Frid case with a marvelous agent named Tom Ballard. Sadly, Ballard and his wife had relocated for his promotion and were currently in Philly. They kept in touch every so often. His son, Richard, had gone to Georgetown after his first year at UNM.

Ballard called Memphis a year earlier to tell him that Richard was now an FBI agent working in the Atlanta field office.

"Yes, we do," Adam said.

"How'd that happen?" Nick asked.

"Our estimable Mr. Geary knows a state senator that knows the FBI director. Need I say more?"

"That guy has juice," Frick muttered.

"Lucky for us," Adam said. "At least we can muster up resources to find the kids."

"If they're still alive," Frack said evenly.

"We need to go with that assumption," Nick said. "A few weeks isn't long enough to write them off."

"Agreed," Memphis said. "What's the fibbie's name?"

"My contact at the field office said he's a transferee and won't be in the office until Wednesday. Meanwhile, let's discuss next steps. There isn't anything more that I can do back home since I've collected as much information as possible. There're detailed notes in my folder that you can have. My next thought would be to head up to San Luis and ask around."

"Our predecessors Dunbar and Abbott did that and got nowhere," Frack said. "However, they didn't have the info on the car that you just gave us so we're going to have to re-scour. That's our job."

"It's our job, too," Nick said. "Both Adam and our firm have been hired to pursue this regardless of whether or not you real cops make any progress." He looked at Adam. "Anything else you've done at your end?"

"Lee's going to put some personal ads in newspapers across the country with the couple's info and car details. Taylor called her dad from various locations, so we have a reasonable geographic travel line to follow. Maybe we can get a tip."

"Isn't this whole thing with both of you guys and the newspapers and all going to cost a fortune?" Frack asked skeptically.

Without replying Adam took out his wallet and handed Frack a picture of an adorable little five-year-old girl with golden blonde hair and huge blue eyes holding a pink teddy bear. "Her father doesn't give a damn about the cost. He just wants his baby girl home."

Frack looked at the photo and handed it to Frick, who nodded and handed it back to Adam. Adam put the picture back in his wallet and pulled a manila envelope from his briefcase. He handed it to Memphis.

"Those are Taylor's dental and medical records. You can keep those copies," Adam said.

"Is there anything special about her physicality?" Sand asked. "You know, like past broken bones or a dental crown?" He glanced over at Frick. "There doesn't seem to be a mention of that in the official cop records." Frick just grunted and Frack nodded his head sadly; their predecessors weren't as thorough as they could have been.

"Excellent questions," Adam said, nodding. "According to her father she never had any broken bones. Her teeth were normally developed with occasional cavities that had to be filled with standard amalgam. Per the x-rays she had fillings in the upper right cuspid and fifth bicuspid, and the lower left second and third molars. She wore braces when she was a kid, but they were removed when she was thirteen."

"What was her blood type?" Memphis asked. Sand threw him a glance. He understood Memphis's obsession with female blood types.

"B," Adam said.

"That's good," Memphis said, nodding absently. He straightened in his chair. "So. We need to develop a plan of action. Nick?"

"I think the first thing to do is travel north and revisit the trail leading down from Colorado to here and see if we dig up anything with our new car information."

"We're going to do that," Frack said crabbily. "That's our job."

"It's our job, too," Nick snapped then immediately said, "Sorry."

"You always were a pain in the ass, even when you were in the slammer," Frick growled without any trace of menace.

"You were in jail?" Adam said, his eyebrows rising theatrically.

"It was a minor matter," Nick said, frowning at Frick.

"Yeah, if you consider being arrested for murder a minor matter," Frack said. He looked at Adam. "He didn't do it, but his questionable character and hippie persona had him at the top of a list of suspects. Actually, he was the only one on the list."

"I'm sorry I bought you lunch," Nick muttered.

"The pie was delicious," Frick shot back.

Adam grinned and said to Memphis, "Looks like an interesting dynamic between you and law enforcement."

"You have no idea," Memphis replied. "My wife, Swan, and her brother Sand, who are both partners in the firm, are ex-cops." He nodded towards Frick and Frack. "And these two hang around like lovesick puppies nipping at our heels." Frack made a snarling face at him.

"You're not an ex-cop?" Adam asked.

"No, worse," Frick said. "He's a lawyer."

Adam bit back a grin. "Sorry to hear that. I think we can work together anyway." He winked at Nick. "I was a hippie, too, in the late sixties. Long hair, beard, pot, commune, the whole ball of wax. Got rousted by the cops when Manson happened. They were hassling all of the undesirables."

"And now you're an upstanding citizen," Nick said.

"I pay my taxes and try to stay on the right side of the law." He glanced slyly at Frick and Frack. "If certain law enforcement representatives weren't within earshot, I'd say I still enjoy a joint now and then."

"Yeah, he fits right in with you outlaws," Frack said.

Memphis nodded, then turned serious. "What can you tell us about Taylor herself? What was she like? Did she take risks? Was she a rebel or pretending to be?"

"Incisive questions," Adam replied as he poured himself another cup of black coffee. "According to her parents she was the perfect child growing up. Obedient, sweet, generous. She had her bad side but was generally a good girl. She started getting a little distant from them as she progressed through high school."

"Completely normal," Sand said, and Memphis nodded.

"Agreed," Adam said. "She was active in school life and on the girls' soccer team, and in the French and Math clubs. She was a good chess player. She was Prom Queen in high school. Her grades were average but managed to get her into college. She was also a good photographer and took dozens of rolls of film all around the city. She lived at home during college although she wanted to live on campus. Her parents didn't think it made sense to live on campus since they lived in the same city. She had a couple of semi-serious boyfriends in college, then in her senior year fate intervened."

"She met Stone," Nick said.

"Yes. One of her friends was a budding artist and she took Taylor to an amateur art show on Fisherman's Wharf. According to the friend it was love at first sight. Thing is, you'd think that she met a bad guy and lost her sense of right and wrong, but that wasn't the case. Stone was a good kid who may have been a college dropout but was devoted to his art. I guess maybe some people could find beauty and meaning in his work, but I'm more of a traditionalist. I like things I can identify and understand." He withdrew a few photos from his briefcase and handed them to Memphis. "Some of his work."

"Wow," Memphis said. "Nice colors, but … what the hell is it?" He turned over the photo, which had the name of the painting on its back. "The evil and influence of the bourgeois society on the proletariat. Good God."

"Yeah, he wasn't selling much," Adam said. "But he loved Taylor and when she urged him to expand his horizons and explore the world, he agreed to go cross country with her so she could snap photos and he could paint pictures."

"Huh," Nick said thoughtfully. "So, it's possible that there may be developed and undeveloped rolls of film and some canvases out there that they created. If they were abandoned or stolen, we might be able to find some and see where the new owners got them and narrow the geographic search."

"That's a great idea," Sand said.

"Yeah, it is," Frick agreed and Frack nodded his head. "Got copies of those photos?"

Adam handed Frick an envelope that contained a half dozen images of Stone's paintings and a dozen photos that Taylor had taken in and around San Francisco.

"Yikes," Frick said. "Rembrandt he ain't. Pretty colors, though."

"She's got an eye for perspective," Frack said as she studied the photos that Taylor had taken of Muir Woods and the Golden Gate Bridge.

"Basically, they're good kids," Adam said quietly. "I'd like to get them back to their families, one way or another."

There was a moment of silence before Sand spoke. "They're dead, aren't they?"

"Yeah," Adam said. "But we still have to bring them home."

CHAPTER TEN

Adolph Francis Alphonse Bandelier was born in Bern, Switzerland in 1840 to an upper-class family. He was eight years old when his family, like so many others, emigrated to the United States in search of a better life. The family settled in a Swiss enclave in Highland, Illinois. His father was a lawyer and hoped that his son would follow in his professional footsteps. Adolph returned to Bern for his collegiate education.

Unfortunately for his father but fortunately for the discipline of archeology, Bandelier studied the writings and research of Alexander von Humboldt and Lewis Henry Morgan, men who were devoted to the study of ancient cultures and natural history. Bandelier returned to the United States and began his long professional career mixing archeology and anthropology at the Archeological Institute of America in New York. He was devoted to proving Morgan's theory of evolution in which the Aztec socio-political structure was based on a democratic system, which would be very similar to the existing one amongst the Iroquois Indians of North America.

Bandelier spent a decade studying and analyzing the Native American cultures of Arizona, New Mexico, and parts of Mexico. Unlike many of his professional/academic contemporaries he adhered to the concept of living research; i.e., rather than simply observing, he lived amongst his subjects and participated in their lives and culture, and had hands-on contact with ruins and artifacts. Some of his research was published in Harvard University's Peabody Museum's magazine. Benefactors such as Henry Villard financed his exploration of South American cultures. His research and writings were a lynchpin in disabusing the white culture of their inaccurate preconceptions about Native Americans.

His name was memorialized not only in his writings and in books that referenced his work and accomplishments, but also in the nomenclature of the National Monument designated by President Woodrow Wilson on February 11, 1916. The park infrastructure was developed in the 1930s by crews of the Civilian Conservation Corps (CCC) and is a National Historic Landmark for its well-preserved architecture.

The Bandelier National Monument is around forty miles west of Santa Fe near Los Alamos. It is set in the rugged cliffs and canyons of Pajarito Plateau and shelters the remains of an ancestral pueblo settlement. The twenty-three thousand acres range in elevation from five thousand feet at the Rio Grande River to over ten thousand feet at the summit of Cerro Grande.

The human presence in the area goes back ten thousand years, with a permanent settlement by Puebloan peoples dating back to around the year 1000 AD. Spanish colonial settlers migrated to the area in the eighteenth century. Adolph Bandelier visited the location in 1880 and stated, "It is the grandest thing I ever saw."

Both before and after President Wilson declared the location a National Monument excavations and upgrades were made to entice academics, scientists, artists, photographers, and tourists. Visitors can roam and enjoy and photograph such park sites as seventy miles of hiking trails, the Cave Kiva, the Big Kiva, the Small Kiva, Tyuonyi, Cave Rooms, Canyon Panorama, Petroglyphs, the Pictograph and Bat Cave, the Long House, and the Talus House. The Visitors Center offers information and souvenirs.

The sites, however, often offer much more. Their beauty and history can provide a balm of sorts to troubled souls who seek to divest themselves—at least for a few hours—of many of the aspects of civilization that rub the heart and mind raw with technology, stress, and competition. Here one can walk past the ruins of an ancient civilization and dream of the simplicity of life (as well as the downsides) and evaluate and perhaps better appreciate their own lives.

Percy first visited the monument after he'd been in Santa Fe for two years. Tansee drove him there because she wanted him to better understand her race and its history. He had been an enthusiastic student, not only because the woman he loved was Indian but because he respected all diverse cultures and believed that every single day was an opportunity to expand one's knowledge of the world and of one's own self. On his first visit she had spent two hours telling him the history of the site. She taught him about the religion the people had, their food, their clothes, the marriage and familial customs. He soaked it all in like a sponge, and now that he had a daughter he planned on becoming a storyteller for her, too. Ever since Elspeth was a baby Tansee would sing songs to her about their people, just as Percy would tell his daughter about his adopted family and the world from which he came. He promised her that someday she could splash in the Atlantic Ocean.

When he was conflicted or particularly anxious, he would sometimes come to Bandelier, sit at a favorite spot, and think. He was used to the stares and now they generally rolled off his back like water off a duck. Sometimes there were stupid remarks, but they were the exception. He worried about the future when his daughter would hear and understand the cutting and cruel verbiage that he had heard all his life as an achondroplasiac dwarf. She had already begun to question why Daddy was so much smaller than Mommy. The simplistic explanation that people came in all colors, shapes, and sizes was only going to go so far. Elspeth was showing signs of a high intellect and pretty soon she was going to demand more. Percy loved that while he dreaded it.

Percy rarely absconded from his office during a normal workday, but he had a lot to think about with this Cameo case and his concern about his partner's well-being. Years ago, he'd have to walk, take public transportation, or ask someone to drive him somewhere where he'd be comfortable to think, away from people. That changed in 1970 on his thirty-fifth birthday. Memphis had driven him home from the office and left for a while before the family returned to celebrate his birthday. Tansee prepared a nice dinner and a homemade cake, and the Grayhawks, Hazelwoods, and Nick and his family were in attendance. The dinner was wonderful, the gifts thoughtful and full of love. Then, Tansee said that the Grayhawks' combined gift was out back. Under protest Percy was blindfolded by his wife and the family swarmed out back. Tansee removed his blindfold.

And there it was, a brand new 1970 Chevy Nova four-door sedan, dark forest green. He just stared at it, then looked up at his wife.

"We had a few adjustments made," she said serenely as she took his hand and led him over to the driver's side door. She opened it. There was a collapsible step that she flipped down, and a booster seat. The pedals' rods were extended to accommodate his leg length. There was a key slot on the driver's outside flank in front of the door for the alarm system.

On cue everyone yelled, "Happy Birthday, Percival."

Memphis said, "Now all you have to do is learn to drive it and get your license."

"Yeah, and stop calling taxies," Sand said, laughing.

Percy just stared at all of them, stared at the car, and stared at his family. He could have bought an expensive car and had it modified; he was rich. But part of him perhaps needed to be somewhat dependent on others for a portion of his mobility. Maybe he was just a little scared because dependence had been part of his identity for his entire life. He had constantly pushed the boundaries of his limitations, leaving this last one dangling. His family and his friends had pushed that final envelope for him.

He did something he hadn't done in years. He cried.

He learned to drive very quickly and after some false starts and administrative bullshit he obtained his driver's license. He was bursting with pride when he opened the passenger door for his wife and took her for a ride. He was the one in the driver's seat when he took Tansee to the hospital to deliver their daughter.

He and Tansee had taken turns driving to various archeological and historic sites in the state, including Acoma Pueblo, Taos, Nambé, Santa Clara, and Jemez. Bandelier, however, was his favorite. He didn't really know why; it just struck a chord in him. The sense of history, geology, and Indian culture was just overwhelming.

Percy parked in the visitors' lot and paid his admission. He ignored the stares as he usually did and took the main loop to stop at the Big Kiva. The kiva was circular and recessed into the earth; in its heyday it would have had a roof made of wood and earth supported by wooden pillars. The mud-packed roof would have been solid enough to support people walking on it since the opening to the kiva was on the roof and down a ladder. The kiva was the center of the community and used not only for religious and other ceremonies but also for education and gathering to make tribal decisions.

Now, it was open and resembled an ancient Roman amphitheater. The stone wall was solid, and the mud seams baked hard from centuries of sun and weather. Percy went to one of the lower edges and seated himself, the sun to the back of his head. He took a moment to survey his surroundings. Thirty feet away, directly across from him, there was an Indian man sitting on a collapsible chair in front of an easel, his paints in front of him, brush in hand. He was studying the cliffs behind Percy before he looked down and made a pass across his canvas. A mother and her son were playing checkers as they sat on a blanket on the hard earth. Two young couples were walking hand in hand along the path, pausing for a moment to take in the ancient site. A few single stragglers were strolling, alternately looking around and reading a visitor's pamphlet.

Percy returned to his own purpose. He was surprised when Cameo revealed that since her stay in the hospital five years earlier, she had been keeping a journal of her thoughts and impressions. She agreed to let Percy read her journals as part of his therapy although she made it clear that she preferred only Percy to read the material.

Percy understood. He sensed that Tucson might be getting too emotionally involved in the young woman's case, and that would compromise his objectivity. Besides, it wasn't either protocol or provocative of the best results for two psychologists to simultaneously treat the same patient. Tucson knew this and knew he needed to back off and let his partner take the lead. They'd talked about an approach Friday and touched base Sunday morning. Percy was interested in Tucson's observations of Cameo at the lake and how she seemed comfortable with nature and fishing—an interesting piece of the puzzle.

The three of them had spent the entire morning Monday in his office watching the video and talking about the visuals and Cameo's reactions and memories. They were all intrigued by her reactions to the ocean photo and the snapshot of memory that it had evoked. Cameo had brought two of her journals with her and explained how she had started them. She was a little reluctant at first to let them out of her possession, but Percy promised that he'd keep them safe. He started to read them Monday night at home after dinner. They fascinated him because they opened some interesting avenues to pursue.

Speech is one aspect of analyzing a person's emotional and intellectual states. The manner of speaking—tone, volume, accent, cadence, slang, contractions, and other aspects of the verbal word—can be used to determine a person's place of origin, education, and emotions. The written word is equally as telling. Percy had learned a great deal from reading only one journal. Handwriting analysis is an art that can tell as much about a person's psychology as a physical examination can tell about flesh and bone. The patterns and characteristics of handwriting are a window into the writer's psychology in general and specifically at the time of the text creation; e.g., wobbly lettering could indicate stress while sure, swift strokes could indicate determination or urgency. Although many academics and scientists consider graphology a pseudoscience, the technique has been used for hundreds of years as a forensics tool.

Cameo wrote in cursive, and her handwriting indicated a righthanded person. There was no indication that she might be ambidextrous. The handwriting was close to calligraphic in its elegance with flowery capital letters and no sharp points on any letter of the alphabet. She always referred to herself in the first person, never in the third. She rarely used contractions, and her punctuation was spot-on. She always spelled out numbers except for dates; she spelled out the month but used numbers to indicate day and year. Her date structure was American English—month, day, year instead of day, month, year. She used complex, multisyllabic words to express a thought; her style was structured and precise but also concise with no wasted words.

She indented paragraphs precisely and never split a paragraph between pages. She numbered her pages, starting at "one" in each journal; the number was numeric, not alphabetic. Her style was tightly controlled, methodical. Her written expressions also made it clear that she was educated either in advanced classes during her teenage years and/or an institution of higher education that expected excellence. This was not a woman who had squandered her academic experience, whether it was in a structured institution or home taught.

Percy noted that there were some words that she used that were familiar to him as a New Englander. She wrote several very descriptive sentences about how she enjoyed a "grinder" at the beach; "grinder" was equivalent to sub, hoagie, wedge, or hero in other parts of the country for the same type of sandwich. She referred to traveling to the beach on the Atlantic coast as "down east" instead of southeast. She referred to making a "hamburg" instead of a "hamburger." She mentioned stopping at a "packie" to pick up a bottle of wine—that was a term that New Englanders used for liquor (package) stores. Those and other unique colloquialisms led him to believe that there was a good chance she was a New Englander. Since she didn't have an obvious accent, he settled on Connecticut or perhaps southern

Massachusetts west of Rhode Island. However, he thought that her accent could have changed after her head trauma.

As he read and interpreted, he spoke into a microphone, recording his impressions.

He was so engrossed in Cameo's journal that he lost track of time. When he checked his watch, he saw that he had been there for over three hours. He had to be getting back. Even as he stared at his watch a tall shadow fell over him and he looked up to see the Indian painter standing three feet away. The man smiled. He had a full set of white, even teeth. His swarthy face was highlighted by sharp cheekbones and thick, black eyebrows. His nose had a slight hook to it. His long black hair was pulled back into a ponytail secured at the nape of his neck.

"I have been watching you," the man said. "Your face is an open book. It hides nothing."

Percy cocked his head. "Really? I've spent a lifetime making sure that my thoughts and feelings are private."

The man said, "Perhaps I am just intuitive. My name is Hashkeh Naabah."

"Percival McBean." Percy nodded at the man's canvas. "Do you work in oil?"

"I do. Occasionally acrylic, but I prefer the basics. I mix my own colors."

"May I see?"

Naabah uncovered the canvas and turned it around. The image of the kiva and cliffs was brilliantly rendered with vivid browns and earth tones. The sky was azure without clouds. The kiva's stone details were rendered with minute precision. What made Percy inhale sharply was the unfinished image of him sitting on the edge of the kiva, reading. The proportions of his head, thorax and limbs were spot on.

"I included you with all due respect," Naabah said.

"But without my permission," Percy replied evenly. "What do you plan on doing with this painting?"

"It is yours," Naabah replied, "once I have finished it. Consider it a gift."

"Why?"

"Because I wish it to be so. I paint what the spirit moves me to. The scene of the kiva and cliffs is beautiful in itself, but with your presence it becomes remarkable." He held the painting up to Percy's eye level so Percy could study it.

Percy scrutinized every inch of the work. At the bottom right he noticed the artist's signature—HashNaa. He recognized the name.

"Your work is in the Evening Star Art Gallery," Percy said in surprise. "My wife and I go there often, as well as to other art enclaves in Santa Fe. You're from Taos, right?"

"I am, but I spend much of my time traveling the state and choosing locations where I can create my art. As you may know I only work on New Mexico images."

"You're a sculpture, too, aren't you?"

"I prefer painting."

"Your paintings are in several galleries. Not to sound obsequious, but your work is stunning." Percy had also noted that the paintings were selling for very high prices.

"Thank you. Perhaps you will allow me to fill in your face and complete this work. I would be honored if you would display this in your home. I have yet to name this piece, but I assure you the title will be appropriate."

"I would be honored. My wife and I have a number of original Native American paintings and artwork and this would be a most welcome addition."

"You like the Indian culture?"

Percy smiled unaffectedly. "Very much so, especially since my wife is Indian. Hopi."

"Ah. Then she will have a deep appreciation for the imagery. Are you aware that there are cultural Indian myths around people of your stature?"

"My wife has told me a few."

"Many Indian tribes have held dwarves to be magical or sacred in many traditions, wilderness spirits that bring good fortune. Have you ever heard of the Teihiihan?"

"No. Is that an Indian tribe?"

"No. It is a mythical creature of several Plains Indian tribes such as the Arapahoe, Crow, Comanche, and Cheyenne, amongst others. The word comes from the Arapahoe for 'strong.' They are also called Hecesiiteihii, which means 'little people.' They were highly revered and feared for their courage and strength. They were said to be fearsome warriors so aggressive that they had to be killed in battle to reach the afterlife. Depending on the tribe these beings may have wings, or one eye. One unappealing aspect of their mythology is that they liked to eat people."

"They sound terrifying."

"You would not want to meet one in a dark alley, as the white man might say."

"No, I don't believe I would."

"I am a man of the present, but I hold to my culture's traditions and beliefs and feel that our paths crossing today was written in fate. Your presence in my painting has made it more than it would have been without you. Are you able to extend your stay here so that I may finish?"

"I wish I could," Percy said, "but I have obligations in my work and I really do need to get back to the city."

"What work do you do?"

"I'm a doctor of psychology. I treat patients in my private practice. I took a little time away from the office to study a particularly intriguing case, but I do need to get back. Would it be possible for us to meet at another time?"

"Of course. I have a small studio in Santa Fe, and I am in the city often."

Percy handed him a business card. "Please call at your convenience."

"I shall. Thank you for your time and your presence. Good day." With that Naabah bowed his head and ambled off down the path.

Percy watched him go, still amazed at the good fortune of meeting a well-known artist. He loved art, and especially Indian art. He had cultivated a sincere and deep taste for paintings, sculptures, wall hangings, and other forms of art that depicted his wife's race. Over the years he and Tansee had accumulated quite a few art pieces, mainly originals. Their overall décor, however, was eclectic, with Indian art sharing space with New England seascapes and photographs of family and places they'd visited. Percy made good on his promise to take Tansee to Paris for their honeymoon, and one wall of the den was devoted just to framed photos from that trip. Percy's favorite was the one a fellow tourist had snapped of him and Tansee under the Eiffel Tower.

This new painting would be an incredible addition to their home. He couldn't wait to tell Tansee about meeting the artist and ask her about cannibalistic dwarves.

CHAPTER ELEVEN

"I don't even think this place should have a name," Frack grumbled as he leaned against the car and scowled at the "San Luis City Limits Elev 7965 Ft" sign by the side of the road. "Christ—it's a half square mile in area. I've seen bigger cactus farms."

"A half square mile is over three hundred acres," Frick countered.

"Like I said—bigger cactus farms. And how many people live here? Ten?"

"According to my research," Sand said, "over three hundred."

"New York City, watch out," Frack said sarcastically.

"Some people like living in small towns," Nick added as he took the last swallow of a bottle of Pepsi. "And why are you so grumbly today? I mean, even more than usual. Haven't had a chance to beat a confession out of a suspect recently? Captain Carraway force you to read the Miranda warning out loud before you could go on duty?"

"I'm hungry," Frack confessed. "I had a small breakfast."

Frick snorted. "Three eggs, four slices of bacon, two slices of toast, hash browns, two glasses of orange juice, and a cup of coffee. It's a wonder you have the strength to stand."

"That was hours ago."

"Gentlemen," Sand said, sighing, "can we pend the subject of food and hit a few places on our mission?" He pointed a quarter mile up the road. "I'm guessing that may be the only gas station in town, so let's go there. We'll check the pay phone to make sure it's the one that Taylor's call traced back to."

"Maybe they'll have snacks," Nick offered.

Frack grunted and got back in the car. Frick was already behind the wheel and Sand and Nick got into their own car and followed the two cops down the road. They parked on either side of the singular gas pump and less than a minute later a middle-aged man in dark green overalls came out of the station and headed towards them. He seemed confused as to which car to service first. Sand pointed at his and the man unscrewed the gas cap.

"What's yer pleasure?" the attendant asked.

"Regular. Fill her up," Sand replied.

The attendant nodded to Frick and Frack. "Be with you gents in a few minutes."

"Don't worry," Frick said. "We're all together. You Jerry Hensley?"

The man looked surprised. "That's me. How do you know my name?"

"You talked to a detective Abbott about a missing persons case."

"Right, right. You a cop, too?"

Frick jabbed his thumb towards Frack. "Both of us." He nodded at Sand and Nick. "Those two are private eyes."

Hensley grinned. "Like Stu Bailey on *77 Sunset Strip*?"

"Yeah, just not as successful or debonair," Frack said. "Mind if we ask you a few questions?"

"I don't mind at all," Hensley said. "I ain't had many customers today. Damn lonely here sometimes." He removed the nozzle from Sand's gas tank and screwed the cap back on. He moved around to the front of the car and began cleaning the windshield. "Lotsa bug juice here," he said laconically.

"You told Detective Abbott that you weren't sure if you'd seen the couple or not. That right?" Frick asked.

"Yes, sir," Hensley said as he picked off a stubborn spot of dried dead insect. "That detective told me the day and date he said they called home, but, honestly, it was a weekend and that's when traffic picks up around here with people going back and forth across the border. I think I might've had maybe six or seven couples that day, and at least a dozen or so single drivers. Not all of them bought gas, you know. Some of 'em just used the pay phone." He pointed to the pay phone at the corner of the station. "The cop didn't know what kind of car they had, either."

"Well, we have the kind of car now," Frack said. He showed Hensley a photo of the Pontiac LeMans.

Hensley took the photo and studied it. "Hell of a car," he said. "Older model but in damn good shape." He scratched his head. "I'd remember that car. I didn't see it. Sorry." He opened the car hood and pulled out the oil dipstick. He glanced at Sand. "Needs a quart." When Sand nodded Hensley went back into the station for a can of oil. Nick walked over to the pay phone to check the number against their records. He looked back at Sand and nodded.

"Shit," Frick said.

"Just because he didn't see the car doesn't mean that someone else didn't," Nick said. "I'm sure there's more than ten people in the area. We could fan out and hit as many as we can." At that moment Hensley came out and added the new oil to Sand's engine. He slammed down the hood and ambled over to Frick's car.

"Fill 'er up?" he asked.

"Yeah, regular," Frick said.

"You got any snacks in your station?" Frack asked.

"Not so many," Hensley said as he wiped Frick's window squeaky clean. "There's Laurie-Ann's grocery shop 'bout a quarter mile east. Plenty to choose from there." He popped open Frick's hood and checked the oil. "Don't need any oil." He closed the hood and finished filling the tank. He looked at Sand. "That'll be five bucks, young fella." He nodded to Frick. "Four-fifty for you." They paid him, he smiled, and plodded back into the gas station.

"That was fun," Frack muttered. "So, how we gonna split this up? You two go east and we go west?"

"I think we should have two teams of one cop and one P.I.," Nick said. "That way, whoever we accost will at least have one official police officer in the mix."

"Calling dibs on Frick," Sand said quickly. He laughed at the sour look on Frack's face. "Your brilliance and splendor would be too much for me. Nick's younger and tougher."

"But not as good a bullshitter," Nick said.

The four men talked for a few minutes, looking at the town map that Skye had somehow produced. She also found an old article in the library from the *Pueblo Chieftain*, a newspaper started in Pueblo, Colorado in 1868. This article, dated June 8, 1872, described the three stores in San Luis as owned by Fred Meyer & Company, Auguste Lacombe, and Mazers & Rich. The article also mentioned a blacksmith, a butcher, a beer saloon, a carpenter, and two hotels. According to Frack, San Luis didn't seem to have changed very much in a hundred years.

The two teams drove to the mom-and-pop store down the road and picked up two six-packs of Pepsi, a bag of ice for the coolers, and a dozen snacks. They agreed to meet back at the store at four o'clock. Then, Sand and Frick headed east, and Frack and Nick headed west. Each team chose which houses or businesses to stop at, and occasionally people walking on the sidewalks. In general, the inquiries were met with friendliness, but none of those approached remembered the couple or the car.

When Frack and Nick returned to the store at four-ten their companions were already waiting.

"Nada," Nick said as he got out of the car. "Total bust."

"Us, too," Sand replied. "I guess we can scratch the cactus farm off our list. The question is, should we hit the surrounding towns like Abbott and Dunbar did, or head south into New Mexico and scour the places there?"

"What time did Taylor call her father?" Nick asked.

Frick checked his notes. "2:30 PM, mountain time."

"If I were just above the New Mexico border before three in the afternoon, I'd head south and get as far into the state as I could before settling in for the night," Nick said.

"That's reasonable," Frack said. He balled up his empty potato chip bag and tossed it into the trash can by the door of the store. "We got enough food for the rest of the day?"

"I think we should find a place to stay in Taos for the night," Sand said. "Maybe Laurie-Ann has some sandwiches that can hold us." He started to go into the store.

"Hey," Frick said, and Sand turned to him. "Did we ask her if she saw the kids or car?"

"I think so," Frack said.

"I don't think so," Nick countered.

"Then let's get that disappointment out of the way and get our sandwiches," Sand said as he opened the door. He greeted the elderly lady behind the counter and asked if she had any sandwiches. She smiled widely and said she'd make whatever they needed. The team ordered roast beef sandwiches all the way around. They picked up a few more snacks and sodas while she made the sandwiches in the back room. While she rang up the purchases and began bagging them, Frick showed her a photo of Taylor and Stone and a photo of the car.

"Ma'am, you ever see this couple or their car in the last month or so?" Frick asked.

Laurie-Ann stopped bagging and studied the photos. "I think that was their car," she remarked as she placed a sandwich in the bag. The men became alert at once.

"You saw them?" Sand asked quickly.

"Yes, sir," she replied as she pulled another paper bag from under the counter for the remaining snacks. "Cute couple. He watched her like a puppy dog. She was a little snippy, though. Maybe a little too forward, but I guess that's the young people of today. Here you are," she finished, handing them the bags.

"Can you tell us about when you saw them and what they bought and said?" Sand asked as he fished a few bills from his wallet.

"Are they in trouble?" she asked nervously.

"We don't know, ma'am," Frack said. "They're missing, and we're trying to find them." He flashed his badge. "Anything you can tell us would help."

"Poor things," she murmured and handed the photos back to Frick. "They were in here for, what, maybe twenty minutes? They bought some sandwiches and pops, and some candy. Chocolate, I think. He paid for them. They left and drove off. I remember thinking that I just loved their car. Grey is my favorite color. It reminds me of turtle doves."

"Did they say anything to you about where they were headed?" Frick asked.

"New Mexico," she said.

"Any particular place in New Mexico?"

"Um … yes. He mentioned that they were going to stop in Taos for the night then head down to Santa Fe. I think she mentioned that they were from California." She frowned. "She remarked that she wanted to take lots of pictures of all the Indians in the pueblo. I warned her that she had to be respectful and not take pictures unless the people said it was okay. Those Taos Indians are persnickety about that. I guess you can't really blame them. After all, the pueblo isn't Disneyland—it's their home. She didn't seem to take that seriously."

"Anything else you can tell us?" Nick asked.

"No, that's it. I hope you find them. So young." She shook her head. "Oh, yeah—I told them that the fastest way to go was south on Route 159, and that turns into Route 522 which would take them right to Taos. They thanked me and left."

"Laurie-Ann, thank you very much," Sand said and shook her hand.

As the men left, she called after them, "Hope you like the sandwiches. I added extra mayo."

Frick pulled his car to the side of the road when they passed the New Mexico border, just outside of Costilla. Sand pulled up behind them. He grinned at Frack, who was halfway through his roast beef sandwich.

"Enough mayo?" Sand asked.

"That woman knows how to make a sandwich," Frack mumbled as he chewed.

"How far are we from Taos?" Nick asked.

"About forty miles," Sand said.

"Do you know where the police department is?" Nick asked.

"It's complicated," Frick said. "Taos is a different bird than Santa Fe. It's not just a 'city.' I mean, there is a city of Taos, but you also have the Taos Pueblo, and that's what complicates things."

"Where's the pueblo?"

"About a mile north of Taos city limits."

"What makes it complicated?"

"How about some background on it for our less enlightened associate?" Sand said, glancing at Nick. Although the young New Englander had been living in New Mexico for nearly ten years, he was really only familiar with the Santa Fe and Albuquerque areas and a few surrounding Indian enclaves. Even as Sand spoke Nick cursed himself for not being as integrated into the state as he should be. He vowed to explore the rest of what had become his forever home.

"Sure," Frick said. "The city of Taos isn't very big, just over five square miles. It goes back to the early 1600s when Spain began colonizing the new world. The pueblo, however, goes back a millennium. It's considered one of the oldest continually inhabited communities in the United States. Now, the city of Taos is pretty well known for hosting a lot of artist communities. That goes back seventy years."

Frack took up the story. "Yeah, it was, like, around 1912 or 1915 when a bunch of artists established the Taos Society of Artists."

"1915," Frick said.

"Right. After that those creative types just kept coming and a lot stayed. I mean, let's face it—the Taos Pueblo and the Sangre de Cristo Mountains are a painter's and photographer's dream. Some of the artists' houses are even listed on the National Register of Historic Places."

“So, if Taylor was really into her photography, this city and pueblo would be ideal for her and her camera,” Nick said.

“Exactly,” Sand agreed.

“It would,” Frick said, “but the Taos Pueblo is a horse of a different color. It’s a … unique place. It has a colorful history and a lot of spoken and unspoken rules for the people that live and visit there.”

“Like what?” Nick asked.

“Well, it’s known for being one of the most private, conservative, and secretive pueblos in the state. Residents tolerate outsiders in order to draw in necessary revenue, but they view them with suspicion and rarely talk to outsiders about their religious and social customs and beliefs. One of the reasons that outsiders know so little about the pueblo and its people is that their Tanoan language has never been written down. History is passed orally. The governing body is tribal, so for the most part although they’ll tolerate some of the white man’s law enforcement, they don’t really recognize federal authority.”

“How big is it?”

“Not too big, only around twenty acres close to a small river, the Rio de Pueblo Taos. However, the reservation surrounding it is close to a hundred thousand acres. I’d say around four or five thousand people live in the rez and pueblo, maybe just a couple hundred in the pueblo itself.”

“You said they were governed by a tribal council,” Nick said. “Any other law enforcement agencies in the area that we should contact?”

Frack nodded as he brushed breadcrumbs off his lips. “Several. You’ve got the Taos Pueblo Tribal Court, of course, as well as the Taos Police Department, the Taos County Sheriff’s Department, and the New Mexico State Police. I say we hit the Taos Police Department first.”

“Works for me,” Sand said. “Even though we could drive back to Santa Fe by late night I suggest we spend the night in Taos so we can extend our search area in both the city and the pueblo.”

“Yeah, I’m not sure that the boss will want us to invoice a hotel,” Frack said.

"Our treat," Sand said.

"In that case, let's hole up at the Hotel La Fonda de Taos."

"You just love spending our money, don't you?" Nick said, amused.

"You guys might not have any class, but we do," Frick said.

"Fine. As soon as we find a pay phone, I'll call in a reservation. But you two are getting a room, not a suite," Sand said. "And no room service."

"Might as well stay at a cheap motel then," Frack muttered as he and Frick got back into their car. "I don't care what he thinks—I'm gonna hit the mini bar."

As Nick slid into the passenger seat and Sand got behind the wheel Nick said, "We're not going to charge the client for their room, are we?"

"Hell, no. I'll pay for it. A few bucks will buy us some good will."

"Can we have room service?"

"Hell, no."

"I'll pay for the room service."

"Okay."

Nick grinned. "I love how well we get along now that you're not beating a confession out of me with a rubber hose."

"I never used a rubber hose. It was a fly swatter."

"It still hurt." Nick smiled to himself as he watched the road rush by as they headed to Taos. It had been Sand, then a detective in Santa Fe in 1965, and his late partner, Cole Garrison, who had arrested him for Stephanie Danvers' murder. They had interrogated him, but he had never confessed. And neither man had laid a hand on him, which is more than he could say for a few other cops. He always respected Sand for that, especially since at the time Nick had been a grimy, arrogant hippie that disdained cops simply on principle. It didn't happen overnight, but over the years they had become not only colleagues but good friends. Relatives, almost, since Nick was married to Sand's significant other's sister. Nick and Yuki had helped Sand and Akiro move into their new house, and Nick himself had painted the living room and kitchen.

The two cars drove past the sign pointing to the Taos Pueblo. Five miles outside of the city center Route 522 turned into Route 64, which took them directly to the hotel after they turned off on Plaza. They parked and went inside.

Frack whistled. "Classy."

He was right. The inside lobby was huge, with giant wooden beams across the ceiling. Hand-carved benches with red leather cushions welcomed arrivals, and the L-shaped lobby desk had a pert, smiling clerk waiting to help them. The walls in the lobby were covered with Indian and southwest art, quite a few pictures devoted to Kiowa artist Robert Redbird. The clerk had their reservations handy and within minutes they were walking towards their rooms. Each pair had a large room with two queen beds and, thankfully for Frack, a mini bar.

The four men reconvened in the lobby a half hour later and since the police station was only a quarter mile away, they decided to walk there to meet with one of the detectives; Skye had called ahead of time and arranged the meeting. Sand and Nick kept up a running commentary as they walked, admiring the buildings and charm of the center of the city. Nick pointed out a small taco place that Sand agreed would do well for dinner.

Frick and Frack preceded them into the station and Frick told the desk sergeant that they were expected by a Detective Garcia. A few minutes later a tall Hispanic man with a pencil-thin moustache and slicked-back dark brown hair walked over to them and shook hands. He led the four men into a conference room and sat at the head of the table.

Frick introduced himself and his associates and explained their missing persons search in great detail. Garcia listened quietly, nodding on occasion and asking for clarification on a few points. When Frick finished, Garcia was silent for a moment, then leaned forward.

"So," Garcia said slowly, "you have a pair of missing young people but there is no evidence of any foul play. Yet you are treating this situation like a kidnapping or major crime, engaging private investigators in a police matter."

Before Frick could reply Sand said, "Detective Smith didn't 'engage' us. The missing girl's father did. Two decent young people have been missing for almost a month, and their families are concerned."

"With all due respect," Garcia said, his tone indicating anything but respect, "this is not a matter for the Taos police. Unless we have evidence that a crime was committed in our jurisdiction, we cannot waste resources gadding about looking for a man and woman who may simply be off on a lark somewhere else."

Frick's response was again stalled by Nick's interjection.

"With all due respect, Detective Garcia, we aren't asking for your help. Our visit was simply a consideration to inform you of our presence and mission," Nick said flatly. "Between our Santa Fe police detectives" —he inclined his head towards Frick and Frack— "and myself and my colleague, we are quite adequate to handle the search." He smiled tightly, the smile never reaching his sharp blue eyes.

Garcia stared at Nick coldly, then produced his own tight smile as he focused on Frick. "Thank you for your … consideration. Please be sure to contact me if you come across anything that would indicate criminal activity in my jurisdiction. Permit me to see you out." With that he rose and walked to the door and opened it. He made a sweeping arm gesture towards the quartet, who exited single file then followed Garcia back to the lobby.

Wordlessly Frick led his partners outside where he stood on the sidewalk balancing on his heels, dead silent for an interminable moment. He turned to Nick.

"Are there any cops between the east coast and California that you haven't pissed off?" Frick said flatly.

Nick pursed his lips, then shook his head. "Can't think of any. It's pretty much a matter of degree between general dislike and outright hatred."

"I'm waffling between the two," Frack growled.

"Right now, I'm not," Frick snapped.

Sand came to his partner's defense. "That man was not going to help us. You could hear it in his voice and see it in his face." He threw a sideways glance at Nick. "Maybe Nick could have been a little more circumspect, but the end result would've been the same."

Frick snorted and began walking back towards the hotel with Frack on his heels. Just before following Sand turned to Nick and said, "Spaz."

Nick shrugged and followed Sand down the street. Frack swerved into the taco shop and they sat at a small table. The waiter brought over ten tacos and a huge bowl of chips plus salsa. Frack ate most of the food as they talked about next steps. They had several hours of daylight left and plenty of time to start canvassing. Sand suggested that he and Nick take art galleries since Stone was a painter while Frick and Frack checked out hotels and other places. Tomorrow, they'd head out to Taos Pueblo.

Sand and Nick made the rounds of the galleries that lined the central plaza. Nick was excited when they were in one that was highlighting the paintings of HashNaa. One dominated the west wall of the gallery, a minutely detailed scene of the Taos Pueblo with the imposing Sangre de Cristo Mountains looming in the background, a lightning storm threatening to break open clouds of rain. The small brass plaque affixed to the bottom of the painting named the work succinctly—"Angry Spirits."

Nick told Sand that Percy had met the artist and the man had painted him into a Bandelier scene and was going to gift him the painting when it was done. Both men were awed by the price of the paintings for sale. In a smaller gallery highlighting black and white watercolor sketches of desert scenes Nick found one that he knew Yuki would love. He ignored Sand's eyerolling as he paid for the framed original.

Neither team had any luck in finding any person or business that remembered the missing couple or their car. They met up back at the hotel after nine, had a nightcap at the bar, and went to their respective rooms.

Nick called Yuki and they talked for a half hour. She was feeling fine and swore that she felt the baby kick. Nick was aching to get home. He kept her gift a secret. He asked her to call Percy and let him know that all was well, and he'd be home tomorrow.

Sand called Memphis and updated him on their progress, and Memphis said he'd call Adam in San Francisco and give him the skinny. Memphis said that he and Swan planned on traveling back east in a few days to try to mine information about Cameo at the hospital and police station and see if there was any trail they could follow. Cameo had given them written permission to talk to the doctors, including the psychiatrist with whom she'd had two sessions. Sand asked about their other open cases and Memphis said that Devon was handling two of them with some assistance from Tucson and he was thinking of hiring another associate. No, he didn't have any candidates in mind. They'd discuss the matter when everyone was back in the office.

Frick called Captain Carraway and updated him on their progress. He made it clear that the hotel was being paid for by the P.I.s. After he hung up, he called Akiro, who was pet sitting his cat and Frack's dog. Akiro said both pets were fine and, yes, he fed Pierre the sirloin steak that Frack had left for him. Yes, he gave Bast a can of albacore tuna.

No one wanted to eat a late dinner and all four men crashed by eleven. As tired as he was Frick was up several times during the night due to Frack's loud snoring. He wondered how Carly had endured it for all the years they were married. He fell into a fitful sleep around three and managed to stay asleep until nearly 8 AM. When he woke up Frack was in the shower belting out a horrendous version of *Bad, Bad Leroy Brown.* Frick stuffed his head under the pillow until the caterwauling died out. He growled and swore as he slogged through a wet, messy bathroom to take his own shower. He wished he had brought his toothbrush and used his index finger as best he could.

They met Sand and Nick downstairs in the hotel's Noula's Coffee Shop. The two P.I.s looked perky and refreshed and had obviously had a good night's sleep. They were drinking coffee and chomping on various pastries. When Frack found out the shop didn't serve "real breakfast food," he started getting crabby, but Sand promised they'd find a nice place to eat before they drove to the Taos Pueblo. Sand called over the waiter who directed them to a good place in the historic district to get pancakes, eggs, and bacon; that seemed to mollify Frack.

Four full breakfasts later the four men piled into Frick's car, the largest, and headed up Route 64 to their destination. The parking lot already had a substantial number of cars. Frick asked to talk to someone in charge and a few minutes later he was explaining that he and his friends wanted to talk to some of the people to see if anyone knew of the couple for which they were searching. The man wasn't too sanguine about that, but he understood and handed Frick a brochure that made the rules of visiting the pueblo clear.

1. Please abide by "Restricted Area" signs. These areas are designated to protect the privacy of our residents and the sites of our native religious practices.
2. We ask to not enter doors/homes that are not clearly marked as businesses. Some of the homes are used as a place of business which are clearly marked with signs. Other homes are not open to the public.
3. Please do not photograph tribal members without permission.
4. Absolutely no photography in San Geronimo Chapel.
5. Please respect our cemetery by not entering, it also holds the ruins of the old church. An adobe wall surrounds this area, this is the boundary.
6. Do not enter the river—our sole source of drinking water.
7. And last but far from least, as we welcome you into our home please respect it as it was your own home. There are rules in place to ensure a great visit for visitors and to ensure the culture and traditions of our home are maintained and kept intact.

Frick thanked him and paid for four admissions. Each man had copies of the photos and they spread out throughout the pueblo as they began investigating.

Sand hadn't had any luck as he meandered towards the cemetery, mindful of the regulation to not enter. An elderly woman was inside cleaning weeds away from one of the grave markers. The remnant of the mission church stood watch over the field of crosses, its top crowned by a large bell; a row of single-story adobe houses rimmed the section beside the expanse of shrub-filled desert leading up to the mountains. He took a minute to watch her. She knelt, then made the sign of the cross, rose, and walked towards the cemetery entrance. He hated to bother her, but he'd had no luck so far and he wanted to touch every possible base.

She was walking towards him, so he took a deep breath and approached her carefully. She stopped and stared at him. He ducked his head and smiled. He had no concept of the Tanoan language, so he spoke in English. "Good morning." He waited.

The Indian woman hesitated for a few seconds then replied in accented English. "Good morning." She had to be in her seventies, her lined face full of the crags and flaws accompanying a long and hard life, yet with eyes as bright and alive as any teenager's.

"May I ask you a question?" he said gently.

She hesitated again, then nodded.

Sand showed her the photo of Taylor and Stone. "Have you ever seen these people, ma'am?"

The woman stared at the photos for what seemed a long time. She finally looked up into Sand's face. She twisted her head quickly and spit on the ground.

"White bitch," she snarled.

CHAPTER TWELVE

"The LeBlanc case takes priority," Memphis said to Devon as they went over the pending cases in his office. "Then the McAllister case, and lastly the background check for Professor Castillo. Any questions?"

"What if something horrible happens while everyone's out of the office?" Devon asked seriously.

"Skye, Tucson, Akiro, Percy in that order. Frick or Frack if you're desperate for police intervention. But I'm sure you can handle anything 'horrible' that occurs. Besides, except for me and Swan the others are expected to be around, just in and out of the office. There aren't any other out-of-town trips planned." He arched an eyebrow. "You're an ex-cop. Surely you can handle anything short of a multi-man shootout. Even then, I wouldn't bet against you."

"Damn straight," she said, straightening in her chair. "I just like to know the rules."

"The rules are you can handle it." He paused a moment, then took out a thin folder and handed it to her. "A couple of days ago I put an ad in the paper looking for a new associate. Those are the five most promising candidates. Study the applications and make notes regarding your impressions. Then ask Skye to schedule interviews. Either Sand or I should be present, but I'd like you to be there, too."

"Me? I'm still a newbie."

"And whoever I hire will be the next newbie, making you one of the oldies but goodies."

Devon flipped through the applications while Memphis watched. She looked at him thoughtfully.

"What are you looking for? I mean, regardless of education or experience."

"Use your instincts. I do. That's why I hired you. Now, go. I've got work to do and so do you."

Both stood at the same time. Devon inclined her head and left the office. She headed into her office, which was set up to hold two junior associates. She thought that whoever was selected would be up close and personal with her on a daily basis, so she had a vested interest in making sure the right person was chosen. Not that it was her call, but she was relieved and proud that the boss valued her opinion and put stock in her instincts.

She had been hesitant when she joined the firm, almost on a whim. She thought that perhaps she should have gone up north with Jamal for his new job in the State Police, but something about Santa Fe drew her to the city. Now, she was glad she stayed since he had cheated on her and they had broken up. Even before that she had thrown herself into her new job. Her comfort level grew quickly once she adjusted to the diverse personalities, skill sets, and backgrounds of her colleagues. Swan and Sand were ex-cops. The firm was clearly family-oriented since most of the building's residents were either related by blood or marriage. Perhaps the most unusual member was the dwarf. She had been shocked at first; the only place she had ever seen such a small human being was at the circus. Her initial impression of surprise quickly dissipated when she got to know him. He was smart, devoted to his family, and a consummate professional. It didn't take long for her to not see his physical limitations at all.

Devon missed her family back east, but they kept in contact over the phone. She thought she'd hate living in the desert surrounded by mountains and peculiar architecture, but after a couple of months she learned to appreciate the desert and the adobe buildings and red tile roofs. She found a studio apartment off the beaten path and furnished it minimally although she'd started to buy southwest-inspired hanging prints to decorate her walls. She had made several friends outside of work but only a couple were black like she was (although her father was white, she considered herself black). The city was mainly white, Indian, and Hispanic. She'd been the recipient of a few nasty racial remarks but always answered them with a raised middle finger or a black power salute. That didn't make her popular, but it was a way of diffusing her natural anger.

She looked over the five applications. All men, ranging in age from twenty-four to thirty-two. Three had college degrees. Two had served in the armed forces. Two were from the Santa Fe area while the other three were from California, Mississippi, and Virginia. Only one application was accompanied by a resumé, a half-page with basic contact information, academic information, and a few lines of job experience that had nothing to do with investigations. She compared that man's application with the others. His was meticulously filled out with symmetrical block letters that never went over the lines or boxes. His signature was bold. The others had filled their applications out with some care, but most of them left some spaces blank or illegible. She put the neatnik's application to the side; he'd be her first interview.

Dante Redwolf. The name intrigued her. Unlike her, obviously not black and Irish. She called Skye and asked her to set up an interview for her, Redwolf, and Sand as soon as possible. She prioritized the other four applications, but she just had a feeling about number one. She wondered if Memphis did, too, since Redwolf's application was on top of the others.

Sand rapped sharply on Memphis's door before entering without an invitation. Nick was right behind him, followed by Frick.

"Where's your better half?" Memphis asked Frick.

"Pierre was due for shots and blood tests," Frick said. "Then he's off to the groomer for clipping, shampooing, and a massage."

"A massage?" Sand said, his eyebrows shooting halfway up his forehead.

"What can I say? He's Frack's baby boy."

Memphis snorted. "Our version of that is to turn on the hose full blast." Beloved family dog Pancakes had passed on two years earlier, but old Waffles was still spry. He was also the mentor and guardian to the black lab, Odin, that the family had adopted last year. For whatever reason Odin had made his parent choice and followed Raleigh around wherever she went. "So, what've we got?"

Sand flipped open his spiral notebook. "The lady at the Taos cemetery was named Elpidia Martinez. She's lived there all her life, a devout Catholic although she does adhere to her people's ancient beliefs and customs in most respects. The day I met her she was visiting her son's grave. He died in Vietnam. Anyway, she identified Taylor Geary from the photos. She spit on the ground when I showed it to her and called her a 'white bitch.' Apparently, what pissed her off was that Taylor and her boyfriend were preening and sitting on the cemetery stone wall and mugging for the camera. Elpidia said it was extremely disrespectful. She called them on it and the idiot girl flipped her the bird."

"Asshole," Frick muttered.

"Yeah." Sand shook his head. "I found the guy who was selling the admission tickets that day and he says he doesn't specifically remember them. He said, 'All you palefaces look alike to me.' That's a direct quote."

"We did find a couple other people who think they saw the kids that day but couldn't say for sure and didn't have any up-front contact with them," Nick said.

"Anything special going on that day that might have bearing on the case?" Memphis asked. "Like, were there any festivals or ceremonies happening?"

Sand shook his head. "The people we talked to said it was a typical day with typical tourists, artists, and photographers. Other than the kids' aberrant behavior it seemed like visitors were respecting the rules and playing nice."

"No one noticed when they left or where they were going," Frick added. "South, I expect, to Santa Fe, but there's no telling how far south they got before they vanished."

"Or, if they even continued towards the city," Nick said. "There's a cluster of pueblos around the area that they might have wanted to visit, like Picuris, San Juan, Nambé. They could've cut off on Route 75, Route 76, any number of offshoots that would have taken them east or west."

"So, we're right back where we started," Frick said dejectedly.

"Far from it," Memphis said, shaking his head. "We found them in San Luis, we found them in Taos, and we know that somewhere between Taos and Santa Fe they were in the area. That's seventy miles north-south, and less east-west if they decided to hit another pueblo. It's not a small area, but it's not like the entire state."

"It's too much for only a few of us to cover," Nick said. "Think Geary will okay additional resources?"

"Probably," Memphis said. "But I'm not sure that throwing bodies at the area will buy us much. We need to come up with a smarter plan."

"Got one in mind?" Sand asked.

"Not off the top of my head." Before he could go on Skye called and said the guy he was expecting had arrived. Memphis told her to wait a few minutes then bring him into the Graceland Conference Room. He ushered his crew out of his office and into the larger space.

"We're expecting a guy?" Sand asked when he sat down.

Memphis nodded. "Our new FBI contact, the one Adam told us about. He drove up here from Albuquerque." He turned on the Mr. Coffee.

"Great," Frick said sourly. "I hate fibbies."

"You didn't hate Tom Ballard," Sand said.

"He was different. He was like a normal person, not a G-Man turd."

"Try to keep an open mind," Nick said. Frick grunted. "I know that doesn't come natural to you but try."

Skye pounded unnecessarily hard on the conference room door and opened it. She made a sweeping arm gesture and a man entered. He turned to thank her, but she was already gone. A few years under thirty, he was a solid six-footer, a freckled redhead with brilliant blue eyes. He had a thousand-watt smile that was clearly genuine, not a trace of artifice on his open face. He was wearing a crisp navy three-piece suit with a white shirt and raspberry tie.

Memphis rose and walked over to him. The man stuck out his hand and said, "Special Agent Richard Ballard."

"Ballard," Sand exclaimed. "Are you related—"

"Tom Ballard is my father." He grinned. "So, I guess I have one up on you as far as familiarity."

"You kind of look like your dad," Memphis said, indicating an empty chair. When Ballard sat down Memphis introduced his associates then said, "Did you just relocate to Albuquerque?"

"A few weeks ago," Ballard said. "My wife is setting up our apartment while I learn the ropes of the new job. I was in Atlanta before that."

"Your dad still in Philly?" Memphis noticed an almost indefinable shadow pass over Ballard's face.

Ballard nodded. "He's retiring next year. I think he and my mom plan on doing some traveling after that."

"Well, maybe he'll visit you out here," Memphis said. "We'd love to see him again."

Ballard's smile was tight. "Maybe." He opened his briefcase and withdrew a manila folder. "Your current case notwithstanding, I have what may be interesting information for you."

"Relating to the case?" Frick asked.

"Maybe, maybe not." He handed a sheet of paper to Memphis, and a duplicate to Frick. "It seems like your San Francisco couple may not be the only missing kids in the state. On that list you'll find eleven names of people that have vanished over the past five years."

"All kids?" Sand said as he craned his neck to see the list Memphis was looking at.

"Nope. They run the gamut. Men and women, youngest was eighteen and the oldest was fifty-nine. Four of them are New Mexico natives and the other seven were from four different states."

"Surely there must be more than just eleven people missing in the state during that time period," Frick said.

"Of course. Some missing persons were found, either dead or alive, but this list seems to locate them in a circular diameter of around one hundred fifty miles in central-northern New Mexico. That includes Santa Fe and Albuquerque. When we compiled the list, we also discounted certain reasons for 'disappearing,' like avoiding child support and alimony, evading arrest, collections, and things like that, things that would prompt someone to deliberately disappear."

"Do these eleven people have anything in common?" Sand asked.

"From what we know about them, not a damn thing," Ballard said, shaking his head.

"Then they're probably completely unrelated to Taylor and Stone," Frick said. "People disappear all the time."

Sand nodded. "True. And, with all due respect to these other people, we weren't hired to find them. It's an interesting aside, but my feeling is that we need to just focus on the object of our investigation."

"But if they are related ..." Nick said, trailing off with the unspoken thought.

"Look," Memphis said. "You're all right. We were hired to look for the Frisco kids. But it wouldn't hurt to spend a day, say, looking at Agent Ballard's list and see if we can intuit anything that might impact our case."

"Rick, please," Ballard said.

"Rick," Memphis echoed, nodding. "So, Rick, how about we update you on what we've discovered over the past week?"

"I'd be grateful," Ballard said. "I'd be even more grateful if I could get a cup of coffee." He didn't wait and jumped up and poured a mug. The rest of the crew lined up to do the same; Frick was ticked when Sand poured the last of the coffee into his cup.

"Chill, Frickster," Sand said casually as he washed the carafe out in the small sink and set a new pot to brew. "It'll take five minutes." He handed his full mug to Frick. "Be my guest."

Frick grunted a semi-thank you and took the mug. Sand stood by the coffee machine waiting for his own brew then reseated himself.

Memphis ran over the investigation done by his crew and the police, with Sand, Nick, and Frick interjecting for clarification and details. Halfway through the door opened and Frack joined the gang. He impatiently shooed Nick away so he could sit next to his partner. Memphis introduced him to Ballard. Frack was surprised to find out that he'd be working with the next generation of the Ballard family.

"Everything okay with the mutt?" Nick asked.

"The rotten beast lives better than I do," Frack said. "His grooming costs more."

"Well, sure," Nick said. "Doesn't cost much to put a soup bowl on your head and clip around the edges."

"You could use a haircut yourself. You're startin' to look like George Harrison."

"Cut these glorious locks? Nah. My wife likes to run her fingers through them."

Ballard grinned widely. He asked Memphis, "Do you charge extra for the comedy show?"

"Freebie for the FBI," Memphis replied. "For others we add on ten percent." He said to Frack, "We updated Rick on your investigation. He's brought us a list of other similarly missing people in the area over the last five years."

"Oh, Christ," Frack moaned. "You're not going to tell Carraway about this, are you? We're run ragged as it is."

"There's nothing to suggest that the cases are related to the Frisco kids," Ballard said. "And from what you've told me, there's still no definitive proof that any foul play was involved in their disappearance." He held up a hand. "But I'm personally inclined to believe that something bad has happened. I'm just not sure what the FBI can do about it, or you gentlemen, for that matter."

"Somewhere between Taos and Santa Fe, Taylor and Stone vanished," Memphis said.

"Do you think they're still alive?" Ballard asked quietly.

"No," Memphis answered just as quietly. "It's just a feeling."

"We still have avenues to pursue," Sand said. "She liked to take pictures, so maybe we should make the rounds of nearby pueblos and any other historical sites. And cars."

"What about cars?" Frick asked.

"We know the car they were driving. We can put ads in the regional papers to see if anyone's seen or bought a car like that. I mean, if someone … killed them it's possible they took the car and kept it and are using it. Or, they might have sold it in whole or in parts."

"We're screwed if it's in parts," Nick said. "Hell, it could be in Mexico by now."

Memphis snapped his fingers. "Swan and I met a good cop down in El Paso when we were backtracking Joanna Frid's activity in the border area. Maybe I'll give him a call and see if he can root around in El Paso and Juárez for the car. It's a longshot, but we've got nothing to lose." He noted the smirk on Sand's face. "Don't even go there," he warned his brother-in-law. Everyone except Ballard burst out laughing.

"Inside joke?" Ballard asked.

"You have no idea," Sand said, laughing. "Look, I'll talk to Swan and get the Texas cop's contact info, and I'll have Skye put ads in the regional papers. Want me to add newspapers from Arizona and Texas?"

"Yeah, do that," Memphis said. "You and Nick make out a pueblo map and we'll go over it tomorrow." He glanced at Frick. "I think our law enforcement buddies would like to get back to their jobs. I'll call Adam and Rick and I'll update him on what we've discussed."

Sand, Nick, and the two detectives left. Memphis got another cup of coffee and called Adam on speakerphone. He introduced Ballard and gave Adam a detailed synopsis of what the investigation had uncovered, and the list of missing persons that the FBI had produced. Adam agreed that there wasn't enough to go on to relate those cases to the one on which they were working. He told Memphis that he'd visit the Gearys and update them on the case.

When Memphis hung up, he sighed and leaned back in his chair.

"I wanted to tell you why I'm not involved in the day to day investigation of this case," he said. "The reason is that my wife, Swan, and I are taking the lead on another, well … sort of missing persons case that's going to take us to the east coast in a few days."

"Sort of missing person?" Ballard said curiously.

"It's confidential, but all I can say is that we're trying to identify an amnesiac client."

"Amnesia. Wow. That's rare."

Memphis nodded. "It is. It's a curious and somewhat intriguing case. My brother, Tucson, is a Doctor of Psychology and his partner, Percy, and he are exploring the psychological aspect of her case."

"Is this the … little Percy my father told me about?"

"He'd be the one. I'll introduce you soon. So, let me ask—do you have everything you need with your relocation? Anything we can do to help?"

"No, but thanks. I lived there for some years before I went off to college back east."

"Right, right. I forgot. Is your wife from back east?"

Ballard flashed an odd smile. "Very back east." He paused at the querulous look on Memphis's face. "My wife, Noor, is from Jordan."

"That really is back east," Memphis said, smiling. "At least she'll be comfortable with the desert weather. How long have you been married?"

"Eight months. I met Noor last year when I was a fresh agent accompanying a senior agent on a fact-finding mission in Amman. I confess—it was love at first sight, at least for me. She was smarter and more cautious. But … the heart wants what it wants, and we fell in love. That opened a can of very nasty worms. Her family was a prominent noble family called the Ayasrah. They trace their lineage back hundreds of years to Banu Hashim, Hashemite descendants of the Prophet Muhammad. The last thing in the universe that they wanted was for their daughter to marry a Christian, and an American Christian at that."

"Your family?"

"Ah … not happy at all. That's probably understating it. But we decided to say we were going to live our lives as we saw fit. We got married here in the States. Her family disowned her and considers her dead. My family in Philly will barely speak to me."

"I'm kind of surprised at that," Memphis said slowly. "I always viewed your father as enlightened and willing to accept things out of his usual realm of comfort."

Ballard shrugged. "I think he changed during his assignment regarding the Middle East. It's been a powder keg for years, and sometimes it's difficult to reconcile tolerance with reality. I'm hoping that he and my mom will come around. Right now, I have a job to do, and Noor has to adjust to a new country and new way of life."

"Does she work?"

"Not right now. Maybe when she gets used to America and New Mexico. She was educated in Switzerland and has a degree from the University of Geneva. She got her degree in social sciences. She loved studying about the challenges of contemporary societies and shifting political and social identities. I don't imagine her parents thought she'd do anything other than be the educated wife of a prominent Jordanian man."

"And then you came along."

"And then I came along."

"Perhaps you can encourage her to study at the UNM."

"Great idea." Ballard checked his watch and took a deep breath. "I need to get back."

"Do you have time for lunch?"

"I wish. Maybe another time. I'd rather get home. Sometimes Noor gets nervous when she's alone for too long."

"How about this," Memphis said as they rose at the same time. "When Swan and I get back from our east coast trip why don't you and your wife join us for dinner? We can dump the kids on a relative so dinner will be relatively calm. You can give us a list of foods to avoid. Neither of us is a great cook but most of what we whip up in the kitchen isn't lethal."

"Well, there's an enticement if ever there was one," Ballard said, laughing. "It's a date."

They shook hands and Memphis walked Ballard out to his car. He waved as the FBI agent drove away.

Yeah, he thought, this second-generation Ballard would work out well.

CHAPTER THIRTEEN

Kim Caine hated his name because "Kim" was generally a girl's name and he was a man's man. His full first name was Kimball, but everyone in his family called him Kim. He gave himself a nickname when he was in middle school, Roy. Why? Because "Kimball" meant Royal Bold. Regardless of how much he protested his parents still called him Kim. His older sister called him idiot. He called her bitch.

After he graduated Stony Brook University, he spent a month at home in Huntington, New York, figuring out what he wanted to do with his life. He had majored in History, an utterly useless discipline according to his welder father. His parents had scraped and saved to put him and his sister through college. She, at least, had become a teacher and had a job with benefits. He was the dreamer of the family, the rebel, the one with vision, or so he told himself and anyone else that would listen.

In July his father told him to get a job and cut his goddamn fucking hair or get out of the house. Mr. Caine had secured an apprentice welder job for him at the place where he worked, but Roy would have preferred death by electrocution. He said those exact words to his father who proceeded to give him twenty-four hours to get his lazy ass out of the house. Roy stuffed a backpack full of clothes and sundries (including six joints), kissed his mother goodbye, flashed his father the finger, and took the train into New York City. He couch-surfed with a few friends until their patience ran out, then he packed up once again. He took the ferry to New Jersey, then hit Interstate 80 and began hitchhiking west. I-80 wasn't a complete, uninterrupted road from one end of the country to the other, but there was enough of a system to get him close to his ultimate goal, San Francisco.

Since he had no job waiting or anything else resembling a defined plan, he took his time traveling. He'd never left New York before and he wanted to soak in the wonderful aspects of the country. The country was changing rapidly, and he wanted to drink it all in; he was thirsty for adventure. He had started college in 1970, and in the past four years so many critical changes had occurred across the globe.

The Vietnam War was officially over although U.S. troops still maintained a presence in Saigon. He was relieved that his student deferment had prevented him from being drafted.

The Beatles had broken up and gone on their separate musical journeys. He thought that John was the most likely to succeed. Ringo was history.

Disco had replaced the British Invasion. He absolutely hated ABBA and had actually smashed a transistor radio when *Waterloo* came on for the millionth time. He screamed when he first heard *Havin' My Baby* by Paul Anka; he'd moan when *The Night Chicago Died* and *Billy, Don't Be a Hero* would hit the airwaves. He closed his eyes and nodded his head in approval when Gordon Lightfoot sang *Sundown.*

Women's Lib was in full force. His stupid sister had joined an activist group that met once a week in Steak and Ale to harp about men and the rising cost of gasoline (it was up to $.55 per gallon!). They also planned their monthly trip to the city to shop at Macy's and Bloomie's.

Hippies were still around but their clothing and attitude had changed with the times. Pot was still big; so was long hair.

He didn't consider himself a hippie; rather, a free spirit. He disdained "the Establishment" and the rules and limitations that concept imposed. He felt free to do his own thing and others' opinions be damned.

He stopped and restarted his hitchhiking in various places so he could take in the sights of his country. He rode the I-80 for a while before swinging south and zigzagging his way west. He got off in Pennsylvania and headed to Gettysburg, at which he found a sense of history that he had studied, and an unusual sense of peace. He decided that wherever he visited he'd take a piece of that place with him. He picked up a quarter-sized rock from the battlefield and put it in his backpack. That was his pattern from that point on.

Roy hit Washington, D.C. then Virginia. He was halfway to Appomattox when he read that Nixon was going to resign, so he hitched back up to D.C. and stood with the crowds outside the White House and clapped and cheered when the crook gave his address on August 8th. He smoked his last joint in celebration, then headed back south. He hit the historical place where General Lee surrendered, picked up a small souvenir, and continued south. He hit Charleston and Savannah. In the latter city he visited the Bonaventure Cemetery. He was about to pick up a small stone souvenir when he had a sudden urge to take a real piece of the magnificent burying grounds with him. He carefully looked around, then used a sharp rock to chip off an edge of an old headstone. He slipped it in his backpack and hurried off. The adrenaline was pumping, and he vowed that from that point on he'd take real pieces from his journeys, not stupid rocks.

He moved west after he visited New Orleans. He had to wait until after dark to nail a tiny piece of the Alamo in San Antonio. While he was in the city he learned from informational booths about New Mexico and the wealth of pueblos clustered in a close area. He had studied the Spanish colonization of the southwest in college and the possibility of visiting these sites excited him. He bought a map and made a plan. He'd start north and work his way down, so Taos was the first stop on his mission. It would be a hell of a mission—New Mexico had nineteen pueblos. In addition to Taos, the northernmost, there were the Acoma, Cochiti, Isleta, Jemez, Laguna, Nambé, Picuris, Pojoaque, Sandia, San Felipe, San Ildefonso, San Juan, Santa Ana,

Santa Clara, Santo Domingo, Tesuque, Zia, and Zuni pueblos. Zuni was the farthest west, so that would be the endgame.

He was in awe of the pueblo. He spent a half day there and managed to collect his souvenir. He thought his backpack was getting heavy. He'd have to chuck some old clothes to make room. He hit the Picuris Pueblo next, then the San Juan and Santa Clara. He swung east to visit Nambé.

Nambé, he thought, was proving to be one of the more interesting pueblos.

Nambé, New Mexico was a tiny town twenty miles north of Santa Fe, just off State Road 503. However, it was not actually a "town," but a Native American enclave comprised of a very small community and the Nambé Oweenge Pueblo. The Pueblo had existed since the fourteenth century and was a member of the Eight Northern Pueblos of New Mexico. These are comprised of Taos, Picuris, Santa Clara, Ohkay Owingeh (formerly San Juan), San Ildefonso, Nambé, Pojoaque, and Tesuque. Taos and Picuris people speak Tiwa; the rest speak Tewa, and both are closely related languages of the Kiowa-Tanoan language family.

Nambé is the Spanish derivative of a similar-sounding Tewa word, which can be interpreted loosely as meaning "rounded earth." The word "pueblo" stems from the Spanish word for "village."

Located in the foothills of the Sangre de Cristo Mountains the pueblo spans twenty thousand acres characterized by immense cottonwoods, juniper, oak, and occasional outcroppings of sandstone. The Rio Nambé, whose headwaters originate high in the mountains, five miles to the east of the reservation boundary, flows through the pueblo and eventually feeds into the Rio Grande. The designated recreation area permits swimming, lake fishing, a remarkable double-drop waterfall, and camping. Each year on October 4th the pueblo honors its patron saint, San Francisco de Asís, who does double duty as the patron saint of Santa Fe. The pueblo plaza is designated as a National Historic Landmark.

New Mexico became an official state in 1912 along with Arizona, but the Pueblos were recognized as federally viable tribes and allowed to keep their life and customs. The Nambé Pueblo tribe was organized under the Indian Reorganization Act of June 18, 1934.

Although Taos had the spectacular architecture and view of the Sangre de Cristo Mountains, Nambé had a stunning falls and lake area. The series of tall waterfalls (the two top tiers were seventy-five and a hundred feet high) were upstream from the pueblo and were crested by the mountains. The water was pure and sparkling clear, the air fresh and enlivening. There was no visitors' official approach to the falls, but many people chose to follow paths and try to avoid the tribal authorities. Roy passed another illicit hiker on his way to the top and they avoided eye contact. He had purchased a camera in D.C. and was recording his adventures not only with his souvenirs but also with photos. The shots of the falls were magnificent.

Roy took note of the construction at the top of the falls; the sign said that a dam was being created and work had started on June 13th. The storage reservoir would provide supplemental irrigation for the Pojoaque Valley Irrigation District and the pueblos of San Ildefonso, Nambé, and Pojoaque. The dam would be located about three hundred feet upstream from Nambé Falls, which formed the sharp break between the Sangre de Cristo Mountains on the east and the Espanola Basin on the west; it would be situated in a five-hundred-foot-long southwesterly trending gorge. The sign specified that completion of the project would take two years. Roy thought it was sheer luck that he was visiting on a weekend so that no one was working on the project.

He hiked down, slipping multiple times on wet rocks, but the effort was worth it. He drank from the falls and the stream below before he hiked downstream towards the pueblo. It wasn't too hot; October seemed to be a perfect month for exploring northern New Mexico. He roamed around the pueblo, garnering curious and sometimes disapproving looks from the residents. His long blonde hair and light blue eyes garnered him a fair share of appreciative looks from several young ladies. He stopped in a trading post and bought a dreamcatcher. He ambled towards the San Francisco de Asis church, a small adobe building that had been built in 1910. He watched as a few Indians went in and came out, and he thought he'd look inside.

The church was small, but quiet and reverent. A dozen people dotted the pews, and the silence inside the building was almost deafening. He was raised Catholic but discounted those teachings before he entered high school. He hated the Latin mass because he couldn't understand it. He walked slowly down the aisle to the candles. He glanced around quickly; everyone had their heads bowed and took no notice of him as he slipped a candle and its red glass holder into his pocket. He dropped a quarter into the box then ambled back up the aisle and out of the church. He grinned; he had snatched the same items from the churches in the other pueblos, and from now on that would be his souvenir signature. When he got to Frisco and found a place to live, he'd buy a couple of joints, sit cross-legged on the floor with the lit candles surrounding him in a circle, and enjoy the mellow feelings associated with smoking primo weed.

Roy decided he'd had enough, and it was time to head out. He walked back to the main road and stuck out his thumb. Two cars passed him, and he resisted flashing them the finger. A third car pulled out of the church parking lot and drove past him for twenty feet then stopped. Roy jogged up to the car and slid into the passenger seat.

"Hey, thanks, man," Roy said to the man who was driving. "How far you goin'?"

Po'Pay glanced over and smiled at him. "All the way, my young friend. All the way."

Kimball "Roy" Caine came awake slowly. The first thing he felt was the pounding headache that threatened to split his skull in two. The second thing was that he couldn't move. A few minutes passed before he was cognizant enough to realize that he wasn't paralyzed but held down by restraints. He tried to turn his head to the left, eliciting a sharp pain in his head and neck. His eyes were crusty, and his vision blurred. He forced himself to focus, and finally he could see that he was staring at a wall about five feet away. He craned his neck to the right.

The man was standing there a few feet away, watching him. Roy tried to speak but his mouth was as dry as cotton and he couldn't even emit a squeak. He blinked repeatedly and focused on the man, whom he realized was the one that had picked him up outside of the Nambé pueblo.

He was Indian, or maybe Mexican. No, something about his bearing and face clearly marked him as Indian. An inch or two under six feet he was muscular running towards beefy; yet, there didn't seem to be an ounce of extra fat on his burly frame. He had long black hair silvering at the temples, parted in the middle, and flowing over his shoulders and down his back. His dark eyes were deep-set with a slightly prominent brow over them, and eyebrows that evinced a sense of wings in flight. His nose was very slightly hooked; his cheekbones were sharp enough to slice a slab of meat.

He was dressed differently than when he was driving the car. Then, he had on faded jeans and a red and white checkered shirt and a thin leather vest. Now, he was wearing clothes that had a traditional Indian style to them. He wore light leather leggings that were loose and partially hidden by a long, fringed, belted leather breechclout; the belt was intricately braided strips of leather fastened by a silver buckle into which was hammered an eagle feather. His soft suede mukluks reached halfway up his calf; the top edge was fringed and there were no soles on the boots, the bottoms conforming to the shape of the foot. The boots and breechclout were heavily decorated with beads, the boot toes displaying single pieces of black-veined turquoise.

His shirt draped over his hips, a dark cranberry cotton garment with tiny white dots all over it in a structured pattern. Over the shirt was an ornate buckskin vest, fringed and beaded, with a row of feathers dangling from the bottom edges. He wore a red headband across his forehead, and several silver and turquoise rings on his hands. He was every inch representative of what Americans would consider the standard for an Indian man. The only things he was missing were a huge feathered headdress and a spear in his hand.

This man was holding a meat cleaver in his hand.

The stillness and silence of the room was broken by the desperate whimpering emanating from the back of Roy's throat. His immobilized body began trembling uncontrollably, and without warning he soiled himself. The man walked over to him slowly and stood above him. Roy was fastened to a wide rectangular table by thick leather straps across his ankles, thighs, midsection, upper arms, and wrists. He stared up at the Indian in absolute terror, tears filling his pleading eyes, the front of his jeans now soiled by urine as well.

"P-please," Roy managed to eke out.

"Do you wish mercy?" Po'Pay said in his deep, measured voice.

Roy's only answer was a mewling and the trembling of his dry lips.

"You are a white man that wishes mercy from a red man," Po'Pay said thoughtfully. "Should I show you the same mercy that your people have shown mine for hundreds of years?"

The mewling increased in intensity.

"Let me tell you about mercy," Po'Pay said flatly as he placed the cleaver down beside Roy's hip. "Mercy is something the invaders from Europe failed to show the indigenous population of what is now New England. They brought with them diseases and social and religious beliefs that they made clear were far superior to the pathetic Indian beliefs. They used heavy-handed and often brutal tactics to convert the 'savages' to that bastion of tolerance and love, Christianity. They called them 'Indians' because that idiot that 'found' the new world thought he'd landed in India. That insulting term stands to this very day.

"They stole their lands, killed their warriors, enslaved men, women, and children, and declared that the land belonged to them. That didn't stop on the east coast. As the white man pushed his way north, south and west he did the same thing to the tribes that were in the way of the white man's manifest destiny. They stole, murdered, butchered, and decimated the native populations and when they were done with that, they stuck those who survived onto reservations that defined the words desperate and poor.

"And reservations didn't shield the Indian from his oppressors. Did you ever hear of Wounded Knee? No? Let me tell you. The Lakota Sioux were herded onto the Wounded Knee reservation in South Dakota when it was established in 1889, the latest result of the government stealing Indian lands. In 1890 Chief Spotted Elk's warriors were armed and resistant to being corralled like animals. But animals they were to the United States government and the 7th Cavalry Regiment commanded by Major Samuel Whitside and Colonel James Forsyth surrounded the Indians' encampment. On December 29th, the U.S. cavalry and their four Hotchkiss mountain guns went in to disarm the Lakota.

"Long story short, the cavalry began shooting and when all was said and done hundreds of Lakota lay dead. Over half of those were women and children. Eyewitness accounts state that women holding babies were chased down over two miles by soldiers and slaughtered. After much of the carnage was finished the soldiers called out to survivors to come out and surrender. When they did, many—including young boys—were cut down. Some survivors said the soldiers simply went berserk. Twenty-five soldiers died, but at least the U.S. government awarded twenty soldiers the distinguished Medal of Honor.

"The Sand Creek Massacre in November of 1864 saw the murders of hundreds of men, women, children, and babies by the 675-man cavalry force under the command of Colonel John Chivington. His men didn't just obliterate a village of Arapaho and Cheyenne, they engaged in soulless, inhuman destruction of the virtually helpless inhabitants of the village. They scalped men, women, and children; unborn babies were cut out of their mothers' bodies. The soldiers decorated their weaponry and garments with the scalps and pieces of the dead. Early in the attack the Indians raised a white flag. That was ignored and the massacre went on.

"Chivington hated Indians with a passion. His famous declaration was, 'Damn any man who sympathizes with Indians! I have come to kill Indians, and believe it is right and honorable to use any means under God's heaven to kill Indians. Kill and scalp all, big and little; nits make lice.' Nits make lice. Chivington was soon condemned for his part in the massacre, but he had already resigned from the Army. The general post-Civil War amnesty meant that criminal charges could not be filed against him. You know, just a few years ago they made a movie based on the massacre. *Soldier Blue*. Unusually, it took the side of the Indians and presented a very horrific cinematic version of the event.

"My people lost their history, their traditions, their lands, their self-respect. Many became victims of alcohol. Suicide is not uncommon. We cling to what we remember and what we do have despite your people's best efforts to erase our culture. We do our best in these modern times to retain our honor, and all we ask of your people is basic respect."

Po'Pay whirled around and walked over to another table and picked up an object. He held it over Roy. "You stole this from a sacred place, a church that means everything to the people of the Nambé Pueblo. I searched your bag and found others as well as a map of our pueblos with several checked off. You stole those, too, from the other pueblos, didn't you? You were on a journey of disrespect. I do not know where the other items that appear to be mementoes of your travels came from, but I imagine they were representative of your ill will towards decency and honor as well."

Po'Pay put the candle down next to Roy's side and walked back to the other table. He gathered the other candles and placed them around Roy's body, and lit the wicks. Wordlessly he tightly fastened a small belt around the middle of Roy's right forearm. He stared down at Roy's terrified face. He stuffed a colorful bandana into Roy's mouth, muffling the continuous mewling.

"There are consequences, my young friend. There are always consequences."

Without another word Po'Pay picked up the meat cleaver, and seconds later brought it down with such force that it cleanly severed Roy's forearm from his body.

Roy's body jerked and he screamed into the gag. His eyes rolled back, and he twisted his head back and forth. A strong hand grasped his chin and forced him to look up. Po'Pay was holding the severed limb in his hand as the blood dripped onto Roy's face.

"I much prefer to acquire undamaged bones for my work, but in this case an exception was warranted," Po'Pay said. He threw the hand on the floor and walked to the table where he picked up a small blowtorch. Without another word he cauterized the forearm stump as Roy screamed and screamed into his gag before he lost consciousness and stopped moving.

Po'Pay picked up the hand and plunked it into a small, five-gallon aquarium. He put the cover back on and sat in front of the aquarium. He smiled benevolently as he watched his diligent beetles start feasting on the first part of his latest acquisition.

He watched the little fellows' repast for hours.

Baked, stuffed pheasant, he thought. Baked sweet potatoes. His mouth watered at the thought of the coming feast.

Then he went to work.

CHAPTER FOURTEEN

Percy settled himself into Pryce Gallagher's guest chair and sniffed his chamomile tea. Pryce had two cups ready for them and explained that he was not a coffee drinker although his wife, Carmen, certainly was. He preferred tea, whether from genuine tea leaves or from herbs such as the one emanating from his cup right now. Chamomile was known for its calming effects as well as its ability to assist in sleeping. Pryce was generally a calm person and rarely experienced insomnia, but he simply liked the flavor and many medical people as well as devout herbalists declared that it had antibacterial, anti-inflammatory and liver-protecting effects. His wife called him a health nut, but there were worst things to be. He was going to do everything in his power to stay healthy for a long, long time to be with the woman with whom he was madly in love. They had met as college teaching colleagues, and a long friendship developed into a long courtship which he prayed would result in a very long marriage.

"Is Tucson joining us?" Pryce asked.

Percy shook his head. "He and I agreed that his professional involvement with the Adams case should be minimal at best and that I'd take the lead in treating her amnesia and its psychological impacts. Besides, he's developing an emotional attachment to her and that—"

"And that is counterproductive to her case as well as his professional skills and credibility," Pryce finished. Tucson had been one of his top students in psychology class at Sangre de Cristo College and he was proud of the young man's accomplishments, especially considering what he had suffered during the war. "How is he handling that?"

"He understands, but he still chafes at being kept at professional arm's length. Fortunately, or unfortunately, depending on one's perspective, he isn't being at arm's length with the client on a personal basis."

"Is he getting emotionally attached?"

"I think so. He knows the risks, but I think he's making excuses to ignore most of them."

"What about her?"

"She's warming up to human contact. She was quite reserved and skeptical when she first came to us, but, honestly, I think … I think he's been good for her."

Pryce nodded thoughtfully. He understood being reserved and nervous about close, intimate relationships. A gawky, odd kid with glasses he'd had a rough childhood with being bullied for his intellect and stuttering. Now, Pryce was a gangly man in his late fifties with a head of thick silver hair that had started to go gray in his early twenties. He wore thick horn-rimmed eyeglasses pushed down on his nose and which he habitually had to push farther up the bridge. When one had an unobstructed look at his eyes, they could see beautiful hazel orbs whose brown rims seemed to pulse. He always seemed happy and enthusiastic, and his students adored him. On rare occasions he still stuttered when he was abnormally stressed or anxious.

He had blossomed in college when he was more independent from other students, finally achieving a decent measure of self-respect and self-esteem. He snagged a position teaching high school for three years in Chicago, then decided to upend his boring life. He applied to a half dozen southwestern colleges and wound up teaching psychology at Sangre de Cristo College in Santa Fe.

It was there that he hit his stride, gained confidence in his teaching abilities, and rose to head the Psychology department. Along the way he had fallen in love with a fellow professor, Carmen Castillo, who taught History. A divorcée with a teenage daughter, she became a friend and then a lover and then, miracle of miracles, his wife. His stepdaughter, Candelaria, had married Troy Grayhawk and three months after she gave birth became his widow. She worked as the indispensable assistant to Percy and Tucson while she went to college part-time to study pre-law. Although her biological father was alive and living in Arizona, she called Pryce "Pops" and he considered Chessie his granddaughter. Candy and Chessie lived with Pryce and Carmen and the four of them made a close, cozy little family.

Pryce nodded his head. "That's good, for both. Now, you said you wanted to discuss her amnesia with me."

"From an objective perspective," Percy said. "Naturally, I'm bound by client confidentiality so I can't get into any specifics save the fact that she remembers nothing before that night she was found and taken to the hospital. I've studied the basics of amnesia and some anecdotal case studies, but Tucson told me that you actually focused on that for your Master's thesis."

Pryce nodded. "I did. It's a fascinating state of mind."

"Pretend I'm a novice and give me your best thoughts on the subject."

"Novice, eh? Sure. The term itself is from ancient Greek and means forgetfulness or, in its basest form, 'without memory.' Most people take the term and its implications with fairly naïve understanding."

"How do you mean?"

"I mean that laymen don't understand that amnesia is a multi-layered condition and cannot be defined or treated with a singular focus. Most psychologists and physicians categorize four basic types of amnesia, but that's just the tip of the iceberg."

"The two types I've seen highlighted in several books are anterograde amnesia and retrograde amnesia."

"Those do seem to be the most commonly understood variations," Pryce said. "Anterograde amnesia prevents the subject from creating new memories due to brain damage. Long-term memories from before the trauma remain intact. For example, a person can suffer brain damage from blunt-force trauma yet remember his high school prom or first kiss. The brain damage isn't related to intense physical trauma, however. It can result from alcoholism, a stroke, severe malnutrition, surgery, or encephalitis, to name a few causes. Any of these causes impact the two brain regions, the medial temporal lobe and the medial diencephalon."

"Can that type of amnesia be successfully treated?"

"The amnesia can't be reversed, but the person can be retrained for behaviors that will help him move forward with life. It's not totally mandatory, but success in this area is dependent on social and emotional support. It's not something a person can do by himself. Now, retrograde amnesia—that's a different story."

"That's what Cameo has."

"Maybe. As I said there are many different types. Let me do an overview and we can see where she fits in."

"You're right. Please go on."

"Retrograde amnesia is the inability to recall memories before the amnesia occurred. New memories can be created just as they would have been had the amnesia never happened. Although it's possible, it's rare for this type of amnesia to occur because of anything other than head trauma or brain damage to parts of the brain other than the hippocampus. As you know, the hippocampus is responsible for encoding new memories."

Percy smiled. "I know. I live with a doctor and she's educated me on the gruesome details of every part of the human body, whether I want to know them or not."

"Lucky you. Her knowledge is a great supplement for your theoretical and anecdotal understanding of psychology. Now, the interesting thing about retrograde amnesia is that the afflicted person remembers general knowledge. For example, he understands language, can read, can write, recognizes different physical aspects of the world, knows who the president is, how many states we have, and the like. Specifics, however, are generally out of their grasp. For example, why a certain song is meaningful in either a positive or negative way. This type of amnesia is usually temporary."

"Is five years considered temporary?"

"Not to me, but that doesn't mean that she won't wake up one day and remember everything."

"From what I read retrograde amnesia can be treated by subjecting the person to memories from the past, like a family member, a favorite book, and specific location. In Cameo's case there don't really seem to be any of those reminders to edge her towards remembering."

"I haven't even spoken to the lady so I can't hazard a guess as to which type of amnesia she might have or how to treat it," Pryce said. "It certainly sounds like retrograde, but there are others. One that might also fit her situation is post-traumatic amnesia. That's generally due to a head injury, and you said she had a concussion when she was found."

"Yes, a severe one, but with no fracturing of the skull."

"Unfortunately, that type of amnesia isn't exclusive of the other two. Based on the little I know her type of amnesia sounds like dissociative amnesia. Unlike the ones we've just discussed, this type plays heavily into psychological causes that may or may not have anything to do with an organic cause. Meaning, her head trauma may not have caused her amnesia."

"Does dissociative amnesia fall into a single category of cause and resolution?"

"Of course not. That would be too easy." Pryce smiled wanly.

"We wouldn't want that. What types are there?"

"There are three. Repressed memory is one. Dissociative fugue is another. The third is post-hypnotic amnesia."

"I hypnotized Cameo once to see how suggestive she would be in a more intense session."

"Since she became an amnesiac well before that, we can almost rule that out."

"Almost?"

"Can you tell me for certain that she wasn't hypnotized before she became a Jane Doe?"

"No, I can't. That's food for thought."

"Don't chew too hard. Let's explore the other two which are far more likely. Repressed memory isn't truly amnesia. Rather, it's that some memories were so traumatic that the mind could only cope by storing them in its farthest recesses of long-term memory. The person's innate psychological defense mechanisms prevent the mind from extracting the memory so that the person doesn't have to relive the horror. It's not impossible to draw those memories out, but there's no infallible method of doing so."

"Would a violent rape be a likely cause?"

Pryce's eyebrows shot up. He wanted to ask but didn't. "Yes, that could be a cause. Seeing someone you love commit a murder or violent act is another common cause. Yet another would be childhood sexual abuse. Often the abused child represses those horrific memories and may live out his life without every bringing them to the forefront, and that can negatively impact his entire life and relationships. The mind is a remarkable thing. It survives in any way it can. Sometimes, it doesn't survive, and sadly many of those people live their lives in psychiatric institutions."

"Tell me about dissociative fugue."

"That, too, is strictly psychological and not the result of a physical injury. Unlike repressed memories or those other types of physical-based amnesias, this one tends to be temporary. It exists outside of medical conditions. And, it can come and go. There are anecdotes of people falling into one of these fugue states and winding up hundreds of miles from home living under new identities. Their basic personalities can vary widely from the basic individual. For example, a virginal young woman might wind up in Las Vegas turning tricks."

"What are the other types of amnesia?"

"Well, there's lacunar amnesia, childhood amnesia, transient global amnesia, drug-induced amnesia, semantic amnesia, Korsakoff's syndrome, and a couple more. Should I go on or is your head ready to explode?"

"It's ticking down to a big boom," Percy said, shaking his head. "Based on my observations and what we've discussed here, I'm of the mind that Cameo is afflicted with either retrograde amnesia or post-traumatic amnesia. I can't get into the specifics, but she did respond to certain visual stimuli when I put her into a light trance."

"That's interesting. No hints?"

Percy smiled. "Sorry. Are there any suggestions you can make based on what we've discussed?"

"It's hard without specifics, but if she responded to certain stimuli you might want to build on that with similar visual aids. If the visual aids have real-life sensory components associated with them, you might expose her to those impressions. For example, if she reacted when you showed her a picture of pine trees, take her to a forest where she can smell the pine scent. It might jog something."

Percy's eyebrows drew together thoughtfully. "Something like that may already have happened. Hypothetically speaking, if someone went fishing and knew exactly how to fish, gut, and descale a trout, mightn't that suggest that she's done that before? Hypothetically, Tucson might have said it seemed to come naturally to her."

"Hypothetically."

"Yes."

"Sounds like a memory eked its way into the present without her being aware. I'd build on that if possible. Hypothetically. You know, you're killing me. This case is fascinating. Kind of makes me wish I went into practice instead of teaching."

"You're training generations of psychologists. You're right where you should be."

"Thank you."

Percy stood. "If I need you for further consultations would you be amenable?"

Pryce laughed. "Just try and stop me. Tell Candy Pops said hello." They shook hands and Percy left, headed back to his office.

Percy drove to his office and parked in his designated spot. Occasionally one of his colleagues would park in his spot just to annoy him, but after a few well-placed dog poops that embedded themselves in tire treads that tactic faded into oblivion. He saw that Tucson's car was already there, as were most of the P.I.s' and lawyers' and the two nannies' vehicles. He stopped in the daycare center and spent a few minutes with Elspeth before heading into his office. He relayed Pryce's message to Candy whose eyes twinkled in affection. She told Percy she'd bring in some coffee and that Tucson was waiting in his office.

Tucson was standing by the window staring outside. Percy said his name, but Tucson remained rigid and unmoving. Percy had seen this before. Sometimes his partner and friend fell into another world, a state of mind where he took a few minutes to come back to normal. Percy called to him again and Tucson turned.

"Get any insight from Pryce?" Tucson asked.

"Yes, some," Percy replied as he walked around his desk and put his briefcase on the edge. He sat down and Tucson followed suit.

For the first time Tucson smiled widely. "Nice bowtie. A gift from Candy?" Percy always wore bowties with his suits instead of ties, and it was a running gag amongst his friends and family to gift him with the most unusual or outrageous bowties they could find. Today, he was wearing one with tiny mariachis all over a red background. Candy always presented him with bowties that had an Hispanic motif.

"That obvious, eh?"

"That obvious."

"Did you get Cameo settled into her new job?" Percy asked.

Tucson nodded. "I think working for Caleb will be a big help for her state of mind."

While reading Cameo's journals Percy was struck not only with the thoughts therein but with the elegance of the prose and the quality of grammar and syntax. If she hadn't gone to school and excelled in English, then she was a natural for writing ability. He knew she was antsy while her case was under investigation, and he approached Caleb Winsted with an idea before he subsequently approached Cameo.

Caleb had lost his top editor five months earlier when the man was poached by the *Santa Fe New Mexican*. He had lost his associate editor when she married and moved to Denver with her new husband. He had advertised for and interviewed several people about an associate editor's position, but no one seemed to meet his standards. He bemoaned the fact over a beer with Nick at the Sweet Revenge Saloon. Nick told Percy, and Percy's mental lightbulb went off. He conferred with Tucson, who agreed that if Cameo had something else to focus on it would improve her mental health. She didn't need the money right now, but she needed another outlet besides thinking and worrying about her past.

Percy discussed the matter with Caleb. He couldn't provide any samples of Cameo's writing since her thoughts were confidential between them, but he was persuasive, and Caleb had faith in his judgment. Caleb agreed to take her on for a trial. Then, Percy talked to Cameo. At first, she was reluctant, but her reluctance was short-lived, and she agreed that having a creative outlet might be the best thing for her. She had settled into a small studio apartment on the east side, bought a car, and settled in. Tucson and his brother Luc had helped move in the scarce furniture she bought. When Percy came to her with the suggestion, she realized that she needed something tangible on which to focus. And, she confessed, she loved the written word.

Percy introduced her to Caleb over lunch at the Pink Adobe and the newsman and woman seeking her identity hit it off right away. To his credit Caleb didn't pry about her past or her present and the investigations. Percy told him only the basics, that she had amnesia and was seeking help in finding her past. Caleb was intrigued as any newsman would be, but he was smart enough to know when to back off. He and Cameo agreed on a salary and starting date, and both were looking forward to the new chapter in her life. He scowled menacingly and warned her he was going to work her like a dog. She scowled back and replied, "Arf."

A spirited relationship was born.

"Good, good," Percy said. "I'm meeting with her in a couple of days, so I hope she'll have some positive feedback on her experience and whether she wants to continue with it."

"She seems more relaxed these past few days," Tucson said. "I think it's been beneficial that she has people who are taking her seriously and making a concerted effort to backtrack her life."

"Did Memphis and Swan leave on time this morning?"

"I dropped them off at the airport around nine," Tucson said. His brother and sister-in-law were flying to New England to dig into Cameo's experience when she was found. "I'll be staying at their house to watch the kids and keep an eye on Luc and Raleigh. Sand's going to stay over as well."

"Is your sister still salivating over that quarterback?"

"More like salivating over the position of quarterback rather than the kid. She's chafing at the fact that they won't let girls on the football team."

"Should they?"

"I will not get into that argument," Tucson said. "I've already been reamed over by my sister for my caveman viewpoint. Besides, she's on the girls' softball team and has a big wooden bat."

"Coward."

"Survivor. So, tell me what you and Pryce talked about."

Percy went into detail about the subject of amnesia, pausing for clarification and checking reference books during a few points. He and Tucson agreed that Cameo had either retrograde amnesia or post-traumatic amnesia. Percy suggested that since Cameo had a response to the images of the ocean that they collect similar images from both coasts and see if they could narrow down her responses.

"Well, we've got lots of reference books in our library," Tucson said. "I'm sure I've seen a few that have pictures of both coasts that we can use. I'll check them out." He glanced at his watch then rose. "Meanwhile, I've got a patient coming in."

"New client?"

Tucson nodded. "Another vet. I don't know all the particulars. The VA center recommended me. He's met with a couple of other psychologists, but they didn't seem to be a good fit. We'll see."

Percy spent a half hour finishing up his reports. Candy buzzed him and said that an Indian gentleman was in the reception area and would like to see him. At the name Percy told her to bring him in. He rose and walked to his office door just as Candy knocked and opened it.

Hashkeh Naabah towered over Candy. He was holding a large rectangular object wrapped in brown paper. She excused herself and Percy welcomed his visitor. Naabah carefully set the package down on its edge against Percy's desk and seated himself.

"Is that what I think it is?" Percy asked affably, already knowing the answer. "And before you respond can I offer you anything to drink?"

"No, thank you, Dr. McBean. I'm good. Yes, this is the finished canvas. I hope it meets with your approval," Naabah said in his deep, modulated voice.

"I can't imagine it wouldn't," Percy replied. "May I open it?"

"Unless you wish to hang it on your wall with the paper covering the image." There was amusement in the Indian's voice as his eyes twinkled.

Percy carefully undid the wrapping paper and withdrew the finished canvas. Naabah had framed it with saguaro cactus skeleton planks two inches wide, and with all the perfect imperfections that made the plant the icon it was.

"It's magnificent," Percy said in a low, hushed tone. "My god." He studied every inch of the painting, every brushstroke, every image, every nuance. He noted that Naabah had signed it as he usually did his works, with "HashNaa" over a small arrow. At the bottom of the frame was affixed a small brass plaque with the name of the painting—*Doo Nidahałtingóó Níłch'i.*

"I believe I have captured your essence, my friend," Naabah said quietly. "The name means desert spirit."

Percy nodded. His features in the painting weren't as a photograph would capture them but were more intimated, yet with enough detail to tell it was Percival McBean. The face and body clearly captured the essence of the man.

Percy turned to the artist. "I am humbled by your work. Thank you. I have the perfect place to hang it in my home. If you are amenable, I'd like you to see it in person."

“I would be honored.” Naabah rose and inclined his head. “I will be in Taos for several weeks, perhaps months, working on my pueblo series. But when I return, I will call you and we can set up a time.” He stuck out his hand and Percy shook it. Without another word the artist left as quickly as he had come.

“Candy,” Percy yelled. “Get in here.”

Candy rushed in seconds later, her eyes wide and worried.

“Look at this,” Percy said in awe and satisfaction.

“Oh, my God,” she exclaimed. “That’s beautiful.”

“It’s amazing,” Percy said quietly. “Think Tansee will like it?”

“If she doesn’t, I have a spare wall.”

“Not a chance,” Percy said. He shook his head as he studied the canvas. “Not a chance.”

CHAPTER FIFTEEN

Frick had indigestion. He should have known better than to pick up a couple of sloppy tacos at a roadside food truck, but he was hungry and pissed off. The truck was parked on the city outskirts in front of another truck with Sonora, Mexico license plates; that one had an open bed filled with bushels of lemons. He purchased a five-pound bag for a buck that he'd split with his partner. Frick liked iced tea, but only if it had lemon in it.

He'd gobbled down the tacos before he pulled back on the road and headed a few miles north to check out a chop shop, one of many he and Frack had investigated to try to find any trace of the Geary girl's car. They hadn't come up with anything, and the trail was feeling as cold as Minnesota in January. Frack was headed south to do the same and they planned to meet up at the Pink Adobe for dinner.

Frick was upset that no progress had been made either in the official law enforcement front or by the private investigators. Taylor Geary and Stone Powell had just plain vanished. There was no doubt in his mind that they were dead, but how, and why? He thought about Ellis Geary and his wife and couldn't imagine losing a child, and their only child. He and his late wife never had kids; she had died two years into their marriage and he'd never remarried. Frack and his late wife, Carly, had two sons who were grown and fathers themselves. Despite their divergent familial lives both men were now on their own, facing old age and retirement. Both hated the fact that their possible last case wouldn't be solved before they left the force. Four weeks from Friday, November 22nd, and for the first time since he was fifteen Frick wouldn't be working a job.

Their buddies on the force had planned a retirement party for them at the Sweet Revenge Saloon. At Frick's and Frack's insistence the crew at Warrior Spirit Investigations and their legal firm were invited. There was still some bad blood between a few members of the police force and ex-cops Sand and Swan, but Frick knew they'd put that aside to help celebrate. He hoped, anyway. After the party Frack was going to head down to Phoenix where his oldest son and his family lived. The other brother, his wife and two daughters would join them for a long Thanksgiving week. Frick volunteered to watch Pierre.

The last chop shop was a bust, so Frick headed back into Santa Fe. It was far too early for dinner and he didn't feel like going back to the station. For some reason he found himself driving towards the P.I. firm. He refused to admit outwardly that he liked those damn people and enjoyed their banter. Besides that, they had the best coffee around, and on occasion Tansee McBean made New England-style crullers, and Frick had become addicted to them.

He recognized a few cars in the parking lot, plus a couple new ones. One had an Arizona plate. Probably a new client, he thought. He knew that Memphis and his crew were doing well. He parked at the edge of the lot and entered the lobby. He could hear childish voices in the back and he smiled; the daycare center for the crew's young kids. On a whim he eased back to the center and watched the chaos through the double glass doors.

Memphis's young twins, Sara and Shea, were engaged in a savage tug of war over a large stuffed bunny that was seconds away from being rent in two. The British nanny, Ansonia, was standing over them trying to disengage their battle but they were ignoring her. He thought that they showed the same intense focus and determination that their mother, Swan, did. Swan would have made a great police detective, but she never stood a chance the ways things were when she was an officer. Memphis's oldest daughter, Sage, was at school, and from what Frick knew of her she was a tough, aggressive little girl just like her mother. Smart, too—she had already skipped a grade in school and was conversant in Spanish. Her parents had signed her up for karate classes and she was already a dead shot with a BB gun.

Frick knew that preparing their daughter in self-defense mechanisms wasn't simply a whim. Seven years ago, a madwoman serial killer had nearly killed Memphis and had injured Sand, Swan, Frack, and Sage. Joanna Frid warned Memphis to stop looking for her or else she'd come back; the threat against Sage was unspoken but very real. Joanna had vanished for the second time and theoretically was still out there somewhere, although by now she was in her early seventies. She had taken a young child with her; many law enforcement people thought the girl was probably dead, but Memphis and his crew didn't think so. The threat of Joanna was real and ever-present in their minds. Despite Joanna's warning Frick knew that Memphis was still covertly searching for Joanna. Frick didn't even want to think about what might happen if he ever found her.

Little Shea was victorious in taking sole ownership of the bunny, which was now missing the soft, floppy ear that Sara had in her hand. The twins glared at one another. Frick didn't want to think about what they'd be like as teenagers. He pitied the boys they'd eventually start dating.

The McBeans' daughter, Elspeth, was sitting quietly in a small white wooden rocking chair, a picture book opened on her lap. Her lips were moving as she tried to say the big words on the pages. Little Mariko Griffin was plopped on a rug in the center of the floor playing pattycake with the other nanny, Whitney. Francesca Grayhawk, the late Troy's and Candy's daughter, was now out of the general daycare and in a normal nursery school for the morning; she'd rejoin her family mates in the afternoon. Next year she'd be starting kindergarten.

Yes, Frick thought, the next generation was growing up. He sighed; and his generation was growing old.

Ansonia spotted him, smiled, and waved. He waved back then took the elevator to the third floor where a chipper Skye was feeding sunflower seeds to a gray parrot. He'd learned from Memphis that Skye was an animal lover and shared her life with a swarm of purchased and rescued animals, including three parrots, two dogs, two cats, a guinea pig, a pair of geckos, and a seven-legged tarantula. Occasionally, she'd bring one or two to work. Today, he guessed, was bring-your-grey-parrot-to-work day. She was cooing to the bird. When she caught a glimpse of Frick, she raised her eyebrows and he replied, "Sand," to her facial question. She impatiently waved him towards Sand's office then put another sunflower seed next to the parrot's beak.

Sand's office door was open, but Frick knocked anyway. Sand was at his desk frowning and he looked up at the sharp rap. He impatiently motioned Frick to sit down.

"That the Geary case?" Frick asked.

Sand shook his head. "We've got other cases, too, Frickster. I was just reviewing the summary before I hand it off to Devon and our newbie."

"You hire another gumshoe?"

"We had to. Surprisingly, it's a name from the past."

"Really? Who?"

"I'm sure you remember the Marcy Ortiz case." Marcy Ortiz was a teenager that had been abducted and murdered by Joanna Frid. Her body had been drained of blood in which Joanna bathed in a desperate attempt to stave off the ageing process. Joanna was groomed to fear ageing by a mother that had given birth to an older sister who died at age three from the hellish disease progeria; progeria rapidly aged the afflicted child, turning a three-year-old into something resembling an eighty-year-old. When Marcy was abducted but before her body was found, Frick and Frack had been assigned to the case.

"As if I could ever forget," Frick said quietly.

"Well, remember that Marcy was enamored of a teenage boy named Dante Redwolf? She wrote about him in her notebook, wrote poems to him."

"I remember. I was the one that interviewed him."

"Well, Dante grew up, went to college, and wound up applying for our open position. We hired him last week and assigned Devon to mentor him and work on a case with him."

"What's he like?" Frick remembered a gangly, tall, copper-skinned young man with unruly ebony hair and sad brown eyes.

"He's intelligent and determined to succeed. I think he may have some self-esteem issues, but those should work themselves out as he learns the ropes and works his cases. Devon will keep him on the straight and narrow."

"She scares me."

"All strong women scare you. Strong three-year-olds scare you. Before we talk about whatever it is you came here for, let me hand this off." Sand dialed and asked Devon to come to his office and bring Dante. A few minutes later—and after Frick got a cup of coffee—Devon entered followed by the newest "spirit warrior" (as Memphis occasionally called his people).

"Devon, you know Detective Smith."

"Yeah," Devon said flatly. "He commented on my hairstyle and asked me if I was related to Angela Davis." Devon's kinky red-brown hair had grown out significantly since she was first hired, and the Angela Davis comparison was on target. Today she was wearing gold wire-rimmed eyeglasses instead of her contact lenses, but her vivid green eyes radiated out like lasers.

"I didn't mean anything by that," Frick muttered. "As I recall you called me a troglodyte."

"If the wooden club and the saber-toothed tiger loincloth fit …"

"Okay, okay," Sand said, sighing. "Enough. Dante, you know the detective as well."

"It's nice to see you again, Detective Smith," Dante said sincerely. Adult Dante was a solid six-footer, slender but not thin, with broad shoulders and layered black hair; jawline sideburns framed his clean-shaven face. His eyes were bright and lively. He was wearing crisp new jeans and a light blue shirt tucked into his waistband. Alligator-hide cowboy boots peeked out from under the bellbottom jeans' cuffs.

"I'm glad to see you're well, Dante," Frick said. "Hope you like your new job."

"I'm sure I will."

Sand handed the folder to Devon who flipped it open to glance at the top summary. "Phoenix?" she asked curiously. "A missing person?"

"An eighteen-year-old that quit college and went down there with a boyfriend that subsequently dumped her. She's being stubborn and refuses to come home, so her parents hired us to persuade her to do so," Sand said. "She's living with a half dozen other dumbbells in some trailer in the desert just north of the city."

"Parameters?" Devon asked.

"No violence, handcuffs, zip ties, valium, or other illegal methods." Sand nodded towards Frick. "We have a real, live cop here so I'm instructing you to behave. Nod your head." Devon nodded her head dutifully. Sand looked at Dante, who did the same. "Good. You leave tomorrow morning. Keep receipts for gas, food, and the motel."

"Can we stay at the Biltmore?" Devon asked.

"Sure," Sand replied, "as long as you're parked at the far end of the lot and sleeping in the car. I won't pay for bail, so be discreet. Shoo."

Devon whirled around and beckoned Dante after her. He flashed a smile at Frick and Sand and shut the door behind him.

"Really?" Sand said. "Angela Davis?"

"I plead the fifth," Frick said. He raised his hand in a black power salute. "Power to the people."

"You are such a fucking dinosaur," Sand said, shaking his head. "So, okay, Dino—what's up?"

"The last of the chop shops was a bust. There's just nowhere to go after this. The case is cold," Frick said succinctly.

Sand leaned back in his chair. He felt the same as Frick, who wore his frustration and anger on his face like a kabuki mask. He and Nick had already agreed that from their point of view there was really no place left to search. They had received dozens of tips from the newspaper ads, but none of them panned out. They talked to Adam every other day and he was as frustrated as they were. He didn't want to give the Geary family false hope, but he also didn't want to give them the worst news unless they could verify it. To date, Taylor and Stone were missing, presumed dead, but that couldn't be verified. So, the hope went on, but now it was time to determine if the Warrior Spirit and Santa Fe police investigations should go on.

Sand tapped his pen absently on his desk and sighed. "I'm thinking I should go out to San Francisco and meet with Adam, and then the two of us should meet with the Gearys and lay out the options."

"What options?"

"Keep spending their money on a futile search or give up the search. I don't want to take their money if it's unlikely we can find the kids."

"You want to give up the search."

"I don't *want* to, but that may be the only reasonable course of action."

"I hate this."

"I hate this, too." At that moment Sand's phone rang. He picked up and listened to Skye, then told her to transfer the call. He handed the receiver to Frick. "Call from the station."

Frick took the receiver and listened, then said hello and listened again. His brow knitted and he hmm'd. He said he'd be back in ten minutes. He handed the receiver to Sand who hung it up.

"Problem?" Sand asked.

"Maybe," Frick replied, standing. "I'll find out the details and call you if you need to be involved."

"Come on."

Frick sighed. "That was Captain Carraway. He wants me and Frack back because it seems like we may have another missing person. That's all I know."

"Where's Frack?"

"South of the city somewhere. If he calls here tell him to get his ass back to the station, okay?"

"Okay. Let me know."

"I will." Frick rushed out and Sand leaned back. Another missing person. What the hell was that all about? He called Nick into his office.

Frick made it back to the police station in eight minutes flat. Carraway was waiting for him in his office, and just as he entered Frack appeared and followed him in. Carraway handed Frick a folder.

"I don't know if this has any bearing on the Geary case, but a detective in New Jersey saw an ad in a regional newspaper about the kids, and he had a similar case in his files. The missing guy was on his way towards our location, so the detective thought he'd throw the case our way to see if it jogged anything. The details are in the folder. Read them, discuss them, then get back here in an hour and we'll see what you think," Carraway said.

"Do—" Frack began but Carraway held up a hand.

"Read, discuss, come back. Go."

"Yes, sir," Frick said and grabbed Frack's jacket and drew him out of the captain's office. He led his partner to a small interrogation room where they sat, read, and discussed.

"It's a single adult," Frick said. "Age thirty-five, a college professor, missing since … huh? 1972?" Frack said, frowning.

"Cold case," Frack said. "Two years."

Frick scanned the facts describing the missing man. "Howard Kensington Carter, a tenured professor of archeology at Princeton. A British expatriate who's been living in the States since 1963. He finished up the spring 1972 semester then planned on crossing the country to explore ancient Native American sites. He left a general map of his expected direction and stops with his colleague." Frick unfolded a U.S.A. map from the folder and spread it out on the table. He searched his jacket for a pen and found none. Frack had a red pen ready; he always carried one. Frick marked an 'X' for each planned stop per the professor's agenda which, unfortunately, only listed the states and not the places within the states.

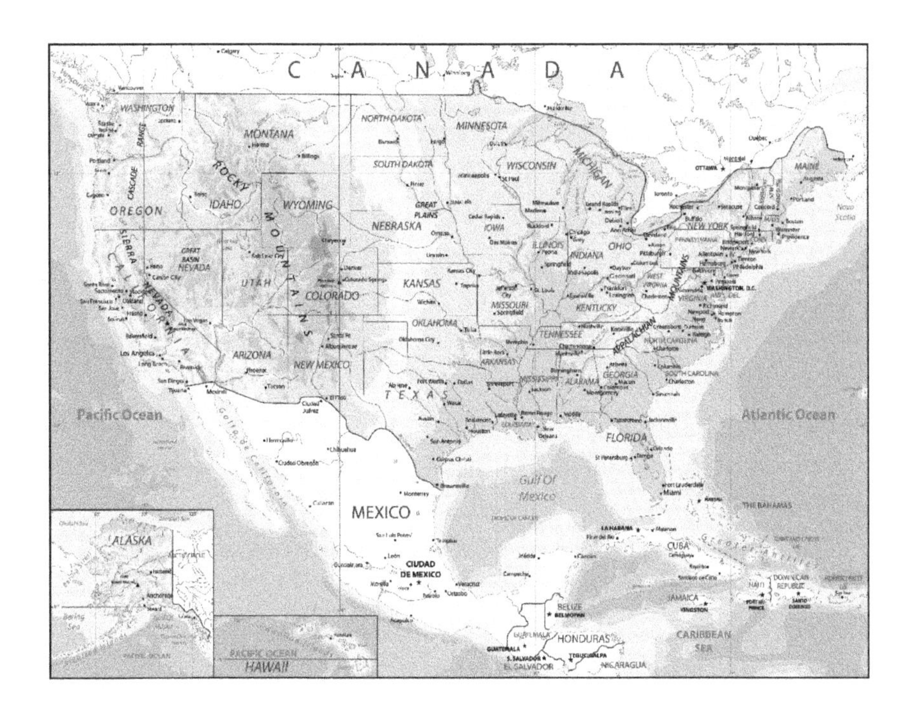

"Looks like he planned an elliptical tour starting down the east coast into the Carolinas, down into Louisiana then over to the west through Texas as far as Arizona, a turn north into Utah, and a return path through Colorado, Kansas, Missouri, Kentucky, back to North Carolina, and then ending back in New Jersey," Frick said thoughtfully.

"Did he list the sites he planned to visit?" Frack asked.

"That's not in the folder, but it's a good question. Write that down." Frack complied.

"Did he contact his friends during the trip?" Frack asked. He rustled the folder's documents and nodded. "I know—write that down." He wrote the question down, paused, then wrote another line. He looked at Frick. "I added a question if the professor sent his friends any postcards or packages. If he did, that'll give a partial trail and timeline."

"Yeah, but I'd think the Jersey cops would have homed in on those possibilities, too."

"We're smarter than any Jersey cops."

"Well, yeah, but don't mention that when we talk to them. Be nice. I know that's hard."

"It's New Jersey, for Christ's sake."

"Be. Nice."

"Fine. What else we got on the dude?"

"It says that he taught archeology, but it doesn't say if he taught general knowledge or focused on any specific aspects or cultures. If he did, then that might point us to associated sites he could have visited." Frick looked at Frack but Frack was already writing the question down. Frick tapped a sentence in the report. "Says here he had an associated interest in anthropology. I wonder what classes he taught? Write—"

"—that down," Frack said. "What's the difference?"

"Huh?"

"Between archeology and anthropology."

"Damned if I know. Write—"

"I got it. Not a moron. He have any family?" Frack asked, pen poised.

"Says here he's single, no kids. Doesn't say if he's divorced or widowed. Parents deceased, no siblings." Frick felt a chill run down his spine. If Frick disappeared, who would look for him? Lots of people—Frack, the Grayhawks and their crew, fellow cops. If he vanished, he'd be missed, and he'd be searched for. His determination at finding not only the professor but the Geary kids filled him with renewed purpose.

"I don't see a medical report in the folder," Frack said. "We gotta get that to see if he had any unusual features or tattoos or something." He put his pen down and stared at his partner. "Is this busy work, or does Carraway really think we can make progress?"

"Why?"

"Because in a few weeks we'll be outa here and someone else will take over."

"I'm good with busy work. And, we might come up with something. The bottom line is that this guy is also missing and whether he has family or friends that want him back or not he deserves to be found."

"We're not going to New Jersey, right?"

"Christ, no. We'll talk to the cops there by phone. Carraway's not gonna authorize travel funds. We're not special like the P.I.s."

"Should we run this by them?"

"When we get additional information. Let's first see what similarities and differences there are to the Geary case. Let's see if our P.I. buddies can point us to a professor at the college who might be able to enlighten us on archeology." He held up a finger then dialed a familiar number on the phone. "Griffin. It's me, Frick. You took classes over at the college, didn't you? Right. I was at your graduation. I tried blocking that out. You happen to know any archology or anthropology professors over there? We got a new case and some questions. Let me write that name down." He snapped his fingers at Frack who handed him the pen and notebook. "Is that a guy or gal? Yes, man or woman," he said, sighing. "Okay, thanks. I'll let you know." Frick hung up the receiver. He showed the name to Frack.

"London Monroe," Frack said. "That a guy or a gal?"

"Woman," Frick replied deliberately. "I'll find her number and make an appointment for tomorrow. We can call the Jersey cop today."

"He might not be there," Frack said. "Two-hour time difference. It's after five in Jersey."

"You know any cops that go home by five?"

"It's Jersey. Who the hell knows how they measure time?"

"Well, we're going to give it a try." Frick dialed the long-distance number and it rang six times before a gruff male voice said hello in an unmistakably annoyed tone. Frick identified himself and started talking.

CHAPTER SIXTEEN

Berkshire County rests on the western edge of Massachusetts. At nearly a thousand square miles its structure is almost a perfect rectangle that stretches from the top of the state to the bottom, bordering New York, Vermont, and Connecticut. Pittsfield is its largest city and its county seat. At forty-two square miles it is the fourth largest city in western Massachusetts, behind Springfield, Holyoke, and Chicopee. By the mid-1970s the population hovered at around fifty-five thousand.

Originally inhabited by the Mohican Indians, the township area morphed into European dominance through war and disease, with the Native Americans migrating westward as the whites moved in. A village began to grow, named Pontoosuck Plantation; Pontoosuck is a Mohican word meaning "a field or haven for winter deer." By 1761 the township was rechristened Pittsfield Township by Royal Governor Sir Francis Bernard after British nobleman and politician William Pitt. At that time, the population was two hundred; however, by the end of the Revolutionary War the population had swelled to two thousand.

The economy was based on agriculture, with mills springing up to produce lumber, grist, paper, and textiles. Sheep farming grew as well. The city's industries were supported and developed by its location on the Housatonic River, which provided boats for trading and receiving and shipping merchandise. The City of Pittsfield was incorporated in 1891. Population and industry growth continued to boom.

William Stanley Jr., who had relocated his Electric Manufacturing Company to Pittsfield in 1890 from Great Barrington, produced the first electric transformer. His enterprise was the forerunner of the internationally known corporate giant, General Electric (GE). With the unqualified success of GE, Pittsfield's population in 1930 had grown to more than fifty thousand.

Pittsfield was noted in history for several events. In 1902 President Theodore Roosevelt and several colleagues were on a two-week trip to campaign for Republican congressmen. The carriage that they were riding in collided head-on with a trolley. The men were thrown to the street; one was killed, bodyguard William Craig, who went down in history as the first Secret Service officer killed in the line of duty. The trolley driver pled guilty to manslaughter and spent six months in jail.

A 1791 by-law prohibited playing baseball within eighty yards of Pittsfield's new meeting house. This was the earliest known reference to the American game of baseball in the country's history. In 1859 the first intercollegiate baseball game was played in Pittsfield; Amherst trounced Williams College 73-32. The Pittsfield Senators, a minor-league baseball team, play in the city's Wahconah Park, which was built in 1919.

Pittsfield lies at the confluence of the east and west branches of the Housatonic River, which flows south from the city towards its mouth at Long Island Sound, some 149 miles distant. The eastern branch leads down from the hills, while the western branch is fed from Onota Lake and Pontoosuc Lake (which lies partly in Lanesborough). The city's climate is continental, with harsh winters that have an average of seventy-three inches of snow. The winters can be bitterly cold, but the summers are warm. The lowest temperature recorded in Pittsfield was –26°F on February 15, 1943; the highest temperature of 101°F was recorded on July 23, 1926. Over the course of a year nearly half of the days have measurable precipitation.

The landscape of Pittsfield is typical New England—lush, green, with tall mountains and hills and large and small rivers and lakes dotting the towns and suburbs. The impressive Berkshire Mountains tower over Berkshire County, dense, dark green, and imposing. North of Pittsfield by twenty miles or so they loom over the state's western edge of the famous Mohawk Trail. A former Indian trading route, it now enjoys a reputation as a tourist destination, particularly in the fall when the hills and trail are lined with trees whose leaves range from brown to gold to red to orange. The length of the trail, Route 2, often has traffic-jam-like lines of cars making the forty-mile sightseeing journey from Greenfield to North Adams and passing quaint, small towns like Shelburne Falls, Charlemont, Florida, and Clarksburg. When the top of the trail opens to a panoramic view of the Berkshires, tourists giddily drive with care around the dangerous Hairpin Turn as they descend to North Adams.

Swan had insisted on taking the scenic route, and she and Memphis had flown into Bradley Airport in Windsor, Connecticut, rented a car, drove up I-91 to Greenfield, then headed up Route 2. They soon found out that the rumors about bumper-to-bumper cars along the road were all too true. Swan had started out driving but after five miles of cursing, yelling, and gesturing with her middle finger Memphis told her to pull over and he'd drive. Grudgingly, she complied and pulled into the Mohawk Trading Post. The parking lot was packed but fortune smiled on them and a car was pulling out as they were pulling in. They went inside and maneuvered around the dozens of tourists. Swan picked up several souvenirs for all the kids and tee-shirts for her and Memphis as well as two pints of maple syrup. He drove when they left.

Swan snapped a few photos from the car as they drove up the road. It took two hours to make the forty-mile journey to the Hairpin Turn where Swan snapped a shot of the amazing Mount Greylock, and it was still slow going down into North Adams. Traffic freed up once they got to the city limits and Swan directed her husband to

Route 8 which took them directly into the Pittsfield. Just southwest of the city they took a side road to the Berkshire Bed & Breakfast, which was a quarter mile from Lake Onota, and checked in. It was past eight o'clock, but fortunately there was a small pancake house a half mile away where they enjoyed breakfast food for dinner. Memphis called Tucson to check on the kids and his brother told him all was well with their daughters and siblings.

Memphis and Swan collapsed on their bed, too tired to even attempt a shower. They fell asleep with their clothes on. When Memphis woke up the next morning, he could hear the shower water running. He also noticed that a third of one of the maple syrup pints had been emptied. Swan came out of the bathroom, still toweling herself dry. She flashed him a salacious grin and casually dropped the towel.

"See anything you like, Geronimo?" she said coyly.

"Maybe," he murmured, throwing his legs over the edge of the mattress. "Come here, white woman." He stretched out his hands. Swan took them and he pulled her down on the bed. She giggled and they kissed passionately for long moments before he pulled away, grinned, and reached over to the bedstand where the partially empty maple syrup bottle was resting. He bit his lower lip and slowly unscrewed the top as his wife lay back on the pillow and watched his intense, handsome face. She inhaled sharply; how she loved that man.

Memphis carefully poured a few ounces of maple syrup on Swan's stomach, then put the bottle back. He leaned over and licked the sweet liquid. Slowly. It struck him that the sticky amber syrup was the same color as his skin.

"Um, you taste good," he whispered. He continued licking until her stomach was clean. Then he straddled her, and their eyes locked with anticipation and passion.

"Get naked, Geronimo," she whispered huskily as she began unbuttoning his shirt.

"Yes, ma'am," he whispered back desperately as he whipped off his belt and pulled his shirt out of his jeans.

An hour and a two-person shower later they dressed and headed downstairs to the breakfast room where the two other guests were being served a remarkably impressive morning meal. They were presented with the same and husband and wife wolfed the food down. It was still early, so they decided to take a walk to the lake before heading off to the police station.

Lake Onota is over six hundred acres in size, and is popular for swimming, fishing, crew rowing, and sailing. Divided into north and south basins it empties via Onota Brook into the west branch of the Housatonic River. In the late 19th and early 20th centuries the elite rich in the area built large summer mansions around the lake. Many of those houses plus much newer ones (including mobile homes) dot the circumference of the lake. The crystal-clear blue water is surrounded by dense trees of many varieties, including ghostly aspen trees, and has a horizon rimmed with high green hills. It looks like a white wonderland in the winter when the water freezes over. Then, quite a few people venture out and chip away to enjoy ice fishing. A few fall in.

The B & B was a short walk to the lake and when they got there they turned north and began to hike the perimeter as far as they could without encroaching on private properties. Swan whispered to Memphis that she'd love to strip her clothes off and plunge into the water. He told her that if she didn't get arrested, she'd turn blue and freeze; this was almost the end of October and the water was most definitely not warm.

They walked for a good hour before returning to the B & B and gathering their things for the day's investigative effort. Skye had arranged a meeting with the lead detective on Cameo's case and they were due to meet him at ten o'clock. Memphis memorized the directions to the police station, and they pulled into the front parking lot at nine-forty-five. The building was typical New England, a two-story, wide brick structure with nothing fancy on the outside except a set of blue double front doors. A few of the windows had portable air conditioners sticking out. A gas lamp-style electric streetlight stood in front of the building as well as all around the quiet street. An American flag flew at the station entrance.

Memphis and Swan walked over to the desk sergeant and identified themselves. He told them to wait over at the benches and Detective Hollister would be with them as soon as he could. They parked themselves on a bench away from the homeless-looking woman at the other end. She coughed a while, then a policewoman came out and gently guided her to an office.

Ten o'clock came and went, and so did ten-twenty. At ten-thirty Swan jumped up and stalked over to the desk sergeant and forced herself to politely ask when Detective Hollister would be available. He stared at her blankly and said he didn't know; they'd just have to wait. Swan snatched a piece of note paper from his desk and scribbled a few words on it. She shoved it at the sergeant.

"Here," she snapped as Memphis came up behind her. "That's the name of our city's preeminent newspaper publisher. He knows a shitload of other publishers including those in your city and nearby areas. I'm sure if he called them to discuss how the Pittsfield police force is treating visiting investigators like crap, they'd be happy to print an article or editorial. Unless, of course, you people have a sterling reputation with the civilians of this town. The last number is where we're staying. Feel free to have Detective Hollister call us for a meeting at our convenience and location. We'll be staying there for a few days. Before we leave, we'll call our publisher friend. Have a nice fucking day."

With that last remark Swan whirled around and shoved past her husband as she stormed out of the station. Memphis grinned at the cop, then sauntered after her. Outside, he grabbed her wrist. She struggled for a few seconds then relented as he drew her to him and kissed her. When he drew back, he grinned at her.

"I couldn't see over the desk, but I wouldn't be surprised if that poor cop pissed himself. You have that effect on people," Memphis said.

"Good," Swan said as she swept up her hair into a tight long ponytail. "I don't like assholes whether or not they're wearing a badge. Ten o'clock means ten o'clock, not ten-thirty." She arched a deadly eyebrow. "You do remember the deadlocks on the doors and windows when you came home three hours late that day you were exploring the Victorian." Memphis, Percy, Sand, and Troy had been inspecting Memphis's inherited Victorian to try to find evidence against Joanna Frid. They found secret compartments and evidence in the massive fireplace, but instead of coming home at seven they came home closer to ten. Swan and Memphis's parents had put new deadlocks on both houses' doors and windows, as well as on Percy's townhouse. They had to dish out significant bucks to spend the night at the La Fonda Inn. From that point on when his wife told him to be somewhere at a specific time, he was never late.

"I remember," Memphis replied, sighing. "Since we aren't going to get anywhere here, let's head over to the hospital and see if we can corral the doctors that treated Cameo."

"You lead, I follow, kemo sabe," Swan said.

"Seriously?"

"It's a term of endearment. Deal with it. Come on." Swan began leading them back to the car when they heard a man yelling at them from the police station door. They turned together and saw a man in a sports coat waving at them and beckoning them back. Memphis and Swan looked at one another and shrugged. They started walking back to the station as the man moved forward and stuck out his hand. Memphis took the offered hand gingerly while Swan folded her arms tightly.

"Detective Harris Hollister," the man said. "And I'm assuming you would be the couple with the publisher friend that could raise hell."

"Yeah, that's us," Memphis said, nodding. "Memphis Grayhawk and Swan Hazelwood. Is that why you came after us?" He summed up the man mentally. Thirty-five to forty, average height, trim, neat, but with a touch of modern fashion with a wide tie and jeans instead of regular pants. His chestnut-brown hair was well past his ears, and he had a Fu Manchu moustache. Half tradition, half disco age.

"Part of the reason," Hollister confessed. "The other part is that I finally finished my last interrogation and rushed out to my late meeting. I apologize for the half hour delay." He flashed the piece of paper that Swan had written on. "Where are you staying?"

"The Berkshire Bed & Breakfast."

"Great place. When my mom visited from Springfield she stayed there."

"Not with you?" Swan asked.

"Ah … she and my wife aren't best buds."

Swan put her hand on Memphis's shoulder. "I worship my husband's parents."

"You two are married?" Hollister exclaimed.

"Seven years," Memphis said. "Sort of. Long story. Are you free to talk now?"

"Yes, I am. Come on back." He narrowed his eyes at Swan. "I'd swerve to the left when we get to the desk sergeant. He's a crack shot. And pissed."

"I could outshoot him with my eyes closed," Swan said flatly as she followed Memphis and Hollister back into the station. When she passed the scowling desk sergeant, she batted her eyes and blew him a kiss.

Five minutes later they were all settling into a small conference room that had a window overlooking the street. Hollister left them there then said he'd be right back. He looked at Swan, repeated that, and crossed his heart. When he returned after ten minutes, he was carrying a thick folder and three cups of coffee.

"Thanks," Memphis said as he sipped. Not too terrible for cop coffee, he thought.

"So," Hollister said, "according to your secretary, this meeting is to discuss the Cameo Adams case. I take it she must have hired you?"

Swan nodded. "She did. She wound up in Santa Fe and someone had given her our firm as a reference. We've taken her on, and she's seeing one of our colleagues for a psychological investigation."

"She had a couple of those here," Hollister said. "She also hired a P.I. from Springfield that cost her a lot of money and produced no results. What makes you think you can solve the case?"

"Because we're better than Springfield," Swan said without any trace of doubt.

Hollister cocked his head and studied her for a moment, then looked at Memphis. "Huh," he said. "Grayhawk and Hazelwood. Those names seem … familiar. You do anything newsworthy?" Before Memphis could answer Hollister snapped his fingers and pointed at the couple. "Goddamn. The vampire serial killer out in—where? Arizona?"

"New Mexico," Memphis said. He shook his head ruefully. "Yeah, that was us and a few of our colleagues and family."

"She got away, didn't she?"

"Yes," Memphis said tersely. "Honestly, we'd really prefer not to relive that. Let's focus on the Adams case."

"Look, I'm sorry. It's just a fascinating case. We'll do the Adams case first, but I'd appreciate any consideration you could give about providing at least a summary, from your viewpoint."

"Fine," Swan said. "Afterwards. Let's deal with Cameo first." She nodded at his folder. "Those the official records and notes?"

"Yes," Hollister said. "I was the lead on the case. My partner, Norm Dickinson, retired two years ago and moved to Florida."

"When did you get the call about her?" Memphis asked.

Hollister took a sip of coffee and flipped open the folder to the first document. "The initial call came in at 9:52 PM on May 4, 1969. May's still spring so the temperature barely made sixty-five by early evening. It wasn't cold, though. Well, it may have been for her. Anyway, a unit was sent out to the Housatonic River south of the east and west branch confluence, specifically a few yards from where Wampenum Brook branches off. There aren't any residences or businesses there, just the river and brook and a thick forest of trees. Pine, aspen, oak, trees like that, with thick foliage that wasn't fully blossomed yet since it was a good month and a half from summer.

"Further down there were houses and a guy from there was taking his son on a night hike to teach the kid about nocturnal creatures for some school project. They heard a sort of moaning and that led them to the girl. She was lying a few yards from the riverbank, naked, and bleeding. The weird thing was a backpack strapped to her back. The guy sent his son back to their house to call the police. After the officers got there they called for an ambulance and she was transported to the hospital. When the doctors found evidence of blunt force trauma and possibly rape, the uniforms called for a detective, and that's how Norm and I got involved. We were on call that night."

"How long before you were able to interview her?" Memphis asked.

"Several hours. She had a concussion and drifted in and out of consciousness until well past midnight. The doctor wanted us to wait until the next day but it's always critical to get as many facts as possible as early on, so we pushed, and he gave in. We got fifteen minutes with her but didn't get much. Couldn't even get her name. She was foggy and her eyes couldn't focus, so we gave up and came back in the morning."

"And that's when you learned she couldn't give you her name," Memphis said.

"So she said."

"You didn't believe her?" Swan asked.

"Honestly? Not at first, but after an extensive interview as well as discussions with her doctors I concluded that she was telling the truth. There was no identification in the backpack, just a shitload of money. And I mean a *shitload.* My first thought was that it was from a bank robbery or something criminal. But the bills weren't brand new and the serial numbers weren't on any lookout list. We had several dozen bills fingerprinted and hers weren't on them, just a few that didn't match up to anything in our files. No, they're not on any list but my gut tells me they're ill-gotten gains. We fingerprinted her but there's no record of her prints, so she clearly hadn't been arrested in the past or had a job where fingerprinting is mandatory. Let me ask you—you have the records about this. Why did you want to meet in person?"

"Because records are only factual documents," Memphis said. "We wanted to get your emotional and intellectual reactions to the case. Those are things that wouldn't be written down."

Hollister nodded. "I get that. You aren't an ex-cop, are you?" He smiled.

"Nope. Just a bar-certified lawyer-cum-private eye." He nodded towards Swan. "My wife was a cop. A damn good one."

Hollister looked at Swan. "Why did you quit?"

"I was fired," Swan said flatly.

"Huh. What did you do?"

"Ball-kicked a couple of detectives that were ragging on my brother. He was a cop, too, but got canned for his personal life. I didn't take kindly to either circumstance. Now, let's get back to the case." Swan folded her arms again and stared at Hollister without blinking.

Hollister turned to Memphis. "She's scary."

"You have no idea," Memphis replied, a smile tugging at his lips. "Tell me—were the doctors skeptical of her amnesia claim?"

"At first, but probably not so much as me. After all, she'd had a severe head trauma and they explained that could easily cause temporary amnesia. While she was in the hospital they brought in a psychiatrist, and after two sessions he confirmed that her amnesia was genuine. She saw him a couple of times after she was discharged."

Memphis flipped through a couple of sheets in his binder (Skye had pooh-pooh'd the idea of keeping records in a folder and changed all their cases' materials into binders with separator tabs). "It says that you and your partner interviewed a lot of people to see if they could identify her. You also put notices in the newspapers. Get a lot of tips?"

"They crawl out of the woodwork on something like this. None of them were viable. We interviewed a few of the tipsters. A couple were decent people who just made a mistake. A few were assholes that just wanted their fifteen minutes. I believe the P.I. that she hired went the same route as we did and came up just as empty." He shook his head. "Can you imagine not knowing who you are? Forgetting your past? Your family? Christ, and not only that but to have been raped, too. At least she didn't get pregnant."

"The doctors said she was raped," Swan said, "but is it possible that her vaginal injuries and other skin bruising were the result of consensual rough sex?"

"We considered that. Her bruises and bleeding, however, pointed more to a nonconsensual violent act. There was semen, and the doctor said it was from only one blood type, type B."

"Did he say whether or not she was a virgin at the time of the rape?"

Hollister seemed startled. "I don't think we ever talked about that. You'd have to ask him. I assume he's on your investigation list?"

"He is. Dr. Kent Danforth, right? The primary physician," Memphis said as he flipped to the medical tab. "Cameo gave us written permission to discuss her medical records with him."

"That's good."

"The records say that you went to several colleges to see if anyone recognized her," Swan said.

Hollister nodded. "We did. She seemed to be the age of a college student. We hit all the colleges around Pittsfield as well as those up in North Adams, southern Vermont, and as far east as Greenfield. We also sent copies of her photo to colleges around Boston and down into Connecticut and Rhode Island. New Hampshire and Maine, too. Nada."

"Only New England?" Swan said.

"Do you know how many colleges there are in the Unites States? Too many. We had newspaper ads with her photo spread as far as the Mississippi. We did the best we could."

"Of course you did," Memphis said. "We aren't meaning to imply anything else."

"And yet here you are, questioning our investigation and, I'm sure" —he threw a glance at Swan— "believing that you can do a better job."

"We didn't say that, either," Memphis said coolly. "It's not something we even considered."

"Okay," Hollister said. "I'll take you at your word. What else do you want to know?"

"We want to know what you think happened. Forget facts, forget evidence," Swan said. "What personal conclusions did you come to?"

Hollister looked her in the eye. "I think something bad happened to the lady, something so bad that she can't allow herself to think about it. Women are raped all the time, but I've never seen a case where that erased their memory. She had a bad knock on the head with a mild concussion. Temporary amnesia? Maybe, but according to you five years later she still doesn't remember her past. Maybe that past is too horrible to remember. And, maybe she's better off not remembering."

"Maybe, but she still wants to know. She wants to know if she left a family behind, or a husband. A life."

"Then why the hell can't she remember?" Hollister said tersely. "If she's got people she loves buried deep inside her mind, why isn't she digging them out?"

"She is—she hired us, and my friend, Dr. McBean, a psychologist. And, he's actually made some progress in unearthing her past."

"How?"

"He used some visual techniques on her to gauge her emotional responses. She reacted to several, including this one." Memphis pulled a copy of the coastline photo from his binder and handed it to Hollister. "Ring any bells?"

"The ocean, obviously. If I had to guess I'd say the Atlantic. Rocky coast, so it could be from Connecticut on north to Maine. Can't say this particular image rings a bell, though. By the way, how is she doing?"

"Physically, she's very healthy. Mentally, she's obsessed with knowing who she is. However, she has toned that down enough to set down some roots in Santa Fe. We even got her a job so she can focus on something intellectual. She's working as an editor on our hometown newspaper."

Hollister frowned. "How did that come about?"

"Well, after she left here in search of herself, she began writing her thoughts down in journals. Incredibly detailed, intelligent thoughts. She let her psychologist read the journals, and he found them replete with incisive sentences, perfect grammar and syntax and punctuation. Wherever she came from, whoever she is she's clearly educated and smart. That tells us a lot about her. We have a publisher friend that needed an editor and he gave her a trial job. They both seem happy with the working relationship."

"Damn," Hollister said softly. "It's too bad she didn't start writing those and sharing them with us before she left Pittsfield. Anything in them to suggest her origins?"

"Dr. McBean didn't think so, but it gave insight into her character, into the person behind the face she presents in daily life."

Hollister looked down at the coastline photo and drummed his fingers on it. He held up a finger then left the room.

"Was it something I said?" Swan asked, an eyebrow arched.

"Maybe the fact that you still smell a little of maple syrup made him desperate for a vending machine snack."

"We have a pint and a half of the stuff left," she whispered, leaning towards him.

"My salacious little pancake," he whispered back. Their lips were a millimeter apart when Hollister came back into the room with another cop in a crisp blue uniform. They both snapped back.

"This is Officer DeVere York. He's from the coast area," Hollister said.

"Portsmouth, New Hampshire to be specific," the young officer said, smiling widely. He had to be a rookie, no more than twenty-two. A handsome black man he had close-cropped hair and a wisp of a moustache.

"Pleased to meet you," Memphis said, offering his hand.

"DeVere," Hollister began, "does this photo give you any idea where the coastline might be?" He handed the photo to DeVere.

DeVere studied the photo and pursed his lips. After a long minute he handed it back to Hollister. "If I had to make a guess," he said, "I'd say it's part of the coast north of Boston and well up into Maine. The coastline is real rocky and you can see the power of the waves. It could be lower, say down towards the Cape and Rhode Island and Connecticut, but I'd put my money on north. Could even be one of the zillions of islands off the Maine coast. Where did you get it?"

Memphis took the photo and looked at it for a second. "A doctor friend of mine found it in an old magazine and used it as a visual aid for one of his client sessions. The magazine didn't specify where it was taken."

"What was the magazine?" Hollister asked.

"*World Seas Journal*. He found it at a yard sale with a few other old ones that had interesting pictures. He uses visual aids in some of his sessions and cut out a few then had them photographed for clarity processing."

"Does he still have the magazine?"

"He does, but a little research determined that it had a fairly short publishing run, from 1967 to 1971. The company's out of business now. Unfortunately, a lot of the images didn't have photographers attributed to the scenes. This was one of them. Also, unfortunately it wasn't in an article specific to a general location but in one that had snapshots of seas and oceans around the United States. We've tried to find some of the editorial names in the magazine but no luck yet."

"Do you have a duplicate of that shot?" DeVere asked. Memphis handed him one. "Super. I know a couple of naturalist photographers back home. I can flash this by them and see if they can pin down the location or if they know any photographers that worked for that magazine."

"That would be fantastic," Memphis said. He handed DeVere a business card. "Thank you."

Hollister nodded at DeVere who smiled widely and ducked out of the room. "He's going to be a hell of cop someday," he said. He looked at Swan. "What else can I tell you about our investigation?"

"Did you determine how she wound up on the banks of the river?" Swan asked.

Hollister shook his head. "Not really. There were any number of ways. With her head wound and other injuries, including the broken wrist, I'm not sure I can see her walking there from a populated area. Possible, but unlikely. My best guess is that she was dropped there from a boat. There weren't any gashes in the bank to indicate that a boat was pressed up against the mud, and any telltale footprints were obliterated by the guy and his son as well as the first officers on scene and the ambulance crew. I had two uniforms go back and search the area for a quarter mile all ways, but they found nothing. It's almost like she was dropped down from the heavens."

"Did you check any surrounding boat docks?"

"Yup. But a lot of people haul their boats to the river on trailers when they want to go boating. Impossible to track all of them down."

"Of course," Memphis said. He looked at his wife. "Anything else from you, honey?"

Swan scowled. "Don't call me honey in front of a cop."

"Sorry, sugar lips." Memphis laughed and turned to Hollister. "I am so doomed when we get home."

Swan ignored him but vowed silently that the couch was going to be inhabited for at least a week when they got home. She said to Hollister, "I think we've got all we need. We're going to hit the hospital next. Any other suggestions?"

"I think you've got it covered with your records and our discussion. If I think of anything else, I'll call you. How long are you staying?"

"A few days," Swan said. "We have to get home before Halloween." She always felt a chill down her spine when she thought of the holiday and what had happened on that night seven years earlier. It was an unspoken determination between her and Memphis that they'd never leave the kids alone without them on that day or the next, the Day of the Dead.

"You got kids?"

"Three girls," Memphis replied. He hesitated a few seconds. "That's not the reason we always need to be home by that date. Got a few minutes? We can give you the short story about the vampire killer."

"Want some more coffee?"

"Please."

Hollister returned a few minutes later with fresh coffee and a few packs of Drake's Ring Dings from the vending machine. He sat down. "I am all ears."

Memphis sighed and took a sip of coffee.

"Once upon a time …"

CHAPTER SEVENTEEN

London Monroe was a proud American, not an expatriate Brit as her first name might suggest. Her grandfather was English and was born and raised in London, so when she was born, he insisted that she be named after his beloved hometown. Grandpa Monroe died when she was ten, and to this day she missed his love, affection, and wisdom. She missed her parents, too, who had died years earlier, only a year separating their funerals in Chapel Hill, North Carolina.

Her father had been a professor of History at the University of North Carolina at Chapel Hill, her mother a professor of Sociology at the same campus. She grew up in an academic world and excelled at her own studies. She snagged a full scholarship to Chapel Hill and took her Bachelor's degree in History there. She wanted to spread her wings and extract herself from her comfort zone, so she went to Rice University for her Master's and then the University of Texas in Austin for her PhD. During her tenure at those colleges she taught as a grad student and acquired a sterling reputation. She settled in at the University of Texas for her post-PhD professorship. She enjoyed her work, but she found herself restless, and when an opportunity arose, she snapped at it.

Sangre de Cristo College was established in Santa Fe, New Mexico by a cabal of four highly placed professors who had convinced a philanthropist with a lot of money and no heirs to fund the building of a new college on a fifty-acre spread of land at the foot of the Sangre de Cristo Mountains to the east of Santa Fe. The college opened to its first freshman class in September of 1958 and was an immediate success. The disciplines offered grew and in 1964 the college offered Master's degrees and in 1969 PhDs. The college had an excellent reputation especially for its History and Psychology departments.

London's proficiency in her teaching career was known past the borders of Texas, and every so often she was solicited by colleges to join their programs. In 1963 Sangre de Cristo offered her a position with the caveats of being able to establish at least one new discipline and a thirty-percent raise in pay. She thought on the offer for a long weekend, then accepted.

She was tough but fair and had a stellar reputation amongst her students albeit some contention with the school administrators and other professors who thought her too abrasive and aggressive. She was criticized for words and actions which her critics would have applauded had she been a man. She had endured the same from all the colleges to which she had gone and handled the contention with respect and aplomb. She taught several standard History courses, but especially loved the one that she had created, Indian Cultures. It was a popular course and each semester students flooded to get in. In 1969 she split the course into two distinct sections, Ancient Indian Cultures and Modern Indian Cultures. She taught both but also had hired another professor to carry part of the load.

Always seeking to expand her horizons London studied for and achieved a Master's in Anthropology, which dovetailed nicely with her History courses. Although there were already three Anthropology professors plus a head of that department, she taught two courses on Indian Anthropology. Like her other courses, students flocked to join her class. That bought some resentment on the part of the other professors, but since the college was growing there was enough to go around. Besides, as the head of the History department she had no intention of changing major disciplines.

At forty-two she was settled into her profession, loved and respected, and happy in her professional and personal lives. She had never married or had children. A few past love affairs left her wary of romance, but she believed in it and didn't discount it for her middle age. She kept herself healthy and well-groomed. Her short salt-and-pepper hair (mainly pepper) never reached past her shoulders, and for the past few years she had been affecting a pixie cut that required little attention. She was slender and at five-eight was shapely and toned in all the right places. She enjoyed traveling, reading, exploring Indian sites around the country, and on occasion lying on a Pacific beach and walking through the surf. She had a wide circle of friends that included a good number of colleagues. She was closest to Carmen Castillo; they had bonded years earlier when they experienced and survived the initial resentment to their hirings and methods. She, Carmen, and Pryce had dinner together at least twice a month.

She checked her calendar again and was thrilled that her eleven o'clock staff meeting had been canceled. That meant that the ten o'clock meeting she was having with the two detectives wouldn't be rushed. She learned that they had been referred to her by one of her former students, Nick Griffin. He was a P.I. in the most respected firm in the city. She had also had one of his colleagues, Tucson Grayhawk, for one of her Indian Cultures classes. As she remembered, they had both done quite well. She had called Nick to get the basics of what the police wanted, although he didn't go into too much detail.

At 9:59 AM her secretary called and said that the two detectives had arrived. She told the girl to send them in. She stood behind her desk, waiting. The door opened and the secretary ushered the men inside then shut the door behind her.

London was good at judging first impressions. The men were physical opposites, with one resembling a lumbering bear and the other, well, maybe a slight doppelganger for Lurch. Lurch had a hangdog face, but his eyes were lively and belied his looming presence. The bear had a real commitment and focus to his facial expression. London thought that because of their physicality and age they might be underrated; she was sure that they were crack professionals. Just a hunch …

"Won't you please sit down?" she said, gesturing to her guest chairs. When they were seated, she sat down, too. "London Monroe, but you already know that."

Frack nodded and said, "Jesse Morgan. This is Bart Smith. We're detectives assigned to a missing persons case. Well, two, actually."

"And … I can help you how?" London asked politely.

"Okay, well, one of these missing persons is a professor of Archeology from Princeton."

"What's his name? Or, her?"

"Howard Kensington Carter."

"Really?" London exclaimed. "I've read his paper on the King Tut discovery and its long-term impacts on subsequent Middle East finds. Very incisive. You say he's missing? When?"

"1972," Frack replied.

"And you're just investigating this now?" London's tone had a thread of incredulity in it.

"Yeah, we are," Frick said coolly, "but the Jersey cops started investigating a few weeks after the guy left on an exploration journey."

"Exploration to where?" she asked.

"A pretty long summer elliptical trip around the country to explore various Indian archeological sites. Who knows—maybe he was thinking of writing another paper or a book? You remember any of his other papers dealing with that subject?"

"Actually, I do. I also read his treatise on the Algonquins and their displacement from western New England due to the encroachment of Europeans settlers. He spent some time at an excavation site and helped catalog various items from the sixteen hundreds and earlier. So, tell me—why did this drop in your laps?"

Frick sighed. "We had another missing person case and part of our investigation was to put ads in papers across the country. Our missing persons—two twenty-somethings from San Francisco—were last seen in Taos exploring the pueblo. They'd started their cross-country trip from Boston and hit a number of historical sites, according to phone calls home and a few postcards. We conferred with the Jersey cop leading the initial investigation and he said this Carter guy had sent a few postcards back to friends. A couple of them were from sites in Texas, and in the last postcard he said that he couldn't wait to get to Taos. When the detective saw our ad, he decided to contact our captain and see if there were any other overlaps. Longshot, but worth a try."

"And, you contacted me because …"

"Just to get a little clarification on anthropology and archeology. We weren't sure about how they differ and whether the Carter guy, who was an Archeology professor, might be exploring both disciplines. We hoped it might give us an insight into where specifically he might have been going when he disappeared," Frick said.

"So," Frack said. "Can you enlighten us?"

"I can, and I will," London said, flashing a genuine smile for the first time. "First, would you like some coffee?"

"Oh, yes ma'am," Frack said enthusiastically. "I'm dry as a bone."

"That would be appreciated," Frick said, his eyes never leaving London's face. *Good-lookin' woman*, he thought. She wore her linen navy pantsuit, silk blouse, and leopard-print neck scarf like a fashion model. He felt a very unexpected stirring.

London called her secretary and asked for three cups of coffee. A few minutes later the detectives and the professor were sipping really decent brew. She finished half of her cup then put it down.

"The disciplines of anthropology and archeology are intricately linked. Archaeology is similar to anthropology in that it focuses on understanding human culture from the deepest history up until the recent past. It differs from anthropology in that it focuses specifically on analyzing material remains such as artifacts and architectural remnants. Just to throw a little more confusion into the mix, there's also the discipline of paleontology, which is the study of fossils through geologic time. Fossils are not limited to animals; plants are also gathered and studied. That study is not part of an archeologist's job, but is critical to understanding the development of species, when they came about, when they became extinct, etc."

"What if the archeologist is engaged in a site that also has animal and plant fossils?" Frick asked.

"An excellent question, detective. If a paleontologist isn't available one can be called in, or the archeologist might gather those fossils and return them to a specialist."

"What's the whole point of these efforts?" Frack asked. His pen was poised above his notebook.

"The point, detective, is to understand human history not only for the sake of the knowledge itself, but to apply that knowledge to understanding and perhaps solving current issues in civilization. Anthropologists use social, biological, and physical science to analyze and interpret human culture, to see commonality and to see differences, and explain how they resulted in the current state of various cultures. Archeology can be seen as a branch of anthropology, the branch that studies physical remnants of past civilizations such as pottery, weapons, stone tools, and bones."

"Bones?" Frick said. "Why bones?"

"Well, because bones can tell us the average size of persons of certain cultures and measure how they've changed today. They can tell us whether a person had a disease, or an injury. Bones have been revered in many cultures, and even used to build monuments and offerings to ancient gods or prominent people."

"Seriously?" Frack said, his eyes wide.

London nodded. "There's the Skull Tower in Serbia that was built out of nearly a thousand skulls of Serbian soldiers that fell to the Ottomans. The Ottomans wanted to make it clear that they would tolerate no aggression. That's simply one example. There are quite a lot across the centuries."

"Do you have any books on that subject?" Frick asked.

"Not offhand, but I can probably find one. Let me root around and I'll give you a call. So, now that we've discussed the disciplines, what else can I help you with?"

"Would an archeologist be particularly interested in exploring living pueblos like, say, Taos?" Frick asked.

"Taos has been explored by both anthropologists and archeologists. There's archeological evidence that the original inhabitants may have been forced to leave. Our state has the Archeological Society of New Mexico, which was founded almost a hundred years ago. They have members and documents that drill back to their finds and interpretations. They've explored Taos as well as other pueblos and non-puebloan sites. I don't believe they have any active investigations of Taos.

"Anthropologically speaking, regardless of artifacts Taos and other pueblos are a goldmine of information for anthropologists. Taos is quite an interesting place. They've been very secretive about their daily life and rituals. They do not like people mucking about without permission or good reason. They don't like it even when there's a good reason. I would say many of the other pueblos are similar but not as stringent."

"How would a person disrespect the Taos Pueblo?" Frack asked.

"Well, taking photographs of the inhabitants without permission for one. Not showing proper deference to the cemetery or chapel. Acting stupid and making faces while they take pictures of themselves if it was a couple or small group. Arguing over prices at the gift shop. Making stupid remarks about Indians. That's just to name a few. I'm sure the Indians there could add other signs of disrespect."

"What happens if the pueblo is disrespected?" Frack asked.

"They would be asked to leave, politely at first and then with more insistence. I've known a couple of residents who snatched cameras out of tourists' hands and smashed them to the ground. However, with his reputation I can't see Dr. Carter breaking any rules there or at any sites. He's shown nothing but respect for the cultures he explores. Was he last seen at Taos or one of the other pueblos in the state?"

Frick shook his head. He took out the map of the Unites States with the elliptical path highlighted in red. He laid it flat on her desk and came around behind her to point out a few sites. Frack stayed in his seat.

"Carter followed an elliptical tour starting down the east coast into the Carolinas. After that he made it to Louisiana then over to the west through Texas. That's where his trail ends based on the phone calls back home and the postcards he sent. The last postcard he mailed was a shot of the Cathedral of San Fernando in San Antonio. On it he wrote, 'Having a blast. Glad you're not here (ha ha). Heading up through New Mexico and then over to Arizona. Will send you a card from Albuquerque and Taos. Hugs to the puppies.' That was the last known contact he had with anyone."

"Any possibility that he simply continued on through those two states with no problems and simply forgot or dismissed the need for contact at those points?" London asked.

"Possibly," Frick said, "but to my mind unlikely. I mean, if you wound up in a pueblo or Santa Fe could you resist sending out a postcard?"

"No, not me. Did he indicate where his first stop in New Mexico would be?"

"Nope," Frack said, draining the last of his coffee. "I think we can make educated guesses, though. If he came through El Paso and up to Las Cruces on his way to Albuquerque and Santa Fe, he might have stopped at …"

"What?" London asked curiously.

Frick smiled. "You tell us. You're the expert. We're just dumb cops." He reseated himself and picked up his coffee cup.

London raised a challenging eyebrow. "Somehow the adjective 'dumb' isn't the first I'd think of you as."

"What would that be?"

"Sly. Smarter than you let on. Okay, let's see. The most southern site to see would be Carlsbad Caverns, but he'd have to swing east to get there. Heading north he'd come across the White Sands National Monument, but he'd have to swing east for that site, too. A fascinating place. Both are, but they really aren't associated with archeology or anthropology."

"Let's assume that he scratched those off a tentative to-do list and headed towards Albuquerque," Frick said.

"Northeast of the route are the Gila Cliff Dwellings. They're ancient residences built into the cliffs. Although it would be exciting for an archeologist to visit that and take his own impression, visitors are not permitted up into the dwellings. No, my best guess is that after he crossed the border he headed straight north into the largest city and capital city area. There, he'd have a lot of sites and pueblos to visit."

"We've been to some for our other case," Frack said. "There's a lot clustered in a tight circumference."

"For sure," London said, nodding. "All of them offer some sense of either anthropological aspects or archeological ones, often both. He could have hit any of them. If he planned on hitting the cluster in an efficient fashion, I would say he probably hit the Isleta Pueblo south of Albuquerque. From there, most likely, the Acoma Pueblo, which is west of Isleta. He could have gone farther west and hit the Zuni Pueblo, but if he wanted to spend as little travel time versus an overall journey, then he probably headed back to Albuquerque and went north towards Santa Fe. He could have hit the Sandia, the San Felipe, and the rest of them. Of course, if he were interested in the archeology of the state in general, he could have visited other non-pueblo sites, like the Bandelier National Monument, or even reservations."

"My head hurts," Frack said.

"Would you like an aspirin?" London asked.

"I don't think that'll help," Frick said. "He always gets headaches when he has to think too much." He was gratified at her wide smile. He ignored his partner's scowl. "You know, we've taken up enough of your time. You've been incredibly helpful. Thank you."

"You're very welcome. I'll get that book on the bone monuments. I'm pretty sure I can have it by tomorrow."

Fuck it, Frick thought, then spoke rashly. "If you can get it by tomorrow, I'd love to collect it and take you to lunch to thank you with a good meal and wine."

She cocked her head. "Wine? Wouldn't you be on duty?"

"Frack—I mean, Detective Morgan—and I are a month from retirement. I'm not too worried about breaking a rule or two."

"I see," she mused. "One o'clock at the Pink Adobe?"

"It's a date—a deal, I mean." Frick stood. He stared down at Frack, who was staring up at him with wide eyes and an open mouth. Frack lumbered to his feet and stuck out his hand towards London.

"Thanks for your time," Frack said. "And don't worry—I won't turn up at your lunch. Some of us have paperwork to do."

Frick took London's hand and held it for a few seconds too long before he reluctantly withdrew it. He ducked his head with a slight smile and led his partner out of the office.

London sat back in her chair and stared at the closed door. She couldn't quite pin down why she felt a slight thrill. Frack—then she remembered that Nick had called them Frick and Frack. So, Lurch was Frick. She laughed.

"What the hell was that all about?" Frack growled at his partner as they left the building and headed towards their car.

"What was what all about?" Frick said.

"You know what I'm talking about."

"Do not."

"Do so. You were ogling her."

"I don't ogle. I was looking at her … appreciatively. She's a nice lady."

"You were ogling. And it's not a 'deal'—it's a date. You're too old to date."

"Am not."

"Are so. You're older than dirt."

"I'm younger than you."

"I'm better preserved."

"It's not a date."

"It's *so* a date."

"So what if it's a date? It's just lunch."

"Lunches lead to dinners and dinners lead to getting to first base and before you know it, you're trying to remember how to use your weenie again without it breaking off."

"I hate you."

"Don't kiss her on the first date."

"What if there's not a second?"

"She was ogling you, too. There'll be a second date."

"You think?"

"I think."

CHAPTER EIGHTEEN

"How much farther, DeVere?" Memphis asked as the young police officer drove the twisting roads leading to the Atlantic coast around Gloucester, Massachusetts. His photographer friend recognized the description of the coastline photo and the grainy fax and told him exactly where to find it. He also stated that his uncle had taken the photo in 1962, but he had passed on a few years later. However, he had inherited his uncle's photos and negatives, and he had a collage of the area he'd duplicate for DeVere's friends. DeVere agreed to drive Memphis and Swan to the coast. It wasn't an inconvenience; the investigation excited him.

"Maybe five miles," DeVere replied, glancing across the road at a new strip mall being built. "He lives at Land's End, which is about five miles from what he believes is the rocky coastline in the photos. Where did you book us rooms?"

"The Atlantis Oceanfront Inn," Swan replied. "Thanks for agreeing to stay overnight while we explore the area."

"It's truly my pleasure," DeVere said. "I love living in the Berkshires, but I grew up close to the ocean and it's a thrill to be back, even for a short time."

"How far is Portsmouth from here?" Memphis asked.

"Maybe sixty miles north."

"Are your parents still living there?"

DeVere nodded. "Yup. My dad works in the fishing industry and my mom's a librarian. Got a brother who's a cop, too."

"How long since you've seen them?" Swan asked.

"A good six or seven months. I've been really tied up with my job. I miss them."

"You know," Memphis said, "we should be done for the day by dinnertime. Why don't you give them a call and see if they can come down and have dinner with us?"

DeVere threw Memphis a look. "Oh, that would be great. You don't mind?"

"Not at all. Our treat," Memphis said. "Got any restaurants in mind?"

DeVere grinned. "We spent a lot of time visiting Salem, and there's a great saloon there that serves perfect shepherd's pie and bangers and mash. It's called the Pot O' Gold Saloon."

"Sounds like a plan," Swan said. "I hope the beer is cold."

"Glacial," DeVere said, nodding. "Should we check into the hotel first?"

"Yeah, good idea," Memphis said. "You can call your parents from there and call your friend."

"Works for me," DeVere said. He glanced at the road signs and took a right towards the Gloucester shore. The coastline was beautiful, and he nodded appreciatively as the hotel came up on his right. It was directly across the street from the coastline, which was a bit foggy. As he parked, he could hear the waves hissing across the rocky shore, and the cawing of seagulls. He could smell the fresh salt air. There were a few people standing on the rocks snapping pictures or walking leisurely on the wide asphalt sidewalk on the east side of Atlantic Road.

Even though it was only late morning their rooms were ready, and they checked in. They agreed to meet in the dining room in a half hour, giving them enough time to make their phone calls. Both rooms faced the ocean and were on the second floor; they couldn't have had a better view. Memphis and Swan were in the dining room when DeVere came in and sat at their table.

"Eddie said he'd come over here instead of us having to drive to his place." DeVere looked around at the open room whose large window opened to a view of the ocean. "We were lucky to get the rooms. They're about to close down for the season."

"It felt pretty cold when we were walking to the lobby," Swan said. She nodded towards the window. "Looks like the wind is really kicking up."

"New England coastal winds can freeze you solid," DeVere said, laughing. "What's that old Mark Twain saying—the coldest winter I ever spent was a summer in San Francisco? Kind of applies here, too."

"Let's order something to eat before the kitchen closes down," Memphis said. He scanned the menu and settled on the Atlantic Corned Beef Hash; Swan chose the Irish Omelet; and DeVere salivated over the Country Breakfast. They all ordered coffee and orange juice.

"Your parents and brother going to make it down for dinner?" Memphis asked.

DeVere nodded. "They're thrilled. I made the reservation for five o'clock for six people. You'll love my folks. My brother is an acquired taste."

"How so?" Swan asked.

"Think Dirty Harry with an afro." Everyone laughed, and minutes later the pert waitress with a heavy Boston accent delivered their food. They were halfway through their meals when a tall, fortyish man resembling a beanpole appeared at the entrance to the dining room and looked around, darting his head quickly like an ostrich surveilling its surroundings and looking for prey. He jerked and froze and loped over to the table. He parked himself in the last chair, glanced around, spied the waitress, and snapped his fingers loudly. People turned to see who would be so crass, but he was oblivious to their disapproval. The girl came over and pleasantly asked what he'd like. She left with an order for two triple espressos. Then, a big, happy grin exploded on his thin face. He stuck his hand out to Memphis.

"Eddie," he said. "Eddie Troy."

"Memphis Grayhawk. This is my wife, Swan Hazelwood, and of course you know DeVere."

"Oh, yeah. I've done some photography for his family. I shot his brother's two weddings. Isn't he engaged again?" Eddie asked DeVere.

DeVere sighed. "Yeah, he's on his way to number three." He looked at Memphis and Swan. "My brother isn't particularly good marriage material. We're hoping this one sticks because my parents want some grandchildren."

The waitress came over with Eddie's espressos and he thanked her politely, then asked for cream. Memphis saw her roll her eyes just before she turned and left.

"Let me see the photo that DeVere mentioned," Eddie said. He put a teaspoon of sugar in each espresso cup.

Memphis had a thin leather briefcase and opened it to withdraw the photo. He handed it over to Eddie, who studied it for a moment. By that time, his cream had arrived, and the waitress fled.

Eddie nodded. "Yes, I've seen this before in my uncle's portfolio. It's part of the collage I made. I also have individual shots as well as duplicate negatives that you can have."

"Do you know specifically where the shots were taken?" Swan asked, finishing her juice.

Eddie laughed loudly, eliciting more nasty looks from other diners. "You're kidding, right?" he asked in amusement.

"Uh, no, we're not kidding," Swan said, her tone taking on a growing pissed-off edge. "Why would you say that?"

Eddie laughed again, took a sip of his creamy espresso, and nodded his head towards the large picture window. "Because this photo was taken right across the street. So were some of the others I have. In fact, the collage is all about the coastline right in front of us." He had a shoulder bag that he rifled through before pulling out a manila envelope. He handed it to Memphis. "Here ya go."

DeVere and Swan moved close to Memphis as he took out the collage and stared at it. The top shot to the left was the one in their photo.

"That's it," Memphis murmured. "So, it's right across the street?"

"So close you can smell it," Eddie said as he finished off his second espresso. "Care to view it in person?"

"Hell, yes," Swan said as she rose and pulled her wallet out of her shoulder bag. She counted off two tens and put them on the table. As they left, she nodded to the waitress and pointed to the table.

Atlantic Road was only two lanes, with a wide sidewalk on the western side. They waited for a couple of cars to pass then walked across the street and continued to the rocky expanse. They stopped about twenty feet in and studied the landscape from right to left. Memphis grunted and pointed to the south and they followed him to a very rocky area. He carefully edged down the slight incline to a big rock and stood there staring.

"There it is," he said as Swan came up behind him.

The tiny low inlet was rimmed on either side by levels of grey rock. The ocean whooshed into the inlet hard, throwing up cold, white spray before the tide sucked the water back to the ocean and did it all over again. The wind was whipping up, and the visibility far out into the ocean faded into a white miasma. Swan shaded her eyes and stared up at the unbroken blanket of white and grey clouds.

"It's going to rain," she said quietly.

"Yeah," her husband agreed. "Let's walk south for a while and then backtrack to the north of here. I want to match the shots against the coastline." He glanced behind him at DeVere and Eddie, who were standing on a slippery wet rock staring out into the water. Eddie had brought his camera and was taking shots.

Memphis recognized each edge of shoreline in the collage. A damn seagull was even sitting on the same rock as the one in the picture. A couple of times he got too close to the edge of the rocks and wound up with a face full of salt water and a snappish comment by his annoyed wife. He led his little group back to the sidewalk and looked back at the ocean. He turned to Eddie.

"Is there anything noteworthy of this particular piece of coastline that would entice your uncle to photograph it?" he asked.

Eddie shook his head. "Not really. He was just fascinated with the ocean and traveled entirely up the Maine coast and down to Long Island Sound taking coast shots. A lot of his shots were just of the water. He was published in a few regional magazines, but he wasn't proficient or well-known enough to warrant a shoutout from the publishers. He got decent pay, though. Now, I've been published, too, and did get a footnote."

"Have wc heard of the magazine?" DeVere asked.

"I dunno. Ever hear of *Life*?" Eddie grinned. Who hadn't heard of one of the most famous magazines in the world?

"I'm impressed," Swan said seriously. She thought about Snow, who was a decent photographer and should have made that her professional career.

Memphis cocked his head. "Eddie, you ever hear of any events that occurred around here? Murders, stuff like that?"

"Nothing I can think of that would be newsworthy on a national level. Like any area we have our crimes, including an occasional murder. And, of course, we're close to Witch City so we get weirdness every so often, like a coven meeting at midnight or a goat or chicken cut up for some ritual. It happens."

Swan took a photo of Cameo out of her wallet. "Did you ever see this woman?" she asked Eddie.

Eddie took the photo and stared at it for a long minute before shaking his head. "Pretty sure I haven't. But …"

"But?" Memphis said.

"There's something about her face, her eyes that seems … familiar. But I'm sure I've never seen the girl. Who is she?"

"Our client," Swan said, pocketing the photo. "She thinks she might have seen that first shot of the coastline. We'll show her the others when we get back."

"Is she from around here?" Eddie asked.

"That's what we're trying to find out," Memphis said. "She's an amnesiac. She lost her memory five years ago. We're trying to find out who she is and why she can't remember her past."

"Whoa," Eddie said and whistled.

Memphis glanced first at Eddie and then at DeVere. He held up a finger and dug into his briefcase and extracted a small handheld tape recorder. Percy had had Cameo read from a book and he taped her. He'd given Memphis a copy. "Listen to this," Memphis said. He clicked on the recorder and Cameo's vivid melodious voice rang our clear and true. After two minutes he clicked off the tape.

"You two are New Englanders, so can you tell me if you can identify any accent?"

Eddie shook his head. "It sure ain't Maine, Vermont or New Hampshire."

"Sure as hell isn't Boston or eastern Massachusetts. Doesn't give off any Rhode Island vibes, either," DeVere said. He drew his eyebrows together in deep thought. He looked at Eddie, who nodded slightly.

"Connecticut," Eddie and DeVere said together.

"You sure?" Swan asked.

"Nope, but that's our best guess," Eddie said. "Of course, that's based on her reading from written text. Now, if she was just talking and maybe said some regional-particular colloquialisms, that might narrow it down. You know, we got specific words that people down south or in the Midwest use differently. Like, up here we say 'soda' while those guys in the Midwest say 'pop.' We eat 'grinders' while uninformed people outside the northeast eat 'subs.' That sort of stuff."

"Are there variations of Connecticut accents?" Swan asked.

"Not sure, but I'd think that people down south in the state probably effect a New Yorkish way of speaking. Those near the Rhodey border probably sound more like that state."

"So, if you don't get a whiff of southern Connecticut or eastern Connecticut, are you thinking central or western?" Memphis asked.

Eddie bobbed his head shoulder to shoulder. "Yeah, I guess I'd go with that, but it's a guess, not a guarantee. I mean, she could've been raised in another state and moved to this area when she was a teenager or adult. She'd've retained her original accent."

Memphis sighed. "All right. Eddie, can you make copies of the photos you or your uncle have taken up and down the coast? We'll pay for them and for the shipping, of course." He handed Eddie a business card with the firm's address on it.

"Sure, no problem. It'll take a few days to get the negatives processed. You know, I can root around the area and see if anyone recognizes her or if they've heard of any odd events."

"Perfect," Swan said, handing Cameo's photo over to the man. "Why don't we drive up the coast and see what it's like there, and then we can head over to Salem for dinner. DeVere made reservations for five o'clock."

"Look," DeVere said to Eddie. "My parents and brother are driving down. Want to join us? We're going to the Pot O' Gold Saloon."

"I'm there, man," Eddie said enthusiastically. "Best shepherd's pie on the east coast."

"Cool," DeVere said. "I'd better call and tell them the table's for seven, not six."

DeVere made a fast stop in his room to call the restaurant then rejoined his new friends and Eddie for a trip up the coast. They piled into his car comfortably and headed towards Rockport—where Eddie made his home—then hugged the coast up towards Plum Island, turning around just before the made the New Hampshire border. They retraced their path south, taking the bridge past Salem and navigating the coast all around the Marblehead and south towards Swampscott. At that point, multiple exposed film rolls in hand, they decided to make King's Beach their ending point of the day and drove back to Gloucester. They huddled in Memphis's and Swan's hotel room to discuss what they'd seen.

At four-fifteen DeVere aimed his car towards Salem. As usual, there were few parking spaces close by the saloon and they wound up walking four blocks. Luckily, the rain held off but there was a heavy mist to the air. They made it in just before five. DeVere identified himself and a roguish lass with a heavy Irish accent smiled brightly and led them to a table where DeVere's parents and brother were waiting. With a lot of hugs and hearty introductions the York family sat down to break bread with their favorite photographer and the New Mexicans.

The saloon was packed, mainly with tourists that had traveled to the city to celebrate the upcoming holiday. The customers were raucous and chaotic, but that didn't bother any of them. They ordered beer, Irish whiskey and other beverages and after ten minutes had given the waitress their food orders. DeVere and his brother bantered, and he let his family know the barest facts about his mission with the P.I.s. Brother ReVere was fascinated and kept asking questions until his father shut him down. The waitress had delivered their food and the delicious Irish fare was wolfed down with gusto. ReVere managed to interject questions in between bites until his father slammed his fork down on the table and said, "Enough. Stop being a cop for one goddamn night."

DeVere leaned to whisper into Memphis's ear. "See? Dirty Harry."

"With an afro," Memphis whispered back, grinning.

Swan smiled at the banter then noticed that Eddie looked like he was feeling a little left out.

"You got any siblings, Eddie?" Swan asked.

Eddie nodded. "Got a younger sister, Sigrid. She was an Army nurse in 'Nam. She spent a year in Boston when she came home in '72, then spent a year in a Newark inner-city hospital. Right now, she's in Denver. I think she's moving her way west until she gets to L.A. or Frisco."[2]

"Takes a lot of guts to be a nurse in war and in the inner city," Memphis said.

"Yeah, I'm real proud of her. Our dad died when she was in 'Nam but our mom is still alive. She lives in Salem. That's where we were born."

"Salem, Massachusetts?" Swan asked. "I know there's a Salem, New Hampshire." She knew that because that was where Percy had grown up with his adoptive parents.

"Witch City. A great place to grow up. Especially around Halloween." He noticed that a frozen look came over Swan's face. "Are you okay? Did I say something wrong?"

"No, I'm fine," Swan said flatly. She met Memphis's eyes.

"We, uh, have some bad memories around that holiday," Memphis said. "We have to be home days before. Just a family rule."

"Oh, right," DeVere said, remembering what Hollister had told him about the vampire killer and her assault on the family on Halloween, 1967. He saw the inquisitive look on his brother's face and shook his head. "Not the proper topic of conversation for this nice meal."

"You're killing me," ReVere muttered.

"Poor choice of words, bro. Not now." With that DeVere launched into a suggested next-day agenda including roaming around the Gloucester area to see if anyone recognized Cameo, then ending their search on the streets of Salem before driving back to Pittsfield. Both Eddie and the Yorks said they'd keep their eyes and ears open, and Memphis handed ReVere another photo of Cameo to show around. Swan made a point of saying that they were going to take rolls of photos of Gloucester and Salem just in case Cameo might recognize a scene.

---

2 Please see the novels *Voices of Angels* and *Out of the Ash* for Sigrid's story.

The meal ended at nine and everyone wended their way through a throng of noisy drinkers, spilling into the cool night air on a crowded street. Memphis said that he, Swan, and Eddie would meet DeVere at the car so he could spend a few minutes with his family alone. He said not to rush.

A half hour later a happy and fulfilled DeVere returned to the car. He drove them back to the inn where Eddie took his leave and said he'd stay in touch. Memphis and Swan headed off to their room, as did their new cop friend.

The next morning, they had a big breakfast, checked out, and headed into Salem. Despite hitting the bricks for hours, they found out nothing. Swan stopped in a spiritual shop run by a sweet lady named Charity Dane and purchased several souvenirs for the kids back home. Swan just loved the Witch City and said that someday they needed to bring their kids here to enjoy Halloween. She made a point of saying that they needed to eventually put that day in perspective and move forward without trepidation. Memphis agreed, reluctantly. On an impulse he bought a Ouija Board. Miss Dane explained the history and how to use it properly.

They rolled into Pittsfield after seven. DeVere dropped Swan and Memphis off at their B & B, told them he'd keep in touch, then drove home.

The next day they drove back to Windsor Locks, dropped off the rental car, and flew home. Memphis was relieved that they made it three days before Halloween.

The family's kids went wild over their presents. Tansee was thrilled with the pint of maple syrup and said it was too bad they hadn't bought another.

CHAPTER NINETEEN

Less than a mile north of the San Miguel Church lies an historic site that was dedicated during the 1920 Santa Fe Fiesta. The site was created to commemorate twenty-one friars that died during the 1680 Pueblo Revolt. Every autumn the fiesta concludes with a mass at the Saint Francis Cathedral; then the worshippers cluster and form a candlelight procession that wends its way up the steep and twisting path from the Paseo de Peralta. At the top people are treated to a beautiful 360-degree panoramic view of the city, beautiful in the daytime, splendorous at night. The Cross of the Martyrs is a Santa Fe legend.

The center piece is a reinforced concrete cross that stands twenty-five feet tall and weighs seventy-six tons. On a splendid night in 1925 the fiesta procession numbered three thousand people that lit bonfires that illuminated the magnificent cross.

Tonight, at ten-thirty, the cross was illuminated with portable floodlights, and the "procession" was a flurry of police officers and detectives plus the forensics and coroner's teams. A man was sitting at the base of the cross, his legs outstretched, his arms dangling at his side, a gun in one hand.

He was dead, dead from what appeared to be a gunshot directly in the middle of his forehead. His dark eyes were open wide, his face in repose seeming fierce despite the lack of animation. An attractive black man, he had a big afro and a bushy beard that fell nearly to his neckline. He was wearing an orange and white dashiki shirt and faded jeans with scuffed ankle boots. He had a pierced left ear with a one-carat diamond stud in it. He wore a wristwatch, but no other jewelry. His nails were ragged, his righthand knuckles slightly bruised.

Abbott wasn't in the best physical shape and even after ten minutes post-hike he was still wheezing. Besides his heavy breathing Abbott was shivering; the cold November night air was too brisk for his liking. Dunbar had preceded him to the crime scene by fifteen minutes, not winded, not a hair out of place. Abbott thought his partner looked like a goddamn model even at crime scenes. Just his luck to be stuck with Warren-Fucking-Beatty instead of Fred Mertz. Dunbar's saving grace was that he was a good cop, pleasant, and loyal to Abbott.

Abbott walked carefully up to Dunbar, who was standing two feet away from the corpse, talking to Carlito Cruz, who was nodding and gesturing towards the surrounding area. Carlito nodded to Abbott then walked away to confer with one of his techs.

"He get anything yet?" Abbott asked his partner.

Dunbar nodded. "He found some footprints close by the dead guy. Smaller shoe, could be a small man or a woman. Still, he can't rule out that the footprints were made by a daytime visitor. He's taking a plaster cast anyway."

"GSR on the guy's forehead?"

"Not too much." Dunbar stepped back a couple of feet and stretched out his arm, jerking it as though he had fired a gun. "Cruz says he thinks the killer was at least four or five feet from the guy when he got blasted. Still, up close and personal."

"Any ID on the vic?" Abbott asked.

"No wallet."

"Any witnesses?"

"Of course not."

"Hmm."

"Hmm what?"

"There's something about his face … I could swear I've seen him before."

"You bust him?"

"No, that's not it. It'll come to me. Maybe something will come up in the autopsy. What kind of gun is that?" Abbott asked. Carlito had left the gun where it was as he and his tech went about taking photos and gathering evidence.

Dunbar squinted. "A .38 special. Revolver. That's why there aren't any shell casings lying around." He slipped on a latex glove and signaled to Carlito that he wanted to pick up the gun. Carlito nodded and walked over with an evidence bag. Dunbar gingerly picked up the gun; the dead man's fingers were splayed out, not grasping the gun. Dunbar held the edge of the barrel with two fingers and brought it to his face. He sniffed, no scent of gunpowder. He gently flipped open the cylinder. "Six bullets," he said. "It hasn't been recently fired." He dropped the gun in Carlito's bag. "Any idea what caliber made that nice round hole in his forehead?"

"I dunno," Carlito grunted. "I'd say a .22, but the autopsy will verify that. Don't look like the bullet exited the skull so we might have a good specimen to compare if we get a suspect or the murder weapon."

"If it is a murder," Abbott mused.

"Yeah," Dunbar said sarcastically. "I've seen dozens of suicides just like it. Kill yourself, get rid of the gun, then slide down a cross with a phony gun in your hand. Clever guy."

"Dope," Abbott said crossly. "What I mean is it could've been self-defense."

"Holy fucking *shit*," came a loud exclamation from behind the three men. They turned simultaneously to see Carlito's intern, the Alfred E. Neuman lookalike whose real name was Elmer Batchelder.

"What's the deal, Elmer?" Carlito asked crossly. He'd told the kid to surveil the desert around the monument for any evidence or clues.

"Don't you know who that is?" Elmer said excitedly.

"Bill Cosby?" Abbott asked.

"That's Jackson Ryder," Elmer said in a self-satisfied tone. He knew something the big dogs didn't.

"Why do I know that name?" Dunbar asked. Before anyone could answer or make another remark he exclaimed, "Holy shit. His face is all over the post office."

Abbott snapped his fingers. "That radical group, the Weather Underground."

"Uh-uh," Elmer said. "Him and few of his cohorts were too radical even for the Weathermen. He broke off into a really radical group called Thunderstorm. He's wanted for the murder of a security guard in a museum they bombed last winter in Virginia. They bombed a couple more buildings, too. They're fucking scary."

"Well," Abbott said, "now he's fucking dead. At least we can verify his identity. We'll contact the FBI and see what info they have on him and his group."

"What the hell was he doing in Santa Fe?" Carlito asked.

"I have no idea," Abbott said flatly. "No fucking idea."

Sand had a full day at the office that spilled over into evening. He spent a couple of those hours trying to avoid having Devon and Dante thrown into jail. Apparently, they broke their promise to Sand to not engage in anything illegal when they went down to Phoenix to find the runaway teenager who'd chucked college and fled with her doper boyfriend. The two P.I.s searched for three days before finding her. She was shacked up with her new boyfriend, and they were living with two other couples in a one-bedroom apartment in Peoria.

Devon and Dante shadowed her for a day before they accosted her coming out of a bakery with a bag of donuts. Devon patiently explained that her father had asked them to find her and ask her if she'd please come home. She explained that Shelby Alameda's father loved her and wanted her home. The girl stared at Devon wordlessly. Then, she burst out laughing and told Devon to fuck off. Shelby sauntered down the sidewalk and turned into the apartment complex, which was obviously a converted cheap motel. Her boyfriend met her at the door and tore the bag out of her hands and dragged her inside, slamming the door.

"Now what?" Dante said.

"Now, we won't be so nice," Devon replied.

They took turns staying close by and monitoring the comings and goings of the people crowded into the small apartment. At eleven o'clock at night Shelby and her deadbeat boyfriend came out and started walking west for a few streets. Devon and Dante hung back by fifty yards as they followed. The young couple went into a parking lot and met some man that looked scary even in the dark. Devon could see the boyfriend and man exchange something, and on instinct from her time on the streets of Hartford as a cop she knew that a drug deal had just taken place.

Devon urged Dante into the alley near a building on the way back to the apartment. When Shelby and her boyfriend started to pass by the alley Devon lurched out and dragged her into the darkness while Dante did the same for the boyfriend. Devon shoved Shelby to the ground, whirled around, and right-crossed the boyfriend, slamming him into the wall. He slid down the wall and lay on the ground unconscious.

Shelby was shocked and silent for the moment it took Dante to stuff a gag into her mouth and handcuff her wrists behind her back. Devon searched the boyfriend and found the baggie of cocaine. She stared down at him them gave him a swift kick in the ass.

"Get the car," Devon demanded, and Dante flew off. A few minutes later he pulled up in front of the alley and Devon dragged Shelby to her feet and shoved her into the back of the car. She got in next to the girl and said to Dante, "Drive."

Dante drove them to their motel and scrambled to gather their things while Devon stayed in the back seat with the girl. By a little after midnight they were on their way up the I-17 to Flagstaff before they'd turn east and head home.

Shelby yelled and cursed and pleaded throughout the drive from Phoenix to Camp Verde. Dante pulled off the highway and gassed up while Devon watched their "companion." Shelby tried to scream but Devon stuffed a bandana into her mouth. Luckily, it was in the dead of night, the gas pump was self-service, and the station attendant was engrossed in his dog-eared copy of *Carrie* when Dante handed him the seven bucks.

They were on I-40 east of Flagstaff when Shelby just wouldn't shut up despite repeated requests. Devon instructed Dante to pull over to the side of the road. There was little traffic, so when Devon dragged Shelby out of the car and stuffed her into the trunk, they were good to go. Devon took over the driving from that point on and made sure she did the speed limit; it wouldn't be a good thing if she were pulled over for speeding and the state cop heard the muffled yelling and banging coming from the rear of the car.

They pulled into Santa Fe just after dawn broke and drove directly to Sand's house. He and Akiro were still in bed when Devon pounded on the door. Sand opened the door—wearing only his boxer shorts—to see Devon standing there looking like she'd been through the ringer. She whirled around without a word and Sand followed her to the car. She looked at him half apologetically, half defiantly.

"I had to do this," she said as she opened the trunk.

Sand stared down at the girl who was glaring at him with furious eyes. Devon shut the trunk loudly.

"Really?" Sand said. "There was no other way to get her back here?"

"Judgment call," Devon said succinctly.

"How am I supposed to keep you out of jail?"

"You're smart. You'll think of something."

"Get her out of there. I'll throw some clothes on and we'll take her home."

"Oh, one more thing," Devon said. She pulled the baggie of coke out of her jeans and dangled it. "We nabbed her when she and her boyfriend were doing a drug deal."

Sand's eyebrows shot up. "She touch the bag?" Devon shook her head. "Make sure she touches the bag. Getting her fingerprints on it may be our saving grace." He went back into the house while Devon got Shelby out of the trunk, tossed her the bag which she automatically caught, then grabbed the bag back and handed it gingerly to Dante.

Sand got into the back seat with Shelby and did his best to calm her down as Devon drove to the Alameda house. A Mexican gardener was out front watering the shrubs and flowers. He tipped his straw hat as Sand pulled Shelby towards the front door. He rang the doorbell.

A minute later the door opened, and Aurelio Alameda stood there. His eyes lit up and his jaw dropped when he spied his daughter; a second later he engulfed her in his arms and murmured, "Mi corazón, mi corazón." Tears spilled down his face. He looked over her head at Sand and said "Thank you" over and over again. Sand nodded.

Shelby pulled away and scowled at Sand before saying to her father, "They kidnapped me! They made me ride in the trunk of the car! I want them arrested!"

"This is true?" Aurelio asked Sand.

"Pretty much," Sand said. "She and her boyfriend were buying drugs when my people, um, 'rescued' her." He pulled the baggie out of his jacket pocket. "Coke. Her fingerprints are on the bag."

"They tricked me," Shelby exclaimed.

Aurelio stared at his daughter, then stared at Sand, and glanced at the two young people leaning against the car. He stuck out his hand and said to Sand, "Thank you."

Sand shook his hand, nodded his head, and went back to the car. Devon dropped him off at home, then drove Dante home. When she got to her apartment, she fell on the bed fully clothed and was asleep in ten seconds.

The next day Sand received full payment from Aurelio along with a heartfelt thank-you card. The day after that police detective Tom Christensen visited him, mentioning a complaint by one Shelby Alameda. Although her father denied her allegations, he still had to check it out. Sand was circumspect about his people's methods. He and Christensen bandied back and forth, each skirting around using words that had connotations of illegal methods and activity. Finally, Sand used his get-out-of-jail-free card and mentioned that he might know of a baggie of coke with Shelby's fingerprints on it. Christensen said he'd relay that to Miss Alameda and see if she wanted to pursue a case. He called back an hour later and said everything was resolved. Sand thanked him.

Sand had a few other cases to review and document, so he didn't get home until after nine. When he entered the house, all was silent. He called out to Akiro saying he was home. No answer.

He called out again. No answer. He quietly opened an armoire drawer in the living room where he kept his spare gun.

The gun was missing.

He inhaled and held a deep breath as his heartbeat increased. He heard a sound behind him, and he whirled around.

He stood frozen as he stared into a pair of icy eyes. Familiar eyes. Eyes he hadn't seen in nine years.

Snow.

And she was holding a gun pointed at him.

"Hey, big brother," she said in a singsong voice. "Long time no see."

Snow was thin, too thin. Her blonde hair was cut haphazardly to the shoulders, and she had long bangs that almost—but not quite—hid her blue eyes. There was a bruise on her upper left cheek. She was wearing an Army jacket with sergeant stripes, faded jeans, and an old tee-shirt that read, "Hell no, we won't go." She was holding a .22 on him, and it was obvious from her stance that she wasn't unfamiliar with guns.

"What do you want?" Sand said coldly. His initial impulse to hug his long-missing sister was tempered by her threatening presence and her cool demeanor.

She countered with a segue. "How's my daughter?"

"You don't have a daughter—Memphis and Swan have a daughter," he replied cuttingly.

"Maybe you're right, but I still gave birth to her. You needn't answer—I've been keeping tabs on you and the family for years. I was surprised when my sister moved in on my man so fast."

"You did Memphis a big favor by taking off. He's with the right woman now, and Sage is with the right mother. Now, where's Akiro? If you've hurt him …"

"He's fine, just locked in the master closet. Good-looking guy. You did good." She smiled sadly. "Unfortunately, I can't say the same of myself."

"Memphis is a damn fine human being."

"I wasn't talking about Memphis." She paused. "How is he?"

"Fine," Sand snapped. "Swan is fine, everybody's fine. Shockingly, no one misses you anymore."

Snow inhaled sharply. "I knew you could be tough. I didn't know you could be cruel."

"Welcome to my world. Now, again, I'll ask—why are you here? And you think you can put the gun down?"

Snow smiled slightly and lowered the gun. She thrust it into her belt on the left side. "Happy?" she asked.

"That's not a word I'd equate with you at this moment. How many times must I ask—why are you here, Snow?"

"You have a nice house. Big front yard, fenced-in back yard. Comfortable. You should get a dog. Labs are nice—they're loyal. I wish I could stay and offer some more suggestions, but I have to get on the road."

"What? You came here to point a gun at me, say a few words, then leave without any explanation?"

"There's an explanation. Akiro knows. As far as my staying, not a good idea."

"Why?"

"I just murdered someone," Snow stated with no trace of emotion.

Sand's jaw dropped, not only at the stunning words but at the matter-of-fact way in which his sister had said them. "I don't believe you," he said slowly when he got his voice back.

"It should be on the news by tomorrow. The cops are probably at the crime scene now. So, I need to hit the road." Without warning she fired her gun, putting a bullet into the fireplace wall. She smiled slightly. "Just in case you need to make a ballistics match."

She nodded towards the coffee table. Sand noticed the envelope on the table for the first time. "Everything you need is in there. Off I go." She made to turn but in two strides Sand was across the floor and grabbed her left arm. A second later he had gun in his face. He could smell the pungent gunpowder. "I don't want to shoot you, big brother, but I will. Take you hand off me." Sand complied. She turned back towards the door, then suddenly whirled around and threw her arms around him for a very fast, very tight hug. A second later she was out the door, disappearing into the night.

Sand stood rock-still for ten seconds before he fled into the bedroom. He saw a chair braced under the closet door handle.

"Akiro," he yelled.

"I'm okay," Akiro said from the closet. "Get us out of here."

Us? Sand thought as he pulled the chair away and opened the closet door.

Akiro was standing in the middle of the closet. He looked fine.

And beside him stood a young child, a little boy that was obviously half-white and half-black. He was four or five, with café-au-lait skin and close-cropped wavy brown hair. He was wearing a Disney tee-shirt and khaki shorts; his eyes were a vivid blue. He looked sad and frightened. Akiro had his hand on the boy's shoulder.

Sand met Akiro's eyes.

Akiro smiled wanly and said, "Meet your nephew, Elijah. Elijah, this is your Uncle Sand."

CHAPTER TWENTY

December 24, 1974, Dublin, Ireland

Trinity College was closed for the holiday, of course, but Cassidy Carr loved the campus and felt a sense of peace whenever she'd walk by the old, hallowed buildings. Despite it being the day before Christmas there were still a few dozen people walking around, some students, some professors, some admirers of the beautiful architecture.

She loved each and every building for its structure and its history, but her favorite was the G.M.B, or Graduates Memorial Building, a neo-Gothic Victorian building designed by Sir Thomas Drew in 1897. It was constructed to celebrate Trinity College's 300th anniversary. The building is divided into three houses; House 28 and House 30, are student residences. House 29 in the center of the building is used by three societies—the University Philosophical Society, the College Historical Society, and the College Theological Society. The University Philosophical Society was well-known for its spirited debating, and Cassidy had joined that union when she matriculated into Trinity College to study for her Master's degree.

The building reminded Cassidy of the Dakota in New York City, a building she just loved. Polanski had filmed some of *Rosemary's Baby* there (renaming it "the Bram" per Ira Levin's book), and just last year John Lennon and wife Yoko Ono had purchased an apartment, somehow making it past the finicky board.

Cassidy loved her studies at Trinity College. It was balancing act, though, between her course load, her job as a reporter for the *Irish Independent*, and her personal life. Too many times she felt that twenty-four hours in a day just wasn't enough. She had been innocent and callow when she experienced her undergraduate courses at NYU, and she'd always regretted not going for her Master's. When she returned to Ireland in January 1969, she decided that she'd fulfill her dream. She moved to a small apartment in Dublin, applied to several newspapers and was offered two positions; she chose the *Irish Independent*, which had been her father's favorite newspaper. She hoped he'd be proud of her, looking down from Heaven above. She hoped her parents were together there.

On occasion she revisited her partial manuscript of the Joanna Frid case. The case was basically solved before she left Santa Fe although the protagonist had escaped a second time and was supposedly out there somewhere. She'd researched possibilities throughout the years but found nothing to suggest where Joanna might have gone. If she went underground, she was almost to the Earth's core.

She was relatively happy in Dublin. She rued the submission to temptation that had thrown the man she loved into another woman's arms, even if only for a night. Tucson apologized sincerely in his letter and begged her to give him another chance. She thought about it, her mind and heart warring between forgiving and forgetting. In the end she decided to cut the heartstrings and go her own way. She moved to Georgia and accepted an offer from a Savannah newspaper. She grew to love the city and to love its sister city in South Carolina, Charleston. She spent fifteen months there, and then it was time to move again.

She'd only been seven when she and her mother had fled Ireland, but she remembered her life there and part of her longed for her homeland. It was a good place to grow up amongst kind, cheerful people, green, green land, and quaint homesteads, not to mention the best beer on the planet. She visited her old town outside of Dublin and came across an old childhood friend, Declan O'Malley, who was visiting his family. He told her he'd moved to Dublin and was working at the Guinness Brewery. Declan was the one that convinced her that Dublin was the "in" place for a lusty young woman. He helped her search for an apartment and showed her the best places to get a meal and groceries. He adored her; she adored him. They knew nothing else could come of their friendship since he was, as he'd put it while batting his eyes, "a gay blade, ready to thrust."

Their friendship deepened over the years until finally for the sake of comfort and economy they took a three-bedroom apartment together on Reginald Street, walking distance from Liberty Market and its plethora of vendors. They'd shop together and pick up the freshest meats, vegetables, and fruits. Declan always managed to bring home a weekly stash of beer. Declan was indispensable on weeknights when Cassidy had to attend some classes or head off to a location for a story. He chided her every so often about getting her manuscript published, but she shrugged him off. He chided her about the other thing, too, but she told him point blank that it was not something she wanted to discuss.

Everything was going well until the day she saw the doctor. She wasn't eating well and was constantly fatigued. Those symptoms didn't really bother her, but then the abdominal pain started. It started small and grew rapidly, making its way to her back. When her flesh started appearing jaundiced, Declan forced her to see her doctor. The doctor put her through a rigorous test regimen, taking samples of her urine and blood. He was pleased that she had never smoked. When the tests were completed and analyzed the doctor called her in. Declan went with her. They listened in stunned horror when the doctor told her that she had stage four pancreatic cancer, and that stage was incurable.

The cancer had metastasized to other organs, and the prognosis was a life expectancy of three to six months, meaning she could expect to die anywhere between August and January. He could refer her to support groups and provide antianxiety and sleep medications. Chemotherapy might help but it could make her remaining life span even more uncomfortable than it already was.

Cassidy walked home in a trance with Declan holding her hand. She glanced over at him; tears were streaming down his face. When they got home, Cassidy dismissed Mrs. O'Riley, sat down on the couch, and sobbed her heart out as Declan held her in a death grip. They both cried most of the night, but by the morning Cassidy was oddly calm. She had aligned in her head all the things she needed to take care of. She was pleasant with Mrs. O'Riley and said she'd be home by noon. She left before Declan was ready to head off to his job.

She took a one-month leave of absence in June; Declan did the same. They went to London and saw the sights. They traveled to Paris, sitting during a mass at the Cathedral of Notre Dame. They went to the Louvre and the top level of the Eiffel Tower. They went to Madrid and Rome, to Athens and Amsterdam before going home to Dublin. The point was to make sweet memories. They snapped hundreds of photos.

She'd achieved her Master's degree in Journalism in 1972, but every so often she walked around the campus, remembering the joy of learning. It was cold and grey this last Christmastime of her life, and she was weak and in pain, but she wanted to walk the campus one more time. The cold, breezy air stung her cheeks, but that made her feel alive. She was thin; bony, even, her cheekbones sharpened with the weight loss she'd experienced over the last few months. Oddly enough, she was calm because she knew everything would eventually be all right after her passing.

Her one true regret was that she hadn't given Tucson a second chance.

The college was two thousand meters from her apartment, but the long walk soothed her both going and coming. When she opened the door to her apartment, she smelled the wonderful scent of shepherd's pie, heard the commotion in the kitchen, and knew that Declan was making a Christmas Eve meal to remember. She glanced over to the corner of the living room and felt such love for the man that had decorated the tree with a long strand of popcorn and blinking blue lights; he knew that was her favorite color, and he said the lights couldn't hold a candle to her eyes. He told her to change and park her shapely butt at the table since he was bringing in the pie. They held hands and Cassidy said her favorite prayer, and then they began piling pie and mashed sweet potatoes on their plates.

One gift each was opened before midnight, and then they settled in their beds. Declan slept badly and checked Cassidy during the night; she was sleeping soundly and breathing evenly. He went back to bed and slept until dawn broke. Declan got up, washed his face, and brushed his teeth. He pulled on his pants and padded barefoot to Cassidy's room. He opened the door quietly. She was on her back. Her big blue eyes were open. Her red hair was splayed out across the pillow. She looked peaceful.

She was dead.

Declan slid to the floor and moaned.

December 31, 1974, Santa Fe, New Mexico

Tucson was propped up on his left elbow as he watched Cameo sleep. She looked beautiful and peaceful in her repose. He noticed that behind her closed eyelids her eyes were flitting back and forth. He wondered what she was dreaming about.

He carefully extricated himself from the bed covers and walked over to the turret window. He glanced down at the front yard where Percy was playing catch with Elspeth. It was barely eight o'clock, but the weather was unusually temperate, and Percy always made sure that his daughter had fresh air and outdoor exercise and play time. Tansee came out of the house and called to them, saying that breakfast was ready. She and Percy each took a child hand and led the little girl back inside the house.

Before Tucson could turn around Cameo came up behind him and slid her slender arms around his chest. She put her head against his back and squeezed,

"Did I wake you?" he asked as he turned around.

"Yes, so feel guilty. You can make it up to me," she said easily.

"Anything."

"I need a hot shower, but I don't want to be lonely."

"I could keep you company."

"Standing there naked, under a cascade of hot water massaging every inch of my body, all by myself."

"I could massage your body."

Cameo ducked her head, grinned, took his hand, and led him to the small shower stall in the turret's bathroom. Minutes later they were standing under the battering cascade, kissing deeply and running their hands up and down their bodies. Cameo moaned as Tucson began kissing her from the neck down her front, winding up on his knees and sending her into spasms of eroticism that crashed over her like violent ocean waves.

When he finished, he rose, and she pulled him to her as she backed against the shower stall. He thrust into her and she made a jump and wrapped her legs around his waist. The ocean waves rushed on and on.

They were both breathing heavily when they climaxed together. They finished the shower and dried each other off, then dressed. Tucson had a five-day beard stubble but didn't plan on shaving until Monday when he'd go back to work. He and Percy had closed the office for the last week of the year. Tansee only had a couple of days off and had to return to the hospital on Thursday. Cameo would return to her job on the *Courant* the same day.

Tucson and Percy planned on taking their ladies out for New Year's Eve to the Sweet Revenge Saloon, where they'd meet the other celebrating couples of the family. The family children would be huddled together at the Victorian under the eagle eyes of Luc and Raleigh. Luc offered a measure of resistance to be stuck at home with a bunch of crazy kids, but Memphis pointed out that he was too young to drink legally and that convinced Luc. That, and a fifty-dollar bill slipped into his hand. Memphis was paying both of his younger siblings to watch the kids, but he knew that a few extra bucks would solidify Luc's performance as a dedicated uncle.

Tucson didn't know how his older brother did it, having a busy career, a strong marriage, and being a top-notch dad. Tucson wondered if he could ever do it. His thoughts had moved that way when he and Cameo had started to get serious.

Memphis and Swan hadn't come up with anything definitive from their trip back east. When they showed Cameo shots of the east coast, she seemed to think she recognized a few places, but couldn't say for sure. Percy put her in another light trance and noted which images provoked a change in her respiration or body language. She reacted mainly to the shots taken around that first image outside the Atlantis Oceanfront Inn.

On a third trance attempt that had become a deep hypnosis session something peculiar happened. Cameo began moving her right hand as though she were writing, while staring straight ahead. Percy quickly put a pen in her hand and a piece of paper on the table and moved her hand down. She kept writing, pausing, writing. When Percy brought her out of the trance, she didn't remember anything about the writing, but the proof was there.

And the proof was written in Latin.

Sed ego elegi mihi multus tecum: Verus est interfectus velut exitio; ipse morte consortio mors mihi vita Sic per vim naturae vinculum est in corde meo sentio me ad hauriendam mea, mea suas in te, quia mea est, quod ipsa es, Seneca separari nos unum sumus Una caro; te perdere perderent me.

Percy engaged a Latin professor from the college, who provided the translation, and told him that it was from John Milton's *Paradise Lost.*

However, I with thee have fixed my lot, Certain to undergo like doom; if death Consort with thee, death is to me as life; So forcible within my heart I feel The bond of nature draw me to my own, My own in thee, for what thou art is mine; Our state cannot be severed, we are one, One flesh; to lose thee were to lose myself.

Cameo was floored; she swore she had no knowledge of Latin and had never read John Milton. Well, she knew that she hadn't read that book in the past five years. It was at that point that Cameo put a halt to both investigations since neither had made any concrete progress. She wanted to let it lie for the time being. She was happy in her job, Caleb adored her, and she had made genuine friends and a semblance of a life in Santa Fe. She thought it might be time to surrender the past and concentrate on the future. Percy and Memphis agreed to suspend the investigation until she told them otherwise, but they wanted to revisit the search in six months.

Tucson was of two minds about the decision. He understood her frustration and desire to build on her new life, but he knew that she never really could until she found out exactly what happened to her and who and what she had left behind.

And he was of two minds because he was becoming deeply attached to her. He recognized a desperate, dark yearning to come to terms with a past too often out of control. He acknowledged to himself that he hadn't exorcized his own demons, and to move forward, he had to. He and Cameo shared hidden wounds and debilitating emotions; perhaps they could work through them together.

As the months passed, they had grown closer, spending time enjoying the city and all it had to offer. They went to the movies every weekend and ate dinner out twice a week. They spent quiet time reading books and listening to music; Tucson loved the Eagles and Cameo had a soft spot for the Carpenters.

They kissed for the first time on Halloween, a gentle peck on the lips. That grew to deep kissing, but Tucson pulled back every time things might have gotten intimate. She had been raped, although she didn't remember it. He was terrified that if he tried to make love to her that memory would come crashing back. When Memphis and Swan had spoken to the doctors in Pittsfield that treated her, they were informed that she had been a virgin when she had been assaulted, so her first foray into carnal intimacy had been a violent, vicious act. They informed Cameo of this fact; she was, after all, the client.

Cameo was the one who broached the subject of intimacy when Tucson failed to make the first move. She told him she didn't remember the act and it had no bearing on what they might have. On Christmas Eve she surprised him in his turret bedroom, and they locked eyes; a minute later they were tearing off one another's clothes and falling, falling on the bed. There were no thoughts, no hints of the past, and afterwards they lay in one another's arms, sated, content, at peace.

Over the week leading up to the new year they spent another night at the Victorian, and the rest of the nights at her apartment exploring their bodies and emotions. By the end of the week, this morning, they felt as though they'd been together forever. They headed downstairs to the kitchen, hand in hand. Tansee was flipping pancakes in the air to Elspeth's giggling delight. Tansee winked at them and said there were plenty of pancakes for everyone.

After a filling breakfast Tucson and Cameo went out back and sat in lounge chairs, enjoying the cold, fresh air and content in their silent communion. They began discussing a film they'd seen two weeks earlier, *Young Frankenstein*, and they both broke down into laughter when they imitated scenes from the film. At noon they decided to go out to lunch and after haggling for few minutes agreed on Malagueña Fiesta. After a filling Mexican meal, they brought takeout to Luc and Raleigh before heading next door to Memphis's house to cavort with the kids. The afternoon passed quickly and at six Memphis stuffed his younger siblings in the car along with Sage, Shea, and Sara and drove them over to the Victorian. Nick had already dropped off Mariko.

Sand was the last parent to arrive with Elijah. The shock of Snow's brief reappearance with her second child was still fresh in everyone's emotions. The boy was introverted and not particularly communicative, but there was gentleness to his personality that shown through the eyes he'd inherited from his mother. Swan had introduced Elijah to her girls as their cousin; it was far too soon and raw for her to tell Sage that he was her biological half-brother.

Luc and Raleigh were given their instructions yet again and were beyond relieved when their family members were finally out of the house.

Nick and Yuki were already at the saloon with Akiro. They'd reserved a large table that would fit the entire family, and by ten everyone was whooping and laughing and swilling down beer, martinis, and champagne—except, of course, Yuki, who was five months' pregnant; she was enjoying a couple of Virgin Marys. At ten on the dot they all watched the TV above the bar as the glittering ball dropped down in Times Square, marking the first moment of 1975 for the United States. Santa Fe was still two hours shy.

At ten-thirty their favorite waitress wended her way through the throng to their table. She leaned over Tucson and whispered something. He looked curious. When she left Memphis asked what the matter was.

"I don't know," Tucson said, rising. "Apparently Luc called here and said to tell me to get home now and that, no, the kids are fine. No need to come with me. I'll call in an hour. If I don't, you'll know that I've been kidnapped."

"We should be so lucky," Nick said.

"Really," Swan said, nodding her head vigorously.

"Such a loving, wonderful family," Tucson quipped as he helped Cameo into her jacket. "I'll call. Have a margarita on me."

"Don't I wish," Yuki said sadly, glaring at her tomato juice.

Tucson rolled down his car window and enjoyed the cold air rushing through the car. Cameo sat pushed up against his side and he had his arm around her shoulder. He pulled up in front of the house where Raleigh was sitting on the front step hugging herself from the chilly night air. She got up and sauntered over to him.

"What's wrong?" Tucson asked.

"Ah … I wouldn't say wrong, just maybe … unexpected?" Raleigh said in a lilting voice suffused with amusement and confusion. "It's probably better you see for yourself."

Raleigh led him and Cameo inside where Luc was standing in the living room with a strange man with big brown eyes almost hidden behind round wire-rim eyeglasses. He was a good six feet and slender bordering on skinny. He was dressed in Jordache jeans, a white shirt, and a tweed jacket. He was wearing a bowtie.

"Meet Declan O'Malley," Luc said. "Straight off the boat from Ireland."

Declan walked over to Tucson and stared at him for a few seconds before sticking out his hand. "I'm pleased to meet you, Mr. Grayhawk," he said. His Irish brogue was almost too thick to understand.

"Mr. O'Malley," Tucson replied. "Have we come across one another in the past?"

Declan smiled. "We've not met, but I know a lot about you. A lot."

"That a fact. And who enlightened you?"

Declan took a deep breath. "Me childhood friend, who became me dearest adult friend over the past five years. Cassidy Carr."

Tucson inhaled sharply and he heard Cameo gasp behind him. He narrowed his eyes at Declan. "Got any proof of that?"

Declan nodded and took a photo out of his jacket pocket. He handed it to Tucson, who stared down at the shot of Cassidy and Declan standing side-by-side with a cliff and a roiling ocean behind them. Tucson handed the photo back.

"Why are you here?" Tucson said flatly.

"I'm here to deliver t' ye some information and a legacy from Cass."

"Why isn't she here to deliver it?"

"Because she's buried at Glasnevin Cemetery in Dublin. She died on Christmas Day," Declan said quietly, his voice breaking at the last few words.

"What?" Tucson whispered in shock. "What? H-how?"

"Pancreatic cancer. She was on borrowed time for the last five months. She had time at least to put her affairs in order and plan for the time after her burial. That's why I'm here, to deliver you her last wishes and a letter. And her legacy." Declan nodded at Luc, who rolled his eyes and left the room.

Tucson sat down hard on the couch and took several deep breaths in and out. He felt Cameo's gentle hand on his shoulder. Raleigh was standing a few feet away with her arms crossed.

Declan said, "I understand that this comes as a shock to you, and that you have a million questions. Cassidy's letter should answer some of them, and I'll be here to answer whatever I can. I can stay as long as you need me."

"Need you?" Tucson said.

Declan smiled shyly. "I'm good at both my jobs, a beer maker and a nanny."

"Nanny?" Tucson repeated, rising. Just then Luc returned, but not alone.

Tucson just stared at the two young children that were obviously twins. They had dark auburn hair and deep azure eyes. They were lighter than Tucson and darker than Cassidy.

Declan straightened and said formally, "Mr. Grayhawk, I'd like to introduce you to your son and daughter. This is Braeden," he said, putting a gentle hand on the little boy's head, "and this is Brianna." He looked down at the innocent, curious little faces gazing up at him.

"Kids, this is your da. Say hello."

BOOK TWO

"The postmodern notion of 'appropriation' is not a good fit. In New Mexico, the 'indigenous' is a syncretic fusion of Native American and Hispano American. Just as Pueblo people who are Catholics embrace their traditional religions, Nuevo Mexicanos who wear Metallica T-shirts also attend mass and clean the ditches. The fact that both good and bad aspects of the larger pop culture are welcomed with open arms in New Mexican villages and pueblos does not belie the passion with which local ethnic culture is embraced."

Lucy R. Lippard, Nuevo Mexico Profundo: Rituals of an Indo-Hispano Homeland

CHAPTER ONE

August 8, 1976, Santa Fe, New Mexico

The nonstop hammering sounded as loud as cannons going off as Tucson blinked his eyes then squinted at the bright sun streaming through the bedroom window. He stumbled out of bed and weaved to the window, pulling the curtains closed. Before he turned around, he moved the curtain back and glanced out at the backyard where three of the contractors were tightly clustered and looking at a set of blueprints. The head contractor promised that the house addition would be finished by mid-September at the latest. Tucson thought that might happen if there was immediate divine intervention. At least the pool had been finished by late May so the kids could dive and swim and splash in the privacy of their fenced-in back yard.

He watched as Cameo approached them waving her arms, and it looked like she and the head man were having a philosophical tussle. By the time she walked away it was clear that she was the victor. He almost regretted the decision to upgrade the house he'd bought fifteen months ago. Almost. But he knew that they had to have more room. They needed at least four bedrooms, and preferably five—one bedroom for him and Cameo, one for the twins, one for Declan, and one for the nursery. Cameo had given birth to their son three months earlier, little Brett Adams Grayhawk, eleven months after they'd gotten married.

Tucson was still coming to terms with the radical direction his life had taken twenty months ago. Twenty months ago, he had a new girlfriend, was single, was living in a friend's Victorian turret, and had no plans to have children in the foreseeable future. Now, he was married, he had two school-age children whose mother had died, an Irish nanny that could never quite bring himself to leave, a new baby, a healthy professional practice, and a new house that needed updating. Oh—he also had a new car, a station wagon that screamed domesticity all over its aqua-blue exterior. He tried to not drive it, and, in his mind, it was the "family" car. He had his Camaro and Cameo had her Cougar to prove that they were still independent, cool adults. Declan had a Beetle and parked it outside since they only had a three-car garage.

Tucson heard Declan yelling at the kids to get their arses in gear, and the kids were yelling back at him in their heavy brogue that their arses *were* in gear.

Declan. *I can stay as long as you need me.* Well, no one expected that to last one year and eight months and counting. It was obvious from the get-go that he was extremely attached to the twins and they to him. They clearly adored their "Uncle Dec." Under the circumstances with the twins being introduced to their new father (and vice versa), a new country, a new city, a new home, and a radical new climate and landscape, they were in a state of confusion and angst. So, Declan stayed for two weeks to get them settled in and help Tucson understand Cassidy's decisions. Two weeks passed, then three, then two months, and here they were twenty months later having formed an unusual household.

Declan missed Dublin, but he'd miss the twins more and he found every reason to elongate his residence. After six months Tucson gave up thinking he'd ever leave and simply adjusted their mutual new world. Declan was wonderful with the kids. He was patient, considerate, and loved them with every beat of his heart, as he'd loved their mother. At first Tucson thought Declan may have been in love with Cassidy, but after a few days he realized that Declan was gay. Sand confirmed this saying his gaydar was giving off massive vibes. Sand deftly let Declan know that he, too, was of that sexual persuasion and was living with his longtime boyfriend. Declan was relieved and began to feel less stressed although he was struggling with his new environment. England was lush, cool, wet, and had small towns with old houses and streets. Now, he was in the high desert, and that was like being on Venus.

He felt like an alien, and, in truth, he was. The only thing that kept him from going back to Ireland for the first six months was the twins. They needed him now more than ever, and he'd never abandon them. He was grateful that Tucson never pressed him for a departure date, and over the months they all seemed to settle into a new if strange normal. When Tucson offered him permanent residency to take care of the kids, he flew back to Dublin, closed up his apartment, spent a long weekend with his family, then flew back to his new life. He made a second trip in April to visit him mum and da, then came home. Mid-flight over the Atlantic he realized that he was going *home*.

A few days after he and the twins first appeared, he sat down with Tucson and they talked for hours. Declan told Tucson every detail he could about Cassidy from the time she returned to the Emerald Isle to her sad death and burial. He knew that Tucson had read Cassidy's letter and had questions. He also knew that the letter had eased some of Tucson's guilt and perhaps mitigated some of his anger about keeping the children a secret from him. Tucson showed him the letter, which Declan had left sealed, not wanting to intrude on Cassidy's privacy.

December 1, 1974

Dear Tucson,

I don't know where to begin. Perhaps with something I feel and have felt for so very long.

To the depths of my soul I regret not forgiving you and giving you a second chance. I was hurt, and I let my emotions overrule my head. You explained what happened and I knew deep down it would never happen again. I don't exactly know what made me run. Perhaps it was the pregnancy about which I'd just learned. I knew that had happened that last time I visited you in San Diego.

I was pregnant, I was hurt, I was angry. I was a mass of roiling emotions. I fled. I thought it might only be for a short time, but when I learned of the Pueblo incident, I was badly shaken, and wondered if you'd survive. If not, I had to make my own way. I've never been dependent on anyone, never had a committed family like yours and that frightened me.

I took a reporting job in Savannah and grew to love the south. As my pregnancy progressed, I learned I was carrying twins. I was terrified. I dug into my new life. When I gave birth, you were still being held captive in North Korea. I was relieved when the Pueblo crew came home, but by then I thought it was just too late for us. I know now that I was wrong.

I wasn't thrilled with the chaos going on in America, and 1968 in particular was a year of turbulence and upheaval. I thought the best place to raise my children was in my home country. After all the years had passed, I felt safe going back. I moved there and started yet another new life. One godsend in that life was my childhood friend, Declan, who became my guardian angel as I struggled to build a life for me and my children.

I gave them Irish first names, but their middle names reflect the two southern cities I grew fond of. Since your family has a habit of naming children after cities, I thought it was a salute to their paternal line.

I know, I know, I know—I should have contacted you and told you about them. I am so sorry. I hope you can forgive me someday. I'd like to think that eventually I would have shaken off my fears and guilt and told you about your son and daughter.

Please take care of our children and bring them up to be decent, honourable, compassionate human beings. Tell them that their mother loved them with every beat of her heart. Tell them that although she ran away for many reasons, their father was the only man she truly loved. Tell them—well, you'll know what to tell them.

I wish you only good things. I wish you love and joy and long life. I hope that you have or will find a woman that completes you. I hope she will love our children.

Be good to yourself. Banish any regrets. Regrets and guilt and shame tie us to the past when we should be looking towards the future.

You will be forever in my heart, and I hope I will be forever in yours.

Cassidy

Declan confirmed that Cassidy had told him more than once that Tucson was the love of her life and she lived with regret every day. Then, he asked Tucson why he hadn't searched for her. Tucson said he had tried searching but Caleb had no idea where she went, and she had few friends outside of the Grayhawk family. Also, it was clear that she hadn't forgiven him, or she wouldn't have left or would have come back after the Pueblo incident was resolved. Not, he added, that she would have found him. Tucson had fled himself after he was released, traversing the country, trying to find some measure of peace. He didn't give any specifics but said that he wound up in some bad places and situations, and it took him a year to be willing to rejoin the real world and his family.

Declan was happy to stay as long as the kids needed him to acclimate themselves to their new life. For the first two weeks they clung to him, shying away from their new father. Even though Tucson had had a great deal of experience with children—his younger siblings and his swarm of nieces—he was wholly unprepared to handle two strange children that were in the throes of grief. He had no clue where to begin.

When Memphis and the rest of the New Year's Eve celebrators descended on the Victorian to collect their children, they were all stunned at the news and the two small new members of the family. Tansee said that for the night the kids could stay in the guest room and Declan could stay with them on a cot or sleep on the couch. He chose the cot, and after midnight the twins were settled in. The nonresidents of the house had departed with promises to return tomorrow morning. Cameo stayed.

No one got much sleep that night. Tucson crept down to the guest bedroom several times. Declan was lying in the middle of the full bed with a child cuddled to each side. Barely audible, the twins were softly crying. They were crying each time Tucson checked on them. He was completely bewildered as to how to go about soothing them and figuring out how the hell to be a father.

Thank God for Memphis and Declan. His brother was an old hand at fatherhood, and his new Irish acquaintance was an old hand at nannyhood. He hadn't studied for the position but had developed the skills as he nurtured Cassidy and her kids. And, to make his presence more enticing, he knew how to make beer.

The morning after Declan's and the twins' appearance the Victorian's living room and kitchen were full of clan members milling about and discussing the situation. The women were focused on trying to comfort the bewildered twins while the men planned for immediate living conditions. It was decided that for the time being Tucson, the twins, and their "nanny" would stay with the McBeans in the current sleeping situation until any legal ramifications were addressed.

Memphis and Akiro scrutinized the documents that Cassidy had sent along. She'd had a will drawn up leaving all her assets to the kids. She had also had a lawyer create a notarized document stating that Tucson Grayhawk was their father (and this was also on their birth certificates from Savannah) and assigning him as their legal guardian. Memphis grilled Declan about Cassidy's life, her state of mind, and anything that wasn't in the documents or the letter. Declan gave every bit of information that he could. Safe to say he was a little intimidated by the six-foot-four, tough Indian staring into his eyes. In truth, he was intimidated by the entire clan, even the little psychologist, Dr. McBean.

The next few weeks saw a flurry of actions associated with bringing the twins into the clan. Surprisingly, Raleigh volunteered for aunt duty whenever she wasn't in class. Other family members took turns acclimating the twins to their new life. Gradually, they started to come out of their shells. They were terribly shy around their new father, but exactly ten days from their appearance they first called him "Da," the name that Irish children called their father. Tucson would have preferred "Dad," but he wasn't about to push that so early in their relationship.

Declan was a godsend, and he kept putting off his return to Ireland. The fact was that he was so attached to the twins that he couldn't imagine life without them. He had been their "uncle" and until now the only father figure they'd had. Every time he brought up the subject of leaving, they'd cry and beg him to stay. He'd stay. He had a shocking thought rolling around in his head and he finally sat down and talked with Tucson. He asked if he could stay on as their nanny, oh, maybe for a year or so, until they were comfortable with their new family. He'd barely gotten the words out when Tucson said yes and thanked him.

That circumstance meant that Tucson would have to find a residence of his own to house the family. He and Cameo talked, and she said she wanted to move in with him. He nearly cried, partly from relief, partly from joy, and partly from terror.

The new family wound up staying in the Victorian for five months before Tucson found the right house, only two miles from his brother's home. Memphis helped with the down payment, and after four weeks of escrow the Tucson Grayhawk family moved in and started building a new life. Parents Hehewuti and Jakub returned home in February from their working cruise to Australia, delighted with their new grandchildren and sorrowful about the doomed Cassidy. Jakub was the mainstay in helping Tucson ready his new home and make upgrades inside; the kitchen was wholly redone and expanded, and Jakub gifted his son with brand new appliances.

The twins started school and after a few bumps (and remarks about their accent) began feeling accepted. A month after the move-in Tucson and Cameo were married quietly and with only family in attendance at the San Miguel Church, where Memphis and Swan had taken their vows. Cameo said that she wanted to be traditional and took Tucson's surname as her own. Shortly thereafter Cameo became pregnant, and eleven months after the wedding baby Brett joined the clan. Cameo decided to indefinitely suspend the investigation into her past. She told her new husband that it didn't seem to mean so much and that she wanted to concentrate on the future. He agreed, but in the back of both of their minds were still the burning questions that had brought them together.

Tucson and his family weren't the only ones experiencing change and moving forward. In early April Yuki gave birth to her and Nick's second child, a boy they named Zenjiro Percival. Yuki decided to take a leave of absence from work and be a stay-at-home mom for at least a year. Yuki's parents were over the moon. Mariko was a little peeved at first to not be the center of her parents' attention, but after a few months she turned the corner and became the doting older sister. Mariko had just started kindergarten along with Shea and Sara, so the childcare center at the office building was currently unoccupied. Memphis let Whitney go with a one-month severance package. British nanny/ex-MI5 Ansonia remained as a part-time investigator for Memphis but he knew she was having rumblings of homesickness for England.

Memphis was enthusiastic about his growing firm, and he had snagged several long-term, large clients. Aurelio Alameda had been so grateful that his daughter was returned to him that he hired WSI as the in-house investigation firm for his business. He threw them a lot of business and recommended the firm to his friends; two of them were CEOs of mid-sized companies in Santa Fe. Memphis and his associates serviced them, too.

Over the years Nick had proved to be a valuable asset to the P.I. firm. In the eleven years since he was once the antagonistic hippie nicknamed "Renegade" he had built a respected professional footprint and a stable, happy personal one. He still wore his hair and sideburns long. As a recognition of that his percentage in the firm's equity was increased. When Memphis legally established his firm with percentages for equity, he retained fifty-one percent of the equity and income. Tucson was given thirteen percent, as were Swan and Percy; Nick came in at eight percent, with the remaining two percent going to a general firm fund.

That matrix couldn't hold out with the changes in everyone's professional duties. Since Tucson and Percy had established their own practice, their percentages were cut down. Memphis was insistent that they retain some points since, frankly, Tucson was his brother and Percy had helped fund the firm with a $5,000 loan. Also, the two psychologists consulted on various cases outside of their own practice. Tucson's and Percy's pieces of the pie were cut down to five percent each, leaving sixteen percent for reallocation. Memphis bumped Swan's percentage up to seventeen percent and Nick's up to thirteen percent. That left another seven percent for the general fund and any future allocations.

Percy and Tansee experienced a heartbreaking loss when she became pregnant in mid-1975 then lost the baby two months later. They focused on their cherished daughter, Elspeth, who was now in kindergarten along with Memphis's twins, Sara and Shea. Tansee finished her residency at Sangre de Cristo Hospital and decided to open her own office, half dedicated to family medicine and half dedicated to genetic research. She had a suite of offices on the first floor of the Grayhawk building adjacent to the childcare center. She hired a secretary and a nurse and began a steady growth in clients. Percy was on the second floor with his psychology practice.

Percy was busier than ever with his clients and his publications. He had published a critically received paper on amnesia, its causes, and treatment, using Cameo's case as the anecdote; her name was never mentioned, nor were the details of her trauma or cross-country journey. With Cameo's okay he had begun a manuscript for a book. He published another paper on the effect of integrating children into an unknown family and was invited to give a lecture at UCLA. The lecture brought on loud applause when it was finished. When he first walked up to the adjusted podium, he heard a few (familiar) gasps and saw a lot of (familiar) surprised looks. By the end of the lecture and the question and answer session those gasps and looks had faded from their progenitors' consciousness.

He took Tansee and Elspeth along and after he'd finished his obligation took his family to Disneyland and Knott's Berry Farm. He had never seen Elspeth so happy. Her pair of Mickey Mouse ears took front and center on her bedroom dresser. A framed photo of her and Minnie stood beside it. Percy looked at it every day.

Frick and Frack retired from the police force on schedule, both unhappy that the cases they were working on weren't resolved. They desperately wanted to find their missing persons. Both considered their last cases failures. Memphis and Sand tried talking them out of their angst but were only minimally successful.

The retirement had an odd side effect. Both ex-detectives were bored, bored to tears. They started hanging around the police station. It wasn't long before the annoyed Captain Carraway told them he sympathized, but they had to find another place to hang out.

They migrated over to Warrior Spirit Investigations and began hanging around there. Skye endured them sitting around in the reception area, drinking coffee, asking questions, and driving her crazy. She complained to Memphis. The next day Memphis came into the area and saw Frick and Frack sitting on the couch talking about the upcoming baseball season. Skye was feeding her tarantula and scowled at her boss, expecting him to throw them out.

Memphis barked at the pair and told them to follow him. He led them to a small but comfortable office with a window overlooking the back parking lot. He told them to make the space their own and not bother his secretary. The next day movers brought in two desks and faced them towards one another (as the pair's station desks had been), two large file cabinets, and a table for the Mr. Coffee machine, toaster, Litton microwave oven, and small refrigerator. The day after that the desks were covered with accouterments like staplers, pencil sharpeners, notebooks, typewriters, and writing instruments. That day the two phone lines were installed. By week's end the pair had a functioning office and a permanent place to go. No one was more relieved than Skye.

Memphis said he couldn't promise them any work. They understood. They still bugged him, and slowly a few small cases were thrown their way just to mitigate the annoyance level.

Frick and Frack were happy.

Frick was even happier now that he and Professor London Monroe were dating. Frack had called it—the lunch turned into lunches which turned into dinners which turned into first base which turned into Frick discovering that, yes, you never forgot how to ride a bicycle. They maintained separate residences but saw each other several times a week. Frick thought it was sweet that she called him Lurch. In their intimate moments he called her Morticia.

After his sister's surprise appearance and delivery Sand's life was upended. He sat down with Memphis and Swan the day after and told them all about the visit, the bullet (which he had dug out of the wall and put in the company safe), and Snow's admission that she had murdered someone. He showed them the morning edition of the *Sangre de Cristo Courant*, which had the top story of a murder at the Cross of the Martyrs. The story identified the victim as the FBI-wanted fugitive Ryder Jackson, and that the bullet seemed to be a .22. Sand told them that their new nephew, Elijah, was half-black, and that Snow had had a bruise on her face. When Sand undressed Elijah for a bath he saw fading bruises on the boy's body. He also saw several healed-over cigarette burns.

None of them felt an iota of sympathy for the dead man, but the question was what to do about the living woman. Snow was their sister, but she was also a self-professed murderer. There were two choices—notify the authorities of what had transpired or keep quiet about her confession. The matter couldn't be decided in a day, so they all stepped back for a week and thought and thought and discussed. Finally, a hard decision was made. Akiro knew the score and he acted as Sand's legal counsel when he called FBI Special Agent Richard Ballard and asked him to drive up to Santa Fe for a meeting. Akiro didn't give him a hint about the subject matter, but Ballard was savvy enough to know that the request was for something significant. He drove up.

Ballard entered the Hazelwood Conference Room where Memphis, Swan, Sand, and Akiro were waiting. He could see the gravity written all over their faces and wondered what the hell was up. Skye put a cup of coffee in front of him and left. He took a sip then said, "Go for it."

Akiro started off by saying this was off the record and hypothetical. Ballard knew that that meant that what he would be saying was the unvarnished truth. Akiro nodded to Sand, who took a deep breath and told Ballard everything. When he finished, there was dead silence in the room. Ballard's lips were slightly parted, and his eyes were wide. It took him a few minutes to compose himself and formulate questions for Sand.

Was she with anybody?

Don't know.

Did you see her vehicle?

No.

Did she say where she was going?

No.

Did she intimate that she'd be back?

No.

Did she leave anything with her son that might point to her location?

No, just a worn blue teddy bear.

Did she show any regret over shooting Jackson?

(pause) No.

Did the boy say anything about Jackson?

No.

We're assuming that Jackson is the boy's father?

Yes.

Was your sister wearing a wedding ring?

No.

Did you get the impression that she was more than Jackson's domestic partner? Was she a member of that so-called Thunderstorm?

(long pause and a whispered response) I think so.

Ballard sat back and asked whether they'd go on the non-hypothetical record. Sand hesitated, then reluctantly said yes. He took the plastic baggie with the .22 slug from his wall out of his pocket and handed it to Ballard. Ballard said a quiet thank-you, then made a phone call to his superiors in Albuquerque.

The next day Snow Noelle Hazelwood was put on the Most Wanted List for domestic terrorism and murder.

CHAPTER TWO

Screamin' Al Demon had been on the AM radio airwaves for less than a year. He had an hour show at 1 AM on a tiny Santa Fe station that operated from 6 PM to 2 AM with a mix of music, advertisements, and two opinion programs. Al's was the last on the schedule before the station signed off until the next evening.

His format was simple; he presented a topic of his choosing, opined on it from his perspective for a half hour, then opened the phone lines for call-in questions and comments. He liked to call himself a provocateur. Occasionally he played the devil's advocate on some issues just to provoke a response from his listeners, but most of the time he held to the radical and often sexist and racist opinions he spewed. He had had similar programs on stations from the east coast to the west coast; he had been fired from each one. Rather than seeing that as a downside, he reveled in his so-called "American right of free speech," and each time he moved to a new station he became just a bit more intolerable.

In Santa Fe there wasn't a single station staff member that even remotely liked him. They tolerated his inane, bombastic comments and salacious leers because their station ratings had slightly risen as more people listened to his show. Then, he grabbed the butt of a young woman acting as a temporary secretary while she made spending money during her freshman year at college. She might have been a callow teenager, but she whirled around and cracked him with a slap so hard that the guys in the next room heard it and came running to the door to stare at the conclusion of the scene. She leaned over his shocked face and said if he ever did that again she would get her brother's shotgun and cut him in half. She stalked out of the room; he watched with dropped jaw, and his face reddened when he heard the laughter from the next room. That Grayhawk girl was a bitch, all right. He never came within three feet of her again.

It was the week of September 16th, the day that the Hispanics would celebrate Mexican Independence Day. He couldn't stand spics. He hated the Puerto Ricans in New York, and the Cubans in Miami. When he hit Texas, his bigotry rose to new levels with his disdain for Mexicans and Indians. They were frequent targets for his bile.

He took careful aim at the Mexicans and Indians when he finally got a job in Santa Fe (at half his pay and half his airtime from his last gig in Sacramento). He roasted both the Mexicans and the French on his Cinco de Mayo show, and the phone lines burned up. He left at 2 AM to find that his car was fully egged and all four tires flat. He wasn't mad—he was thrilled and railed about the "sub-humans" that had injured his vehicle.

On his July 4th show he denigrated the Indians, saying that they were too primitive and stupid to have formed any decent civilization until the white man came onto the country's shores and semi-civilized them. He segued into a raucous and vicious tirade against the Africans, saying that if it weren't for the white Europeans colonizing their jungle, they'd still be swinging from trees and sniffing one another's butts. After work he found that all his car windows had been shattered. He bullied the station owner into springing for a new car. The owner suggested that he tone down his vitriol, but that was Screamin' Al Demon's style, even when he was Alfred Cohen of Jamaica Plains, New York.

On the night before Mexican Independence Day he fired off a wild rant about the issues at the New Mexico State Penitentiary that had been bubbling over for years. The prison housed far too many prisoners, the cells were dank, oppressive, and unsanitary, the educational and rehabilitative courses were suspended, and the food was abominable. The prison kitchen produced slop, with roaches and mice prevalent; intestinal issues were rampant. A visiting warden stated that the prison conditions were the worse he'd ever seen.

In 1976 the prisoners' frustration led to a work strike that was organized by inmates as a response to the prison's poor conditions. Deputy Warden Robert Montoya decided to subjugate the complainers by authorizing the use of tear gas against the striking prisoners. As they exited the dormitory coughing from the gas, they were stripped naked and run nearly a hundred yards down the central corridor through a gauntlet of officials who beat them with ubiquitous ax handles. Called "the night of the ax handles," the incident was corroborated by several eyewitnesses, including some officials themselves, and resulted in serious injuries as well as a federal lawsuit, naming Deputy Warden Montoya and a senior guard captain among the assailants. After this violent response to prisoners' concerns, inmate Dwight Duran drafted a 99-page handwritten civil rights complaint to the U.S. District Court of New Mexico, Duran v Apodaca.

Screamin' Al had no patience with anyone who broke the law. He railed against the prisoners, and asked his audience—what did they expect? The prison was filled with Mexicans and Indians, and we know how *they* are. The Mexicans were barely civilized, but the Indians—they were savages still. They lived in poverty, begging for handouts. They lived in mud huts like the pathetic pueblo buildings in Taos. Those ugly mud huts should be torn down and the people there forced to build real houses and pay for the supplies. They could afford to buy lumber if they'd hold off on buying fire water to get drunk every night. They didn't want to advance themselves. His last comment before opening the phone lines was that perhaps the country would be better off if the redskins were rounded up and relocated to Guatemala.

The phones lit up with half the callers agreeing and half suggesting certain anatomical fornication acts and threatening Al's life. He was eating it up with a spoon. A station manager in Albuquerque had caught his show a week earlier and wanted to talk about a place on his station's roster. The station was in the state's largest city and had a huge audience. He knew—he *knew*—he was on his way to fame and fortune. He could move out of his ratshit trailer and set fire to his cheap car. Babes would be hanging all over him.

He answered and agreed with and insulted his callers and slammed the phone down on the last one. He grabbed his jacket and sped out of the station. Maybe one or two bars were still open, but he could drink for free at home. He had a bottle of Jose Cuervo that was begging to be opened. His fucking blender had kicked the bucket a couple of days ago so there was no frozen margarita in sight. America didn't make quality products anymore.

The trailer park was dark; virtually all the residents were asleep. He turned smoothly into his small dirt driveway on the side of the trailer. He slammed on his brakes as his headlights revealed a tall, broad man standing beside the steps to his front door. He put the car in park, leaving the headlights on. He cautiously got out of the car, keeping his distance.

"Who are you? What do you want?" he asked the stranger warily.

"Peace, friend," the man said. "I came here to thank you for your many true words about my people."

Al squinted. Yup, the guy was an Indian. "Thank me?"

The man nodded. "Your words are harsh but painfully true. My people are badly flawed. They need to own up to their weaknesses and stop being a drain on white America. It is time that we picked up our share of the load and contribute to society instead of dragging it down."

Al relaxed just a little. "Really? That's what I've been saying." Al eagerly walked over to the man and extended his hand. "Screamin' Al."

The man grasped his hand and smiled. "Po'Pay."

"I can't believe I wound up on Boardwalk," Frack grumbled as he moved the shoe on the Monopoly board.

"And what's even worse is that I own it," Frick crowed. "Hand over the money, Frackster."

Frack muttered something uncomplimentary as he handed over the play money. He looked down at his pile; he was almost broke. Thank God they didn't play for real cash.

Frick put Frack's money in his thick pile, sat back, and flashed a Cheshire Cat grin.

Frack threw his remaining money at his partner. "I surrender. I'm hungry. Let's get lunch."

"I could use a burger," Frick said just as Skye opened their office door.

"You got visitors," she snapped. She looked at the board game. "You're such a loser, Frack."

"Who are they?" Frick asked.

"Fuzz. Active ones, not sitting around on their lazy asses like you."

"Names?"

"Abbott and Dunbar. Should I send them in?"

"Yeah, thanks." When Skye left, he looked at Frack and they both shrugged. They respected those two detectives but were never really close with them. He wondered if it had something to do with the wanted Hazelwood woman since they'd pulled the Ryder Jackson murder case.

Skye led the two detectives into the office then closed the door and left without another word. Abbott and Dunbar stood waiting for Frick and Frack to invite them to sit down. After a minute Dunbar rolled his eyes and plopped down into a guest chair; Abbott did the same.

Dunbar looked around the office. It was far more colorful and interesting than when the retired detectives first moved in. There were framed movie posters on the west wall—1973's *Dillinger*, 1941's *The Maltese Falcon*, 1967's *Bonnie and Clyde*, and 1931's *The Public Enemy*. Frick even had a plant on his desk, a small barrel cactus.

"Nice digs," Dunbar said.

"Thanks," Frack said. "So, is this a social call or can we help you professionally?"

"So, have you two become actual P.I.s?"

"Unofficially. The real ones come cryin' to us when they can't figure something out."

"Okay," Dunbar said. "We're here because, well …"

"Because we have a missing person that might relate to that old Frisco kids' case. Maybe not," Abbott said.

"Who's missing?" Frick asked.

"You read about that radio prick on KHFN who didn't come into work last week?"

"The Screamin' Asshole?"

"Screamin' Al Demon, AKA Alfred Cohen."

"Why is *anyone* looking for him?" Frack asked.

"An ex-wife in Newark that's pissed about a missing alimony check for one. The station manager was pissed when he didn't show up for work, but after a couple of days that turned to worry. He had to scramble to fill the time slot. After he got a call from the ex-Mrs. Cohen, he filed a missing persons' report. Guess who the lucky bastards were that got the case?"

Frack chortled. "Guys, you are the next Frick and Frack of the Santa Fe police department."

Frick grinned. "So sorry for your troubles."

"Yeah, I can see that," Abbott grumbled. "So, how's about we tell you why we're here?"

"Please do," Frack said imperiously. "You said you think there might be a link to our old case."

"It's possible," Dunbar said. "Your Frisco kids seemed to have pissed off some members of the Taos Pueblo, right?"

"Right," Frick said. A Taos resident had seen the missing kids preening and disrespecting the cemetery. She called them on it and the girl had flipped her the bird. *White bitch*, Elpidia Martinez had said.

"Well, we got to thinking, and from your report and our case file, it seems that Screamin' Al was far more disrespectful. Have you ever listened to his show?"

"I'm asleep after midnight," Frick said. "I've heard about it, though. He's pretty much a racist asshole, right?"

"That's putting it mildly. He viciously puts down Mexicans, blacks, Indians, hippies, liberated women, and any other group that isn't white bread conservative and male. He's had his car egged and tires slashed, and a number of death threats on his life."

"That didn't scare him into restraint?" Frack asked.

"Hell, he thrived on the controversy. The station manager said another station in Albuquerque was talking to him about a move to a bigger forum. That alone makes me think he didn't just take off on his own."

"Is his car missing, too?" Frick asked.

Abbott nodded. "It is. We searched his trailer and found nothing. His clothes were still there. There was only one set of fresh tire tracks around his driveway. We went door to door, but no one heard or saw anything. He left work, drove home, and fell off the face of the earth."

"So," Frick said thoughtfully, "we have at least three missing people who disrespected the Indian culture and turned up missing. Do you think that their words and actions were the catalyst to their disappearances?"

"I wouldn't rule it out," Dunbar said. "In fact, I'd put it in the top five reasons."

"What are the other four?"

"Um … actually, that's the only one we've got. Making it one of five makes it look like we have more ideas than we do."

Frack shook his head. "You two will never be another Frick and Frack."

Frick said, "Are there any telltale physical or psychological aspects of his body or character? I mean, besides being a jerk."

"Well, we know he's a jerk. Physical?" Dunbar flipped through his documents. "Says here he's five-eight, skinny, got some pock marks on his face from a teenage bout with acne, a tattoo of the

Statue of Liberty on his upper left arm and … ah, he had a hip replacement five years ago so he's got metal in his body. According to his dental records he's missing a molar on the top left. Got three crowns and lots of fillings."

"Am I under the correct impression that you haven't a clue as to what happened or where he is?" Frack asked.

Dunbar nodded. "The only thing we came up with was the thin link to your old case which, by the way, our estimable captain has also dumped on us when we posited our theory."

Frick cocked his head thoughtfully, then held up a finger. He hit his speed dial for #4. After two rings Nick picked up. Frick asked him to come to his office. He knew that Sand was in Las Cruces wrapping up a fraud case. Nick came in and frowned when he saw the two detectives. He didn't wait for an explanation.

"What are these two morons doing here?" Nick snapped. Dunbar and Abbott had been two of the interrogation cops when Nick was arrested for murder. They were verbally and, once, physically abusive. Sand and his late partner, Cole Garrison, had been loud but never crossed the line.

"Do we really have to have the hippie as part of this discussion?" Abbott said coolly.

"Yeah, we do. It was his case when we started, so he needs to be here. Plus, he's a partner in this firm."

"Why *am* I here?" Nick asked flatly as he sat back against the short bookcase that held Frick's massive volume of paperback novels. The first shelf was lined with Frick's favorite author's books. Leon Uris's novels like *Battle Cry*, *Exodus*, *Mila 18*, and *QB VII* had the place of honor. Uris had published a new novel just this year, *Trinity*, about the battles between the faiths in Ireland.

Frack said, "The morons have a new missing person case and they think there may be a link to the Frisco case. Maybe the professor case, too."

"That right? Enlighten me."

Frick gestured to Abbott, who proceeded to go over the Alfred Cohen case bit by bit. When he finished Nick stared at him neutrally.

"Huh," Nick said. "Interesting. Yeah, that could be a link. So, do you have any theories as to who the abductor might be?"

"Gotta be an Indian," Frack said. "Sure, the boob insulted lots of groups, but the only group that he had any overlap with the Frisco case is the Indians. That is, if it is a real link. Right now, it's just a suspicion."

"And if that is the link, it very well may be related to Professor Carter's case. He was on his way to the pueblos when he vanished," Frick added. He made a mental note to talk with London about this possibility. And, no, it wasn't just an excuse to spend more time with her. "It's not likely that he would somehow disrespect the cultures he was studying, but it's all in the perception."

"Exactly," Nick agreed. "He may have said or done something innocuous that someone misinterpreted." Nick cocked his head at Dunbar. "You know of any radical Indian groups that might take offense?"

"We haven't explored that yet," Dunbar replied.

"We can compile a list," Frack said quickly. He wanted in on the case and not stay on the peripheral. He hated the fact that the Frisco and New Jersey cases were unresolved when he retired. He addressed Nick. "When will Sand be back?"

"Late tomorrow," Nick said. "But we shouldn't wait for him. I'll update Memphis. Meanwhile, you two get going on the radical groups' list." He nodded to Abbott. "Think we can get a copy of your case file?"

"I guess," Abbott said, sighing. He still didn't like Nick even though he was innocent of all suspected crimes, here and back in Rhode Island. Nick held out his hand and Abbott put the folder in it. Frick called Skye, who grumbled as she left the office with copying duties. She brought back the originals and the copies and as she handed the folder to Abbott she snapped, "Two dollars and twenty cents."

"For what?" Abbott snapped back.

"Ten cents a page. Only members of the firm get copies for free."

"They're the ones that wanted the copies," Dunbar exclaimed.

"Copies of *your* material. Hand it over."

"Not a chance."

Skye grabbed the copies and tossed them in the trash can. "See how well they do in covering your asses without the background material," Skye said icily.

"Just give her the fucking money," Abbott said.

Dunbar grumbled but took out two singles and two dimes and handed them to Skye. She retrieved the copies from the trash and handed them to Nick. Then, she flounced out of the office, slamming the door behind her.

Dunbar and Abbott stood up. Abbott said, "Call us tomorrow to let us know your progress on the list. Meanwhile, we're going to re-canvass his trailer park and the blocks around the radio station."

"Have fun," Nick said as they left. He looked at Frick and Frack. "Hey—Raleigh had a summer job at the station, and I'll bet she could give you some up close and personal, unvarnished opinions on Cohen. I can't say why, but this feels like it could be something."

"I agree," Frick said. "I'm going to head over to the college and talk to London for her input."

"I'll hit a few contacts and see what I can come up with," Frack added.

Nick smirked at Frick. As he left the office he started softly crooning, "Frick and London, sitting in a tree, k-i-s-s-i-n-g."

"Twerp," Frick muttered, scowling.

"Yeah," Frack said. "He should know you could never haul your uncoordinated ass up a tree."

"I hate you."

"I know."

Nick finished his stuffed acorn squash at dinner that evening with his brother and sister-in-law. Beside those two, Nick, and Yuki, there was another adult guest at the table. Hashkeh Naabah, the Indian artist that had painted the beautiful picture hanging over the McBean fireplace, sat at the opposite end of the dining table. This was the first time that Nick had met him. Percy had commissioned a portrait of Elspeth the previous year, but it taken a while to complete since Naabah had other artistic commitments, including finishing his pueblo series of paintings for the Evening Star Art Gallery. The painting was still wrapped, with the unveiling to be "dessert."

Nick found the artist charming although not overly chatty. He exhibited wit and deep thought. Naabah asked Nick about his work, and Nick brought up the Frisco case and briefly told them what was being researched and how the case might be linked to the missing Cohen. The meal finally ended, and the family retired to the living room where Naabah stood next to his painting.

He smiled. "I was very fortunate to have a splendid subject for this painting," he said, nodding at antsy little Elspeth, who sat between her father and mother on the couch. "Your daughter is a treasure." With that he carefully undid the brown wrapping paper. The painting was turned to the back. He slowly turned it around.

Tansee gasped. Naabah had done a remarkable job of capturing Elspeth's lovely features. Her long black hair cascaded over her shoulders and down her back. Elspeth had posed in her usual clothes, but the artist had painted her with traditional Navajo dress, including a headband with an eagle feather and a carved turquoise star in the middle. She was wearing calf-high fringed moccasins and wore small turquoise earrings and a ring. Behind her was the image of a Taos Pueblo building with the mountains off to the right and a hint of the river. The azure sky had a puffy white cloud in the shape of a wolf's head; there was the slightest hint of a partial rainbow. The colors on Elspeth's clothes were vivid and bright, red, copper, bright yellow, and luminescent blue. The frame was a cactus saguaro skeleton, just like Percy's. The brass plaque read, "Sǫ' Áłchíní"—Star Child.

Percy slid off the couch, holding his daughter's hand. "My God," he said. "That's … magnificent."

"I believe it captures her essence, her spirit, her soul if you will. She is a true daughter of the Navajo and the Hopi. I had a shaman bless the portrait to keep her safe and well."

Tansee impulsively hugged Naabah then just stared at the beauty that was her child.

Nick shook his head in wonder. "It's just … I have no words," he said.

Percy shook hands with Naabah. "Thank you, Hashkeh. This will have a place of honor in our lives forever."

"It is always a pleasure to paint an image of something special. Your daughter qualifies. And now, I must get going. I have a long drive to Gallup tomorrow to meet with a prospective client. Thank you for the lovely dinner and company."

Percy and Tansee escorted him to his car and bid him goodbye before they went back in to stare at the portrait.

Naabah drove up to Taos and pulled into his driveway. He was tired and had had a long day. Tomorrow there'd be a long drive and a busy day. Still, he had to check on his project.

He descended to the basement where he opened the metal coffin and stared at the nearly completely eaten form of Screamin' Al Demon. He scowled at the metal hip, but that was part of his prey and so should be considered special. He had cut off a section of skin before he committed the body to his beetles. He had a project for that.

He slammed the lid down and went upstairs. He sank into his recliner and sighed. He smiled to himself, his eyes closed, wondering what his new friends would say if they knew that he was an avenger of white injustices.

When he finished the special canvas on which he was working, he'd sign it with his soul name.

Po'Pay.

CHAPTER THREE

Rockport, Massachusetts

Eddie Troy was duct-taped to a wooden chair in the basement of his small Cape Cod house on Summer Street. His right eye blinked rapidly; his left was swollen shut from the dozens of hits with the fly swatter. As painful as that was it paled in comparison to the two-inch nails shot into his legs with the nail gun, and the baseball bat that reduced his toes to mush.

He was terrified, in agony, and baffled. The two people in the basement with him hadn't asked any questions. He had come home from a photo shoot in Boston, and a split second after he switched on the light in his kitchen, he felt a strong arm around his neck and a hot needle plunging into his neck below the arm. The arm tightened for a few seconds before he lost consciousness and slid to the floor.

He awoke in his basement, immobilized in the chair, duct tape tightly affixed across his mouth. He noticed that the basement window was plastered over with cardboard so that no light was visible from the street. A man was standing in the corner watching him, his arms crossed, his face bland. The second man whom he sensed somehow was in charge stood in front of him, two feet away. He was dressed entirely in black, jeans, turtle-neck shirt, jacket, and shiny shoes. He was tall—at least six-two—well-built, Caucasian, with longish black hair, and fathomless black eyes. Dead eyes. Merciless eyes.

Evil eyes.

Devil eyes.

The man said nothing to him. He picked up the fly swatter and began beating Eddie's left eye with rhythmic precision and timing. After two dozen hits the eye was swollen shut and bleeding. Then, the corner man walked over to the devil man and handed him a nail gun. The man looked down at him and without warning put a nail into his upper thigh, missing the femoral artery. Thirty seconds later another nail pierced his other leg. Every thirty seconds for three minutes another nail was sent into his bleeding lower limbs, piercing the flesh deep enough to only show the nail head.

The corner man knelt and pulled off Eddie's shoes and socks, then walked back to the corner where he picked up a baseball bat. He handed it to the devil man. Unlike the swatter and nails, which were timed and measured, the devil man began to smashed Eddie's toes in a terrifying frenzy. Eddie moaned and screamed behind his gag, his undamaged right eye flooded with tears of pain and terror. The moaning and screaming dissolved into mewling and sobs.

The devil man stood back and studied the mess he had created. He lay the bat gently on the floor then took a step closer to Eddie, looming over him. He gently cupped Eddie's chin and forced his face to look up. His voice was modulated, calm, and frightening. There was no humanity within his tone, or his words.

"I have questions for you," the man said. "Rather than asking them and having you answer falsely or hold back a response, I wanted to show you what would happen if you failed to convince me of the veracity of your answers. Now, you may think that my actions thus far have been inhumane, so I would like to enlighten you. What I have done to you is just the beginning. I have many more creative and pain-inducing acts that I can visit on your body. For example." He nodded to corner man, who walked over and revealed a pair of hand-held hedge clippers. "These are very sharp, and highly effective in removing testicles, ears, noses, and fingers. Nod if you understand."

Eddie managed a singular nod. Even before the man asked his questions Eddie knew he was doomed. Neither assailant had bothered to mask his face. They had no intention of letting him live. That was his certainty. Still, if he could stave off any pain before the devil man would take his life, he would do his best to try to minimize the horror.

"I'm going to remove the tape from your mouth," the man said. "One single sound from you other than answering my questions and the first testicle will be removed. However, let me provide a tiny glimpse of what could be your immediate future." He grasped Eddie's bound hand and snipped off his right pinky. "There. I believe we have an understanding." With that the man ripped off the duct tape covering Eddie's mouth. Blood issued from his mouth from the deep bite he'd inflicted on his tongue. He looked up at the devil man with pleading, terrified eyes, but he held his tongue.

"Good," the man said in his oddly melodious, baritone voice. He held up a photo. "Do you recognize this woman?"

Eddie stared at the photo of Cameo Adams that the New Mexican detectives had given him. He nodded vigorously. He had made a dozen copies and handed them out to people in the nearby area. He hadn't written Cameo's name on the back of any of them.

"Good. Where did you get this photo?"

"DeVere," Eddie whispered hoarsely. "York."

"DeVere York. Who is he?"

"A, a cop. Pittsfield."

"Pittsfield …" the devil man said slowly. "He came here?"

"Y-yes."

"Why?"

"She, she recognized a shot of the coast in Gloucester. Her psychiatrist showed it to her."

"Interesting … Anyone else visit you besides the cop?"

"Water … water, please."

The devil man picked up a bottle of water, unscrewed the cap, and poured the warm liquid down Eddie's throat. "Must I repeat my question?" he said as he brandished the hedge clippers.

Eddie shook his head and coughed. "He was with … he was with a couple of detectives. Private investigators."

"From Pittsfield?'

"Arizona," Eddie whispered, praying his lie would be believed. He knew he was doomed.

"Arizona? Very interesting. Names?"

"I … I can't think. I can't remember. I swear." Eddie's mind was roiling with terror and pain. He tried desperately to extract the names but his ability to think was hampered by his fear and agony. He prayed the devil man wouldn't see through his lie about the state.

Devil man tapped the photo. "And her name?"

Eddie shook his head back and forth. "I dunno. Candy … Carrie something. Maybe. I don't remember. I swear to God I don't remember. It wasn't that important to me."

"I see. Anyone else know about the photo?"

Eddie shivered and trembled and managed to shake his head. He remembered that DeVere's family knew, but he had already sacrificed DeVere and he wasn't going to compound that action by pointing this madman towards his family. He prayed that the madman believed him.

"What did this cop and his companions say about the woman in the photo?"

"He said … he said that she had amnesia. Couldn't remember who she was or where she came from. They were trying to find clues … to her past. Please. I don't know anymore. Please."

"I believe you," the man intoned seriously. He nodded to corner man. The man came over and put a pile of kindling near the captive and lit it on fire. Eddie froze; his heart was a split second from jumping out of his chest. If they were going to burn him why was the fire not closer? He tried to focus his good eye on the kindling. He could see that the cut part of the wood was green; it wasn't seasoned. After a few minutes, the fire began to smoke. He knew that when the wood wasn't seasoned and dry the water in the green wood would evaporate and begin smoking.

Devil man suddenly dragged Eddie's chair close to the fire and leaned it over so that Eddie's face was in the middle of the smoke. Eddie coughed and pleaded and coughed again as his lungs filled with the smoke.

Just as suddenly devil man righted the chair and corner man thrust a plastic bag over Eddie's head. A minute later, Eddie slumped dead in the chair, asphyxiated. Corner man quickly unfastened all the duct tape and moved Eddie's body close to the wood stove, which was already roaring with flames from seasoned wood. He took a moment to pull the nails out of Eddie's legs and stick them in his pocket. He used a cast iron poker to drag a burning log from the stove and onto the floor. He dipped a stick with a wrapped rag into the flames and handed it to devil man, who went upstairs to touch the flames to strategic places in the house. Corner man stayed back and did the same in the basement before running up the stairs. By the time he got there the devil man's efforts were burgeoning with pockets of flames crackling and burning the first floor.

Devil man nodded and both men slipped out the back door of the kitchen into the night. They wended their way through the backyard on Summer Street until they reached Pleasant Street, where their car was parked. As corner man started the car, they could hear the distant fire engines. Corner man drove a quarter mile down Pleasant Street with his headlights off; he turned them on then headed down Route 127 to Route 128, taking the cutoff to Route 1. That took them to Boston and the devil man's house.

The next day the two men plus an additional compatriot got into the car and headed to Pittsfield.

Santa Fe, New Mexico

"He was a first-class asshole," Raleigh said. She was slouched in Nick's office chair with one long leg flung over the arm and rhythmically kicking the air. She was wearing a pair of cut-off denim shorts which showed her slender, tanned legs to their best effect. "You know, when he heard my last name, he leered at me and said he could make me one happy squaw."

"You didn't tell your brothers about that, did you?" Frick said.

"If I had he wouldn't be missing. His defleshed head would be sticking out of the desert floor next to a swarm of red ants picking their teeth." Raleigh flipped her long, straight hair over her shoulder with a touch of arrogance. She was tall, like her brothers, and slender without being skinny. She had broad swimmer's shoulders and those and her arms were as tanned as her legs. She was wearing a star-spangled tank top that read "Carter 1976."

"He ever talk to you without leering?" Frack asked.

"Nope. I tried to avoid contact with him especially after he grabbed my ass."

"He what?" Nick exclaimed, leaning forward with shock on his face.

"I'm guessing that your brothers don't know about that, either," Frack said, fighting back a grin. The Grayhawk brothers might be forces to be reckoned with, but their little sister was no slouch in the toughness department.

"I cracked him across the face and told him I'd get Memphis's shotgun and cut him in half with it. He never bothered me after that," she said.

"Did he have anyone at the station that didn't hate him?"

"Nope. Pretty sure he didn't have any friends outside of work, either. Definitely no chicks—he would have been bragging about that nonstop."

"Anyone there want him dead?"

"Besides me? On general principal?"

"Yeah, besides you," Nick said.

"I don't think so."

"Did you ever hear anyone on the phone making threats? Maybe someone came to the station irate and loud?" Frick asked.

"No and no. And you know what? Even if I did, I wouldn't tell you. I'd love to help the guy get away if he did anything bad to that dick."

"Hard to argue with that logic," Nick said, sighing.

"Do you or your family belong to any Indian groups?" Frick asked.

"You mean tribes, paleface?"

"Very funny. No, I mean any groups that promote cultural awareness, activism, that sort of thing."

"My mom belongs to a group of medicine women who gather monthly to talk about illnesses and cures. Me and my brothers are pretty much apolitical. I do know of a few."

Nick handed her a notebook and pen. "Can you write the names down and any members you might know?" Nick asked.

Raleigh squinted at him. "What exactly is this all about?"

"It's kind of confidential," Frack said.

Raleigh tossed the notebook at him. "So's my help." She stood up and turned to leave.

"All right, all right," Nick said. "Sit. Listen." Then, Nick gave her the summary version of the possible link between the disappearance cases and said they wanted to interview any Indian groups that might have input.

Raleigh arched her wing-like eyebrows and sighed. She wrote down a few lines. "I'm out of here," she said. "Got two classes at college and I have to study for my other offsite courses."

"What other courses?" Frick asked. "Aren't you going for a degree in Anthropology at Sangre?"

"I am, but I'm hedging my bets," she said. "I know this will come as shock to you, but the world is changing. It's becoming more reliant on technology, on computers. I don't plan on being left behind."

"Where and what are you studying?" Frack asked curiously. This girl had smarts, he thought.

"Last year a couple of guys who used to work for IBM came to town and established a school called the Computer Processing Institute. They teach programming, keypunch machines, loading and running tape drives, and how to create and execute computer programs. They teach a language called COBOL. I plan on mastering that."

"COBOL?" Frick said.

"It's an acronym for Common Business-Oriented Language. It's semi-English with specific structure for communicating with the big mainframes."

"Mainframes?" Frack said.

"Argh," Raleigh said. "I don't have the time to teach a course here and now. Suffice to say I'm studying something for the future, not rooting around in the past. You're not going to find me joining my mom's medicine group. I've gotta go. If you have any more questions, find another Indian. Ciao." Raleigh wriggled her long fingers and departed.

"I pity the poor bastard that marries her," Frack said. "She'll eat him alive."

"With barbecue sauce," Frick intoned seriously.

"All right, Raleigh's culinary habits aside, I think you should split up and talk with these various groups. Divvy them up and hit the road," Nick said. He handed the notebook to Frick. "Have Skye make a copy for me."

When Frick and Frack reached the office door Frick turned to Nick with a sly smile. "See? Wasn't keeping us close by beneficial?"

Nick shrugged. "We had a spare office. Putting you there keeps most of the rats out."

Frick turned back to the door and flashed a wide grin. Once outside, with the door closed, he turned to his partner and said, "They need us so bad."

"For sure," Frack said, nodding.

Frick had conferred with London before he went out to talk to a few of the groups that Raleigh had written down. She insisted on coming with him, and he had no reason to protest. Besides being knowledgeable about Indian culture she was always a great companion. They hit two of the groups and had long talks with them, but nothing turned up. Frick took her to lunch at the diner, then they drove over to a small adobe building outside of Taos. That housed the group named Native Americans For Progress. The receptionist was busy typing and frowned when they entered; clearly, she was wary of white people. Frick identified himself as a private investigator (he wasn't yet; his license application was still under review) and asked to speak to someone in charge.

The teenage girl behind the desk said coolly, "What makes you think I'm not in charge?"

Frick was tongue-tied but London rescued him. "You are in charge, but the people who think they are are oblivious. It's pretty much that way with most women."

The girl replied, "Ain't that the truth. Our two group leaders aren't on site today. Luke Blackwolf is in Gallup on personal business, and Hashkeh Naabah is in the pueblo."

"Will he be back soon?" Frick asked.

"You never know. I think he's working on a painting. He tends to lose track of time when he's working. You could go up there and see if you can find him. Otherwise, I'll take a message and give it to him when he comes in."

"That's okay," London said. "It's a nice day to drive. We'll go up there. Thanks."

"You're welcome," the girl said. As they left, she went back to her hunt-and-peck typing.

On the drive up to the pueblo Frick said, "I know about that artist. He painted the canvas of Percy at Bandelier and the new one of Elspeth in buckskin clothes. He's a pretty good painter."

"Famous, too," London said. "He's a mainstay of the Evening Star Art Gallery and his paintings hang in big galleries in Arizona, California, and Texas."

"How do you know so much about his art?"

"I make it my business to understand both ancient and modern Indian cultures including various forms of art. So many of the tribes make remarkable pottery, like the Santa Clara black clay. The Acoma

Pueblo pottery is world-renowned. You've seen some of those in my den and my office."

"I never paid much attention," Frick confessed. "Sorry. I'm a guy."

"I forgive you. But I'm going to give you a show-and-tell lecture soon on the art of the Puebloans and other southwest tribes."

"I look forward to that."

"Yeah, I can tell." London put a hand on Frick's thigh and purred, "There are other show-and-tell subjects on which I can enlighten you … Lurch."

Frick inhaled sharply. Nope, no problematic bicycle in his life.

Frick pulled into the Taos Pueblo parking lot and a few minutes later he bought admission tickets for them. He asked one of the security officers where he might find Naabah. Luckily, the officer had seen him earlier by the chapel with his easel set up. That was three hours ago but they should try there first. No, he hadn't seen the artist leave.

Frick knew his way around and headed to the chapel. London walked beside him admiring the pueblo and the landscape. A civilization stuck in time, she thought, so much of it indistinguishable from what existed two hundred years earlier. A beautiful testament to time and tradition.

Frick stopped and pointed towards the mountain side of the chapel. Sitting in a lawn chair with an easel in front of him and a small table next to him, he was holding a paint brush and gently guiding it across the top of the canvas. As Frick and London moved closer, they saw that his chapel painting suggested a vivid sunset, with elements of peach, orange, and purple spread across the fading blue sky.

Naabah sensed company and turned to see the man and woman approaching him. He recognized the man from newspaper stories about the missing young couple. He smiled slightly; it should be an interesting conversation.

CHAPTER FOUR

"We need to talk, Dad," Sage said with seriousness written all over her oval face.

Memphis thought that his oldest daughter was ten going on thirty. She had been precocious ever since she learned to walk. Once she started talking, she never stopped. She asked question after question, some on point and some nonsensical. After numerous attempts to deflect some of the latter Memphis and Swan gave up and answered as best they could even if they had to make something up.

"So," Memphis said slowly as he brushed the croissant crumbs off his desk, "what is it this time? Dating advice?"

Sage dumped herself into his guest chair and threw him an owlish glare. She had gotten out of class early due to a teachers' conference, and rather than going home or to a relative's she descended on her father. Swan had the joy of corralling their twins in her office.

Sage rolled her eyes. "I'm too young to date. No, I want to ask you and Mom something."

"Should we get her in here?"

"I can ask you and if you need clarification you can confer with her."

"What the hell kind of language is that? 'Clarification?' 'Confer?' How old are you?"

"Grandma says I have an old soul."

"That was probably educated at Harvard. Okay. What do you want to know?"

"Is Mom my biological mother?"

Memphis stared at his daughter, then hit speed dial and told his wife to get her butt into his office.

Sage arched her delicate eyebrows. "I'm going to take that as a no." She grinned. "You've got a bead of sweat on your forehead."

"It's hot in here."

"No, it's not."

Just then Swan came into the office and looked at her husband and her daughter. "What's up?" she asked warily.

Before Memphis could speak Sage turned towards Swan and asked, "Are you my biological mother?"

Before Memphis could butt in Swan replied, "No, I'm not. I'm the mother that raised you, wiped your butt, fed you, clothed you, and kissed your booboos."

"A simple no would have done, Mom," Sage said, sighing. "I know all that. Of course, you're my mother. I was just asking for—"

"Clarification," Memphis interjected.

"Exactly," Sage said, nodding. "Since I look just like you, I'm assuming that bio-mom is your twin sister, Snow."

"That's correct," Swan said.

"Can I get a word in here?" Memphis asked.

"No," Swan and Sage said together. Memphis put up his hands in surrender.

"Let me enlighten you, daughter mine," Swan said. "Yes, your dad was once engaged to my sister. She ran off before they could get married."

"She dumped him," Sage said.

"I wouldn't say dumped," Memphis muttered. Swan scowled at him. "Okay, she dumped me."

"Why?" Sage asked.

"She wanted to forge a different path in life other than being a wife and mother," Swan said. "We searched for her and Nick finally found her. She gave birth and sent him home with you. After your dad and I got married I legally adopted you. Questions?"

Sage paused for a beat. "Did she ever explain why she left Dad and gave me up?"

Swan nodded. "She sent a letter home with Nick. You can read it tonight. She wanted the best for you and knew that Dad would raise you with love and care."

Sage ran her tongue along the inside of her mouth and squinted. She said, "Okay. So, this leaves me with an issue."

Swan looked at her husband. "Why does she talk like that?"

Memphis shrugged. "Beats me. Mom said she has an old soul." He looked at his daughter. "What's the issue?"

"Elijah," Sage said succinctly. "He's not my cousin, is he?"

"No," Swan said. "He's your half-brother."

"So, am I supposed to think of him as a cousin or brother?"

"You're going to have to figure that out," Memphis said. "Whatever you decide will be the right decision."

"Does he know?"

"I doubt it," Swan said. "You know, you don't have to decide right now. Read the letter, ask questions, take it in, and come to a conclusion in your own time."

"Snow killed her husband, his father, didn't she?"

"Yes," Swan said quietly. The pain was always fresh when she thought about her sister murdering Elijah's father, who turned out to be her legal husband. "He was apparently not only a crazy radical, but he abused her and their son. She killed him to protect herself and her child, and she left Elijah with our brother to raise."

"She gave up both her kids," Sage said sadly. "She must be a very unhappy woman."

"I think so," Swan said. "Now let me ask you a question—how did you come to the conclusion that I wasn't your biological mother?"

"A lot of whispering when Elijah came to stay. Furtive glances, that sort of thing."

"We were going to tell you when we felt you were old enough to understand and deal with it," Memphis said quietly.

"Like, my college graduation?"

"Somewhere along those lines."

"Parents," Sage said in exasperation. "You don't give kids enough credit for brains and flexibility."

Memphis looked at his wife. "Yet another high school big word. She'll be in Harvard by next year."

"Not my kid," Swan said. "I want her closer. Stanford."

"Do I have any say in this?" Sage asked.

"Of course, sweetheart," Swan crooned. "But try to remember that we're paying the bills."

"What if I get a scholarship?"

"Do you have an answer for everything?" Memphis grumbled, secretly thrilled at his daughter's maturity and pizzazz.

"In this family you have to. But I promise to take your opinions into consideration."

Memphis shook his head. "I'm not even going to argue with her anymore. My brain would explode."

"It's only going to get worse when the twins enter adolescence," Swan said. "And it could start all over again if we add to the brood."

"I forbid you to get pregnant again," Memphis said.

Swan smiled slyly. "Too late, Geronimo."

"Huh? No … You *are*?"

"I am." She looked at Sage. "Looks like you're going to be a big sister again."

Sage whooped and threw her arms around Swan's neck, nearly strangling her. They both looked at Memphis, whose face had morphed into a semblance of shell shock.

"Dad's so happy that his face is frozen," Sage said.

Swan nodded. "Ecstatic that his diapering days aren't yet over."

"I need a drink," Memphis muttered.

"Well, while you are acquainting yourself with that bottle of tequila in your bottom drawer, Sage and I are going out for a milkshake. The twins are in the daycare center with the other kids. Come on, honey. I'm thinking chocolate."

Sage jumped up and said, "Strawberry." She wriggled her fingers at Memphis. "Bye, Dad. Later."

"Later, gator," Swan said in a singsong voice as she ushered their daughter out of the office. Memphis poured a good, stiff drink into his "World's Best Dad" shot glass.

Sand and Akiro took the day off. Instead of picking Elijah up before the conference they decided to let him play hooky and spend the day with his uncles. The six-year-old was a serious child who rarely smiled even when he was happy. He had spent the first few years of his life hiding his emotions from his father, who had little tolerance for a gentle, thoughtful kid. Ryder Jackson was a force of nature, alternately charming and kind and angry and abusive. Elijah had seen his father hit his mother several times, and then inflicted his frustration and passion on their little boy. That changed his mother who was a mama bear with her cub, and although she might tolerate some physical abuse from her husband there was no way she was going to let him make their child a target.

Elijah was coming out of his shell, but it was taking a long time. He shied away at first from affectionate hugs by his mother's brother and sister, and the man-friend that his uncle lived with. He liked the house in which they were living. It was warm and comfortable and ... stable. He had a big room that his uncle(s) helped him decorate. They'd even put a small TV set on his dresser. They bought him new clothes, and a baseball and bat. Uncle Akiro took him out to the back yard on weekends to practice. Uncle Sand would read him stories at night and answer his questions on why the Grinch hated Christmas and were there really green eggs?

When his father was alive Elijah rarely socialized with other children. He and his mom were always moving around as his father did his work, whatever that work was. When he asked Daddy about his work Ryder smiled at him, patted his head, and said he was making the world a better place. Now that he was living with his Uncle Sand, he had a swarm of family kids to play with, and then kids he met in school. He had never gone to a school; it was a new experience. He was teased at first but slowly the other kids came to accept him. On occasion one of them would make a comment about his murderous dad and mom, and he learned to push back.

Of all the family kids he liked Sage the best. She was the oldest, and besides being beautiful she was smart, and nice, and protective of her sisters. He liked the other kids, too, and maybe his second favorite was Elspeth. Her father was short, but he was compassionate and loving towards his only child. The more Elijah saw inside the family interactions the more he realized that maybe his father wasn't as nice. He missed his mother, though, and it was weird seeing Aunt Swan since she looked just like Mom.

Besides the real cousins and the unofficial cousins Elijah was overwhelmed with aunts and uncles. Uncle Sand, Uncle Akiro, Uncle Memphis, Uncle Nick, Uncle Percy, Uncle Luc, Uncle Tucson, Aunt Swan, Aunt Tansee, Aunt Yuki, Aunt Raleigh, Aunt Candy, and Aunt Cameo. Uncle Memphis's mother said he could call her Gram and her husband Gramps.

Today was a special day. His uncles played hooky with him and they drove him east of the city to a small horse farm where he was given a pony ride. He'd never had one, and he was so excited that they let him take a second ride. On the way home they stopped at a diner and had milkshakes. They saw Aunt Swan and Sage there also drinking milkshakes and sat with them. He wondered why Sage was giving him a funny look. He blushed; she was so cool.

Back home his uncles played baseball with him for an hour, then they sat on the couch and watched TV. He enjoyed *The $20,000 Pyramid* but didn't get the whole *One Life to Live* show that Uncle Akiro called a soap opera. Uncle Sand made tacos for dinner and in the evening they all cuddled and watch *The Life and Times of Grizzly Adams* before he was shuffled off to bed. Uncle Sand said it was a great Hump Day, but, confused, Elijah didn't ask what the day had to do with a camel.

Tansee was spending the day at Sangre de Cristo Hospital as a favor for her old mentor. He was interested in genetics, too, and had guided her through that specific discipline, engaging in heated and fascinating back-and-forth discussions about the part genetics played in the development of humanity. She promised to be home by five at the latest so that she and Percy could take Elspeth to her favorite restaurant for dinner, Malagueña Fiesta. Elspeth was addicted to their enchiladas, a passion she shared with her father.

Percy glanced down at his office floor where Elspeth was sitting on a blanket trying to fit Legos together with a decent amount of success. She was totally focused on her efforts, frowning and opening her eyes wide and trying alternate ways of fitting the plastic pieces together. Percy watched his daughter, pleased with her obvious intelligence and determination. She looked like her mother, but she had a good percentage of her father in her, too. Her beloved Maltese, Pookie, was sitting patiently by her side, guarding her with adoring eyes.

He thought about Tansee's most recent miscarriage and wondered if they should abandon any chance to produce a second child. Each miscarriage took its toll on both of them although they forced themselves to focus on the joyful child they had. Also, Percy was worried that if she did carry another baby to term the child would suffer from his form of dwarfism. Tansee professed no concern that this might be the case, but Percy knew what it was like to grow up "different." True, the times were different from the 1930s and 1940s in which he grew to young adulthood, but their civilization wasn't enlightened enough for the condition to not be a significant factor in a child's or adult's life.

Percy considered a vasectomy. He brought the subject up carefully with his wife; she shot it down without considering his arguments. She wasn't a super religious person, but she believed that nature knew what it was doing, and that people should take what comes and make the best of it.

"Enough," Percy said to his daughter who looked up at him curiously.

"I didn't finish, Daddy," Elspeth said. She held out a red plastic Lego. "I have to put this in."

"Well, put it in and then we're going to go somewhere really cool."

Elspeth scrambled to her feet. "Where?" she asked eagerly.

"We're going to visit the Taos Pueblo. That's where that painter lives. You can see the real building in your portrait."

Elspeth looked flustered and stared at the plastic in her hands. She looked up at her father pleadingly. "Do I have to finish the red thing?"

Percy smiled at her. "Yes, but not right now. Let's go for a ride."

Elspeth jumped up and down. "Yea," she exclaimed. Pookie spun around and barked.

Tucson was sitting in his office chair with baby Brett cuddled snugly in his left arm while he made notes on a case file he was working. He had been treating a Vietnam vet named Ralph Mancini for six months and had made only minimal progress. He hadn't expressed the thought to anyone, even Percy or Cameo, but this guy had been a prisoner of war in the Hanoi Hilton and was exhibiting far too many similar characteristics that Tucson was experiencing. Unlike Tucson, Mancini's side effects of his war experience were consistent; Tucson experienced the most severe psychological events on a sporadic basis. Unfortunately, Tucson's experiences were becoming more frequent.

Mancini experienced repetitive nightmares. Tucson had nightmares, too, but even worse he was afflicted by night terrors, or sleep terrors as they are sometimes called. Nightmares take place during REM sleep and are basically defined as frightening dreams. Sleep terrors are classified as a parasomnia—an undesirable behavior or experience during sleep. Sleep terrors are a disorder of arousal, meaning they occur during N3 sleep, the deepest stage of non-rapid eye movement (NREM) sleep. When the person awakes from a nightmare very little of the dream is remembered. Night terrors are an entirely different animal, several levels in intensity and psychological effect above nightmares. Night terrors are characterized by screaming, intense fear, and violent flailing while asleep. Generally occurring during the first third or half of the night but rarely during naps, night terrors can lead to sleepwalking.

Symptoms of a night terror experience often follow a common path:

- Screaming or shouting in fear
- Sitting up in bed and appearing frightened
- Staring wide-eyed
- Sweating, heavy breathing, a racing pulse, flushed face, and dilated pupils
- Kicking and thrashing
- Difficult to awaken, and confused if awakened
- Being inconsolable
- Having no or little memory of the event the next morning
- Possibly getting out of bed and running around the house or having aggressive behavior if blocked or restrained

Tucson had experienced them all. The first time a night terror happened when he and Cameo were sleeping together scared the hell out of her, but to her credit she talked with him, held him, and told him that she loved him and they'd get through this together. She had her own nightmares that were intense but evaporated as soon as she woke up; she remembered nothing of the bad dream. Since they started living together his night terrors had diminished but not entirely disappeared. He experienced one the night his twins were dropped on his doorstep, and four since. He mentioned the first one to Percy who abandoned his let's-see approach and strongly urged Tucson to see him professionally. Reluctantly, Tucson agreed to see his partner in a professional capacity weekly and that was helping to blanket his psyche with a comforting relaxation and acceptance of the past. He was doing his best to create an intimate and safe environment for his kids.

Cameo had the twins today, picking them up after school and driving them to her office to show them around the newspaper. She told them that their mother had once worked there and was considered a top-notch reporter and writer. She dug into the archives and came up with several articles that Cassidy had written, and she sat cross-legged between them and read what their mother had written. She was making slow progress with the twins accepting her as their stepmother, but little by little the ice was cracking. There was no doubt that their beer-making nanny, Declan, was a big influence. He had become indispensable to the family, especially when Brett was born.

Tucson put down his pen and stared into the scrunched-up face of his sleeping son. *I am so blessed*, he thought. He kissed Brett's soft forehead.

Yuki had taken her and Nick's kids and her parents to San Francisco for a couple of days. There was a Japanese festival going on and she wanted to expose her kids to their maternal culture. Her parents hadn't been back since they were ripped from their lives and shipped off to the Santa Fe internment camp in 1942. They agreed that it was past time to face their ghosts and catch up with any old friends that might have survived the war and moved back to their homes.

Nick had wanted to go with them, but he had an obligation to stick around and be involved in the new possible clue to the disappearances. Frick and Frack had interviewed people from the various Indian activist groups, but no new clues turned up. He was surprised that the artist Hashkeh Naabah was a member of a group up near Taos; surprised because he simply assumed that art was the entire focus of Naabah's life. The artist had spent a full hour talking with Frick and Frack and explaining the roots of so many groups and how the persecution and neglect that Indians had endured since the white man first landed on the country's shores had been endured and suppressed for centuries. Now, he said, Indians were demanding change, accountability, and, perhaps, punishment.

Naabah's words rang true and Nick thought he understood, but as a white man he knew he never really could any more than he could fully absorb the enormity of how the Japanese-Americans had suffered during World War II. His wife, Yuki, had been born and lived the first part of her childhood in the Santa Fe internment camp. Her brother, Akiro, had entered the camp as a baby and spent nearly four years incarcerated.

Nick missed his wife and kids. He thought, case be damned, it had waited this long. He called Skye and asked her to get him on the next plane to San Francisco. He couldn't spend another night without his wife in his arms, or another breakfast without Mariko and Zenjiro.

Candy had worked a full but easy day at her job. Percy and Tucson didn't have any clients today and both left the office by three. She packed up her schoolbooks which she studied on her breaks and down time. She was studying pre-law, taking a half course load each semester. She had her sights on becoming a lawyer and knew that there would be a place for her in Akiro's firm.

Until six months ago she was focused on two things, school and motherhood. She had been crazy in love with her late husband, Troy, and never dated after he was killed. Oh, she was asked, but nothing felt right.

Until Dante Redwolf.

They saw each other frequently since they worked in the same building, and he was always pleasant and nice to her. To everybody, really. Memphis told her that Dante was turning out to be an excellent investigator. Gradually their paths crossed more frequently, and one day he stopped by her desk with flowers and asked if she'd like to see a movie with him.

Candy stared at him, then smelled the flowers. She closed her eyes and let a gentle smile cross her lovely face. To Dante's apparent surprise she said yes. They went on a Saturday to see *Gable and Lombard.* They shared a tub of popcorn. Halfway through the film

Dante took her hand and they remained linked that way for the rest of the movie. Candy felt a sharp pain in her heart when Carole Lombard died on screen.

They took their courtship slow, and even today they still hadn't been intimate. Candy was conflicted by her lost love for Troy and the potential for a new love and future. Her conflict lessened as Dante showed how caring he was towards Chessie. She probed Memphis for his opinion of the young man, and her brother-in-law gave him the green light.

When she left work, she picked up Chessie at home and Dante arrived to take them to a picnic at the park. It was obvious that Chessie adored her mommy's friend. Chessie was playing with jacks when her mother and Dante met eyes over her head. Suddenly, Candy knew it was time to grab ahold of the future and go for it.

She reached out her hand and caressed Dante's cheek. There was no mistaking the love in his eyes.

CHAPTER FIVE

"Thanks for helping me clean the shed out," Swan said to Cameo. "I've been holding onto this stuff for too long."

The two women were in the backyard of Swan's house going through a large metal shed which held tools, two bicycles, and a dozen taped-up boxes. The boxes were labeled "Snow" and were the lost sister's possessions from her old spiritual store. Swan had donated her sister's clothes and a few household items she didn't want around, but she and Sand had simply boxed up the store stuff and stored it in various places until she and Memphis had moved into their own house. After eleven years it was well past time to get rid of some of the past.

"No problem," Cameo replied. "I like to keep busy on my days off. I'm so glad Hehewuti is easy about taking care of the baby." The twins were at school and Brett was with his doting grandmother. Grandpa Jakub was up at the cabin building a new firepit. "What's in these boxes anyway?"

Swan grunted as she tried to move a box that was heavy as hell. "Books, candles, other shit. I don't even remember it's been so long. I know I should have labeled them, but I was pissed and just wanted to pack everything up."

"It must have been hard," Cameo said quietly.

"Not as hard as having your sister on the FBI's Most Wanted List," Swan said flatly. "Or being hauled into a police station because someone thought you were her." Swan had been subjected to stares and suspicion in several instances that resulted in having to prove her identity. One time when she was investigating a case in Flagstaff she was arrested and held overnight despite her driver's license and growing aggravation at being mistaken for a deadly fugitive. Thank God for Richard Ballard who drove from Albuquerque to Flagstaff to set the record straight. After that Swan had an intricate swan tattooed over her right shoulder and photographed for FBI records to prove who she was if need be.

Swan threw a guilty look at Cameo. "Sorry. I didn't mean to be so negative. Sometimes it just bubbles up."

"No apology necessary," Cameo said, flashing a genuine smile. Despite their rocky beginning over the past two years the women had come to an understanding. They were sisters-in-law now, loved the two Grayhawk brothers, and were devoted to their lives and their families. They respected one another's professional abilities as well.

Cameo flicked open her box cutter and slit the tape from the top of the heavy box Swan had wedged out of its resting place. "Huh. Books," she said as she picked up the top book and glanced at the cover. "Hesse's *Steppenwolf.* Heavy reading."

Swan slit open another box. "Books here, too." She began taking them out and laying them on the floor.

Cameo did the same, but more slowly. Her box seemed to have a stockpile of spiritual- and occult-themed books. She paused and studied the titles, almost as though in a trance. *Demonology and Witchcraft* by Sir Walter Scott; *The Book of Ceremonial Magic* by Arthur Waite; *Satanism and Witchcraft* by Jules Michelet; and *A Separate Reality* by Carlos Castaneda were just a few at the top of the box. She put them down and picked up the next one.

The Secret Grimoire of Turiel.

Swan looked over at the book Cameo was holding motionlessly in her hands. "What's that?" she asked.

"A grimoire," Cameo murmured absently.

"What's a grimoire?"

"It's a book of spells. It … explains how to create talismans and amulets, and create spells, charms, and divinations."

"Like witch stuff?"

"It's more than that. It can be … dangerous. It shows you how to summon or invoke supernatural entities, like angels and spirits."

"That doesn't sound too dangerous."

Cameo glanced at Swan. "It can also be used to summon demons."

"Is Turiel a place?"

Cameo shook her head. "No. Turiel was a fallen Watcher in the ancient apocryphal text known as the Book of Enoch. He was one of the twenty leaders of two hundred fallen angels. The name is believed to originate from tuwr, 'rock' and El, 'God,' meaning 'rock of God.'"

"How do you know that?"

"I have no idea."

"Maybe you read about this grimoire thing after you got out of the hospital?"

Cameo shook her head. "Do you mind if I keep this book so I can read it?"

"Take whatever you want. What you don't want I'll donate to the library. I'm not sure if they'll want to put this stuff on their shelves, but it's worth a try. I want to put a few things aside for Sage and Elijah so that whatever happens in the future they'll have some things that belonged to their birth mother."

"Thanks. I'll pick out a few."

Two hours later all the boxes had been opened and Swan and Cameo had put aside the things they wanted. Swan repacked all the books to be donated and she labeled them and put the other non-literary stuff in two more boxes for donation to Goodwill. Swan yelled for Luc to come out and put the boxes in the back of the station wagon. The youngest Grayhawk son reluctantly lumbered out of his house and did as he was told. He was a typical college student, devoted to anything other than hard manual work. He had managed to slime out of going with his father to the cabin, so he thought he had the best deal helping his sisters-in-law with their little project.

"Anything else?" he grumbled.

"Yeah," Swan said tartly. "Get your lazy butt in gear and drive those boxes over to the library and then the thrift store. Get receipts."

"Receipts?"

"For tax purposes. Nothing wrong with being practical," Swan said defensively as Luc rolled his eyes. "Just do it, please."

"Fine," Luc said, sighing. Swan threw him the keys and he got into the car and took off without another word.

Swan shook her head. "We still think he's going to wind up behind bars someday, but until then we're keeping him busy."

"How's he doing in college? This is his last year, right?"

"Right. He's studying History and making A's and B's. He's smart enough to make straight A's but he gets distracted easily. Now Raleigh, she's making straight A's in her freshman year."

"Tucson said she's the smartest of all the siblings."

"No argument there."

"Well, if you don't need me for anything else, I think I'll get Brett and head home. I need to polish an article for the paper."

"Where's Declan today?"

Cameo grinned unaffectedly. "He and Akiro are checking out an old warehouse on the north side. You know our nanny worked in Guinness making beer, right?"

"Uh-huh. Love me some Guinness."

"Me, too. But his talents are wasted on just his nanny duties, so Memphis and Tucson made a deal with him to open a microbrewery and make his own custom brand of beer."

"That's fantastic! But I'm going to kill my husband for not telling me."

"It wasn't a done deal until today when they signed the contracts. There's a lot of cost and tasks to do the startup but Declan's thrilled. He actually cried."

"He is sensitive."

"Grill Memphis when he gets home. I think they're still bandying about names for the beer, so you have the chance to put in your two cents. I'm staying out of it."

"Sounds like a plan." Swan winked at Cameo and helped put her stuff into her car while she retrieved Brett. Swan waved goodbye and watched the car recede thoughtfully. Her curiosity had spiked at Cameo's reaction to that weird book. She remembered that in one of her hypnosis sessions with Percy she had written a phrase from Milton's famous book, *Paradise Lost*. Percy hadn't broken the seal of confidentiality; Cameo had told her. Swan decided to find out more about it. Maybe Carmen knew something about the subject or could point her in the right direction.

When Memphis got home, Swan blasted him about not telling her about the brewery. He apologized profusely. She forgave him, then threw out a few possible beer brand names. He agreed that every one of them was fantastic (being wary of spending a night on the couch), but Declan had to make the final call. Wordlessly she turned around and went into the kitchen to make dinner.

The next day Swan dropped the kids off at school but instead of heading directly to the office she drove over to Sangre de Cristo College and knocked on Carmen Castillo's office door. Carmen was happy to see her and ushered her in.

"What can I do you for, Swan?" Carmen asked pleasantly. She was in the middle of grading papers and was thrilled for the interruption. She had to give the last one a "D." Too many students just didn't seem to get the sociopolitical implications of the Spanish Inquisition.

"Well, I'm looking for information on a book. It's not a history book but seems to relate to the occult."

"Really? That's a fascinating subject. There are significant implications throughout history of the occult, even up to today. Did you know that Hitler was into the occult?"

"No, I didn't. That's weird."

"He was a nutjob that used any tools at his disposal to hold onto and spread his power. And the interest in the occult is growing with all the books and movies that have come out. *Rosemary's Baby*, *The Exorcist*, and *The Omen* for example. Anyway, what kind of book?"

"Is there a professor here that knows a lot about the occult, or teaches a class in it?"

"We're not that progressive yet. I've probably got most of the academic knowledge about it here. I know that Professor Peden has studied spiritualism and is knowledgeable, but, honestly, I think I can better answer your questions. I also know a few non-academics in the area that could fill in some blanks. Wasn't your sister into it a little bit? She had that shop."

Swan nodded. "And that's why I'm here. Cameo and I were clearing out some old boxes of Snow's stuff for donations and she came across this book that seemed to affect her. The name of the book was *The Secret Grimoire of Turiel*. She gave me a brief explanation of what a grimoire was and who Turiel was."

"Sounds familiar. A fallen angel, I believe. My parents were devout Catholics and we read more than just the Bible in our home."

"So, you know what a grimoire is? Any chance you can immerse me into its history and usage?"

"I can try," Carmen said. "Basically, it's a book of magic. How to cast spells, raise spirits, that sort of stuff."

"Cameo said it could be used to invoke demons."

Carmen nodded. "There's that. Some say the physical book itself may have supernatural powers."

"Is it a single book?"

"Heavens, no. There are grimoires all over the history of man. The title of the one you said is the grimoire specifically of that fallen angel." She held up a finger and walked over to her bookcase and scanned the titles. She pulled one out, flipped through it, put it back, and did the same for two more. On her fourth try she said, "Aha" and walked back to her desk. "This is a book that has a chapter devoted to spiritualism in Medieval times. I knew I'd read that name somewhere." She showed Swan the book cover with the title *Spiritualism in Medieval Times*.

"What does the chapter say?" Swan was intrigued.

Carmen flipped through a couple of pages before going back to the beginning of the chapter. “The book is supposed to give the magician the means of contacting Turiel. Supposedly it was written in 1518, but it might have been copied from a manuscript even older than that. Some guy named Marius Malchus got ahold of it in 1927. It was an English translation of a Latin work that was sold to him by a defrocked priest. The English version was only published in 1960. There seemed to be a lot of contention as to whether some of the parts were plagiarized from other books, but the matter was never settled.”

“What about these … grimoires in general? How far back do they go?”

“Way back. Magical incantations were found on clay tablets from Mesopotamia that archeologists excavated from the city of Uruk in what’s now present-day Iraq. They dated them to around the fourth and fifth centuries BC. Around the same time the Egyptians had similar tablets. The ancient Greeks and Romans believed that magical books were devised by the Persians. Pliny the Elder believed that magic had been first discovered by the ancient philosopher Zoroaster around the year 647 BC but that it was only written down in the fifth century BC by the magician Osthanes. Even Christians were all over magic and the spirits. King Solomon was associated with magic and sorcery.”

“I’d think that Christians were against that type of magic.”

“Oh, in later periods, yes. After the fall of the Roman Empire such books were suppressed by the growing faith and its leaders. The New Testament records that after the unsuccessful exorcism by the seven sons of Sceva became known, many converts decided to burn their own magic and pagan books in the city of Ephesus in what’s now Turkey. This attitude and action were adopted on a large scale after the Christian ascent to power. That didn’t stop the propagation of new grimoires even by Christians. Finally, the faith had to accept some form of grimoire to pacify and control the masses. The Church divided books of magic into two categories: those that dealt with ‘natural magic’ and those that dealt in ‘demonic magic.’”

“And Turiel’s book?”

"I've never seen any text from it but considering that the point was to summon a fallen angel, I'm thinking it would be in the latter category. Since you've got a copy you can look for yourself. I'd love to read it someday."

"I gave it to Cameo but I'm sure she'd have no problem lending it back to me. Are there any more recent grimoires available?"

"Sure. They've been produced for hundreds of years. I think they've become much more accepted and popular with the new taste for horror movies and books. I think *Rosemary's Baby* started the current modern taste for the supernatural."

"I saw the movie. It's all about witches."

"No, it's not," Carmen said with a touch of frustration. "It's not about witches."

"That's what was said in the movie and the book."

"Because the author didn't understand the two concepts and write about the correct one."

"Which two concepts?"

"Witchcraft and Satanism."

"They're not the same thing?"

"Absolutely not. They share some outward affectations, but their intrinsic purposes are poles apart. Witches, or Wiccans, draw their spiritualism from the earth and celestial bodies. There are bad witches just like bad Christians or Jews, but basically, it's a pacific, respectful religion. Satanism, on the other hand, is anything but. Satanists worship Satan, the devil. By the very nature of their 'god' they're evil and desire to perpetrate evil in the world. It's a malignant religion."

"You don't really believe there's a devil, do you?"

"Do you believe in God?"

"Yes."

"Then you have to believe in Satan. They're flip sides of the spiritual coin."

"I never thought of it that way."

"Here," Carmen said, handing Swan the book. "Take it home and read it, and I'll root around and see if I can find any more information. No hurry in getting it back."

Swan took the book and they both stood. “Thanks, Carmen.” She smiled. “How’s it going with Candy and Dante?”

Carmen laughed. “Slow but sure. She still holds onto her past love for Troy, but I think she’s coming around to realize that she has a life to live and Troy would want her to go on and find love and joy.”

“I hope so. She’s overdue. I’ll get this back to you soon.” Swan winked at Carmen and left the office. Carmen sighed and made mental notes about contacts for more background, then she went back to grading papers. She smiled in satisfaction; her best student got a well-deserved A+. She wrote it across the top of the paper with a big red marker.

Cameo didn’t have time the day before to read through the book. She had to get dinner ready, finish her article, and … No, those were just excuses. Something inside of her didn’t want to open the book, didn’t even want to touch it. She put it in a desk drawer in the den and went about her business. She put the other books and items in her salvage box in the garage.

Tucson came thought the front door at six; Declan bounced through the front door right after him. Cameo had never seen him so happy. Clearly, the contracts and warehouse had gone well. Declan picked baby Brett from the crib and plunked him down on his lap as he wedged himself between Brae and Bree on the couch. Tucson planted a kiss on her ready lips and asked if she needed any help with dinner. She shook her head and asked him to set the table.

Declan had taught her some Irish dishes and tonight she’d made corned beef and cabbage. The twins loved that and finished every morsel on their plates. Without her asking they carried their plates to the kitchen sink. Tucson did the dishes (i.e., stacked them in the dishwasher), then took his youngest son into the living room to watch the evening news. Declan chattered endlessly about his plans for the brewery and threw out a few names he was considering. She told him that she liked the last one, Desert Dream Brewery.

The rest of the evening went by as usual although she had to forcibly put the book out of her mind. Luckily, Tucson wasn't in an amorous mood and fell asleep quickly. She stayed awake staring at the ceiling. He started twisting and turning and talking in his sleep in Korean; he'd done it before. He had picked up quite a bit of the language during his captivity. She elbowed him and he simmered down. She fell asleep two hours before dawn.

Cameo got up and made coffee and sipped a cup in a solitary, silent communion with just herself. She heard activity and knew Declan was on his way into the kitchen for his tea before he'd wake up the twins, get them dressed, and take them to school. She made his tea and they exchanged a few words. She asked him casually if he'd take Brett to the firm's daycare center. She had a lot of work to get done and needed complete solitude. He didn't mind at all.

By eight the men, children, and baby were out of the house. Cameo called into work sick. Then she went into the den, took the book, and headed down to the basement, a rarity in the desert southwest and one of the buying points for the house. Tucson had paneled it with walnut planks and added a wood stove. A couch, a recliner, a coffee table, plus a console stereo added to the relaxed ambience. She sat cross-legged in the middle of the carpeted floor, took several deep breaths, and opened the book.

Slowly, page by page, she read the text and studied the images. When she finished, she closed the book and closed her eyes. She swayed ever so slightly. Like TV static an image was forming in her mind until it came together and was as vivid and clear as a movie screen.

Three books, three black candles, two yellow candles on top of a wooden table.

She could smell the incense.

She could feel the stifling heat ripping through her body like blood fire.

She could hear the soft chanting.

She could feel the discomfort of being restrained on a large stone slab.

She could feel the silky black robe encasing her body.

She heard the ominous chanting of the people rhythmically swaying in the dark night.

She could feel the rough hands holding her down.

She could feel herself being lost in a pair of fathomless, pitiless black, black eyes suffused with victory and rage.

Suddenly Cameo jumped up and the book went tumbling across the floor. She stuffed an end of a knitted afghan into her mouth as much as she could then she flung herself on the couch face-down into a pillow and clutched it to the sides of her head.

She screamed.

And screamed and screamed and screamed.

Because she remembered everything.

CHAPTER SIX

"Some good-looking black guy wants to see you, boss," Skye said as she stood under Memphis's door jam.

"That's a pretty hefty compliment coming from you," Memphis replied as he leaned back in his chair. "And this coming from someone who said that Paul Newman was overrated."

"Stunning blue eyes aside, I prefer them dark and mysterious."

"This guy mysterious?"

"Maybe. Should I bring him in?"

"No, let him sit out there just being good-looking."

Skye rolled her eyes and huffed off, returning in a moment with the dude she thought put Billy Dee Williams to shame.

"DeVere," Memphis exclaimed as he jumped up. He grinned and walked around the desk for a hearty handshake. He noticed that Skye was still standing at the door. "You may leave now," he said politely to her. He smiled again. "Sit, sit. It's good to see you." He frowned at the serious look on DeVere's face. "I think."

DeVere sat down. "I don't suppose I can get a cup of coffee?" He eyed the Mr. Coffee machine with a half carafe full of coffee he could smell from his seat.

Memphis filled a mug and refilled his own and put them down. "Not that I'm not glad to see you, but I'm guessing this isn't totally a social call."

"Not exactly," DeVere said. "Couple of things that I thought you should know about. They may mean nothing, but I don't like coincidences."

Memphis leaned forward. "Tell me. No, wait." He rang up Swan who appeared a minute later, as surprised as her husband had been at their guest. DeVere rose and hugged her, then Swan sat down next to him.

"What's up?" she said. "This a social call? Vacation?"

"Not really," DeVere confirmed. "Some news from back east."

Swan leaned towards him. "Someone recognize Cameo's photo?"

"I don't know. It's Eddie Troy."

"The photographer?" Swan said. "He have any news?"

"No," DeVere said. "He's dead."

Both Memphis and Swan were shocked into dead silence. Memphis finally found his voice. "How?"

"His house burned down with him in it."

"Holy shit," Swan exclaimed. "What happened?"

"The fire investigator said it looked like he was in the basement when it started—there was smoke in his lungs, and it seems like the wood stove down there got out of hand and before he could stamp out the start of the flames the smoke inhalation knocked him out. The house was old, and the wood frame was very dry, so it went up like a tinderbox. There wasn't much left of him before the firemen could put out the flames. But there was enough flesh left to do the autopsy that found the smoke in the lungs."

"So, he couldn't have been dead before the fire started," Memphis said.

"Apparently not."

"But …" Swan said, seeing the odd look on DeVere's face.

"But the medical examiner found something odd on his corpse."

"What?"

DeVere pulled out an autopsy photo of a long nail. “The doctor found this near the back of his thigh.”

“He had a nail in his leg?” Swan exclaimed.

DeVere nodded. “A nasty one. It was so far in his leg that the head wouldn’t show, the shaft was completely encased in the flesh, and the point scratched the bone. It didn’t go in by hand.”

“Nail gun?” Memphis said.

“That’s what I’m thinking,” DeVere said, nodding. “And, the M.E. said there were a couple of muscle tears that could have been the result of other nails. If so, then whoever put them there tried to take them out to mask what had to be torture. Apparently, a large part of the drywall ceiling fell on his body’s midsection and provided enough of a shield to prevent him from being burned to a crisp. His arms and legs were pretty much incinerated. The medical examiner specified the cause of death was accidental death by smoke inhalation, but I’m not so sure. It’s kind of coincidental that someone we conferred with about your case winds up dying in a fire with a nail in his leg. I talked to some of his friends and neighbors and they all said he was a very responsible homeowner and was meticulous about keeping his house clean and safe.”

“How’d you find out about Eddie?” Swan asked.

“My brother saw the story in the *Portsmouth Herald* and called me. I drove out to check on the investigation. I stayed a couple of days. I met his sister, Sigrid, and went back to Pittsfield right after the funeral. My brother said that he’d keep me posted about anything that comes up.”

“You said a couple of things,” Memphis said.

DeVere nodded. “When I got back to Pittsfield, I got the sense … I don’t know, that I was being watched. Nothing concrete I could put my finger on, but just a sense.”

“You’re a good cop,” Swan said. “You think you’re being watched, you’re being watched. Any ideas who? Or why?”

“Not a clue. But coupled with Eddie’s death I thought I should let you guys know what’s going on. I mean, if this does have to do with Cameo, and Eddie was targeted, he might have led someone to me, or to you. And, ultimately, to her. If that's true, then someone deadly and sadistic is looking for her."

Memphis looked at Swan. "I think we need to bring Cameo, Tucson, and Percy into this discussion. If someone's out there that may be dangerous to us, we need to take precautions and try to determine who they are." He looked at DeVere. "Do you have to go right back, or can you stick around for a few days?"

"I took a week's vacation. Thought I'd see some of the sights. I've never been west of the Mississippi. And, I've never eaten Mexican." He smiled.

"You're in for a treat," Swan said. "We know the best Mexican restaurant in town. We'll take you there for dinner. I don't want to bring Cameo and the others in to talk about this for a day or two until we do some more research and brainstorm. I don't want to panic them."

"I'll put security around Cameo and Tucson. Devon will be perfect for the job. Devon's an east coast girl so you'll have something in common."

"She pretty?" DeVere asked.

"Beautiful," Swan said. "Smart, too. She used to be a cop."

DeVere threw his hands up. "What—is everyone in this firm an ex-cop?"

"Just three of us," Swan said. "Me and my brother and Devon. You'll meet everyone in the firm before you have to leave."

"I'm looking forward to it. Where should we start?"

"Let me start by grabbing Devon and bringing her into the loop. I'll tell her as little as possible, but she'll have to know about Eddie's death and your stalker. By the way—have you told your family about this?"

"I told ReVere to be cautious. He always is anyway."

"We need two people watching the families," Swan said. "Dante?"

Memphis shook his head. "He's a smart kid but he's still green around the edges. I'm thinking Sand or Nick."

"Nick."

"Okay. Get him and Devon in here and we'll start planning."

Swan whipped out of her chair and left the office. She came back ten minutes later with a good-looking white guy in his early thirties and a gorgeous mixed-race woman in her late twenties. Yeah, DeVere thought. He could work with her. He smiled, flashing his perfectly straight white teeth at Devon. She looked at him balefully.

"Keep it in your pants, Poitier. We're all business around here," Devon said pointedly.

DeVere's mouth dropped open and he was at a complete loss for words. His ears burned when everyone in the room started laughing.

Harlan Barrett and Francis "Frankie" Conway had been best friends since the first grade when they attended the same elementary school in San Ramon, California. Their families lived three houses away from each other on a quiet street. Each had a sister and a stay-at-home mother. Frankie's father worked at a nearby country club as a groundskeeper while Harlan's father worked in Oakland as a bank security guard. Both boys did well at school and each entertained thoughts of college. Neither set of parents could afford to send their son to even a public college, so they worked part-time after school and all day on Saturdays. Their dream was to attend Merritt Community College and transfer to a four-year college if they proved to be academic material. Their long-term dream was to open some sort of business together.

Like most children born in the 1950s and raised on TV they were psychologically immersed in the fantasy world of westerns. They had a steady diet of *Maverick*, *Cheyenne*, *Gunsmoke*, *Bonanza*, *Have Gun Will Travel*, *The Big Valley*, *The High Chaparral*, and so many more. When they were little, they'd sit too close in front of their black-and-white TV sets with cowboy hats and plastic holsters on and fall into the world of cowboys and Indians. They gorged on films that highlighted the magnificent west, especially John Wayne movies with Monument Valley as a backdrop. They swore that someday they'd explore those hills and mountains and deserts just like the Duke and his buddies did.

Harlan was accepted into the college, but Frankie's grades fell a little short. They decided that they'd take a year off and try again in the fall of 1977 to get into another college together. That would give them time to save up some money and investigate where they might matriculate. There was never a question of one going to college and the other not. Harlan's parents begged him to reconsider, but he stuck to his guns. Instead, they decided to explore their dreams after high school graduation for six months, then return home, get jobs, save money, and try again in the spring. Harlan's parents asked him how he planned on seeing the sights without a car, and Harlan stuck out his thumb and grinned.

Three days after graduation Harlan and Frankie hauled their heavy backpacks onto their shoulders, kissed their families goodbye, and started on the first leg of their journey. Harlan's dad drove them to Daly City where they caught a ride on Route 1 south (Frankie wanted to stop in Carmel and see if they could find one of the famous residents, *Rawhide*'s Clint Eastwood). The plan was to hit the I-10 in L.A. and head through Arizona to New Mexico, then north in that state to Colorado and back west into Nevada before heading home to San Ramon.

They never caught a glimpse of Clint but loved the little town and spent a night sleeping under the stars. They decided against visiting any tourist sites in L.A. and instead concentrated on hitching to Phoenix. Frankie had heard about the fabled Lost Dutchman's Mine in the Superstition Mountains, and they delayed their journey for two days camping in those daunting hills but never finding any cave or mine entrance that might make them millionaires. They bought a map of southwestern gold mines from a local vendor and noted with glee that there were mines all along their projected route. Suddenly, with the exuberance that only naïve eighteen-year-olds can muster, they decided that was going to be their goal, to explore old mines along their route.

They stopped in Tucson where they went about exploring old mines like the Old Yuma Mine, the Gila Monster Mine, and the Gould Mine. Those sites weren't necessarily open to the public, but they were determined and managed to get in during dusk or first thing in the morning before residents and tourists could interrupt their fun.

They thumbed their way into New Mexico where they took a mine break and visited the Carlsbad Caverns. They had never seen anything like it, and now exploring caves and mines started bubbling up as a passion. They pushed north into New Mexico and found a few out-of-the-way old mines like the Hayner Ruby Mine in the Organ Mountains. Once they had a scary experience when they were inside an old shaft and a rumble of dirt and rocks scared them shitless as they dug their way out. Once out, they looked at one another, broke into laughter, and gave each other a high five. They were having fun. They were amateur spelunkers. Harlan said they should find a place to make custom tee-shirts saying just that. They had spelunked caves back home in northern California, but nothing dangerous and their dads were always with them.

Northeast of Albuquerque they explored the mining ghost town of Hagan. They visited several pueblos including Taos and were in respectful awe of this culture they had once only seen in cinematic but unrealistic glory. They were beginning to appreciate the reality of the Indian, Mexican, and melded southwest cultures.

Best intentions aside, by October they were getting tired of living without a bed, indoor plumbing, and mom's home cooking. They decided that they'd explore a few places once they entered Colorado then make a hitchhiking beeline home. Along the way since they had started, they had done short, odd jobs to line their pockets and make enough money for food. Their parents had given them a hundred dollars each and told them to try to make it last.

They weren't in too terribly a hurry to get to Colorado, though. Both young men had fallen in love with the magnificent Sangre de Cristo Mountains and decided to camp out and hike for a week or so before continuing their journey. They had one collapsible fishing pole and knew how to find bait, and gut and roast fish; their fathers had taken them fishing ever since they were kids. In the mountains there were always streams where catching dinner was possible.

They had been camped near some hole in the wall called Questa at the western base of the Taos Mountains for two nights and were enjoying their hikes. They found a couple of small caves which they crawled into, hoping to find something special. Once, they found a shard of pottery that looked old and Harlan stuck that in his backpack.

Late that morning they were exploring the area near a steep, craggy rock outcropping deep into the mountains. Harlan noticed that there seemed to be a rudimentary, narrow path that looked manmade. Finding the path was sheer luck; a fox had darted across the trail they were following and when Frankie jumped back, he literally fell into the new path. They followed its winding trajectory for a good mile until they came to a dense part of the mountains that abutted a steep, rocky cliff face. Frankie shoved some thick, sharp branches aside and was startled when he saw what looked like a dark entrance to what could be a cave. He excitedly yelled to his friend to come closer.

They moved branches and squeezed through an opening that tore tiny scratches on their hands and Harlan's cheek. Harlan cursed softly and took out his flashlight; Frankie did the same.

"Shit, look," Frankie exclaimed. "It is a cave."

"Damn," Harlan said softly. "What if it's a bear's den?"

"I don't hear anything. I don't smell anything, either. Don't bears stink?"

"All wild animals stink. Okay, let's go inside. But be ready to run."

"I wish we had a gun."

"You'd shoot yourself in the foot," Harlan said. "Then I'd have to carry you back to camp." Harlan took a deep breath and pushed aside the last heavy bush branches hiding the cave entrance. He smelled the dankness as soon as he made it through the cave entrance, Frankie right behind him. He flashed his light around the entrance. "Huh," he said.

The cave walls near the entry were smooth rock that went back at least ten feet, the distance that his light would illuminate. Frankie flashed his light at the other wall and nudged his friend. It was then that they noticed the paintings on the wall, primitive figures, humans and animals, seeming not especially random but positioned almost as though to tell a story.

"I saw cave art like this in a book on France," Harlan whispered.

"You think Indians did this?" Frankie whispered back.

"No, dumbo—African pygmies. Of course, Indians did this. Wow. We should've brought our camera with us."

"It takes sucky indoor pictures anyway. Let's go farther."

"You sure?"

"No, but let's go anyway. I'll lead." Frankie cautiously moved forward, wishing they'd brought bigger flashlights. They illuminated the walls with what they had and were stunned into silence at the wealth of cave art that was almost as dense as a tapestry on each side of the cave. About ten feet in they noticed that the walls were widening as though opening to a large chamber.

They were. Twenty feet in both teenagers stopped dead in their tracks as their flashlights illuminated a huge circular chamber.

The huge chamber wasn't empty.

"Holy Mother of God," Harlan whispered hoarsely. "Holy Mother of God."

"Jesus friggin' H Christ," Frankie expelled. His mother would have been appalled at his language, but maybe in this case she would have said the same.

Except for those excited utterances the boys were struck speechless. The silence hung heavy in the still air. They felt the breath sucked out of their lungs as they held their flashlights, the only motion the soundless sweeping back and forth of the beams that revealed the contents of the chamber.

"Yá'át'ééh."

Harlan and Frankie whirled around in unison at the voice behind them. Their beams illuminated the form of an Indian man who was standing in a non-threatening, relaxed stance, his hands at his sides, no weapon in sight. For a split second, Harlan wondered how the man had come so far in the dark cave with no sign of a flashlight or lantern. There was something like a gym bag on the ground. He had a slight smile on his face.

He spoke again. “Yá’át’ééh. That is hello in Navajo.”

Harlan found his voice, but his words came out strangled with uncertainty. “Uh, uh … hello. We … we didn’t mean to trespass. Uh, is this your cave?”

“No man can own the earth,” the Indian said.

“Um, okay. We were … we were just exploring,” Frankie said. “We don’t mean any harm.”

Po’Pay smiled. “I believe you. Are you camping around here?”

“Yes, sir,” Harlan said quickly, eager to dispel the man of any misinterpretation of their presence. “We’ve got a camp about a mile down near that crooked stream with the beaver dam.”

“I see. What do you think of this place?” There was genuine curiosity in Po’Pay’s voice.

“It’s incredible,” Frankie said enthusiastically. “Oh, my God. Did you do all this?”

“This is my work. I’m sorry.”

“Sorry?” Harlan said, confused.

“I’m sorry you had to discover it. You seem like decent boys. Wrong place, wrong time.” Without a second’s hesitation Po’Pay pulled a Bowie knife from the rear of his belt and flung it at Harlan, hitting him dead center in the heart. Harlan stared at his killer for one second before tumbling to the ground, dead.

Frankie sobbed and backed up against the wall, his head thrashing back and forth in terror.

Po’Pay stopped and pulled the knife from Harlan’s heart and walked to the cowering young man who had wet his face with tears and his pants with urine. Po’Pay’s face was almost kindly as he ran the blade across Frankie’s throat. A minute later the boy joined his best friend in death.

There would be no feast for these young men, Po’Pay thought. He would give them a decent burial and pray for their innocent souls.

CHAPTER SEVEN

It was unseasonably cold that late October night. Despite the chill the skies were clear except for a blanket of billions of stars; it was a new moon so there was no lunar illumination to accentuate the dots of light that twinkled and formed constellations and random patterns. Even with the darkness the thousands of simple white headstones were bright enough to recognize as they rested there solemnly in their neat rows. During the day, the Santa Fe National Cemetery was solemn; at night, moon or not, it was eerie and more than a little soul-wrenching. When a snowstorm hit and covered the green lawns with a blanket of white, the graveyard was other-worldly.

The cemetery encompassed nearly eighty acres and was established in 1870. Administered by the Unites States Department of Veterans Affairs, it was created after the Civil War to inter Union soldiers that died fighting there, particularly at the Battle of Glorietta Pass, the decisive battle in New Mexico during the war; some dubbed it "the Gettysburg of the west." Basically, the Union kicked the Confederates' asses.

In addition to those Union soldiers interred there the cemetery is the resting place of many well-known personages and/or Medal of Honor recipients. One of the earliest residents is Captain George

Nicholas Bascom, a Union officer killed in 1862 at the Battle of Val Verde. Those interred come from the Civil War, World War I, World War II, the Korean War, and now the Vietnam War. Albuquerque native Daniel D. Fernández, who grew up in nearby Los Lunas, received the Medal of Honor for his selfless act on February 18, 1966 when in Vietnam in the Hậu Nghĩa province he threw himself on a grenade to save his fellow soldiers.

The Grayhawk family was all too familiar with the cemetery since Troy Grayhawk was buried there. His headstone rested under an immense fir tree, the last in the line before the roots. A good six feet away from the next rows, there was room to stand or sit, and his family did just that on his birthday (January 25, 1949) and the date of his death (September 13, 1970). The last time Tucson was there was a month ago.

He wasn't sure why Cameo wanted to visit the grave at night, but he humored her and watched as she spread a blanket over the lawn between Troy's row and the next. She said she just wanted to spend some private, alone time with her husband, away from work, away from kids, away from family. He suggested a picnic during the day, but she seemed to want the night. Maybe there was something on her mind and she just needed an odd place to bring it out. She had been on the road a few times in the last month for work, heading down to Phoenix twice and once to Las Vegas. Caleb was working her butt off, but she seemed to thrive on it. She was oddly electric in the past couple of weeks.

Cameo sat down on the blanket, smiled up at Tucson, and patted the ground. He dropped down next to her and before he could say a word, she pulled him to her and kissed him long and passionately. He started getting aroused but pulled himself away before he could desecrate his brother's resting place. Sex in a graveyard was just not his thing.

She smiled; her eyes closed as she lay on her back with her hands behind her head. Tucson lay next to her staring up at the stars. There was a strong breeze that rustled the fir branches close to them, making a pleasant background noise to the general silence. Far in the distance a coyote clan howled up a fast but loud storm before settling down. Husband and wife were quiet for a long time, watching the stars, touching sides, holding hands.

Tucson gently nudged her, and Cameo opened her eyes and looked over at him. He pointed to the sky and she looked up.

"See the constellation?" he asked, still pointing.

"Um-hum," she murmured. "Orion."

"Look at the three stars in the belt. See them?"

"Yes."

"Now follow their path upwards to the v-shaped pattern of stars."

"It's the face of Taurus the Bull. The bright star is Aldebaran."

Tucson was surprised. "You really know your constellations."

"I've always loved astronomy." Before he could query her on when she studied it she said, "And there at the bull's shoulder are the Pleiades. The Pleiades cluster rises into the eastern sky before Aldebaran rises, and sets in the west before Aldebaran sets. It's best seen in North America during the winter season. Some consider it magical, clinging to the dome of the night."

Still surprised, Tucson said, "That's right. They call it the Seven Sisters. It comes from the Greek word meaning 'to sail.' Navigators used it to traverse the seas."

"It's beautiful," she said softly.

"I'll bet you didn't know that there are Indian legends about its creation," he said, nudging her again.

"Tell me," she whispered close to his ear, her hot breath tickling the lobe just before she gently bit it.

"My mom told me the legends. She's been all over the country with my dad visiting various tribes and learning their cultures. She inevitably brought the information home to us and drilled it into our skulls."

"She was a good mother," Cameo said absently, hoping Tucson wouldn't discern the trembling in her voice. "Tell me the legends."

"There's a Cherokee myth that tells of seven boys that were playing a game with sticks and stones. The game was called gatayu'sti. They played and played it all day instead of doing their chores, like weeding gardens and tilling the crops. They were having too much fun and no matter how often or loud their mothers called to them to stop they kept on playing. They did this every day. Their mothers became so frustrated that one day they gave the boys boiled gatayu'sti stones instead of corn.

"The boys were angry at their mothers and decided to get back at them. They danced in a circle and prayed to and called the spirits to come to them. Their mothers found them and begged them to stop, but the boys kept dancing and with every circle they made their feet lifted higher and higher off the ground. The mothers cried and grabbed for their legs, but the boys kept going higher and higher, and finally rose into the heavens where they became the Pleiades. The Cherokee still call the star cluster Ani'tsutsa, which means 'the boys.'"

"How sad," Cameo said. "The mothers lost their sons."

"But the heavens gained them. The Dakota in the Midwest believed that the cluster is the abode of their ancestors, called the Tiyami. It's considered their afterlife like we consider Heaven ours. One of their myths is how seven maidens were being hunted by a bear. The girls prayed to the gods to save them, and the gods answered their prayers by raising the ground under their feet high into the air. The bear clawed angrily at the earth, leaving claw marks, but finally gave up and left. The maidens were saved and turned into stars and placed in the sky for eternal safekeeping. The place where they were risen is what we now call Wyoming's Devil's Tower, complete with huge vertical striations thought to be bear claw marks."

"I love your legends," she said softly. "They're full of passion and beauty."

"Violence, too, if you're a fair young maiden being chased by a hungry bear."

"You can leave that part out when you relate those stories to our kids." Cameo linked her fingers with Tucson's. "You're the best father," she said quietly.

He laughed. "Hardly. I'm still trying to figure it all out, to say nothing of dealing with my own flaws."

"We all have flaws."

He noticed her distant tone. "Are you all right?"

"Of course. Why?"

"Well, we're lying on a blanket at night in a cemetery, for one thing."

"It's peaceful." Suddenly she rose on her side and put her hand gently on his cheek. "I love you, you know."

"I love you, too. But even so, I'm not going to get all hot and bothered in a graveyard. Especially near my brother's headstone."

"Brothers are special beings," she said seriously. She shivered, violently enough for him to notice.

Tucson sat up and stroked her arm. "What's wrong? Are you worried about what DeVere told us a few weeks ago?"

She shook her head. "No. I'm sure it's just bad luck and coincidence. I don't sense anything amiss around us."

"He called Memphis yesterday and said he hadn't sensed anyone following him since he got home."

"That's good." Cameo sat up and gently reached over, cupping Tucson's cheeks. She kissed his lips lightly. "Thank you for the Indian legends," she said.

"I've got lots more where those came from. I'll regale you next time we're not in a cemetery. Ready to go home?" Without waiting for any answer, he rose and pulled her to her feet. He folded the blanket, put a gentle hand on Troy's headstone, and walked hand in hand with his wife to their waiting car.

He may have been disinclined for intimacy in the cemetery but in their bed, they made love wordlessly and as passionately as they ever had. He fell asleep with her head on his chest.

Tucson had a full client calendar the next day and was so busy he barely had a chance to say hello or goodbye to Percy. Normally he'd call home at noon to check on Brett, but he was swamped and knew that if anything were wrong Declan would call him. When he walked through his front door after six, he smelled a pot roast coming from the kitchen and he could hear the twins talking over one another as Declan sought to make peace. Tucson walked in and saw his nanny at the stove frowning over a pot while Bree was tugging at his sleeve and Brae was stamping his foot.

"What's going on here?" Tucson said mock-angrily.

Brae rushed at him and said, "He won't make potatoes, Da. We asked for potatoes."

"Well," Tucson said, bending down to talk to his son eye to eye, "Declan can cook what he wants and we'll be grateful and eat it, right?"

Brae kicked his toe into the tile floor. "But we wanted potatoes," he muttered truculently.

"Well, yer not getting potatoes you daft silly thing," Declan said. "You're getting carrots, and carrots you'll eat."

"I hate carrots," Bree said, stamping her foot.

Declan looked Tucson in the eye. "Might I use your phrase, sir?"

"You may," Tucson said, fighting back a grin. He reached down into the small crib by the window and rubbed Brett's tummy while the baby gurgled happily.

Declan leaned down and looked Bree in the eye. "Tough shyte."

Tucson grinned and said to Declan, "Where's the lady of the house?"

"She isna home yet," Declan said. "She said this morning she'd probably be home late. Oh—she left a note for you in your den. Put that *down*," he said crossly to Bree as she quickly withdrew her hand from the plate of cookies resting on the kitchen table.

Tucson went into the den and put his briefcase on the desk. He saw the sealed envelope with his name on it in the middle of desk. It was Cameo's cursive handwriting. He picked it up and felt that it had at least two pages in it. He frowned; odd, that. Usually she just left him fast notes. He stared at the envelope for a long moment then slit it open. He sat at his desk and read the letter.

Declan finished cooking dinner and settling the twins down after he promised them roasted potatoes for tomorrow's dinner. Potatoes—they were Irish to the core. Brett was getting crabby and was obviously hungry. Luckily, Cameo wasn't nursing him, so Declan prepared a bottle of formula and settled Brae into a chair with the bottle and his baby brother on his lap. Brae was careful with the baby. Bree stood close by watching. Declan felt they were safe enough for him to leave the kitchen and extract their father from his den.

He rapped sharply on the closed den door and called out quietly for Tucson to come to dinner. There was no answer. He knocked again. He hated disturbing Tucson, but he gently opened the den door. He saw Tucson sitting rigid and motionless at his desk, a letter in his hand, his eyes staring unblinking into space. Declan very quietly closed the den door and walked back into the kitchen. With one eye on the kids he dialed Memphis and asked him to come over, please. Yes, something might be wrong.

Memphis was there in ten minutes. Declan told him briefly what had transpired. Memphis nodded and went to the den while Declan fed the kids. Memphis didn't bother knocking but opened the door slowly. Tucson was in the same position as he was when Declan had entered. Memphis didn't say a word, just walked over and carefully took the letter out of his brother's hand. The other page was on the desk, so he picked that up and sat on the wing chair near the window and began reading.

October 16, 1976

My Darling Tucson,

Let me say first that I love you. I love you with all my heart. And as much as I love you, I love our son a thousand times more.

That being said, I must leave you both, for now. You would only understand if I could tell you everything, but right now I cannot. There are things you are better off not knowing.

What I can tell you is that I remember.

I remember who I am.

I know my name.

I know where I came from.

I remember what happened.

My past is not past. I must return to that past so that we can have a future. There are things I must do, things that may not be successful, things that may allow me to return to you or to abandon you forever, for your sake.

There are things I have done that may be unforgiveable, and what I must do may be even more so.

Of course, you will try to find me, but don't, please don't. Live your life, care for your children. I have made every effort to cover my tracks in order to protect you. For that purpose, I cannot even tell you my real name. And, in truth, "Cameo" is my name as far was our life together goes.

When this is all over, I will try to come back, and maybe you can find it in your heart to forgive me. I will understand if you cannot and be assured that I would never try to reclaim Brett away from you.

Buddha once said, "No one saves us but ourselves. No one can and no one may. We ourselves must walk the path."

I am walking the path, and I will save myself.

Be well and safe, beloved.

Cameo

Memphis put the letter on the desk. Tucson was watching him closely for his reaction. Memphis finally shrugged.

"Could be worse," he said.

"How?" Tucson asked in disbelief.

"She could have taken off with no letter and left you hanging like Cassidy did. At least she had the decency to try to explain some of the … unexplainable."

"That's little comfort." Without warning Tucson swept his arm angrily across his desk knocking over almost everything on it. He jumped up, his fists balled, fire in his eyes. "What the fuck could be so bad that she had to leave?" He looked around wildly then picked up a small vase of flowers and threw it against the wall. The crash and tinkle of the glass mixed with the water and crystalline shards dribbling down the west wall.

He was hyperventilating when he asked his brother, "What's wrong with me that the women I love run away from me?"

Memphis grasped his brother's arms and drew him close. He whispered harshly, "Seems to me Cameo's trying to run to you through the obstacle course of her past. You're still the end game. Don't you get that?"

Tucson pulled away. "She could have told me the truth, all of it."

"Maybe she was afraid it would be too much for you to accept," Memphis said quietly. He thought about Snow running away from him days before they were to be married. She left a note that made it clear she didn't want him, wasn't in love with him. He was broken from that for a while, but Swan put him back together. Now, he was grateful for the betrayal and pain that led him to the woman he really loved.

"She's my wife, the mother of my children. I love her. I'd never reject her. She should know that."

"Maybe what she said is true, that keeping you in the dark is protecting you."

"From what?"

"From whatever the hell it is she ran away from."

"And is running back to."

"To finish it, like she said."

"I'm not just going to stand back and do nothing."

“Of course not. We’ll do our best to find her and help her.”

Tucson leaned back against his desk. There was a look of anguish on his face. “She could have told me her real name.”

“For your life together, Cameo is her real name.”

CHAPTER EIGHT

"All right," Frick said as he flipped open his pocket notebook. "I spent an entire day roaming around Phoenix, checking hotels, other places, to see if I could backtrack Cameo's movements down there."

"She was on assignment for Caleb," Tucson said. "I checked with him."

"So did I," Frack replied. "Caleb said that she really only needed to go down there once for background on the story she was doing, but she went back, according to her, to talk to a few people she missed on the first go-round."

"That sounds legitimate," Memphis said. The men were huddled in the Hazelwood Conference Room. They'd been there for an hour while Frick and Frack grilled Tucson about Cameo's flight and actions in the weeks before she left. Percy was drawn into the search as well since he had been the one treating her psychologically.

"It does," Frick agreed, "but when I talked to the names she had on that visit number two list they said she'd talked to them the first time she was there."

"Why then would she go back?" Tucson asked.

"That's what I asked myself," Frick said. "Then, I came up with a wild hair."

"Which was?" Memphis asked impatiently. Frick and Frack were always thorough in their investigations, but sometimes they over-explained things and wasted time.

"The time it takes to do a background check on someone trying to buy a gun," Frick said.

"Are you serious?" Tucson said. "Cameo won't even hold the guns I have in our home safe."

"Well, she's holding guns now," Frick replied. "To be specific, a 9mm Luger, a .357 Magnum, a .22, a rifle, a shotgun, and three exceptionally large knives courtesy of Chuck's Gun Emporium in Apache Junction. Oh, and lots of ammo. She bought them under her name and Chuck confirmed her photo. Do you want the rest of the bad information or do you want to chew on just that for a few minutes?"

"The rest," Percy said quietly in his deep voice, wondering how the hell he could have missed Cameo's iron side during their sessions.

"Chuck sent her to a shop in Phoenix on Northern Avenue that sells martial arts and spy shit. I showed her photo to the owner and he said, yeah, she was there. She bought a lot of stuff."

"Such as?" Tucson said tightly. His stomach was churning.

Frick flipped over a notebook page and read from his notes. "Surveillance equipment, nunchucks, shurikens—"

"What the hell's a shuriken?" Frack asked, frowning.

"It's those little metal throwing stars you see in ninja movies," Frick responded. "Nunchucks are those short baton thingies with a chain link. I saw Bruce Lee use them in one of his Dragon movies. She also got a utility belt, a face mask, non-slip gloves, and some other stuff that James Bond might envy. Also, the guy said that he remembers her not only for what she bought but what she was wearing. He said she was dressed all in black, like a tight black shirt down to her knee-high black leather boots."

"The fuck?" Tucson whispered.

"Honestly?" Frick said. "I wouldn't want to meet your wife in a dark alley. No offense."

Tucson placed his hands flat, palm-down on the table. He shook his head in disbelief. "I don't …" he began, "I don't even know the woman you're describing. That woman isn't my … wife."

"Yeah, she is," Memphis said slowly, "but obviously a hell of a lot more than just the Cameo we know." He looked at Percy. "Did you ever suspect that she was capable of getting involved in something like this?"

Percy shook his head. "Not in word or deed. I can't think of a single clue that would have made me suspect her recent actions. But, that's neither here nor there. Right now, we have to figure out where she's going and what she plans on doing."

"My guess?" Frack said. "She's going after someone, or a few someones. You don't pack heat like that to expect a civilized conversation over coffee and donuts."

"Then I'm guessing that she's headed back east, where we believe she most likely came from," Memphis said.

"Pittsfield?" Percy asked.

"More likely the coast of Massachusetts."

"But you think she may have a Connecticut or thereabouts accent," Frack opined.

"Accents can change," Percy said. "She seems to have one now, but what's the potential for her accent to have been different before she was injured? I've been exploring the psychology of dysprosody, and that may very well apply to Cameo."

"What's dypsody?" Frack asked, frowning. He didn't like weird words.

"Dysprosody," Percy corrected. "It's a disorder that's also known in some circles as foreign-accent syndrome. Basically, people have what are called prosodic functions, which relate to one's spoken language in terms of melody, intonation, pauses, stresses, intensity, vocal quality, and accent. Dysprosody is generally attributed to neurological damage, such as brain tumors, brain trauma, brain vascular damage, stroke, and severe head injury. Dysprosody's most common expression is when a person starts speaking in an accent which is not their own. It doesn't have to be foreign, like starting to speak in a Cockney or French accent."

"So, someone with an Alabama accent can suddenly start speaking like they were from Jersey?" Frick asked.

"Exactly," Percy said, nodding. "Cameo might have had a strong Boston accent then after her head trauma began speaking like someone from a different state."

"Can the condition be reversed?" Frick asked.

"Hard to say," Percy replied. "From the papers I've read it seems like speech therapy is the way to return a prior accent, once you know what the accent is. Now, whether Cameo has reverted to her previous accent since she's recovered her memory is anyone's guess." He shrugged. "In the past couple of weeks, I haven't noticed any change in her verbal cadence. Have you, Tucson?" Tucson shook his head. "So, either she hasn't reverted accents or she has but is clever enough to disguise them with the way she speaks now." He addressed Frick. "Did you ask the gun shop and spy shop owners about her accent?"

Frick shook his head. "It never occurred to me. I can call them and ask."

"So, where should we start looking?" Frack asked.

"Considering that she reacted to a photo of the Massachusetts coast," Memphis said, "the most feasible place to start looking for her is there. Also, Eddie Troy died close by. His death was ruled accidental, but I have my doubts."

Frack said, "I checked the flights out of Albuquerque and there weren't any for a passenger Cameo Adams or Cameo Grayhawk."

"Maybe she got a phony ID and booked under her real name," Frick said. "Whatever that is."

"We know about when she left so if we can get ahold of the passenger lists for the east coast, we can whittle down the female names," Memphis said.

"Unless she used a real phony ID with a new name," Percy said.

"Well," Memphis said, "we've gotta start somewhere. Frack, you get ahold of the passenger lists from Albuquerque and Phoenix. She might have driven elsewhere and boarded, but we start with the most logical."

"The airlines ain't gonna hand over their lists just like that," Frack said.

"Fine," Memphis said. "We'll use leverage. I'll call Richard Ballard and see if I can wheedle his help. I'll give DeVere a call and see if he wants to head over to the coast with me and Swan."

"Why Swan?" Tucson snapped.

"Because she was with me when we first explored that area," Memphis said patiently. "She knows the investigation best."

"And maybe you need a fresh eye," Tucson said coldly. "I don't care whether Swan goes or not, but I sure as hell am."

"The hell you are," Memphis said equally coldly. "Need I remind you that you have three kids at home that need their father now more than ever?"

"Declan's there. Mom and Dad are there. A shitload of family and friends are there. I'm going with you. You can talk until your vocal cords give out, but you won't dissuade me." He looked sharply at Percy. "What do you think, partner?" The challenge in his voice was blatant.

"I think you should follow your heart," Percy said, deliberately keeping his eyes averted from Memphis.

"Since, apparently," Memphis added, "your head isn't working. Fine. You can come. But you'll damn well follow my lead." He arched an eyebrow. "Since you're tagging along, I think Swan can stay here and hold down the fort and be prepared to support any research or tasks we might need."

"And, she's pregnant," Frick said. "She shouldn't be roaming around."

"Does London like your face?" Memphis asked. "Because she won't if you wind up having it ripped off by an angry, knocked-up P.I." He sighed. "You're still a dinosaur."

"A proud old reptile and glad of it," Frack said.

"All right," Memphis said, sighing. "We've got a general plan, so we just have to pin down precise tasks. I'll talk to Swan, Sand,

and Nick and update them on the situation and what they need to do while we're gone."

"Where are Sand and Nick?" Frack asked. "I thought they might have been part of our powwow."

"Abbott and Dunbar asked for a meeting. They should be glaring at one another over food at the diner," Memphis said. "And, no, I have no idea why."

Abbott was over-salting his French fries. Sand shook his head as he poured a half bottle of ketchup on his fries. "That's going to kill you," he said to the sodium-addicted detective.

Abbott looked up from his plate. "I like salt," he said defensively.

Dunbar jumped in. "If Rocky was eating a plate of salt, he'd put more salt on it."

"You're going to have a heart attack," Nick said.

"Then my wife will have a big insurance payout and live happily ever after," Abbott said as he stuffed a half dozen fries into his mouth.

"Not that we aren't grateful for the free food," Sand said, "but how about you tell us why we're here?"

Dunbar nodded, held up a finger, and took a large bite out of his bacon cheeseburger. He had barely swallowed the masticated manna when he said, "Got a couple more missing kids."

Abbott added, "Harlan Barrett and Francis 'Frankie' Conway from San Ramon, California." He handed Sand two photos that were obviously the standard high school graduation shots included in a yearbook. Both had long hair common for the time. Harlan's eyes were dark, Frankie's, light, perhaps blue. They had identical looks on their faces, wonder mixed with hope. One couldn't tell from a photo, but Sand had the feeling that these were good kids.

"What makes them missing?" Sand asked as he handed the photos back to Abbott.

"After they graduated high school, they decided to take a year off before trying to get into the same college. They decided to spend their time seeing the country and took off on a hitchhiking tour of what they called 'the wild west.' They called home occasionally and sent postcards to their families, but somewhere after they sent a postcard from Santa Fe, they dropped off the face of the earth. According to their parents they were headed up to Colorado and then would swing back west to California. The postcard was sent three weeks ago. According to their schedule they should be in Colorado and sending a card or calling from the Denver area," Abbott said.

"And since it looks like they vanished in the same area as those Frisco kids, we thought we'd like to get your input," Dunbar said.

"This is too coincidental," Nick said.

"Yeah, that's what we thought," Dunbar said. "We asked the State Police to search between Taos and the Colorado border, but that's a lot of acreage to search for two backpacking teens. We're checking the hospitals and clinics, too."

"Any idea where they mailed the postcard from?" Sand asked.

Abbott shook his head. "No such luck. We've got, what, a dozen ZIP codes in Santa Fe? But the only code was the one belonging to the recipient. The post office stamp only has Santa Fe, the date, and AM or PM."

"What was on the face of the postcard?" Sand asked.

"Ah, didn't ask," Dunbar confessed, embarrassed. He understood the implication right away.

Nick went on. "Because it might tell us where they were when they wrote it out and mailed it. Like, if it was a postcard of the plaza, or of one of the pueblos."

"Even so," Sand said, "those postcards are available anywhere. You can get a Taos postcard right here, and vice versa."

"Were these the kind of kids that might be involved with something dicey, like drugs?" Nick asked.

"Not according to their parents," Dunbar replied. "They were good kids. From the people I've talked to nothing suggests otherwise."

"They could have accidentally walked into the middle of something," Sand said. "Like a drug deal. They could just have been collateral damage."

"Hell of an epitaph," Abbott murmured. He roused himself and took a deep breath. "So, what do you think? Any ideas?"

Sand said, "As far as where to look for them, I think you've got that covered. As to the motive? There doesn't seem to be one any more than there was for the Frisco couple. Any indications that the boys might have been disrespectful to Indian traditions or sites?"

Abbott shook his head. "Their parents said that they revered the 'wild west' and were eager to experience the white and Indian cultures. It's possible, of course, that they might have inadvertently done something untoward to the Indian culture, but if I were a betting man, I'd bet against that. So, where does that leave us?"

"I think," Nick began slowly, "that these disappearances are related. We can't pin down any definitive clues, but my gut tells me we're dealing with the same reason and cause of the vanishings. We talked about this before with Frick and Frack. We even interviewed some Indian groups but came up with nada."

"It's an Indian," Sand said flatly. The other three men looked at him. "No, no proof, but it figures. The Frisco kids showed disrespect to Taos. Professor Carter was on his way to visit pueblos, and these California teens were on a search for wild-west America. Screamin' Al was blatantly disrespectful towards Indians as well as all non-white races. Somehow, they crossed paths with someone who took exception to their actions or intentions."

"Someone's paying back the white man for perceived injuries," Abbott said slowly. "Christ almighty."

"He's an injustice collector," Nick said. "Percy and I talked about that. It's not a concept that's widely held yet, but many psychologists hold to it as a legitimate psychological aberration."

"What is it, exactly?" Abbott asked.

"It's someone who nurses grudges, however slight, and acts to avenge them. The so-called 'injustice' could be a look, a word, an action, anything that pricks at the collector's soul. There's virtually no forgiveness on his part; he holds grudges forever. He never forgets, he never forgives, he never lets go, and he always strikes back. Revenge fantasies feed his mind and heart. There are quite a few in history.

One was an electrician named Andrew Kehoe, who lived in Bath, Michigan. Those who knew him considered him unpredictable, rigid, demanding, self-righteous, and perceiving of virtually anything as an injury against him."

"What happened to him?" Dunbar asked, intrigued.

"In 1927 he lost his job, he lost a local election, and he and his wife were having marital problems. He wired explosives inside a school and blew up forty-five people, including thirty-five children. Before he set off the bomb, he'd killed his wife and their farm animals, and later killed himself."

"So, there are signs that might pinpoint this injustice collector?" Sand asked.

Nick nodded. "Most of the time, but the psyche is so complex that it's possible that all of the negative personality traits can be well-hidden."

"So, not necessarily easy to spot," Abbott said thoughtfully.

"Nope," Nick agreed. "He could be your next-door neighbor, or even a close relative. Your pastor."

"Wonderful," Dunbar murmured. "I love my job."

"Me, too," Sand said as he noisily drew the last of the milkshake through his straw. Since Abbott and Dunbar were paying, he ordered another one.

Logan International Airport was busy as hell. It was the peak of the foliage season in New England, and people flocked not only from nearby states but from far-away ones with the promise of a spectacular visual experience. The car rental counters were busy, and Cameo had to wait twenty minutes to complete her reservation and get the paperwork for the fire-engine-red Chevy Camaro. She had purchased her ticket and the car rental with the phony ID she'd acquired in Phoenix, Mary Kay Randall, as innocuous a name as possible. A sweet car rental young man offered to help her with her luggage since she had not only a carry-on but two large padlocked suitcases. He loaded one in the trunk and wedged the other one into the back seat. She thanked him and handed him a five-dollar bill.

She made her way carefully out of Logan and headed south to Quincy where she had a reservation at the Best Western Adams Inn. She had requested a suite with a water view, and that was exactly what she got. The suite was large, with a queen bed, a sitting area, and a bathtub with jets. The view was spectacular from the huge window. She'd almost forgotten how much she missed being close to the ocean and its waterways.

She left the suitcases on the bed and went out for a half hour to a nearby grocery store where she picked up a six-pack of Pepsi plus cookies and other snacks. She saw a package store and braked sharply, going inside for two bottles of Merlot and the necessary bottle opener. She put the beverages in the suite's mini-fridge, then headed into the shower and took a long, long hot one. She washed and conditioned her short hair; she had cut it into a pixie look and dyed it black when she left New Mexico, ruing the loss of the mane that had flowed halfway down her back and through which her husband would sensually run his fingers. She had various contact lenses and had worn the dark brown ones before she had boarded her plane in Las Vegas.

She was thoroughly refreshed when she padded naked into the suite and threw herself on the bed next to the suitcases. She stared up at the ceiling, breathing in and out deeply, then turned over and unlocked the padlock on the first suitcase.

That one had half her weapons' supply as well as new clothes she had purchased; the second suitcase contained her remaining weapons and sundries. Wordlessly she picked up the Luger and quickly disassembled then reassembled it, satisfied that she hadn't lost her touch. She stored the suitcases by the sitting area, then turned off the lights, leaving the drapes open so that she had the view of the water and the twinkling lights of the banks' businesses.

Still naked, she slipped under the sheet and put the loaded gun—its safety clip on—under her pillow. She sighed; she was bone-tired but excited.

She was going to make him pay.
That was her certainty and his.
She closed her eyes and fell asleep immediately.
She slept like the dead.
She didn't dream.

CHAPTER NINE

Swan was decidedly pale when she returned to her office from a desperate bathroom run. Her morning sickness had kicked into high gear with a vengeance. She was crabby and snappish on a good day, and the bump in her hormones only accentuated that part of her personality. She sat down and took a swig of her warm iced tea and rolled her eyes at Tansee, who had taken a break from her medical clients.

"The joys of motherhood," Swan muttered. "This is it, the last one. Memphis said it better be a boy, but I really don't care. I'm going to have him fixed."

Tansee laughed loudly. "Good luck with that. Manly men won't allow themselves to be snipped."

"If he ever wants to have sex again, he will." Swan arched a curious eyebrow. "There's that sly look on your face. What aren't you telling me?"

Tansee bit her lower lip and fought back a grin. She leaned forward conspiratorially. "Elspeth is going to have a baby brother or sister," she whispered, her face alight with joy.

"Oh, honey," Swan said and whipped around the desk to engulf her cousin-in-law in her arms.

Tansee reveled in the embrace and her face was glowing as she pulled away. "I'm three weeks past where I miscarried the other babies, so the doctor is hopeful."

"Does Percy know?"

Tansee shook her head. "I want to wait a few more weeks. Two, at least. You know," she said slowly, "this wasn't a happy accident."

"What?"

"I went off my birth control deliberately. I want a second baby so bad, Swan," Tansee exclaimed. "I feel it, I just feel it that this baby will come to term." She squeezed Swan's hand hard.

Swan brushed the back of her hand gently along Tansee's cheek and said a silent prayer that this baby would survive. She didn't know how Tansee or Percy could endure a fifth miscarriage. If anyone deserved a second chance at parenthood it was Tansee and Percy.

"Honey," Swan said gently, "you should tell him now. Remember how shocked and guilty he felt when you miscarried that first time and he knew nothing about the pregnancy. I know this baby will be born, but if it isn't, he needs to be prepared."

Tansee nodded slowly. "You're right. I need to tell Percival now. I'll do it tonight."

"Good," Swan said and squeezed Tansee's hand. "Why don't you make him a nice romantic dinner, candles and all? I'll take Elspeth for the evening so you two can have some privacy."

"That would be great." Tansee paused. "Clams. I need to find clams. He loves chowder."

"Um, good luck with that. Better have a Plan B just in case. I'll pick the kid up at four."

Tansee nodded happily, hugged Swan one more time, and went downstairs to her office.

Swan sat down and contemplated what Tansee had told her. She hoped to hell that her friend didn't lose this baby. If she'd had as many miscarriages as Tansee had she would've had Memphis fixed for sure. As it was Swan had had one miscarriage in 1973 when she was six weeks pregnant. She tried to pretend it was no big deal, but when she came home from the hospital, she had cried in Memphis's arms for two hours. She knew he'd like a son this time around, but she was hoping for another girl. Four daughters. Memphis would be so outnumbered. She liked that thought. It wasn't going to be easy thinking up a four-letter female name beginning with "S," though. If it were a boy, they'd give him an "M" name and that field was wide open. She hoped to God it wouldn't be a second set of twins.

Damn—she'd sell her soul for a glass of wine.

Or a shot of tequila.

Or a shot of tequila in a glass of wine …

Sand was reading over various brochures for summer camps for next year. Elijah was doing well and had made a lot of friends, but Sand wanted to socialize him with more fun activities that didn't necessarily include family members. There were a few wilderness camps in the Santa Fe-Albuquerque area as well as some in northern Arizona and southern Colorado. He wanted any camp to be within driving distance from home in case he had to burn rubber to pick up his nephew for whatever reason. Akiro liked the idea and agreed that their nephew needed to expand his horizons; it was time and would be more than two years since his mother had dropped him off and gone on the run.

Elijah had had a hard time adjusting for the first six months, but Sand felt that the boy was settled and comfortable in the knowledge that he was in a safe, stable, loving home. And Sand had learned to adjust to becoming a father, something he never thought he'd be. Luckily Akiro was flexible and didn't resent the insertion of a small child into their lives. They were fortunate that in 1975 New Mexico had decriminalized homosexuality so they weren't at risk for breaking any laws that might cause them to lose custody. Even so, it was months before the courts designated Sand as Elijah's legal guardian. Sand planned on legally adopting Elijah, hopefully in the next year. Akiro was working on the legal documents.

Sand had pretty much decided on a camp in nearby Pecos when Frick came in without knocking. He looked solemn.

"What?" Sand asked.

"Would you happen to be in the mood for a road trip?" Frick asked.

"Depends. Where?"

"Trinidad."

"Don't you have to fly there?"

"Trinidad, Colorado. Just over the border."

"What's in Trinidad?"

"Two dead kids from San Ramon."

"Let's go," Sand said, jumping up. Pecos was going to have to wait.

Trinidad, Colorado is located one hundred ninety-five miles south of Denver and just twenty-one miles north of Raton, New Mexico on the historic Santa Fe Trail. Founded in 1862 when a vein of coal was discovered it became a bustling town with the influx of immigrants that hoped to make their fortune in mining. By the late 1860s the town's population had swelled to twelve hundred, and in 1876 it was incorporated just before Colorado became the thirty-eighth state in the Union. The state's nickname is the "Centennial State" since it was admitted to the Union one hundred years (and twenty-eight days) after the Declaration of Independence was signed.

Despite its tiny size and innocuous beginnings, Trinidad has seen several events that led to it being a notable footnote in Colorado's history. In the early 1900s Trinidad became nationally known for having the first woman sports editor of a newspaper, Ina Eloise Young. On August 7, 1902, the Bowen Town coal mine, six miles north of Trinidad, was the scene of a horrific gas explosion that killed thirteen miners. One of the worst mining disasters in the state, the mine's terrible working conditions and deadly consequences provided the impetus for subsequent labor strikes. Trinidad became a focal point for the United Mine Workers of America strike of 1913-1914 against the Rockefeller-owned Colorado Fuel & Iron company. The event was known as the Colorado Coalfield War. The Colorado and Southern Railway stop that connected Trinidad with Denver and Walsenburg made the town strategically important for both the strikers and the Colorado National Guard.

On April 20, 1914, just eighteen miles north of town, the Ludlow Massacre occurred. A militia of anti-strikers attacked a mining camp and brutally killed twenty-one members of strikers' families including children. John D. Rockefeller, Jr, was excoriated in the press for having instigated the action.

More recently, Trinidad became known as the "Sex Change Capital of the World" because of the renown of Dr. Stanley Biber. Biber performed his first sex reassignment surgery in 1969 after a trans woman asked him if he would be willing and able to do so. At first, he had no clue as to how to perform the procedure, but he learned by studying diagrams from Johns Hopkins Hospital. He kept his first few surgeries secret from the Catholic nuns who operated the hospital, due to concerns that they would react negatively.

And now, Sand thought ruefully as Frick pulled his car up in front of the Trinidad police station, the town would be known for the discovery of the bodies of two missing young men from California. He unfolded himself from the back seat of Frick's car since Frack claimed shotgun. The ride up was uncomfortable but to his credit Frick drove like a bat out of hell. It was sheer luck that a State Trooper hadn't pulled them over, but since they were tailgating Abbott and Dunbar who had their siren and lights on for the drive that was unlikely anyway.

Sand studied the two-story red-brick building that held the small police force. It was an unassuming building in contrast to the three-story blond stone building across the street, which was the Las Animas County Courthouse. Kitty-corner to the station was the similar two-story brick building that housed the BPO Elks club.

Dunbar warned the Warrior Spirit team to keep their mouths shut since this was an *official* Santa Fe police matter and *official* Santa Fe detectives would be handling the matter. Frick, Frack, and Sand agreed wholeheartedly; everyone knew they were lying.

Dunbar told the desk officer who they were and a few minutes later a middle-aged man with steel-grey hair and a square jaw walked up to them and shook hands all the way around. He introduced himself as Detective Rudy Batista and led them to a small, windowless conference room.

As he seated himself Batista said, "I didn't expect a swarm of law enforcement from your town." He was obviously expecting an explanation.

"Actually," Abbott said casually, "it's really just me and Dunbar who are the official reps from our corner of heaven." He nodded at Frick, Frack, and Sand. "This happy little trio are P.I.s that are just tangential to the case. So, you can address your official comments to me and my partner."

"Ouch," Frick muttered.

Batista grunted. "Works for me. Okay, here's the lowdown. A hiker up at Fisher's Peak saw a coyote pawing the ground. He tossed common sense to the wind and threw sticks at the beast and ran him off. Moron. Anyway, when he got close, he saw what looked like fabric peeking out of the ground, and upon further examination he brushed away dirt and uncovered a decomposing hand. He hauled ass down to a pay phone and called us. We sent an officer up and he confirmed that we were looking at a body. When our team went up, we found two bodies, buried side by side."

"Where's Fisher's Peak?" Frick asked. Abbott threw him a nasty look and Frick had the decency to look abashed.

Batista smiled at the interaction. He addressed the P.I.s. "Any of you guys ex-cops?"

"All of us," Frack answered. "Me and Frick, here, retired. Sand, well, decided on a career change."

Batista cocked his head. Then, he nodded. "I remember now. Heard your names associated with that vampire woman case a few years back."

"We'll never live it down," Frack muttered. "Notoriety sticks around forever."

"That it does," Batista said. "To answer your non-official question, Fisher's Peak is a mesa maybe ten thousand feet or so in elevation just south of here. You would have seen it on your way into town. Rumors say it might have once been an active volcano, but geologists say it was created around a million years ago by horizontal lava flows. Early maps called it Raton Peak."

"Anything special about it except its unusual flat shape?" Dunbar asked.

"No, not really. It's pretty, though. Highest elevation of any peak east of its longitude. Anyway, when we dug up the two bodies yesterday, we were surprised to find that they had identification. We had a bulletin about those two missing guys from California and lo and behold, the IDs matched. The bodies are too decomposed to make a facial identification, but we requested dental charts from the San Ramon police and the medical examiner matched them. Pretty weird, though."

"What?" Sand asked.

"Normally when you kill someone and bury the body you do whatever you need to do to disguise the identity to make it difficult to find clues. Whoever killed these kids wanted them to be identified. Maybe wanted them to be found."

"Why do you say that?" Abbott asked.

"Besides leaving their wallets in their backpacks, which were buried with them, they weren't buried too deep. It was almost foreseeable that they'd become uncovered."

"How were they killed?" Frick asked, ignoring Abbott's scowl.

"Harlan Barrett was killed by a single stab wound to the heart. Francis Conway had his throat cut. M.E. says they died at the same time."

"Were there any signs of torture or sexual abuse?" Dunbar asked.

"Not according to the M.E."

"Have their families been notified?" Sand asked quietly. A chill washed over him; he thought about Elijah, and how he would feel if anything happened to the boy.

"I talked to the San Ramon cops this morning and they'll do the notification. Gonna have a member of each family fly out here for personal identifications." Batista narrowed his eyes at the quintet.

"Correct me if I'm wrong, but I get the feeling that this case has deeper implications for you guys."

Sand nodded. "It does. Our firm was handling the case of two missing young people from San Francisco a couple of years ago. They seemed to have disappeared between San Luis and Santa Fe while they were traveling the country."

"You find them? Alive or dead?" Batista asked.

Sand shook his head. "We never did. They're still missing. We've had a few more missing persons cases that might or might not be related."

"You think this one is related?"

"We don't know," Sand said, "but they disappeared after they left Santa Fe. That's kind of coincidental."

"Do you have any clues as to the perp?" Dunbar asked.

Batista shook his head. "Not so far. I had a team scour the area leading up to the burial site and around a one-mile circumference, but so far nothing. No tire tracks, fabric, broken branches, anything that would point to someone dragging a body up from a vehicular location to the burial site. We're still looking. Oh," Batista said, snapping his fingers. "There was one oddity. They were buried with a shovel between them, one of those collapsible, small shovels."

"A shovel?" Abbott said incredulously. "What does that mean?"

"It sounds like the graves were dug with the shovel, but the earth was pushed back over them manually or with another shovel. That doesn't make any sense," Dunbar said, confused. "And there was nothing to indicate that before the shovel was dug up?"

"Nope," Batista said.

"Sounds like someone who knows how not to leave spore," Sand murmured, mulling over the oddity of the buried shovel. "Any clues on the shovel?"

"No, just covered with dirt. No fingerprints or blood."

"Stranger and stranger," Frack said under his breath. "Maybe the killer had two shovels."

"Can we see the bodies?" Dunbar asked.

"Sure. I'll take you to the M.E.'s lab. Follow me."

Batista drove the men to the coroner's office and the Santa Feans observed the remains. The bodies had been divested of their clothes and bore the common v-shaped chest incision that was an autopsy mainstay. Their clothes and personal items were in plastic evidence bags.

"We're counting on the family members to tell us if anything is missing from their effects, like a ring," Batista said. He picked up a small evidence bag. "There are two high school rings in here. They're silver. Also, the boys had a few bucks in each wallet, so I'm thinking this wasn't a robbery gone bad. Other than that, there's not much I can tell you. I'll let you know what we find out from the families. Might be a couple of days."

"Were the bodies washed before they were buried?" Sand asked suddenly.

"Huh?" Batista said. "I don't know how you could tell since they were covered with dirt."

"Maybe the M.E. could check for sweat and grime that would have been there before they were buried," Sand said mildly. "Just a thought. Just to be thorough."

Batista shrugged. "I'll ask him. Anything else you want to see here?"

"No, I think two decomposing dead bodies is enough for one day," Dunbar said. "Could we see your reports and crime scene photos?"

"Sure. It's almost two. You gents up for a late lunch?"

"I'm starving," Frack said.

"How could anyone ever tell?" Sand remarked with a grin.

"There's a restaurant not far from here where we can chow down, then we'll head back to the station. This is a mi casa, su casa situation, right?"

"Hmm?" Abbott said.

"I show you mine, you show me yours. About the other disappearances."

"Of course. I'll have the material faxed to you when we get back to Santa Fe."

"Perfect. Let's eat. Best chili on the planet."

Sand thought the chili was decent but couldn't match up to Akiro's. He and his friends spent the rest of the day with Batista going over the crime scene photos. It was getting dark when they arrived at the actual burial site. The only thing that told him was that whoever had buried the boys knew how to traverse rugged mountain country and cover his tracks.

Batista drove after them to the Trinidad city limits and waved as they headed south. They were across the state border just outside of Costilla where they had stopped after their earlier foray into San Luis. Dunbar and Abbott were following and pulled behind Frick's car.

"What?" Dunbar barked as he got out of the car and walked over to Frick. "It's late. Let's go home."

"Keep your panties on," Frick growled. He turned to Sand. "What was all that about the boys being clean or not when they were buried?"

Sand blew out a hard breath. "The answer plays into the possibility of the boys' killer being the same one responsible for the disappearances we've been investigating."

"How so?" Abbott asked.

"How much do you know about Indian burial practices?" Sand asked.

"Not a damn thing," Dunbar confessed.

"They vary amongst tribes, but in the Navajo nation, for example, the dead are buried with the implements used to bury them."

"Like the shovel," Frack said, understanding dawning.

"That, and they are washed and dressed in burial clothes. These kids had their own clothes on because any Indian garments would be a clue. But if their bodies were washed before they were buried, well …"

"What does that signify?" Dunbar asked.

"It tells me that whoever buried them did so with reverence and ritual, and respect. Which goes to the theory that maybe these boys weren't doing anything wrong but were in the wrong place at the wrong time. Whoever killed them regrets having to do so and showed that regret by giving them a decent burial."

"So, we're talking an Indian killer," Frick said.

Sand nodded. "Yeah, we are."

CHAPTER TEN

Chris Komansky was drunk as a skunk as he stumbled out of Burke's Bar at two in the morning. He would have crashed to the sidewalk if he weren't being supported by the skanky blonde that was stronger than she looked at first glance. It was Friday night and he had no commitments, so he hit his favorite drinking hole on a side street a few blocks from the New England Aquarium and proceeded to drink his favorite Irish whiskey until his sight blurred. He never expected a svelte blonde to sidle up to him and offer to buy him another drink. Her long blonde hair with eye-length bangs swished as she moved her lean, athletic body in the skin-tight spandex tank top and micro-mini skirt she was wearing above her stiletto heels. She was wearing a pair of huge stylish designer eyeglasses that were lightly shaded, but not dark enough to hide her cobalt blue eyes.

He tried to sloppily kiss her, but she turned her head and said, coyly, that she preferred intimacy in a private place. He could feel himself getting an erection as they walked down the street west of the bay. He had no idea where they were going, but he had a slight moment of clarity when he realized that they were in the exclusive Beacon Hill section of Boston. Wow, he thought—the bitch was not only hot but rich, maybe. His head was still fuzzy, and he tried to shake himself away from the vagueness that had been increasing since they left the bar. Suddenly, they stopped.

"We're here," she said softly as she strengthened her tight hold on his body, which was relaxing into a state of unconsciousness. He blinked and tried to lick his lips, but his mouth was like cotton. He squinted at her, then squinted at the front of the luxurious red brick townhouse on Chestnut Street. He couldn't quite put his finger on it; the façade seemed familiar. The white-trimmed bay window, the black double door with the shiny brass street number and knocker in the shape of a dragon head flanked by small, ornate brass letters; "D" on one side and "S" on the other. The four-story townhouse … the townhouse …

Komansky jerked straight for a second trying to focus. The woman was smiling at him. She had seemed familiar, sort of, in the bar but he was so pickled that he could have been sitting on a bar stool next to Linda Fucking Ronstadt and not have recognized her. Now, he did, but before he could speak her name the drug she had put in his last whiskey finalized his loss of willpower and movement; that, and without warning she slammed his head against the door and he slid to the ground.

Cameo glanced both ways, but the street was quiet and empty. She felt under the hidden ledge of the flowerbox and breathed a sigh of relief as the spare key was still in its place. She quickly unlocked the front door and dragged Komansky into the dark foyer. She knew that the townhouse's owner was out of town, so she wasn't nervous about encountering her target while she was unprepared. She left Komansky on the foyer floor while she retrieved the small backpack she had hidden in the bush outside the house earlier that evening.

She took out the night goggles she had purchased at the Phoenix spy shop and put them on. She wouldn't have to turn on any lights to perform her tasks. She opened the small syringe kit and checked the cc's in the tube. Enough to knock Komansky out as though he were anesthetized but not enough to kill him. She didn't want that to kill him.

She dragged Komansky into the spacious living room and laid him near the ultra-expensive antique Persian rug. She laid out her tools on the Louis XIV coffee table.

She stared down at the unconscious man for five long minutes, thinking, remembering.

Then she went to work.

It was close to dawn when she left the townhouse carefully, checking the street for any late or early passersby or residents. Up one side of the street a man was jogging away from her position, his lively lab galloping by his side. She walked quickly down Brimmer Street to Beacon then swung over to Arlington Street to a side street where she'd parked her car. She cursed silently at the parking ticket under her windshield wiper. She shook her head; the city of Boston could try to collect their fine from Mary Kay Randall, but since she didn't actually exist, good luck with that.

The sun was peeking out of the eastern horizon when Cameo returned to her hotel room. She stripped and showered, made sure the "Do Not Disturb" sign was on the door, drew the drapes, and slipped naked between the sheets. Right now, she would have sold her soul to have Tucson wrapped around her, making her feel warm and safe. She cried herself to sleep.

DeVere York waited patiently for the plane to taxi and disgorge its passengers. He was standing at the entrance to the disembarkment gate, scanning the crowd for Memphis and his brother. At six-four Memphis tended to tower over most people and DeVere spied him quickly and waved wildly. Memphis caught the movement and picked up his pace as he and Tucson weaved through the crowd. DeVere stuck his hand out and grinned.

"You made it. How was the flight?" DeVere asked.

"Crowded," Memphis said. "We had a slight delay changing planes in Dallas but luckily we still arrived on time."

"Are you hungry?" DeVere asked as they made their way to the luggage carousel.

"Starved," Memphis said.

"We'll stop at a little place ReVere told me about on our way to the Atlantis Oceanfront Inn. I got you guys a double room and one for me right next door. We lucked out again with the timing since they'll be closing up for the winter season in a week or two."

"Sounds like a plan," Memphis said as he grabbed for his suitcase as it rounded the end of the carousel. They had to wait a few more minutes for Tucson's suitcase but by four-thirty they were pulling out of the airport garage. Memphis was glad he wasn't driving since the rush-hour Boston area traffic was insane. For a lengthy part of the drive it felt like constant stop and go, and he was relieved when DeVere pulled onto the coastline road that would take them to Gloucester.

It was close to six when DeVere pulled into the parking lot of The Gloucester House, a well-known restaurant that had been serving hungry diners for nearly twenty years. It was a simple white building with black shutters.

As DeVere parked the car he grinned and said, "Doesn't look like much, but it's a favorite with locals and visitors. It boasts a great menu of authentic seafood. It has one little claim to fame."

"And that is?" Memphis asked as he got out of the car.

"The TV show *Bewitched* filmed an episode here around 1972 or 1973. There's a picture hanging inside of the TV crew with the employees. I recommend the Gloucester House Baked Haddock if you like fish."

"They have anything else?" Tucson asked tightly. He rarely ate fish; he never ate rice. He never forgot the rotten fish and rice that the North Koreans fed the prisoners of the *Pueblo* during that hellish year.

"Sure," DeVere said. "Steak, chicken, pasta, you name it."

The men had to wait ten minutes before they were seated but lucked out with a table that wasn't close to others and had a modicum of privacy. Both DeVere and Memphis ordered the Gloucester House Baked Haddock and Tucson settled on the Chicken Piccata.

"It's delicious," Memphis said as he nodded his head and chewed a succulent piece of baked haddock.

"I knew you'd love it," DeVere crowed in satisfaction as he attacked his own fish. "How's the chicken?" he asked Tucson.

"Good, very good," Tucson said. The fowl was tender and juicy and seasoned exactly right. His stomach tightened; Cameo had learned to make the dish a few months earlier. She had taken a gourmet cooking class and was using her new talents to experiment on her family. He quelled his fear that the experiments might never happen again.

"So, I got permission from Eddie's sister, Sigrid, to visit the remains of his house. Next week the ruins are being removed so the lot can be sold. There's not much to see there but I thought you'd probably want to take a gander. I also got an interview with the M.E. to discuss his COD. The detectives on Eddie's initial case are willing to talk to us, but they think it's still an accidental death."

"Despite the nail?" Memphis said skeptically.

DeVere shrugged. "They say he could have been doing some work and accidentally hit himself with a nail gun."

"Did they find a nail gun?"

"No, but the fire was so intense that it could have melted a nail gun and melded it into other parts of the ruined house and furniture."

"He was murdered," Tucson said flatly.

Memphis nodded. "I agree, and the only reason has to be tied up with Cameo's past. He was passing around photos of her, wasn't he?"

DeVere nodded. "Yeah, I talked to him a few weeks after we left, and he said he'd made copies and was passing them around. Think someone saw one of the photos and recognized her, then found out where the photo came from?"

"I do," Memphis said. "So, from that it's logical to think that whoever killed him is deadly dangerous and is now on Cameo's trail."

"The guy that raped her?" DeVere said.

"Probably. And if you really were being stalked then Eddie might have told him about you and the guy or guys were hoping to either abduct you for information or hope you'd lead them to her."

"Did he write her name on the back of the photos?" Tucson asked.

DeVere shook his head.

"He might have said her name while he was being tortured," Memphis said.

"Maybe, maybe not," DeVere said. "He obviously told them my name, but if he had mentioned your names or hers and where you came from I'd think he would have traveled to Santa Fe instead of Pittsfield. We may have lucked out."

"I wonder why Eddie didn't tell them everything," Memphis said.

"Maybe he knew they were going to kill him anyway and he decided to not drag everyone down with him," Tucson said quietly.

"That took guts," DeVere said just as quietly. He raised his glass of white wine. "To Eddie. May he rest in peace and may we find the fuckers that killed him."

"To Eddie," Memphis and Tucson said together and clinked glasses.

"So, you think Cameo would've flown into Logan if she was headed back here?" DeVere asked.

"Best option," Memphis said, "but if she wanted to hide her steps she could've flown into Hartford or New York, rented a car, and driven here."

"She probably rented a car anyway," Tucson said. "Under whatever name she was traveling."

"Did you try to find out if she left from Albuquerque?" DeVere asked.

"Nothing under her own name, and since we don't know what her real name is we can't verify that. I had an FBI friend get a list of women that were traveling alone out of Albuquerque and my team back home is trying to track them down."

"Maybe she wasn't traveling alone," DeVere mused.

"What do you mean?" Tucson asked curiously.

"Well, if she's as cunning and smart as she seems to be, based on what you told me about her recent purchases, maybe she, well, 'rented' somebody to fly with her and then turn around and go back. If it were a man she'd just seem like one half of a typical couple."

"Shit," Memphis said in a low voice. "I hadn't thought of that. Be right back." He got up and walked over to a waiter, who then pointed him towards the pay phone near the restrooms. He came back immediately and looked abashed. “Got any change?” he asked his brother. Tucson dug into his pockets and handed Memphis a handful of change. Memphis came back again after ten minutes and sat down. “I called Devon and told her call Ballard and see if he can revisit the flight lists.”

DeVere pretended to be casual. “So, how is Devon? Still sniping at unexpected guests?”

“She’s a sniper all right,” Memphis said, smiling.

“She, uh, ever mention me?” It was completely impossible to miss the hope in his voice.

“Nope,” Memphis said.

“Oh,” DeVere replied, clearly dejected.

“Dope,” Memphis said affectionately. “She might have worked your name into a conversation or two. She did mention that she missed the New England foliage season and thought it would be a good idea to visit her hometown and take a ride north. She specifically mentioned the Yankee Candle store and Gould’s Sugar House.”

DeVere’s face lit up. “Cool. I mean, oh, that’s nice.”

“Don’t ever play poker,” Tucson said, flashing a genuine smile, the first in a long time. Then he sobered. “Okay, where should we start looking? Here?”

“Let’s visit the site of the fire and ask around,” Memphis said. “Maybe the killers flashed Cameo’s photo around the neighborhood. Can we head over when we’ve finished here?”

DeVere nodded to his left towards a window. “Late October, gets dark early. We can hit it first thing in the morning.”

“Okay,” Tucson said reluctantly. It would give him and Memphis time for the rest of the evening to go over their search plan yet again. Both Grayhawk brothers were all too aware that they were shooting blind, and all too aware that Cameo might not have even gone back to New England. Still, they had nothing to go on except her reaction to that snapshot of the Gloucester coast.

Memphis paid for the meal and DeVere drove them to the inn where the same girl who checked them in the year before widened her smile and welcomed them back. They agreed to meet in the dining room when it opened and headed off to their respective rooms.

Tucson called Declan when they settled in and talked to the twins for a few minutes. Declan put Brett up to the phone and Tucson crooned a hello and I-love-you to his youngest son before he had a few more words with Declan and hung up. Memphis called Swan and talked for about ten minutes while his brother took a fast shower. Tucson came back into the bedroom with a blue towel wrapped around his waist, his long damp hair letting droplets fall on his shoulders and cheeks.

"Everything okay at home?" Tucson asked.

"Everything's fine," Memphis said. "Swan told me in great detail how she threw up three times today and that there was a snip and stitch in my near future."

"You actually thinking about that?"

Memphis shrugged. "Maybe. Four kids are more than enough."

"Cameo and I talked about a fourth kid somewhere in the future. That'll probably never happen now."

"You don't know that."

"I know my wife isn't even close to the woman I thought she was. I know that she doesn't trust me enough to tell me the truth—hell, to tell me her goddamn name."

"Did you ever think she was trying to protect you? Like, from the bastards that hurt her and may still be looking for her? You think it was easy for her to abandon her kids and the man she loves? And, little brother, she does love you. I see that in her face every time she looks at you." Memphis's voice was hard even though he sympathized.

"Yeah, well, her actions paint a different picture. Maybe. Christ, Gracie—I just want my family back the way it was." Tucson's anguish was impossible to miss.

"That's not going to happen," Memphis said quietly. "However this plays out we're going to be living in a different normal than before. Not saying it's better or worse, simply different. It will be what you make of it."

"And if I don't get my wife back?"

"Then you still keep moving forward. You've got three kids depending on that, not to mention a big family that needs you. Now, I've spent enough time soothing your roiling soul, so I think it's my turn in the shower. That is, if you left any hot water for me."

"Plenty," Tucson murmured. A moment later he could hear his brother in the shower. He draped the damp towel over the footboard and got under the thick bedcovers. He was bone-tired and had to fight to alleviate his dispirit. There was little more than foreboding in his mind and heart as he closed his eyes and listened to the battering cascade of hot water. After a few moments, the water stopped, and finally Memphis came out of the bathroom naked and dry.

The elder Grayhawk saw his brother's closed eyes but sensed that he was still awake. He turned off the light and slipped into his own bed. After a few moments he said, "We'll find her."

Tucson kept his eyes closed and nodded.

The Chestnut Street neighborhood in Beacon Hill was elegant, quiet, and private, but in one respect, annoying—parking. The residents and visitors had to park on the street and places were at a premium virtually 24/7. At ten o'clock at night all parking spaces for a full block up and down on either side were taken, and he had to park his Porsche on an adjacent street and walk to his townhouse. It was a chilly evening, brisk, but not unpleasant. He relished this time of year when the sultry humidity of summer was long gone, and the frostiness and frigidity of winter had not yet made its dastardly appearance. That, and the celebrations and rituals associated with the Wiccan holidays like All Hallow's Eve that were perverted by commercialism and stupidity, and really had little to do with his religion.

A few people were meandering up and down Chestnut Street, and he cursed silently as a car pulled out of a parking space just twenty feet from his front door. He knew that by the time he returned to his own car and circled around the space would be occupied once again, so he didn't bother. He fished in his pocket for his house key and unlocked the two deadbolts in his front door.

A split second after he entered the foyer he froze and inhaled sharply. He had already registered the excessive chill in the house and knew that the air conditioner had been turned onto its highest setting. Even so, that didn't eradicate the scent with which he was all too familiar. He quietly and slowly opened the drawer in the small table beside the door and withdrew a gun. He moved like a wraith through the foyer towards the living room where the smell intensified.

He paused, and froze, and listened. He sensed no one moving about or breathing. All of his senses were finely attuned to the world in which he lived, and his gut told him that no one was waiting to waylay him. He moved to the arch at the start of the living room and reached left to flip on the light switch. A second later the room was bathed in light. He studied the scene, which had been meticulously designed and left for him to find. He knew, he knew right away who had been there and why.

He had traveled to Tehran, Iran in 1960 and bought the fifteen-by-twenty-foot Persian Qum-style rug from a dealer whose family had been in the rug business for five generations. Woven under slave-like conditions by downtrodden women and pre-teen girls in 1935, the rug was a miasma of colors, symbols, and images that bespoke of its country of origin and that country's history and mythology. The red was as vivid as blood, the blues ranging from a deep sapphire to a perfect sky-blue, the brown as lush as the pelt of any sable being groomed as the eventual coat for a rich woman who shrugged off murdering innocent animals to put on an elite façade. The weaving, at seven hundred knots per square inch, was absolutely impeccable.

The images and colors were now distorted. Only an inch or so on the shorter side separated the edging from the rim of the circle of blood that any layman's eye could see was nearly perfect. The five points of the pentagram drawn inside the circle neatly touched the circle's inner edge. The lines were exceptionally clean, not jagged at all; it had taken time to create a perfect star image inside a perfect circle image.

But not just any circular image. The blood circle and design were clearly representative of the Sigil of Baphomet, the official insignia of the Church of Satan. A "material pentagram," it represented carnality and earthly principles. The Hebrew letters at the five points of the pentagram spelled out Leviathan, a frightening sea creature in Jewish belief. The body of the pentagram was an image of a goat, the animal's riveting eyes directly in the middle of the pentagram. The eyes, however, were assumed since the pentagram was partially obscured by the body on top of it.

The body on the star in the circle was far from perfect, but meaningful in its ghastly way.

Chris Komansky was naked.

And dead.

Sticking up high and straight from where his heart had once beat was the ceremonial Lord of the Underworld Serpents Satanic Skull King Sword, its mirror-polished, stainless-steel blade smeared with dried blood. Komansky's head lined up with the top point of the star; his arms and legs were splayed to line up with the other star points. Twelve-inch steel spikes were driven into his wrists and ankles to secure him to the mahogany wood floor. His hands were palm-up; one held his tongue, and one held his penis. His eyes were open and staring at the ceiling, no longer the vivid blue they once had been but the milky orbs of the dead and decomposing.

The living eyes of the townhouse's owner scanned the living room and came to rest on the fireplace; rather, on the fireplace mantle. The two silver candlesticks that held the handmade black tapered candles were placed carefully on their sides, pointing to one another. In between them was a standard piece of writing paper that was draped down towards the floor.

The paper was affixed to the sleek wooden fireplace mantel with a nail driven into the wood so deep that only the head showed. He recognized the handwriting.

I'm coming for you.

Despite himself, Damien Savage felt a deep chill run up his spine.

CHAPTER ELEVEN

"Lava."

"Lava?"

"Lava."

"You mean the kind that spews out of volcanoes?"

Carlito Cruz sighed heavily. "No, I mean the soap. Lava soap. That's what the Trinidad M.E. found on the boys' remains. Although, to be honest, one ingredient of the soap is pumice, which is a byproduct of volcanic activity. I'm assuming that's why the company gave it that name. The granularization in the soap is an excellent exfoliant and would not only clean a body but scrape off dead skin cells for an extra-clean result."

Sand nodded. That aspect of the autopsy could prove his theory about an Indian killer adhering to some burial practices. According to the Trinidad police Harlan's buried backpack had a half-used bar of Irish Spring soap inside it, not Lava soap. Frankie's backpack had no soap at all. Lava was a strong soap, a heavy-duty cleaner, rough in its physicality and not particularly fragrant. It was doubtful that Frankie had used Lava and run out but rather more likely that both boys used the fragrant and milder Irish Spring. That pointed to the possibility that the killer had used the Lava to clean the boys' bodies as best he could before burying them.

"Are there any special purposes or professionals that would choose that soap over others?" Frick asked.

"Probably," Carlito replied, shrugging. "I didn't ask the M.E. but I could find out. Anything else you need from me right now?"

Sand shook his head. "No, Carlito. Thanks for following up. Talk to you soon."

"Adios, muchachos," Carlito said, saluting as he left Sand's office. Just before he made the door he snapped his fingers and turned around. "Got this list of soap ingredients from the M.E. and made you a copy." He handed the list to Sand and left.

Sand scanned the list and read off a few ingredients. "Pumice, glycerin, coconut acid and palmitic acid, teterasodium etidronate, and a few others that I've never heard of and won't try to pronounce."

"I got a few ideas," Nick said. "I mean, if it's a heavy-duty cleanser then it would probably be used by professionals that deal with strong dirt and grime in their typical lives."

"Like?" Frack asked.

"First one that comes to mind is car mechanic. They deal with oil and grease all the time and that Irish Spring isn't going to cut it."

Sand nodded. "Makes sense. Maybe gardeners, contractors, oil derrick workers, painters, sculptors, road crews that work with tar, people like that."

"That doesn't narrow it down much," Frack grumbled. "And it could be a red herring."

"How so?" Sand asked.

Frack shrugged. "Maybe the killer just used it for this purpose, to clean the bodies, and doesn't actually use it in his everyday life."

"Thanks a bunch," Frick said sourly.

"Just sayin'," Frack retorted. "We have to look at every angle."

"Frack's right," Nick said. "This killer is smart and precise. There's no reason to think he wouldn't throw us a curve ball in analyzing his actions and methods."

"Can I throw another red herring in?" Frack asked.

"No," Frick said.

"I'm going to anyway," Frack said. "We are going under the assumption that this killer may be an Indian who's collecting these so-called 'injustices' done to his people by the white man."

"Yeah?" Sand said.

"So, what if it ain't an Indian but a white man who sympathizes with them and wants to help make things right? Or, he might simply be using a ploy to make us think he's an Indian," Frack said.

"I hate you," Frick said.

"So, find someone else to be your best man," Frack countered. Frick had finally gotten up the nerve to ask London to marry him two weeks earlier and to his stunned disbelief she said yes. He actually blinked and asked her, "Are you sure?" She responded, "Well not *now*." It took profuse groveling and apologies to get her to accept the diamond ring.

Nick decided to swing the team back on track. "Is there any usefulness in trying to track down where the Lava soap was bought?"

"Nah," Frick said. "It's sold in every store that sells soap."

"And I suppose it's almost as pointless to try to root out any professional that might use the soap," Nick said dejectedly.

"I have another red herring," Frack piped up. Despite the glares from his three colleagues he went on. "What if there are two killers at work, and they have no relation to one another? One guy who happened to kill our San Ramon hikers and the other who's responsible for the various missing people."

Sand sighed. "Caleb has agreed to a front-page story about the San Ramon guys and the other missing people to see if it jogs any thoughts or tips. Maybe someone knows something that can move this investigation forward. Right now, we're stuck like a mastodon in the La Brea Tar Pits."

"Hey," Frack said to Frick. "You could take London there for your honeymoon. She could probably relate to a dinosaur."

Frick stared balefully at his best friend. "I hate you."

Naabah read the *Courant*'s front-page story twice, focusing on every word, every nuance, every fact, every implication. He had thought that taking the boys' bodies across the state line into Colorado was one means of throwing suspicion off of any New Mexico connection. He had been to Fisher's Peak several times and had even done a painting of the mesa at sunrise. He considered it a reverent, beautiful place, and with a mixture of compassion, respect, and, yes, guilt he decided to bury the boys there. He thought he'd buried them deep enough after he bathed their bodies, put their clothes back on, and wrapped them in blankets they had brought with them. He had found their campsite easily enough and gathered all of their belongings and made sure the site looked undisturbed. They had camped in a remote spot so the likelihood of someone coming along and finding any evidence of their presence was negligible.

He was good at covering his tracks. The talent hadn't come naturally but with the tutelage from his father, a Pueblo Indian who preferred to live off the land, hunting and fishing and, occasionally, crossing the line into less than legal methods of taking care of his large family.

Naabah was the only boy; there were five sisters, three older and two younger. Naabah had been born in 1930 and his family in the Taos Pueblo had seen the worst of the Great Depression. His mother was Navajo and had left her family behind in Gallup for the love of a dour but compassionate Puebloan who promised her the moon and gave her a tiny adobe home in a desolate, poverty-ridden place. Their oldest daughter married an abusive man when she was fifteen; she and her firstborn died in childbirth nine months later. The family's youngest daughter died in her crib at the age of two months.

Naabah first went hunting with his father at the age of eight and learned how to track, aim, and kill within a short year. The training served him well; his father was shot to death in a drunken brawl by a white man from Albuquerque when Naabah was twelve and he became the man of the house. He supplemented his food-finding skills with odd jobs to keep his mother's and sisters' stomachs from rumbling too much. He found good husbands for his two older sisters, who moved away to other pueblos to start their own families. His mother died when he was eighteen and his remaining younger sister was seven. He wheedled his way into the good graces of a church group that took in his sister and put her in a good school where she thrived. She was the first in both her maternal and paternal lines to go to a community college and graduate with an Associate's degree in History. She was hired as a teacher on the Navajo reservation where she thrived, married, had three children, and continued teaching her people. They had very infrequent contact.

He had dropped out of school at fourteen. A bright student, he saw no future in furthering his academic education, especially since he had an innate talent for art. He kept his paintings hidden at first, but after his last sister left the nest he forged ahead with his chosen profession. At the same time, he changed his name to reflect his Navajo heritage; Hashkeh Naabah meant "angry warrior." He combined syllables from the first and last names to create his artistic signature. As the years passed people who knew him by his birth name faded away, and no one remembered what name he once went by.

He managed to sell some crude paintings to tourists; the funds allowed him to buy better supplies and enhance his abilities. Sometimes he drank too much and got into fights, but never enough to warrant arrest. He bedded any number of one-night stands and a few weeks longer, but he swore to himself that he'd never recreate the familial situation in which he had grown up. He had helped raise his sisters and wasn't sanguine about wanting to propagate and raise his own children. That determination was hardened by the way he saw his people treated, particularly by the white man. His resentment simmered, simmered for years until that first time.

He was thirty-five. He was celebrating his birthday in a cheap tavern north of Santa Fe. There was a mixture of whites, Indians, and Mexicans drinking and rebel-rousing. The place was noisy and filled with the stench of cigarette smoke and cheap whiskey and body odor. Somewhere near midnight a couple of Indians got into an argument with a pack of white guys. The argument escalated into violence and long story short the white pack beat the shit out of the two Indians while a mixture of whites, Indians, and Mexicans egged them on. Naabah tried to intervene but was traduced by the crack of a whiskey bottle on the back of his head. When he came to he stumbled out of the tavern and saw the two Indians lying in a pool of blood, one's face battered beyond recognition. Virtually everyone fled before the police arrived, including Naabah. He watched from a distance as the tavern owner spoke with the cops. Two ambulances arrived to carry the victims to the hospital; one died on the way.

Naabah waited for an arrest. It never happened even though any number of witnesses could have fingered the perpetrators. He knew that if the races had been reversed the perps would have been arrested, tried, and sent to prison. That didn't sit well with him.

He waited a month before he cornered the white ringleader one dark night. He knocked him out, tied him to his truck's bumper, and dragged him until the man was a dead mess of flayed flesh and broken bones. Naabah stared down at the bones peeking out of the decimated flesh and thought about his mother, who had imbued a deep sense of reverence and respect for their ancestors and race. She told him many stories about various Indian people, and some of those stories involved bones, bones of humans and bones of creatures briefly or long gone.

Many tribes found and revered fossils. The Plains Indians collected iridescent marine fossils and used them in ceremonies to summon buffalo herds. Some tribes were lucky enough to collect large fossilized dinosaur bones. They held them in deep respect and not a small measure of awe. Rocks were often seen as spiritual "bones" and many traditional Indians saw the unearthing of rocks as the desecration of Mother Earth. In the Indian worldview, the land and everything that composes it, including stones and fossils, are hallowed, vital entities.

In 1890 a Paiute shaman named Wovoka declared, "You ask me to plow the ground! Shall I take a knife and tear my Mother's bosom? Then when I die, she will not take me to her bosom to rest. You ask me to dig for stones! Shall I dig under her skin for her bones?" George

Armstrong Custer's Crow scout, Curly, voiced similar sentiments in 1907: "The soil you can see is not ordinary soil—it is the dust of the blood, the flesh, and the bones of our ancestors and relations." Naabah's own maternal people, the Navajo, feared that excavation of dinosaur fossils would interfere with the resting places of the Indians' ancestors' bones.

Bones, Naabah thought. Bones could be used for other than fertilizing the earth. They could be used to make an artistic statement. That night, he found his true calling. That night, he began to clean and prepare his first set of bones.

His initial efforts were trial and error on removing all flesh, muscles, and ligaments from the bones he collected. He decided to confer with someone who might offer suggestions; of course, he'd have to make sure that said person believed he was talking about animal bones. He hit paydirt with his first visit to a taxidermist. He learned of dermestid beetles, where to get them, and how to use them. After a few more victims he mastered the art of defleshing bones. Once he had the clean bones he sanded them and applied a preservative lacquer. Then, he used them to create his special art, art that the unlucky young men from San Ramon had stumbled upon and for that mistake lost their lives.

He felt no guilt towards his victims; each in some way had disrespected his race and culture. He wouldn't admit to himself that he had developed a taste for his special art and, perhaps, he sought out victims. He also sought out reading material on the subject and became quite adept at identifying every single bone in the human body. He also sought out historical information on the mythology of bones and found a wide range of reading materials. He was especially enamored of the various ossuaries across the globe. He promised himself that someday he would visit Paris and Rome.

In the last two years he had developed a hunger for a particular set of bones to add to his collection. The problem was that the person was completely respectful of the Indian culture. Naabah's personal code of injustice and retribution prevented him from acting on his desire, but that desire ached since that day at Bandelier when he saw that both maligned and marvelous expression of nature.

The dwarf would be his crowning achievement.

Someday.

All he had to do was wait, wait for Dr. Percival McBean to make some tiny mistake that would fit his criteria for taking action.

He thirsted, but he was patient …

Percy finished up with his last patient of the day. He felt that they had made some progress in changing the woman's agoraphobia, if only because she was not as reluctant to come into the office. Her anxiety disorder made her fear leaving her house or putting herself in any situation where she might feel panicked, entrapped, helpless, or embarrassed. They had had five therapy sessions so far and Percy could see that she was less tense than the first time she entered his office when she stood for the entire time, taut and looking like she'd run for the hills if he so much as blinked at her. Gradually, she was learning to trust him.

His day was particularly busy since Tucson was off on his hunt and Percy took two sessions with his partner's patients. He tried to call Tucson's most difficult patient, Ralph Mancini, the Vietnam vet and Hanoi Hilton POW that had many of the same symptoms of anxiety that Tucson had from his similar wartime experience. The man hadn't answered his phone, but Candy said that he turned up just as the office opened, demanding to see Tucson. She had to calm him down and tell him gently that Tucson was out of town, but she was sure that Percy could see him. Mancini left without saying another word. Candy told Percy that he was all keyed up and had an odd look in his eyes.

Percy tried calling Mancini one more time, but the phone rang and rang. He sighed; nothing more he could do about the situation today, but maybe he'd pop over to the guy's apartment first thing in the morning. It was late, he was tired, and he needed to get home.

The aroma of potato soup assailed his nostrils when he came into the house and he smiled; Tansee knew just how to season it and make sure the soup part was thick and creamy. His mother hadn't made it any better. He wondered where Elspeth was since usually she ran like a bat out of hell when he came home and flung herself into his arms. Pretty soon that flinging was going to result in him hitting the floor hard and fast, and soon after that there wouldn't be any flinging at all. His little girl was growing up.

"Tansee," he called out as he tossed his suit jacket over a chair and began rolling up the sleeves of his shirt. He removed his bowtie just before he went into the kitchen where he saw his wife at the stove tasting a spoonful of their dinner. She looked over at him and winked, then put the spoon down and kissed him on the lips.

"Hungry?" she asked.

"Starved," he replied. "Where's the little one? No smart remarks."

"She's spending the night at Nick's. I thought we could have a nice dinner and evening just by ourselves."

"That would be lovely. Anything I can do to help?"

"Set the table, please."

Percy complied, even lighting a candle, and placing it between their plates. Minutes later Tansee ladled a hefty portion of soup into his bowl, an antique pattern of a set his mother had used when he was growing up.

They ate slowly and talked about her day and his day and whether to sign Elspeth up for ballet class (yes). They talked for a solid ten minutes about Tucson's quest and whether Cameo would be found and, if so, would she come home? Tansee said that no mother worth her salt would abandon her child. She quickly apologized but Percy said she'd said nothing wrong. They were both aware that Percy's birth parents were horrified at their dwarf baby and had dumped him in an orphanage before he was a week old.

Tansee smiled and asked if Percy was ready for dessert and he answered with an enthusiastic yes. He carried the plates into the kitchen and saw Tansee pick up two small plates with half-circle shiny covers on them. Back at the table she placed one in front of him and smiled brightly. She had chickened out that night that Swan took Elspeth for the evening.

He narrowed his eyes. He knew when his wife was being coy. He carefully removed the cover from his plate and looked confused. Instead of a piece of cake or pie the plate contained a small new baby rattle. He inhaled sharply and met her eyes. She nodded and her smile widened.

"I'm weeks past where I lost the other babies, Percival. There's a good chance this baby will be born. Aren't you happy?"

Without a word Percy slid off his chair and rushed to his wife for a tight embrace. He could feel her joy; he was glad that she couldn't see the fear in his face. Before either could start talking the phone rang. Percy disengaged and walked away to answer the phone. He spoke quietly, listened, and Tansee could see his face pale. He nodded and said he'd be right there.

"What is it, sweetheart?" she asked.

"One of our patients—one of Tucson's patients—committed suicide tonight. That was Detective Abbott. He wants to talk to me at the scene. I may be gone a few hours. I'm sorry."

"That's okay," she said softly. "I'll wait up."

He nodded and grabbed his car keys. Just as he reached the front door he looked back at Tansee. "I love you, baby," he said quietly. "And I'm overjoyed about our new son or daughter."

Her face broke out in a wide grin. "A son. I just know it."

"A son," he murmured as he left the house for the drive to Ralph Mancini's tiny apartment where he had hanged himself from a rafter and ended forever his emotional torment.

CHAPTER TWELVE

"Well, I have some good news and some bad news from back home," Memphis said over a fast lunch at a Gloucester seaside restaurant.

He was pigging out on fried cod and chips while Tucson was sticking to his cheeseburger and onion rings. DeVere was shoveling deep-fried scallops into his mouth, washing them down with a frosty glass of Pepsi. His brother, ReVere, had driven down from Portsmouth to add a fresh eye to their search and spend some time with his younger sibling. He was eating a Caesar salad in deference to the ten pounds he'd put on since his latest marriage.

"Good news would be a nice change of pace," Tucson said dourly.

"It would," Memphis agreed. "Anyway, Richard Ballard called me just before we left the inn. He was able to check out flight manifests from the days after Cameo left."

Tucson leaned forward eagerly. "Did he find something?"

Memphis shook his head. "Nothing of note from Albuquerque, Phoenix, or Denver. But, he checked the Santa Fe Regional Airport."

"Santa Fe doesn't fly to the east coast," Tucson said. "It's a small airport."

"True, but Ballard checked it out and found something interesting. A woman named Mary Kay Randall took a flight from Santa Fe to

Las Vegas, and from there she took a flight to Logan with a quick layover in Atlanta. He showed the desk clerk a photo of Cameo, but the girl didn't recognize her. It'd be even less likely that an ID could be made in Vegas with the volume of customers. She would want to be anonymous and provoke no events that would make her memorable to anyone."

"And she was probably wearing a wig and special makeup," ReVere said as he glowered at his pathetic excuse for a meal. "Maybe contacts. Probably too many variations to get an affirmative ID."

"True," Memphis said, nodding. "But maybe we can check out the name in various hotels and car rental places and see if we get a hit. We can start with the places around here and then hit Salem and go down to the Boston area."

"She'd likely rent a car right at Logan," DeVere said. "We can start there."

"What if she's going by a second phony ID?" DeVere asked.

"Then we're back at square one after spinning our wheels," Tucson said. He picked up his last onion ring, stared at it, and threw it back down on the plate.

"So," DeVere said to Memphis, "what's the bad news?"

"My wife has become a hormone tornado and is driving the entire office crazy. Our oldest daughter packed a bag and went next door to live with my parents until, as Skye repeated, 'Mom settles the hell down and stops acting like a psycho woman.' The twins, supposedly, are on the verge of following their sister."

Tucson smiled automatically. "You need a Declan."

"Given the opportunity, I'd steal him from you," Memphis said, half seriously.

"That the only bad news?" DeVere asked.

Memphis absently toyed with his straw then said, "Actually, I need to talk to my brother privately for a few minutes."

"We know when we're not wanted," ReVere said mildly as he rose and DeVere followed. "I'll make a call to the Logan car rental places and see if they have a customer with that name."

Memphis scribbled down a few lines on a napkin and handed it to ReVere. "That's the flight number and date and time the plane landed. I don't know if car rental places log that info but maybe it'll help."

"Thanks," ReVere said. DeVere followed him out to the pay phone.

"Okay," Tucson said slowly. "What's up?"

Memphis looked at Tucson's face and knew his brother had enough to deal with, but Tucson would be furious that such important information was withheld from him. Neither Memphis nor Percy should have to deal with the reactive anger of that delay.

"I talked to Percy last night. Something happened two days ago. He didn't know whether he should tell you or not and left that up to me, the damn little scamp."

Tucson's lips parted. "Are my kids okay? Declan?"

"They're fine. It's … one of your patients. Ralph Mancini."

"Ralph? Is he okay? Did he have a breakdown and require hospitalization?"

Memphis bit his lip and shook his head. "I'm sorry. Ralph … took his own life. He's dead."

Tucson sat back hard in his chair and just stared at his brother for a long, silent minute. Then his eyes overflowed with tears and he shook his head. "I should have been there for him. Oh, my God—I wasn't there for him and he killed himself."

"Let's focus on the part that he killed himself—not you. You can only do so much. There's every possibility that he would have done the same thing if you were still back in Santa Fe."

"We'll never know that, will we?" Tucson asked bitterly. He scraped his chair back and shuddered. "I need some fresh air." He turned towards the door.

Memphis jumped up. "Wait—I'll go with you."

"No," Tucson said sharply. "I need some time alone. Just … leave me alone." With that he walked quickly through the restaurant door and jammed his hands down on the rim of a metal trash can and vomited out his cheeseburger and onion rings. A few second later he felt a reassuring pat on the back from Memphis and he flung himself around and Memphis held him tightly.

"I'm so sorry," Memphis whispered. He felt Tucson's head nodding tightly against his. After a minute they broke apart and Tucson savagely wiped the tears from his eyes. He took a deep breath and narrowed his eyes just as the York brothers came up from behind them.

"I can't deal with this now," he said. "I need to find my wife. That's all I'm going to focus on. Maybe you should go on home?"

"The hell I will," Memphis said.

"It's two days to Halloween and you need to be home for that holiday," Tucson replied quietly.

Memphis shook his head. "I've let that fear take hold of my mind and life for nearly ten years. It has to end. Swan's there as well as all family members that know how to use a gun. I'm okay staying."

"Why do you have to be home for Halloween?" ReVere asked curiously as he and DeVere joined their friends.

"It's a long story," DeVere said quickly. "I'll tell it to you later. Anyway, we have news."

"Good news?" Memphis asked.

"Well, it has nothing to do with hormonal funnel clouds, so, yeah, I guess."

"One Mary Kay Randall rented a fire-engine-red Chevy Camaro for one week with an option to extend. I'm got the VIN and license tag if we need to track the car down," ReVere said, patting his jacket pocket.

"So, she's using that name," Tucson murmured.

"Maybe," Memphis said slowly. "We're making a leap that Cameo is using that alias, but it could be coincidental that a real Mary Kay Randall flew from Santa Fe to Boston and has nothing to do with Cameo."

"Except," DeVere interjected, "if this 'real' Mary Kay wanted to go from Santa Fe to Boston why didn't she just take a flight out of Albuquerque? No reason to hop to Vegas to catch a flight except to throw anyone off her trail."

"Good point," Memphis said. "So, we should start tracking down Mary Kay."

"That's the plan, man," DeVere said brightly. He hated to admit that he was having a great time accompanying the Santa Feans on their quest. The effort was exhilarating, a hell of a lot more so than his work as a patrolman back in Pittsfield. And Pittsfield didn't have Devon … They'd made a connection when he visited Santa Fe. She was abrasive, smart, tough, and she made him feel like a teenage boy. She took him to dinner that first day and lunch the next, and spent her day off shuttling him around the various tourist sites around the city. The night before he flew home she, well … banged his brains out. They'd been having a long-distance romance ever since. Wanting to see her again was an ache in his heart.

"So, gumshoes," ReVere said in his raspy baritone, "where do we go from here?"

"Well, we don't need to check car rental places, so we need to start hitting hotels, motels, and B&Bs from here down to Boston."

"We'll make better time if we split up," DeVere said.

"Excellent idea," Memphis replied. "Why don't you and your brother take the Gloucester/Salem area while Tucson and I drive down to Boston?"

DeVere handed Memphis his car keys. "You take my car, and we'll use ReVere's. Be careful driving around that crazy place—I just got it detailed." ReVere scribbled out the VIN and tag of the Camaro and handed the paper to Memphis.

Memphis crossed his heart and grinned. He watched as the York brothers walked to ReVere's car then slid behind the steering wheel as Tucson parked himself in the passenger seat and fastened his seat belt. He turned to Memphis.

"We're going to find her, aren't we?" he asked.

"Bet your ass we are, Cochise," Memphis said in a strong, determined voice.

Damien Savage studied his living room, pleased that his friends had cleaned up the mess so that it looked and smelled like it had never happened. He regretted the loss of the Persian rug, but not the loss of his increasingly erratic henchman, Chris Komansky. In the early days, a decade ago, Komansky had been a trusted, loyal associate. He had failed in a few assignments, but Savage gave him some leeway because under the nervousness, drinking, and insecurity Komansky was bloodthirsty and could be called upon to assist in the most heinous of crimes. He had helped torture and kill that dolt, Eddie Troy.

He had also helped to hold down Maeve Kiara Riley when Savage raped her on their wedding night.

And now, Maeve was on the hunt.

And she was a force to be reckoned with.

A force to be broken.

His first name was from the Greek and meant to tame or to subdue. He had needed help in taming her the last time. He admitted only to himself that he had failed. He blamed the failure on his underlings who had let her damn brother spirit her away in the night, taking her to who knows where. He instituted a search, of course, but made no headway. That wasn't acceptable, certainly not acceptable for a scion of the Savage family from Beacon Hill.

The Savages had been rooted in Boston's fabric since the late 1600s. From the moment the first Savage set foot in the new land the dynasty of prevarication, crooked dealings, betrayal, and an endless thirst for power grew and thrived. Amadeus Savage fortunately picked the right side in the Revolutionary War and made a fortune supplying troops with muskets and gunpowder. He made even more money selling weaponry on the sly to the Redcoats.

The War of 1812 and the Mexican-American War filled the coffers, but the Civil War sent the family fortunes into the stratosphere. Of course, there were other methods of making a buck, and in 1920 the Savages joined the ranks of bootleggers. By that time various family members had their fingers in pies all over New England, but Damien's grandfather and father stuck with illegal booze. Damien's great-grandfather was the first in his nuclear family to go to college, graduating Harvard as valedictorian. Simeon Savage was brilliant, and as debauched as the Marquis de Sade. Even so, he was smart enough to understand the sensibilities of a decent civilization and actively developed and promoted an impenetrable veneer of sophistication and respectability.

Simeon's son, Balthazar, continued the family fortunes and that veneer. His mother was a weak-willed, subdued woman permanently under Simeon's thumb. Balthazar wanted none of that and meticulously looked for a woman that would match his own strength and purpose. He found her in Artemis Bennett, a direct descendant of one of the Salem Witch Trials witnesses, Elizabeth Hubbard. She had left Salem after the trials, moved to Gloucester, and married a man named John Bennett. They had four children, one of whom was Artemis's ancestor. She was tall, blonde, blue-eyed and educated, and threw off an aura of superiority without fail. She produced six children, one of whom was Damien's father, Barnabas.

All of Balthazar's children radiated entitlement and made good marriages. Barnabas and his brother, Jeremiah, although as smart as any member of the family, had dark sides that went beyond sketchy or illegal business practices. Barnabas opened a series of brothels in and around Boston; he used his power to rape all of the girls that worked for him. Jeremiah delved into the illegal drug trade and became one of the most powerful drug lords in the city. He initially cut prices until more people were hooked, and there was a rumor (true) that he had three of his rivals murdered; their bodies were never found.

Both were truly the spiritual children of the Marquis de Sade. Since they were children they were drawn in by the dark arts, perhaps because of their distant ancestor but more likely because they were emotionally and mentally damaged. Jeremiah whored around in his brother's houses of ill repute as well as taking advantage of powerless serving girls and streetwalkers. Barnabas married well, to an introverted girl name Gillian Riley, the daughter of another seamy Boston entrepreneur. Her father was a major player in the bootlegging industry and even ran illegal booze with the inimitable

Joe Kennedy, another Boston mainstay who had perfected the art of supercilious veneer.

While Jeremiah dabbled in dark arts, only, really, to serve his base physical needs, Barnabas immersed himself into said arts as a matter of servicing similar needs but principally to increase his power and wealth. He made a point of studying the history of black magic from ancient to modern times and read every book he could get his hands on regarding Satanism as opposed to more benevolent witchcraft. On a business trip to Germany he procured an ancient grimoire book and considered it his most cherished possession. He studied it and decided to start his own coven. On a trip the year after he found a magnificent 1800s version of Milton's *Paradise Lost*, printed in Latin. He learned Latin to be able to read it.

But not just any coven, one that would be comprised of the higher echelons of society that were as powerful as he but were compliant enough to accept him as their leader. He cherry picked each of the twelve members, one of whom was his father-in-law, Cillian Riley. To set the atmosphere for his first gathering he chose Salem because of its history and mystery. Fortunately, Cillian Riley was an ocean-loving man and had a summer home in Gloucester, an old two-story, clapboard whitewashed house set back on three acres of land right across the street from the rocky coast. He brought his extended family of children, in-laws, and grandchildren there during every season, and for a solid month in the summer. He hosted Barnabas and a few other coven members in the house as they planned for the ceremony.

Barnabas had purchased a five-acre plot of barren land near a forest outside of Salem and that was where he planned his first foray into Satanism. He didn't really believe in the devil—or God, for that matter—but religion was a powerful tool to subdue people and keep them in line. Fear and skullduggery were just icing on the cake.

The ceremony was somber, and the coven members were riveted as Barnabas invoked Satan with words from his grimoire book. There were gasps when Riley's youngest daughter, Regan, was led out in a diaphanous white gown. The ten-year-old's long brown hair fell down her back. Her eyes were dull as her father took her hand and led her to the altar. He lifted her up and positioned her body prone on the granite slab large enough to hold a tall man. He bound her wrists gently then stood back, looked at Barnabas, and bowed to him.

Barnabas led an ancient chant, then read several passages from his Latin *Paradise Lost*. John Milton's poem, written in 1667, was divided into two arcs, one following Satan (or Lucifer) and one following Adam and Eve. Divided into ten books it encompassed ten thousand lines. He kept to Satan's story, and he repeated what he thought was the most integral part of the text—Potius est regnabit apud inferos, quam in omnibus in Caelo.

Better to reign in Hell than to serve in Heaven.

One could hear a pin drop when he finished his oration. Then, he walked to the head of the altar and withdrew a long stiletto from his black robes and raised it above his head. Everyone assumed that he was using the gesture symbolically and were stunned when he plunged it down into little Regan's heart. She let out a squeak then stopped moving as the blood issued from her chest. Barnabas stared into each set of eyes, then spoke.

"Longum iter est difficile ex inferno prouehit lucem."

Long is the way and hard, that out of Hell leads up to light.

He paused then said, "Our daughter Regan has joined the light. Born blind, deaf, and dumb her human life here in this world served no purpose. Today, she served the purpose of bringing us together as one unit, bound forever. Her father generously allowed her rebirth as an angel of Hell. We should not mourn her, but should joyously celebrate her sacrifice, and our future together. You may begin."

The equal number of male and female coven members paired off and shed their clothes, falling on the rough earth as they fornicated. Barnabas watched for a few minutes, then let a sly, evil smile play across his lips as he mounted the altar and had vigorous sexual relations with the little girl's corpse.

By the end of the night he was assured of the loyalty and fear of his congregation. Riley carried off his daughter's murdered, defiled body and took steps to vanish her from the face of the earth.

Barnabas continued his reign of "Satan," drawing more acolytes and binding the original twelve to him even more tightly. With his wife, Gillian, he spawned six children of his own; first son Damien was born in 1940. By the boy's seventh birthday he was attending his father's ceremonies and grew to become a passionate acolyte and when grown, a purveyor of the same religious beliefs and craven behaviors as his increasingly demented father, perhaps even more so. There seemed to be a wide streak of sadism encompassed in his six-foot-two, athletic, well-structured body. His ebony hair, pale complexion and unfathomable black eyes gave off a vampiric aura, and his own family was frightened of him.

Except Barnabas, who as the years passed became jealous of the son that might eclipse him. They began to quarrel as Damien entered his teens and demanded more power in their devilish little klatch. In 1958 that mutual anger came to a head and had a consequence that Barnabas never saw coming. During the Satanic rites on that night Damien begged off the gathering, which didn't displease his father. The rituals and chants had ended, but before the sexual debauchery could begin Damien stepped out of the forest behind his father and deftly slit his throat. The gasps of the coven settled down immediately as the eighteen-year-old held up the knife dripping with his father's blood.

"I am your new leader," he said in a deadly, low voice. "Does anyone say otherwise?" There was not a single sound, a single gesture to resist his coup. "Good. Mackenzie, Goodson, take his body and place it in the car. Follow me home." He turned to Riley. "You and I must talk."

The rest of the night was a blur to most celebrants and there seemed to be no desire to indulge in carnal efforts. Riley and Mackenzie met Damien at the family home where they carried Barnabas's body into the foyer and placed it at the bottom of the long, curved staircase. Mackenzie snapped his neck then left and Riley stayed. Just ten feet away from the body the two men sat on silk sofas and Damien laid out his plans. Cillian had a son married to the daughter of a Boston banker who was also a coven member. The girl, Maeve, was a beautiful, intelligent ten-year-old with a heart-shaped face, long, luxurious chestnut hair, and luminous hazel eyes. When she grew to womanhood she would make an exceptional wife and mother of his dynasty.

They haggled, but not much—Riley was genuinely afraid of Damien and his brutal ruthlessness. The plan was for the child Maeve to be exceptionally educated and prepared as Damien's eventual bride. To date she had played no part in the satanic rituals, but Damien wanted her to be educated in that religion so that she'd understand and accept it when her time came to become a pure, innocent bride of the devil. Because, as Damien explained in neutral terms, he was Satan, and someday it would be time to rise up and claim his kingdom. Riley was in awe of Damien's stated purpose and even more so that this callow teenager seemed like a fifty-year-old man in terms of determination and purpose. Damien insisted in signing the agreement in blood and used a razor to cut each of their thumbs and blend their blood.

Then he wrote a check on the family account for ten thousand dollars and handed it to Riley, saying that there would be more to come to finance the costs of his future bride's education.

The following Monday Riley registered his granddaughter in a private girls' academy with boarding outside of Danvers. He demanded a rigorous curriculum and got it. Young Maeve pleaded and cried to come home but her father told her this was for her future. She could see her older and younger brothers when she came home for Christmas.

Maeve stayed in the boarding school, which accelerated her education so that at the age of sixteen she was ready for college. She hoped that she'd be allowed to go to a Boston college. She was shocked when her grandfather collected her from the school on her last day and instead of driving her home to her parents' tony townhouse on the Charles River in Back Bay he drove them to Logan where they boarded a flight—first class, of course—for Geneva.

She was horrified when her grandfather told her that she'd be spending her college years in that foreign country and that it was expected of her to excel in her studies. He had engaged special tutors to teach her about religion. He left her in the care of a lovely governess in a small town outside Geneva until the school year started. She was there only a day before the first tutor turned up, a dour German with a heavy accent and the absolute belief that his ethnicity was the best on the planet. She thought he looked and acted like a Nazi.

Maeve was inundated with tutors that drilled into her the history of the Catholic Church, its evils, and the backlash through the centuries. One tutor made her read *Paradise Lost* out loud and explain what the stanzas meant. After he was satisfied with her progress he introduced her to several grimoire books which he said were the bibles of God's enemies. She was taught astronomy, physics, chemistry, English, three languages—Latin, French, and German—and the usual course plethora of a Liberal Arts curriculum.

In addition, a great deal of emphasis was put on athletics and she was coached for the swim team, the tennis team, and a series of in-depth martial arts courses. By the time she was eighteen she could hit dead center of a target board with shurikens that were tightly clustered in the middle. She was taught to shoot as well, with a pistol, a rifle, and a shotgun. She went on hikes and learned to fish. Her college adventure took five years since Damien wanted her to achieve a Master's in Religion as well as her Bachelor's degree. Then, she would be ready to become his bride.

Cillian Riley died two years into Maeve's college years, but she wasn't permitted to fly home for the funeral. In truth, she had become essentially estranged from her birth family except for her younger brother, Aidan, who wrote her covert letters and established a post office box to get smuggled letters from her. He told her of the growing presence of the strange Damien Savage in family events and how he seemed to have a hold over their grandfather and parents.

She was getting a very disturbing feeling as the years went by. She had her nose to the grindstone for her academics, but once or twice tried to break away and have some semblance of a normal life. The new wave of music was hitting hard and fast and she loved the songs of the Beatles, Stones, Animals, and the American Motown stable. She wasn't allowed to have a record player, but she'd manage to covertly buy a transistor radio and listen to its low sounds whenever she could.

One time in her senior year she snuck out to go to a bar with a school friend who had a crush on her. He was sweet, and smart, and she enjoyed their bantering in class and in the hallways. Two days after their date he was found dead in the back alley of the same bar, his head beaten in. Her shock was compounded by the thought that his brutal murder might be related to her. She knew somehow that she was always under surveillance. She never dated again and became more apprehensive as the time for her to return to Boston approached.

Two months before she boarded her flight from Geneva to Boston her father made an unexpected visit in March and told her that she was going home to a wonderful life of privilege, wealth, and power. She was to marry her first cousin, Damien Savage. She was dumbfounded and just stared at him. She asked him if he were insane. She said she barely knew her cousin and what she did see of him she didn't like him very much. Her father smiled at her then took her hands and rose. Without warning he twisted her arm so hard that she screamed. He twisted her arm behind her back and leaned into her neck, whispering harshly that she would do as she was told because her family's position necessitated her compliance. He told her to accept her fate. There was no other option. Then he boarded a plane and went home.

Maeve was nauseous for the final two months and she thought about absconding and not flying back to the States. She sighed in resignation when her older brother, Callan, and one of Damien Savage's friends, Chris Komansky, arrived to "escort" her home. She'd have to make her break once she landed in Boston. She never got the chance.

A sleek, long black limousine was waiting to drive her and her guards home. She was coolly greeted by her parents, but her younger brother, Aidan, could barely restrain himself from flinging his arms around her. When he did he whispered into her ear, "We have to talk. Midnight, same place." That meant their attic.

Maeve pretended to be happy to be home and didn't let a negative emotion wash across her face. She was tired and went to bed at ten o'clock. The rest of the house was silent and locked up by eleven. At five minutes to twelve she slipped silently out of bed and crept up the stairs to the attic where Aidan engulfed her in a bear hug.

And then he told her.

He told her about Damien's extracurricular activities, which he had learned about over the years and through mainly covert channels. He said he even found Damien's hidden house key and used it to search his townhouse where he found a secret room designed with evil images and props; there were a number of books paying homage to the Prince of Darkness and Hell.

Her horror increased minute by minute as her brother detailed the coven, the Satanism, the sadistic things he had done including the rumor that he had murdered his own father to gain control of his coven. The last thing he told her was the worst—she had been bought from the Riley family to be his mate and the mother of his children. It was Damien that had paid for her education and instructed its agenda. It was he that designed her life from the time she was ten years old.

Maeve was frozen to the rocking chair on which she'd perched. Her blood ran cold, and her arms exploded into goosebumps. Aidan knelt in front of her and told her he'd help her get away. They could go away together, maybe to Canada. He clutched her hands and she hugged him tightly.

The next morning Aidan wasn't at breakfast; their mother said he had an early class. Maeve felt chilled to the bone. She wasn't allowed to leave the house all day and her disquiet grew hour by hour. At dinner she barely had any appetite, but her mother urged her to eat all of her shepherd's pie and cornbread and to drink her chocolate milk, a beverage she had always loved. She smiled weakly and finished her meal. She had barely stood up from the dinner table when she felt dizzy and swayed. Her eyes fluttered and it seemed like a bad dream when Callan threw her over his shoulder and headed to the door to the garage. She lost consciousness right after she recognized

Chris Komansky in the driver's seat of that same limousine. Callan dumped her in the back seat. That was the last thing she remembered.

Until she woke up on a cold granite slab in a field north of Salem. Little by little she registered fire, candle aromas, strange, low music, and people chanting. She realized that she was wearing a black dress that covered her legs down to her ankles. She sensed makeup on her face. She tried to move but her wrists and ankles were bound. She twisted and gasped as she tried to wriggle free. A moment later a face appeared above her and she found herself staring into the black eyes of Damien Savage. The devil's eyes, she thought. She twisted her head to the right and her eyes lit upon a small wooden table on which were three books, three black candles, two yellow candles, and a strong tower of incense suffusing the air with cloying sweetness. One of the leather book covers had a raised pentagram on it; another had an evil eye staring upward.

He put his hands on her cheeks and leaned over her and whispered, "Are you ready, my bride, to join your destiny?"

"Fuck you," Maeve snarled and desperately tried to free her wrists. Her efforts paid off when she broke the binding on her right wrist and tried to reach over and unfastened her left one. Suddenly Damien grabbed her hand and slammed it back down on the slab and she could hear the crack as it broke. She screamed and seconds later a cotton cloth was stuffed into her mouth.

Damien stared down at her in fury then raised his eyes towards his enraptured audience and said, "I declare this woman my wife." He looked down at her. "Until death do us part." He swatted away her free hand, still moving despite the broken bone, then frowned and nodded to Chris Komansky who grinned evilly and leaned over her upper body and held down her wrists. She twisted her torso maniacally and wasn't even aware that Damien had summoned her brother, Callan, and another man over. Damien slit her ankle bindings, and each grabbed an ankle and pulled her legs apart.

Maeve screamed at the top of her lungs as Damien pushed up her skirt and mounted her, and a moment later she arched her back in sheer pain as he rammed himself into her again and again while his acolytes chanted. After a moment something happened to her; she drifted away from her body and fixed her soul on anything but the horror of her "wedding night."

Damien finished his forcible consummation and climbed off the altar and raised his arms to cheering. He turned back towards her with a sheer evil, salacious grin on his face but before he could assault her again a wild screaming came from the forest as Aidan ran out shooting a rifle at Damien and into the crowd, all of whom scrambled away from the enraged brother. He reached his sister and dragged her off the slab towards the forest after firing off a few more shots.

Brother and sister ran for their lives through the forest. Maeve stumbled repeatedly, enduring bruises and deep scratches from the rocks and tree branches. One time she crashed hard into a large rock and slammed her head against its unyielding girth. After that she was barely conscious of her brother dragging her to his hidden car. He stuffed her in the back seat and careened off. He told her that they were going to Canada but not up through New England where Damien had many cohorts. He said they would head west to the New York border and continue on to Niagara Falls where they'd cross into Ontario. He had opened their father's safe and taken all the cash inside (gained illicitly) which he stuffed into the backpack resting of the back seat.

Aidan entered the Massachusetts Turnpike and breathed a sigh of relief as he headed west precisely doing the speed limit. He looked back several times and saw that his sister seemed to be unconscious. He choked up at the glistening blood smeared on the front of her dress. For many miles he drove with his eyes flooded with tears. He vowed vengeance.

As the miles passed Aidan became a little paranoid, thinking that cars were following him, members of the coven ready to pounce. He was about eight miles from the New York border when he suddenly got off the Pike and headed north on Route 7. He thought he'd feel safer on back roads and cross over to New York farther north, perhaps when he made Vermont. He pulled over to the shoulder, cast a fast glance at his unconscious sister and pulled out a worn map of New

England from the glove compartment. He studied the border and thought that he'd modify their escape route, going north through Vermont and crossing into Quebec just north of Highgate.

First, however, he'd have to stop in Pittsfield and gas up, and maybe if he could find a place open at these wee hours of the morning get something to eat and drink. Maeve was no doubt dehydrated. Just south of the main drag on South Street he found a small Texaco gas station open. There were no cars around. He parked near one of the two pumps and got out of the car, walking leisurely to the station where a teenager was engrossed in a textbook as he fulfilled his red-eye shift. He looked up and nodded. Aidan asked if he had any snacks or drinks and the kid slid off his stool and walked him over to a small refrigeration unit where Pepsis, Cokes, and Ginger Ales abounded. Right next to the drinks was a stand that had popcorn, chips, and candy bars. Aidan stocked up and brought them to the register. He said he needed gas and could pump it himself. He paid for the gas and snacks and went back outside. When he opened the passenger door he went ice cold—Maeve wasn't in the back seat, nor was the backpack of money. He whirled around madly trying to spot her in the vicinity but didn't. With shaking hands, he filled the tank then drove slowly to the other side of the road and parked.

He inhaled sharply when he found one of her shoes just before the tree line. He slowly went in the same direction as the shoe indicated, and a thousand feet in he found her torn, bloody dress lying on the ground. He picked it up and choked and kept going. It was dark as hell and he didn't have a flashlight. Panic had set in, drenching his heart and mind with terror. After another five hundred feet he found himself on the banks of a river. He walked north and then south searching for Maeve but found no trace. He called to her but got no answer. He got close enough to one section of the bank where he slid on mud and nearly fell in.

Then he heard a couple of voices, one an adult and one a child. He bolted back to the car and sat in the driver's seat hyperventilating and wondering what the hell to do. After about ten minutes he heard police sirens that seemed like they were headed to where the voices were. He was torn between staying or fleeing, but he sensed that his sister had been found and now would be taken to a hospital. He'd stick around the area and see how the matter fell out. He'd keep his eye on the news. He pulled away and found a tiny motel and checked in. He fell dead asleep and stayed that way for twelve hours.

He never expected the denouement to the flight. According to the newspapers a woman had been found severely injured on the banks of the Housatonic River. Two days later a follow-up article stated that the woman had no memory of who she was or her life. Aidan felt a sense of angst mixed with relief. Maybe she would be safer if she was no longer Maeve Riley. He stuck around for weeks following the story, and when there was no sign of a memory return or someone claiming her, he relaxed a little. Perhaps she could make a new life and use the money to find a future. He'd taken the money for her, so it didn't matter. She had been released from the hospital and was living in a small hotel while the doctors and police did their thing. After a month, she left town. He thought it was time for him to bolt, too.

He didn't know where she went or what name she went under, so he continued heading north into Vermont and settled down in Bennington where he changed his name and started working as a garage mechanic. He bided his time because he knew—he just knew—that someday they'd be together again.

Someday.

Damien called his latest henchman and told him that a dangerous foe was back and claiming retribution. He told his man to find her, or else.

The man took off. He knew what "or else" meant.

CHAPTER THIRTEEN

Callan Riley was pissed and tired from a long day's work as an investment banker. His wife had left him and taken the kids back to her family's Newport mansion a week earlier, and his mistress had bid him goodbye as she flew off to Milan for a modeling gig. He was horny as hell and that itch wouldn't be scratched unless he obtained the services of one of the high-class escort services he frequented.

He tossed his Corvette's keys on the side table as he entered the kitchen from the garage door. He tore off his suit jacket and tossed it across a kitchen chair then opened the fridge. He'd worked through lunch and was hungry. Not a goddamn thing to eat. He slammed the door shut and grabbed the wall phone receiver and dialed the well-known number. He barked out an order for a full slab of ribs with all the trimming, including cole slaw and a couple bottles of Pepsi. He dialed another number he knew by heart and ordered a tall blonde, no more than one-twenty in poundage and no older than twenty, and a submissive that didn't mind a little S&M.

He strode into the den and went up to the liquor globe, one of those kitschy things whose top opened to reveal bottles of booze and glasses. He studied the contents and chose an imported Russian vodka. He poured a full tumbler and raised it to his lips as he stared at his reflection in the wall mirror behind the globe. He was thirty-four, just a tad above average height with a fast-receding brown hairline that seemed to be a staple in his family line. His father had gone nearly bald before he was forty, and it was likely that he'd follow in those footsteps. Even so, he had money and class, and women generally overlooked the physical for the possibility of latching onto that type of man.

Callan closed his eyes and took a deep swig of the vodka and sighed deeply at the warm feeling melting though his body. He slowly opened his eyes and froze at the image in the mirror; he wasn't alone. He whirled around, dropping the tumbler, and gasped. She was standing there, dressed all in black, wearing black leather gloves and boots, a black sweatshirt, and tight black jeans. Her hair was cut into an auburn bob and her eyes looked … blue, but that was her, his sister.

Cameo's lips curled into a sly smile. "Hi, big brother. Long time no get held down by."

"Maeve," he whispered. "You … you're here."

Cameo's smile widened. "I certainly am."

"Wh-where have you been? Are you okay?" he said in his most conciliatory voice that didn't even fool him.

"Perfectly fucking fine," she replied brightly, then lifted her arm, revealing the 9mm Luger with a silencer on it. "I came back to settle some scores. You're one of them."

Callan was about to lie and tell her that he was brainwashed and was sick about what he had done, and he was so, so sorry—

Two quiet phtts broke the silence as two bullets entered his heart. He dropped to the floor, dead.

Cameo walked over to his body and stared down for a long moment. An image of them at ages ten and four flew past her mind as Callan pushed her giggling on a backyard swing. The second image was of him helping to pull her legs apart that monstrous night. As she took a moment to stare at what had once been her brother she realized that she felt nothing. That scared her.

She left his body where it had fallen and walked back through the kitchen where she grabbed his car keys and entered the garage. She opened the garage door then started the car, backed it out into the street, and closed the garage door with the clicker. She drove in the night to Chestnut Street where she parked twenty yards away from Damien's townhouse. She got out and walked five blocks to her own car. The night was young.

Brandi Lewis arrived at the Riley townhouse at the same time as the food delivery service. She smiled coyly at the man then rang Callan's doorbell. No answer. She rang again and knocked, then called out his name. The delivery guy was getting antsy, so she paid him for the food and took hold of the large box. He ran to his truck and sped off to his next delivery.

She was a little peeved and tried the doorknob which, surprisingly, was unlocked. She didn't know that another visitor had left it unlocked so that someone could come in. She put the food box down on the end table near the door and called out Callan's name. She felt a peculiar chill run up her spine, but she moved into the townhouse, still calling his name. She saw a light coming from one of the rooms and found herself in the den.

She choked and froze at the dead body on the floor.

And then she began screaming.

Dolan Welsh ran a sightseeing/fishing boat out of Boston and made a decent living in the summer but not so much in the fall, winter, and spring. October had been a particularly cold month and November was promising to roll in with heavy winds and icy temperatures. It wouldn't be too long before he'd have to dry-dock his boat and turn to another profession to make some money that would carry him over to spring. Luckily, his brother-in-law had a lumber yard and reluctantly allowed him to work there in the off season. Welsh wasn't too happy about that. At forty-two he had problems with his legs and back and the work was hard. Still, better than starving.

Tonight, at least, he had an unexpected job to take some broad out into the Atlantic to disperse her late husband's ashes. She was willing to pay him double his rate in cash. Maybe he could wheedle a few extra dollars out of her once they were seabound.

He had arrived at the marina a half hour early to check out the boat and get ready to shove off. He checked his watch; she was two minutes late. He was about to light a cigarette when he saw a woman dressed all in black with shiny auburn hair and lightly shaded eyeglasses walk down the gangplank. She had a large shoulder bag thrown over her left shoulder and he could see that there was something bulky inside. He forced a pleasant smile, which never came naturally to him. Just as she reached his boat she stuck out her hand and he shook it.

"I'm sorry I'm late, Mr. Welsh. I was held up in traffic," she said in a deep voice with the common Boston accent.

"No problems, missy. I mean, Miss?" She had only given him her first name on the phone call.

"Randall. Mary Kay Randall. I appreciate you doing this so late."

He waved his hand. "Pish. It's barely eight o'clock and the waters and weather seem good enough for a boat ride. How far did you want to go out?"

"My husband's will said he'd like his ashes spread at least twenty miles into the Atlantic. I need to respect his wishes. Is that all right?"

"You're da boss." He took her hand and helped her into the boat then cast off the moorings. He focused on his speed and direction while she sat on the back bench enjoying the salty air and the occasional spray of salt water that hit her face. There were a number of boats in the bay as they made their way out into the ocean. The city lights receded and twinkled like stars as the boat engine whirred loudly as the boat cut through the water.

Welsh checked his navigation and looked back towards the shore where the city lights had vanished from the horizon. He had the boat lights on, and he could see the water and the woman easily as he decreased speed and came to a lull in the movement.

"We're twenty miles out," he said to the woman.

"Wonderful," she murmured as she carefully stood up, not moving forward as the boat swayed and settled into relative calmness. She bent down and opened her shoulder bag. Instead of removing an urn she removed her Luger. Welsh was startled and froze until she smiled and tossed the gun into the ocean.

"Whoa," he said. "What's this all about? That's what you wanted to throw into the ocean?"

"One of the things," she said casually as she smoothly withdrew a large hunting knife and without a second of hesitation hurled it hard at Welsh's chest, nailing him dead center. "You would be the other one."

Welsh was wheezing as his blood issued from the chest wound. He stared up at her with terrified eyes and gasped, "Why?"

Cameo squatted beside him and said, "It's the cost of pledging your allegiance to a monster like Damien Savage and helping him to rape an innocent girl not much out of her teens."

"You're Maeve," he gasped.

She put a hand on his cheek and said gently, "Don't think of me as Maeve, just as your executioner. Like I was for Chris Komansky and Callan Riley."

Welsh sobbed. "Please don't kill me. Please. I'll … I'll testify."

Cameo said, "I don't think so. Besides, don't you think I know he has contacts in the legal system including prosecutors and police? I'm already on the hook for two murders, so three isn't a big deal. But thanks for the offer."

She stood and nudged his hand with her foot. "This hand helped hold me down." She turned around and stuck her hand into her shoulder bag once more and pulled out a hatchet.

"Nooooooooooo," he moaned. He tried to push her away with his left hand while she grabbed his right hand and held it flush against the deck of the boat. Without a word she brought the hatchet down with all her force and severed the hand. He howled. She tossed the hand into the ocean.

"I thought about chopping off your cock, but I already did that to Chris, and I don't like to repeat myself. By the way, did you help Damien get rid of his body? Will it keep you company out here?"

Welsh sobbed weakly as his lifeblood vacated his body.

"Okey dokey. Upsy daisy." Cameo looped her arm under his and hauled him up, dragging him over to the edge of the boat. She sat his butt on the edge, smiled, and said, "Buh-bye." She pushed him over and took great satisfaction in the large splash. He floundered in the water for less than a minute before his damaged heart gave out. She watched as he floated for a bit then began to sink. When he was no longer visible she threw the hatchet and shoulder bag over the edge after she took out a longish black wig with short bangs and stuffed the auburn one into the bag. Then she put on the black wig.

She pulled on the padded pants and shirt that made her seem bulky and disguised the curve of her breasts. She zipped up the heavy black sweatshirt with the Harvard logo on the back. She slipped on the black boots with the lifts and tossed her other ones into the ocean. The last thing she did was to take the three sections of clear packing tape from their container and transfer the fingerprints she had lifted from Savage's townhouse to three locations on the boat, including the steering wheel. She crumpled up the sticky pieces of tape and threw them overboard, watching them float away on the choppy waves.

"Okay," she said out loud. "Back to the marina." She had studied boating in preparation for her journey of vengeance and knew how to operate the boat she was on. She washed the blood off the deck and tossed the towels overboard, then pushed the accelerator and turned back to shore.

She made good time as the city lights grew bigger and bigger. There were people milling about the marina, but she had pulled her black sweatshirt's hood over her head and kept her focus on docking and tying up the boat. She walked calmly and straight up the gangway in long strides, making no eye contact. No one paid attention to her. She walked out of the marina and a mile away to her parked car.

She was ravenous and needed food, New England food, fish food. She rued the fact that her favorite seafood place, the No Name Restaurant on Fish Pier Street, was probably closed at this hour; most of the high-end eateries were. She'd have to wait until lunch tomorrow to get her scrod fix. On the way back to the hotel she went through the drive-thru line at Mickey D's and picked up two cheeseburgers, a vanilla milkshake, and a large order of fries. She didn't even wait to get back to the hotel; she wolfed down the food parked there in the lot.

She was calm as she returned to her hotel, all the while thinking of home and her husband and kids and Declan's superb culinary talents. By the time she parked her car, tears were flowing from her eyes as she wondered if she'd ever see them again.

She stood forever under the battering hot cascade of her shower; her skin was clean and warm and smooth as she dried off then slipped under the covers. She fell asleep almost immediately; her last thought repeating over and over in her mind.

Three down, one to go.

Three down, one to go.

Three down, one to go.

I'm coming for you ...

CHAPTER FOURTEEN

"This is cool," Elijah said, his eyes wide and alert.

"I thought you might like it," Sage said as she picked off the four sets of marbles from the Chinese Checkers set, leaving only the red marbles and the blue marbles positioned across from each other on opposing star points.

"The Chinese play checkers this way?" Elijah asked as he watched her deft hands prepare the wooden board. It sure didn't look like a checkerboard.

"Well, sometimes. Truth to tell, this isn't really a version of checkers and it didn't originate in China," Sage said.

"Where did it come from?" Elijah was only six years old, but he was smart and curious, and seemed older than his years once he came out of his shell. He'd heard his Uncle Sand say that Sage was ten going on forty. He didn't know what that meant, but he thought it was probably a really good thing.

Sage knew the history of the game because like any game she played she insisted on understanding how it came to be and why. Her Uncle Luc was a master at chess and had started teaching her that game although after the first session he told her to shut up with the questions. She did, for perhaps two minutes, then battered him again with incisive questions and opinions.

"It came from Germany. That's in Europe. They didn't call it Chinese Checkers back then but Stern-Halma. Stern means star in German."

"What's Halma mean?"

"It's from Greek, meaning jump. So, the original name was Star-Jump. Chinese Checkers came from a toy company in Texas during the Roaring Twenties. They first called it Hop Ching Checkers. I guess they wanted an exotic name that wasn't associated with the Germans."

"Why?"

"Because they were our enemies during World War I. And as it happened, World War II."

"How many World Wars have we had?"

"Just those two … so far."

"What are the Roaring Twenties?"

Sage frowned at her cousin-brother. "I'm not going to give you a history lesson. Do you want to play this game or not?"

"I want to play."

"Okay, look," Sage said. "You're going to be red and I'll be blue. We each got fifteen marbles in our starting space. The point is to get your marbles into my star and mine into yours. You know you can jump in checkers? Well, you can here, too, but it's called hopping. You can move one space if it's empty or hop over a marble if it's in your path. Understand?" Elijah nodded. "Okay. I'll start."

Sage moved one of her top-row marbles then Elijah did the same. They made progress quickly, moving and hopping. Sage sat back and let a slow, appreciative grin across her pretty face as Elijah managed to get his marbles into her starting space; she was one move off. She loudly applauded him.

"Congrats, kiddo. You done good," she said.

"Who done good?" Swan said from the door of the den.

Sage gave her an owlish look. "Elijah kicked my butt in Chinese Checkers."

"Good," Swan said. "Sometimes you need your butt kicked. Good job, Elijah."

The little boy grinned at his aunt. Once he got over his skittishness of having his aunt look exactly like his mother, he warmed to her and felt safe in her presence. He felt a little guilty that he didn't miss his mother as much as he probably should. It didn't take him very long to accept his new uncles and feel safe in their home. Uncle Akiro was doing some legal stuff so that Uncle Sand could be his new father and he'd be a Hazelwood like his uncle, his mom, and his aunt. The whole family seemed to accept him and for the first time he had open space and lots of kids to play with. He had a crush on his English teacher, Miss Smiley, who said his penmanship was excellent. He had even snagged a place on the soccer team.

"What's in the bag, Mom?" Sage asked as she gave a once-over to the large shopping bag on the floor next to Swan.

Swan smiled. "Halloween costumes for the pack. Three days to go, so if you don't like what I've picked out—tough tamales." She handed the bag to Sage, who had scrambled off the floor and lunged at the bag.

Sage unceremoniously dumped the bag contents on the floor. Four costume packages fell out. She quickly picked out the largest size and grinned.

"I'm a ninja," Sage exclaimed.

"Well, someday," her mother said. "We'll start training you next year."

"What am I?" Elijah asked eagerly. Swan picked out her nephew's costume and handed it to him. His face broke out into a wide smile.

"Zorro," he yelled and jumped up and down.

"Where's his hat?" Sage asked. Swan nodded and bent down to the outside side of the door and showed them the Zorro hat and plastic sword.

Elijah impulsively threw his arms around Swan's legs and hugged her tightly. "I love you, Aunt Swan," he said.

"I love you, too, baby," Swan murmured and hugged him back.

"What about Uncle Tucson's twins?" Sage asked.

"Declan is on the hunt for their costumes," Swan said. "Uncles Nick and Percy are handling their kids' stuff. Aunt Candy has already picked out a fairy outfit for Chessie."

"Is Dad gonna make it home?" Sage asked.

Swan shook her head. "Nope. He and Tuse are staying back east to keep looking for Aunt Cameo. He thinks I can handle anything that comes up."

Sage bent her head and said coyly, "I could help if I had a gun."

"Um, yeah, that's not gonna happen," her mother replied in a firm voice. "Maybe when you hit your teens."

"Dad and his siblings could shoot BB guns when they were kids."

"Tough. Anyway, are you home to stay or do you still plan on living with your grandparents?"

"The latter, Mother, until I get some respect." She raised her chin defiantly. "Grandma said I should learn to track in the wilderness right now and Grandpa said he'd take me next month."

"Then I guess I can use your ex-bedroom for the new nursery, daughter. Thanks. We'll still save a plate for you at Thanksgiving."

"You're just plain mean," Sage said, jamming her fists into her waist.

Swan nodded. "It's the hormones. Someday you'll experience this, and I'll be sitting in a rocking chair drinking wine and cackling about Karma."

"What about Karma?" Sand said as he came up behind Swan. He was wearing a natty three-piece navy suit with a light blue shirt and dark blue tie.

"I'm waiting for it to strike my daughter when she has a kid of her own," Swan replied. "Payback's a bitch."

Sand laughed then motioned to Elijah. "Ready?"

Elijah rushed over to Sand. "Ready," the boy declared, grinning. Today was the day he became a Hazelwood. He grabbed Sand's hand and looked up at him in eagerness and love.

Sand said to Swan, "We'll see you in the courtroom in an hour." He winked at Elijah. "Then we'll head over to Malagueña Fiesta for a celebration."

"Can I have a margarita?" Sage asked.

"Of course," Swan said sweetly. "Just as long as there's no tequila in it. Go get your sisters ready." Sage grumbled off and Swan said to her brother, "See you in court."

Sand buckled Elijah into the passenger seat and drove to the office where Akiro was finishing up last minute reviews of the adoption papers. Candy took charge of the little boy while Sand went into Akiro's office. His life partner was sitting at his desk with his jacket off and his sleeves rolled up as he squinted at a document and flipped over a page. Sand sat down.

"Everything okay?" Sand asked.

"All in order," Akiro said. "In less than two short hours you'll be Elijah's legal father."

"And you'll be his other father in everything but name. Wish it could be otherwise, but the country isn't that enlightened and probably won't be in our lifetime."

"Still, we're making progress. At least we aren't 'criminals' anymore. We've come a long way from Stonewall." Akiro was referring to the Stonewall riots in New York City in June of 1969. The police rousting of a gay bar began nights of protests and rage and propelled homosexuals out of the shadows and into the faces of America.

The Stonewall Inn was a well-known gay bar that was frequented with gay men and women who felt safe in their own environment. The night that the protests exploded the place was rocking with loud music and dancing couples, around two hundred patrons that were mostly men but with a decent number of gay women also in attendance. At around 1:30 AM on that fateful morning of June 28th, the great time ended with an unexpected police raid; the unspoken custom between the gays and the police was that a raid would be announced. All parties benefited from this rule, the police who showed themselves to be tough on "perversion," and the patrons who knew they might be shaken down but would generally come out of the experience with little short- or long-term effects. Hell, it was an open secret that the Mafia owned and operated the bar and made more money off blackmailing wealthy patrons than in selling liquor.

Deputy Inspector Seymour Pine led the raid and announced loudly, "Police! We're taking the place!" The Public Morals Squad waited outside for their part in the evening's entertainment. The standard procedure was to line up patrons and review their identification; women and men dressed as women were "handled" by female police officers. It was a fairly well-known, standard process. That night, however, the raid didn't go as planned.

Patrons began resisting the identification checks and began taunting the police, who became rough; lesbians complained that they were being touched inappropriately. Handcuffs were used freely, and police pushing, shoving, and hitting degenerated the raid into what would become a free-for-all. Violence broke out, and what was once a simple raid became a complex riot. Garbage, bottles, rocks, and bricks were hurled from the street at the building. Fires were started. The police tried to use fire hoses to hold back the growing, furious crowd of patrons, spectators, and people who were sick of police brutality, which had also manifested itself in anti-war demonstrations.

People were arrested. People were injured; some had to be hospitalized. Four police officers were injured. Everything—*everything*—in the Stonewall Inn was destroyed.

Sand was there. He had never told anyone, even Akiro, but he was a witness to history. He had taken a vacation long overdue (and forced by Memphis, who sensed his need for relaxation) and spent a week in the Big Apple seeing the sights. At another bar he met a handsome young British guy named Wilde[3] who had long auburn hair, sea-blue eyes, and an accent to die for. They hit it off and talked about spending the night together. They moved to the Stonewall Inn on someone's suggestion. During the melee Sand was injured and taken away in an ambulance and he never saw Wilde again, or even

---

[3] Please see the novel *Saguaro, Volume One of the Arizona Trilogy* for Wilde's story.

learned his last name. Sand gave a phony name to the Emergency Room doctor, got patched up, paid the bill in cash, and fled.

Maybe it was time to tell Akiro about that time of his life. But not today—today was all about Elijah. He wondered briefly about his sister Snow and whether or not she'd approve of what was transpiring. Not that he gave a damn—she had surrendered her right to be a part of Elijah's and Sage's lives by her life choices. Still on the FBI's Most Wanted list she was a confessed murderer and domestic terrorist. Apparently she was leading Thunderstorm now that Jackson was dead. The group was responsible for three small bombings, one in New York and two in California. Thankfully, no one was killed or badly injured, and even more thankfully she had stayed out of New Mexico. Every time the group acted out their rebellion against "the Man" the FBI and other law enforcement groups had paid him and Swan a visit. Occasionally they sensed they were under surveillance but it never last long.

Snow never attempted contact, but Sand had learned a great deal about her life before she dropped Elijah off. Richard Ballard provided a lot of information. Snow had met ex-Black Panther Ryder Jackson at a violent protest rally in Berkeley in late 1968. He had been a member of the Black Panther Party since its inception in 1966 and rose quickly in the ranks. In late 1967 he had a falling out with the leaders of the party and broke away, determined to start his own but it never got off the ground. He tried to recruit men and women as radical as he was and succeeded in gathering an eclectic group. He was charismatic and well-read and educated and drew people to him naturally. Why Swan found him irresistible was something only she could explain. He joined the Weathermen but found that group too mild for his tastes, so he did establish his own tiny group, Thunderstorm.

Swan married him when she was six months pregnant and found out that being the wife of a violent man was somewhat different than being the free girlfriend of such a man. People interviewed said that he hit her on more than one occasion. That made Sand's blood boil. How his smart sister could let a man dominate her like that was beyond the pale. Perhaps she had gotten enough of his abuse and decided to end it and his violence once and for all. Perhaps his bombing of a museum in Virginia in late 1973 that resulted in the of murder of a security guard was the last straw. Perhaps she was protecting Elijah the only way she thought possible. Sand hoped that someday he'd have answers.

Akiro stood and clipped on his bowtie that Elijah had given him for last Christmas and slipped on his suit jacket. He stuck the documents in his briefcase and said, "Ready."

Candy reluctantly released "my little man" to his uncles and watched with a smile as they left the office. When she was alone she studied the engagement ring on her finger. Dante had made a lovely, tasteful choice, a simple one-carat princess-cut diamond with a tiny diamond on each side. She was over the moon at the thought of getting married again to a man she loved and who loved her and her daughter. Memphis and his family had given her their blessing, and she promised that Chessie would always know about her real father. She also promised that although Dante would help raise her she'd keep the Grayhawk name.

It seemed like a busy day at the courthouse but there were parking spaces not too far from the entrance. Elijah walked between his uncles up the steps and into the hallowed halls where they were directed to the judge's chamber. When Sand knocked and was told to come in the chamber was filled with family. Every nuclear and extended family member was present, except Memphis, Tucson, and Cameo, dressed in their finest and holding balloons that read "Hazelwoods Rule!"

Elijah grinned ear to ear as the judge solemnly asked the young man to take a seat. The usual questions were asked and responded to, and then the judge picked up a new Cross pen and signed the adoption papers. He handed Sand the papers and he handed the Cross pen to Elijah. Then he said, "Ladies and gentlemen, may I introduce Elijah Houston Hazelwood." Houston, for Sand's father.

There was cheering and hugging and crying and it took a bit to exit the judge's chamber, but the swarm managed to edge out into the hallway and start moving out to go to the celebration. Sand held

Elijah back and Swan did the same with Sage. Sand squatted down next to his new son.

"Elijah, we think it's time we told you something very important," Sand said.

Elijah looked at Sand with uncertain eyes. "Am I in trouble?" He paused for a split second. "Dad?"

"No, no, of course not," Sand said quickly. He glanced up at his sister. "It's just that, well … we have a complicated family. Do you know what that means?"

"Weird?"

"No argument there," Sage muttered. Her mother mock-scowled at her.

"A little weird, but who wants to be normal, right?" Sand said easily. Elijah nodded and smiled. Sand looked around and noticed a door open to an empty conference room. He rose and said, "Let's go in there and we can explain."

Sand led Elijah, Akiro, Swan, and Sage into the room and closed the door.

Ten minutes later people in the hall were startled by a loud whoop and an exclamation, "I've got a sister! Cool!"

CHAPTER FIFTEEN

October 29, 1976
10:03 PM

Cameo had spent the late afternoon and early evening in the forest surveilling the ritual location which she knew Damien would use on October 31st for his satanic rituals. Several acolytes had been there cleaning the brush and tall grass and washing the granite slab. She recognized one or two but obviously he had recruited some new followers. One of them seemed familiar and then she remembered that she had known the woman back in grade school. Her father had been present that night when Cameo had been bound and sacrificed and raped. Cameo wondered if Damien had recruited her to his bed as well.

Cameo had done a significant background check on Savage, or as much as she could without bringing anyone else into the matter. He had never "remarried" or had children, but his social and professional positions had increased by leaps and bounds in the intervening years. Right now, he was one of the golden boys of the Boston District Attorney's office, the Harvard graduate that had made Law Review.

Imagine that, she thought—a man of pure evil supposedly upholding law enforcement. It would be funny if it weren't so monstrous.

She left after a few hours. She was antsy and nervous for some reason. Up until now she was as cold as ice, as fastidious and focused as anyone could be. She literally felt nothing when she killed Savage's three henchmen, including her own brother. Perhaps because she was coming up on the endgame.

It was dusk when she got back to Boston and sludged her way through the traffic, which was unusually high given the fact that it was late Friday. She had always loved Boston when she was a child and young teenager, but the city had grown and had such bad memories that she could never see herself living there. She realized that she loved Santa Fe and her life there. She loved her husband, her kids, their family and friends, her work. And she had thrown it all away for vengeance. Part of her rued her decision but part of her was stalwart in her need to make the devil and his minions pay.

She cleared the Boston hub and drove into Quincy but swerved east before she reached the hotel. She felt a need to be near the water, to watch the sun set. She drove to the Captains Cove Marina, a deep-water marina located in a protected inlet of the Quincy Town River, nestled in Boston Harbor. She parked and walked on a boardwalk, relishing the dark eastern horizon. She found peace and renewed purpose and shoved regret and guilt to the far reaches of her mind. She didn't know what the future would bring, but she'd face whatever came.

The breeze off the water rushed across her face as a random seagull squawked and water lapped noisily against the moored boats. She closed her eyes and breathed in deeply, and pictured Brett's sweet little face. She flashed back to the moment she gave birth to her son when that one last push and scream brought a new human being into the world, at that time the only human being to share her blood. Tucson was holding her hand and cried with her as the doctor put the newborn on her chest. From that moment on she knew who she truly was, her son's mother, and no other identity or history really mattered.

She spent hours just being in the moment. The sky was dark, and the marina lights twinkled as she walked back to her car and drove to the Best Western Adams Inn. She found a space close by the inn entrance, parked, and locked the car. She was unaware of the eyes that watched her enter the building.

Cameo greeted the desk clerk pleasantly and made her way to her suite. She unlocked the door and entered, flipping on the light. She stopped cold and all the breath rushed out of her body.

"Hello, Maeve," Tucson said quietly from the chair in the sitting area near the window.

October 29, 1976
7:08 AM

"I'm running out of dimes," Memphis said, sighing. "We need to stop at a bank."

"Okay," Tucson said absently as he flipped through the morning newspaper. They had taken a room the previous night at an inexpensive motel outside of Boston rather than traveling back and forth to Gloucester. They'd check out today having used it on and off as a rest stop during their searches and calls and head back to Gloucester. Unfortunately, the cheap motel didn't have phones in each room and Memphis was forced to use the pay phone to call around looking for Mary Kay Randall. Luckily, it was right outside of their room. Unluckily, because of the shrieking teenage couple across the hall, it was right outside of their room. If Memphis heard one more rant to "Daddy" about how awful Allen was he'd tear the phone off the wall.

Memphis fell back on the bed, tired. He rubbed his eyes then blinked a few times. "Anything going on in the world besides our quest?"

"A few things," Tucson said. "Polls are saying Carter's going to kick Ford's ass next week. If he does he'll be the first president from the deep south since the Civil War."

"Boring."

"Patty Hearst's lawyer is whining about letting her out on bail while she appeals her conviction and sentence. She's been suffering some medical problems in prison and now she's in solitary confinement. She's been arraigned on other charges along with the Harrises."

"Whip out the violins."

"I never thought she should have been convicted of the Hibernia bank robbery."

"I agree there but those other things while she was on the run, well …"

"People get brainwashed."

"Enough of Patty. Anything else exciting happening in the world?"

"Um, not really. Well, after forty years they finally got around to granting a pardon to Clarence Norris."

"Who?"

"The last living Scottsboro boy. In the 1930s a bunch of black boys were accused of raping two white women and they were railroaded even though testimony was recanted. Forty years late."

"Is he alive?"

"Yeah, and if you can believe it, it was George 'segregation forever' Wallace who pardoned him." Tucson frowned. "Hmm. There was a murder in Boston of a prominent investment banker. He was found shot to death in his townhouse. I'm reading between the lines, but it looks like his body was discovered by an escort."

Tucson continued reading the article, which had a decent photo of the dead man. He glanced at it and continued reading then stopped and went back and stared at the photo. The photo was of course in black and white, but the man's hair was dark, and he had a widow's peak. There was something about his eyes that made Tucson think of Cameo. He read on, then suddenly jumped up and threw himself on the bed next to Memphis.

"What?" Memphis said grouchily.

"Listen to this," Tucson said as he read from the newspaper. "Callan Riley's family has seen tragedy before. Seven years ago, his younger sister, Maeve Kiara Riley, was tragically killed in a boating accident and their younger brother, Aidan, ran away from home and hasn't been seen since. Police state that the investigation is still early but an inside source says that there are no real clues yet as to the killer's identity or motive. ADA Damien Savage has said unequivocally that the perpetrator will be brought to justice. The Savages and the Rileys have a long history together and are longtime stalwarts of Boston society."

Memphis sat up and sighed. "So?"

"So, look at this photo. Look at his hair."

Memphis took the paper and studied it. "He has a widow's peak, like—"

"Like Cameo."

"Tuse, lots of people have widow's peaks. It's not unusual."

"There's something else. Look at the sister's name."

"Maeve Kiara Riley. So?"

"The initials. MKR."

"Okay, so—" Memphis stopped short. "Mary Kay Randall. MKR. No. That's a coincidence. Even if it's not, she wouldn't come back to kill her own brother, would she?"

"Depends on what that brother did. We need to call ReVere and have him find out about the sister. Meanwhile, we should start calling those same hotels and use the name Maeve."

"Not a good idea. There may be people looking for her. Let's keep doing our checking and I'll have ReVere find out what he can. Give me a dime."

Tucson handed over a dime and Memphis went out to call ReVere and his brother, who were at the inn waiting for a lead to come in. When Memphis got back he said, "I asked him to check about the sister and also if he could find out the dead guy's hair and eye color. It's a longshot."

"We've been successful at longshots before—remember Canada?" Tucson referred to Memphis's investigation into Joanna Frid's background in her hometown of Hamilton, Ontario.

"I told him we'd drive back up to Gloucester in a couple of hours and finish our calls from there. By then he should have some info with his police contacts. There's a bank two blocks down. I need those dimes."

"It won't be open—it's too early."

"Fine. Then I'll go out and find some decent coffee." With that Memphis grabbed the car keys and took off while Tucson reread the article and searched for any related ones about mysterious deaths. He noted a couple of one-paragraph stories near the back page about a missing boater and an unidentified charred body that was found in an old crematorium outside of Danvers. No, Cameo couldn't have anything to do with those deaths, and if she really were Maeve Riley she wouldn't have killed her brother.

On the other hand, she was locked and loaded for bear ... She hadn't come to Boston to sip afternoon tea.

Tucson fished out one of his last dimes and made a collect call home, forgetting the time difference and waking up Declan. The kids were fine, they were sleeping, everyone was well. Tucson made the call short because he didn't want to get into what they might have found out. Declan excitedly told him that some of his beer production equipment was being delivered Monday and so was the sign for the distillery that read, "Desert Dream Brewery" above an Irish shamrock.

Tucson made another collect call, waking up Skye who lambasted him. He apologized tersely and asked her to make a call for him to Richard Ballard. He explained the information he needed. She snapped at him and slammed down the phone.

Memphis came back with two large coffees from Bess Eaton. He triumphantly flashed a roll of dimes that he'd gotten from the salesgirl. Tucson sipped the coffee and was relieved that it was strong and scalding hot. His stomach was growling but he pushed that away as he watched his brother read the article.

"Interesting," Memphis murmured as he put the newspaper down. "You find anything else?"

Tucson turned the paper to the next to the last page and pointed out the small stories on the cremated remains and the missing boater.

"I mean, it's unlikely these have anything to do with Cameo, but I found it interesting that all three deaths took place so close together."

"The boater's only missing, and the cremated guy might have been turned to ash long ago. Doesn't say anything about that. Let's forget about these fellas and concentrate on what ReVere can tell us about our same-initialed long-dead sister of the newly dead banker. I also asked him if he could get a photo of the dead girl." Memphis's voice was calming, and Tucson seemed to settle down.

"Okay, then let's head out for breakfast and finish our list of hotels and motels. Since we've called the ones we could find in the Yellow Pages for Dorchester, Mattapan, and Ashmont, let's focus on Milton and Quincy. I think we should probably go as far south as Braintree."

"Yeah, we can't call every single hotel or motel in the state, and the Yorks have north of Boston covered. Breakfast it is."

After Memphis paid the bill the girl behind the check-in desk pointed them towards a breakfast diner a mile away and within a half hour they were foraging plates of pancakes, toast, bacon, and sausages; they split a bacon omelet. They monopolized the two pay phones on each side of the diner for a half hour and called a few dozen motels starting in Milton. After some dirty looks by people who wanted to make their own calls they abandoned the pay phones and got in the car.

"Where to?" Memphis asked.

"Let's head into Quincy and start calling around there," Tucson replied as he broke open a bottle of water and took a drink.

Memphis sighed. "Quincy, here we come."

Tucson told his brother to find someplace near the water where they could find some phones and make their calls. Despite his torturous experience with the Navy he loved the water and didn't have as much chance to see an ocean or bay living in the desert.

Memphis pointed to a sign for the Captain's Cove Marina and drove there, passing Sprague Energy and the Greater Boston Chinese SDA Church. He turned into the parking lot from Cove Way. The sky was clear, and the morning air was chilly but refreshing, and both could smell the aromas associated with salt water and boats. Memphis followed his nose and the signs, and they found themselves near the marina entrance where there were three separate phone booths waiting for a roll of dimes.

They garnered more than a few curious looks as they ran through the torn Yellow Pages of Quincy-based hotels, motels, and an exclusive resort here and there. Tucson was on the line with a particularly snarky young woman when Memphis snapped his fingers loudly and pointed to his phone. Tucson hung up on Miss Snarky. Memphis held up his hand. He spoke a few sentences quietly then thanked the person on the other end of the line after he said, "No, no message."

Memphis looked his brother in the eyes. "Best Western Adams Inn, 29 Hancock Street. It's five miles north of here. Interesting that she holed up in a hotel with her last name in it. Coincidence, probably." Memphis had barely gotten the last word out when Tucson whirled around and began running to the car, Memphis hot on his heels.

As he drove Memphis said, "We can't just bust in there. For one thing, we still don't know if this Mary Kay is Cameo, and second, if it is the last thing we want to do is spook her and send her on the run."

"Yeah, yeah," Tucson said irritably. "I'm not stupid. The desk clerk say she was in?"

"No, she said she was out but would take a message. I told her not to bother. Let's hope she doesn't mention the call if she sees Mary Kay."

"Cameo."

"Maybe."

"What do we do?"

"Park in an unobtrusive place and surveil. A hot red Camaro won't be hard to spot. I wonder why she didn't rent a less obvious car, like a beige Ford?"

"We'll ask her. Over there—see the sign?"

Memphis nodded. "Nice location. Great river view."

"How are we gonna find out what room she's in?"

"I could try to charm the desk clerk."

Tucson frowned. "That's not going to work."

"Thanks," Memphis said dryly.

Tucson dug his wallet out and withdrew two twenties and a ten. "I'm sure some poor maid could use a few extra bucks. Drive around back."

Memphis complied and drove slowly to the back of the inn where the garbage bins and utility vehicles were. He parked near the corner and Tucson got out and headed over to a young Hispanic maid that was dumping huge bags of trash she'd collected from the guest rooms. She looked nervous at his approach, but Memphis knew his brother could turn on the charm when he wanted to. Memphis watched as they spoke for a few minutes. The girl's demeanor changed, and she ducked her head and smiled and nodded and even laughed. He saw Tucson hand her the folded cash then kiss her cheek gently. Even at this distance Memphis could sense that the girl blushed. He rolled his eyes as Tucson got back in the car and the girl disappeared into the inn.

"You used charm, didn't you?" Memphis said, his voice light.

"Since Luc and I got all the Grayhawk charm it seemed the natural course of action—plus the fifty, of course. Room 313, top level facing the river," Tucson said. "She'll have to go in through the front lobby. Inner hallways so it'll be easy to pick the lock and go in."

"Not until we know it's her."

"Fine. So, we wait."

"We wait." Memphis parked the car kitty-corner from the entrance at the end of the parking lot. They waited.

For hours. Both had to sneak out of the car and find a bush to relieve themselves discreetly, and Memphis managed to make one phone call to DeVere to let them know their progress. DeVere said that his brother had contacted a reporter he knew to find out about the Rileys and also a cop contact in Boston. Memphis said they hoped to be back at the inn before nightfall.

When he got back to the car after the call Memphis had just settled in as Tucson was crunching on their last bag of potato chips. Memphis grabbed a few, ate them, then licked his greasy fingers when suddenly he smacked Tucson on the shoulder and pointed.

A bright red Camaro had entered the parking lot and was pulling into a space close by the entrance. A few seconds later a tall figure dressed all in black smoothly threw her legs out of the car and stood. She locked the car and then scanned the parking lot; the brothers scooched down below the dashboard. A second later Tucson peeked out as the figure walked to the inn entrance.

Memphis sat up. "Hair's different but I'd make an educated guess and say that's your wife."

Tucson stared where his wife had left the scene. He said softly, "Cameo." He started to get out of the car, but Memphis stopped him.

"It's too soon to confront her. We need more information. Let's head back to Gloucester and see what the Yorks have."

"What if she checks out?" Tucson asked. Then he remembered. "The maid said she was staying until next week."

"There. See? Let's head back. At least we know she's okay. Looking like a ninja, but okay."

Tucson nodded as Memphis started the car and pulled out discreetly, heading north.

The York brothers were waiting at the inn when the Grayhawk brothers arrived. Memphis and Tucson had agreed to hold off on telling them that they'd seen Cameo.

After DeVere shook hands he said, "It's chilly but why don't we go out to the rocks and talk there. We could use the fresh air."

The four men crossed the road and found an outcropping of dry flat rocks and sat down. ReVere had a slim folder in his hands and opened it.

"I called a buddy of mine who reports for one of the lesser Boston newspapers and discreetly asked him about the Riley family and the dead daughter mentioned in the article. He looked back in his paper's files and found an article about this Maeve's death in 1969. Tragic. She was only twenty-one."

"Did she die here?" Memphis asked.

ReVere shook his head. "No, apparently she had been going to college in Switzerland and died in a boating accident there. She'd been there since her mid-teens after going to a private school near Boston."

Memphis and Tucson looked at one another and were thinking the same thing, that her going to school out of the country might explain why the Pittsfield police were unsuccessful in finding her at any regional colleges when they showed her photo around.

"When did she die?" Tucson asked.

ReVere consulted his notes. "Um, May 2nd. Odd, though."

"What?"

"She was buried in Switzerland. I would think they'd want to bury their daughter here so they could visit her grave."

"The article said another brother ran off," Memphis said. "Anything on that?"

"That would be eighteen-year-old Aidan Riley. He apparently took off around the time his sister died. Maybe he was so distraught at her death that he just had to go away. My buddy said there's no indication that he was ever heard from again."

"Your buddy get any photos of the two kids?" Memphis asked.

ReVere shook his head. "The brief obit on the girl didn't include any pictures. Oh—I don't know why you want to know, but my friend said that the dead guy had dark brown hair and hazel eyes on his driver's license."

"Just getting all the facts," Tucson murmured as the wind brushed his cheeks and he stared out into the ocean where the waves were really starting to kick up. He had only glimpsed his wife for a few precious seconds, but he had taken in every aspect of her body and body language. She was thinner, but then she had started losing weight before she left Santa Fe. She seemed taller but that was because she was wearing what had to be three-inch heels on her slim leather boots. Her clothes fit her like a glove, black jeans and a tight spandex top under a black windbreaker. Her hair was boyish-short and black. He couldn't see her eyes, but he wondered if she was wearing contact lenses. She moved with purpose and confidence. This was not the woman he married, but he knew it was sure as hell the woman he wanted no matter what her past was, what she might have done. His protective impulse shifted into high gear.

ReVere snapped his long fingers. "Oh—one more thing. About an hour ago the cops found the dead guy's car on a street in Beacon Hill. Oddly, it wasn't far from his friend's place. You know, in the article, the D.A. named Savage?"

"I doubt that the dead sister has anything to do with my wife," Tucson said slowly, avoiding Memphis's eyes. "It's just a coincidence about the initials. You know, I think we're at a dead end."

Memphis picked up on his brother's direction immediately. "He's right. I think you boys should go back to your lives while we finish up here. We've exhausted our search through the various hotels and haven't found this mystery woman who probably has nothing to do with my sister-in-law. I think we need to wrap it up and go home and hope she calls or contacts us. Maybe she just needs time to work some stuff out." He stood up and the other three men followed.

DeVere frowned. "Your sister-in-law stocked up on weaponry and headed out of town covertly. I don't think she's just thinking 'things' over. She's got a purpose."

"Yes, but we don't know what that is. We can't go off in a dozen different directions trying to find her," Tucson said evenly. He met DeVere's eyes. "We think it's better if you two end your participation here."

The York brothers looked at one another and then at their friends. ReVere spoke slowly. "We're both cops, and if there's a chance that there may be some mayhem coming …"

"If there is then it won't concern a cop from Pittsfield and a cop from Portsmouth," Memphis said flatly. "Guys, we're grateful for your help, but—"

Before he could finish DeVere said, "You're right. We'll back off and go home. There's a small car rental place at the edge of town where you can get a short-term rental and I can get my car back. Big brother, time to go home."

"I'm not sure I like this," ReVere said slowly, but at the look on his brother's face, he shrugged. "Fine. We'll go home." He turned to Memphis and stuck out his hand. "I wish you both well and hope you find what you're looking for. Stay out of trouble." The last few words were clearly a warning.

"Thank you both for everything," Memphis said.

ReVere smiled slightly. "It's been an experience. Hope you find what you're looking for."

They walked back to the inn where ReVere collected his things, talked quietly to his brother for a few minutes, then waved and drove back towards New Hampshire. DeVere took the Grayhawks to the car rental place where Memphis rented a nondescript economy Ford.

"Hey, DeVere," Memphis said. "We can't thank you enough for your help."

DeVere grinned. "Like my brother said, it's been an experience. Look. I don't know why you guys specifically wanted us gone, but just be careful. I'd hate to see anything bad happen to you. I've gotten kind of fond of you."

"Of us, or of Devon?" Memphis asked, returning the grin.

DeVere laughed. "Both. Call me when you can. Be careful." Instead of a handshake he gave each of the Grayhawks a hug then got in his car and headed off to Pittsfield.

The brothers Grayhawk watched him drive off then went back to the inn. The room phone showed a message blinking and Tucson picked up and dialed. He listened to the message then hung up and quickly dialed Skye's number. Memphis stood over him while he talked to Skye and listened a lot, then wrote down what looked like a name and address. He thanked her and apologized again for waking her up so early. He looked up at Memphis from the bed.

"Ballard came through for us again. I had Skye call him to see if he could find out if a Maeve Riley flew from Switzerland to Boston around the beginning of May. She did, arriving in Boston on May 3rd."

"That's interesting considering that according to the news she died on May 2nd in Switzerland."

"Isn't it, though?"

"Whether or not their Maeve and our Cameo are the same woman that family's hiding something."

"You think? Ballard did us one better and found out the name of the private school she went to as a kid. It's Friday so someone's got to be working there. Let's head up and see if we can sweet-talk anyone into opening her file. Bet there are photos in it."

"No bet. Let's go."

They got good directions from the desk clerk about the area of the private school and an hour later pulled up in a half-filled parking lot. Tucson sighed in relief when he saw people going in and out of the administration building. He told Memphis to wait in the car and he took the front steps two at a time. There were signs in the lobby, and he followed them to a relatively busy office with several secretaries and clerks bustling about. One came over and he identified himself as a detective and quickly flashed Memphis's ID and asked about an old student. He used a mixture of charm and subtle intimidation to get the young woman to get the Maeve Riley file and take him to a small conference room to review it.

Tucson read the transcripts and thought Maeve was one smart girl. She had an exceptionally well-rounded curriculum and her worst grade was a B+ in Advanced Chemistry when she was thirteen. He flipped through the sheets then stopped as he came across a five-by-seven shot of a girls' tennis team. There was Maeve, right in the middle of the first row. He didn't need to check the names on the back; he recognized his chestnut-haired, hazel-eyed, heart-shaped-faced wife even at the tender age of about twelve.

He stared at the photo and ran his thumb across her face. Maeve. Cameo was Maeve Riley. He stared for what seemed an eternity before he reluctantly put the photo down and went through the rest of the records in the folder. He stopped short at a financial record. It listed payments for her education. It specified the bank and the payor—Damien Savage. He remembered the name from the newspaper article on Callan Riley. From what he had read both the Savage and Riley families were well off and although "close friends for decades" why would one family pay for another one's daughter to attend a private school?

He wrote down facts and figures from the financial papers and a few notes on Maeve's tenure at the school. He pondered whether or not to take the photo, then stuck it in his jacket pocket. He returned to the clerk and thanked her and said he wouldn't need any further information. She smiled but he could see she was distracted and that was a good thing. He watched her go to her desk and toss the folder on it before she hurried over to another clerk and started discussing a document she was holding.

"Find out anything?" Memphis asked as his brother got into the car.

Wordlessly Tucson handed the photo to Memphis whose eyebrows arched high. "That's Cameo," he said.

"Maeve," Tucson said flatly. "I finally know my wife's real name."

"Maeve," Memphis said. "Based on the Riley part I'm thinking it's Irish. Funny how you ended up with two Irish loves."

"Hysterical," Tucson said. "I found out some other things." He updated Memphis on the notes, grades, and the oddity of who was paying for the school. "So, somehow this Savage guy is involved. I just know it," Tucson said hotly. "Riley's car was found close by his residence, he was paying for her education, and who knows how else he's tied up in this whole ball of chaos."

"Do you think she killed her brother?" Memphis asked slowly.

Tucson looked at him and slowly nodded. "I think so. And I think maybe she's going after this Damien Savage for whatever reason."

"You think he's the guy that raped her?"

"I wouldn't bet against it."

"We need to confront her."

"I need to confront her. Tonight. I'm not going to take the chance that she bolts ahead of schedule for some reason and we have to start looking again."

"I'm going with you."

"No, I—"

"I'm fucking going with you. This woman, this … Maeve or Cameo or Mary Kay or whoever the hell she is is dangerous. She's well-armed. She may have already committed murder. You think you know her mind and heart? Well, obviously you don't. None of us do. She may write that she loves you, but she might view you as an obstacle to whatever her endgame is, and obstacles by the very definition are something that need to be removed."

"I need to talk to her alone. Okay, you can come but you stay in the car."

"What? Until I hear a gunshot?"

"Then you can stand over my grave and tell me you were right. Yes, until you hear a gunshot, or I come out."

"I don't like it."

"I don't care. So just suck it up and let's get going. It'll be dark by the time we get back down to Quincy."

Memphis held up his hands in surrender then did what his brother told him to. The traffic around the Boston circle was unusually heavy for a Friday night and they had a long delay at a two-car accident that merged two lanes of cars into one. After they hit South Boston it was open when they cut off the highway and took Route 3A down to Quincy. Memphis slowed as they approached the inn. He rolled slowly through the parking lot; no red Camaro.

"She went out," Tucson murmured.

"Hopefully, she'll be back. Hang on." Memphis parked in his previous space and walked over to the pay phone. Tucson watched him drop a dime and start speaking, then nodding. He came back to the car.

"I asked if Miss Randall was still resident and they said yes," Memphis said.

"Okay," Tucson said as he opened his car door. He looked at Memphis. "You stay in the car and I'll go to her room."

"You don't have a key."

Tucson rolled his eyes. "How many times have we broken into places without the use of a key ever since we were kids?" He patted his jacket. "I'm all set." With that he ambled over to the entrance and went inside as though he belonged there. Memphis stayed in the car and waited and watched. It was going on three hours when the Camaro pulled into a space unfortunately not too far from Memphis's car. He threw himself under the passenger dashboard until he heard the car door slam and sharp footsteps walking away. Cameo was dressed the same and moved swiftly to the inn. Memphis wished he could be a fly on the wall in that hotel room.

Fuck it, he thought. He could listen in at the door. He got out of the car after a few minutes and went inside.

October 29, 1976
10:03 PM

"Hello, Maeve."

She couldn't move; she literally couldn't move, and her limbs felt like they had been dipped in liquid nitrogen.

Tucson stood and faced her from five feet away. He waited. Their eyes locked, neither of them blinking. Finally, some of the ice in her frame melted enough for her lips to move.

"You found me," she said inanely.

"I did," he replied mildly. "Had a lot of help."

"You know my name."

"It's a beautiful name, Maeve Kiara Riley."

"You don't know what happened to me."

"Tell me."

"You don't know what I've done," she whispered harshly as a fat tear rolled down her left cheek. "You don't know what I'm going to do."

"Tell me."

"I want to."

"What's stopping you?"

"This," she said in a low, throaty voice as she launched herself at her husband and wrapped her legs around his waist while she thrust her tongue into his mouth and crushed him to her and desperately whined at the back of her throat.

Tucson held her against him as he awkwardly moved them to the bed, and they fell with a dull thud and a creak of the mattress.

Memphis sighed outside their door from his leaning position against the wall. He shook his head and pulled a MacDonald's receipt from his wallet and scribbled a note on it and stuck it under the door.

Pick you up tomorrow morning.

He headed off to the Atlantis Oceanfront Inn hoping the Boston traffic had died down.

CHAPTER SIXTEEN

October 30, 1976
12:13 AM

"Tell me about my wife," Tucson murmured in the dark, the only lights those twinkling from buildings across the river. The drapes were open providing a panoramic nighttime view of the water and the land beyond it. He ran his hand over Cameo's bare shoulder and arm as she lay peacefully with her head on his chest and one leg thrown over his lower body. She ran her hand gently over his chest and hugged him tightly. He took her hand and they linked fingers.

"You know everything you need to know about your wife," she said softly. "But let me tell you about someone you never knew, an innocent young girl whose life shattered into a million little pieces. Let me tell you about Maeve Riley."

With that she began her story and left out no details, bringing him from her early family life through her adolescence through her faraway education and to that one terrible night that changed her life forever. He asked no questions but occasionally held her tighter and fought back tears. Her voice was modulated and even, even when she described her rape and the mad flight with her brother.

"I wish I knew what happened to Aidan," she said almost inaudibly. "I pray he wasn't caught and punished by them."

"The newspaper said that he was still missing." He kissed the top of her head. "And you're dead and buried in Switzerland." With that he told her all about the search and how he and Memphis fit the pieces together.

When he finished there was an oddly comfortable silence between them, the only sounds a distant boat whistle and the dull, faraway sound of cars passing by on the bridge. A soft voice in the hall dissolved as the person walked away.

Cameo snuggled closer to her husband. "Think your brother is asleep in the car, or did he head back to Gloucester?"

"He's smarter than he looks. I'm sure he went back to the inn," Tucson said, smiling in the dark. He had heard Memphis outside the door and then heard his footsteps depart even as he was pulling off Cameo's clothes. He sobered. "We have to talk. I … have to ask you something I'm not sure I want the answer to."

"I will never lie to you again. Ask me anything."

"The newspaper said your brother Callan was shot to death." He let the unasked question hang heavy in the air.

Cameo hesitated. "I don't want to involve you in this. If I tell you it could be construed as you being an accomplice after the fact."

"I'm your husband. I can't be compelled to give testimony against you. Even if we weren't married I wouldn't betray you."

"I know." After a pregnant pause Cameo said very quietly, "I shot him."

Tucson was silent for a long minute before he said, "Is there anything else I should know about what you've been doing here?"

It was Cameo's turn to be silent for that long minute. "The other two men that held me down—Chris Komansky and Dolan Welsh—I killed them, too. Do you want to know how?"

"Maybe later," he said slowly. "Did you leave any possible evidence behind?"

"I don't think so. I always wore a wig and gloves and had virtually all of my body covered."

"Where did you get that … talent?"

"I've been living in the company of private investigators and cops for a couple of years. I've picked things up." She paused. "I … I spent a little time with a survivalist group in North Carolina a few years ago when I was making my way south trying to find my past."

"Seriously? Survivalists?"

"I wanted to learn how to protect myself. I learned to shoot and use a knife, and track, and do hand-to-hand combat. A little bit of martial arts with Asian weapons. When I remembered who I was, I also remembered that in Switzerland I had some shooting lessons. I learned to ride a horse."

"You can ride a horse? We need to do that together someday. What else did you learn?"

"I learned to never trust anyone, but to trust my instincts. I learned to strike without warning or delay. You know these movies you see, about crime or westerns, things like that?"

"Yeah?"

"The bad guy always takes time to tell the good guy what he's doing, giving the good guy time to turn the tables. I was taught to never take those extra seconds to give the other guy a chance. Are you shocked?"

"Um, yeah, that would be one of the words."

Cameo pushed herself up on her elbow and studied his face, which was illuminated by the light coming from the window. "What would be others?"

He sat up and stuffed a pillow behind his back and studied her expressive face. She sat on top of his thighs and leaned over and gently kissed him, then drew back.

"Proud," he whispered. "I am … in awe of you. You're tough, tougher than I could ever be."

"That's not true," she said softly. "After what you went through in the war—"

Tucson grabbed her upper arms. "We're both broken in our own ways. We're both … damaged. The only way we make sense and survive is … each other. We're … whole with each other." There was wonder in his voice as though something suddenly became as clear as a star-filled night sky during a cloudless new moon. Suddenly he flipped over so that she was under him and he stared into her eyes. "I'll never let you go."

"I don't want you to," she said as she wrapped her arms around his neck and kissed him frantically. As they made desperate love Cameo gasped out the details of her murders of Komansky and Welsh, eliciting only groans and raspy murmurs from her husband who finally fell back sated and exhausted. They dozed, wrapped around one another, awakening before dawn.

Tucson opened his eyes to see Cameo studying his face and gently tracing the length of his lightning-bolt scar from a North Korean bayonet with her finger. She smiled slightly.

"It makes you look rakish. Dangerous. It's a perfect imperfection," she said, then kissed his damaged cheek and laid her head on his chest.

"It's funny," he said against her hair. She looked good with a short cut, but he missed her glorious, silky mane that she would whip across his face when she was on top of him.

"What is?"

"The case back home, the one Sand and Nick are working on."

"The missing people?"

"Yeah. For a lot of reasons, they've determined that whoever is disappearing these men and women is what Percy calls an injustice collector. It means that he's taking and harming these people because he feels they have been disrespectful or damaging to the Indian culture in some way."

"The guy's an Indian?"

"Probably."

"Why is it funny?"

Tucson twisted his head as she looked up at him. "It's kind of what you're doing," he replied quietly. "Making bad people pay for their trespasses. You're … dispensing your own brand of justice." Suddenly his temper turned, and his voice rose. "Damn it, Cameo—why the hell didn't you just tell me? We could have gone to the police and had them arrested. It's been seven years so the statutes of limitation on rape, kidnapping, assault and whatever the hell ever are still valid."

"You don't understand," she retorted, flinging herself off the bed. She stood by the window, glancing at the lightening sky, and said, "He's got those people under his thumb. It's their word against mine. They'd never get convicted even if they were prosecuted. He's a fucking ADA. They stick to their own. What would they find? That he was nice enough to get me a good education? That he paid for my schools?"

"Did their crimes warrant the death penalty?" he asked flatly.

She stared at him, then nodded her head slowly. "They murdered Maeve Kiara Riley. She is dead, as dead as any corpse decomposing in a graveyard. In fact, didn't you tell me she's buried in Switzerland? And, do you think it's their only crimes? Aidan told me that he believes the rumor that Damien murdered his own father in a power grab. I'd never live to testify, and that's not what I care about. There's you and Brett and the twins. They'd be in danger, too. I just know it. There isn't even the slightest doubt in my mind that Damien would kill our kids just to get back at me."

"So, you're going to take out the threat."

"You're goddamn right I am."

"Okay, then. Let's take out the threat."

"What?" Cameo said, startled.

In two strides Tucson made his way to where she was standing and took her in his arms. "Let's take that fucker down."

Cameo pushed him away roughly. "I said I won't drag you into this."

"For better for worse, for richer for poorer—"

"Our vows never said anything about prison cells or Death Row."

"I'm improvising."

"I'm not going to make you complicit in tearing your soul apart by committing a mortal sin."

"It's my soul, and it's my family. So, do you have a plan for this Damien Savage?"

She hesitated. "I do."

"Does it include death?"

"It does, but … if I play it right I might get away with it."

Tucson grabbed her shoulders tightly and searched her face. "Let's focus on that part. Before we discuss next steps, let's wait until my brother gets here. I'm pretty sure he'll be amenable to helping."

"I don't know … maybe." She smiled slyly. "It's barely dawn. Think we have time?"

"Time for what?"

Wordlessly she took his hand and led him back to the bed.

October 30, 1976
07:22 AM

Memphis trudged up the stairs since a pack of giddy Japanese tourists had stuffed themselves into the elevator near the lobby. He felt like Godzilla towering over them. That they were whispering and pointing to him and giggling didn't help matters. He took the steps two at a time and swerved around two maids' carts before he stopped at Cameo's room. He leaned in and listened and didn't hear any sounds that might indicate bed action. He knocked sharply. A moment later the door opened, and he found himself looking at his sister-in-law.

"Not sure what to call you," he said laconically as he moved into the room. His brother was nowhere in sight, but he heard the shower running. He put the bag of breakfast food on the small sitting table by the window.

"The same name you've been calling me for two years," she said easily. "Hope there's black coffee in there."

"Three large. Croissants, egg and bacon sandwiches, coupla hash browns. Tucson in the shower?"

"Yup," she said as she withdrew a cup and took a careful swallow; it was scalding hot. She fished around for an egg sandwich and breathed in the wonderful aroma. She noticed Memphis studying her. "Like the hair?" she asked.

"Not really," he replied as he got his own coffee. "I like a long mane." She was dressed in white clam diggers and a sleeveless blouse which showed her tanned, well-toned arms to their best view. She had on leather sandals. He noted that she wasn't wearing her wedding ring.

"Tough shit," Tucson said from the now open bathroom door. He was damp and had a towel around his waist. His hair was plastered to his forehead and neck and still dripping down the back. "I like it." He winked at her. "Besides—it'll grow back." He quickly added, "If she wants it to."

"I take it you two have resolved your differences and come to some kind of understanding?" Memphis asked as he parked himself in the chair and started to unwrap his hash brown. He rifled through the bag and found the pepper, salt, and ketchup.

"Yeah, we got a few things straight," Tucson said as he pulled on his boxers then jeans and shimmied into a dark blue polo shirt. Cameo handed him a coffee. He took a sip. "We need to talk to you about that."

Suddenly, Cameo put a hand on her husband's arm. "Tucson—maybe not. It's one thing between a husband and wife, but Memphis doesn't have the legal protection of marital privilege."

"Yeah," Tucson said thoughtfully. He looked his brother in the eye. "You could be in a very precarious position—and we could, too—if you know what's been going on the last week."

"Seriously?" Memphis said as he stuffed the last bite of the hash brown into his mouth and chewed. "Like, you think I wouldn't lie to protect family? Do *anything* to protect family? Idiot." He pointed at Cameo. "You may have explained yourself to your husband, but I've got a vested interest in your past, too. I spent a hell of a lot of time trying to uncover it, and, quite frankly, I want answers."

"Ask your questions," Cameo said evenly as Tucson took her hand and they sat on the bed beside one another.

"Are you Maeve Kiara Riley?"

"Yes. Next."

"Did you kill your brother?"

"I did."

Memphis inhaled sharply. "Anyone else?"

"Two more. There's one to go. Damien Savage. He's the one that destroyed my life, raped me, and sent me on the journey of the past seven years."

Memphis unexpectedly snorted and laughed.

"What?" Tucson asked.

"Her accent. She drops her R's. Sounds like the guy in *Jaws*. 'They're in the yahd not too fah from the cah.' It'll take some getting used to. So, what's your plan for your next victim?"

"Damien Savage isn't a victim by any stretch of the imagination," Tucson said. "Let her tell you her story and you can judge for yourself."

Memphis took a sip of coffee and a bite of a croissant. "I'm all ears."

For the next hour Cameo told Memphis the same story she'd told Tucson, adding in the three killings and her plan for Savage. She looked completely drained when she finished. Memphis hadn't said a word during the tale, keeping his face neutral and his mind open. He could feel his brother's eyes on him intently as Tucson tried to discern Memphis's thoughts and reactions. There was a long, pregnant silence before he spoke.

"Joanna Frid shot me twice, my brother-in-law, a couple of cops and guards, drugged my wife, held my cousins hostage, and kidnapped my baby daughter. She made me watch as she extracted blood from my child so she could have a special Christmas present made for me to remind me of her power and crimes. If I were in the same room with her right now I would put my hands around her throat and squeeze until her last breath wheezed out, even if it meant spending my life in prison. I understand the difference between the law and justice. Christ, I'm a lawyer, but I for one would like to come down on the side of justice. What I'm trying to say is that I understand what you did, and I have no problem with it."

Cameo visibly relaxed and let out the deep breath she was holding. She squeezed Tucson's hand then jumped up and threw her arms around her brother-in-law's neck.

Memphis held her close for a minute then said, "So I guess forever after you're Cameo?"

"Maeve is dead," she said, searching his face. "Even if I could become her again I wouldn't. I'd never give up what I have. I'd never give up Cameo's life." She looked shyly at Tucson. "Cameo's love."

"Okay, then, let's figure out next steps so we can all go home. You still have all of your weapons except the ones you threw in the Atlantic?" Memphis said.

"Yes. I may have overstocked but better prepared than needing something at a critical time. I'm, um, missing a couple of items I planned on buying today."

"Tomorrow is D-Day," Tucson said. "Halloween." He frowned at Memphis. "Are you going to be all right with that?"

"Life goes on," Memphis said with more ease than he felt. Right now, he wished he were home watching his wife and kids like a hawk.

"Do you think we should tell anyone back home?" Cameo said.

"Oh, hell no," Memphis said. "They'll find out fast enough if this all goes south. We're keeping the Yorks out of this, too. We didn't tell them we found you."

"We're not sure whether DeVere is in any danger or not," Tucson said to Cameo. "He came out to tell us about Eddie and said he felt like he was being stalked. He even flew out of Albany instead of Hartford to throw anyone off his trail. Luckily, none of us have felt any eyes on us since he left, so maybe no one knows that he went to New Mexico and that we're out there. Maybe Eddie didn't tell his killer that."

"You got a list of what you need?" Memphis asked abruptly.

Cameo nodded. "I can write one up," she said. She walked over to the desk and took out a pad and pen and started making a list. She handed it to Memphis who scanned the items, his eyebrows arching. He stared at one item then looked at her and shrugged.

"Okay. I can pick these up somewhere not too close. I'll pay cash. How far is Worcester from here?"

"About sixty miles," Cameo said.

"Okay, good." Memphis ripped off the bottom third of the list. "You two can get this stuff. It shouldn't take you long. Head down to Taunton. May I make a suggestion?"

"Sure," Tucson said a little warily.

"We don't know how this is going to play out. There's a good chance it might result in our incarceration or worse. Why don't you two spend the known part of the future together and just enjoy being husband and wife. Find a beach to walk on. Eat hotdogs. Smooch. And be grateful for those hours. Don't think about tomorrow or yesterday, just today. Just today," Memphis echoed. He thought of Swan and their girls. There was nothing in the whole fucking world that he wanted more than to be home with them and crush them in his arms.

"Sounds like a plan," Tucson murmured as he nuzzled Cameo's cheek.

"We'll meet up back here later, say, five o'clock?" Tucson and Cameo nodded. Memphis swallowed his last ounce of coffee then picked up Tucson's cup, saw it was half full, and carried it out of the suite along with another hash brown.

Tucson took Cameo in his arms and kissed her. "Let's take a walk across the bridge and enjoy the morning air before it's clogged up with traffic sounds and smells."

"That's an enticing offer," Cameo said, "but how about we take a short drive to Wollaston Beach? We can take off our shoes and wade through the surf and throw leftover croissant crumbs at the seagulls. The concierge here told me about a seafood place a half mile away called the Clam Box. I can't think of a better place to have lunch, then we can head out to the store."

"I love that idea," he said quietly. "I love you."

"I love you, too, Cochise."

CHAPTER SEVENTEEN

October 31, 1976
08:26 AM

Memphis, Tucson, and Cameo were hidden in the woods outside of Salem where she believed Damien Savage would hold a Satanic ritual that night on Halloween. She had taken them there just before dawn broke so they could reconnoiter the forest and perimeter. She couldn't miss the frozen look of rage on her husband's face when his eyes fell on the granite slab; that was where the woman he loved had lost her virginity in a violent, brutal rape.

Memphis surveilled the area with a practiced tracker's eye, picking up where the best hiding places would be, and the best places to initiate an attack. He mentally marked out four of the best paths along which to retreat. When he was checking out the last path Cameo came up beside him and pointed to a large rock. She told him that was where she had crashed down and sustained her concussion. He put a strong, comforting hand on her shoulder.

They were standing about twenty feet inside the forest, hidden from the ritual area, when Tucson heard a tiny snap of a branch. He froze and put a finger to his lips. He motioned to Memphis and the brothers started in opposite directions in a wide circle. Cameo stood unmoving and waited, and then she heard a noise and some yelling and crashing of men scuffling and branches breaking. Her heart was beating hard and fast like a bass drum. She absently fondled the knife resting in a sheath on her side.

Suddenly Memphis and Tucson emerged from the left with a man held tightly in between them. The man was a solid six-footer and slender, in his mid-twenties. His sable hair was layered and long with one errant lock falling over his left eye. He had high cheekbones and a Roman nose and couldn't be considered anything except handsome although at the moment there was a surly cast to his face. His faded bell-bottom jeans fit him like a glove; so did the clinging black shirt that failed to hide his strong, well-toned shoulders. The Grayhawks stopped about ten feet from Cameo, both still holding the man's wrists and arms tightly.

"Let him go," Cameo commanded evenly, her eyes never leaving the man's face.

Tucson cocked his head in wordless curiosity but did as she said. Memphis took a few seconds longer. The man took one long stride forward and stopped. He and Cameo stared at one another for about ten seconds before they both ran forward and threw their arms around each other. Cameo sobbed and started crying. Memphis and Tucson looked at one another in confusion.

"I take it you know this guy?" Tucson asked.

Cameo disengaged and nodded her head. She touched the man's cheek then said, "This is Aidan, my brother. The one that saved me." She looked at Aidan. "My baby brother," she whispered. They hugged again. This time he was crying, too.

"You look ... you look beautiful, Sis," Aidan choked out. He brushed his long lock of hair away from his eye and the Grayhawks saw that he had the same vivid hazel eyes as Cameo did.

"Introduce us, Cameo," Memphis said.

Aidan stared at Memphis. "Cameo?"

Cameo brushed the backs of her fingers against her brother's hot cheek. "It's my new name. My forever name. It's such as long story, but first you need to meet my … family." She reached out her hand and Tucson walked over and took it. "This is my husband, Tucson Grayhawk. That's his brother, Memphis."

"You're married?" Aidan asked in wonder.

Cameo nodded. "And I'm a mother. I gave birth to my first biological son a few months ago. His name is Brett. And I have two wonderful stepchildren, a boy and a girl. Braeden and Brianna. And … a ton of other relatives by marriage. We all live in Santa Fe, New Mexico." Her brow furrowed. "Where have you been?"

"Before he answers that," Memphis said, "how about we relocate to a more private place for this family reunion?"

"Good idea," Tucson said. "Let's go to the Gloucester inn." He looked at Aidan. "You got a car?"

"Yes. Which inn is it?"

"The Atlantis Oceanfront Inn. It's on—"

"I know where it is," Aidan said. "It's a short distance from our grandfather's seaside house." He looked at Cameo. "He left it to Callan."

"We'll talk about Callan when we get to the inn," Cameo said. She turned to Tucson. "I'll ride with my brother and we'll meet you there."

"You sure?" Tucson asked, keeping one eye on his brand-new brother-in-law.

"I'm sure." She kissed Tucson's cheek. "See you soon."

Memphis and Tucson watched the brother and sister walk off through a dense patch of forest.

"She'll be fine," Memphis said.

"I know. Let's go."

Memphis pulled into the inn a half hour later. He noticed that the sky was cloudy, and the waves were really kicking up. The spray from the water hitting the rocks shot up ten to twelve feet before the waves hissed back into the suction of the ocean. A dozen seagulls were perched across the rocks for nearly a quarter mile, the targets of photo-mad tourists walking along the road. Memphis was about to swing towards their room when Tucson stopped him.

"I need coffee," Tucson said.

"I could go for some," Memphis agreed, and they headed into the half-empty dining room where they were able to sit at the table next to the window which showed a panoramic view of the coastline and ocean. The waitress took their order and handed them a breakfast menu.

"You know what?" Tucson said. "I'm hungry again. I'm going to have the Irish omelet."

"I'll take the Country breakfast and bacon. Are you going to order something for Cameo?"

"She and her brother can make their choices when they get here." He looked out the window and nodded. "That's them now." He called the waitress over and ordered two more coffees. She just returned with the coffees when Cameo and Aidan came into the dining room and sat down.

"We ordered you coffees," Memphis said, handing Aidan the menu. "Pick your meal."

Camco studied her menu, smiled, and put it down. "Definitely the Irish omelet," she said.

"Stuffed French toast," Aidan said then took a sip of coffee.

The waitress came back and took their orders and refilled the half-empty coffee cups.

"So," Tucson said to Cameo. "Did you two talk about everything that's happened?"

"A little," Cameo admitted. "We have a whole lot more to discuss."

"Curious," Memphis said to Aidan. "How is it you're down here at this particular time?"

"The murder of a Boston brahmin even makes its way to the wilds of Vermont," Aidan said. "I saw the article in the *Bennington Banner* and just sensed it had something to do with what happened all those years ago. I threw a few clothes together and drove here, hoping to find out more information." He looked at his sister shyly. "I was hoping that I might find Maeve. I'd lost track of her after she left the Pittsfield hospital."

Cameo touched Aidan's hand. "I'm Cameo now. Maeve is dead and gone."

"Yeah," Aidan said quietly. "So is Aidan Riley. I've been going by Connor Donnelly since I settled in the Green Mountain State."

Cameo smiled. "I like that name. I guess we both had pasts that are better left buried."

Aidan grinned. "New Mexico, eh? I don't think we ever talked about seeing the southwest let alone living there."

"Santa Fe's wonderful," Cameo said. "You have to come back with us and see it, see if you like it enough to resettle."

"Can you buy maple syrup there?"

"We even have electricity and horseless carriages," Memphis said curtly. He mentally shook his head—New Englanders. The only thing worse was New Yorkers.

"Maeve—Cameo—told me that you two are half-Indian. What's the other half?"

"Polish and gypsy," Tucson said. "Did she tell you what's going on here regarding both your brother and … others?"

"Not exactly," Aidan said. "Just, maybe, a hint of discovering the past and accounting for it." He looked at Cameo. "Did you … did you have anything to do with what happened to Callan?"

Memphis cut off the response. "Not a place to discuss this. We can use the hotel room for that. Here's our food."

They fell silent as the cheery waitress put their plates down then refilled their coffees. There wasn't much conversation as the meal progressed. Both Tucson and Memphis were very cognizant of Aidan's facial expressions and body language, and both relaxed when they came to the same conclusion, that Cameo's brother loved her and was no threat to her. Memphis left a good tip and they headed to the Grayhawks' room.

"Okay," Memphis said. "Now's the time to talk. So, Aidan Riley—where have you been and what have you been doing since that night you rescued Cameo then lost her in Pittsfield?"

"I had no idea where she went after she left the hospital," Aidan said. "The newspapers weren't full of details. Also, I was afraid of calling attention to myself or her by prying. I didn't want any information to get back to Savage or our family. I sure as hell didn't trust our family after what they did. I knew she had the money, and I knew she was strong. When I couldn't find her I also knew I couldn't go home, not that I wanted to. I had the distinct feeling that I'd wind up dead. So, I headed north into Vermont and settled down in Bennington. I've worked as a car mechanic and found I'm good with machinery."

"Are you married?" Cameo asked, looking at his ringless left hand.

Aidan shook his head. "Never came close. I just kept my head down and lived a quiet life. I rarely saw anything in the local papers about Savage or our family. He was involved in a high-profile drug case a few years ago and that trickled to the *Banner*. Nothing about our family. But when I saw the story about Callan's murder, something just prompted me to come home and see if I could find you. I was afraid maybe Savage had found you and was going to take you back to the ritual place and kill you. That's what I was doing there, scoping out the place."

"What do you think about Callan's death?" Cameo asked.

"I never liked the cocksucker. Blood doesn't necessarily make family. Maybe I should feel grief or something, but all I feel is … relieved, and a sense of satisfaction. He got what was coming to him."

"I gave that to him," Cameo said, searching Aidan's face.

Aidan broke out into a grin. "Right on, girl. I always knew you were tough as nails. A stone fox *and* a Charles Bronson rival. Did he know it was you?"

"I looked him right in the eye when I pulled the trigger." She glanced over at her husband and brother-in-law. "I, um … he wasn't the only one. Chris Komansky and Dolan Welsh."

"Scum," Aidan said, his lips curled. "You'll have to give me the details later. Now, what about Savage?"

"He's the last on my list."

Aidan grabbed her shoulders tightly. "I'm here now. I'll help you." He glanced at the Grayhawks. "Are they cool with this?"

"Yeah," Tucson said mildly. "We're cool."

"Groovy, even," Memphis added with a touch of sarcasm. "Cameo can explain in detail, but so far she's been extremely careful about leaving any clues or evidence when she was … administering justice. The same needs to be done with Savage. Cameo, why don't you explain the last plan to—do you want to be called Aidan or Connor?"

"Connor."

"Explain the last plan to Connor. Tonight's the night, and we have a lot of stuff to do."

Cameo pulled Connor down on the bed and took his hand. Then, she started to explain the previous three kills and the final one that would sever the past forever.

October 31, 1976
01:36 PM

Damien Savage wanted to slam the door hard enough to turn it into a pile of splinters, but he knew he had to pretend to be civilized and respect the two police detectives that had just darkened his door. He thought they had low-class accents and looked like trailer park trash, but he forced himself to treat them as equals. Hah—as if they could ever be.

He answered their questions and was certain that they couldn't detect the times he was outright prevaricating or twisting the facts to lead them off the trail. They had spent two hours asking him questions about the late and unlamented Callan Riley—when did he last see Riley? Did Riley have any enemies? What was his normal professional and personal routines? Did he have any vices, like gambling? The peppering questions were along those lines, ending with a few surprise queries.

"Where were you the night Riley was killed?"

"When was the last time you were in his townhouse or car?"

"Why was his car parked on your street?"

"Did you have any beef with him?"

Then they caught him a little off guard when they brought up the names of Chris Komansky and Dolan Welsh. Savage admitted that he knew of the men and might have met them once or twice, but they were hardly friends and he knew nothing about Welsh's disappearance or Komansky's death. One of the detectives asked when was the last time he was on Welsh's boat? Savage said he never was. The other detective asked how he knew that Komansky was dead—the identity of the cremated body hadn't been identified in the press. Savage shrugged and said in the D.A.'s office news floated around quickly. They didn't mention that the old crematorium was on property he owned; his rerouting of real estate through a half dozen dummy companies would hold. He hoped. But if they kept digging …

There was something secretive about the two detectives and he was relieved when they left. Their last questions were odd. He didn't like feeling he was being accused of anything. If they had any proof that he was they would have dragged him to the station and read him his rights.

Savage knew that Callan, Dolan, and Chris were dead by Maeve Riley's hand. Callan was in a morgue awaiting embalming; Chris was a charred skeleton at the coroner's lab; and Dolan was probably being eaten by cod at the bottom of the ocean. He was as certain of that as he was that the sun would rise in the east. He couldn't very well tell the detectives that since they would have wanted to know why she went on a killing spree and what his involvement was. He wondered if he were under surveillance. Damn—he might have to cancel the night's festivities. No, that would make him look weak in his followers' eyes. He could never appear weak. The rites would go on.

Savage made a few phone calls to followers and helpers to ensure that the ritual location was ready. He hadn't been out there for months. He walked over to his rolltop desk and opened the secret drawer and withdrew his 9mm gun. He studied it and made sure it was in working order and loaded.

If the bitch did show up, she was going to become intimately acquainted with hot lead.

October 31, 1976
08:42 PM

Savage was not pleased as he ran his eyes over his congregants. Four key members of the coven were missing. *Bastards*, he thought. There would be consequences for their failure and defiance. He decided to nix his usual speech and intonation and instead delve deep into Anton LaVey's teachings. LaVey had established his infamous Church of Satan on April 30, 1966 during Walpurgis Night. Proclaiming the date as "Year One" of Satanism his teachings and writings relied heavily on "superman"-ideologist Friedrich Nietzsche. His ideas caught on with too many people and up until 1975 he had supported the growths of "grottos" of Satanists across the country; a grotto was a clandestine association or gathering of Satanists within geographical proximity for means of social, ritual, and special interest activities. When he abolished the grotto system informal organizations continued to spring up from coast to coast.

Savage's coven was an informal "grotto" that he had established simply to grow and consolidate his power. Point of fact, few people engaged in supernatural pursuits rarely knew the different between the grotto and the coven; they tended to use the nomenclature interchangeably. He didn't believe in God, so he certainly didn't believe in Satan; his group was just a means to an end. He relished the power he felt, the orgiastic sex he had, and the manipulations of members who could further his professional aspirations. Someday, he planned on seeing himself seated as the first (albeit unknown) Satanist Boston District Attorney.

He took LaVey's famous book, *The Satanic Bible*, from his satchel and opened it. Although he was not a believer he did appreciate many of the tenets of the book. He wholeheartedly agreed with the Nine Satanic Statements.

1. Satan represents indulgence, instead of abstinence!
2. Satan represents vital existence, instead of spiritual pipe dreams!

3. Satan represents undefiled wisdom, instead of hypocritical self-deceit!
4. Satan represents kindness to those who deserve it, instead of love wasted on ingrates!
5. Satan represents vengeance, instead of turning the other cheek!
6. Satan represents responsibility to the responsible, instead of concern for psychic vampires!
7. Satan represents man as just another animal, sometimes better, more often worse than those that walk on all-fours, who, because of his "divine spiritual and intellectual development," has become the most vicious animal of all!
8. Satan represents all of the so-called sins, as they all lead to physical, mental, or emotional gratification!
9. Satan has been the best friend the church has ever had, as he has kept it in business all these years!

All of his acolytes had gathered, and the bonfire was blazing ten feet in front of him as he stood on a raised platform with a podium on which his open book rested. Those looking at him saw an image of a black-garbed man rising out of the flames of Hell, exactly the image he wanted to project. Savage waited until the crowd was silent and he had all eyes on him before he spoke.

"Our great prophet, Anton LaVey, has often said that our religion is based on the universal traits of man. We are inherently carnal and animalistic, and those so-called seven deadly sins are part of man's natural instincts and should be lauded and encouraged, not feared and denied. There is nothing wrong with Machiavellian self-interest."

He paused for effect, but just as he opened his mouth to continue there was a shriek from the audience. He saw a couple of people move towards a woman who was clutching her face and screaming. He heard her moan, "My eye, my eye."

Savage moved swiftly down from the podium and hustled over to the injured woman. He inhaled sharply as he saw a small metal star embedded in her right eye. Suddenly, there was another shriek and that was quickly followed by another. He saw the second screamer, a man, who seemed to have a similar star embedded in his right cheek. He didn't bother looking around for the third screamer. Out of the corner of his eye he saw a streak of light which seconds later proved to be a flaming arrow that embedded itself in the shoulder of one of his henchmen. A couple of men furiously patted out the flames, but the arrow was still embedded.

Then a volley of gunshots rent the air, and at that moment the crowd turned around as if one entity and began running towards the hidden patch of land where their cars were parked. Savage was momentarily shocked, long enough for the three dark figures to burst from the forest and head straight towards him. They were dressed head-to-toe in black and wore black ski masks. He whirled around while he reached for the gun in his belt and stopped dead in his tracks at the sight of a fourth black-garbed figure standing six feet away from him.

"Hi, honey. I'm home," Cameo said then discharged the taser. The double dart-like electrodes were attached to the weapon by thin copper wire, and when they hit Savage's chest they discharged an electric shock that knocked Savage over onto the ground where he convulsed and twisted until he was unmoving and silent. He was definitely incapacitated but not fully unconscious. His eyes were open wide so he could see Cameo kneeling down next to him and withdrawing some tube from her zipped-up jacket. He registered that the tube was a syringe and a second later she jammed it into his neck and depressed the plunger hard.

Memphis ran over to the bonfire and began hitting it with foam from his fire extinguisher; Tucson helped by stamping on the edges of the flames. A minute later the fire was out, and the unconscious Damien Savage was hauled over Connor's shoulder. Cameo grabbed Savage's satchel and books, then the four swept into the forest and headed down the twisted path, passing the unconscious henchman that Cameo had taken out with her nunchucks. They reached Connor's seafoam-green 1969 Chrysler Road Runner and stuffed Savage into the trunk. Connor roared the engine to life then screeched off, the

Road Runner barreling out of the forest and onto the road with its powerful 383 engine and 4-speed transmission. They knew that the coven acolytes wouldn't be screeching anywhere; Connor had stabbed all of their tires with his knife. They were in for a long walk home and a lot of towing bills, and a few medical bills thanks to Cameo's shuriken talent and Tucson's tried-and-true bow and arrow.

October 31, 1976
10:15 PM

Damien Savage awoke and took a few seconds to realize that he was being slapped across the face repeatedly to bring him back to consciousness. He felt a hard surface beneath his body and craned his neck to the side to see that it was a wooden floor. He twisted his head the other way and saw that he was in a small cabin. His eye caught a pile of bricks by the fireplace, which was roaring with brilliant orange flames. He groaned and looked up to see four dark figures standing over him. Unlike their presence at the ritual site they weren't wearing their masks. He thought that didn't bode well if they weren't afraid of being identified to the police.

He homed in on Cameo's face. Obviously older than the callow twenty-one when she escaped his clutches, she was slender with short, black hair; her cheeks were thinner and seemed higher. She was—what? Twenty-eight? And she still looked remarkably beautiful, but this time with a defiant seriousness and maturity to her face and body language. He felt his wrists bound behind his back, but his legs were unencumbered. He sniffed and used all his will to sit up.

His lip curled, he said to her, "You look good, bitch. Who're your friends? I see you hooked back up with your pathetic younger brother." He winked at Connor who glared at him balefully.

Tucson had made a move forward at the bitch remark, but Cameo held him back. She nodded at Tucson.

"This is my husband. That's his brother," she said blandly.

Damien narrowed his eyes at Tucson for a few seconds, then laughed. "I'll bet it frosts your balls that I fucked her first."

Damien didn't get more than five seconds to enjoy his shot when Tucson's pointed boot made violent contact with his genitals. Damien howled and squirmed and balled up in a fetal position as the pain raged through his nether regions. "Fucker," he hissed.

Memphis squatted down next to his face and said, "And he has a very fucker-ish brother, so I'd choose your words carefully from this point on unless you want your pecker to turn into Cream of Wheat." Memphis stood and backed away, letting Cameo take the lead. This was, after all, her vengeance.

"You'll never get away with this," Damien hissed to Cameo.

She smiled benevolently. "You know, I think I will. So far I've gotten away with exacting justice on Chris, Dolan, and Callan."

"The cops will find the evidence," Damien spit out.

"I believe they already have found some of the evidence that I … planted. Do you have any idea how easy it is to use clear tape to lift fingerprints and then transfer them to another hard surface? Like, a boat steering wheel and the edging by the stairs? A bourbon bottle in Callan's den? By the way—did you happen to notice that your cleanup of your drawing room might not have been as thorough as you might like? I refer specifically to a corner in the fireplace where Chris's house key found its way under a burned log. A thorough search warrant by the cops would no doubt find that.

"If not, then maybe they'll uncover the fact that the crematorium land is owned by you through a few dummy companies. Did I mention that when I was staking Chris out on your Persian rug I had time to rifle through your desk and other cabinets and found a great deal of information you'd prefer to keep hidden? Including several false passports. I nicked one of them." She looked at Tucson. "Did I mention to him that I can simulate virtually every cursive handwriting?"

"I don't believe you did," Tucson said politely.

Cameo smiled wickedly. "And I may have left a short letter buried in your papers asking a friend in Europe to provide you with false papers and an identity? Why, shockingly, you decided that the cops may find the evidence to convict you and you fled the country."

Damien curled his lip and snarled, "Get this over with, bitch. I'm getting bored." He glared up at Tucson. "Then you and your pussy-whipped hubby can go back to domestic bliss."

Tucson made a menacing step towards Damien, but Memphis held him back and waggled a finger at him. Then without warning he let loose a savage kick that broke Damien's jaw and sent a dozen bloody teeth flying. Damien gagged and spit out blood and a couple of other broken teeth. He glared up at his execution squad.

"Well?" he asked with difficulty. "Which one of you is going to strike the death blow? Maeve? You got the guts?"

"I believe I do," Cameo said casually and without hesitation aimed her .38 and blew a hole in the middle of his forehead. For good measure she aimed a second time and made hamburger out of his genitals. She looked at her family. "Okay. I'm good now."

Tucson walked over to the door where a large satchel rested. He pulled a small electric chain saw out of the bag and plugged it into the wall closest to the body. He turned it on, but Cameo patted his arm and shook her head.

"This is my job. Beat it, all of you," she said as she took the saw out of her husband's hands.

"You sure, baby?" Tucson asked.

"I'm sure."

Memphis patted Tucson's shoulder and walked him out of the cabin with Connor following. The cabin was a small getaway in the New Hampshire forest near Kingston and the Webster Natural Area, only a mile from Powwow Pond. It had been in the Riley family for two generations but very rarely used. Cameo remembered being there when she was five or six for a weekend. She didn't remember too much about the cabin or area, just that she'd been eaten alive by mosquitoes.

The men stood twenty feet from the cabin. The still air was broken with a familiar whirr; the chain saw had been turned on. Memphis decided to make ridiculous small talk while Cameo finished her work.

"So," he said to Tucson. "I recommend that you never piss off your wife. I certainly won't."

Tucson shrugged. "I dunno. I wouldn't mind seeing a chain saw battle between our wives. No bets, though—it'd be too close to call."

"I can't wait to meet the rest of your family," Connor said. "I can't wait to meet my nephews and niece." He glanced at the cabin when there was a short spike in the whirr.

"You'll fit in," Tucson said. He cocked his head and studied his new brother-in-law. "So, I guess you'll be staying Connor Donnelly. We'll have to figure out a back story to present you as Cameo's brother."

"Will you fly back with us when this is all over?" Memphis said.

"I'd like to, but I need to make arrangements for my car to be transported. I love that car, and I'd rather not drive it three thousand miles," Connor said. "It'll take me a few days to arrange everything."

"Sounds good," Memphis said. He lit up a thin cigar and puffed while they fell into a semi-peaceful silence, the only sound the constant whirr of the saw.

A half hour later the cabin door opened, and Cameo stood there. She was covered with blood.

"All right, gentlemen," she said. "Time to wrap this up." She smiled at the irony of her words.

The men picked up the bags full of plastic garbage bags and went inside while Cameo stripped naked, turned the rusty but still working hose on, and cleansed her body. She stuffed the bloody clothes in a garbage bag along with the disconnected hose. She pulled on simple dark clothes and waited for the men to be done with their tasks.

It was a beautiful, cool night. The stars shone down, crickets cricked, and owls hooted. As the car drove away she looked back at the cabin, now shooting flames through its windows and roof. She thought the fire was beautiful.

November 1, 1976
01:23 AM

The *Slice of Life* rocked under the pressure of the ocean waves thirty miles out in the ocean. Tucson had driven up to Portsmouth and rented the boat for two days under a false name. It was docked at Portsmouth Marina on Sagamore Creek. The journey to the ocean went up the creek and under the bridge of Route 1B, opening up to the Piscataqua River. The river emptied into the Atlantic Ocean. Cameo and her companions parked at the marina and made several discreet trips from the car to the boat, each trip resulting in a large Igloo cooler being wheeled down the gangplank to the boat. When they loaded everything, Tucson revved up the boat and headed to the ocean.

Halfway out they paused to dump the disarticulated chain saw and the remainder of Cameo's weapons (and the bow and arrow) into the drink. Ten miles later they dumped the contents of one of the Igloos, and then headed out to their projected limit of thirty miles.

Cameo stood on the deck of the boat watching her family dump the heavily wrapped packages into the water. Each package had a half dozen bricks to weight it down. Connor picked up the last, bulky round package but Cameo stopped him and took the package from his hands. She stared down at the wrapped head for a long moment then walked over to the edge and heaved the last piece of Damien Savage into the Atlantic Ocean. She mouthed, "Bye-bye, fucker," then turned to her men and said, "Let's go home."

Memphis drove the boat while she and Tucson sat beside one another and held hands. Suddenly she laughed.

"What?" Tucson said.

"Today. It's after midnight." Her lips curled in a satisfied smile. "It's the Day of the Dead."

Tucson kissed his wife's cheek and squeezed her hand.

"I can't think of any way better to celebrate," Tucson said.

"Damn straight, Cochise. Damn straight."

CHAPTER EIGHTEEN

January 1, 1977

"Come on—this is bullshit," Sand yelled at the TV as the third quarter of the Rose Bowl ended with no score for that quarter. The same thing had happened in the first quarter although the Michigan Wolverines and the USC Trojans had both managed to score in quarter two. He fumed on. "This is the best they can do? It's bullshit."

Memphis leaned over and said loudly to Connor, "He's like this for every football game. You should have seen him during Super Bowl last year when his beloved Cowboys fell to the Steelers. It wasn't pretty."

"Kind of been a Patriots fan because of my roots," Connor said, eliciting a scowl from Sand and Akiro.

"You're not ingratiating yourself," Sand growled. "Patriots. Ugh. Sam Cunningham's a decent Fullback, but I don't think Sam Adams is a memorable Right Guard."

"You're wrong," Connor said flatly. "And before you start quibbling just remember that New Mexico doesn't even have a professional sports team." He took a swig of beer and pasted a shit-eating grin on his face.

Sand grunted; he had no answer for that. He certainly wasn't going to admit that he liked Cameo's brother, who had quickly integrated into the extensive clan. Sand knew the real story about the east-coast trip, and Swan did, too. Memphis and Tucson had decided to keep the truth from the rest of their family and friends and cooked up a story about Cameo finding her roots, which were a middle-class family near Boston. Her parents were dead but her brother, Connor, was still there and they reunited. They gave her name as Mavis Donnelly. She never remembered who had attacked her and how she'd gotten to Pittsfield, and the protective weapons she'd brought with her proved to be pointless; they were discarded. Connor added that the money was a legacy from their parents, and she had taken it and left town to start a new life.

The story was iffy, but it seemed to hold as long as it wasn't put under a microscope. She said that she was Cameo now and that's how she'd live out the rest of her life. Percy seemed skeptical but restrained himself from probing further in respect to Tucson and his family. Still, the story itched at him.

Connor moved in temporarily with his sister, and that move provided an unexpected opportunity for him and for Declan. The beer brewery was in the process of having all the equipment installed and Declan wasn't happy with the team doing that. They had run over schedule and budget, and in a frustrated huff Declan had fired them shortly after Connor made his appearance. When he found that Connor was mechanically inclined he impulsively hired him to finish the installation. Declan was ecstatic when Connor fixed the problems, installed the remainder of the equipment, and tweaked the internal processing to make it quicker and more efficient. He hired Connor immediately to become the operations manager, and their relationship was sealed with a firm handshake.

With the addition of one more family member Tucson commissioned a contractor to build a small casita in the back of his house. Until it was completed sometime in February Connor bunked with Declan in the room addition that had been completed in November. Fortunately, the two men got along on a personal as well as professional basis. Declan brought Connor out of his shell, and Connor tempered down Declan's wild personality to more of one suited for a new businessman. Connor also fell quickly into the role of uncle to Tucson's three children. For the first three weeks Cameo couldn't pry Brett out of his new uncle's arms.

While Memphis, Sand, Connor, Tucson, and Luc were watching the game and Sage was riding herd on the family children in the den, the women along with Percy and Nick were out back having what Memphis daringly called a "hen party." He knew he'd regret that remark. He planned on making himself scarce until he could figure out the best way to get out of couch sleep for the next week.

What was going on out back was hardly a hen party. Nick and Yuki had their heads together and were giggling and canoodling with little interest in the others around them. Percy sat next to his wife studying a case file for a new client. Swan and Tansee sat side-by-side half-gabbing about their five-month pregnancies and half-mesmerized by the taekwondo training that Cameo was imparting to Raleigh. Cameo moved like a ballerina while Raleigh was still immersed in her awkward stage. Still, the youngest Grayhawk sibling was learning fast and exuded menace as she and her sister-in-law circled one another waiting for an opening.

"Wait. Stop," Cameo snapped. "Take a breath."

"What?" Raleigh said, breathing hard, her arms still extended for attack.

"This discipline has tenets. Rules. It's not just how hard and often you can kick or punch an opponent. So. Tell me the tenets."

Raleigh rolled her eyes and relaxed into a non-aggressive stance. "Fine," she said, sighing. "There are five tenets. Courtesy, integrity, perseverance, self-control, and indomitable spirit. Happy?"

"Not with your attitude but at least your memory's on solid ground. Now, recite the student oath." Cameo folded her arms and stared at her sister-in-law balefully.

"Oy. Okay. Observe the tenets of Taekwondo. Respect all seniors and instructors. Never misuse Taekwondo. Be a champion of freedom and justice. Help to build a more peaceful world."

Nick snorted. "Yeah, like that's gonna happen." Raleigh turned to him and flashed both middle fingers.

"I could kick your ass with one hand tied behind my back," Raleigh said.

"In your dreams, little girl," Nick said, laughing.

"So," Percy interjected, speaking to his brother. "Your estate all in order so Yuki doesn't have to go through probate?"

The banter went on as Swan retreated from the conversation and scoured the set of east-coast newspapers that had been sent to the office every week since the team had returned home and arranged for their delivery. The first few issues of the *Boston Globe* focused on the disappearance of ADA Damien Savage as the police were focusing on him for the murder of Callan Riley and the assumed murder of missing Dolan Welsh. They were also investigating the death and cremation of Chris Komansky. The police had a search warrant for Savage's townhouse and found trace evidence of blood and a scorched set of car keys hidden in the fireplace. Savage's fingerprints had also been found on a bottle of bourbon on Riley's den desk and on several points of Welsh's boat. Several issues later an article stated that the crematory location where Komansky was found was owned by Savage through a set of dummy companies.

Damien Savage was still nowhere to be found. The police stated that they had found multiple phony passports, and a letter indicating that he was thinking of fleeing. There was an all-points bulletin for his apprehension. They'd interviewed a number of associates and friends who were reluctant to talk about him and pleaded ignorance about his last known day.

Swan smiled slyly at the thought of Savage lying in pieces at the bottom of the ocean. He deserved it. She couldn't help but admire the hell out of Cameo for righting a terrible wrong. When they first met she didn't care for Cameo, but the woman grew on her, especially after she married Tucson and became a caring, devoted mother to his children by Cassidy and their son. Now, they were very good friends.

Cameo bowed to Raleigh, who bowed back. Cameo dropped down in a chair next to Swan and Tansee and wiped the sweat off her face then finished a 20-ounce bottle of cold water waiting for her in the Igloo. Raleigh drank a bottle, too, then went inside to finish watching the football game.

"She's good," Cameo said, nodding and reaching for another bottle. "A regular Bruce Lee."

"And she can shoot a gun like Dirty Harry," Swan replied. "Did she tell you that she wants to apply to the FBI? Now that J. Edgar is dead they've opened the force up to women. They already have a few. I warned her that she'd be in for hell, but I think she's tough enough to survive it. As it stands we need a new FBI contact since Ballard left." Richard Ballard had transferred to Phoenix in November with the hope that shortly thereafter he and his wife could make their home in San Francisco. When they settled in he called Memphis and told him that Noor was pregnant, and they were ecstatic. Memphis hoped the baby would help bridge the estrangement between Richard and his father, Tom.

"Well, she's got a few more years before she takes that drastic step. She's still a freshman. Chances are she'll change her mind and find something less daunting," Tansee offered.

"Did you?" Swan asked.

"Oh, God, no. I always wanted to be a doctor, ever since I was a kid."

"Some role model you are."

All of a sudden Cameo spoke up. "Nick, Percy, could you leave for a short while?"

"Why?" Nick said suspiciously.

"Girl talk," Cameo said succinctly. "Shoo." She watched as the two men grumbled their way into the house and shut the glass slider. Raleigh came right back out rolling her eyes and muttering, "Men."

"Okay, girl," Swan said. "What's up?"

"C'mon, spill," Yuki said eagerly.

Cameo smiled, a shy look on her face. "I'm pregnant." She barely got the last word out when the females all whooped and started clapping.

Tansee hugged her and asked, "Was this planned?"

"God, no. I never envisioned having another child until Brett was at least in pre-school. I'm pretty sure it happened in Boston, or just when we came back."

"Does Tucson know?"

"No. I planned on telling him today. I just couldn't keep it a secret anymore being here with you guys." She looked at Raleigh apologetically. "I'm sorry, but this is our last training session for now. I can't take the chance of an errant kick harming the baby."

Raleigh snorted and rolled her eyes. "Of course not. I'll find another trainer, probably one better than you."

"Ouch."

Raleigh laughed. "Just kiddin'. You are the best. We'll pick up after you lose the baby fat."

"So … how did you break it to Percy about your baby?" Cameo asked Tansee.

"I served him a dessert plate with a cover over a baby rattle. He was stunned and, I think, more than a little scared considering my history of miscarriages."

"What about you?" Cameo asked Swan.

"I made an off-the-cuff remark when we were filling Sage in about Snow. In the middle Memphis said he forbad me to get pregnant again. When I told him I was, he said, 'I need a drink.'"

"Why is it men think everything can be fixed with booze?" Raleigh said.

"Same reason women think everything can be fixed with ice cream," Tansee said. They all looked at her. She shrugged. "It's French vanilla for Percival, preferably drenched in caramel sauce."

"So, do you want a boy or a girl?" Yuki asked Cameo.

"I absolutely don't care, but maybe it would be nice to have a girl, so we have two of each."

"Hehewuti and Jakub will be thrilled to have another grandchild," Swan said. She grimaced as the baby threw a few solid kicks inside the womb. "They won't find out until they hit a port of call and call home." The Grayhawk parents were on a three-month cruise to Australia and New Zealand on one of the favorite lines; they'd be back in early April. They had the biggest house outside of Percy and Tansee, so the clan had gathered here to enjoy New Year's Day.

Suddenly there a loud roar from inside the house.

"Somebody made a touchdown," Swan said sardonically. She put down the Boston newspaper and picked up the *Courant*. Cameo had resumed her editorial duties a couple of weeks after they came home, and Caleb had charged her with writing an "End of the Bicentennial Year" summary of 1976. Cameo was a structured, detailed writer and had broken up the year by highlighting events month by month. She started each month with a quick summary of events then wrote about them in detail. Caleb had given her two full pages for the story.

January: Jimmy Carter won the Iowa Democratic Caucus. Sara Jane Moore was sentenced to life in prison for her attempted assassination of President Gerald Ford. The Philadelphia Flyers creamed the Soviet Union's hockey team 4-1. The Lutz family fled their new home in Amityville, New York, claiming supernatural forces drove them out. In Super Bowl X the Pittsburgh Steelers defeated the Dallas Cowboys, 21-17 in Miami.

February: The Winter Olympics took place in Innsbruck, Austria where the Soviets garnered twenty-seven medals followed by East Germany with nineteen and the United States and West Germany tying with ten. Actor Sal Mineo was stabbed to death outside of his home. Former Supremes singer Florence Ballard died of heart failure at thirty-two in her hometown of Detroit, Michigan. Nearly 2,000 students became involved in a racially charged riot at Escambia High School in Pensacola, Florida; 30 students were injured in the four-hour fray.

March: A cable car crash in Calavese, Italy resulted in forty-three deaths. Patty Hearst was found guilty of the Hibernia bank robbery in 1974. The New Jersey Supreme Court ruled that the patient in a persistent vegetative state in the Karen Ann Quinlan case could be disconnected from her ventilator. Foreign Service officer Bradford Bishop allegedly murdered five of his family members in Bethesda, Maryland. The crime went undiscovered for ten days and the suspect was never caught. Two coal mine explosions at the Blue Diamond

Coal Co. Scotia Mine, in Letcher County, Kentucky claimed twenty-six lives.

April: In what was called "The Great Bookie Robbery" in Melbourne, Australia bandits stole A$1.4 million in bookmakers' settlements from Queen Street. In the largest prison break in Spain since the Spanish civil war, twenty-nine political prisoners escaped from Segovia prison. The United States Treasury Department reintroduced the two-dollar bill as a Federal Reserve Note on Thomas Jefferson's 233rd birthday as part of the United States Bicentennial celebration. Millionaire businessman, aviator, and notorious recluse Howard Hughes died at the age of seventy.

May: A 6.5 earthquake hit the Friuli area in Italy, killing more than 900 people and making another 100,000 homeless. U.S. President Gerald Ford defeated challenger Ronald Reagan in three Republican presidential primaries in Kentucky, Tennessee and Oregon. The Judgment of Paris pitted French vs. California wines in a blind taste-test in Paris, France, where the California wines won the contest, surprising the wine world and opening the wine industry to newcomers in several countries. Johnny Rutherford won the Indianapolis 500-Mile Race, the shortest race in the history of the event at 102 laps.

June: In Phoenix, Arizona reporter Don Bolles was killed by a car bomb. The Teton Dam collapsed in southeast Idaho, killing eleven people. Francis E. Meloy Jr., the newly appointed U.S. Ambassador to Lebanon, along with two others, was kidnapped and killed in Beirut, Lebanon, and as a result hundreds of Western tourists were moved from Beirut and taken to safety in Syria by the U.S. military. Savage thunderstorms rolled through the state of Iowa, spawning several tornadoes, including an F-5 tornado that destroyed the town of Jordan, Iowa.

July: The United States celebrated the United States Bicentennial in memory for the 200th anniversary of the American Revolution (Cameo included a large color photo of the ships in New York harbor). In June Palestinian militants had hijacked an Air France plane in Greece with 246 passengers and 12 crew and flew it to

Entebbe, Uganda; on July 4th Israeli airborne commandos freed 103 hostages being held by the Palestinian hijackers at Uganda's Entebbe Airport. Jimmy Carter secured the nomination for U.S. president at the Democratic National Convention in New York City. Twenty-six Chowchilla schoolchildren and their bus driver were abducted and buried in a box truck in a quarry in Livermore, California; the captives dug themselves free after sixteen hours and the quarry-owner's son and two accomplices were arrested for the crime. The Summer Olympics took place in Quebec, Canada where Nadia Comăneci of Romania earned seven perfect scores of ten.

August: A sniper rampage in Wichita, Kansas at a Holiday Inn resulted in three deaths and seven wounded. A gunman murdered twelve-year-old Andrea Wilborn and Stan Farr and injured her mother, Priscilla Davis, and Gus Gavrel, in an incident at Priscilla's mansion in Fort Worth, Texas. T. Cullen Davis, Priscilla's husband and one of the richest men in Texas, was arrested for the crime. Actress Anissa Jones, famous for playing Buffy Davis in the TV series *Family Affair*, was found dead of an accidental drug overdose in Oceanside, California; she was eighteen.

September: Beginning with the Night of the Pencils, a series of kidnappings and forced disappearances followed by the torture, rape, and murder of students under the Argentine dictatorship took place. Frank Sinatra brought Jerry Lewis's former partner Dean Martin onstage, unannounced, at the Jerry Lewis MDA Telethon in Las Vegas, reuniting the comedy team for the first time in over twenty years. Patty Hearst was sentenced to seven years in prison for her role in the 1974 Hibernia bank robbery. Mao Zedong, the general secretary of China, died at the age of eighty-two from a heart attack. *The Muppet Show* was broadcast for the first time on ITV.

October: The United States Commission on Civil Rights released the report, *Puerto Ricans in the Continental United States: An Uncertain Future,* documenting that Puerto Ricans in the United States had a poverty rate of 33% in 1974, the highest of all major racial-ethnic groups in the country. Cubana de Aviación Flight 455 crashed due to a bomb placed by anti-Fidel Castro terrorists, after taking off from Bridgetown, Barbados; all seventy-three people on board were killed. The Mississippi River ferry MV *George Prince* was struck by a ship while crossing from Destrehan, Louisiana to Luling, Louisiana, killing seventy-eight passengers and crew. Clarence Norris, the last known survivor of the Scottsboro Boys, was pardoned. The Cultural Revolution in China concluded with the capture of the Gang of Four.

November: On November 2nd Jimmy Carter defeated incumbent Gerald Ford, becoming the first candidate from the Deep South to win since the Civil War. The New York Yankees signed free agent Reggie Jackson to a five-year, $3 million contract setting the precedence for lucrative multi-year contracts for Major League Baseball players. Microsoft was officially registered with the Office of the Secretary of the State of New Mexico. The first megamouth shark was discovered off Oahu in Hawaii.

December: The Viet Cong was disbanded, and its former members became a part of the Vietnam People's Army. Angola and Samoa joined the United Nations. Jamaican singer Bob Marley and his manager, Don Taylor, were shot in an assassination attempt in Kingston, Jamaica. Richard J. Daley, the mayor of Chicago for twenty-one years, died. The Eagles released *Hotel California*. Sir Douglas Nicholls was appointed as the 28th Governor of South Australia, the first Australian Aboriginal appointed to a vice-regal office.

Cameo added a bordered section for the entertainment industry listing the top ten songs and movies of 1976. *Silly Love Songs*, *Don't Go Breaking My Heart*, *Disco Lady*, *December 1963*, *Play That Funky Music*, *Kiss and Say Goodbye*, *Love Machine*, *50 Ways to Leave Your Lover*, *Love Is Alive*, and *A Fifth of Beethoven* occupied the top positions in Billboard's Top 100 chart. The top-grossers in box office revenue were *Rocky*, *To Fly!*, *A Star Is Born*, *King Kong*, *Silver Streak*, *All the President's Men*, *The Omen*, *The Enforcer*, *Midway*, and *The Bad News Bears*. The movies raked in over $600 million.

Swan thought it had truly been an exhausting year, both world-wide and in the family's own little corner of Santa Fe. Three new babies had been conceived, Cameo's past had been revealed along with her actioning of genuine justice, and the family's businesses were running fast and true. Still, the Indian injustice killer had not been found and at least in the past few months he seemed to have taken no known victims. Oh, and possibly the most precious thing that happened was when Frick and London had married quietly in the San Miguel Chapel on Christmas Eve, and then headed off to a honeymoon in Hawaii. Frack had stood up as best man, and Carmen Castillo had been the matron of honor.

Life was good, Swan thought, and she hoped that the rest of 1977 would be as peaceful as today was. She rubbed her tummy and smiled at the baby's movement. She hoped it would be a boy.

CHAPTER NINETEEN

May 18, 1977

"Push," Memphis ordered.

"What the hell do you think I'm doing, moron?" Swan wheezed just before another contraction ripped through her body. She screamed and clutched Memphis's hand so hard his knuckles turned white.

"Just breathe, honey," Memphis said through gritted teeth.

"Don't tell me what to do," Swan snapped. She scrunched up her red, damp face and gave another push her all. "Fuck it," she said, seething. "You're getting fixed as soon as this kid is out." Another contraction prompted another scream.

"We're almost there," Dr. Osten said cheerfully. "One more push should do it."

"Go to hell," Swan replied. "What's this 'we' bullshit?"

"The baby's crowning," Dr. Osten said.

"Pull it out," Swan shrieked. She gave one last push and realized that the baby was out. A few seconds later she heard its first cry.

"It's a boy," Memphis said in a hushed tone. He squeezed her hand. He watched as the baby was wiped off and the umbilical cord was severed, then Dr. Osten put the baby on Swan's chest. She held her son as Memphis nuzzled her neck and kissed her. "Good job, Mom," he said.

"You're still getting fixed," Swan said.

Two rooms down a similar scene was playing out as Tansee went through labor. She was two weeks late and Swan was a week early, and somehow they wound up going into labor on the same day. Percy was propped up on her bed with one arm under her head and the other hand holding hers as she struggled with fifteen hours of labor. She rarely screamed, part of her stoic approach to life. Percy was sweating and occasionally chuffing as he tried to soothe her until their child was ready to make its appearance.

Tansee was in significant pain but, as she thought, it was a good pain because it would bring her new daughter or son into the world. The doctor said she had crowned, and she knew it would only be moments, but the moments felt like hours. She and Percy were all too aware that the baby could suffer from his dwarfism. She didn't care; she'd love her child no matter what, and so would Percy. But she understood the struggles and turmoil of growing up a dwarf and fighting to be accepted as a "normal" person in a visually bigoted world. He had beaten all the odds.

She gritted her teeth and gave one last push and felt the baby slide out of her body. The doctor and nurse were attending the newborn and she couldn't see what her baby looked like. She felt Percy kiss her forehead as both anxiously waited for word. The doctor turned to them, smiling.

"You've got a beautiful son," Dr. Dearing said. "Congratulations."

The nurse had cleaned and wrapped the baby, then carefully handed him over to his mother. Tansee stared down at the baby with a head of dark hair and his father's riveting blue eyes.

Percy looked at his son and hissed in a loud breath. "He's normal," he said as tears edged out of his eyes.

"Yes," Dr. Dearing said. "No dwarfism at all. Do you have a name for him?"

Tansee looked at Percy and smiled. "Benjamin Nicholas."

Dr. Dearing smiled and nodded. “That’s a fine name. Now, we’ll take you to recovery and log all of little Benjamin’s measurements and blood type. We’ll bring him to you shortly.” He signaled the nurse who gently pried Benjamin from his mother’s arms. Percy jumped off the bed and the nurse and orderly wheeled Tansee away. Percy was breathing hard, his heart beating a mile a minute. He decided to go and see if the Grayhawks had their baby, and then he’d head to his wife’s room.

Memphis was standing outside of the birth room door when Percy approached. He grinned. “It’s a boy.”

“Mine, too,” Percy said. “We’re calling him Benjamin Nicholas. You got a name?”

“We’re still arguing,” Memphis said. “Tansee okay?”

“She’s fine. We’re all fine.”

“I guess we’d better head off to the lounge and let the family know.” Memphis’s eyes lit up as a nurse approached and put his son into his arms. He lowered the baby so Percy could get a good look.

“He’s beautiful,” Percy said. “He’s got your black hair and brown eyes.”

“About time. My girls all have their mother’s coloring. Let’s go get your kid and head down to the lounge.”

They went to Tansee’s room where she was sitting up in bed. One of the nurses had brushed her hair and she was taking a sip of water. She saw that Memphis was carrying his baby and she stretched out her arms and said, “Gimme, gimme, gimme.” Memphis put the baby in her arms, and she cooed over him just as the nurse came in with Benjamin. The two fathers and one mother ooh’d and ah’d, then the men took their respective children and headed off to the lounge where a swarm of Grayhawks and McBeans and friends were waiting for the appearance of the new family members. Tansee grimaced in pain and her eyes opened wide as a flower of blood began staining her lower blanket.

Hehewuti extracted the baby from her son and tucked him into the crook of her arm. She whispered something in Hopi and kissed his soft forehead before relinquishing him to Memphis. The only child present was Sage; the others were under the eagle eyes of Frick and London at their home except for Tucson's kids, who were at home with Declan and Connor. Sage contemplated her new brother very seriously. She nodded then looked at her father, a hint of decision on her pretty face.

"Mom and I have been talking, and we decided on a name, Dad," Sage said.

"Don't you think I have any say in this?" Memphis asked with a highly arched eyebrow.

Sage shrugged. "Not really. Want to know your only son's name?"

Memphis sighed theatrically. "Hit me."

Sage looked into the baby's face and gently brushed a lock of his silky hair across his forehead. She smiled at her father. "Maximilian Sebastian. It's a mouthful, but we'll just call him Max."

"Max," Memphis murmured as he looked down at his seven-pound-twelve-ounce son, who, Jakub said, looked just like he did as a newborn. He looked at his daughter. "I can live with that. We're going to talk about the middle name, though."

"It has to start with an 'S,'" Sand said. "Your girls are all 'S' then 'M,' so reverse it. Sand is a good middle name."

Cameo was holding Percy's new son. She couldn't wait to give birth to her own child, somewhere around the end of July. These first months of 1977 she felt a peacefulness and calm in her mind and heart now that her past was resolved, and she didn't have to look back anymore. She was about to hand Benjamin back to his father when the doctor rushed through the lounge door followed by a young nurse.

"Dr. McBean," he said urgently, "you need to come with me. It's your wife."

Percy went ice cold. "What's wrong?" he asked flatly.

"She began to bleed after you left her room. She's … she's in the operating room right now. Please come with me. Nurse Sisti will take the baby."

The nurse gently took the baby from Cameo's arms and followed the doctor and Percy out.

"What the hell?" Nick growled. He had already fallen in love with his nephew and was terrified that something was badly wrong with Tansee. He made to follow but Tucson grabbed his arm.

"Wait, just wait. They'll come back when they know something. Let's not get in their way."

Nick inhaled sharply and nodded.

Memphis said, "I'll take … Max back to his mother. I'll be back as soon as I can but if you hear anything come get me. Room 413." He took the baby from Hehewuti and left the lounge.

Twenty minutes later Memphis was back but there was no sign of Percy or the doctor that had delivered Ben. Everyone was anxious and the men in general seem to be nervously pacing around. A half hour later Percy returned. Everyone jumped up and clustered around him.

"First, Tansee is going to be okay," Percy said to a collective exhale from his family.

"What happened?" Nick asked.

"Uterine inversion," Percy said. "And before you say, 'what the hell is that,' I'll tell you. It's a condition during childbirth. Normally, a placenta detaches from the uterus and vacates the vagina about a half hour after birth. If it doesn't detach from the uterus it turns the uterus inside out. Most of the time the doctor can manually detach the placenta and push the uterus back to its natural state, but with Tansee somehow she began bleeding badly and they took her into the operating room. They couldn't reposition the uterus because it was torn and bleeding, so they … they performed a hysterectomy. She's in post-op and will be moved to the ICU soon."

Memphis laid a comforting hand on Percy's shoulder. "She's got you, Elspeth, and Benjamin. Like you said, she'll be fine."

"And we're all here for you," Yuki added, squeezing Nick's hand.

"I know," Percy said quietly. "You all should go home. I'll stay here with Tansee. Really, go." He went out as a lot of eyes followed him.

"I got nothing to do at home," Sand said. "Think I'll stick around."

"Well," Akiro said, sighing, "I've got to get some sleep since I'll be in court all day tomorrow. I'll pick up Elijah on the way home." He gave Sand a fast peck on the cheek. "See you tomorrow morning."

"Nick will stay, and I'll pick up our terrible two," Yuki said. She put out her hand. "Car keys, please." Nick complied, she gave him a hug, and walked to the elevator where Akiro was awaiting.

The group argued about going or staying and when the dust settled the only ones left in the lounge were Memphis, Nick, Sand, Tucson, and Cameo, although Tucson called her a taxi an hour later and made her go home.

When Tucson came back from walking his wife to the taxi Memphis asked, "So, little brother—you picked out any names yet?"

"We've been bandying a few names about," Tucson said, "both for a girl and a boy."

"Come on—let's have 'em."

"We thought we'd stick with a 'B' name since the other three start with that. If it's a girl, Belinda Charlotte, and if it's a boy, Beckett Memphis." He winked at his brother.

"I like them," Sand said. "Maybe work on the boy's middle name." He dodged a swat from Memphis.

"At least I'm not named after desert dirt," Memphis said.

The brothers bandied jovially for a while, and shortly before dawn Percy came back, surprised and not surprised to see the smaller yet devoted group in the lounge. Tucson was stretched out on one couch sleeping; Sand was looped over a chair snoring. Nick jumped up and walked over to his brother.

"Tansee?" Nick asked anxiously.

"She's awake and doing fine," Percy said. "They want to keep her for a day or two before they release her."

"Me and Yuki will take care of Elspeth," Nick said. "If they let you take Ben home before they release Tansee just bring him over to our house."

"Thanks, brother," Percy said quietly. "Now, all of you home, please. I'm going, too, to take a nap and change before I come back. Let's go."

Percy hustled his family and friends like a swarm of chicks towards the elevator.

Benjamin Memphis Grayhawk made his screaming, kicking appearance on July 22, 1977 after his mother went through only four hours of labor. He had his father's coloring and black hair. He was the center of attention when his parents brought him home to his brothers and sister; Bree immediately claimed her baby brother as hers; she was fascinated with the baby and adored him. Brae was a little more aloof since he was so much older, and Brett was too young to understand the concept of siblinghood anyway. Tucson knew they'd grow into it.

Declan was spending less time at home as he readied his brewery for its opening on Mexican Independence Day, September 16th. He had designed four types of beer and their names—lager beer (Irish Dream), prickly pear cactus beer (Desert Sunset), dark ale (Midnight Oasis), and light beer (Santa Fe Sunrise). He had hired additional workers and Connor was overseeing their work as well as creating a tasting room/bar per Declan's requirements with a dark walnut bar, tables, and chairs. Connor and Declan had become fast friends and Connor was reveling in his new life and his reunion with his big sister.

Luc had graduated college with a 3.9 GPA but hadn't yet decided on a career path, or so his family thought. He had actually decided what profession he wanted to enter, but he wasn't sure his family would support him. He didn't really have to tell them for a few months, and he kept himself busy running errands for Memphis's and Akiro's firms and helping his father sand and construct commissioned violins and guitars. He was good at that, and Jakub hinted around about having them work together on those efforts permanently. He sloughed off the hints and said he hadn't decided on the future yet.

Raleigh had finished her freshman year of college and was scheduled to start her sophomore year at Sangre de Cristo College in August. She had grumbled about that since the beginning of the year. The college was all well and good but hardly the kind of preeminent school that would make the FBI look twice at her when she applied. She secretly applied to Georgetown, Yale, and Columbia; Yale said no but the other two approved her transfer.

Her parents, however, did not. Besides the excessive cost of tuition, room, and board, there was the matter of her being only the tender age of nineteen. She and her parents argued and, frustrated, she sought out the support of her brothers. Tucson was leery, but she got a semi-enthusiastic nod from Memphis and Luc. Still, she was overruled by the people that held the purse strings and that had led to a lot of tension during the summer. Finally, however, she got the tentative okay from her parents to transfer for her junior year, but only if she maintained a GPA of 3.5 or higher. Piece of cake, she thought; she had ended her freshman year with a GPA of 3.7.

The summer was filled with dealing with new babies and a lull in investigative cases. There was no movement on the missing persons front, and so far no other tourists had disappeared. Sand took Elijah, Sage, Shea, and Sara to Disneyland while Memphis and Swan held down the fort and looked after Max. Akiro didn't go with them since he was engrossed in his second murder case and one of his associates had left to take a job in Los Angeles. Tucson's twins had wanted to go but their father promised that they'd have a family trip around Christmas time. Brae stamped his foot and scowled, and Tucson told him that that attitude would get him excluded from the trip.

Tansee was back at work and had to back-burner her genetics research to handle her family-practice clients. Percy and Tucson found they had an inordinate number of clients that were suffering from PTSD. Tucson hadn't gotten over Ralph Mancini's suicide, but he was rational enough to know that he wasn't responsible. Percy noticed that Tucson was calmer and seemed to have reached a plateau of acceptance and perspective. He was certain that whatever had transpired with Cameo back east was a big part of that. She was heavily on the job at the *Courant* and had moved up the ladder.

Candy and Dante set their wedding date for Friday, September 16th, Mexican Independence Day. She demanded a small, tasteful wedding, and her mother convinced her that, yes, she could wear a white gown.

As Labor Day edged towards them the family and extended clan were on a peaceful plane where they were looking forward to the future.

Sometimes hopes and dreams and simple things came true.

Sometimes they didn't.

CHAPTER TWENTY

September 23, 1977

The priest solemnly intoned the Bible passages at the cemetery under a cloudless blue sky. The wind was eleven mph, and at mid-morning the temperature leveled at 70°F with the forecasters' projections of the day's high at 82°F. The air was comfortable, but no one really cared; the crowd of black-garbed mourners shared no comfort, only grief. The peaceful, beautiful cemetery was sometime a balm to the soul, but not today. Not today.

The Rosario Cemetery on North Guadalupe Street was built in 1868 although the Rosario Chapel was built in 1807. The chapel was intended to receive the statue of La Conquistadora which originated in Mexico. During the annual novena, the statue makes its way in a procession from the St. Francis Basilica to the chapel for masses before it is returned to the Basilica. La Conquistadora is a thirty-inch sacred wooden relic of the Madonna and child that arrived by wagon train in Santa Fe in 1626 through the efforts of Fray Alonso de Benavides. The statue was stolen from the cathedral in 1973 by two teenage boys and was later recovered, along with a stolen statue of San Miguel, from an abandoned mine shaft in the Manzano Mountains near Los Lunas.

The cemetery itself is Catholic, spanning multiple acres of green lawns that rival Ireland's lushness, dotted with huge old trees towering over many simple white headstones as well as private family mausoleums. Several burial sections are dedicated to Christian Brothers, Sisters, and Priests who were a mainstay of servicing the religious needs of people who sought to make northern New Mexico their home. The chapel's parishioners were mainly Hispanic, with a few whites and Indians dotting the overall complexion.

The Redwolf family were amongst those Indian parishioners or had been until Dante's parents moved down to Las Cruces. He rarely attended mass after that, and when he started courting Candy he would accompany her to her family's church. They married there on September 16th and spent their wedding night in the La Fonda Inn's most luxurious room. The next day they drove down to Albuquerque to catch their flight to Madrid, Spain to enjoy a two-week honeymoon in the land of Candy's distant ancestors.

They never made it.

Seventy-year-old Robin Fain was driving north to Santa Fe. She was a lifelong alcoholic with a failing liver, and she decided to force her son to let her see the grandkids just one more time before she'd kick the bucket. She'd had three stiff drinks before she left Albuquerque and had filled a thermos with as much cheap whiskey as it could hold. By the time that she reached the La Cienega area the thermos was empty, and she was filthy drunk. Her car was weaving all over the two north lanes, barely missing a half-dozen vehicles and sideswiping one before she lost complete control of her car.

At seventy-five miles per hour the cream-yellow 1973 Ford Bronco torpedoed into the highway divider, went sailing in the air, flipped over and hit the median train tracks, flipped again then flew into the southbound lane, crushing the brand new, pearly white Mustang that Dante was driving. The husband and wife of less than twenty-four hours were killed instantly, crushed into a mass of intermingled flesh and bones and blood and metal that exploded seconds after impact.

The southbound lane of I-25 was closed for two hours as the state police and the fire department extinguished the flames and began to process the scene. Miraculously, the Mustang's license plate was torn off and thrown to the side of the road, basically undamaged except for a deep dent in the middle. One of the troopers traced the registration to Dante Redwolf. The next of kin listed his parents in Las Cruces. The trooper made a call he hated to make but had to make all too often in the course of his work. He had barely made the notification when Dante's mother at the other end of the line began screaming and wailing; she handed the phone to her husband who had the same reaction.

Mr. Redwolf could barely dial with his trembling hand but managed to call Candy's mother. Carmen had the same reaction as she collapsed into Pryce's arms and babbled out the horror. Pryce managed to hold it together long enough to call Memphis, who subsequently got ahold of Sand and Frick and barreled down the highway to get to the accident twenty miles away. Frick's status as a former cop got them a little consideration, and soon enough the three men were staring at the smoking heap of what had been a car. All three bodies had been removed and were on their way to the Santa Fe medical examiner. The trooper said he believed they were killed instantly and didn't feel a thing.

The next week saw the investigation unofficially conclude and the funeral arrangements made. Carmen was a zombie during this time and Memphis took Chessie into his home for the duration. Memphis and Pryce made the burial plans, picked out coffins, arranged for a gravesite, and acquired a priest. Tucson made the notifications to their family and friends, and on the morning of the seventh day after the young couple were married they were laid to rest side-by-side. Carmen could barely stand, propped up by her grieving husband. Candy's biological father never bothered to show up.

The Redwolfs declined the invitation to go with their deceased daughter-in-law's family to a private memorial gathering. They spent an hour with Chessie, then left to drive back to Las Cruces. The extended clan drove to Percy's Victorian to grieve together and give each other support. Tansee had been cooking and preparing all night and the food was spread out from the kitchen to the living room. Memphis assigned Sage to watch over her cousin Chessie. Sage was so mature for her age and she nodded seriously at her father's request. She took Chessie by the hand and led her into the den where they sat down on the floor to play Chutes and Ladders.

Pryce asked Memphis quietly to go out on the porch to talk. They both grabbed a beer and headed out, parking themselves on the white wrought iron patio set. They were silent for five long minutes.

"It's about Chessie," Pryce finally said. "About her future."

"No worries there," Memphis replied. "She'll never want for anything."

"Except a mother and father," Pryce said bitterly.

"She's got you and Carmen to take care of her."

"We're getting older, Memphis. Oh, we're not exactly ancient, but it's tough raising a kid at our ages. That's not the issue. It's what's best for Chessie. She needs parents, not grandparents."

"What are you getting at?"

"You know that Candy had a will made out just after Troy died, right? I believe it was Akiro that designed the estate plan."

"Yeah, I know that. I don't know the specifics." Memphis frowned. "What *are* you getting at? She designated Carmen as the kid's legal guardian, right?"

Pryce swallowed the last of his beer then studied the empty bottle. "No, no she didn't. She named you as legal guardian."

"What?" Memphis exclaimed.

"She did, and Carmen and I have talked about it and feel that you should take up the reins of parenthood. Seriously—in your household what's one more daughter?"

"Whoa," Memphis said, putting his hands up. "This isn't something I can decide by myself. My wife has a say in this. We have to … we have to discuss this."

"Of course. Naturally, as grandparents, Carmen and I would have full access to her."

"Well, yeah, of course." He was about to say something else when Swan came on the porch and sat on Memphis's lap. She put her arm around his shoulder, took the bottle from his hand, and slurped down the last few ounces of beer. She nuzzled her husband.

"What's up, Doc?" she said.

"Um, Pryce was just telling me … asking me … it's …"

Swan squeezed her husband. "You're so articulate," she said, laughing. "By the way, I already told Pryce and Carmen that we'd do it."

"What?" Memphis exclaimed. He looked at Pryce. "You talked to my wife before you approached me?"

"Pryce knows who wears the pants in our family. Chessie is family. She's your dead brother's only child. You have an obligation. We have an obligation. Anyway, it's settled, so get used to it. I talked to your parents and we agreed that since our family has grown by two kids this year that their house would be a better place for our family. They agreed to move into our house next door and take Luc and Raleigh with them."

"You've got it all figured out, haven't you?" Memphis said in a mixture of grumpiness and admiration.

Swan took his face in her hands. "Oh, baby, I've had it all figured out since I ravished you in that tent in the mountains." Right after Snow dumped Memphis and left town days before their wedding on January 1, 1966 Swan tracked him down to his camping tent in the forest where he had absconded to lick his wounds. They confessed their love for one another and were soulmates ever since.

Pryce guffawed and Memphis scowled at him. Then he shrugged. "Fine. What's one more kid? You, however, can figure out the logistics. I'm just an innocent bystander."

"Innocent? Oh, baby, I don't think so."

Naabah whistled an old country tune as he rumbled along the road in his used Ford truck. Dusk was falling and the eastern sky had darkened considerably although there was a wide swath of blue on the western horizon. He liked the night, he felt alive in the night. His windows were all down and the evening breeze blew through the truck and felt as cold as an air conditioner. There was nothing like camping out under the stars on an early fall night, staring up at the sky, snuggling in his sleeping bag, listening to the symphonic music of the night, the howling coyotes, the rustle of avian predators whispering low in the sky, the crickets singing their songs in harmony. No human sounds; he liked that.

He passed the stretch of road where he had damnably lost three of the bones from his victim in the late summer of 1974. He had blown a tire and careened over to the road's shoulder. Stopping short his bag of preserved bones had been thrown violently against the side of the truck bed and a few had flown out. He hadn't realized that the bones—a femur, an ulna, and a rib—had been thrown quite a few yards into the desert until he reached his destination and unbagged the bones for a final count. His blood ran cold at the missing bones but thought it unlikely that anyone would venture into the desert at that desolate point and find them. He was also dismayed that the skeleton wouldn't be perfect for his needs, but he managed to make do without too much angst.

He realized that he was wrong about the bones not being found when he read a short article in the *Courant* about a tourist's discovery of the bones. So far, the police had no leads and after one more tiny follow-up article the matter seemed to dissolve. He laughed to himself—dissolved like the flesh had been on those bones.

He was more careful transporting his bones after that, like the batch in the large Igloo cooler in the small back seat of the truck. He had gone to a popular bar on Mexican Independence Day and was enjoying a few beers when the place became raucous. There was shouting and boozing and singing. He could tolerate that although he didn't like it. What set his nerves on fire was when a young, skinny Mexican college student wearing a Sangre de Cristo College tee-shirt jumped up on the bar carrying a genuine Indian feather headdress. He put it on and began mimicking a war dance and making tomahawk chopping motions and demanding a squaw—a lot of squaws. His mistake—other than the obvious—was that he tried dragging a poor young Indian waitress up on the bar with him. She barely escaped his clutches.

The college student had sealed his doom. He and his buddies left the bar after 2 AM and stuffed themselves into someone's car and roared off towards the campus. He followed them and parked a dozen cars away at what apparently was their dormitory. Three of the buddies fell out of the car laughing, drunk as skunks, and half-crawled, half-stumbled towards one of the dorm buildings. The student helped the last buddy out of his car and looped an arm around him as they ambled back to the next dorm. The buddy fell down, out like a light; he probably didn't even feel the impact of the rock on the grass that clipped his forehead. That was Naabah's opportunity.

He jogged over to the student and said he'd help him get his friend to the hospital. They'd take Naabah's truck. The student was semi-truculent but when Naabah mentioned that his friend might sue him if he didn't get him medical help, the student grudgingly helped his friend over to Naabah's truck. He was surprised when Naabah let go and he and his unconscious buddy hit the ground. He was about to castigate Naabah when a sap made contact with his temple; a minute later he was loaded into the back of the truck and Naabah was driving slowly away from campus. There was no one else in that dead of night to see what happened.

The rest was rote: the execution, the beetles, the lacquering, the feast. Now, a week after it all went down Naabah was tooling towards his cave, his life's work.

The night sky settled into ebony black as the truck moved smoothly down the road while its driver continued humming a favorite Hank Williams tune, *I'm So Lonesome I Could Cry.*

Hear that lonesome whippoorwill
He sounds too blue to fly
The midnight train is whining low
I'm so lonesome I could cry ...

BOOK THREE

"I grew up in New Mexico, and the older I get, I have less need for contemporary culture and big cities and all the stuff we are bombarded with. I am happier at my ranch in the middle of nowhere watching a bug carry leaves across the grass, listening to silence, riding my horse, and being in open space."
Tom Ford

CHAPTER ONE

August 8, 1978, Santa Fe, New Mexico

"Shit," Raleigh hissed through her gritted teeth as the police cruiser behind her blasted its siren. She glanced in the rearview mirror and saw the black-and-white closing in on her and the revolving red light announcing to the world that for whatever reason the cops were after her. She slowed down and pulled to the shoulder of the road, stopped the car, and turned it off. She steamed as the police car pulled up twenty feet behind her and a uniformed cop got out and started walking towards her. "Nazi," she muttered under her breath, staring straight ahead, and crossing her arms tightly. The cop reached her and leaned on her open window.

"License and registration, please," came that mellow, familiar voice.

She looked up, startled, and scowled. "Figures it would be you," she snapped at the grinning face of her older brother, Luc. "Were you stalking me to make your ticket quota, Lucifer?"

"Yes, ma'am," he replied. "You were going over the speed limit by ten miles."

"Oh, for the love—it's an open road with hardly any traffic," she exclaimed.

"Still against the law, ma'am."

"Stop that."

"Yes, ma'am."

"You've been insufferable ever since you went over to the dark side and joined the police force. I hate that uniform," she said. "Why couldn't you go into a more respectable profession, like drug dealer?"

"That's my weekend job. So, where are you going?"

"None of your business. I'm twenty years old and I don't need anyone's permission to go anywhere."

Luc pulled out his ticket book and began writing.

"All right. Fine, fine. I was visiting my late classmate's mother on my way to the library to read up on forensic techniques."

Luc put the ticket book away. "Chuy Castaneda?"

"Yeah," she said quietly. "Next month it'll be a year since his disappearance. I won't be around then, so I wanted to make sure I spent some time with her. I gave her a few memories I had of him in and out of class. I don't think she'll ever get over this, especially not knowing if he's dead or alive."

"That's the worst," Luc agreed. "Look. I'm heading back to the station to end my shift. Why don't you follow me, and I'll treat you to an early dinner and a margarita at Malagueña Fiesta? I won't have you around to zing in a few weeks and I need to get my shots in."

"Works for me. So. Am I getting a ticket or not?"

Luc stood straight, smiled, and tipped his hat. "Just a warning this time, ma'am." He winked at her then sauntered back to his patrol car. He pulled out and Raleigh followed him to the police station and waited in the car while he signed out. She closed her eyes and leaned her head back, thinking about what he'd said. Yes, in three weeks she'd be relocated to Northeastern University in Boston where she'd study for her last two years of college. The school had a highly rated Criminal Justice program and making the grade there would help propel her into acceptance into the FBI.

The admission requirements for Northeastern were exceptionally high. Out of a possible perfect SAT score of 1600 Northeastern's 75th percentile rested at 1540. As high as one might view a 1390 score for many other colleges, that score placed an applicant at the below-average level; below 1390 an applicant was very unlikely to be considered. Raleigh scored a 1550.

Although a high school graduation GPS of 4.0 seems perfect, extra credit and advanced courses could bring that up and Northeastern's average for applicants was 4.04. To achieve that an applicant would have had to achieve straight A's through high school in both standard classes and advanced, extra-credit classes. Raleigh achieved a 4.03 in high school but brought that up to a 4.06 in her first two years of college, surpassing her parents' demanded 3.5.

In addition, the school looked at recommendations and extra-curricular activities. Raleigh always had the latter going on from tutoring low-income students, volunteering, and political activism during the 1976 campaign. She had no problem getting recommendations from her high school teachers as well as Sangre de Cristo College professors. She even had one from Richard Ballard, the family's favorite FBI agent. She wrote a heartfelt personal statement about who she was, who her family was, and why she wanted to attend.

Even if all of the basic expectations were met there was still only an 18% chance of admission. When Raleigh applied she was disappointed to be put on a waiting list and assumed that she'd have to find another school. After she applied to two others she received a letter saying that she was off the list and had been admitted. She spent the summer enjoying the last taste of home that she'd have for a while, although she planned on flying home for Thanksgiving and Christmas. Memphis paid her first semester tuition, room, and board and decided to give her a monthly allowance for "stuff." Her parents and all of her siblings pledged to chip in for her expenses.

She was stoked about going, and although she'd never admit it, terrified. But the one thing Raleigh never showed was fear.

She was startled out of her thoughts when Luc opened the passenger door and slid in.

"Off to Margaritaville," he said blithely, and Raleigh drove to the restaurant, parked, and followed her brother inside.

Luc fought back a grin as he noted the awestruck faces on most of the men in the bar, who were staring at his sister. A shade under six feet, with an athletic body, a high-cheekboned face with deep-set, milk-chocolate-brown eyes, and glossy black hair swinging down to the small of her back, Raleigh turned heads wherever she went. The older and more beautiful she grew the more concern her brothers felt about protecting her from the big, bad wolf. She didn't need their protection; she was a strong athlete and well-versed in martial arts and hand-to-hand combat. She'd had a few boyfriends over the last four years but none of them ever got to first base or lasted very long. Most were a little intimidated; a few were downright scared.

"A nice, cold pitcher of margaritas, Selena," Luc said as the waitress plunked down a huge basket of chips and a dish of salsa. She winked at him and sauntered off.

"She's sweet on you," Raleigh teased as she scooped a big pile of salsa on a chip and stuffed it in her mouth. She wiped away the dribble from her chin.

"She just likes the uniform," Luc replied.

"You're not wearing it now and she was making goo-goo eyes at you."

Luc was about to make a cutting comment when Selena brought over the pitcher and poured each of them a glass before she whirled around and left.

"Hey," Raleigh said. "She didn't ask us for our orders."

"Does she really have to? Neither of us orders anything except the cheese enchiladas for me and the pork chimi for you."

"Well, she could *ask*."

"Drink your damned margarita."

Raleigh drank half her glass in one gulp as her brother shook his head. They were silent for a few minutes as they drank and crunched chips, and then Selena brought over their meals.

"You should ask her out," Raleigh said, swirling around the icy tequila drink.

"I'm busy with my career."

"It's been almost a year since you joined the police force and I don't think the family's still gotten over it. We kind of expected to be visiting you monthly in the New Mexico Penitentiary by now. Unless you were in solitary, of course. Or had escaped towards Canada with bloodhounds on your trail."

Luc grinned. "Sorry to disappoint you, baby sister. But, a new decade's right around the corner so don't give up hope."

Raleigh grunted and cut a chunk of her chimi, dipping it into the green sauce and chewing vigorously. She became solemn. "Mrs. Castaneda seems so bereft. I mean, she's got her husband and another son, but it seems her whole world revolves around Chuy. You know, Sand and Nick are convinced that their unknown, suspected 'Indian injustice collector' is responsible. They brought that up to Dunbar and Abbott and they agreed that it was possible. Still no clues as to who the guy is."

"If he even exists," Luc said. "It's all just supposition. Reasonable supposition, but supposition, nevertheless. You know, Abbott's a pretty cool guy when you get to know him. He's been acting as kind of rabbi to me since I joined."

"We're not Jewish."

"Not that kind of a rabbi, twit. In cop talk it's like a mentor, someone who guides you and helps your career along. He knows that my goal is to make detective in a few years. I've been trying to insert myself into this Indian killer investigation. If I could come up with a helpful suggestion or take action, it could cut down on my uniform time."

"Slow the hell down. You're twenty-three. Still a baby."

"Oh, this from someone rabidly and maniacally barreling towards FBI-dom. You know if they accept you in three years—"

"I'm graduating in two years."

"They don't accept an applicant until they're twenty-three. Or didn't your research come across that little point?"

Raleigh grumbled, “Yeah, okay, I may have read that. It just gives me another year to possibly get a Master’s degree or take other courses that will make them salivate over me.”

Luc sighed. “It’s shame you lack so much self-esteem.”

She blinked at him rapidly and stuck her tongue out. Selena came over to see if they needed anything and Raleigh told her to hold up.

“Selena, my brother’s too shy to act on some of his desires, so I’d like to ask you for him.”

“Raleigh,” Luc said in a deadly warning voice.

Raleigh ignored him. “Luc was hoping you’d take in a movie with him this weekend. He’s dying to see *Animal House* at the Rivoli. Are you free?”

Selena practically jumped up and down. “Oh, oh yes, I’m free.” She smiled down at Luc with eyes a-twinkle. “I’d love to go.”

“Great,” Luc said forcing a reasonably realistic smile on his face. “I’ll, um, pick you up here after work on Friday and we can head over.”

Selena danced off and Luc shot eyes of fire at his sister. “You’ve seen *The Godfather*, right?”

“Nine or ten times.”

“Then just remember—revenge is a dish best served cold.”

Raleigh laughed. “I’m out of your league, big brother. Come on—finish your food and I’ll drive you back to get your car. The library’s closed by now so I think I’ll head home and bug our firstborn Grayhawk about his case.”

Luc grunted, finished up his meal, and put cash on the table with a huge tip for Selena. Raleigh drove him back to the precinct then sped off. He thought he really should have ticketed her.

Memphis sat back in his recliner with his eyes closed and Max nestled on his lap. The house was ripe with the cacophony of an adult woman and four young girls arguing and yelling and pleading and demanding. The demanding, as usual, was coming from Sage, who at the age of twelve was a whirlwind of demands, opinions, energy, and toughness. He was thrilled that his daughter was so tough and opinionated; he didn't want his kids to be wimps afraid to voice an opinion. Sara was following in her older sister's footsteps; Shea was a tad more reserved and thoughtful.

Chessie was only now coming out of her shell after the death of her mother and the drastic change in her life and home. She still cried a lot and every so often would exhibit a withdrawn personality. She was a basket case for the first two months after Candy and Dante died, but Memphis put her under Percy's psychological care. His reasoning wasn't only because Percy was a top-notch psychologist, but his small stature would be less intimidating for a traumatized seven-year-old than, say, Percy's six-foot-two partner, Tucson. They had two sessions per week for the first two months, and now the therapy was ongoing at weekly sessions. Percy was making progress with her, and in the last few months she had even started smiling and laughing. She worshipped Sage and followed her around whenever she could. Sage was extraordinarily patient with her young cousin.

Memphis sniffed and groaned; time to change Max. He managed to get out of the recliner and hustled Max off to the bathroom where he deftly changed Max's diaper, washed his lower body, and fixed another Pamper on his son's soft, clean bottom. As he returned to the living room Raleigh was coming through the front door and a few seconds later she scooped her nephew out of his father's arms and parked her butt on his recliner.

Raleigh cooed and cuddled the baby for a few minutes then looked up at Memphis, who was standing over her. "Your rotten baby brother tried to give me a speeding ticket today."

"Did he?" Memphis asked.

"No, but I got back at him anyway. Let's just say he has a date with Selena the waitress this weekend that I arranged for him."

"What did Selena ever do to you?"

She laughed. "Don't worry—he's already sworn revenge." She sobered. "So, I want to ask you about the Chuy Castaneda case."

"That's Abbott's and Dunbar's case. We aren't officially engaged."

"You're deflecting. And you're as engaged as they are. So, tell me what's been happening since Chuy disappeared. I know some of it since I was interviewed as one of his classmates, but you guys have been playing it close to the vest."

Memphis sighed. "I'll tell you what I know if you agree to babysit the kids Saturday."

"Why?"

"I want to take Swan for the day to the cabin so she can decompress and relax."

"Then shouldn't you let her go by herself?"

"Ha-ha. So witty. You were a mouthy kid and now you're a mouthy adult."

"Learned from the best. So?"

"I can't tell you anything you don't already know except for the police investigation itself. We were only interviewed by Abbott and Dunbar after the fact. And, considering what happened the next day, we weren't too interested in the case."

The day after Mexican Independence Day, the day that newlyweds Candy and Dante met their tragic fate, a college student named Cruz Castaneda was reported missing by his college roommate, Douglas Mackintosh. The roommate woke up on the grass with a splitting headache and a rancid taste in his mouth. He managed to drag himself upright and leaned against Chuy's car. He thought it weird that the car was parked by the lawn instead of in its designated parking space. He dragged himself up to their dorm room, which was empty. He fell face first on his bed and slept for another five hours.

When Douglas awakened he glanced out the window and saw that the car was gone. He didn't know at the time that it had been towed by the campus police and that Chuy was nowhere to be found. When he learned about the tow he went to the campus police station and filed a missing person report. The police weren't initially helpful since Chuy had been missing for less than twenty-four hours, but they grudgingly contacted his family and did cursory interviews in the dorm. One of the cops wrote in his notebook, "Ain't no one saw or heard nothing. Shocker."

By September 19th Chuy's family was panicked and the police were taking the case much more seriously. They interviewed more of his classmates, including Raleigh, who attended a 19th Century European History course with him. She said they weren't "friendly," but he seemed nice enough and was regularly the class cut-up. He had never made any racist remarks about Indians within earshot of her, but that might have been because he knew he'd wind up scalped; Dunbar laughed outright at that observation. Abbott spent a few hours with Memphis, Nick, and Sand to review the case. What he told them about Chuy's last night sent their spidey senses into overdrive.

Chuy was drunk as hell when he pulled off his shirt in the saloon where people were crushed in celebration of Mexican Independence Day. He spied a young Indian man who was carrying a war bonnet (that, it turned out later, he had made and brought with him to show his friends) and whooped and ripped it out of the young man's hands. He pulled it on lopsidedly and climbed on the bar to do a war dance. He was cheered and egged on by his friends and quite a few of the bar's patrons. He tried to grope a young Indian girl who was waitressing to make money she'd need for her next college semester. He left soon after with his group and they made it back to campus. Shortly thereafter, he disappeared.

Sand said there was little doubt that he had been taken by the Indian injustice collector, and that being the case their suspect had been in that bar that night. Rounding up all the patrons would be a massive headache; there were around two hundred. Also, as Nick pointed out, someone who witnessed the war dance might have told someone else who wasn't there but later took action.

Memphis said that the cops did their best to round up the patrons for interviews, but they fell short at just over one hundred. They also found out that some patrons had come from Albuquerque and other cities and pueblos. In the end they found no definitive clues as to a suspicious patron. Most people were half drunk for the evening that ended at three in the morning. They checked around campus and found no witnesses. The roommate, Douglas, didn't remember most of the evening and didn't even remember blacking out.

Memphis said, “So, there’s been no progress made in the last six months. Nothing to go on.”

Raleigh was silent for a moment, then said, “It’s horrible for the family to never know. And imagine if some of those who disappeared didn’t even have people searching for them.”

“If you disappeared, we’d all search for you forever. And we’d find you,” Memphis said quietly.

“Even Lucifer?” she asked sardonically.

“With a passion like the raging fires of hell. You are going to call home at least every other day, aren’t you?”

“Once a week?” she asked hopefully.

“Every. Other. Day,” Memphis reiterated. “Call collect. Promise?”

She sighed loudly. “I promise. Here. Take your kid.” She handed Max off to his father and walked towards the front door. She turned. “Can I come over for dinner?”

“Alone. No other brothers.”

Raleigh saluted smartly. “Aye, aye, sir.” She left the house laughing.

At that moment Swan came into the living room and glowered at her husband. “Did I just hear you invite your sister for dinner?”

“She invited herself.”

“Fine. Then you can get your ass in the kitchen and help make dinner, Geronimo.”

CHAPTER TWO

Memphis rustled the newspaper as he relaxed that Friday morning, anxious about leaving work early and packing up his wife to head out to the family cabin at Spirit Lake. They'd spend the night and come home late Saturday. He had finished all of his paperwork and reviewed the status of the cases that the rest of the firm members were working on. Dante's death had left a big hole in the heart and workings of the firm; part-time investigator and former nanny Antonia Fairfield had resigned and gone back to England. Memphis had dawdled for months after Dante's death to fill an empty investigative slot. He only half-heartedly put an ad out for applications and he always found something wrong with the applicant. Sand finally barked at him that if Jesus Christ had applied Memphis would have turned him down, too. Memphis agreed.

Then, one Monday morning in late January Devon knocked on his door and stood in the hall.

"What?" he barked as he threw the last batch of applications in the trash can.

"I may have an applicant for our open position," she replied affably. Before he could ask who she stepped to the side and DeVere stepped into view.

"I'll be a son of a bitch," Memphis said sweeping from behind his desk to clasp the Pittsfield cop's hand. "What are you doing here?"

"I need a job. Figured you owed me, and I came to collect," DeVere said as he parked himself in one of the guest chairs while Devon sat down in the other. As Memphis reseated himself he didn't miss the discreet handholding between the two young people.

"A job, eh? I thought you were a die-hard New Englander."

"I love New England," DeVere said. "It's always going to be home. I love the landscape, the mountains, the lakes, the ocean, the people, the culture, the clam chowder."

"Then why leave?" Memphis asked curiously.

DeVere glanced to his left. "Because I love Devon more," he said simply.

"What about your career as a cop? Weren't you hoping to make detective someday?"

"The culture there wasn't particularly conducive to that direction, especially after we got a new captain that seemed to think *Birth of a Nation* was a wonderful depiction of reality. The writing was on the wall that I'd be a uniformed patrolman most if not all of my career. I wanted more."

"Well, what about trying to get on the force here?"

"I'd have to start all over. As a P.I. I can get to do investigative work—"

"Boring paperwork," Memphis said.

"I do that now."

"Divorce case stakeouts."

"People gotta get a fair shake."

Memphis squinted at him and shook his head. "You know I won't always assign the two of you to work together on a case, and both of you damn well better keep it professional in the office."

"But, Boss," Devon said innocently, "you let your wife sit on your lap and kiss you."

"The operative words are 'wife' and 'Boss.' Okay. I'm willing to give you a trial period. What were you making in Pittsfield?" DeVere told him. "Well, I'll add ten percent to that for starters. And, yes—Devon makes more than you will."

"I'm cool with that," DeVere said grinning.

"When can you start?"

DeVere looked at his watch. "Five minutes soon enough?"

Memphis groaned and rolled his eyes. "Make it Wednesday morning at nine. We'll work out the details then." He pointed a finger at Devon. "He's your responsibility. He screws up, you pay the price."

Devon scowled. "That's not fair."

Before Memphis could throw his weight around DeVere said quickly, "I won't screw up." He stood and pulled Devon up. "Thanks, Memphis," he said sincerely.

Just as the young lovers and now colleagues were out of the office Memphis called after them, "Make me proud."

DeVere did make Memphis proud and dovetailed into the team as though he'd been born to it. He worked well with Devon and the other team members and was sharp and dogged. The team—excluding Devon and DeVere—had a pool on when he'd propose. He had moved in with her right away.

Devon and DeVere were out of the office on their way to Flagstaff for a drug case; a young man had been arrested for dealing and he swore he wasn't guilty. His father was from Santa Fe and hired the team to prove his son innocent. Only Skye was in the office this morning, so Memphis felt relaxed and peaceful. Not so much when he read the newspaper. There was a front-page story about another serial killing down in Tucson, Arizona.[4] Since last year someone had been using a variety of axes to dispatch people, and just two days earlier he had claimed his tenth victim, one Sydney Mackay, an Australian expatriate and a Fine Arts graduate from the University of Arizona. His goal was to become a Hollywood actor and after he graduated in 1974 he made the rounds of New York City and Hollywood. After two small parts in commercials his prospects seemed to dry up, but

---

4 Please see the novel *Saguaro, Volume One of the Arizona Trilogy* for the story of the Tucson, Arizona Ax Murderer.

as luck would have it a friend snagged him a position as a drama teacher at a private school in Tucson; a year later he was thriving in his new career and life was good.

Until August 9th, when someone plummeted a hatchet into his forehead, splitting the skull, then did the same to the back of his skull when he turned over. Like the previous nine murders the police were still baffled.

Memphis felt guilty; he recognized the consequences of the horrific crimes, but that was a juicy serial murder spree that got his investigative juices flowing. He was surprised at the story in one of the article's paragraphs—an FBI agent from San Francisco named Richard Ballard had provided some support and background to the Tucson police as well as a private investigations firm that was also involved. Union Jack Investigations was an integral part of the case if only because one of the partners, a guy named Michael Quintana, was a victim: his uncle, aunt, and cousin were three of the ax murderer's victims. Memphis knew all too well what it was like to be the victim of a mad killer. He hoped they'd find the maniac soon.

He read a couple of other articles that intrigued him. A man named David Berkowitz had been arrested the day before in New York City, and it was rumored that he was the infamous serial killer that called himself "the Son of Sam." The first shooting attributed to him took place on July 29, 1976 when he shot two female teenagers, killing one and wounding the other. Over the year between that attack and the last one before he was arrested Berkowitz was believed to have killed or wounded thirteen men and women.

Ted Bundy was still in a Florida jail awaiting trial, scheduled to begin in the middle of 1979. He had kidnaped, raped, and killed dozens of women over the course of his thirty-two-year-old lifespan, spanning many states but thankfully ending after a blitz of horrific attacks in Gainesville that saw his capture and arrest. The thing Memphis found most sickening was that fact that Bundy received hundreds of love letters and marriage proposals,

Memphis thought of his own personal serial killer, Joanna Frid, who was known by the scintillating appellation of "the Vampire

Killer" because of her propensity for extracting blood from her victims. Her identity was known but she had successfully fled from authorities after her last attack, which happened to be on him and his family. She was still on the FBI's Most Wanted List. Memphis had a feeling in his gut that they'd meet again.

Now, Santa Fe had another killer that no one really knew about except the police and his firm. All they had was circumstantial evidence that crimes had taken place, but nothing definitive and no real suspect. They believed he was an Indian that was collecting injustices done to his race. And, yes, Memphis and his team were convinced that the missing Chuy Castaneda was one of his victims. If only there had been a clue through interviewing the patrons and employees of the bar that night.

His thoughts were interrupted when the phone rang. Swan was on the line telling him that she'd forgotten a field trip she was supposed to take Sage on for a school Art paper. She said to pick the kid up in an hour at the library and take her to the StarRise Gallery a block from the plaza. Before he could object she hung up.

"Argh," he growled as he finished up filing his papers and then took off. On the way out he told Skye to take the rest of the day off. She whipped her purse from her desk drawer and followed him out, chattering about heading to the Desert Dream Brewery for Declan's superb lager beer, Irish Dream. Then she had an appointment at an animal rescue to pick up a three-legged gecko. Sadly, her seven-legged tarantula had died many months ago.

Memphis headed over to the library. Sage was sitting with her book bag on the front steps and she rushed over to the car. Memphis smiled; most of the time when he picked up a kid it was Luc at school, who was waiting in the principal's office because he'd done something against the rules. And now his wild, irreverent brother was a cop.

Sage jumped in the car and said, "Hi, Dad."

Memphis pulled carefully away from the front curb. "So, what's this art project you need to go to the StarRise Gallery for? And, why are you doing a paper? It's summer."

"My Art teacher assigned it just before summer break for extra credit. It's almost done. I got the background I needed and now I need to view paintings by a series of artists to indicate what the common denominators are and what the artist is trying to say with his subjects and talent. The gallery has been having an exhibition of well-known artists that use the southwest culture as their subjects."

"Okay," he sighed. "But you've got one hour to do your thing. Mom and I are heading to the cabin."

"Ninety minutes," Sage countered.

"One hour."

"Seventy-five minutes and that's my best offer." Sage arched a challenging eyebrow and stared at her father.

"Jesus," Memphis breathed in resignation. "Seventy-five minutes and not a second longer." Out of the corner of his eye he could see the victorious smirk on his daughter's face. Yeah, it was like an encore of Raleigh. On steroids.

Memphis paid the entrance fee and Sage walked over to the first exhibit, a half dozen beautifully framed prints of paintings by Deborah Hiatt. Memphis came up from behind her and watched as Sage wrote down the paintings' names, the subject matter, and impressions of the technical continuity.

"What do you see?" Memphis asked.

Sage pointed to the middle painting, called *Time of Tranquility*, and said, "She's a minimalist in terms of her subject matter. Simple, clean, sleek lines of buildings and rock formations. She uses variations of white to impart a sense of peace while she uses a small variety of pastel colors to paint her people. All but one of these paintings shows the people from the back. She seems to prefer singular people, mainly women, mainly anonymous since their faces are turned away. The background of homes and rocks diminishes the person, making her seem small in relation to nature and manmade creations. I think the women are secondary in terms of the painting itself but are primary in her estimation."

"Nice," Memphis murmured. "Which one do you like best?"

"That one." Sage pointed again to *Time of Tranquility.* "It's magnificent." The subject was two Indian women walking into a white home, above which was a sky of light turquoise. The print was bordered by double mattes of white and turquoise, cut with sharp edges to give a little pizzazz to the actual artwork. The print was encapsulated by a sleek white wooden frame. She took in a deep breath then moved to the next exhibition, seven paintings by Georgia O'Keeffe. Five were of vividly colored flower closeups, one was of a ribbon-like, deep pastel view of Lake George in New York, and the last was the most familiar southwest image of a steer skull hovering against the roiling grey clouds over a mountain silhouette. Sage pointed out the flowers and said she thought the artist was most comfortable with extremely close-up imagery. She liked the skull but didn't love it. She made the insidious comment that she thought O'Keeffe was a tad overrated.

Memphis followed his daughter as she came to a corner exhibit where the paintings covered two perpendicular walls; a free-standing wall three feet away held paintings on either side. These ten paintings were the work of Naabah. The exhibition was called the Pueblo Series, and the subject of each painting was one of the pueblos in the central and northern New Mexico area. Memphis recognized the Taos Pueblo right away, and the Acoma Pueblo as well. He noticed that Sage was taking more time studying and writing notes on each painting. Occasionally she moved closer and squinted, and cocked her head before drawing something on her pad next to a few sentences.

"You like his style?" Memphis asked. "You seem fascinated by his work more than that of the first two."

"I like his work, but somehow it unnerves me. I don't know why." She shrugged. "Maybe it's the bones."

"What bones?" Memphis asked curiously. The paintings were of pueblos with a person in three of them.

Sage pointed her pencil tip to a tiny rock grouping at the Acoma Pueblo. Memphis squinted. He couldn't see what she was getting at. Sage groaned theatrically and pointed the pencil close.

"See?" she said. "It looks like a rock on first glance but if you look really close it looks like a finger bone." She traced the image in the air.

Memphis squinted, then saw it. Yes, it did look kind of like a finger bone, but it could still easily be a long, crooked thin pebble. "What else you got?" he asked.

Sage walked over to the Taos Pueblo painting and pointed her pencil at the ground near the chapel. "This one looks like a femur." She moved to a third painting. "This one doesn't have anything, but this one does." She pointed at a small rock outcropping by the desert's edge near a residence at the Zia Pueblo. One of the rocks half-tucked behind another looked like the right side of a skull. All three of the "bones" were very tactfully incorporated into the overall picture, and it took a very meticulous scrutiny to uncover the hidden component. Sage pointed out that the color of the "bones" was a shade off the areas against which they were placed, with a very, very faint off-white, semi-shiny color.

Sage walked to each of the paintings, making her notes and finding only one more hidden bone in a picture, one that looked like a vertebra.

"What do you think the bones mean, Dad?"

"Dunno. Maybe it's just a personal signature to his work."

"Not all the pictures have it. Do you think it means something special to the subjects where there is a bone? Maybe he's just using them to incorporate a sense of humanity into the picture."

"That's very astute."

"Hey—you know what we should do? Go over to Uncle Percy's place and check out his painting."

"That's a good idea. Another time, though. Finish your reviews so we can get going."

Sage meandered towards the four-picture Robert Redbird exhibit, then moved on to the last one, the famous Navajo painter, R.C. Gorman. Sage thought Gorman's technique showed similarities to Hiatt's, but she still preferred the clean, minimalistic lines of Hiatt's work. Sage looked around for her father and saw him chatting up one of the art gallery's hostesses. She jogged over.

"I'm ready, Dad," she said.

"Good." He turned to the lady. "We really enjoyed your art exhibits. Thank you."

"Come back anytime," she said brightly then moved off towards another potential buyer.

Memphis and Sage got in his car and headed off home. Swan was standing outside the front door tapping her foot.

"You're screwed, Dad," Sage whispered.

"Language," he warned.

Sage bounced up to her mother and smiled as widely as she could. "It's my fault, Mom. I begged and pleaded for extra time and Dad just caved."

"Shocker," Swan said. "Your sisters and brother are next door so go over to Grandma's." She looked balefully at Memphis. "Suitcase in the living room. Let's get cracking. Move it," she snapped.

"Yes, ma'am," Memphis said, sighing. He didn't envy any of his future sons-in-law. He grabbed the suitcase, opened the passenger door for Swan, threw it in the back of the car, and took off for the cabin. He thought, *Happy wife, happy life.*

The next morning there was a knock at the front door and Hehewuti found herself staring at a delivery man from the StarRise Gallery.

"Delivery for a Miss Sage Grayhawk," the man said.

"Um, okay," Hehewuti said. "Bring it in."

The man went back to his truck and a few minutes later came back carrying a large rectangular object wrapped in brown paper. Hehewuti stepped aside and the man rested the article against the couch, got her signature, then left.

She studied the item then called for her granddaughter. All four of her granddaughters barged into the living room.

"What's that?" Sage demanded.

"I have no idea. It's for you."

"Open it, open it," the twins chanted in perfect sync.

"Pipe down, insects," Sage said to her sisters as she clawed away the brown wrapping paper. When the paper was off she gasped. It was the framed Deborah Hiatt she loved at the gallery.

As she stared at the print she whispered, "Love you, Dad."

CHAPTER THREE

The Zia Pueblo is one of the lesser New Mexican pueblos off to the west of I-25 off Route 550, around thirty-five miles northwest of Albuquerque. It is situated in the steep mountain slopes and canyons of the Sierra Nacimiento Mountains. The gently sloping flood plain of the Jemez River, and the large Pajarito and Jemez Plateaus establish the setting for the Zia Indian Reservation. Sitting on a rocky knoll 5,472 feet above sea level the twenty-seven-square-mile pueblo blends seamlessly into the rough terrain. Inconspicuous, it has survived six hundred years despite the toll that nature and man has placed on it. The pueblo suffered dire losses of people and property during the Pueblo Revolt, decimating its population through the loss of six hundred residents.

A small, tightknit community of agricultural workers and raisers of livestock the population of the pueblo has a strong sense of cultural identity, expressed in its famous pottery and other arts. Prominent among Zia crafts is that pottery, unpolished redware with white slip; decorations in brown or black are produced often with a bird motif. The Zia tradition is faithfully adhered to; innovation is avoided. The traditional language of the Zia Pueblo is Keresan, but many may speak Spanish, some speak Navajo and most also speak English.

The principal festival of the year for the Zia Pueblo, the Corn Dance, takes place in August on the feast day of Our Lady of the Assumption. Colorful, meaningful traditional costumes and ceremonies make this an important event in the life of the pueblo and one which attracts visitors.

Frick pulled over to the Big Chief Gas Station to fill up since his tank was almost empty flitting to and fro between pueblos north of Albuquerque. The rundown station had a big chief's head painted on a side wall; the same image rose high above a post that one could see for a mile or two. Plopped down in the desolate desert one could see for miles in any direction, a bleak land with few cars passing by. Low, distant mountains bordered the horizon. When he finished he and Frack got back in the car and drove another thousand feet northwest before they cut off on the road that would lead them to the pueblo, Indian Service Route 78.

They passed well-distanced single-story houses that were rough-hewn, with plenty of space for rundown cars and trucks. An occasional fenced-in yard exhibited farm animals like goats, sheep, and chickens. Two houses had small, old-looking burros standing perfectly still as they endured another day of life with no variety, comfort, or genuine care, just marking time until they lost their legs, fell to the ground, and breathed their last breaths. The farther they drove on the road the denser the clusters of houses became. Women and men ambled about their homes and dusty children played simple games like kickball to amuse themselves and break up the monotony of the day. A few kids were sitting cross-legged on the earth playing jacks or marbles. Women were hanging newly washed garments on their clotheslines. The wind was kicking up and Frick could imagine the beautiful fresh smell of those clothes when they were taken down.

Frick pulled into a small building with a "Zia Pueblo Cultural Center" sign in front. He turned off the ignition but didn't make a move to get out of the car. He reached in the small Igloo between him and Frack and took out a bottle of warm water. He drank half of it down under the curious eyes of his partner.

"What's wrong?" Frack asked.

"I'm just tired. We've been driving all over the place for hours since we started out this morning."

"At least we spent the night in Albuquerque and got a fresh start yesterday for the pueblos around there. Wish we didn't have to go as far as Zuni. But Sand told us to hit 'em all. You gotta admit we had a great dinner last night. Best tacos I've ever had."

"I guess. I'm just missing London. And Bast."

Frack grunted. "You've been so domesticated. It's revolting." Frack knew that Frick would understand that he was joking.

Frick grunted back and pulled the map of pueblos out of his satchel and studied it.

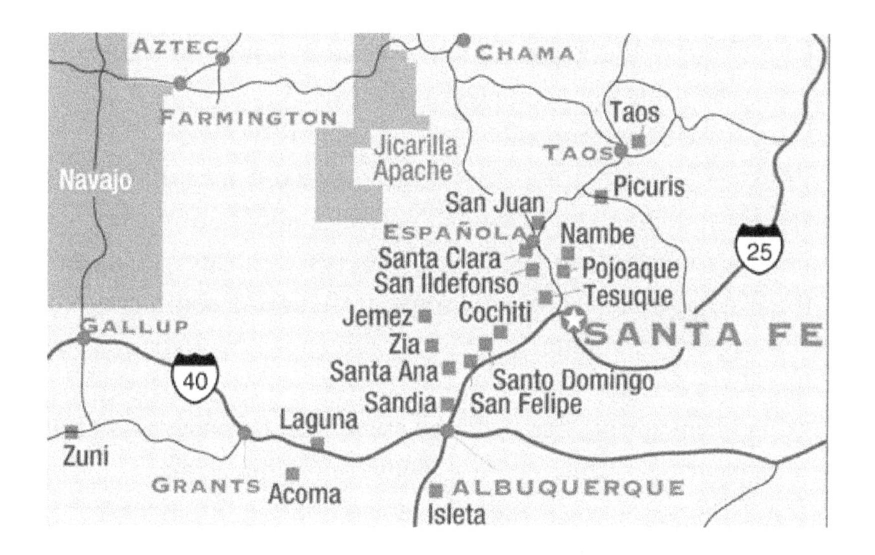

Yesterday they had hit the Zuni, Acoma, Isleta, Laguna, and Sandia pueblos. This morning they had already hit San Felipe and Santa Ana before rolling up to the Zia Pueblo. After that they'd hit Jemez, Santo Domingo, and Cochiti before returning to Santa Fe. Thankfully, Sand and Nick would take the pueblos north of Santa Fe. Memphis had sent the New England lovebirds (as Frick called Devon and DeVere) on some special search mission.

"This is a longshot," Frack commented as he took a swig of tepid iced tea. "The cops made a cursory pass at most of these pueblos when Professor Carver first disappeared."

"Memphis said it was a wild card, but something just tingled at his spidey senses about his kid's comments on those Naabah pictures. When he went over to Percy's house he checked out the Bandelier painting and sure as shit there was a tiny bone image nestled next to the rocks near Percy's feet. Remember those three bones that New York hiker discovered and Carlito analyzed?"

"Yeah?"

"Memphis thinks that Naabah's inclusion of the almost undetectable bones must mean something to the artist. And since the paintings of many of the pueblos had that—what did he call it? signature—and we know that some of our missing people were present at several of the pueblos, he thought it was a path we should explore. He feels that even if there's a one in a million chance that there may be some remote danger to Percy."

"Hey—we're getting paid so no complaints. Let's go."

Frick and Frack exited the car and walked into the Cultural Center. It was a small building, but perfectly maintained inside with extreme attention paid to cleanliness. There was no air conditioning, but three stand-up fans provided some draft albeit a warm one. They walked up to the counter where a smiling young Indian woman greeted them enthusiastically.

"Can I help you gentlemen?" she asked. Her nametag read "Lily." She was wearing a white peasant blouse and faded jeans.

"Hi, Lily, yes," Frick said. He showed her his P.I. license. "My name is Bart Smith, and this is my partner, Jesse Morgan. May we ask you a few questions?"

"Um, sure, I guess."

Frick showed her a photo of Professor Howard Carver. "Ever see this guy?"

Lily studied the shot then shook her head. "Never seen him."

Frick showed her an 8X10 photograph of Naabah's painting of the Zia Pueblo. "Do you recognize this? The artist, I mean."

Lily broke into a wide smile and nodded. "Of course. That's HashNaa's work." She pointed to the east wall of the center. "He had a print framed and sent to us. Isn't it beautiful?"

"It is," Frack agreed. "Do you happen to know when he painted that picture?"

"Um, no, I don't think so. I think I know where he might have positioned himself while painting it by the angle. It's about a mile down the road. Maybe someone around there could help you."

"Thanks, Lily," Frick said. "One more question—is there a part of your culture or ceremonies that use bones?"

"Bones? Not really. I mean, most Indian tribes use animal bones for some ceremonies or art. Like this." She bent down and withdrew a rattle from under the desk. "See? The body is a tortoise shell and the handle is a deer horn. I guess technically those are bones."

"Are you selling those?" Frick asked.

"Oh, yes. It's five dollars."

"I'll take it."

Frick took out a ten-dollar bill while Lily wrapped the rattle. She handed it to him, and he gave her the ten. "Keep the change," he said, gratified at the wide grin that split her pretty face. He winked at her as he and Frack left the building.

"What are you going to do with that?" Frack asked.

"It's an I'm-home-baby gift for London."

"Totally, fucking domesticated," Frack muttered, shaking his head.

They headed up the road or a mile or so and both agreed that their position looked like the angle from which the picture was painted.

They spent the next two hours knocking on doors, getting receptions ranging from polite to hostile. Several doors were slammed in their faces. One ancient old man bent over and barely balancing himself on a cane spit at their feet.

After the last unhelpful response Frack said, "I don't think they like white people."

"Can you blame them? White folks stole their land, murdered their people, raped their women, infected them with diseases, introduced them to the devil alcohol."

"Well, when you put it like that …"

"Look, I think we've exhausted our investigation here, so let's head over to Jemez and then knock that one and the last two before we go back to Santa Fe. It's probably gonna be dark before we get home."

"Sounds good," Frack agreed. "but I need food."

"There was a food stand just before we made the gas station. We'll stop there. Pick up some sandwiches and soda."

They picked up their food and ate it as Frick drove to the Jemez Pueblo, where they had as much lack of luck as they did at Zia. They hit the last two pueblos with similar luck although a couple of people in Cochiti Pueblo said that Naabah had visited there several times and was seen painting the cliff formation that looked like fat stalks of asparagus pointing at the sky. They made it back to Santa Fe after 8 PM. Frack had left his car at Frick's and London was babysitting Frack's French bulldog, Pierre. He grabbed his pet and went home. Frick gave London her new turtle rattle and she welcomed him home appropriately.

"This is just icky," Devon said, frowning, as she and DeVere got out of her car in front of the small, rickety adobe building in Nageezi, one hundred and twenty miles northwest of Santa Fe. At 7,000 feet above sea level, encompassing fourteen square miles which was home to around two hundred people, Nageezi was in the middle of a desolate area and in daytime and night seemed forlorn. The closest decent-sized town was Farmington, about forty miles away. Just before that was the smaller town of Bloomington where the children of Nageezi were bused to school.

"Icky about covers it," DeVere murmured as he got out of the car and surveyed the horizon for 360 degrees.

Devon put her hands on her waist and scowled at the exterior of the building, which was decorated with Indian art, pottery, odd metal animals, and two live chickens. She shook her head. "Definitely it could pass as Uncle Willie's place."

"Who's Uncle Willie? A relative?"

"Naw, he was a character in an old TV movie. Well, not so old—early seventies. It was called *Gargoyles*. This anthropologist and his daughter visited this place near Mexico to see some special archeological find this old guy wrote him about. It turned out to be a gargoyle skull."

"And …"

"And the gargoyle flock attacked, killed Willie, and burned his house down. Then they spent the rest of the movie chasing the anthropologist, who had salvaged the skull."

"Happy ending?"

"Not for the gargoyles. Anyway, Uncle Willie's place was as weird as this. I hope we don't have a Navajo Willie inside."

"I just hope we don't have a flock of gargoyles in any rock caves around here."

"I'll protect you, sugar," Devon said then kissed his cheek and winked at him and opened the creaky front door and went inside. "Yikes," she said. "It is Uncle Willie's."

The room was thirty-by-fifty feet and was packed to the gills with "stuff." It had a familiar musty smell that most old overstuffed, never dusted, unsanitized display rooms had, but this smell was particularly pungent. The designated "aisles" were narrow and haphazard with no rhyme or reason to their location. There was barely enough room for a full-grown man to move by. Just inside on the right was a huge terrarium that contained a couple of young rattlesnakes that were hissing and rattling their tails. A terrarium right next to the snakes had a variety of lizards; tortoises had their own smaller terrarium on the left side of the aisle.

There were two stuffed deer heads high on one wall surrounded by a couple of bows and arrows and a dangling raccoon tail. The perpendicular wall was dotted with shadow boxes containing dead, pinned tarantulas. There were tarantula snow globes and one that had a family of pinned scorpions in it. DeVere nudged Devon and pointed to a small, filthy-looking refrigerator.

"How much you wanna bet that's filled with coffee cans full of mulch and worms?"

"No bet," she replied.

DeVere almost tripped over a dozing dog that looked about a thousand years old. The dog opened its eyes and stared up at him and weakly wagged its tail. For the life of him he could not figure out what blend of breeds had created the sad old mutt. He had big, sweet brown eyes.

"Hello?" Devon finally called out. A jangling bell atop the front door announced their entrance but no one had come forward and they heard no noises except the whirr of a fan. "Hello?"

Ten seconds later the rear door opened, and an old Indian man shuffled through it.

"Sweet Jesus," Devon whispered to DeVere. "It is Uncle Willie."

The old man must have been seventy if a day and was no more than five-foot-five with a squat body and round face. Unlike most Indian men he wasn't clean-shaven; he had a wispy, sparse white beard. Memphis had told Devon that Indian men could grow facial hair, but not to the extent that non-Indians could. Most Indians considered facial hair a vulgarity and removed it as soon as it began to sprout, even using such painful techniques as plucking each hair out individually. Most men—and women—tended to pluck their eyebrows, too, if they were particularly unsightly.

This man had long, long thin, stringy grey hair pulled back in a ponytail, and he was wearing a wide-brimmed straw hat that appeared to have been chewed on by vermin. His fingernails and teeth were tobacco-stained. His facial skin looked like well-worn leather, and there were prominent saddlebags under his eyes. Still, when he smiled at them (showing his four missing front teeth) the smile seemed genuine. Devon thought that he probably didn't get much company out here and that even a black couple was thrilling.

"Mr. Begay?" DeVere asked.

"That's me. What can I do for you?" He was staring at Devon.

"Something?" she asked archly.

"Don't see many black folks out here. You sure are beautiful for a white girl."

"I'm not white."

"If you ain't Indian then you're white to me. How can I help you?"

"You know a man named Jakub Kosmicki?"

"Sure, I know Jakub. He comes here maybe two, three times to stock upon supplies when he goes hunting."

"He gave us your name as a possible reference. We're looking for a particular item."

"Can I get you kids a Coke?"

"Um, sure," Devon said. "That would be nice." Begay opened the small fridge and took out two bottles of Coke. Devon was sure that she had glimpsed coffee cans inside. He handed one to each of his visitors.

"That'll be a dollar," he said, smiling.

DeVere pulled out his wallet and handed him a dollar, trying not to laugh.

Devon was a little leery of drinking a Coke that might have been rubbing elbows with a can of worms, but she didn't want to insult Begay. She popped the top and took a swig. It tasted fine and was icy cold.

"So, what are you kids looking for?" Begay asked as he popped his own bottle of soda. Apparently, he liked Tab.

"Dermestid beetles," Devon said. "You sell them?"

"Might," Begay said casually. He sipped his Tab. "How many you looking for?"

"Enough to chow down on a big-ass buck and leave nothing but the bones," DeVere said.

"That's a lot of beetles."

"It's a big deer. Do you have that many?"

"Might—if'n you tell me the real reason you're interested. I may be an old redskin, but I got a brain."

"Sorry," Devon said. She pulled out her P.I. credentials and showed them to him. "You're right—we don't want to buy beetles. We want to buy information."

"That costs more," Begay said.

"I figured," DeVere replied. "How about we tell you what we want, you chew on it for a few minutes, then you present us a cost for your assistance. Maybe we dicker, maybe we don't."

Begay grunted what seemed to be assent.

Devon said, "We're looking for someone who bought enough beetles to decimate that buck, and anyone who might have made more than one such purchase. Names and dates."

DeVere added, "And any names of other beetle sellers in the northern New Mexico area."

"Why?" Begay demanded.

Devon thought about saying a big, fat lie, but she decided that Begay would probably sense that and consider it disrespectful. "We're trying to find someone that may be using beetles to clean a special set of bones."

"What kind of bones?" Begay asked suspiciously.

"Human bones," DeVere said flatly. "Coupla years ago, the police found three human bones by the roadside in Santa Fe. They were perfectly clean and lacquered. During the last few years, a number of people from all walks of life have disappeared from the northern New Mexico area. There's nothing to link these together, and it's a longshot that they might be related, but we're grasping at straws."

"So," Begay began slowly, "if someone was using beetles to clean human bones, why? What is he doing with them?"

"Not a damned clue," DeVere said. "Like I said—a longshot. Can you help us?"

"Could." Begay paused and seemed to be thinking hard. He sighed. "Fifty bucks—and pretty girl sits on my lap for a minute." He grinned salaciously at Devon. He suddenly cackled and slapped his knee.

"Fifty bucks and I don't sit on your lap," Devon said coolly. "And DeVere doesn't kick your horny old ass."

Begay nodded his head sagely. "I believe we have come to an agreement. Give me ten minutes."

With that he went through the rear door, leaving Devon and DeVere to fight off the laughter they wanted to expel. Devon wandered through the room alternately shaking her head or rolling her eyes at the kitsch she found. She turned over a pretty piece of pottery that still had a "Made in China" label on the bottom. She held it up to DeVere. "Made by those Chinese Indians."

"Hey, hey," DeVere said excitedly. "Look at this." Devon wandered over and made a face.

"I hate spiders," she exclaimed. "They're … evil. Ugly."

"Yeah but look at this one closely."

Devon came a little closer and scrutinized the tarantula. It had only seven legs. She looked into DeVere's excited face. "Oh, no. We are not taking this back to Santa Fe."

"Didn't Skye cry her eyes out when she lost her last spider?"

"Yeah, but I'm not … I'm not driving over a hundred miles with that thing in the car. No way."

"Look, he's selling small five-gallon aquariums. We'll buy one and keep the hairy sucker safely inside until we get home. Think of how happy Skye will be. Come on. Be brave. Be a brave black white woman."

"I hate you," she muttered, grimacing at the arachnid. She made a face and said, "Eew."

Twenty minutes later Begay came out and handed them a short list. He stuck out his hand and wriggled his fingers. DeVere handed him two twenties and a ten.

"We were thinking of buying your tarantula," DeVere said casually. "What're you asking?"

"He's a pretty prime specimen," Begay said laconically, sensing another opportunity. "Couldn't let him go for less than, say, twenty?"

"Twenty dollars for a friggin' spider?" Devon exclaimed. "No way." With that she stormed out of the building and the two men could hear a car door slamming.

DeVere smiled at Begay. "Let's dicker."

Ten minutes later DeVere walked outside holding a five-gallon aquarium with a cover and an agitated seven-legged tarantula inside. Also inside was a small mason jar with a top that had holes poked in it; it held a half dozen beetles. He slid into the passenger side and held the aquarium on his lap. “Home, James,” he said lightly, averting his eyes from her menacing scowl.

For fifty miles she castigated him while trying to keep one eye on the road and the other on the spider. He and the spider spent the night in the living room, he on the couch and the tarantula he’d dubbed “Scamp” on the end table.

He was certain the critter was watching him all night.

CHAPTER FOUR

"So, we have a list of names that might possibly be Indian injustice collectors," Sand said at the Tuesday morning staff meeting in the Graceland Conference Room. Normally they were held on Mondays, but yesterday had been Labor Day. "Not that all of them have done anything we know about, but people who have been very verbal, angry, or agitated about mistreatment from the white man."

"Or black white men," DeVere muttered, receiving an immediate shot in the ribs by Devon, who was sitting next to him.

Sand went on. "And we don't have any proof that any of these men might be using dermestid beetles to clean bones. After all, all we have are those three bones and because they're lacquered there's no way to determine if beetles were used to clean off the flesh. And, if so, so what? There's also nothing to indicate that our Indian Killer is doing anything with bones. If he's killing these missing people then he's probably burying them, just like he buried the San Ramon kids."

"And just because Naabah paints hidden bones in some of his landscapes that doesn't automatically link him to the guy disappearing our people," Nick said. "But I don't like the fact that he painted a bone in Percy's Bandelier painting. Why? And why wasn't there one in Elspeth's?"

"Elspeth was a portrait, for one thing," Swan said.

"Look," Memphis said in frustration. "We have a list of potential perps, so I suggest we dig into their backgrounds and find anything that might solidify suspicions—or dispel them. But first, we still have open and backlogged cases that we can't abandon, so let's find out the status on them and assign personnel as needed. Skye," he said to his executive assistant sitting opposite him at the big rectangular table, "read the open case roster and let's get some statuses." He cast a baleful eye at the small two-gallon terrarium housing her new pet, Scamp, positioned at her left side on the table, a scant foot away from a repulsed Frack. Memphis was on edge more so than usual for the past week after he drove Raleigh to Albuquerque to catch her flight to Boston. He hated having his only sister so far away. On the sly he caught his mother crying.

Skye pushed her eyeglasses down on her nose and frowned at the case summaries. "Miss Devon, besides bringing home my wonderful new pet—"

"Don't blame that on me," Devon snapped immediately. She scowled at DeVere. "This ninny bought the beast and made me ride over a hundred miles with it in the car hoping it wouldn't get out of its tank and scuttle between my legs."

Skye sighed. Her crew could almost never get through one of these status meetings without most of the team veering off on tangents. "Miss Devon. How is the divorce case for the Esparzas going?"

"Thankfully just about over. Yesterday I followed the scumbag all evening and finally caught him doing the dirty at a motel off I-25. Got some nice shots."

"She pretty?" Nick asked. Devon handed him a small stack of photos. "Holy shit! I guess *he*'s pretty."

"It's a guy?" Sand exclaimed and Nick handed him the photo. "Yeah, that's a guy."

"A guy that's going to translate to an excellent settlement for Mrs. Esparza," Devon said.

"I don't like the idea of deliberately outing someone for material gain," Sand said quietly. He had been outed by Joanna Frid to destroy his career and throw him off her scent. He had been tossed off the police force; his whole world had changed, except for the love and support he unwaveringly received from his best friend, Memphis, his sister, Swan, and the host of other friends and family that never gave a damn about his sexual orientation.

"We're not going to out him," Memphis said. "We're going to inform him of the information we've acquired and let him make the decision about the right thing to do for child and spousal support."

"And if he doesn't do the right thing?" Sand asked.

"We'll dig deeper and mine every foul piece of his life that will get his wife the settlement she deserves. Next."

Skye straightened and peered at Frick, who looked decidedly uncomfortable. "Mr. Smith. You were supposed to get the paperwork done and signed off for the Rizzoli case. I've been waiting ten days for that. Starting tomorrow if you don't provide the paperwork you'll be docked $10 per day."

"I've been a little busy, here," Frick growled. "Up and down and across and backwards across this godforsaken state chasing down pueblos."

"Try chasing down beetles and tarantulas," DeVere said smoothly.

"So, let me reiterate," Skye said firmly. "Mr. Smith will finish his paperwork or pay the financial price." She narrowed her eyes at Frick. "Clear?"

"Clear," Frick muttered.

"Excellent. Nicholas. Any progress on the arson fire of the restaurant?" A popular Chinese restaurant had burned to the ground three weeks earlier. The Fire Department judged it as accidental, but the owner was convinced that it was arson.

"Actually, some," Nick said. "I narrowed down a list of potential professional and personal enemies of Mr. Cho and I've been making the rounds of stores that might have sold them incendiary material. The fire department said that the accidental fire started on bad electrical wiring in the kitchen, but Mr. Cho had the electrical wiring upgraded six months ago. I've been talking to several electricians to see what they think could cause a fire that seemed accidental but was deliberate. Stay tuned."

"Is he going to rebuild?" Swan asked.

"He doesn't know," Nick said. "He had some insurance but not enough to replace the building and equipment. He's still considering his options." Nick stopped and looked thoughtful. "Hmm. I might have an idea. I'll let you know."

"Well, that's mysterious," Swan said. "Want my update, Miss Skye?"

"I have an agenda here in a specific order," Skye said mildly.

"By all means—let's go with the agenda," Swan said with a tight smile.

"Thank you. Swan—may we please have your update?" There was an unmistakable satisfaction in Skye's eyes.

Frack guffawed and Swan shot him a dirty look. "Happy to do so," Swan said. She placed her hand down on a piece of paper in front of her. "These are the names our group has acquired from bug world. I cross-referenced the names and found four that seemed to have bought beetles from more than one dealer." She scowled down at the paper; Memphis was right—she needed to consider getting reading glasses. Yeah—when Hell froze over. "Charlie Whitedog, Barry Frost, Antonio Quará, and Ashkii Tahoma. We also have a second list of possible suspects like that Indian agitator that leads a protest every Columbus Day and burns the explorer in effigy."

"Are we really going to go any further with this?" Nick asked. He held up his hands. "Just asking."

"Maybe another mile or so," Memphis said. "It bothers the hell out of me to have made no headway on our own missing persons cases and if there's a one in a million chance there's a link I say we spend some time on it."

"Nick and I should progress on this," Sand said. "The San Francisco couple was our case. Chuy Castaneda was also our case. We'd like to see it through."

"Fine," Memphis said. "You two take the four beetle names, Swan will take the agitator, and Frick and Frack can handle the other names on her suspect list. Everyone okay with that?"

There were a few mumbles, but no one objected, and Memphis nodded to Skye to finish the meeting. Twenty minutes later all the agenda items had been put to bed, but Skye told them to hold up; she had an announcement. Without a word she dialed a number and asked someone to come up. A few minutes later Akiro came into the conference room.

"Hey, gang," he said cheerfully.

"What's up?" Sand asked. Akiro motioned to Skye and all eyes were on her. She stood.

"I've been working with you crazy people for eleven years now, and I've enjoyed ninety percent of that time," Skye said.

"What about the other ten percent?" Memphis asked.

"That would be when you let Frick and Frack on board. May I continue?"

"Are you quitting?" Nick asked.

"Yes," she replied succinctly. "But I'll be close by." She glanced at Akiro. "I like to keep my private life private, so I'm sure most if not all of you had no idea that for the past nine years I've been attending college classes at night and on weekends."

"What?" Swan exclaimed. "Where? For what?"

"The University of New Mexico. I've been driving down to Albuquerque around three nights per week. I got my undergraduate degree in Political Science. And then … I went further." She winked at Akiro.

Akiro picked up the tale. "You are looking at the newest member of the New Mexico bar," he said proudly.

"You're a lawyer?" Nick exclaimed in disbelief. "What the hell happened to that sweet, ethereal, anti-establishment hippie girl I once knew?"

"Same thing that happened to that wild, pot-smoking renegade I used to know, who cut his hair, put on decent clothes, and changed into a respected P.I., married man, and father of two. I grew up."

Memphis scowled at Akiro. "Are you hiring her away from me?"

"Yup," Akiro said. "Done deal. But we've agreed that after her two weeks' notice she can work a couple hours a day until you find a new executive assistant."

"Party time," Devon declared.

"Thank you for volunteering to set that up," Memphis said politely to Devon. He grinned at the surprised look on her face. "Money is no object." He looked at Skye thoughtfully, then got up, walked around the table, and hugged her close. "Congratulations," he said quietly. "I'm so incredibly proud of you." That was followed by a round of hugs and quite a few tears before a shout startled them.

"Scamp got out of his box," DeVere exclaimed as everyone's eyes flew to the now empty terrarium whose top was askew.

"Don't step on him," Skye shouted, and everyone froze, then began eyeballing the floor for the fleeing tarantula.

"There's the little shit," Frack blurted out and pointed to a spider leg disappearing behind the mini-fridge. Skye dived to the floor and crushed herself against the wall trying to peer at the back of the fridge. DeVere got on the other side.

Standing over her boyfriend Devon said, "I told you not to buy the damn thing."

Memphis glanced at Akiro. "Sure you want the insect woman in your crew?"

Akiro grinned. "I surely do."

It was the first week of September and the various festivals and art fairs were already in full swing. This year, a small circus got permission to set up outside of town. They had a substantial Big Top and two smaller ones, and a nice variety of rides and fun booths where gullible people could spend twenty bucks trying to win a two-dollar prize. It was more of a carnival than circus, but there were a few wild animals that performed.

Naabah was bored for the past few weeks and hadn't had much of an urge to paint. He was antsy about his special art projects, which were unfinished. He didn't know if one would ever be finished. The carnival was crowded on Saturday and his senses were assailed by the smells of hotdogs, cotton candy, and popcorn, and the whoops of people who thought they'd won an expensive prize. Every few minutes the air was punctuated with a child's wail or yell. Some people had brought their dogs as evidenced not only by the barking but by the impressive poop piles one had to circumnavigate to prevent shoe damage.

Naabah bought a chili dog, a Coke, and a big bag of kettle corn and sat on a bench to eat. He enjoyed people-watching and was always on the lookout for another victim. He hadn't taken one since the derelict three months ago. Something caught his eye and he turned to his left and saw a trio of dwarves ambling towards the Big Top. One was dressed like an old-west cowboy; two were dressed like stereotypical Indian war chiefs, bonnets, tomahawks, war paint, and all. He narrowed his eyes, then got up, tossed his trash, and bought a ticket to the show. The tent was spacious and had considerable height. The benches were crowded together to support as many people as possible, four deep with increasing levels like bleachers. The center ring had a thick carpet of sawdust and above it was a high wire. Naabah climbed up to the top-level bench and squished himself against the end with a thick rope as the only security for not falling off.

A large clown cartwheeled into the center ring and began honking his nose and gesturing wildly. The kids in the audience laughed and tittered. Naabah had never liked clowns; they gave him the creeps. Another clown joined him, and they began chasing one another around and whapping each other with Styrofoam bats. The audience was eating it up. The ringmaster made an exuberant entrance and used a booming voice to lay out the show. Up first—the high wire act. Naabah had to admit that the two men and one woman were skilled acrobats. They finished their set to an appreciative round of applause.

Then the ringmaster announced, "General Lickety-Split and Chiefs Little Big Man and Big Little Man" and the miniature cowboy and Indians ran into the ring and began performing an obviously frequently performed act of two Indians doing a war dance and threatening the cowboy with their tomahawks. Naabah wondered if their costumes were supposed to represent a particular tribe, since from his perspective they had a mishmash of styles, from plains Indians to the Apaches of Arizona to … something he had no idea about. Their actions and facial expressions were badly exaggerated but provoked raucous laughter from most of the audience.

After a few minutes, the cowboy shot one of the Indians, who fell down on his back and comically convulsed before he "died." The other Indian tomahawked the cowboy and did a victory dance around his body while screaming, "Woo! Woo! Woo!" and clapping his hand over his mouth. A few seconds later the "dead" dwarves stood up and bowed to loud clapping before they hopped out of the tent. Naabah didn't clap and quietly and carefully climbed down from the bench and slipped out of the tent from a side opening. He could hear the ringmaster announcing the next act, the lion tamer. He would have liked to have seen that.

He caught a glimpse of the three dwarves walking side by side towards their tent where they'd probably hang out until the next show. It was about fifty feet away at the edge of the carnival perimeter. Naabah's heart was beating like a throbbing bass drum as he dared contemplate something, well, daring. He looked around towards the various souvenir booths and one caught his eye. Three people were ahead of him and he was antsy and impatient, but he held his temper. When it was his turn he pointed to a large carry-on bag with the carnival's logo and a picture of the three dwarves on it, dressed in their costumes and grinning widely. There were others with a lion, a clown, a llama, and a Big Top; he thought the selection was propitious. He bought the lion version, too, handed over his money, and headed off to his car.

He sat behind the wheel gripping it and releasing it repeatedly as he hyperventilated. The cautious part of him knew it was best to wait until nightfall; the impulsive and reckless part of him said, *Now*. He got out of the truck carrying the dwarf bag. He also had chloroform with him, and he soaked a rag thoroughly and put it in the bag. He was unremarkable as he ambled around the perimeter of the carnival until he reached within twenty feet of the back of the dwarves' tent. His heart was beating so furiously that he couldn't hear the sounds from within the event. He moved up silently behind the tent, which had slits every six feet like the Big Top. Out of the corner of his eye he saw the cowboy leave on the arm of a female dwarf. He would have liked to study her.

He heard the other two men talking in the tent and he gently pried open a slit and eyed the inside. The dwarf that had played the first Indian was within arm's length of the tent wall. The one that had done the repulsive "Woo! Woo! Woo!" victory dance was naked and sitting in a small tub of water, his eyes closed while he soaked and smoked a fat stogie. In his head Naabah ran over the best option to incapacitate the one he didn't want and then snatch away the one he did. He came up with three fast scenarios but before he could act the clothed dwarf jumped up and said he was going for a beer. He left the tent.

The gods were on his side, Naabah thought as he eyed the bathing man, the one he truly wanted. Like a wraith he wedged his body sideways between the tent flaps without making a sound. He walked over to the tub and stood still for a moment as he stared down at his target. Then he took the chloroform-soaked rag in one hand and clasped it over the man's mouth while he held his head immobile with the other hand. The man struggled and splashed for few brief seconds before he lost consciousness. The cigar fell out of his hand and floated in the soapy water.

Naabah wasted no time in pulling the man from the tub and stuffing him into the bag. Seconds later he slipped through the tent flaps and walked leisurely to his truck. A few minutes later he was on the road to home.

As Naabah drove he felt a mixture of giddiness and relief; giddiness, because now he had the small person he craved for his art, and relief because now he didn't have to take Percy. He liked the little psychologist. He was glad he didn't have to debone him.

CHAPTER FIVE

"I don't talk to pigs," Chelan Chee spat out at Swan from the door jamb of the Indians for Freedom headquarters in north Santa Fe. "Even private pigs."

Swan sighed and just stared at the fiery activist that was clearly not going to cooperate with any "white man" questions. She hadn't known anything about either the person or the movement when she headed off to the interview. She went on the assumption that she'd encounter a tall, belligerent older man when instead she found herself facing a petite, slender young woman who couldn't be more than twenty or top five-feet-tall. Her long sable hair spilled across her shoulders and her dark brown eyes spit fire. Hehewuti had told Swan that the name "Chelan" meant "deep water," and this Chelan, although looking more like a puddle, presented herself as a vibrant tsunami of passion, resentment, and commitment to her people.

Swan fixed an annoyingly neutral stare on her face for a moment, then shrugged, and turned to leave. Over her shoulder she threw, "We're looking for someone who might have a grudge against white people but who can also subdue a full-grown man or two. Your grudge is apparent, but you couldn't subdue a pigeon. Hágoónee'." A split second later the recalcitrant woman grabbed Swan from behind to make a point of how strong and determined she was. Two seconds later she found herself flat on her back with Swan standing over her, a smirk on her self-satisfied face.

Chelan stared up at the victor. She pushed herself off the ground and smacked her hands against her butt to remove the layer of dust on her jeans. Her lip was tightly curled as she said, "Where'd you learn to say 'goodbye' in Navajo?"

"From my mother-in-law," Swan said coolly.

"You're married to an Indian?"

"A half-breed. I guess you'd call our kids quarter-breeds."

Chelan harrumphed. "Where'd you learn to fight like that?"

"Before I was a private pig I was a real one, and I've always strived to perfect hand-to-hand combat and martial arts. That, and I'm just naturally a bitch."

"Yeah, you got that characteristic down pat. What do you want?"

"I wanted to ask a few questions about your organization and members."

"Why?"

"Looking for answers. Yes or no?"

Chelan narrowed her eyes and contemplated the white woman for a long moment before she gave a terse nod and led Swan into the building. The large room was a bit chaotic on the décor side, with two battered old metal desks holding heavy manual typewriters and papers scattered over the tops. A gangly young man with Coke-bottle eyeglasses was sitting at one desk hunched over his typewriter and hunting and pecking letters very slowly.

Chelan nodded towards him. "Jimmy Black Crow. He's working on a high school history paper. Come into my office." She led Swan to a door and then her office, which was small, particularly neat, and seemed like a display case for pride in the American Indian. There were Indian artists' prints on the walls, two woven wool mandalas highlighted by eagle feathers, an intricate woven Navajo rug with the Zia sun symbol at the center, and various artifacts that looked ancient and were placed in strategic locations on her desk and the other tables and bookcases. There was a single guest chair and Swan carefully parked herself on it. The chair seemed sturdy enough, so she relaxed a little as Chelan slipped behind her desk.

"So, why are you asking these questions?" Chelan asked as she popped open a bottle of water. She could have offered a bottle to Swan, but she decided not to.

"We're working on a couple of cases that may have the same person involved."

"What kind of cases?"

"Missing persons. We were engaged a few years ago to try to track down a missing couple from San Francisco."

"You ever find them?"

"No. We're pretty sure they're dead now, but they seemed to be the tip of the iceberg. There have been a series of other missing persons cases, too. In several cases the apparent motive for the disappearances may be a show of disrespect for the Indian culture. We've had the FBI as well as our own psychologist come up with a profile of a possible perpetrator. We think this man may be—"

"An injustice collector," Chelan finished.

Swan was surprised. "That's right. How do you know—"

Chelan scowled. "I'm not some damn ignorant squaw who's staying home cooking for my warrior and popping out papooses. My education wasn't first-class, but I have a brain and I read and study."

Swan held her hands up in surrender. "It was just a question. Okay, so you understand the concept. Is there anyone you might know of who could fit the profile? An Indian man forty to sixty, well-muscled, stable, has his own home. He may be married but it's more likely that he's single. If he is married he's a 'perfect' husband and father, and no one would ever suspect him of criminal actions. He may have a second residence far away, and probably has a truck or SUV. He probably has a job that requires strength and meticulous process. He's very devoted to his race and culture and hates the things the white man has done since Columbus landed on these shores. There's a rage simmering beneath the surface, but he rarely lets anyone see that rage."

"That it?" Chelan said cheekily.

"A few more refinement points but, yes, that's basically it. Know anyone that might fit that bill?"

"Have you got a few hours? That fits a shitload of people I know or have heard about. Even if I knew of such a man, why would I want to help you?"

"Because this man is taking the lives of innocent people in the name of some quest to punish the sinners. And all these so-called sinners have done is maybe show disrespect intentionally or unintentionally towards Indian culture. They haven't killed, or raped, or committed arson, or anything that would warrant genuine punishment. They are being targeted for their race."

"Tell me about it," Chelan replied sarcastically.

Swan slammed her hand down on the desk, startling Chelan. "Damn it. I am well aware of Indians' legitimate gripes. I live with Indians of one percentage or another, and my kids carry that blood."

"Who's your mother-in-law?" Chelan suddenly asked.

"Hehewuti Maasikiisa. She—"

"I know of her. She's a medicine woman and a respected member of the Hopi and Navajo tribes. Who's her son?"

"Memphis Grayhawk is the oldest and my husband. His brother, Tucson, is one of the psychologists that helped compile the profile of our suspect." Swan removed a folded piece of paper from her fanny pack and handed it to Chelan. "Do you know any of these men?"

Chelan skimmed the four names. "A couple." She frowned. "These your suspects?"

"Yes and no. The reasons they're on this list is because they purchased large quantities of dermestid beetles from multiple sources."

"What the hell do beetles have to do with an injustice collector?"

"Maybe nothing. It's just a wild hunch. It may have to do with another case. Can you think of why anyone would need to have human bones for some religious or artistic reasons?"

"Bones? You're a crazy white woman."

"So, which two on the list do you know?"

"I don't know them—I know of them. Charlie Whitedog, Barry Frost—harmless hunters. No real grudges against you people." She cocked her head. "That other name—Antonio Quará. It seems familiar, but I can't place it. I'd need to think."

"Does he live around here?"

"I'm thinking … it's a name from the past. Not my past, but perhaps my people's past. I'd have to think about it."

Swan stood and tried to hand Chelan a business card. When Chelan didn't take it Swan flipped the card onto her desk. "Thanks for the hospitality and lack of information. Maybe someday I can return the favor." With that she turned on her heel and stalked out of the office. Chelan picked up the card and studied it thoughtfully. Then she walked over to her bookcase, scanned the titles, and pulled out a thick book on pueblo history. She pulled out another one on peyote culture. She spent the next hour cross-referencing certain information and made a few notes. Maybe she'd visit the arrogant white woman on her own turf.

Sand and Nick enjoyed the shade under the big tree near the Taos Pueblo visitor's center. It was ten o'clock in the morning and the temperature was cool because of the September averages and the slightly lower elevation that was complemented by the wind rolling off the Sangre de Cristo Mountains. They had been there a few times before seeking the whereabouts of the San Francisco couple, and the woman manning the cash register at the snack counter, Blue Corn, smiled and remembered them by name. They asked her if she recognized the four names on their list and she shook her head. They bought Cokes and potato chips and sat on the shaded bench to chow down. They were about to start canvassing the various residents and tourists when Blue Corn rushed out of the center. She was short and pudgy and in her mid-fifties, but she had a thousand-watt smile.

She reached them and smiled broadly. "I remember something," she said.

"About the names?" Sand asked.

"Si, Mr. Sand. One of the names." He showed her the list and she put her finger on a name. Antonio Quará.

"Do you know him?" Nick asked.

"No, no, but many years ago there was a family here with that last name. They gone now, but maybe one of them was Antonio."

"Who might we ask about them?" Sand said.

Blue Corn furrowed her meaty brow and said. "Maybe the Peñas or the Lujans or the Looking Elks. They still have old grandmas and grandpas around who might remember."

"How long ago do you think this Quará family lived here?" Nick asked.

Blue Corn shrugged and thought. "Don't know. Maybe thirty, forty years?"

"Where are these families you mentioned?" Sand asked.

Blue Corn pointed to the left section of pueblos. "They all live there. Just ask."

Sand took Blue Corn's hand and kissed it respectfully. "Thank you, Miss Blue Corn. You have been a great help."

Blue Corn giggled then whirled around and rushed back to the center to spell her register replacement, who happened to be her granddaughter.

"So," Nick said, chucking his empty chip bag and bottle into the trash can, "shall we?"

"We shall," Sand said, and they began walking towards where Blue Corn had pointed. They spent three hours interviewing members of the three families and compiled a lot of information. One piece of info was a revelation, and it made Sand's heart beat faster.

They were nearly back to the car when Sand said he wanted to call in to the office before they hit the road. He waited a minute as a tourist finished his call on the pay phone then called in. Skye answered, shot off a few clipped sentences, then hung up. Nick was parked in the driver's seat waiting, and Sand got into the car. Nick could see that he was excited.

"Everything okay?" Nick asked as he turned on the engine.

"With our folks, yeah, but Abbott and Dunbar are at the office huddling with our colleagues."

"What's happened?"

"Another person was abducted. He's been missing for two days."

"They think it may be our guy?" Nick pulled onto the main road into the right lane.

"Maybe." Sand glanced sideways. "This new missing person is a little different than the others."

"How so?"

"The missing person is a dwarf."

Nick accelerated and flew down the road, passing slower drivers at an alarming rate. They made the Santa Fe limits seventy miles away in just over an hour.

The Hazelwood Conference Room was littered with empty soda cups and pizza boxes. Memphis was there; so were Swan and Frick as well as Detectives Dunbar and Abbott. Frack was making the rounds with his list of names and Devon and DeVere were working a new case of multiple background checks for a small company north of Albuquerque. The detectives had descended on Warrior Spirit Investigations around noon and laid out most of their information on the missing person, Chief Big Little Man, AKA, thirty-eight-year-old Milton Steinberg of Queens, New York. They were still talking about the exact timeline when Sand and Nick arrived.

"The pizza's all gone?" Nick said dejectedly.

Swan pointed to the phone. "Feel free to order another."

"Where's Skye?"

"Our newly minted lawyer is downstairs working on a project for Akiro. You're on your own for now."

"We need another Skye," Nick replied. He picked up the receiver and dialed the number he knew by heart. He ordered two pizzas.

"There'll never be another Skye," Memphis said, sighing.

Sand looked at Dunbar and said, "So tell us about this missing person."

Dunbar nodded. "His name is Milton Steinberg, late of New York City. He's been with the circus for three years crisscrossing the country and playing several parts, mainly as an Indian in the cowboy act. He worked with two other dwarves, one Danny Crockett from Helena, Montana, and Lancelot LaPointe from New Orleans, Louisiana."

"Lancelot?" Sand exclaimed. "Seriously?"

"Any friction between them?" Nick asked.

"Some, according to Lancelot. Didn't get much from Danny. He and his girlfriend were singularly unhelpful. I've asked Lancelot to come in tomorrow for another interview here so you could sit in," Dunbar said.

"When did he vanish?" Sand asked.

"Two nights ago, the three of them did their silly cowboy and Indians routine in the Big Top then went back to their own tent to relax before the next show. Crockett and his girlfriend left for some nookie, and Lancelot stuck around chatting with Milton while he took a bath. Lancelot left shortly thereafter to get a beer. When he came back to the tent Milton was gone."

"How long was Lancelot gone?" Nick asked.

"Fifteen minutes, tops, he said," Abbott replied.

"Was he alarmed at Milton's absence?" Swan asked.

"Not really. He only became concerned when it was a half hour to showtime and Milton still hadn't returned to the tent. He found the circus owner and let him know that Milton was nowhere to be found. The owner was pissed, and he told Lancelot and Danny to perform as a duo. The owner thought maybe Milton had gone off on a drunk since it had happened a couple of times before. When Milton didn't show up yesterday the owner told Lancelot to tell him that he was fired."

"So, what was it that made Lancelot suspect there might be foul play?" Frick said.

"For one thing," Dunbar said, "Milton's precious Cuban cigar was floating in the bath water. Lancelot said he smoked those stogies down to the nub. And, all of Milton's clothes and costumes were still in the tent. There was nothing missing."

"So, are you saying that he left the tent wet and naked?" Sand said in disbelief.

"That's the supposition we're working under," Abbott said.

"Don't you think someone might notice a naked dwarf walking around the circus or outskirts?" Nick said skeptically.

"Sure—if he were walking," Abbott said. "Flying, even. But not if he were stuffed into something and carried out like luggage."

"Did anyone … see luggage around?" Memphis asked.

Abbott shook his head. "We haven't had the chance to interview everyone, but that would stand out. You know what wouldn't stand out?" With that he picked up a large nylon bag with the circus logo on it. "This. They sell them at one of the kiosks and according to the vendor he sold maybe thirty or forty that day. Cash, no receipts, no names."

"Yes, a dwarf would fit in there. But he'd have to be sedated to prevent yelling or movement," Nick said.

"The most likely scenario is that someone very quietly slipped between the tent flaps and came up on Milton from behind and clasped a cloth of chloroform over his mouth. Small dude, it wouldn't take long to incapacitate him, pull him out of the tub and stuff him the bag."

"That's what we were thinking," Abbott said.

"What made you think he could be a victim of our injustice collector?" Swan asked.

Abbott seemed embarrassed. "I took my wife and kids to see the shows a few days earlier and the trio was performing their schtick. It was … kind of embarrassing for even a white guy. The costumes, the whoops, the makeup—it was over-the-top stereotypical, and I can see where it would royally piss off an Indian who was reverent about his culture."

"So, we're making the rounds of interviews and that's where we are right now," Dunbar said. "We brought this information to you because it has strong similarities to the Chuy Castaneda case, and we wanted to pick your brains."

"Have you laid out a scale map of the circus area and analyzed which areas someone with a carnival bag might pass by discreetly towards the parking lot?" Sand said.

"Huh. No," Abbott confessed.

"We can work one up," Swan said. "I can take a run out there and make some sketches and we can get together tomorrow to review it."

"That'd be a big help," Abbott said. "Thanks." He checked his watch. "We gotta get going. Back here at 9 AM?"

"9 AM," Memphis confirmed.

With handshakes all around the two detectives left just as the pizza delivery guy came in and handed off the aromatic, hot pies. Memphis tipped him well and looked back to see Nick already breaking into one and dripping a hot, cheesy slice onto an inadequate napkin.

Memphis said, "So, before Swan heads off to do her sketches did you gents make any headway up in Taos? Anyone recognize the names or the people themselves?"

"We might have made a little progress," Sand said smoothly as he selected the cheesiest slice of the pepperoni pie and took a bite, burning his tongue. He hissed loudly and took a fast drink out of his water bottle.

"We went into the visitor's center and asked the register lady about the names. She's a sweet soul," Nick said. "Her name's Blue Corn. Anyway, Blue Corn didn't recognize the names at first but after we left she came running after us and said one of the names was sort of familiar. Antonio Quará."

"He live in Taos?" Frick asked.

"No, but she thought that a family with that surname lived there many years ago. She pointed us to a few well-established families that we could ask," Sand said. "We had no luck with one of them, but two of the families had some memory of the Quará family. They were a small unit that broke apart gradually by the 1920s, leaving only one nuclear family. The patriarch was named Antonio. He was puebloan and the mother was a Navajo. There were five or six kids with one boy in the middle. They were surviving during the Great Depression and were as dirt poor as they come, even for Indians. A couple of the daughters died young."

"So, are we thinking that this Antonio might be the guy we're seeking?" Memphis asked.

Nick shook his head. "The father was killed in the early 1940s in a drunken brawl with a white man. But, that middle son was named after his father, the second Antonio Quará. At ten or twelve he became the man of the house and was charged with taking care of his mother and sisters. He did odd jobs to make money, and somehow he scraped by. His mother died a few years later and somehow he got his older sisters well married and his younger one into a church school. They think she might live in the Gallup area."

"What happened to the son?" Memphis asked, intrigued.

"He dropped out of school a couple years after his old man died. He was bright but didn't see the point. The Looking Elk guy told us he remembered the boy being artistic and did some cheap paintings to sell to tourists. He left the pueblo and traveled around but came back on occasion. He never married or had kids, and he became quite adept at his art and grew in professional prominence."

"I've never heard the name," Swan said. "I'll ask Sage if she knows about him."

"Oh," Sand said, "I'm sure she does know his work." He nodded to Memphis. "So do you. We all do."

"Yeah?" Swan said suspiciously.

"Yeah. Oh—did I mention that the young artist took another name for his identity? He took it from his Navajo mother's language and culture. His name means 'angry warrior.'"

"And that would be?"

"Hashkeh Naabah, AKA HashNaa."

There was dead silence before Memphis said, "Are you shitting me?"

"I shit you not."

"Where do we go from here?" Swan asked quietly.

"You go do your thing at the circus, and tomorrow morning Sand and Nick will drive to Gallup to see if they can find the sister. Do we know anything about her?" he asked Sand.

"A little. Supposedly she's a rez teacher and is married and has kids," Sand replied. "I guess we could look up marriage records and make the rounds of whatever schools are around there." He looked at Nick. "We should start out by seven." Nick nodded.

"This seems very interesting," Frick said, "but even if the Antonio guy is our HashNaa, that doesn't prove anything."

"Painting artists don't generally buy flesh-eating beetles," Swan said. "And, even if they did, that doesn't mean that flesh was human and not a big buck. It's certainly not enough to haul him in as a legitimate suspect. And, keep in mind that there is a chance that our Antonio Quará, AKA HashNaa, might not be the same guy buying the beetles. Quará's not an extremely unusual puebloan name, and they could be two different men."

"But we can keeping building circumstantial evidence as a point that might tip the scales for legal action," Memphis said. "We've got three ex-cops in this room so I'm sure you know the rules and limitations."

"Yeah, but we're all renegades," Sand said with a grin. "We break the rules."

Swan looked at her husband and smiled. "We should add that to our business cards."

Memphis rolled his eyes.

CHAPTER SIX

In 1946, actor, jazz pianist, singer, and songwriter Bobby Troup and his wife, Cynthia, drove across the country to Los Angeles. He loved their journey and decided to memorialize the experience by writing a song about traveling on Route 66. The song told people they could have fun, could get their kicks, on Route 66. In Los Angeles, Bobby Troup took the song to Nat King Cole. The song was originally performed by Nat King Cole and the King Cole Trio, and a second version was performed by Bing Crosby and the Andrews Sisters. Both versions of *(Get Your Kicks On) Route 66* were huge 1946 hits. Chuck Berry later covered the song, too.

If you ever plan to motor west
Travel my way, take the highway that's the best
Get your kicks on Route 66
It winds from Chicago to L.A.
More than two thousand miles all the way
Get your kicks on Route 66
Now you go through Saint Louis, Joplin Missouri
And Oklahoma City looks mighty pretty...
You'll see Amarillo, Gallup, New Mexico
Flagstaff, Arizona...

The song did encourage some families to take a road trip and many followed the route that Troup did. In 1960 Route 66 was further memorialized in the travels of two handsome young men in the TV series *Route 66*. Tod Stiles, played by actor Martin Milner, and Buzz Murdock, played by George Maharis, set women's hearts a-fluttering and men's hearts into a whirlpool of desire to roam the roads free and adventurous and unencumbered with a nine-to-five life cluttered with responsibilities, wives, kids, and invisible social chains. It didn't hurt that Tod and Buzz tooled down the road in a spiffy Corvette convertible.

More than thirty years later another flashy Corvette was tooling down Route 66 to Gallup. Nick had treated himself to the midnight-blue, convertible 'Vette for his thirtieth birthday three years ago. The seating wasn't terribly comfortable, but the car was a head-turner and he loved the panache. It was early in the morning and with the top down the wind whipped through his long hair and Sand's and dusted their cheeks with a chilliness that brought the skin to a light rose. They barely spoke, simply enjoying the tranquility of tearing down the road.

The signs began to specify the number of miles to Gallup, which was one hundred thirty-eight miles from Albuquerque. They passed Thoreau; thirty-two miles. Not too far from Thoreau they saw the signs stating that they were on the Continental Divide. Jamestown; twenty miles. Making the Church Rock city limits they were almost to their destination at ten miles. They were welcomed into Gallup's city limits by a big billboard that read, "Gallup – Heart of Indian Country." Fifteen miles away—a hop, skip, and a jump—lay the

Arizona Border. Around ten more miles northwest was Window Rock, Arizona, the capital of the Navajo Nation.

The small city was on the edge of the Navajo reservation but was home to many other tribes as well including Hopi and Zuni. The county seat of McKinley County (named after President William McKinley), Gallup's area was a modest thirteen square miles with a population of around 17,000. Gallup itself was established in 1881 and named after David Gallup, a paymaster for the Atlantic and Pacific Railroad. Route 66's parallel road, Route 666, angered a number of people who associated that number with Satan and devil worship, the Number of the Beast. So far, petitions to have that road's name changed had been unsuccessful. The *Southwest Chief* train line opened in 1974 and runs like Route 66 through Gallup from Chicago to L.A. It is considered one of the most scenic train lines and provides spectacular views of the Painted Desert and the Red Cliffs of Sedona, as well as the plains of Iowa, Kansas and Colorado.

Besides being a hotspot for Indian residents and culture, Gallup lays claim to a large number of notable buildings, people, and events. Film director D.W. Griffith's brother built the historic El Rancho Hotel, which opened in 1937 as a base for movie operations. Films included *The Bad Man* (1940), *The Streets of Laredo* (1948), *Ace in the Hole* (1951), and *The Hallelujah Trail* (1964). Famous guests included Ronald Reagan, Jane Wyman, Spencer Tracy, Katharine Hepburn, Alan Ladd, and the king of western movies himself, John Wayne.

Gallup has an historic lack of sustainable economic development, and much of its economy came from the surrounding mines. Mine closures dominoed one after another, leaving a large portion of the population living in very low-income conditions. Along with the often poverty-level existence of too many people, crime shot up and Gallup was sadly infamous for its number of serious crimes like rape, murder, robbery, and aggravated assault. However, it was also known as the name of three Navy ships commissioned between 1917 and 1977. Unlike Santa Fe, in World War II Gallup fought successfully to prevent Japanese-Americans from being interned; it was the only New Mexico city to do so.

With a semi-arid climate, Gallup has most of its rain in the summer, but today the dew and puddles were still drying out after a midnight thunderstorm. The air smelled heavy with moisture, but at the same time the coolness was refreshing. The sky was still a little overcast, but the clouds were breaking up rapidly and the day promised to be sunny with bright blue skies. Winter was another matter, with Gallup's elevation of 6,500 feet above sea level often enticing snow that could fall up to several feet.

There were many small businesses and shops and eateries on the outskirts coming into the city and Nick pulled over into the parking lot of a pancake house. He and Sand hit the restrooms before sliding into a booth and ordering an immense breakfast. All of the employees seemed to be Indians and their waitress could have been Blue Corn's daughter with her size, gait, and welcoming smile. They took a good hour to eat and discuss their plan for the day. Sand agreed with Nick that searching public records would be time-consuming and their best bet was to hit the reservation and see if they could find a female teacher with the married or maiden name of Quará.

The waitress gave them directions and they headed back to the road and kept moving towards the city proper. They took Exit 20 and headed north on Munoz Boulevard until they reached the Overpass Intersection of Highway 491 and State Route 264, around seven miles north of Gallup. They saw the signs for the reservation.

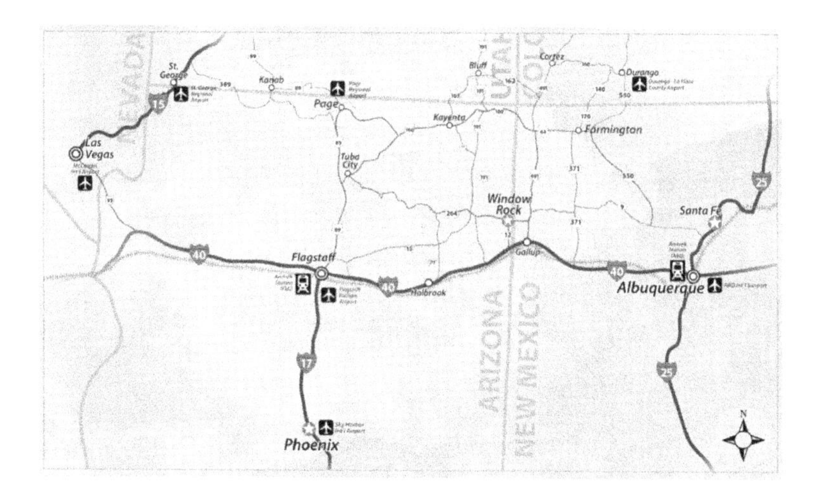

"Hehewuti told me the rez is 27,000 square miles," Sand said. "It's larger than a lot of states and hits two states besides New Mexico—Utah and Arizona."

"I never thought about it," Nick said, "but is 'Navajo' an Indian word?"

"Not according to Memphis's mom. The Navajo people call themselves the Diné, which in their language means 'the people.' When those adorable Spanish conquerors invaded the southwest they began calling them Navajo. Between the Spaniards and the U.S. government the Navajo have put up with a shitload of cruelty, betrayal, disrespect, and land theft. Hehewuti told me about the Army forcing more than 8,000 Navajo on the Long Walk to Bosque Redondo near Fort Sumner, where they were incarcerated for four years before being allowed to return to their homeland. The Navajos and the U.S. government signed the Treaty of 1868. I'll leave it to you to figure out if the government kept all of their written and verbal promises."

"Pretty sure they didn't," Nick replied, shaking his head.

"The Indians have a lot of reason to hate us," Sand said. "Hehewuti was born on the rez and she and Jakub met in a bar in Gallup when she was nineteen. She knew him maybe two hours before she dumped her fiancé and ran off to Hollywood with a perfect stranger. That was nearly forty years ago."

Sand turned off the 264 onto 491 and headed west, following signs that pointed to cultural interests and businesses such as the reservation information center. Sand pulled into the parking lot and they went inside. The man behind the desk wasn't outright hostile, but there was definitely no welcoming smile. Sand walked up to the counter and smiled, then nodded.

"Yá'át'ééh abíní," Sand said, hoping his Navajo words and inflection were correct or at least not offensive.

"Good morning to you, too," the man said in perfect English. "You speak the language of the Diné?"

"A few words," Sand said. "A friend taught me some basic phrases."

The man switched to his birth language. "Haash yinílyé?"

"My name is Sand Hazelwood. This is my partner, Nick Griffin."

"Yá'át'ééh," Nick said, stumbling over the vowels and pauses. He looked abashed. "That's all I know."

The man grunted. "Peshlakai Ahiga yinishyé."

"How would you like to be addressed?" Sand asked politely.

"Call me Ahiga. Now, what can I do for you?"

Sand pulled out his identification and showed it to Ahiga. "We're from Santa Fe and we're trying to track down a woman who supposedly was educated here and may work as a teacher on the rez. All we have is a possible last name."

"Why are you looking for her?" There was a touch of suspicion in Ahiga's voice.

"We're trying to get some background on her brother. He's involved in one of our cases and much of his past seems to be a mystery."

"Perhaps a mystery that should remain such."

"Perhaps. If she doesn't want to talk about him we'll respect that and go away. We mean her neither disrespect nor harm."

Ahiga kept his eyes locked with Sand's, taking in the measure of the man. He read truth in Sand's face. "We have many schools not only in Gallup but all over the Navajo Nation. Are you sure she's teaching on the rez and not in the city?"

Sand shook his head. "All we have is a Taos Pueblo citizen's distant memory. We're not sure about anything. We believe her maiden name is Quará."

"She's from Taos?"

"Pretty sure," Nick said.

"How old is she?"

"We're not positive, but I'd say in her mid- to late-thirties."

"Well, that could narrow it down. We keep records of our educators and where they originated from. I need some time to make a few calls and see if I can get a list. I'll need a couple of hours. Come back at one."

Sand stuck out his hand and Ahiga shook it. "Thank you. Thank you very much. Any suggestions as to cultural places around here we could explore and grasp a better understanding of your culture?"

Ahiga took out a map and unfolded it. It was a fifty-mile-by-fifty-mile sightseeing map of the Gallup area and places of interest. He took out a yellow marker and highlighted several places. "Window Rock's not a bad drive and you can see the Navajo Nation Museum and Library, Ch'ihootso Indian Marketplace, Navajo Nation Zoo, and the tribal headquarters. That should keep you busy for a few hours. Why don't you make it two o'clock instead?" He handed the map to Sand and the two P.I.s thanked him again and left the building.

Sand and Nick narrowed the list to two places since it would take time to drive across the Arizona border and back, and they didn't want to give them short shrift. They headed to the Navajo Nation Museum, which was fascinating beyond their expectations. The museum collects items that document the culture and history of the Navajo people, including selected materials from tribal and non-Indian neighbors. Its extensive holdings include artistic, ethnographic, archaeological, and archival materials. These include over 40,000 photographs and a wide variety of documents, recordings, motion picture film, and videos. The archives are heavily used by authors, researchers, and publishers as a source for historical photographs. They are definitely an eye-opener for any white person who is ignorant of the beauty of the indigenous people living and developing before Columbus first hit the shores of "the New World."

They spent more time than they had anticipated and had to rush to experience the Ch'ihootso Indian Marketplace. The marketplace was huge and had vendors from multiple tribes with every cultural object that anyone could want to buy. There were booths for silver jewelry, blankets, rugs, weapons, turtle rattles, mandalas, totem poles, handmade furniture, headdresses, cheap tchotchkes that were obviously made overseas, and anything else a person could imagine. Both Sand and Nick loaded up on gifts for their kids and other family members, and Sand bought a beautiful silver and turquoise necklace for Hehewuti.

They made it back to the cultural center at three-ten, apologizing profusely to Ahiga. He just smiled; nice guys, but their white proclivities for obtaining material objects was clear as glass. He pulled out two cold water bottles from the mini-fridge under the counter and handed them off.

"I have good news and better news," Ahiga said cheerfully.

"What's the good news?" Sand asked as he swallowed half a bottle of water.

"Through my contacts I've found five currently active teachers that have either their maiden or married names as Quará. Three are in their thirties but the other two are in their sixties."

"What's the better news?" Nick asked eagerly.

"Only one of those three is from Taos. Aponi Nez, née Quará. She's thirty-seven, married to a full-blooded Navajo man—also a teacher—with three kids, twelve, eleven, and four. She teaches English and Indian History at a small school a few miles west of here."

"What does Aponi mean?" Sand asked.

"Butterfly," Ahiga replied. "I've never met her, but my friend says she has a stellar reputation." Ahiga handed Sand a piece of paper with a name, a phone number, and an address with directions on it.

Sand nodded and said to Ahiga, "Is there anything we can do for you or your people to thank you properly?"

"There's a donation box at the school. You could drop a few bucks in. As for me, you can level with me about what you're truly seeking."

Sand's eyes locked with Ahiga's and slowly nodded. "We're exploring the possibility that the brother may be responsible for multiple disappearances in Santa Fe and northern New Mexico. We're trying to find background on him to prove or disprove our theories."

"Interesting," Ahiga murmured. "I'm not sure whether or not to wish you luck, but I wish you good health and safety in your journey." He offered his hand and Sand and Nick gave it a vigorous, hard shake. He contemplated them thoughtfully as they left the building.

"Think she'll still be at the school this late in the day?" Nick asked as he shifted gears and pulled carefully out of the parking lot.

"Might as well check," Sand said as he studied the silver and turquoise money clip he'd bought for Akiro.

"Down the road we go," Nick said and headed west.

The directions were straightforward except for a few short turns once they got off the main road. The landscape was rather desolate, and all of a sudden there was a brightly painted adobe building with a school sign. Over to the side was a parking lot with a dozen cars or so, and in front of the building a rickety old yellow school bus was being infused with Indian children ranging from five to twelve. The bus driver was a middle-aged man with long salt-and-pepper hair and a leather vest. Two women and one man were helping the students to board. Sand and Nick waited until that was done and the bus began rumbling away before they cautiously approached the three teachers.

"Yá'át'ééh," Sand said to a full complement of suspicious faces. "We're looking for Aponi Nez."

"What do you want with her?" the man asked crossly.

"To ask her a few questions. We're not cops or FBI and we have no intention of causing trouble. We just want to talk."

The man scowled and made a short move forward before the taller woman put a gentle hand on his arm and nodded to the white men.

"I'm Aponi Nez. And who are you?" She was clearly not intimidated by them. She was very tall for an Indian woman, five-eight in flats, and had shoulder-length ebony hair parted in the middle and draped plainly down the sides of her head. Her deep-set brown eyes were focused on them and Sand thought that there was very little this woman would miss.

Sand and Nick took out their P.I. credentials and she studied them carefully.

"You said you weren't cops," she said with a hint of accusation.

"We're private, and the cops we do know would be insulted if we put ourselves in the same category," Nick said with a genuine smile. She didn't smile back.

Suddenly she turned to her two colleagues and spoke softly to them in Navajo. They both scowled at the visitors but turned to go back into the school.

Aponi crossed her arms tightly. “What kind of questions did you want to ask me?”

“About your family,” Sand said.

“My husband and children?” She didn’t mention that the man who had just left was her husband, Aditsan Nez.

Sand shook his head. “No. Your birth family.” He could see that she froze at those words. Her eyes bored into his and a veneer of hostility passed over the glorious brown orbs. When she didn’t respond he added, “Specifically, about your brother, Antonio, otherwise known as Hashkeh Naabah.”

Aponi blinked then uncrossed her arms. “Let’s go inside,” she said quietly and turned towards the front door.

“You can’t park there, ma’am,” Officer Luc Grayhawk said to the turned back of Chelan Chee.

Chelan turned slowly and flashed him the most derogatory look he had ever encountered, even deadlier than the look Miss Finn had given him when he’d poured Aunt Jemima syrup in her classroom desk. “My car’s parked legally,” she spat out.

Luc whipped out his ticket book and began writing. “You’re barely three feet away from the fire hydrant. License and registration please.”

“Fuck off, pig,” Chelan shot back.

Luc stopped writing and tucked his ticket book away. He pulled out his handcuffs. “Turn around, please,” he said very politely. He stepped towards her then clapped his hands over his ears.

“Police brutality,” she screamed, waving her arms in the air. “Police brutality.”

People stopped on the sidewalks and watched the weird scenario play out. A few of them had wide grins plastered on their amused faces. A few weren’t sure who to root for, the cop or the fierce Indian girl.

Luc sighed and reached into his patrol car for his walkie-talkie. He identified himself to the dispatcher and ordered a tow truck.

Chelan hissed. "You are not towing my truck, you goose-stepping Nazi," she snarled.

"Yes, ma'am, I am," Luc replied very evenly. "But I'll give you a choice—a ticket, or a trip to the pokey. What'll it be?"

Chelan was seething and actually bared her teeth. She hissed in a loud breath and said icily, "Give me the fucking ticket."

Luc nodded. "Yes, ma'am. License and registration, please."

Chelan stood there steaming as he wrote out the ticket, finishing just as the tow truck appeared. The tow guy jumped out and deftly hooked up her car and began driving away. Luc smiled, ripped the ticket out of the book, and handed it to her.

"Have a nice day, ma'am," he said, tipping his hat and getting back in his police car.

Chelan watched him drive off and shot out both arms, flashing the back of his police car with double middle fingers. She whirled around and stalked into the building.

She checked the occupant list and saw that Warrior Spirit Investigations was on the third floor. A doctor's clinic and a psychology practice were on the first floor and a law office on the second. She eschewed elevators (the white man's invention) and took the stairs. When she got through the staircase door she saw an old guy near what looked to be a receptionist's desk and she walked over to him.

"I'm looking for Swan Hazelwood," Chelan demanded.

"Good for you, Pocahontas," Frack said.

"Are you the secretary?" she snarked.

"No, I'm the French chef they imported from Paris. Can I get you a plate of snails?"

Chelan was taken aback by the man's quick wit and refusal to back down under her nasty onslaught. She calmed herself and asked semi-respectfully, "Is Swan Hazelwood available for a meeting?"

Frack grunted and moved towards the offices' hallway. "I'll check on my way to see if my frog's legs have finished broiling. Bon appetit." He shuffled off to Swan's office, leaving Chelan standing in the middle of the room with her mouth open.

He knocked briskly on Swan's door then opened it. She looked up from her desk. "Some snotty Indian girl wants to talk to you."

"She give her name?" Swan asked.

"I didn't ask."

"Why not?"

"I didn't care. Should I send her in?"

Swan gave him "the look" then nodded. A few minutes later Frack deposited Chelan into Swan's office.

Swan's eyebrows shot up. "Never thought I'd see you again and that you'd come here. Aren't you worried about being in enemy territory?"

"I've survived worse than you," Chelan said as she parked herself in a chair.

"Why are you here?"

Chelan grunted and took out a folder she had in her shoulder satchel. "I thought I'd heard the name Antonio Quará before and I went digging." She flipped open the folder. "The name was from way back in the early eighteenth century, around 1720 to be exact. The governor of New Mexico, one Antonio de Valverde y Cossio, signed a punishment edict against a Juan del Alamo, who brought peyote he'd gotten from the Hopi into the pueblo. He sentenced Juan to fifty lashes and expulsion from the pueblo."

"Are we talking about the Taos Pueblo?"

"Yes. This Juan had given some peyote to a couple of other Puebloans and encouraged them to use it. One of the men was named either Cristobal or Aristoval Teajaya. The other man was named Antonio Quará. These two men consumed the peyote and supposedly had visions. They tried to entice the Taos population to revolt against their Spanish overlords as well as prepare for an attack against the Ute. The tribal leaders rejected their prophecies and condemned them as crazy. They turned the men over to the Spanish for trial."

"Were they subjected to fifty lashes, too?"

"I couldn't find any documents to verify that. But, I think it may be safe to assume that this Antonio might be an ancestor to the guy on your list." Chelan handed over the folder to Swan.

Swan glanced at the pages then looked up. "Thank you. How can I repay you?"

Chelan's lip curled. "A Nazi cop ticketed me and had my car towed. I need to get it out of impound. I'd appreciate a lift."

"You got it," Swan said, standing. She checked her watch. "It's almost noon. How about lunch then I'll drive you over? My treat."

"As long as it's not a plate of snails," Chelan muttered, rising. She saw the curious look on Swan's face. "Don't ask."

Swan stopped in the hallway and rapped sharply on Memphis's door then went in with Chelan following.

"Buttercup," she said sweetly, "I'd like you to meet Chelan Chee. She brought us some background on Antonio Quará."

Memphis stood up and walked around the desk, extending his hand. Chelan looked up and felt like she was a midget; she was five-foot-nothing and he had to be around six-four. Also, he was drop-dead handsome and looked like an Indian warrior. She was tongue-tied.

"Pleased to meet you," Memphis said. "Thanks for the information." He looked at Swan.

"I'll tell you later," Swan said. "Right now, we're going out to lunch. I'll be back in a couple of hours. The folder is on my desk if you want a look. Ta-ta."

When they got to the parking lot Chelan said, "Your husband is …"

"One damned fine Injun," Swan finished.

They had a great lunch at a hole-in-the-wall that served American and Indian food. Afterwards Swan drove Chelan to the impound lot where she went in to pay the towing fee. Swan stood near her car, sticking around in case there was a problem. Suddenly a pair of strong hands covered her eyes and that shit-eating voice said, "Boo."

"Turkey," Swan said crossly to Luc. "What are you doing here?"

"Checking on a couple of cars I had towed," he replied.

"Towed?" Swan repeated, then broke out into a grin. "One wouldn't happen to belong to a tiny female Indian with a mouth like Lenny Bruce?"

"Sounds about right. Do you know her?"

At that moment Chelan stalked out of the office with her car keys and paid slip. She stopped dead in her tracks at the sight of Luc.

"That's the Nazi cocksucker that towed my car," she spat out, her eyes firing off laser bolts of distaste that might have cowed a lesser man.

"Nice to see you, too, ma'am," Luc said tipping his hat.

"You know this prick?" Chelan said to Swan.

Swan fought back a laugh. "This prick is my brother-in-law. Chelan Chee, meet Luc Grayhawk."

CHAPTER SEVEN

Naabah had been holed up in the cave for three days now, feverishly working on his two projects. He used the dwarf's bones as a special centerpiece and was pleased with the result. He was hesitant about using those bones as a focal point in his other art, which he began to paint from the outside edges inwards instead of vice versa. The canvas was six-foot-by-four-foot, and it was somewhere around ninety percent completed. Eventually it would be completed although the bones had nearly an infinite amount of space remaining to capture their essence. He felt a dreaded sense of urgency, but he pushed that to the back of his mind and concentrated on getting as much done as possible.

He leaned in and studied the edge of the empty central space, came to a decision, then dipped his brush into a dove grey palate and meticulously drew a very thin outline of the dwarf's skull smack dab in the middle. This man's skull was shaped differently than Percy's with a much more elongated jaw and prominent skull top. At least the dwarf was a quick defleshing and was a very unusual addition to his art, although the bowlegged guy he took in Gallup a few years earlier had a certain panache.

He very carefully drew the outline of the skull before he began filling in the details, shading the eye sockets to provide depth. He used four different paint brushes, each thinner with a smaller brush to minimize errors outside the clean lines. Unlike his pueblos and landscapes, he couldn't use broad strokes to simulate reality and impressionism. Rather than painting a singular line for the edges, he decided to try a new technique wherein he'd do dashes of paint a sixteenth of an inch long and the same for the width to form an impressionist outline of the skull. When he finished covering the initial thin outline with his paint dashes, he sat back and studied his work, pleased with the outcome.

Naabah checked his watch and saw that he had been working on the painting for five hours, which had flown by. The cave was well illuminated with electrical wiring and lights hooked up to a gas generator, but by now it would be dark outside. He thought about returning to his campsite close by, but he was tired and decided to spend the night in a sleeping bag here in his "studio."

He was hungry so he broke out a large can of tuna fish in oil and scarfed it down with water. He walked the perimeter of the cave walls and noted a few areas that had to be repositioned for best effect. He stood in front of the painting for ten solid minutes, taking in the precision and symmetry. He turned the light down low and snuggled into his sleeping bag. He stared up at the ceiling for a long time, thinking. The beauty of his art was something he greatly admired—*he*. He found himself wanting to share his accomplishments with someone who could appreciate his talent and vision.

The problem was that whoever he shared his art with couldn't be allowed to tell anyone about it. That person would have to die. And except for that unlucky bout of collateral damage with the two young men, he'd prefer to keep to his code. So, he would have to select a victim that deserved inclusion, but beforehand could be exposed to the cave and the painting. Now, the painting he could take home with him because he could explain it away as a concept he was compelled to actualize. He needed to finish the painting; the other art would always be wanting for completion.

He fell asleep contemplating the options. He slept for eight hours, awakening to a glorious fall day with blue skies and cool breezes. He'd work for a few hours and then return home. Perhaps he'd have an epiphany. He had a few peyote buttons and those would definitely help. Sometimes they gave him visions that impacted his art.

"I asked Mrs. Nez if she minded being recorded and she was reluctant at first but then agreed," Sand said as he placed the small recorder on the conference room table. The full contingent of partners were there, along with Frick and Frack. Tucson and Percy were also in attendance to provide any psychological insight. Sand and Nick had returned from Gallup two days earlier and had briefed Memphis on their journey and meeting, but they wanted time to listen to the recording themselves and make careful notes.

"What was your impression of her?" Tucson asked.

"Smart woman, intelligent, organized, proud of her culture. She had several framed prints on her walls from Indian artists but, oddly enough, not one of Naabah's. She was taller than many Indian woman, with an athletic build and every hair in place. Minimal makeup. I can't pinpoint my finger on it, but she seemed tightly wound," Sand said.

"Did you get any impressions by the way she talked about her brother?" Percy asked.

"Besides some of what she said we got the impression that they weren't close and liked it that way," Nick replied.

"Let's hear the interview," Swan said.

Sand turned the volume up and hit Play. His voice came on first.

SAND: Today is Tuesday, September 12, 1978. My name is Sand Hazelwood and my partner is Nick Griffin. We represent the Warrior Spirit Investigations firm and are interviewing Mrs. Aponi Nez in her office at the Gallup Progressive School northwest of the city. Mrs. Nez—are you amenable to having this conversation recorded?

APONI: Yes. You may call me Aponi.

SAND: Thank you, Aponi. We'd like to start with the basics. Was your maiden name Quará?

APONI: Yes.

SAND: Were you born and raised in the Taos Pueblo?

APONI: I was.

SAND: Do you have a brother whose birth name was Antonio Quará?

APONI: Yes.

NICK: Can you tell us about your nuclear family? Parents and siblings?

APONI: My parents were Isabella and Antonio Quará. My father died in a barroom brawl when I was eleven months old. My mother died of liver cancer when I was around seven. My brother Antonio was the only boy in the family. I had three older sisters, Alisha, Anika, and Amara. My oldest sister, Anika, died in childbirth, and an older sister by twelve months, Amoli, died in infancy.

NICK: Are Alisha and Amara still alive?

APONI: I believe so, but I haven't had any contact with them since I was a kid. Antonio found them husbands and one moved to the Zia Pueblo and the other moved to Acoma.

SAND: What was your brother like as a child?

APONI: I never knew him as a child. He was twelve when our father was killed and from that moment on he became the man of the house and his childhood evaporated. For all intents and purposes, he acted as a father to me. He didn't show much affection and was always serious and focused on providing for us. He didn't have time to be a kid. Maybe that's why he never married or had children—he'd already fulfilled those purposes with our family.

SAND: Did he ever have any girlfriends?

APONI: I don't think so. Sometimes he'd come home in the middle of the night smelling of perfume, and I assume those were simply one-night stands.

NICK: After he married off the other sisters he found a church group to educate you, didn't he?

APONI: How did you know that?

SAND: We interviewed a few people in Taos who remembered your family.

APONI: Interesting. Yes, he found a church group and left me with them while he went back home.

SAND: Was that an acceptable experience?

APONI: In the long run, yes. I got a good education and became a teacher. I met my husband during my first teaching year. A few years later we married. We have three children.

SAND: Have your husband or kids ever met your brother?

APONI: No. I tried to get ahold of him for our wedding but couldn't.

NICK: Do people know that you're Hashkeh Naabah's sister?

APONI: Very few. My husband, of course, and one or two close friends, but that's it. I just … I just felt like keeping my private life private without being associated with a well-known painter.

SAND: When's the last time you spoke to him?

APONI: I can barely remember. Maybe … five years ago?

NICK: You're not close?

APONI: No. Our family just … split apart after my father was killed. I've learned to put the past in the past.

SAND: What can you tell us about your brother? Anything—his thoughts, actions, beliefs, prejudices, anything like that. How does he feel about white people?

APONI: I'm not sure what to say. That's an odd thing to ask.

NICK: Anything you can remember will be helpful.

APONI: Well, he grew up through the Depression where dirt-poor was the norm. The forties when I grew up weren't much better. We were uniformly looked down upon by white people. Even those that were tasked with helping our culture rarely moved past bare tolerance. We had the misfortune of having our father killed by a white man.

SAND: What happened in the bar?

APONI: According to my brother many years later a white guy drunk to the gills started calling the Indians in the bar ugly names and particularly homed in on our women. Someone threw a punch and fifteen minutes later my father lay dead on the floor with his head caved in by a baseball bat. All the white guys said our father started the fight. No one was arrested let alone prosecuted. And that situation played out many other times. Justice was not a familiar commodity for our people.

SAND: Did Antonio ever evince any hatred of whites to the point where he wanted to pay them back for the injustices?

APONI: Sure. He spoke ill of them and said the time was coming for retribution. Many of our men did. But Antonio at least had an outlet for his anger.

SAND: His paintings.

APONI: Yes. He was good at art from the time I understood the craft. He'd sell some rudimentary paintings to tourists to make extra money.

SAND: What else did he do to make money? (long pause) Aponi, it's okay if you don't answer.

APONI: It's a sore subject, but sometimes he … ran drugs to bring in fast cash. Alcohol, too. Those were the last things my people needed but Antonio was determined to provide or his family with little regard for anyone else's.

SAND: What kinds of drugs?

APONI: Marijuana, some peyote buttons, a few magic mushrooms. Nothing hard like heroin.

NICK: Did he ever use the drugs himself?

APONI: He'd smoke a joint on occasion, and he liked the peyote. He said it gave him visionary clarity, whatever that means.

SAND: In his art, did he ever work with bones?

APONI: Bones?

SAND: Yes. Did he ever put bones in his paintings?

APONI: I don't … think so.

SAND: Ever know him to buy dermestid beetles?

APONI: What? What are those?

SAND: Not really important now. It's just an organic method some artists use in their work.

Sand stopped the tape and took out a few photos of Naabah's paintings. "I showed her these and pointed out the hidden bones."

APONI: That's peculiar. Maybe he felt it was a signature he wanted to adopt for whatever reason.

NICK: Why did he change his name from Antonio Quará to Hashkeh Naabah?

APONI: I asked him that once and he said he wanted his past to be anonymous and establish himself with a fresh perspective, including his name. It means angry warrior in Navajo.

SAND: Was he an angry warrior?

APONI: Maybe. He hated the trials we went through as Indians and the death of our father, and the way the white culture has treated Native Americans since they invaded our country.

SAND: Did he think of white people as invaders?

APONI: We all do. But most of us have come to grips with the fact that you're not leaving.

SAND: This next question may seem strange, but I've got to ask it. Would Antonio ever physically harm someone he thought was harming or disrespecting your culture?

APONI: Why are you asking that? Do you suspect my brother of some violence? (voice hard and suspicious)

SAND: You've been honest with me, so I'll be honest with you. Yes. We think that he may have harmed people he thought were disrespecting your culture.

APONI: Harmed how?

NICK: We're investigating multiple disappearances of people who may have riled his cultural pride. Two missing people vanished after a visit to the Taos Pueblo.

APONI: And you think Antonio is responsible?

SAND: Certain aspects suggest it, but we have no proof. (pause) Can you honestly say Antonio would never hurt another human being?

APONI: (long silence) No. No, I can't. I've seen him angry, and once I saw him beat the shit out of a teenage white boy that hurled a squaw insult at me. But kill someone? I don't … I don't know.

SAND: Would you be willing to help us find out?

APONI: How?

SAND: Do you know of any places he might take someone? A second residence, maybe? A special camping spot?

APONI: I don't think he has any secondary living place. He has a house close by the pueblo that he's had for ten or fifteen years. He actually put my name on the title in case anything ever happened to him.

SAND: You're on the title?

APONI: Yes, why?

NICK: As a legal owner of the house you could give us permission to search it.

APONI: I don't know … It seems like an invasion of privacy. And you have no concrete proof that he's done anything criminal.

SAND: We would search it while he's away and leave it exactly as we found it. And if we find nothing incriminating then he drops off our list as a suspect. But if we do find something … these people deserve justice.

APONI: I don't know.

NICK: Please.

Sand stopped the tape and took out a half dozen photos of missing persons, including the San Ramon teens and the San Francisco couple. "We showed her these."

SAND: These people had families that loved them, and they'll never have closure until we can find out what happened to them and hopefully bring them home. Imagine if one of your kids went missing.

APONI: That's a shitty way to solicit my help.

SAND: We're desperate. I'm sorry. Look. I've got an eight-year-old son and if he vanished I'd spend every second of my life searching for him. Those are not the types of losses that ever heal. (Long pause and then the sound of typewriter keys clattering, and moments later a piece of paper being torn out of the typewriter)

APONI: You have my permission to search the house. If Antonio ever finds out what I've done he'll hate me forever for breaching his privacy.

SAND: If we find nothing it'll never come to light.

APONI: And if you do?

SAND: Then justice will take its course. I think we're done here.

APONI: You'll let me know what happens before anything goes public?

NICK: Absolutely. Thank you.

APONI: I pray you find nothing.

SAND: I know.

Sand shut off the tape and leaned back in his chair. "What do you think?" he said.

"I think," Memphis said slowly, "you hit paydirt. You come up with a plan for getting into Naabah's house?"

"We went up yesterday and discreetly scoped it out so we could get the lay of the land," Nick said. "It's a little out in the open but there are a dozen or so houses close enough to be considered neighbors. We hid out a few miles away until after midnight and when we drove by his house it was dark and so were most of the others. Early to bed, I guess. Two houses had dim lights over their front doors, but none of those doors opened up to the back of his house."

"We parked a half mile down and walked to the back of his house and found two rectangular windows apparently in the basement that we could enter," Sand said. "I didn't see any evidence of electronic security like an alarm system."

"We didn't hear any barking, either," Nick added. "We've come up with a tentative plan."

"Before we confirm any breaking and entering plans," Memphis said, "let's take a crack at the psychological impacts of that interview and information. Percy—got any insight?"

"Based on my past knowledge of him, talking with him, seeing his art, and what the sister told us, I'm not sure I could make a definitive evaluation," Percy said.

"If you throw certainty to the wind, what would be your tentative analysis?"

"Well, he certainly fits into our previous profile of the perpetrator, and what his sister said confirms that. I'd say that besides being an injustice collector he also sees himself as an overall avenger for his people, and that works into narcissism. He's full of himself and feels his actions are totally justified. Do I think he's finished with his work? No. I think there'll be more victims unless he's stopped."

"How do the bones fit in?" Frick asked.

Tucson said, "Trophies, but perhaps something else. Perhaps he uses bones in some private ritual to celebrate his victories over bad white people."

"He's having the beetles eat the dead bodies so he can used their bones," Frack said quietly, with a touch of horror.

"This is all just speculation," Memphis said. He nodded at Sand. "Tell us your plan."

Sand rolled out a hand-drawn map of Naabah's home and neighborhood.

"Here's what we plan to do," Sand said as all eyes fell on the map.

CHAPTER EIGHT

It was a full moon Saturday night, with the desert soon to seem like it was lit by floodlights even though the sun hadn't set at 7 PM. The blanket of stars popping out in the sky would add to the soft contrast of light and dark once night had fallen. People were out celebrating Mexican Independence Day in bars, restaurants, and homes, reveling in the rich Spanish culture and richer Spanish food.

The side porch of the McBean Victorian was set with a table and fine linens and heavy brown stoneware plates decorated with red kokopellis. There were several white candles illuminating the table and the outline of the porch itself was rimmed with white lights not only to provide light but to increase the festive nature of the dinner. The water glasses were cut crystal, and the flatware was silver. Several platters of food were already set in the middle, and then Tansee brought out the last dishes, which held traditional Indian food like stuffed squash blossoms. Despite the fact that the day should have been centered around Mexican food she stated that this was a half-Indian household and as such she reserved the right to add a little bit of her culture's traditions, too. No one who ever had Tansee's cooking would even want to disagree.

Baby Ben was in his crib just inside the house, ten feet from the table. The table was set for four—Tansee, Percy, Elspeth, and Hashkeh Naabah. Percy had invited the artist and been insistent that he join the family for a nice, quiet dinner and good conversation. Naabah had been hesitant, but he decided to come out of his privacy shell and enjoy the company of people he genuinely liked. He had met Percy for coffee several times and he found the dwarf an intelligent conversationalist.

Tansee placed the last bowl down on the table and seated herself. She smiled at their guest. "I'm sorry that we don't know any puebloan prayers, but Elspeth has been practicing one from our Navajo people. I hope you will enjoy this." She nodded to her seven-year-old daughter, who stood and put her hands together. Elspeth's voice was true and rarely hesitant as she spoke English and Navajo words.

"In beauty I walk
With beauty before me I walk
With beauty behind me I walk
With beauty above me I walk
With beauty around me I walk
It has become beauty again
It has become beauty again
It has become beauty again
It has become beauty again
Hózhóogo naasháa doo
Shitsijí' hózhóogo naasháa doo
Shikéédéé hózhóogo naasháa doo
Shideigi hózhóogo naasháa doo
T'áá altso shinaagóó hózhóogo naasháa doo
Hózhó náhásdlíí'
Hózhó náhásdlíí'
Hózhó náhásdlíí'
Hózhó náhásdlíí'
Be blessed!"

She smiled brightly when she finished. Naabah leaned towards her and took her hand. "That was beautiful, Elspeth," he said. "You are truly a wondrous credit to our people."

"Thank you. Mr. Naabah," she said shyly then sat back down. She glanced across from her and smiled at her father, who was looking at her with eyes full of love and pride.

Tansee said, "We want to be sure that our daughter and son understand the beauty of their maternal culture and understand that they are representatives of their race when they speak or act. My mother lives in Gallup and when we visit she teaches Elspeth how to say prayers and how to dance. After dinner, if you have the time, we'd love to have you watch her version of the Basket Dance. It's a ceremony of blessing and also lays out the history of the Navajo people."

"I'd be privileged," Naabah said.

"Okay, folks," Percy said. "Let's dig in. Elspeth, pass me your plate, please."

Percy filled his daughter's plate and watched as Naabah dug into the delectable food. He kept his facial expression neutral and hoped that he didn't give away the fact that his task in "Operation Pueblo Bones" was to keep Naabah away from Taos. He was supposed to keep Naabah occupied and away from his home until at least ten o'clock. That would only give the "A Team" less than two hours to search the house since sunset wasn't until 7:09 PM, and even then it took at least a half hour longer for true night to fall. Percy was to call Naabah's home phone and let it ring four times, hang up, then dial again and let it ring twice if the painter was on his way home.

"Hashkeh," Percy said, "tell us about how you choose your subjects and select the perfect colors." The ploy worked; Naabah slowed his eating as he waxed about his techniques and subjects. Percy smiled approvingly. Three hours. He needed to keep Naabah here for at least three hours.

Sand and Nick were finishing up a late dinner at a diner on the outskirts of Taos. Nick kept checking his watch until Sand snapped at him to knock it off. They planned on driving to Naabah's house after eight-fifteen. One aspect of their original plan was modified when Aponi surprised them by Federal Expressing them a copy of a house key that her brother had given her years ago. They wouldn't have to break in through the basement window, but they still kept that as Plan B. Aponi had had the key for years and in that time Naabah could have changed the locks.

"If you check that watch one more time," Sand growled low, "I'll rip it off your wrist and throw it in the iced tea pitcher."

"Typical Nazi cop practices," Nick said, scowling. "You haven't changed your core values in all these years."

"Says the smelly hippie called Renegade," Sand shot back, almost smiling. If anyone had ever told him that he and Nick would one day be partners in a P.I. firm, he would have said they were crazy. In 1965 as a detective Sand had arrested Nick for the murder of a young hippie girl called Starbird. Nick had worn-out clothes, long hair and an unkempt beard, and smoked pot while he lived in a commune on the outskirts of Santa Fe. Sand was a button-down detective hiding the secret of his sexuality. Nick was released when it was clear that he hadn't murdered anyone; Sand had been kicked off the police force when the infamous serial killer Joanna Frid had outed him to his captain. Now, the ex-hippie and ex-cop were partners, working in sync, respecting each other, and having each other's back.

Nick rolled his eyes and pulled his sleeve over his wrist. "Happy?" he asked.

"Thrilled beyond words. So. What time is it?"

"Seven-fifty."

Sand signaled the waitress and ordered two helpings of Dutch apple pie. They finished and paid for the meal at 8:05 PM then headed out to the car. They were using Sand's car, a black Ford Bronco, since in the rarified neighborhood where their target lived a flashy Corvette would've stood out and be remembered.

Sand turned off the main road onto the long dirt road that led to Naabah's house. He drove a mile past the house to the end of the dirt road where there weren't any residences. To Sand's and Nick's shock there was an SUV parked at the end, its engine and lights turned off. Sand heard Nick's gun click and he reached for his own. As they slowly got out of the car the SUV's driver's door opened and a tall figure dressed completely in black stepped out. They were dressed in black, too. Sand relaxed and groaned when he recognized the unexpected visitor and car.

"What are you doing here?" Sand demanded quietly.

"I lost the coin toss," Memphis said. "Swan got to stay home with the kids."

"Don't you trust us?" Nick said with his eyes narrowed.

"Without reservation," Memphis replied. "But this is dicey, and I wanted to make sure you had backup. This is your operation."

Sand nodded and said, "Let's go."

The three men jogged quickly down the road for the mile that brought them to the back of Naabah's house. Several houses down—more than a half mile—there were a couple of dim lights but no sign of people walking around. They stopped walking around fifty yards from the house and finished the journey by belly-crawling over the sand and rocks (and a prickly cactus or two) before reaching the back door. When they stood they simultaneously snapped on latex gloves. Silently, Sand pulled Aponi's key from his vest pocket and very carefully inserted it into the lock.

It didn't turn.

"Shit," Nick hissed. A second later Memphis smacked his shoulder and held up a small bottle of WD-40 lubricant spray he had in his backpack. Sand grinned and sprayed the lock then reinserted the key. They all held their breath while Sand turned the key. With a little jiggling, the lock opened and there was a collective sigh. They entered like wraiths and closed the door behind them. All three fixed the night goggles on their faces, and the kitchen was illuminated with the green glow that semi-simulated daytime, at least enough to move through the house with confidence and some clarity.

"Where do we start?" Nick whispered.

"Don't you have a logistics plan?" Memphis asked.

"The plan was to get in and search the house," Sand whispered. "We planned on playing it by ear once we got in. Any suggestions?"

"Start from the ground up. Let's search the basement first." Memphis pointed to a door at the edge of the kitchen. "Let's try that door."

Sand gently tried turning the knob, but the door was locked. He tried the key but clearly it wasn't the same lock as the outside doors. Without missing a beat Sand pulled out his B&E tools and jimmied the lock. The door opened.

"You make a good burglar," Nick whispered. He winked at his partner.

Sand took a couple of steps down, followed by Nick then Memphis, who closed the door and felt around for a light switch. He was about to flip it on when Nick stopped him.

"Wait," Nick said.

"What?" Memphis asked.

"What if he's got this place booby-trapped? You remember what happened at the bunker. My brother almost died." Percy and Akiro had been exploring a hidden bunker that Joanna Frid used for her evil deeds; it was booby-trapped with a bomb and the two men barely escaped with their lives. Percy spent months in casts.

"We have to go on the assumption that he hasn't set any traps. Still, be careful," Memphis said. He moved to switch on the light when Sand said, "Wait."

"Now what?" Memphis growled.

Sand pointed west. "There are two windows over there. The light will shine through." The windows were made of thick frosted glass that let light in and out but prevented anyone outside from seeing into the basement.

Memphis rolled his eyes and looked around. He spotted several broken-down cardboard boxes leaning against a wall. He pointed to them. "We'll tape those over the windows. Search for tape."

Ten minutes later duct tape helped cover the windows with cardboard and the team moved to different areas of the large basement to search.

Sand had barely made it into his section when he stopped dead and said under his breath, "What the fuck? Guys—come over here." Memphis and Nick stood at his side and all three men looked down at the object set on cinderblocks.

"It's a goddamn coffin," Nick said. "A metal coffin." He glanced up to his left. "That looks like a small room. Pretty rudimentary and probably homemade."

"There's no lock on it," Memphis said as he turned the door handle and opened the door. There was an overhead light and he pulled the chain. They peered in.

There was an off-the-ground firepit made of cinderblocks. On the raised grate there was a big kettle with a cover on it. The firepit was linked up to a propane tank whose reading said it was half empty. Memphis carefully removed the top and stared down into the damp emptiness. "Something was boiled in here. Can you smell the bleach?"

"Yeah," Sand said as Nick snapped photos of the room. "Over there." He pointed to a cluster of bleach gallons near a corner of the tiny room. "Let's go look in the coffin."

"I'm not sure I want to," Nick muttered.

Sand stood over the coffin and took a deep breath, waited for Nick to take pictures, then popped the lock and threw the lid against the back.

"Eew," Nick said in disgust. "What are those?" He snapped five shots of the inside of the coffin.

"I'm not an entymologist," Memphis said, "but I'm thinking dead beetles. I'll put my money on dermestids."

"Do you hear that?" Nick said.

"What?" Sand said.

"I dunno. A kind of soft rustling. Over there."

Memphis and Sand followed Nick over to three large metal cannisters. Nick began shooting. One's top was open, and it was empty. He noticed that there were tiny air holes punched into the lids. Nick grunted as he tried to open the middle one, and finally the tight lid gave way. That one, too, was empty. Sand nodded at his partner and began unscrewing the third lid. As it came loose the rustling increased in volume and he paused.

"Open it," Memphis said impatiently.

"You open it," Sand said, backing away.

"Wuss," Memphis muttered then gave the lid a final rotation and pulled it off. He yelled as a dozen beetles flew out of the container, several landing on his legs as he frantically brushed them off. Dozens more began exiting before Nick slammed the lid back on and frantically turned it clockwise.

"Get the little fuckers," Memphis shouted, and all three men found themselves stomping and crushing.

"Disgusting," Nick said as dozens of beetles lay squashed on the floor. He snapped a dozen pictures of the floor and closeups of the beetles. He turned and looked at Memphis who was holding up a small jar in which a half dozen beetles were shimmying about. Nick grimaced and shuddered.

"All right, kids," Memphis said. "Let's clean up this floor." They used bandanas and paper towels that they'd brought with them and did a decent job of cleaning up. They cleaned the bottoms of their shoes so they wouldn't smear dead bug corpses over the floor.

They began searching every inch of the basement and Sand opened a cabinet in which there were lacquer and brushes. He carefully opened a lacquer bottle and dunked his handkerchief into it then put the bottle away. He put the handkerchief in a plastic evidence bag and tucked it into his backpack. Nick found several hairs that had been swept or misplaced against the wall and put them in another plastic bag.

They took a solid forty-five minutes to search the basement, then moved up to the first floor. The house was single-story and small, not more than a thousand square feet. Sand took the kitchen, Memphis took the spare bedroom and living room, and Nick searched the master bedroom and single bathroom. He found a floor safe under the nightstand, but there was no way to figure out the combination. He tried Naabah's birth date; no go. He tried Aponi's birth date; no luck there, either. He tried a few prominent dates in Indian history, but the lock stubbornly held.

Memphis came into the bedroom and stood over him, watching. "Try Columbus Day," he suggested. Nick nodded and turned 10-right, 12-left, and 92-right. There was a soft click and he grinned up at his friend. Memphis squatted and they looked into the safe, careful not to touch anything. Nick clicked off closeups, then shut the safe door, set the lock back to the number at which he started, and dragged the nightstand back over it.

Sand was standing at the bedroom door when they were all startled by the ringing phone. One, two, three, four, stop. Pause. One, two. Stop.

"He's on his way back," Memphis said. "We still have time, but I think we've gotten all we can out of the house. So, like the shepherd said to the sheep, let's get the flock outa here."

Sand and Nick groaned then laughed. They left by the rear door and crawled fifty yards before they rose and ran back to their cars. Before he drove off Memphis said, "We'll meet up at the office first thing. We'll develop the photos and analyze what we know or suspect."

He took off, then Sand drove carefully down the dirt road and minutes later was on the highway heading back to Santa Fe.

The cold night air whipped through the driver's window as Naabah drove home from his lovely evening out. He always enjoyed talking with Percy, and he was proud that Tansee was raising their daughter to appreciate her ancestors. The Basket Dance Elspeth did after dinner was adorable even though she missed few steps as she twirled and stomped in her traditional Indian costume. Afterwards she begged him to tell her a story about his people and he was thrilled to comply.

He told her that the Pueblos were a sedentary people who lived in towns and sustained themselves by planting corn and hunting small game. Scattered across hundreds of square miles, they spoke different languages and observed distinct customs. Their religious rituals, beliefs and practices were deeply embedded in their culture and way of life. In elaborate ceremonies, they honored the kachinas, the spirits of ancestors, in underground chambers known as kivas. These religious ceremonies were essential to sustaining the Pueblo way of life. He told her that the entire world was the Pueblos' religion from the very moment they wake up in the morning to the moment they go to bed; even when they are asleep, they are practicing their religion.

He promised that the next time he'd tell her about their gods and rituals. He could see she was excited and disappointed when Tansee hustled her off to bed. He commented on her spirit while he and Percy imbibed a final brandy. Tansee and Percy stood at their front door waving goodbye as he drove off.

The drive was fast and comfortable with the influx of fresh air and the peacefulness in his soul. He turned off the highway onto his dirt road and parked his car to the side of his house. He went inside and turned on the living room light. He stopped and frowned. Nothing was amiss but he sensed that someone had been in his house. He withdrew his Bowie knife from his belt and moved cautiously through the house, checking every room. There was no physical sign that anyone had been there, but he still had that nagging feeling.

He descended to the basement. Everything seemed to be in order. He shook his head; he was just imagining things.

Then he saw a beetle skitter across the floor.

CHAPTER NINE

Percy stopped dead in his tracks and stared at the man staring back at him from outside the elevator on the second floor. He was headed up to the Warrior Spirit offices and apparently this man was going there, too. The thing that stopped them both was the fact that the strange man was also a dwarf. Percy's rapid-fire ability to evaluate another person raked in the important details.

Early- to mid-thirties, an inch shorter than Percy, ash-blond hair with the back edges touching his collar and layered bangs reaching his eyebrows, long sideburns. He had a longer face with a sharper chin than Percy, and his eyes were deeply set with a prominent brow. He was dressed neatly in a cheap suit, shirt, and shoes; his tie was plain medium red with a few frayed edges visible. He was carrying a small leather satchel over his shoulder, and he had a wary look on his face. His eyes were fiery, a dark blue, alert, and challenging.

Percy nodded and the man entered the elevator. They stood side by side without speaking as the elevator ascended to the top floor. When the elevator door opened Percy gestured with his arm and the other small man preceded him into the reception area. Percy expected him to amble towards one of the team's offices, but instead the man went around what had been Skye's desk and hopped up on a raised chair that made his chest level with the desk top. He folded his hands and looked Percy in the eyes.

"May I help you?" the man asked politely. The words were polite; the tone was not. He flipped a long hank of hair back from his forehead, but the straight locks simply fell back to nearly cover his left eye.

Percy cocked his head and asked equally politely, "Who are you?" He allowed a touch of arrogance and annoyance to seep into his response.

Before the man could answer Memphis's deep voice came from behind him and said, "This is Lancelot LaPointe, Skye's replacement—for now." Memphis addressed Lancelot. "This is Percival McBean, my cousin-in-law and a partner in the psychology practice on the first floor. Say hello, gentlemen."

"Hello," Percy said evenly.

"'Lo," Lancelot muttered.

Memphis said to Percy, "We're working on his attitude problem. Come into my office." Memphis turned and Percy followed him into his office.

Percy parked himself on the chair and said, "Okay, the story, please. *Reader's Digest* version."

Memphis laughed. "Lancelot was one of those performers at the carnival."

"Not the cowboy and Indian troop," Percy groaned.

"You bet. Indian number two, Chief Little Big Man. We had him come in for an interview a few days after Steinberg's disappearance. He was belligerent and reactive, but as the interview wore on I had a wild hair."

"You always have a wild hair."

Memphis grinned. "So, we asked him questions about the performance, his discussion with Steinberg while that fellow was bathing, and what happened before a missing person's report was made. He answered the questions tersely, to say the least."

"Were there any signs that Milton was unusually nervous or stressed before his disappearance?" Memphis asked Lancelot when they were in the conference room with Sand and Swan.

"No," Lancelot said in a clipped voice with a thread of annoyance glaring brightly in the tone.

"Nothing?" Sand asked.

"Didn't I just say no?"

"Look, shrimp," Swan snapped. "We're trying to find your friend. If you were missing wouldn't you want someone to do everything they could to find you?"

"No one would miss me, except maybe a pack of six-year-olds that like tiny Injuns."

"Well," Memphis said, "you're going to tell this tall Injun everything you know, or we'll let the cops drag you in and interrogate you. I guarantee they won't be so nice." He addressed Sand. "Do your Nazi buddies still use leather straps and batons?"

"Sometimes," Sand said, nodding. "I think they prefer electric shock these days. It doesn't leave external marks."

The team could see that Lancelot was still steaming but there was an unmistakable touch of fear in his face. Memphis used that as leverage. "Are you ready to start answering our questions like a normal person?"

"But I'm not normal," Lancelot hissed. "I'm far from normal. I'm a fucking freak that makes peanuts acting out sickening tableaus in a circus. You don't know this, but I graduated Tulane down in N'Orleans with honors as an English major. I was bullied and called names and had ugly pranks played on me from the time I was in kindergarten. You should have heard the laughter when I walked across the stage to get my degree. The guy behind me even tripped me as I was walking across the stage and I fell flat on my face. They roared.

"Find a job? I can't even count the number of interviews canceled or cut short when they saw who had submitted an application. My brains and credentials meant nothing—I was, as Miss Hazelwood said—a shrimp. So, I eventually wound up dressed in a cruddy costume and acting the clown to stupid people that were amused and couldn't conceive of any measure of respect for the dwarf. Got any idea what that's like?"

"Not really," Memphis said. "The worst I was ever called was a half-breed bastard. Both are true."

"Look," Lancelot sad trying to keep his temper, "I don't know anything else. I've told you and the cops everything. Can I go now? I have to find a ride to L.A."

"You're quitting the circus?" Sand asked.

"Yeah, my stomach's as full of that shit as can be. Maybe I can find a slightly less humiliating job in Hollywood."

"That what you want?" Memphis asked. "A slightly less humiliating job?"

In a rare bout of emotional honesty Lancelot said, "It's all I can hope for."

"How fast can you type?"

"Huh?"

"How fast can you type? Can you type?"

Lancelot wriggled his finger in front of his face. "Stubby digits like these won't put me in the top percentile. But, yeah, I can type. I typed my college papers. Maybe … thirty, thirty-five words per minute. Why?"

"What was your GPA in college?"

Lancelot squinted suspiciously. Were they trying to make fun of him? "3.2."

"Are you good at research?"

"I'm great at research," Lancelot said with his heart beating faster.

Memphis got up and left the room, confusing everyone.

"Sorry I called you a shrimp," Swan said.

"Been called worse," Lancelot replied, shrugging. "Freak, midget, Munchkin—you get the picture."

"Yeah, we do," Sand said. "We know someone who went through the same thing."

Before Sand could elaborate Memphis returned carrying a typewriter, paper, and the newspaper. He put the typewriter down in front of Lancelot and handed him the paper and newspaper. He sat back down.

"Look at the front-page article on the Camp David Accords. When I say go type out as much of the second paragraph as you can." Memphis waited until Lancelot threaded the paper. He took out a stopwatch. "Go," he said.

Lancelot clattered the keys madly and the minute went by far too quickly.

"Stop," Memphis said. Lancelot pulled out the paper and handed it to him. Memphis scanned the results and nodded. "Thirty-two words and only one typo. Not bad."

"Is this interrogation turning into a job interview?" Lancelot asked.

"Looks that way," Swan said. "Are you comfortable speaking on the phone?"

"Sure. It's not like they can see me."

"Can you make good coffee?" Sand asked seriously.

"As long as I have a good brand, like Maxwell House or Folgers."

"Interested in a real job?" Memphis asked.

"Depends. I don't have to wear clown makeup, do I?"

"Only on Halloween," Memphis replied. "So. Would you like a trial at being an executive assistant?"

"Sounds nicer than secretary," Lancelot said. "Okay, yeah. Yes, I'd like a trial job."

"Can you start tomorrow?" Memphis asked. Lancelot nodded. "Okay, I'll get the paperwork started and you can meet me back here tomorrow at nine. I value promptness."

Lancelot shimmied off the chair and shook hands with each of them. He left with a briskness to his step.

Swan shook her head. "You are such a big, fat, fucking marshmallow inside, Geronimo."

Memphis shrugged. "Everyone needs a break once in a while. I leave it to you to tell Skye who she'll have to train."

"She'll be thrilled."

"And that's how we got our new executive assistant," Memphis said to Percy.

"We need to upgrade his fashion sense," Percy said.

"Let him get used to us before you start hounding him about a charcoal three-piece suit and magenta bowtie like you're wearing."

"I'll give him a week."

"So generous." Memphis called Sand, Nick, and Swan into his office and the five settled in to discuss "Operation Pueblo Bones." Before they could start talking Frick and Frack barged in with chairs and parked themselves to the side.

"Carlito Cruz got back to us with an analysis of the lacquer smear I took," Sand said. "He says it's compatible with the lacquer found on those three bones, but he can't say with an absolute certainty that it's a one-hundred-percent match. The lab doesn't have the best equipment to verify that."

"What about the beetles?"

"He verified that they are dermestids and that they are capable of defleshing bones like that. When he did his original analysis of the bones he found no nicks or scrapes that might come from a knife or a razor, but he can't rule that out completely."

Frick picked up a pile of photos of the basement and grunted. "He may be a good painter, but these tell me he's got some SF genes weighing in."

"SF?" Nick asked.

"Sick fuck."

"Look," Frack said. "Everything we've uncovered points to an odd duck but isn't remotely concrete proof that he's responsible for any disappearances or anything else nefarious." He looked at Percy. "What was your take on him during dinner?"

Percy took a thoughtful breath. "He seemed very at ease and personable. He showed no reticence and was particularly affable with my daughter. Unlike many people he didn't talk down to her and treated her as a thinking human being. He even told her a story about the history of the Pueblo people. He evinced no hostility at white people that I could discern. He's very intelligent in his speech and comprehension of topics. If you're asking me to make a definitive diagnosis of whether or not he could be a serial killer, I can't."

"So, we're back at square one," Frick said dejectedly. "Where do we go from here?"

"What if we set a trap?" Percy said quietly.

"What kind of trap?" Sand asked.

"Something that will lure him into taking action so we can nab him in the act."

"Nab?" Frack said in amusement. "You been watching late-night reruns of *The Untouchables*?"

"I'd like to point out how that worked out the last time when a nincompoop tried to lure a serial killer," Sand said looking directly at Memphis.

"The plan worked," Memphis said defensively.

"You, me, and Frack almost died, and a few other people did. And she still got away," Sand said evenly.

"But basically … it worked. And, hey—she shot me twice—you only got one bullet."

"One bullet and puffer fish venom."

"I almost died," Frack said.

"Yeah, yeah," Memphis snapped. "You didn't and your mutt got a year's worth of Omaha Steaks."

Percy decided to cut off the argument. "Let's say it's unlikely that anyone will get shot this time. This may be the best way to nab the guy." He scowled at Frack. "And, yes, I watched the entire *Untouchables* series when I was a young man."

Frick tuned out the argument as he used a magnifying glass to view the photos Nick had snapped of the floor safe. He squinted and tried to focus in, then stopped. He looked at Memphis. "You still got the file that San Francisco guy gave you about those two kids?"

"Sure, why?" Memphis asked.

"Can you get it?"

Memphis dialed nine. "Lance? Bring me the file on Taylor Tiffany Geary and Stonewall Jackson Powell. Thanks." He arched an eyebrow at Frick and Frack. "You haven't met our new executive assistant. Be nice."

"We're always nice," Frack said.

"Most of the time," Frick added.

A few minutes later the office door opened and in walked Lancelot with a thick folder that he handed to Memphis, keeping his eyes from straying to the other dwarf in the room.

"Holy crap—another one," Frick exclaimed.

"Another what?" Percy asked mildly.

"One of you people."

"It's not like we're a race that all live together in a cave and are trying to infiltrate the world of tall people," Percy said sardonically.

"He didn't mean anything," Frack said. "He's just a Neanderthal. He's still trying to come to grips with push-button phones."

"Lancelot LaPointe, meet Frick and Frack. Frick's the one that insulted you. Don't feel too special—he insults all of us at one point or another."

Lancelot grunted and started to leave. He stopped near Frick, looked him directly in the eye, and said, "I bite." Then he left.

"And bear in mind how tall he is," Sand said.

Memphis handed Frick the folder. "What are you looking for?"

"Something," Frick murmured as he scanned the documents. Then he stopped and tapped a page. He handed it to Memphis. "Paragraph two," he said.

Memphis scanned the paragraph and frowned. "It's a list of items their families last saw them wearing before they took off."

"Look at the item marked number six."

"Small silver peace pendant on a silver chain. One-inch diameter."

"Look at this," Frick said, handing Memphis the photo and magnifying glass. "Right in the middle. What does that look like to you?"

Memphis squinted and studied the middle of the photo. "A peace sign," he replied slowly. "Could be a pendant. Can't tell for sure."

"Serial killers tend to take trophies from their victims," Percy said. "Maybe the floor safe is a stash for just that."

"I don't suppose we can sneak back in and examine the safe contents?" Nick asked.

"We were lucky to get out without detection the first time," Memphis said. "That's not an option."

"Besides," Sand said, "how do we lure him in? It's pretty clear that none of our friends and family are bigoted against Indians. What would we use as bait?"

"I haven't worked that part out yet," Percy said.

"Got an idea," Frick said. "We got the Santa Fe Artists Market going on and off most of the year, but once during the year they hold it at Cathedral Park instead of the Railyard Park. It usually takes place there from September 30th through October 1st."

"We take the kids and go several times during the year," Swan said. "The number and talent of the juried artists are stunning. We have a lot of paintings and pottery we bought from New Mexican artists. Tucson takes his kids, too."

"We take Elspeth every year and let her pick out one special item," Percy said.

"Ditto Elijah," Sand said.

"What are you thinking, Frick?" Nick asked.

"I'm thinking pick someone to act as bait and within eye or earshot of Naabah we have our bait loudly diss Indians and make himself a target," Frick said.

"And if Naabah tries to nab him," Percy said, emphasizing the word 'nab,' "we catch him in the act."

"What if we don't catch him?" Frack asked. "Our bait could become beetle poop."

"And who would we use?" Nick asked. "It can't be one of us. He knows everyone in all of our firms. A cop?"

"He probably knows by sight most of the cops in the city," Sand said. "But a cop would be more likely to survive an abduction."

"How about a P.I.?" Memphis said. "From elsewhere."

"Who did you have in mind?" Swan asked.

Memphis smiled and flipped open his rolodex and plucked out a card. He dialed. "Adam Manzone, please. Memphis Grayhawk from

Santa Fe." He waited a few minutes then smiled. "Adam? Hi. I got a lot to tell you … and a lot to ask you. Can you fly out? Day after tomorrow? Fantastic. Let me know your flight and I'll pick you up. Bye." He grinned.

"Methinks we have our bait," Sand said.

CHAPTER TEN

Memphis drove down to Albuquerque by himself in his SUV. The ride was fast and uneventful, and the mixed-song cassette tape he stuck in the dashboard player brought musical soothing to the stark drive, heavy on the British Invasion and completely lacking in any disco tunes. Swan stayed home to help Hehewuti get her guest bedroom ready since all the bedrooms in Memphis's next-door house were taken by a swarm of kids. He was thinking of building an addition as a dedicated guest room, and he had an initial meeting with the architect that designed Tucson's expanded living space.

The traffic around the airport wasn't too bad at 10 AM and he slid into a parking garage spot close to the entrance. He walked over to an American Airlines kiosk and verified with the woman behind the counter that the plane was on time and he could wait at Gate 22-A. He thanked her and dodged people coming and going in a hurry until he got to the gate and sat down and waited. Someone left a folded copy of the day's *Albuquerque Journal* and he passed the time reading the stories.

He shook his head when he read about the death of Pope John Paul I, née Albino Luciani, who died of a heart attack just thirty-three days into his papacy. Now, the Catholic church was going to have to go about choosing a successor while Catholics across the globe mourned and perhaps wondered what the hell God was doing when he called the pope home.

The African National Congress, formed in South Africa in 1912, was being accused of a savage event in their country. On April 8, 1960, the administration of Charles Robberts Swart banned the ANC in South Africa. After the ban, the ANC formed the Umkhonto we Sizwe (Spear of the Nation) to fight against apartheid utilizing guerrilla warfare and sabotage. The ANC reacted to the possibility of having an infiltrated enemy agent in their ranks by trying to eliminate him by poisoning five hundred of its own members. The world was shocked and demanded justice.

The FAA investigation of the collision on September 24th of a Cessna 172 light aircraft and Pacific Southwest Airline Flight 182, a Boeing 727, over San Diego was ongoing with no resolution expected for many months. One hundred forty-four people were killed, seven of them on the ground, two of whom were children. The two people in the Cessna died, and twenty-two homes were destroyed or damaged by the impact and debris.

California Angels outfielder Lyman Bostock, who was shot to death at age twenty-seven while visiting friends in Gary, Indiana, was buried with grief and decorum at the Inglewood Park Cemetery. Part of the eulogy was printed, a loving tribute from teammate Ken Brett: "We called him Jibber Jabber because he enlivened every clubhouse scene, chasing tension, drawing laughter in the darkest hour of defeat. When winning wasn't in the plan, Lyman knew the sun would come up the next morning…. There's only one consolation: We're all better persons for having him touch our lives."

He was about to start the article projecting that Vietnam might invade Cambodia when a familiar voice yelled at him. He looked up and grinned at the sight of Adam Manzone and his wife, Norah Maguire, walking towards him pulling large rolling suitcases. Memphis shook hands with Adam then Norah and led them out of the terminal to the car. Memphis focused on getting out of the garage without being sideswiped by idiots tearing in, and he relaxed when they were on the road north.

"Glad you were able to come with Adam," he said to Norah. "He's talked about you so much that I feel we know each other. My wife can't wait to meet you."

"Likewise," Norah said. She was riding shotgun and Adam was in the back seat.

"You two just got married, didn't you?" Memphis asked.

"June 24th in our hometown of Hartford," Norah said. "St. Cyril's church in the south end close by where we grew up."

Adam laughed. "In some ways it was traditional but in some ways my rebel wife went her own way. I'll show the pictures when we get to your place." He chuckled to himself; his female relatives had bullied Norah into a traditional white gown, but he knew she hated it. So, the day of the wedding he brought her a dress that was totally Norah—a form-fitting, long, red satin gown whose low-cut neckline was held up only by thin spaghetti straps, and whose sides were slit to the hips, revealing long, shapely legs that ended in red satin shoes with four-inch heels. Her maid of honor, Toni, had wiped away the tasteful soft pink lipstick that Norah had been wearing, replacing it with the brightest red in her extensive makeup case. She slathered emerald green eye shadow on her friend, and hurriedly brushed out Norah's elaborate 'do in favor of a long top ponytail that swished back and forth with each step; it was garnished by a big red rose. Adam's family went into collective shock.

They talked about Adam's practice and Norah's magazine and newspaper. She was devoting the next issue to the gay pride movement since it was coming up on ten years since the Stonewall riots. For the upcoming June 1979 issue, she was devoting the entire magazine to gay rights.

As they rolled into the Santa Fe city limits Norah said, "This town is beautiful."

"It has its charm," Memphis agreed. "We're expanding the culture and bringing more artists and musicians into it. Unfortunately, a lot of people we'd rather keep out think of it as a laid-back sanctuary. I don't mind their philosophies but too many of them leave footprints of garbage behind and disrespect the land and people."

"Hippie communes?" Adam asked, thinking of his own hippie days when he had once hooked up with members of the Manson family.

"A few. There were way more in the 1960s, but new ones have tapered off and old ones have vanished. One of my partners, Nick Griffin, was an anti-establishment hippie during the mid-sixties. Now he's part of the establishment."

"I know the type," Adam said. Norah swiveled her head to look at him and he winked.

"You guys like Mexican food?" Memphis asked.

"Like you wouldn't believe," Adam replied.

"Then you'll enjoy dinner. Just the four of us so you won't be inundated by Grayhawks and Hazelwoods. Here we are," Memphis said as he pulled up into the driveway of his parents' house. "You can drop off your stuff and freshen up, then head over to my house."

"Are you close by?" Norah asked.

Memphis inclined his head. "Next door. Long story."

Memphis entered the house and Hehewuti and Jakub were waiting. Introductions were made and Jakub took the Manzones to their bedroom. Memphis said to send them over when they were ready, and he went home.

Twenty minutes later Adam knocked sharply on the front door and Swan opened it and smiled. She introduced herself as, "Geronimo's long-suffering wife."

Swan led them into the kitchen where a flock of Grayhawk children were waiting, ready to pounce.

"You will not pounce," Swan warned them. She knew her kids' proclivities. Her facial expression froze her daughters into silence. She turned to the Manzones. "Left to right, Sage, Shea, Sara, and Chessie. Max is in his crib."

"Do you have any kids?" Sage asked, ignoring her mother's narrowed eyes.

"One son. Connor. He's twelve," Norah replied.

"Hey—Aunt Cameo's brother is named Connor, too."

"All right. All of you to your rooms. Do your homework," Swan said, clapping her hands.

"I finished my homework," Sage said. "The insects don't have any."

"What did I say about calling your sisters names?" Swan said crossly. Sage rolled her eyes and sighed loudly. "Go. All of you. Beat it before I get out the nail-studded leather belt."

Dragging their feet, the four girls ambled out of the living room. Swan turned to Norah. "I just can't wait for them to hit puberty. Sage is teetering on the edge. Sit down, please."

The four adults settled in comfortably and Memphis updated them on his family and business. He told them that they'd meet most of the crew tomorrow at the office where they'd talk about the plan. Memphis had given Adam the overview the previous week when Adam flew out for the first time.

At five-thirty Memphis drove them to Malagueña Fiesta, where the hostess led them to a private table near a window. The busboy descended on them a minute later with a huge bowl of chips and two large bowls of salsa, one regular, one extra spicy. They ordered a pitcher of frozen margaritas and different entrées so they could sample and share. One pitcher turned into two, and after a couple of hours they ended their meal with dessert sopapillas. Before he paid the bill Memphis used the hostess's phone to call Sand to come and drive them home. Ten minutes later Akiro dropped Sand off and he took the driver's seat in the SUV. Memphis introduced him to Norah then rode shotgun while his wife and guests squeezed together in the back seat.

Sand pulled into Memphis's driveway. Akiro was waiting by the curb. Sand waved goodbye and said he'd see them at the office. Memphis and Swan walked their guests to his parents' front door and let them in and said to come over for breakfast at eight.

At eight sharp Adam and Norah came in through the sliding back doors and smelled a miasma of aromas that were enticing down to the tiniest taste bud. Swan had set up a small buffet in the kitchen and told them to chow down. The kids were eating in the dining area although Sage made a couple of efforts to invade her parents' breakfast; she was kicked out both times. While they ate Memphis discreetly evaluated Norah. She was a slender, tall woman with a lovely face and bright, happy eyes, which could have been that old newlywed glow. She exuded confidence and competence, and he could understand why she was such a successful businesswoman both with her magazine, *Seraphim*, and her small newspaper, the *Voice of Angels*. Adam had showed Memphis and Swan a photo of Norah in her wedding dress, and Memphis thought that she was drop-dead gorgeous. In turn Memphis had shown them the polaroid of his and Swan's first wedding in Mexico, and the Manzones had nearly fallen off the couch laughing.

Memphis drove his wife and guests to the Warrior Spirit offices. Lancelot was already at his desk. To their credit neither Adam nor Norah did a double take.

"The Graceland Conference Room is all set up," Lancelot said to Memphis.

"Thanks," Memphis said and nodded to his guests to follow him.

When they got to the spacious room Memphis was surprised to see two plates of bagels and four tubs of cream cheese set in the middle of the table, along with pitchers of water and orange juice. Paper plates and napkins were set at each chair. The twelve-cup Mr. Coffee had a full complement of French roast. The blinds were raised, and sunlight streamed into the room.

"Your secretary do all this?" Adam said, smiling.

"Executive assistant. I reckon he did. He hasn't been on the job long but he's fitting in."

"I didn't see him last time I was here," Adam said. "Where did you find him?"

"At the carnival." Before he could elaborate Tucson walked into the room, spied the bagels, and fell on them like a ravenous hyena.

"Didn't your wife feed you this morning?" Memphis asked.

"She had to head into the office early for some editorial deadline. Declan and Connor were swarmed with the kids so I left before they could drag me into their breakfast chaos," Tucson replied.

Adam and Norah seated themselves after they got cups of coffee and Adam reached for an onion bagel. The four of them chatted while waiting for the rest of the group, and by nine-thirty the room had its full complement—Memphis, Swan, Tucson, Sand, Nick, Percy, Adam, Norah, Frick, and Frack.

"So, now that we all have our bagels and cream cheese, let's review the plan we're putting into action," Memphis said.

"This still makes me very nervous," Percy said.

"I get that," Memphis said, "but we have to do something to lure the person we suspect is responsible for multiple disappearances and, possibly, murders."

"And I'm the bait, huh?" Adam said affably. "The worm on the hook."

"You are," Memphis said, nodding. "So, here's the plan. We believe this person is an injustice collector that is taking justice to the extreme for slights against Indians. Based on a number of factors and research we've narrowed it down to the Indian artist named Hashkeh Naabah." He handed Adam several photos of Naabah and his pueblo paintings.

"Who else is on your list?" Norah asked. She was taking notes and had come along with Adam to investigate what could be a huge story if it panned out. She studied each of the photos thoughtfully.

"No one," Memphis confessed.

"So, what we plan on doing is presenting an 'injustice' to him that he'll feel compelled to act upon," Sand said. "You, Adam, will be the bad guy."

"I can do that," Adam said.

"Every year Santa Fe hosts the Santa Fe Artists Market multiple times a year. It's fairly small but has dozens of juried artists selling their wares. This year they're holding it at Cathedral Park. The Cathedral Park area is bounded on the north by Palace Avenue, on the west by Cathedral Place, on the south by St. Francis Cathedral, and on the east by Marian Hall. It was originally purchased on May 26, 1856, from José Francisco Baca y Terrus by Bishop Jean Baptiste

Lamy for $1,000. Bishop Lamy sold this along with adjoining parcels to Sister Mary Vincent, Superior of the Sisters of Charity.

"Cathedral Park is the site of the original St. Vincent Sanatorium that opened in 1883. Now, it's a peaceful place where people can walk and enjoy the outdoors, and where the festival is held once during the year, usually the first full weekend of October. The other times the festival takes place at the Railyard Park on Saturdays," Memphis said.

"Since the first full weekend isn't until October 7th this year they're holding it a week early," Swan said, "and for two days instead of just Saturday."

"We'll take you there later today so you can get the lay of the land," Nick said.

"Naabah has apparently attended every year although he doesn't present any of his paintings," Memphis said. "He enjoys the artistic expressions of his people and culture."

"So, if a belligerent white dude shows disrespect in front of him, he may take action to punish said dude," Nick said.

"Said dude being me," Adam said.

"He knows all of us but you're a stranger so he shouldn't suspect anything," Sand said. "This may not work, but it's our best shot." He hesitated. "Probably our only shot."

"You'll be under surveillance every minute of the time," Frick said to Adam. "Frack and I will be discreetly parked close by and if it comes to that we can initiate pursuit."

"This man could be innocent, though, with just odd coincidences surrounding him," Norah said.

"Very possibly," Percy said.

"Well, how do I piss him off?" Adam asked, warming to his part of the plan.

"We locate him and move close by but not within direct eyeshot. You are going to be a loud, obnoxious paleface drunk that makes derogatory remarks about the Indian culture. I'll try to calm you down, then you call me a fuckin' redskin and throw a punch," Memphis said.

"You want me to really hit you?" Adam asked.

"It won't look real otherwise," Memphis said, sighing. "Just don't break my jaw. We'll scuffle then I kick you in the butt and tell you to get lost and you stumble off towards the parking area making nasty comments. Someone will be watching you at all times. If he takes the bait and tries to abduct you, we'll close in."

"What if he grabs my husband and gets him in a car before you can stop him?" Norah asked, real concern in her voice.

"We'll have cars ready around the full perimeter of the festival. Someone will be able to follow no matter which direction he goes in."

"And if he doesn't take the bait or isn't there?" Norah asked.

"We try again Sunday with a different team member. If he doesn't take that bait, we're shit out of luck," Memphis said. "Are you both okay with this?"

Adam and Norah looked at one another then both nodded.

"Okay," Memphis said. "Let's go over all of our evidence and then every single detail minute by minute of our tableau. Afterwards we'll take you to the park, and then a special lunch at the Desert Dream Brewery."

"My … Irish nanny opened the brewery and has some fantastic beers and ales. He also recently set up a dining area for some of the best Chinese food you'll ever eat," Tucson said. Their client, Mr. Cho, had been unable to rebuild his restaurant and entered into a bargain with Declan to open up a small Chinese bistro at the brewery.

"Chinese food and beer?" Adam said. "Sounds good to me. We have a superb hole in the wall restaurant in Frisco called the Mandarin Garden that you'll have to try out when you visit."

"Hey," Sand said, grinning. "My partner Akiro and I went to Frisco for New Year's 1968 and ate there. Food magnificent, waitress downright scary."

Norah laughed. "She could stare down Godzilla."

"Okay," Memphis said. "Let's look at the evidence." He opened several thick folders and began to go through the timelines of their investigations.

CHAPTER ELEVEN

Sunday, October 1, 1978
5:58 AM

The sky was still dark; dawn was an hour or more away when the sun would spill over the eastern horizon and warm the cold air. The new moon was almost complete, but stars blanketed the sky. However, the house and neighboring area were as bright as day with the floodlights and police cars illuminating the house as law enforcement walked around the property and went in and out of the house. Taos police, Santa Fe police, an FBI agent from Albuquerque, and members of the Warrior Spirit Investigations team were milling about as the residence was searched and mounds of evidence were being carried out for laboratory analysis.

Memphis, Swan, Sand, Tucson, Adam, Norah, and Frack were standing at the crime tape perimeter as Dennis Dunbar walked over to them and broke police rules by showing them some of the items removed from the floor safe. Adam was wearing gloves as he took and examined the peace-symbol necklace that was in grainy photos that Nick had taken. He closed his eyes for a few seconds then nodded and confirmed that the necklace had belonged to Taylor Geary. The last shred of hope he'd had for her still being alive vanished under the glare of reality.

Frack glanced around and saw the arrival of a news truck and he curled his lip. He hated reporters; well, not Cameo—she was family. He was still a little creeped out by her new accent—she sounded like a Kennedy. He was glad that Abbott was waving them off and making sure they didn't cross the tape.

Tucson was standing as stiff as a statue. His stomach was turning from the outcome of their Saturday plan. One person was in the hospital in the ICU and another was missing. He felt as cold as death inside.

Saturday, September 30, 1978
1:45 PM

Team members were positioned around the perimeter of the art fair as discussed in the previous day's planning meeting. Nearly all of them were out of sight since they didn't want Naabah to suspect anything by seeing too many people he knew milling about. Memphis spied him around noon as he walked over to a Hopi artist that had a superlative display of sand paintings. Memphis had browsed the artist's tent and found a couple he liked for his twins' room. He paid the artist and asked if he could keep the paintings until Memphis could pick them up later.

Adam was close by, waiting in the wings for his part in the play. As Memphis walked up to Naabah he pulled on his left ear; that was Adam's cue.

Memphis shook Naabah's hand. "Fancy meeting you here," he said. "Are you exhibiting?"

Naabah smiled and shook his head. "No, I'm just here to enjoy the beauty of my people's work. Whitewing does wonderful sand paintings."

"I know. I bought two for my kids' room. He's keeping them for me until we leave."

"Are your children here?"

"No, they had an issue with their mother and all of them are grounded. I came here with Sand and Akiro. They brought Elijah. I think they're over by the dreamcatcher booth." He nodded over his shoulder.

"Ah," Naabah said. "Raven does wonderful work with feathers and wool."

"Well, I've gotta go and find my partner. We should have coffee sometime."

"I'd like that," Naabah said.

As Memphis turned he was nearly knocked over by a teetering guy that had clearly drank too much. In fact, he was holding a nearly full bottle of tequila.

"Watch where you're goin', redskin," the man growled, his words slurred as he took another swig of tequila (which was actually tea). "Get the hell outa my way." His eyes were red and his beard stubble made him look like a derelict.

"Easy buddy," Memphis said tersely.

"Don't easy-buddy me," Adam snarled. "Shoulda gone to California. They got white people there. It ain't full of savages. But, no—my stupid bitch old lady wanted to see real Indians. Get outa my way, Sitting Bull." Adam tried to push his way past Memphis, deliberately bumping him.

"Hey," Memphis exclaimed. "What the hell's wrong with you?"

"Nothin' that this won't cure," Adam said as he swung and decked Memphis with an impressive right cross. Naabah grabbed Adam from behind and pinned his arms to his sides and a couple of other guys moved in to help. Memphis dragged himself off the ground and grabbed the tequila bottle and smashed it to the ground.

"Get out of here, lowlife," Memphis said in a low, deadly voice.

"Unless you want to get scalped," Naabah added coldly.

Adam tore himself free of Naabah and another man and spit on the ground.

“I’m going,” Adam spat out. “Can’t stand the stink anymore.” He whirled around and started weaving towards the north end of the park.

“I should have taught that prick a lesson,” Memphis said.

“Oh, I’m sure someday he’ll get his just desserts,” Naabah said. “Forget about it. Go find your friends.”

Memphis dusted off the seat of his jeans, nodded, and walked off into a pathway of food booths as Naabah watched. Naabah smiled slightly, then turned around and started walking north.

Sunday, October 1, 1978
7:32 AM

The sun was up with not a cloud in the sky. Sand was leaning on his car hood studying a map of New Mexico. He had mapped out several routes going north, south, east, and west. He was having a little trouble concentrating since part of his mind was back at the hospital. They said they’d get in touch through the police department if anything changed. Cameo was there to keep personal tabs on what was going on.

Memphis leaned over him and fingered the northern route, then tapped the tiny town of Trinidad which just showed above the state’s border. Adam leaned close and traced the eastern route. Swan tapped the southern route—Mexico was a solid bet. In truth, they had no frickin’ idea which way the fugitive would head. The search moved past critical and went into the realm of desperation. Finding Naabah was imperative, not to capture him, but to rescue his captive.

Terror saturated each of the families and friends.

Terror that Naabah would reach some remote hidey-hole that no one could ever find.

Terror about what he had planned for his captive.

Terror that if they found him, they would be too late.

Saturday, September 30, 1978
1:57 PM

Adam pretended to weave to the borrowed truck, careful not to check behind him to see if anyone was watching. There were people scattered about, but he had parked in as remote a space as he could find. He reached his car and fumbled with the car keys. Suddenly a strong hand clapped him on the shoulder and he automatically whirled around to stare into Naabah's face. A chill ran up Adam's back and he weighed whether or not he could manage to get the gun from his glove compartment if the man were armed. He was wearing an ankle holster, too.

Naabah suddenly took Adam's car keys. "I'll leave these at the information booth. You can pick them up when you're sober."

Adam was taken aback by the unexpected turn of events. He tensed, and muttered, "Um, thanks. Sorry about the rant. Way too much tequila."

"Fire water will do that to you," Naabah said breezily. He patted Adam on the shoulder, winked, and walked off towards the fair, leaving Adam completely perplexed but still on edge. He couldn't follow Naabah back to the fair; that would be suspicious. He spotted Nick sitting slouched in his car a hundred yards away and shrugged. He got into the driver's seat and relaxed, thinking. All of a sudden he saw a battered old truck drive fast towards the street and he recognized Naabah. He tried to turn on the engine, cursing when he remembered that Naabah had taken the car keys. He got out and began running back to the fair. Out of the corner of his eye he saw Nick pull out of his space and follow Naabah. Nick was the only one on that side of the fair so no one except Adam knew that he was in pursuit.

Nick didn't care if Naabah realized that he was being followed. Nick had a feeling, a bad feeling. Where the hell was Naabah heading at such a speed?

Nick matched Naabah turn for turn. He finally realized where Naabah was going—the McBean Victorian. He cursed himself for not having his damn car phone repaired.

Sunday, October 1, 1978
7:56 AM

Carlito Cruz was supervising the removal of the drum of beetles to his van. He couldn't wait to dissect a few. Memphis had given him one from DeVere's stash, but since Carlito was branching off into etymological forensics he was eager to experiment. He wondered how they'd taste salted and roasted …

Abbott suddenly came rushing over to the group and handed Memphis a piece of paper. Memphis scanned the document and paled. He met Abbott's eyes.

"He's got nothing to lose," Memphis said as he handed the paper to Sand.

Saturday, September 30, 1978
2:15 PM

Naabah pulled up short in the McBean driveway, sending a storm of gravel flying through the air on both sides of the car. Seconds later Nick screeched up behind him and flew out of his car yelling, "Hold up, Naabah. What are you doing here?" Nick reached behind him and was about to pull out the gun in his belt when Naabah whirled around smoothly and without a second's pause fired his gun.

Nick was blown back off his feet and whipped around, his head slamming into the front windshield of his car. He slid to the ground unconscious as the red blossom in his chest spread on his white shirt. Naabah stuffed his gun in his jacket pocket and turned around. He saw Tansee running out of the house yelling. She tried to run around him to get to Nick but he grabbed her wrist and pulled her to him and a second later she screamed as her eyes burned with the pepper spray he let loose in her face. He shoved her to the ground and bounded to the front steps. Percy was on the other side of the door locking it. He backed away just in time as Naabah threw himself against the front door, splintering it and knocking it open.

Percy rushed to the sideboard near the door where he kept a pistol. Naabah grabbed his arm and twisted it, then sent another heavy pepper spray into his eyes. Percy screamed in pain, blinded. Naabah heaved him across the room where he crashed into the coffee table.

Naabah looked around and stopped as he saw Elspeth clinging to a door jamb, her eyes wide in fear and shock. He smiled at her, then walked over to her. She fled into the kitchen where he caught up with her and grabbed her arm. He knelt down in front of her.

"Shh, shh, pretty girl. I'm not going to hurt you, but you need to come with me," he whispered then stood and swept her up into his arms. She struggled and cried as he fled out the back door.

Tansee was on her knees leaning over Nick, her hands flat on his chest as she tried to examine the bloody wound, her eyes still burning from the spray, the skin around them red and stinging like a thousand bees had attacked her face. She could barely make out the figure running towards her, carrying something. She thought at first it was Percy but realized that Naabah was carrying Elspeth. She scrambled to her feet and stumbled towards the man carrying off her daughter.

"Mommy, Mommy, Mommy," Elspeth screamed.

"Don't you fucking touch my child," Tansee shrieked at Naabah, who swept her to the ground as he reached his truck. Her hands had managed to claw at his face and he felt a fire of nails grooves down his left cheek. He tossed Elspeth into the small back seat, jumped in the truck, and tore off, sending a cloud of dirt and gravel into the air as he floored it and headed east.

Percy stumbled out of the house and weaved towards his wife and brother, holding his sprained wrist close to his body. Tansee threw herself into his arms sobbing, "Percival, Percival" over and over again.

"I called 9-1-1," Percy gasped. He dropped down next to Nick and leaned his head on his brother's chest. "He's still breathing."

In the distance they could hear the approaching sounds of ambulance and police sirens.

Sunday, October 1, 1978
9:42 AM

Cameo pulled up in front a uniformed cop that was holding up a hand. She identified herself and he let her park and join her family. She hugged Tucson then gave them an update.

"Nick's in the ICU and they're considering upgrading his condition from critical to serious," she said. "Tansee and Percy are getting their vision back and the doctor doesn't see any likely permanent effects, at least not for Percy. The ophthalmologist is concerned about Tansee's left eye, which seems to have gotten a significant dose of the pepper spray. Yuki's parents are caring for Ben and her kids since she won't leave Nick's side."

"At least some good news," Sand said. "There's still no sighting of Naabah or Elspeth or the truck. It's been almost twenty hours. They could be anywhere." He stared down at the map. "Anywhere."

Norah touched Cameo's arm. "While we're waiting, do you think you and I can talk shop for a few minutes?"

Cameo looked at Tucson, who nodded. The two women moved to Cameo's car and sat inside talking.

"I feel so damn helpless," Tucson said in frustration. "We ought to be doing something. Anything."

"Do you think he'll hurt the kid?" Frack asked. Out of the corner of his eye he saw that Frick had arrived and was talking to a Taos detective. His partner nodded and walked over to the group.

"I don't know," Memphis said. "Except for Nick, who posed a legitimate threat to him, he didn't kill Tansee and Percy. He immobilized them with a non-fatal method." He looked at Frick. "What do you got?"

Frick waved a large rolled-up beige paper. "Got this from the college's cartography section. It's a detailed map of the state with roads, mountains, rivers, and all that other land shit. London knows the administrator and begged a favor."

Sand helped Frick open and secure the map on the hood of his car with small rocks at each corner.

"Detailed is an understatement," Memphis said as he scanned the colorful three-foot-by-three-foot map.

Just then Dunbar ran over to them and said, "They found his truck."

"Where?" Swan asked urgently.

Dunbar noticed the map, studied it for a few seconds, then tapped. "Here. Corona." He pointed to a tiny village. "Seventy-five, eighty miles southeast of Albuquerque near the Salinas Pueblos Mission National Monument. About a mile down Mayeux Road off the 54. I'm making a wild guess that he's on his way to Mexico. 54 takes him directly to El Paso and the border."

"Any sign of Elspeth?" Tucson asked. He hesitated for a second. "Any blood?"

"No and no," Dunbar said. "The State Police are swarming the place. I sent Detective Christensen down."

"Wish we had one of our people going," Swan said.

"Covered," Dunbar said. "I had Tom swing around to your office and pick up DeVere." He shrugged. "It's not protocol, but I get that this is very personal." His eye was caught by a forensic tech waving him over. "Gotta go." He walked back towards the house.

Memphis cocked his head thoughtfully. He looked at Swan.

"What?" she said.

Memphis shook his head. "He's smart. Somehow he figured out that we were homing in on him and he acted. Not on the spur of the moment, but I'm betting it's a well-thought-out plan."

"Meaning?" Tucson said.

"Meaning I'll bet my beloved blue Mustang that he's headed north." He drew a big blue circle around the Taos area up through the Colorado area, stopping at Trinidad. He drew an arch of green east of the circle, from Corona up to Trinchera, Colorado. "We need to plot every possible roadway that he could use within this circle, and every hiking path as well. Concentrate on possible hiding places like mines, caves, or abandoned Indian ruins."

"He could have headed west," Sand said.

"The State Police already sent someone to his sister's place in Gallup," Frack said.

"I'm betting he won't head east to Texas," Sand said, "so let's concentrate on north, like Memphis said." Everyone murmured yes or nodded, then they huddled around the topographic map and began theorizing.

Saturday, September 30, 1978
6:31 PM

Naabah pulled over to the side of the road with a lot of bushes. Elspeth said she had to pee and was squiggling around in the front seat, her head barely visible over the dashboard. She'd had to go once before and when he pulled over and they got out of the car she bolted down the dirt road for a few yards before he caught her. He led her back to the truck and took out a roll of toilet tissue, then led her to a cluster of bushes. He told her to do her thing and if she tried to run away again she would be very sorry. He never specified a punishment or a direct threat, and she had no way of knowing that he wasn't going to hurt her. He turned around and a few seconds later he heard a tinkle. She came from behind the bush, her lower lip stuck out, and handed him the tissue. She climbed silently back into the truck, slouched in her seat, and folded her arms tightly. He pulled back on the road and in an hour made Corona.

He was careful to drive the speed limit and had planned for a long trip with a pile of supplies including a case of water and plenty of snacks a child might like. He also had an Igloo full of sandwiches. He pulled off on desolate Mayeux Road and drove for a mile to a large copse of tall bushes behind which he'd parked a relatively new forest-green Ford Bronco two days earlier. He transferred his unwilling companion, all the food and water, the sleeping bags, and the suitcases full of clothes and sundries like soap and toothbrushes. He drove the Bronco to the front of the copse and drove the truck behind it. Before he took off he broke open a cold bottle of Pepsi and handed it to Elspeth. She drank it down without taking a breath.

He drove a couple of miles back north on the 54 then turned east on Route 247 where he spent the next fifty miles until he hit U.S. Highway 285 headed south. He was a solid hundred miles or more from Albuquerque as he tooled down to the connection to State Road 20, which took him up to Fort Sumner so he could catch U.S. 84. About halfway up that road he cut off on a small, desolate road, County Road 2F. An hour later it was after nine when he made the State Road 156. He drove a few miles east then cut north on an unmarked dirt road. He drove off the road into the desert and parked the Bronco.

He looked over at Elspeth, who had fallen asleep, slouched in the front seat, her mouth open slightly, a rumble of soft snoring emanating from her lips. He thought he had never seen such a beautiful, innocent creature, a worthy descendant of their people. He very gently tied a thin rope around her left wrist and then his right one. He slouched, too, and fell asleep in five minutes. He woke up sometime after midnight with Elspeth tugging on his sleeve.

"I gotta pee," she mumbled in her sleepy voice.

Naabah grunted and untied their wrists, then grabbed the toilet paper and a flashlight and helped her out of the car. He waited in front of a bush while she did her business, then they went back into the car. He retied their wrists and they fell back asleep until just past dawn. Naabah went outside to relieve himself as the sun turned the eastern clouds into a horizon of pastel pink, gold, and purple. He felt the spirit of his people rise in his soul as the golden orb breached the horizon and promised a magnificent day. He heard a small sound and turned to see Elspeth exiting the SUV, holding the toilet tissue in her hand. She tramped across the sand to a large bush then reappeared a few minutes later.

"Can I wash my hands?" she asked him.

He nodded and took out a bottle of water and poured it over her hands then gave her a paper towel. "Hungry?" he asked. She nodded. He took out a roast beef on rye sandwich and a half pint of milk. She ate in the passenger seat while he did the same in the driver's seat.

When she finished she looked at him. "I want to go home."

"Soon enough, Amitola," he replied, smiling kindly.

"That's not my name," she said crabbily.

"It should be your Indian name. It means rainbow, a beautiful, colorful expression on nature."

She dug in her heels. "My name is Elspeth. It was my daddy's mother's name."

"And it is lovely. Sit up straight. It is time to go." With that he started the SUV and went back down the dirt road and pulled back to State Road 156 where he headed east until he turned north on Route 209 which took him directly into Tucumcari after he crossed Route 66. He saw the sign for the northeastern section of Route 54 and got on the road, heading upwards to the northwest corner of Texas. He was feeling less stressed since he doubted that any law enforcement or P.I. team member would figure out his zigzag route back to Questa.

He turned off the roadway at Dalhart, Texas, onto the northeast Route 87. Thirty-five miles and he'd be back in New Mexico. At Clayton he'd get on his penultimate road, Route 64, which would take him to the vehicle's endpoint on Route 38 at Red River.

He felt a tug on his sleeve and looked over at Elspeth, who was handing him a carton of milk. He smiled at her and took the offering. She smiled back.

Elspeth turned towards her window and watched as the road and landscape rushed by. Ever since they changed vehicles in Corona she had forced herself to be calm and think, think about how she was going to get away. She wanted to go home to her mommy and daddy and baby brother. She had been collecting things each time she went to the bathroom. Her right pocket had a half dozen sharp cactus spines, and her left back pocket had a three-inch sharp rock. Mommy had started teaching her about desert survival, and how simple things could be used as weapons. Mommy said driving a cluster of cactus spines into someone's eye could temporarily disable them.

She sighed and closed her eyes as she listened to the engine rumbling and the man softly singing a Navajo song.

Maybe clusters of spines in both eyes would work even better.

CHAPTER TWELVE

Monday, October 2, 1978
7:30 AM

Percy was sitting in the chair beside Nick's bed, watching his brother sleep. Akiro had forced his sister to go to their parents and although Yuki resisted he hustled her into his car and drove her there. He promised that someone would always be sitting with Nick, 24/7. 5 AM to 10 AM was Percy's watch, then Skye would take over. Tansee and Ben were bunked down with Memphis's parents.

The rest of the team were still trying to track down the direction and purpose of Naabah's flight, and the problem was that there were far too many variables to be sure of anything. Complicating matters was the fact that they didn't know what kind of car or truck Naabah was driving since he had abandoned his truck. The Motor Vehicle Department was contacted to see if they could find a registration under his current name or birth name. However, he could have bought a car in a private sale and not yet registered it. Memphis was betting on that possibility.

Percy's mind was roiling like volcanic lava. As much as he was concerned about his brother's health (which had thankfully been upgraded from serious to stable), his daughter, his beloved daughter, was somewhere out there with a serial killer. God only knew what plans he had for her. His stomach twisted at the possibilities. He wanted to scream but he couldn't. Snapshots of their lives together blinked across his mind. Watching Elspeth enter the world with Tansee's final scream and push. Holding his daughter in his arms for the first time. Celebrating her first birthday. Her fifth. Watching her perform in dance class. He couldn't imagine life without her and he pushed that horror to the back of his mind.

He fortified himself with words and thoughts he'd read of great, expressive men, many of which helped him get through his early life. He closed his eyes and visualized a poem that had made a lasting impact on the way he went through life and was now making his heart and soul sturdy enough to face the uncertain present. In 1875 English poet William Ernest Henley wrote the immortal *Invictus*, a life-affirming and soul-bolstering ode to man's inner strength. Percy recited it silently, his lips moving, his heart beating fast.

Out of the night that covers me
Black as the pit from pole to pole,
I thank whatever gods may be
For my unconquerable soul.

In the fell clench of circumstance,
I have not winced nor cried aloud.
Under the bludgeonings of chance
My head is bloody, but unbowed.

Beyond this place of wrath and tears
Looms but the horror of the shade,
And yet the menace of the years
Finds, and shall find, me unafraid.

It matters not how strait the gate,
How charged with punishments the scroll,
I am the master of my fate:
I am the captain of my soul.

I am the master of my fate, Percy echoed in his mind.

A sharp knock at the door startled him and he looked up to see Skye standing there.

"I thought I'd spell you a little earlier," she said. "Go home to your wife and son." She dropped her crocheted shoulder bag on a chair and walked over. "Shoo," she said gently.

Percy looked up at her with grateful eyes. He leaned as far as he could towards Nick and kissed his cheek. "Love you, little brother," he whispered. He grasped Skye's hand tightly then left hurriedly without looking back.

8:30 AM

They'd slept in the car overnight with the Bronco well-hidden off Route 38 just short of Red River. They were just about out of food but still had enough water for a few days. Red River was only eleven miles from Questa, but if one were to draw a protractor circle extending out with a diameter of twenty miles the area would contain a large number of natural places and manmade places that people enjoyed through hiking, fishing, bird-watching, camping, and other simple relaxations. There were fewer such people as autumn wore on towards winter, but there were quite a few skiing slopes like Angel Fire and a number of people even enjoyed hiking in the snow.

The mountains were the resting places of many defunct mines and was where Naabah had his special place and studio. There were many mountain peaks which attracted tourists, like Black Mountain, Bear Mountain, Schaefer's Peak, Sawmill Mountain, Touch-Me-Not Mountain, Elephant Rock, and a couple of well-known ex-mines, Caribel Mine and Bunker Hill Mine. Naabah knew every inch of the land between the two towns and sought out and chose a forgotten, hidden old mine that was well off the beaten track and unlikely to attract visitors. The two teenage boys unfortunately found the cave and paid the price for their inquisitive natures.

He followed his familiar route, tensing every time a car passed him going in the other direction. There were few, perhaps three or four. When he got to his endpoint he drove the Bronco off Route 587 into the forest at a mild upward elevation, sideswiping a few trees and putting a long, deep scrape in the passenger side door. He had chosen his Bronco because it was a deep green and would blend in best with the trees and shrubs. Not perfectly, but better than a fire-engine red one would.

He handed Elspeth the toilet tissue and a backpack and told her to change into the clothes inside. She asked for a bottle of water to wash with and he handed her that and a small towel and told her she had ten minutes. While he listened for any suspicious sounds coming from behind the huge pine tree where the child was washing and changing he broke open his own large backpack and changed his clothes. He stuffed the old ones into a paper bag and shoved it under the front seat. He checked his watch—twelve minutes. He called out to her using her newly dubbed Indian name. He tensed for a few seconds before she rustled the bushes and walked out from behind the tree.

Naabah smiled in relief and satisfaction. She had donned the clothes he brought for the hike—sturdy jeans, mid-calf hiking boots with thick soles, a dark green checkered shirt, a green wool sweater, leather gloves, and a baseball cap for the Pueblo Elementary School Hoot Owls. She walked over to him and looked up expectantly. He grunted and fixed the small backpack to her back then put a water bottle and a small bag of potato chips and some Kleenex tissues into it. He strapped a nylon water bottle belt around her waist snugly and stuck a water bottle in it. He stood and nodded his head. He had changed into similar clothes but his large backpack was heavy with water, medical supplies, and tools, and he put a wide-brimmed straw hat on his head. He slipped on sunglasses and handed Elspeth a pair. He stuffed her old clothes into another bag and jammed it into his backpack.

"Let's go," he said and stuck out his hand. She took it and he led her through the forest to the road. He waited and scanned both ways, then crossed the road. They disappeared into a thick patch of wide, tall pine trees as they made their way to the last point on their journey.

Elspeth grinned to herself knowing that the crazy man was unaware that she had been wearing an undershirt and had ripped it into tiny strips, leaving one behind the tree along with a tiny, crushed up piece of toilet paper with her urine on it. It was the best she could do to mark her territory like Uncle Memphis had taught her. She didn't know how long they were going to walk before they came to wherever he was taking her, but she'd try to covertly drop another piece of toilet paper and strip of undershirt. The balled-up sections were stuck in her underpants with a few shoved as deeply as possible into her jeans' pockets. She hoped he couldn't smell them down there.

9:45 AM

"Why are you here?" Memphis asked Percy semi-crossly.

"Tansee and Ben are being guarded by your parents," Percy said. "I don't think a Panzer division could get past them. I spent some time holding my sobbing wife but I'm useless there. I want to help here."

Memphis grunted and rose from behind his desk. Percy followed him into the Graceland Conference Room where a substantial number of the clan were reviewing evidence and maps and talking about theories. Swan and Sand were there, along with Tucson and Luc, Frick and Frack, and Cameo. Adam was present, too, although Norah had to reluctantly return to San Francisco to handle a magazine conflict between the managing editor, Bruce Peterson, and his rival and girlfriend, Donna Pallone.

Cameo grabbed the four-inch-thick hard seat cover and put it on the chair next to her, then signaled Percy to sit by her.

"How's Nick?" she asked.

"He's … he's better. They're listing him as stable now. His color's good," Percy said. "Where are we on finding my daughter?"

"Abbott said they searched the truck inch by inch and found nothing to trace where it had been or where it was going. There was no evidence that Elspeth had been harmed. They know he must have had a car hidden nearby that he switched to, but they have no idea of the make, model, or color. There were tire prints close by that didn't match the truck tires. They were large and wide, something more than a normal-sized car tire," Memphis said.

"Perhaps he was using a truck or car that he'd expect to use off-road?" Percy asked.

"Maybe. So far we haven't come up with any possibilities for a private sale, but Abbott has asked the newspapers here and down to Albuquerque to run a front-page article with his face and asking if anyone has recently sold a vehicle to him. Got a couple of calls and Dunbar interviewed them but it didn't pan out."

"The bones," Sand murmured, drawing everyone's eyes. "What the hell is he doing with the bones, and if we can figure that out, maybe we can figure out where he is."

"Well, we think he may be lacquering them based on the material we found at his house," Swan said. "It matches the coating on those three bones we found years ago, but, again, Carlito couldn't say for certain that it was the same lacquer. He's sent samples of the bone lacquer and the sample we took to the FBI lab in Albuquerque."

"So, where is he going?" Frick asked quietly as he scanned the map for the fiftieth time.

Before anyone could respond there was a soft knock at the door and it opened to reveal Lancelot standing there with a rolled-up, wide piece of paper in his hand. He looked nervous.

"What's up?" Swan asked.

"I did … I did some research that I thought might help you," Lancelot said. He was well aware of the intense gaze Percy was boring into him. A bead of sweat popped out from under his forehead hairline.

"What kind of research?" Sand asked.

"I was looking for a cluster of places that might be used as a hideout," Lancelot replied. "I kind of narrowed it down to the northern part of the state, like, between Taos and Trinidad, where those boys were found."

"What did you come up with?" Frack asked gruffly.

Lancelot hesitated then moved next to Memphis and spread out an old topographical map that looked like it had been created in the early part of the century. It was a xeroxed copy, and obviously hand-drawn and hand-written.

"Where is this area?" Memphis asked.

"The northern part of the state not too far from Colorado," Lancelot said, "maybe twenty miles. I got this from a mining archive that the geology division of the college has practically hidden away. Miss London contacted the archivist and persuaded him to open up at five. He was grumpy, but he understood the urgency. The guy there said the map was drawn in the late 1800s to mark out the gold mining points. He said that the mines are all defunct now, but they're probably still there. Maybe hidden by overgrown trees and bushes. Definitely not too safe."

"Any other hidey-hole possibilities in this area?" Adam asked.

"He said there were a lot of caves, and probably some hidden cliffs that could cause a fatal fall if you didn't know where you were going. He said that there were a large number of established hiking trails to various lakes and streams as well as mountains, but he said that there was a vast portion of the mountain area that was off-trail and not usually approached by hikers."

"A good place to hide," Percy said, frowning. He suddenly addressed Lancelot. "Thank you. Thank you for your help."

Lancelot blushed. "You're welcome. Let me know if I can help in any way. I … I sure hope you get your kid back safely. Um, I'm going out to pick up some more bagels and donuts."

"Don't forget the cream cheese," Luc said. "And butter." He flashed a smile as Memphis rolled his eyes.

"That's a good idea, about the mines," Swan said as she leaned on the table scanning the handmade map. There were bright red dots all over the area, denoting the known mines. At the bottom of the page in cursive handwriting was the caveat, "Some mines still unknown."

"It's still a hell of a big area to search," Tucson said.

"We need more people to search. The cops and fibbies are busy with their plans and methods," Memphis said.

"What if he's not there?" Frack asked. "We'd be wasting our time."

"We're wasting our time here," Frick countered. "You got a better place to be?"

"I didn't say there was anything wrong with wasting our time," Frack said peevishly.

"So, there's everyone in this room, plus Devon and DeVere," Memphis said. "I think we still need more."

"I've got an idea," Luc said brightly. "I'll bet that Indian chick—what's her name? Chelan? —could round up a few men and help us."

"Indian chick?" Memphis said balefully. "Were you planning on asking her?"

"I could."

"She hates you," Swan said flatly. "Is your will up to date?"

"I could charm her," Luc said, with a Cheshire Cat grin.

"You're more likely to come back without a scalp, little brother," Memphis said. "But give it a try. We'll plot out teams and sectors to search and round up supplies."

Luc jumped up, saluted, and flew out of the room.

"He's lucky if he comes back with a head," Tucson said, grinning.

"You are including me in this search, aren't you?" Percy said in a quiet voice.

"Well …" Swan said slowly, trying to find the right words.

"Maybe you should hold down the fort. We'll keep in constant contact. Walkie-talkies and by phones if we can find any booths," Tucson said.

There was an uncomfortable silence in the room for a long minute before Percy took a deep breath and said in a low but measured and determined voice, "I would think after all these years you would know that I'm capable of almost anything. My size inhibits some functions but hiking and searching aren't two of them. I'll match my skills and commitment with any of you tall people any day of the year." He held up a hand. "I understand your concern. Maybe some of it's warranted, but the simple fact is that my child is out there and nothing short of all the demons in Hell could stop me from going. Got that?"

"Got it," Memphis said nodding. He picked up Lancelot's map and taped the edges to the rolling whiteboard. He searched a drawer and found a blue marking pen. Everyone gathered around the board. "So, what do you think? A square area maybe thirty-five by thirty-five miles from the border down to Eagle Nest?"

"Sounds about right," Sand said.

Swan scratched a few numbers on a pad. "That's twelve hundred and twenty-five square miles. Too big."

"Okay," Tucson said. "What about dropping ten miles off each side border? So, below the border, above Eagle Nest, still encompassing Questa but cutting off east to, say, Morena?"

Swan calculated. "That's six hundred and twenty-five square miles. If we break up into six teams—"

"That's about a hundred square miles each," Percy said. "We need to get the square miles to fifty per team. Three hundred square miles total."

Memphis used his blue marker and decreased the search size, then blocked off six fairly equal sections totaling around eighteen-by-eighteen miles. He stood back and considered the result. He sighed. "It's a start. We can expand if we finish the sectors and have to go back to square one."

Swan sat down and began making a list. She noticed that her husband was looking at her quizzically. "I'm making a list of supplies each team needs to take, like compasses, walkie-talkies, flares, flashlights, batteries, stuff like that."

"Good idea," Sand said. He had always admired his sister's meticulous attention to detail. He asked Memphis, "Who'll lead the six teams?"

"Let's see," Memphis said. "Me, you, Swan, Tucson, Frick, and Luc. Percy, you're with me. Cameo with Tucson. If Luc can convince Chelan Chee he'll go with her. Swan, take Devon. Frick, DeVere. If

Chelan agrees and brings in some of her friends then we'll add them to our teams and maybe make a seventh. Adam—are you in?"

"Try and stop me," Adam said.

"Good. Then you can tag along with Sand."

"What about me?" Frack asked.

"We need someone back here to react to any issues and keep in touch with the cops. You'll have a phone—we won't."

"Use Akiro and his people for anything you can," Sand said.

"And Lancelot," Swan added. "Let's not underestimate him."

Frack sighed. "All right."

Swan cocked her head then called Lancelot in. He had an eager look on his face as he tried not to be intimidated by the eyes that were all over him. "Lance, we've devised a search plan and we'll let you know the details soon. Bottom line, you'll be holding the fort down with Frack. But, we need you to do something."

"Anything," Lancelot said quickly.

"Great. I want you to book us motel rooms in Questa and Red River. Three rooms each town, big enough to hold four people or so. Book them for tomorrow night and the night after. Book one for tonight since Memphis and I will drive up late instead of first thing in the morning. Use my American Express card to hold the reservations."

"Yes, ma'am," Lancelot said and started to run out of the room. He stopped and said, "By search teams you mean you guys are going out and actually looking for her, right?"

"Ycah?" Memphis confirmed.

"Well, if you're going on foot maybe you should bring some bloodhounds or other sniffing dogs with you. You can used the kid's scent."

There was silence for a few pregnant seconds before Swan said, "Well? Get going. Rent us those rooms and find us some dogs."

"Yes, ma'am," Lancelot said and bolted from the room.

Swan smiled at Memphis. "He's working out nicely."

"He's short," Percy said tartly, and everyone burst into raucous laughter that they all needed.

2:52 PM

Elspeth sat on a flat rock and eyed Naabah, who was sitting on the ground, back against the thick trunk of a fir tree. He was sweating and looked tired. He closed his eyes and took a drink out of his water bottle, giving her enough time to sneak a urine-drenched piece of tissue and an undershirt strip from her pocket and tuck them near a tiny sapling near the rear of the rock.

She was tired, too. They had been hiking for hours, but not on trails, on the floor of the forest where no one would think to trek. There were zigzags and trips over exposed roots and the occasional sight of a snake although none were rattling. Elspeth did like the family of quail that strode across the path in front of them just as startled as Elspeth and Naabah were, causing them to take flight amongst the trees. Elspeth let out a giggle, and Naabah smiled at her. He had been pointing out various bushes and trees and giving her information on them, as well as various forest animals like ground squirrels (which he said were delicious when roasted), owls, hawks screeing overhead, and a scary-looking bobcat that hissed at them from a low tree branch. He said he would make her squirrel stew when they reached their final destination.

Naabah was careful to take breaks at least every half hour so as not to tire out the seven-year-old. Once, when her little legs were too tuckered out he carried her in his arms for another half hour before he, too, needed rest.

Elspeth was fascinated by the beauty and scariness of the dense forest. It made her think of the fairytales her mother would read to her at night. Her Uncle Memphis had mentioned that he wanted to take her, his kids, and Tucson's twins camping next year to familiarize them with the natural environment. She was excited, but never thought she'd wind up by herself with a strange man that had taken her away from her family. She was kind of scared of him, but he had done nothing to hurt her, and was interesting in his own way. Nevertheless, she had her plans for maybe getting away or leaving a trail. She didn't doubt for a second that her family was coming after her. She had to be calm, be smart, and be patient. Mommy said that Daddy had the patience of a saint. Elspeth didn't know exactly what that meant, but she'd do her best to be a saint, too.

Naabah groaned and stood, stretching his body enough for his joints to crack. He took a deep swig of water and glanced down at his little captive. He extended his hand wordlessly and she took it, and he pulled her off the rock. He let go of her hand and zagged west through a copse of pine trees so tightly together that he had to turn sideways to move past them. She followed and threw a glance behind her, relieved that he hadn't found the spore she left.

They moved slowly; she could sense that he was tired. About a half hour later he reached into his heavy backpack and took a bottle out and swallowed what looked like a pill. She frowned; that reminded her that she hadn't had her vitamins in two days. Mommy insisted that she always take her vitamins. Daddy made her drink orange juice every morning. Something about a C vitamin.

The sounds that accompanied their trek fed her enjoyment of the natural environment and kept her mind a little bit off her homesickness. There were crickets cricking, chicken hawks screeing, small animals rustling the brush, and birds flying and landing on branches and twittering above the ground. Because the trees were so high and dense it was cool near the ground and would get cold as evening fell. The man promised her that they'd get to where they were going before the sun went down.

After a long walk Naabah stopped and drew her attention to the sky. "See there? See the sun?" he said.

Elspeth squinted up and nodded.

"Do you know what time it is?"

"I don't have a watch," she said.

"A true Indian doesn't need one. You read the time by knowing the path and height of the sun."

"What time is it?"

"Between five-fifteen and five-thirty."

"When will we get to where we're going?"

"Another hour. We'll be there before dark. Come."

He turned and began walking and she quickly pulled out a tissue and dropped it on the ground behind her. She skipped ahead of him and giggled, and reached out her hand, leading him down the path for a short while.

Naabah was spot-on about the timing, and she followed him up a small incline to what looked like a large expanse of tangled bushes and branches against a cliff face. She noticed that in the last fifty yards or so the path seemed well-worn and used recently. She spotted a few footprints that she thought might be his. She waited quietly while he pushed aside branches and other flora hiding the entrance. When he was satisfied he turned to her and nodded. She came closer and followed him into the opening.

He used his flashlight to locate a switch and flicked it. The mine was illuminated more than enough to see, but not terribly brightly. Her eyes took in everything (Daddy: "Always be aware of your surroundings."). There were at least a dozen large cardboard boxes lined up against the right wall. A few of them were marked "Cans." She saw a generator about ten feet from the entrance and all the wires linked up with the light. There was faintest smell of gasoline, and a five-gallon red can next to the generator.

There was a cot with a thin mattress, a blanket, and a pillow pushed up against the left wall. There was a small hotplate on a cinder block and a few stacked dishes next to it. There were a few more boxes, one labeled, "Paint."

"We're going to spend the night here before we go to the cave."

"We're going to a cave? Like, a bat cave?" Elspeth said, confused.

"It's a nice cave filled with special art. There are no bats, I promise. Are you hungry?"

"Yes, Mr. Naabah."

"You don't have to call me that."

"What should I call you?"

"My Indian soul name. Po'Pay."

CHAPTER THIRTEEN

Tuesday, October 3, 1978
Questa, New Mexico
6:30 AM

Swan stretched and groaned as she willed herself awake. She could hear the motel room shower going and knew that Memphis was probably up for at least an hour. They had driven to Questa late the previous night, arriving after eleven, and promptly fell into bed, exhausted from the last few days. Swan heard a low whine and looked over the edge of the mattress to where the coal-black German shepherd was lying on the floor, his head on his big paws, looking at her with melting brown eyes. She quickly scanned the floor and breathed a sigh of relief that the dog hadn't done his business.

She swung her legs over the edge and stood; the dog did the same, his tail wagging madly. His name was Smokey, and after only a few hours of acquaintance she was very fond of him. She quickly pulled on her tank top and shorts and slipped into flipflops, then leashed him up and took him outside. She followed him over to the side of the parking lot where he proceeded to take an impressively large dump then a pee stream that made her wonder if he had two bladders. She picked up the poop with a napkin and took him back to the hotel room.

Memphis was out of the shower, a towel wrapped around his waist and his hair still dripping wet. He grimaced when he saw the poop. She threw the leash at him and walked into the bathroom to flush her smelly handful. She left the door open as she stripped and headed into the shower, reveling in the hot cascade. A moment later her clean husband slipped in with her and they proceeded to lather each other and run their hands up and down their flesh and kiss and finally consummate their desperate desire. After all their years together, they still had a red-hot passion that emanated from their very souls and drove their lives and love.

When they dried off and went back into the bedroom they saw that Smokey had managed to reach up to the dresser top and drag down the leftover hamburger and French fries. He chomped down his last bite and wagged his tail.

"Bad dog," Swan scolded. "Very bad dog." Smokey wagged his tail even faster, his jaw opened; he looked like he was grinning. Swan shook her head. She looked at her husband. "What are we going to do with him?"

"What do you mean?" Memphis asked as he pulled on his jeans and threaded a leather belt through the hoops.

"Well, as you very well know Lancelot was only able to rent three dogs. He had to buy three others, Smokey being one of them." Swan had pulled on her own jeans and was shrugging into a long-sleeved dark blue turtleneck shirt. She gathered her long blonde hair up into a ponytail.

"Are you insinuating that we should take him home?"

"No, I'm stating it outright." She squatted and Smokey rushed over to her and began licking her face.

Memphis rolled his eyes in resignation. "Fine." *Happy wife, happy life*. He sat down at the built-in desk and studied the topographical map for the hundredth time. Just as he began scanning his own search area there was a knock at the door. Swan opened it and there stood Percy, Sand, Adam, Luc, and Devon. Sand held out a cup of steaming coffee to her and she mouthed, *Thank you*. She could see the others getting out of their cars and soon the motel room was filled with a cluster of searchers. Just when she thought no more could fit in there was pounding on the door. Devon was closest and opened it, and there stood Chelan Chee and four big, strapping Indian men loaded with backpacks, and packing rifles.

"Where are the dogs?" Swan asked Sand.

"In the cars chowing down on Egg McMuffins," he replied, brushing a small egg scrap from his lower lip.

Swan turned to Chelan and said sincerely, "Thank you for coming. We appreciate your help more than you can know."

Chelan shrugged and pasted a bored look on her face. "I don't like the fact that one of our people is avenging our injustices with murder. That does nothing but hurt our cause. That, and he has an Indian child hostage, and that is unacceptable." She glanced at Luc and frowned. "Not particularly thrilled with being paired up with the Nazi, but I'll do what it takes. So will my brothers."

"These are your brothers?" Frick said.

Chelan nodded at each one in turn. "Ata'halne', Gaagii, Shilah, and Jack."

"Jack?" Memphis said in amusement.

"You got a problem with that?" Jack said in a menacing baritone. He was a solid six-foot-six and without doubt could take down a grizzly bear with one hand, or maybe just the fierce look in his deep-set, hooded eyes.

"Not at all," Memphis said, enunciating every word clearly. "Okay. Let's get started." He handed out copies of the search map.

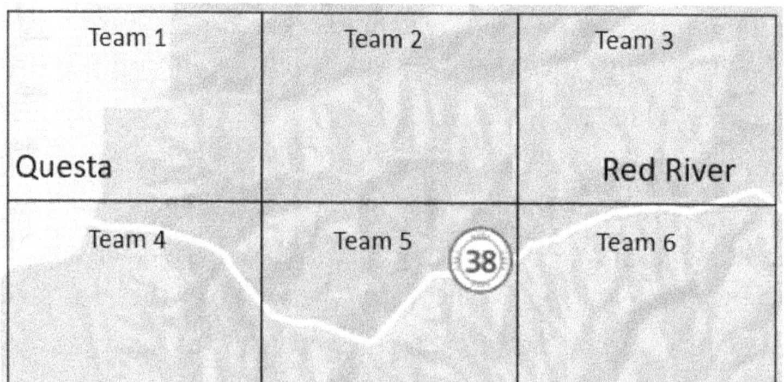

"As you can see," Memphis said, "the area is broken up into six sections. We'll have six team leaders along with one dog per team and adding in members so we can be relatively even in search capacity."

Chelan frowned and asked, "Who are in the teams?"

Swan smiled. "Luc will be leading Team 3. You're his second-in-command."

Memphis said, "I'm leading Team 2 with Percy. Sand's got Team 5 with Adam. Team 4 is Swan's charge, and Devon will go with her. Frick, you and DeVere are Team 1, and Tucson and Cameo are Team 6. Now, that leaves us with the four Chee brothers." He looked at Chelan expectantly. She turned to her brothers.

"Jack, with me. Ata'halne', Team 6. Gaagii, Team 5. Shilah, Team 4."

"Good. Sounds good," Memphis said. "Teams 1, 2, and 4 will have rooms here. You can get the keys from the front desk. Teams 3, 5, and 6 have rooms reserved at the Red River Inn in Red River. You've all got your assignments, your rooms, and your maps. Check into your rooms and then, well … start searching in your quadrant. We realized that walkie-talkies are useless over the scope of our ranges, so for the most part each team will be flying blind with no way to contact any other team. We search until 6 PM, then regroup in our rooms and call each other."

Sand was about to ask a question when there was a knock at the door. They weren't expecting anyone else, so Memphis opened the door curiously.

She was in her late thirties, above-average height, long black hair, Indian to her very core. She was dressed in loose jeans, hiking boots, a checkered shirt, and a thin leather jacket. Memphis recognized her, of course, from photos.

"May I come in?" Aponi Nez asked quietly.

"Um, sure," Memphis said and stepped aside.

She was well aware of the eyes on her, some compassionate but some wary and judgmental. She couldn't blame them. Her brother had been revealed as a madman who had taken a child hostage, committed assault and attempted murder, and may very well be responsible for the disappearance of many innocent people.

Swan asked coolly, “Why are you here, Mrs. Nez?”

“I asked her to come,” Percy said.

“I want to help,” Aponi said. “Please.”

“Team 2,” Memphis said to Percy’s relieved nod.

8:23 AM
The Cave

Elspeth scraped the last oat from her bowl of oatmeal and drank down the last few ounces of powdered milk. That was horrible, but better than nothing. She was still a little hungry, that fact made worse by missing her mother’s special French toast with agave syrup. She was sitting on the edge of the cot where she’d slept the previous night while this “Po’Pay” had slept in a sleeping bag blocking the cave entrance. Right now, he was sitting on a tall stool painting the huge canvas that was set up in the middle of the cave. The picture was so weird—there were nothing but skeletons and individual bones painted on the canvas, with what looked like a dwarf in the middle. It reminded her of her father. In between skulls and other bones were Indian symbols like the Zia sun. Now, the cave walls—that was downright scary. He promised he’d tell her stories as soon as he went on break from his painting. He had been at the easel for two hours.

With his back still towards her he asked, “Did you have enough to eat?”

“I’m okay,” she said. “Are you going to tell me a story?”

He twisted his head to look at her. “Yes, it’s about time to take a break. Come—sit on the floor over here.”

She scrambled off the cot and parked herself on the ground, sitting up straight and crossing her legs. He got off the stool and sat down in front of her, legs crossed. He raised his arm and moved it clockwise from one side of the cave to the other.

"I will tell you the history of our people through the artifacts you have looked at in awe and fear. Do not fear them. They tell the story of how our people sprang from the gods and grew their civilization and endured conquest and the horrors of the land's invaders, and how we reclaimed our pride and will go on through eternity.

"But first, let me tell you about my soul name and how I chose it. This was not the name I was given at birth nor the same I chose for myself when I grew to be a man and an artist."

"I like that painting you did of me," Elspeth said.

Po'Pay smiled. "I'm glad. Our people came to be many eons ago. They grew, they thrived, they built homes and families and lived mainly peaceful lives except for inter-tribal rivalries. But then, the white man came and claimed our land as theirs and brutalized and enslaved our peoples in the name of their king and god. It took much time before our people could take their oppression no longer, and they began to rebel. The great Pueblo Rebellion of 1680 was inevitable and well overdue. There were many brave men and women, but the leader of the rebellion was a Tewa religious leader from Ohkay Owingeh. His name was Po'Pay, and many called the rebellion Po'Pay's Rebellion.

"Po'Pay first appeared in history in 1675 as one of forty-seven religious leaders of the northern Pueblo. They were arrested by Juan Francisco Trevino's government for 'witchcraft.' Three were executed and one committed suicide. The others were whipped, imprisoned in Santa Fe, and sentenced to be sold into slavery. But the people didn't take this sentence lying down. Seventy Pueblo warriors showed up at the governor's office and demanded, politely but persistently, that Po'Pay and the others be released. The governor complied, no doubt in part because the colony was being seriously targeted by Apache and Navajo warring parties and he could not afford to risk a Pueblo revolt. Po'Pay was described as a 'fierce and dynamic individual who inspired respect bordering on fear in those who dealt with him.'

"After his release, Po'Pay retired to the remote Taos Pueblo and began planning a rebellion. Po'Pay's message was simple—destroy the Spanish and their influence and go back to the old ways of life that had given the Pueblos relative peace, prosperity, and independence. He coordinated with other Pueblo leaders and they were at first successful, driving the Spanish out and retaining their independence for twelve years."

"What happened to him?" Elspeth said, lapping up the fascinating history.

"Alas, Po'Pay had his human flaws. Po'Pay had succeeded in expelling the Spanish from New Mexico and according to later accounts he set himself up as the sole ruler of all the Pueblos. He attempted to destroy every trace of the Spanish presence in New Mexico. 'The God of the Christians is dead,' he proclaimed. 'He was made of rotten wood.' Unfortunately, Po'Pay's craving for dictatorial power doomed the long-term prospects of his revised world. There was contention amongst the pueblos, and by the time he died in 1688 they were weak and ready for the Spanish reclamation, which happened in 1692.

"Nevertheless, Po'Pay had good ideals, to reclaim their heritage and sweep away the invaders and punish the injustices inflicted upon them. Sadly, the injustices go on today. The Indian people do not have the rights and prosperity they should have." He tapped her gently on the forehead. "It is up to your generation and those to come to restore our people to glory, to be the standard bearers for a revitalized life. Do you understand?"

Elspeth furrowed her brow and said, "Some of it. I don't get some of those big words. But I get that he was trying to help his people."

"Good, good. Do you like this painting?"

"I dunno," she said. "It kind of reminds me of Halloween. Why did you paint all bones?"

"Bones are the very foundation of a human being. They support our flesh. We stand upright because of bones. We are born with bones, and we die with them. To strip away the flesh reveals the very essence of a man. Bones have been revered throughout time and are used in many ceremonies to show respect and beg the spirits for a favor. They are sacrificed to appease the gods. I have used bones to produce a history of our people, on canvas, and on these walls."

"You've got a little person like Daddy in the middle. How come?"

"Your father has an unusual body and bone structure. I admire the difference and wished to commemorate it on the canvas. I did not want to hurt your daddy so I painted and … used someone else."

"Are you finished with the painting?"

Po'Pay nodded. "Another hour and few tweaks and it will be done. Would you like to do a few brush strokes?"

"Yes," Elspeth exclaimed excitedly. She frowned. "How come you brought me here to see this?"

Po'Pay was thoughtful. "I have never had a wife and children. Had I offspring I would have left my legacy to them after I explained the beauty of their history. You are a special Indian child. You will be my legacy. I will teach you."

"Then can I go home?"

"Yes. Then you may go home. But first, I have new clothes for you before I begin our history." He went over to the pile of backpacks and removed a package from one, a bulky item wrapped in a velvet-soft deer shammy. He handed it to her. "Go behind the divider and put on these clothes. When you come out I will fix your hair and regale you with my story."

Elspeth scrambled off the floor, took the package, and went behind the rickety wood divider.

Po'Pay quickly stripped off his cotton shirt and shimmied into a deerskin shirt with heavy fringes along the arms and front. He wrapped a heavily embroidered decorated band around his head. He dipped his fingers into red-hued clay and drew two long lines across each side of his face. He heard the child come out and he looked at her. She was dressed perfectly in traditional Indian clothing from the mid-calf-length buckskin dress to the soft moccasins. He beckoned her over and she stood in front of him. He told her to turn around and sit with her back to him.

He picked up a porcupine-tail hairbrush and began to gently brush her long, thick black locks, humming as he made each swift, smooth stroke. When he was satisfied with the smoothness and texture of the hair he put down the brush and picked up a thin cedar stick, making a perfectly symmetrical part in her hair. He took hold of one of the two sections and began braiding very slowly, weaving into the hair tiny ribbons of shell beads he had whittled for just this purpose. He finished one braid and tied it off with a thin suede ribbon. He worked the other side exactly the same, and when he was done he told her to turn around. She did, and he nodded in satisfaction. He affixed an elaborately embroidered headband across her forehead.

He picked up a hand mirror and gave it to her. She gazed at her reflection and thought she looked pretty cool.

"You are a beautiful Indian princess," Po'Pay whispered. "And now I shall tell you about our people."

11:52 AM
Team 3

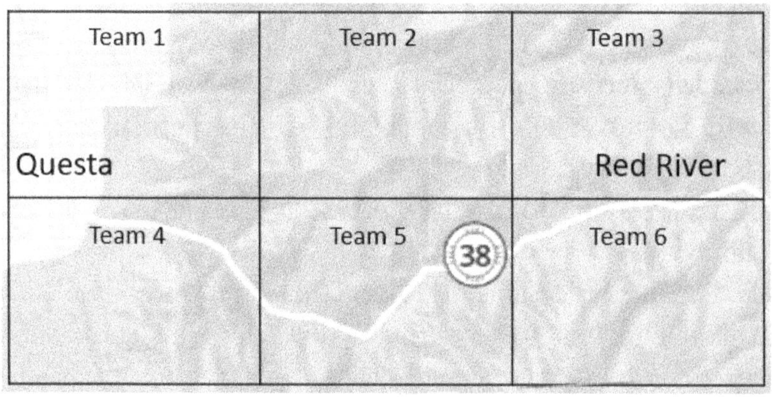

"Hey," Chelan exclaimed. "You did that on purpose." As she walked behind Luc a leafy low branch smacked her in her face as he pushed past it and was careless in preventing it from hitting her.

"Sorry," Luc said breezily, fighting back a grin, not particularly successfully.

"You know my brother can beat the shit out of you and leave nothing but pulp for the vultures."

Jack was standing behind his sister, looming a good foot and a half above her. Luc thought that there wouldn't even be pulp left if the dour man decided to whale on him.

Chelan shoved past him and took the lead, and Jack shoved him hard against a tree trunk as he and the chocolate lab swept past him. They hiked for another thousand yards before they came to a wide but shallow creek. The water was crystal clear, and one could see the rocks on the bottom. A few small fishes wriggled their way down the fast current. Chelan moved ten feet upstream where several big rocks dotted the width of the stream. She used them to traverse it and her brother and "the Nazi" followed.

Luc admired the way she moved, the way she thought. It was clear that her brothers were under her thumb, under the thumb of a tiny but fiery young woman who blustered forth in life without fear or lack of confidence in herself.

Luc wondered if you could fall in love this fast. His thoughts were interrupted by two loud, sharp barks and he watched as Chelan and Jack bolted through the brush. He tore out after them and in a minute they were all standing beside a dark green Bronco with a savage dent in the passenger side. They took a few minutes to search the area then started searching the car.

"Fuck all," Luc said harshly. He held up a small pink sock that had been stuffed under the front seat. It was embroidered with the initials EKM—Elspeth Kaiah McBean. Chelan snatched it from his hand and rubbed it on the lab's nose.

"Find," she snapped.

The dog stiffened, then began galloping towards the road. In the distance Chelan could spot Sawmill Mountain. She admired the stunning beauty of the peak, which was nearly 11,000 feet above sea level. The sides of the mountain were cluttered with tall pine and fir trees and others such as the copse of white-barked aspen trees where they were standing. The trees were dense with bright green leaves, but a few leaves had started to turn orange and yellow, and in a month or so the forest would burst with a canopy of autumn colors that put New England to shame.

Located within the Carson National Forest, the road to the mountain summit is gravelly and rocky and could be treacherous to traverse. Forest Road 597 is totally impassable in winters, often until July 4th or later. The road runs entirely over a mile and a half above the sea level.

The dog sniffed at the road's edge, then followed the scent across it to the other side. He plunged deeper into the forest, followed by Luc and the Chees. Luc was pissed that he had no way to contact his brother, but Memphis was leading Team 2 "next door" and perhaps they'd meet up. Perhaps they'd found their own scents.

12:08 PM
Team 6

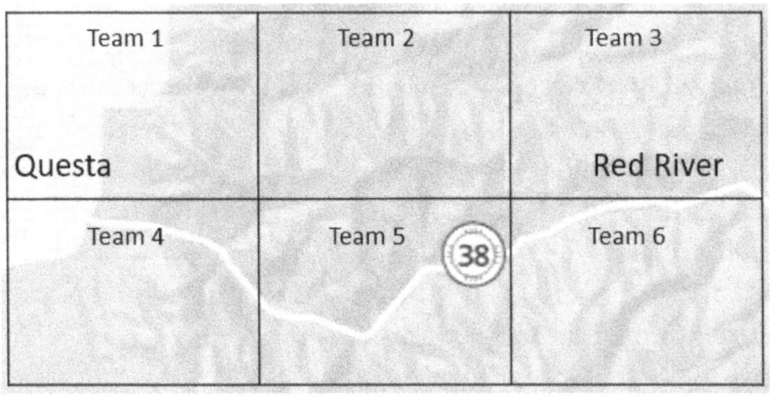

Ata'halne' squatted and examined the earth. He picked up pine needles and studied them, then threw them down. He ran his fingers gently across the ground. He turned around three hundred and sixty degrees, checking for any broken branches that would indicate someone had passed by. Branches were broken all the time, but if a live branch were broken the ends would show live, moist green strands beneath the outer wood. He didn't see any. Wordlessly he rose, adjusted the rifle slung over his shoulder, and continued hiking in a southwesterly direction. He hadn't said a single word to either

Tucson or Cameo from the time they checked into their motel room and left to hunt.

Tucson knew how to hunt and had been in heavily forested areas for much of his youth and adult life. Even so, he admired the stealth and certainty with which Cameo took every step. *Must be that survivalist training*, he thought. He was suddenly struck by a thought he hadn't actually considered before—he was hunting a serial killer with another serial killer. True, Cameo's killing of the four men in Boston was morally justified, but in truth that's exactly what she was. Rather than making him queasy, it made him excited. He was married to a serial killer. Maybe there was something wrong with him, but he didn't care. For the first time in many years he felt whole, happy with his life, and eagerly anticipating the future. He quelled the desire to ravish her right on the forest floor.

Cameo's eyes were alert and she took in everything, every sound, every nuance of the forest, every movement from her husband and the silent Indian. Tucson was ahead of her and she admired his form and determination. He could track although not on the plane of Chelan's brother.

She heard a very slight crackle of a branch and froze, every sense on the alert. She scanned the trees and ground. Apparently Ata'halne' hadn't heard the sound or dismissed it as normal for their location. She sniffed and looked up towards the tree where the men and dog were passing. Without a sound she loaded an arrow into her crossbow and whipped it upwards just as the bobcat snarled and poised to jump. Tucson and Ata'halne' had barely a nanosecond to react to the sound when the bobcat lunged from the tree, screeched, twisted, and fell at their feet dead with the arrow deeply piercing his heart.

Cameo arched her eyebrows in amusement at the shocked looks on the men's faces.

"What's the matter, Kemo Sabes? Cat got your tongue?" she asked as she moved past them and snapped her fingers at the dog who followed her immediately.

4:13 PM
Team 1

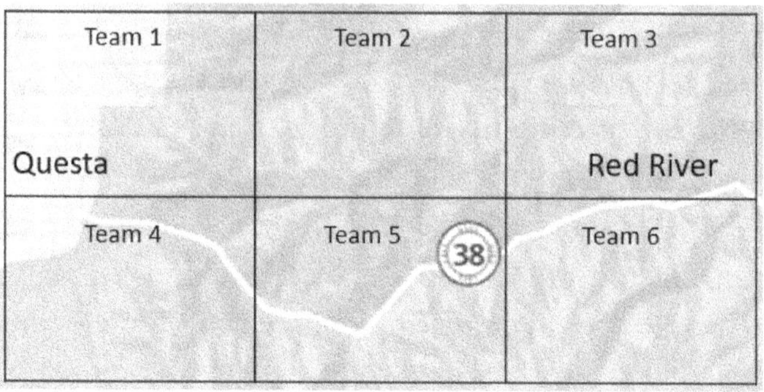

“We had to get the biggest, stupidest, slowest dog on the planet for our team,” Frick groused as he stared down at the bloodhound lying on the ground, his head down and his front paws crossed under it. “He’s napping,” Frick said. “Look at that—he’s fucking napping.”

“Give Pecos a break,” DeVere said, reaching down to scratch the dog’s big, floppy ears. “He’s tired. We all are. Let’s just take a half-hour break and get our wind back. You want an apple?” DeVere held out a Granny Smith.

Frick grunted and took it, then sat on the ground and pulled out his bottle of warm iced tea. He took a large swig and bit into the apple.

DeVere took out his remaining half a sandwich and chewed it with lackluster. So far they had come up with zero, the only excitement in the drudgery when a fat skunk ran across their path and froze them like statues. They breathed a huge sigh of relief when they weren’t sprayed and the critter snuck away under the underbrush.

They were frustrated at not finding any clues or evidence that Naabah and Elspeth had traversed through their section. They had decided to head back to Questa and try to find places that might know Naabah’s face, like a gun shop or a sports shop that specialized in camping gear. They were on their way back to their car now.

Frick groaned and pushed himself off the ground. He cracked his neck and sighed. “I’m getting to old for this shit,” he said.

"Ah, you're barely hitting your stride, old man," DeVere said. "You got a few good years left."

"Yeah, maybe. Not sure this mutt has more than a few months."

"Lancelot had to buy him. What happens to him when we finish the search?"

"Grind him up and make hotdogs."

"You are a sick man." DeVere said. He bent down to scratch behind Pecos's ears. "Maybe I'll take him home."

"Devon'll shoot down that idea."

"Nah, I got an ace up my sleeve to sweeten her up."

"Like?"

DeVere pulled out his wallet and pried a small object from a zippered compartment. He showed it to Frick, who whistled.

"That's some rock," Frick said. "How long have you had it?"

"Coupla months. I've been working up the nerve."

"Think she'll say yes?"

"Maybe."

"What if she doesn't?"

"I'll keep asking her until I wear her down."

"Atta boy."

4:23 PM
Team 4

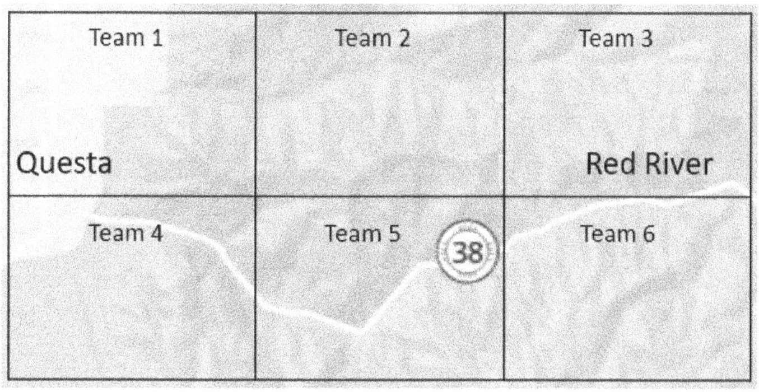

Team 1 Questa	Team 2	Team 3 Red River
Team 4	Team 5 38	Team 6

Swan and her team had started out at the edge of Questa and moved inward section by section; she had gridded her own grid into manageable, logical search areas. She, Devon, and Shilah had walkie-talkies and made a pact to never be out of range as they split off. Every ten minutes they checked in and gave a status.

Disappointingly, they only discovered one mine and no caves. The brown and black German shepherd accompanying them evinced no trace of scent that he'd been given from one of Elspeth's unwashed sweaters. They encountered a half dozen hikers but none of them had seen an Indian man and child or anything odd.

They kept on going, regrouping into a single team around 4 PM. Swan suggested that they move two miles north, then start heading back to where the car was parked. That would bring them to the edge of sunset. She was anxious to get back to her motel room and hoped her husband was there. She was worried sick that they might never find Elspeth. But, they planned on resuming the search tomorrow so there was still hope.

5:12 PM
Team 5

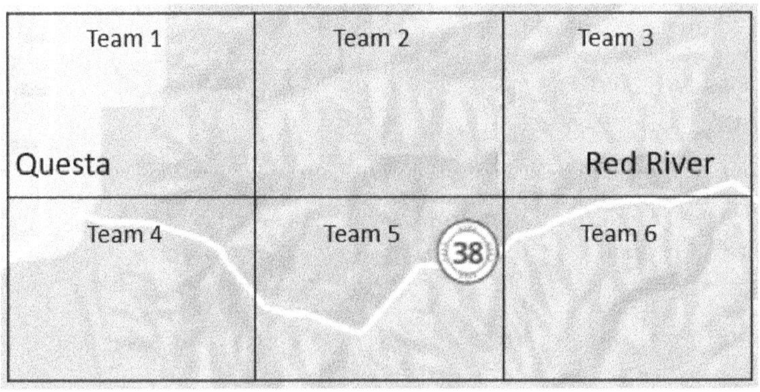

Sand, Adam, and Gaagii stood at the foot of Gold Hill, a 12,711-foot mountain range peak and well-trodden hiking route covered in meadow and pine forest. Huge patches of the top were a rocky, uneven ground with rocks dotting the land in a tight pattern and seemingly hosting dozens of scampering ground squirrels that paid no attention to giant intruders that couldn't run as fast as they could.

During their trek they had come across three abandoned mines with no evidence that anyone had been in them for decades. They found a small cave, but when they heard a low growl coming from inside they backed away quickly. Gaagii told them it was probably a black momma bear with cubs and, no, the last thing on earth they wanted to do was disturb her.

A few off-trail hikers waved to them and kept going. A few minutes after one couple hiked off there was a scream. Sand hightailed it towards the scream and reached the couple who were standing dead still, the woman's hands clasped tightly over her mouth, her eyes as wide as saucers. The man was whispering, "Oh, Jesus, oh Jesus," over and over again. Sand rushed up to them with Adam right on his heels. The two men stared down at what caused the woman to freak out. There it was, partially under a mound of damp leaves, partially uncovered, white on dark green.

A skeleton, its eyeless sockets staring at them, one bony hand stuck out to the side, palm up. The other hand was missing, and so were the feet.

They heard the woman drop to the ground, retching, as her shaking husband held her hair back. Adam and Sand looked at one another, wondering if the dead person was someone they once sought.

CHAPTER FOURTEEN

Tuesday, October 3, 1978
4:44 PM
Team 2

Team 1 Questa	Team 2	Team 3 Red River
Team 4	Team 5 38	Team 6

They were resting in the shade, exhausted from all the hiking and searching. Memphis knew that the hike was difficult for Percy whose short legs hindered their speed. He purposely slowed down a little bit, but he couldn't negatively impact their progress with too much personal compassion. Elspeth's life was in danger. Percy knew that, too, and he pushed himself to keep up as he relentlessly pursued their efforts to find his daughter.

Smokey, the black German shepherd, evinced no sense of finding an olfactory track of the child in the last hour. Memphis wondered if that was because there was no scent, or the dog just wasn't up to snuff. Still, like Swan, he found the beast attractive and affectionate.

They hadn't spoken much since they started into the forest, just a few words to indicate one direction or another. Aponi was mostly silent, unsure of what she could say that wouldn't exacerbate the situation. The man whose daughter her brother had abducted asked her to come in case they met up with their prey and her siblinghood might convince him to surrender or at least give up the child. When they took a break around noon to eat and drink she spoke a little, telling them that Antonio had camped and hunted in this area when he was a young man. He liked exploring the old mines and caves. He felt at home here, she said, but she had no idea where he had camped and where he might be.

Aponi finished her fruit. She had been avoiding Percy's eyes since they stopped; she didn't quite know what to say to him. She rummaged around in her shoulder satchel and took out a small wallet. She withdrew three snapshots, looked at them, and silently handed them to Percy.

"My sons and daughter," she said shyly. "Mingan, Niyol, and Chimalis. They are my whole life, my whole heart, my whole soul. If I lost one of them I would want to die but I would have to go on living for the other two."

"What do their names mean?" Percy asked, handing her back the photos. Chimalis looked very much like Elspeth had at that age.

"Chimalis means bluebird." She smiled broadly and looked at Memphis. "Mingan means grey wolf. Niyol means wind." Her smile faded. "I am so very sorry about what my brother has done. None of what he is accused of reflects the big brother I once knew. I do not know the man we are hunting."

"We're grateful for the help you gave us on his background and the key to his house," Percy said quietly. "You are not responsible for another's sins. Were that the case no human would be without blame."

"You're a kind man," she replied.

Percy thought, *Not so much when I find your brother.*

Memphis stood and brushed the pine needles off his butt. "Okay, we've got about an hour and a half before we need to head back to the car and regroup." He nodded east. "Let's start up that incline and make a wide circle back towards Questa." He whistled sharply at the dog who stood at attention, his ears perked. "Get going, Smokey. Earn your keep for a change."

The dog panted and wagged his tail, then began striding quickly, his nose sometimes in the air, sometimes to the ground. About fifty yards up the dog stopped suddenly and barked twice sharply. He stuck his nose near a tree stump, rooting around.

"Watcha got, boy?" Memphis asked urgently. He pulled on the dog's collar and scanned the area around the stump. "Damn," he said, squatting down and gently prying a dried, balled up tissue from under the end of a rock. He sniffed then looked up at his companions. "Urine," he said. He held the tissue to Smokey's nose and the dog whined then barked. Percy examined the tree stump and the earth around it. He was breathing hard when he slowly picked up a scrap of pink fabric. He closed his eyes and touched the strip to his cheek. He opened his eyes and said to Memphis, "Elspeth was wearing a pink undershirt." He held the strip to Smokey's nose and was rewarded with another whine and bark.

Memphis grasped his friend's shoulder hard. He didn't waste any time. He rubbed the dog's snout with the tissue and strip and said, "Find Elspeth. Find Elspeth."

Smokey barked, froze, then took off in a northwesterly direction with the men and woman hot on his paws.

5:01 PM
Team 5

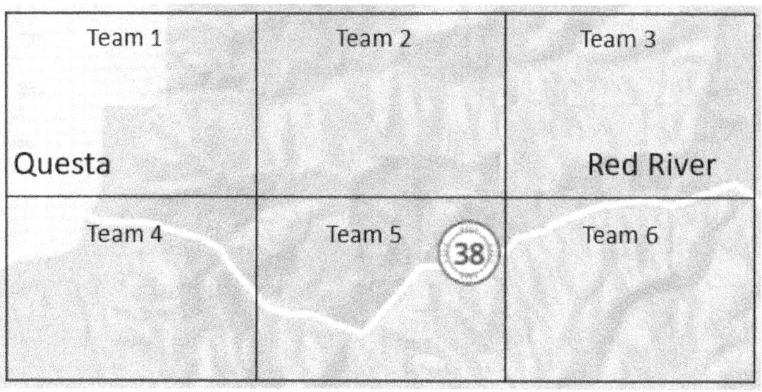

Adam managed to get the husband and wife calmed down; at least she'd stopped sobbing and blowing her nose. The couple's car was parked a solid two hours away from the gravesite, and Sand's borrowed jeep was parked even farther. He and Gaagii quietly discussed the best course of action and they decided that Gaagii would accompany the couple back to their car and drive to the nearest phone and call the State Police. Sand told Gaagii to call in to Frack and let him know what was going on. He and Adam would stay with the skeleton.

It still took a solid twenty minutes for the woman to compose herself enough to make it through the forest, but at least Sand knew the couple would be safe with Gaagii, who was the second tallest and first widest Chee brother. He kept the dog and when Gaagii and the couple disappeared over the horizon Sand dropped to the forest floor and leaned back against a tree. He glanced over at the skeleton. Adam dropped down beside him.

"Think this is one of the missing people?" Adam asked.

"Dunno," Sand said, sighing. "It's not out of the realm of possibility that this could be some random hiker that got lost and died from the elements."

"Hmm," Adam murmured, then crawled over to the skeleton.

"What are you doing?" Sand asked.

"A half-assed, non-medical autopsy." Adam gingerly explored the skull, carefully moving it from side to side. "Hmm," he said. "He died from an element, all right."

"Which element?"

"Lead. Bullet hole in the back of his head. Two, actually. Double tap."

"That sounds like a professional execution."

"Sure does. I'm going to root around and see if I can find any wallet or ID. I'll try not to snap any bones." Adam slowly and carefully felt around under the skeleton. His fingers caught on some kind of stiff fabric and he thought he felt a belt. He moved his hand and then stopped and said, "Aha." He withdrew a stiff, small leather wallet and waved it at Sand.

"Can you open it without it disintegrating?" Sand asked. "Maybe we should wait for the cops."

"I'm an impatient kind of guy." With that Adam gently opened the wallet, grimacing at the crack of stiff leather. The two sides of the wallet came part in his hands.

"The cops are going to be pissed with you tampering with evidence."

"Sand," Adam said. "Sand, Sand, Sand. Obviously, you've mistaken me for someone who gives a damn."

"My mistake."

Adam saw what looked like a driver's license behind a yellowing plastic slot and he extracted it but cracked the plastic which fell into brittle pieces. He held it up and squinted at it. "Andy Denison. The license expired last year." He examined the wallet further. "One Master Charge card, and about thirty, forty dollars. It wasn't robbery, then."

"He doesn't fit our profile," Sand said. "I think we just stumbled across an unrelated crime."

"Well," Adam said thoughtfully, "maybe he had a family that never knew what happened to him, and now we can give them closure." He hesitated for a few seconds then said, "I was, um, wondering."

"'Bout what?"

"Cameo. She and Norah talked a few times, and Norah mentioned that there would be a good true-crime book in this case, but Cameo seemed uninterested in writing it. From the feedback Norah got on her from Caleb Winsted and a few colleagues it seems like she's a smart, articulate person that has a mastery of the English language and writes well. Norah thought it was kind of odd that she had no desire to capitalize on a matter so entrenched in her family and professional world."

Sand told himself to calm down and ease into a plausible explanation. He couldn't very well tell Adam about Cameo's past and her resolution of it. They had made a good job of framing then disappearing Damien Savage, but no one wanted any scrutiny that might get people—particularly law enforcement—to wondering. He shrugged. "She's a very private person. She went through a terrible rape and lost her memory, and only got it back last year. She just wants to lead a quiet life. Family is everything to her. She loves her job on the *Courant* and isn't interested in spreading her wings into the world of true-crime books."

"I guess I get that. Anyway, Norah didn't push."

"Maybe she could write it. Damn fine nonfiction writer, your wife."

"Thanks, but she's occupied with her magazine and newspaper and our son. I'm sure she'll put the story in one edition of *Seraphim*."

Sand shifted his body into a more comfortable position. He stretched his arms above his head and cracked his neck and knuckles. "So, we're stuck here for a while with a dead guy. How are we going to pass the time?"

Adam smiled slightly and took a swig of water from his canteen. Christ, he could use a double shot of Irish whiskey. He leaned back against the tree and closed his eyes and said, "Once upon a time there was a disaffected young vet that was discharged in California and got a little lost. He wound up spending some time with the wrong people."

"How wrong?"

"Ever hear of Charlie Manson?"

5:12 PM
Team 3

Team 1	Team 2	Team 3
Questa		Red River
Team 4	Team 5 38	Team 6

"The kid is leaving her spore," Chelan said as they came across a third balled-up tissue and a second pink fabric strip. "Smart, smart kid." She glanced at Luc. "Has to be her Indian blood."

"Hey. In case you hadn't noticed I'm half-Indian, too," Luc said in annoyance.

"Yeah, but your white blood diluted it. Whoever heard of a half-Polish Indian?"

"Ah," said Luc with a smirk on his face. "You checked me out."

"I like to know the enemy."

"I'd be happy to let you get to know me better." Luc had barely gotten out the last word when a hard hand came down on his shoulder, nearly knocking him off his feet. He turned and looked up at a fierce face. Jack's look could frighten off a pack of starving werewolves.

"Stay away from my sister," Jack said flatly, menace saturating each word.

Luc bravely countered, "And if I don't?"

"I'll tear off your right arm and beat you to death with it, then roast your heart over a campfire and eat it."

Luc held up his hands. "Chill out, Sasquatch. Didn't mean anything by it." Another hard hand smacked his shoulder and spun him around. Chelan glared up at him.

"Insult my brother again and I'll rip your other arm off and eat your liver," she said icily. She stalked over to the dog and rubbed the tissue against his nose and sent him off. Jack followed her while throwing nasty looks at Luc, who trailed behind them thinking it was just his luck to fall into a cannibal family.

6:30 PM
Team 2

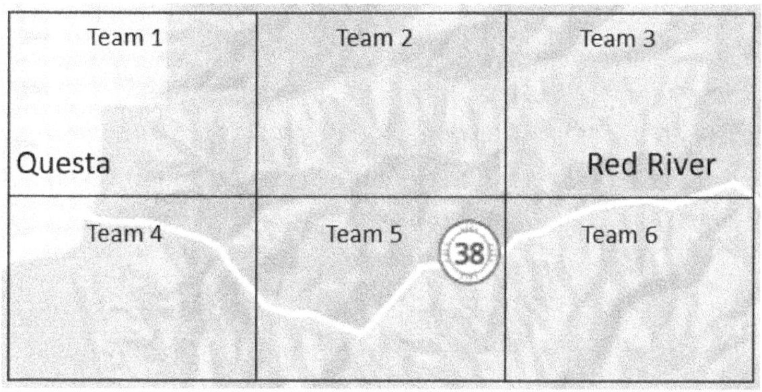

Team 1 Questa	Team 2	Team 3 Red River
Team 4	Team 5 38	Team 6

Smokey stuck his nose into the leaves and pawed at the ground. He pulled back with a pink strip in his mouth. Percy extracted it and held it tightly in his fist. He handed it to Memphis who examined it and put it in the zippered compartment in his backpack.

"We're close," Percy said in a low voice. "I feel we're close."

"Maybe," Memphis said. "We don't know how far in they've gone." He glanced skyward. "It'll be dark soon. Sunset's in about a half hour. Perhaps we should mark our location and go back to—"

"I'm not going back," Percy said flatly. "I'm not going back without my daughter."

"Percy, I understand—"

"No, you don't," Percy replied angrily. "A madman stole my daughter. He—"

Memphis cut him off. "Maybe you're forgetting what a madwoman did to my daughter. You were a witness to that, so, you little bastard, don't give me any shit about not understanding."

Memphis and Percy glared at one another for a moment before Percy closed his eyes and clasped his hand over his mouth. "I'm sorry," he whispered fiercely. Memphis moved swiftly and hugged his friend and they were silent for a long minute. Their moment was interrupted by Aponi.

"I can track in the dark," she said quietly. "And worst comes to worst we hunker down and sleep until dawn and pick up the search then."

Percy was about to thank her when they heard a loud crack of a branch. Without hesitation both men pulled their guns and pointed in the direction of the sound. Memphis groaned and lowered his gun.

"How did you guys get here?" he asked Luc as his brother and the two Chees approached.

"We found Naabah's Bronco," Luc said. "It was hidden off-road and when we searched it we found Elspeth's sock jammed under the seat along with a bag of man's clothes." He handed the sock to Memphis who handed it to Percy. "We scented the dog and he took off and led us here. We picked up a few scraps of a shirt and some urine-soaked tissues."

"We've found the same," Percy said, pocketing the sock.

"So, we're going in the right direction," Memphis said. "The question is, how much farther? It's going to get dark real fast."

"We can track in the dark," Chelan said coolly. "Unless you want to go back and start up again tomorrow."

"I'm not going back," Percy said.

"*We're* not going back," Memphis elaborated. "Aponi?" She nodded immediately.

"I wish there was some way we could get word back to the other teams," Luc said. "They'll go nuts if we don't turn up."

"There's nothing we can do about that. They'll likely converge on our sections tomorrow morning," Memphis said. He addressed Chelan. "Who's the better tracker—you or your brother?"

"Jack," she said.

"Okay, Jack. You'll take the lead when the sun sets. Until then I'll lead and we'll follow the two dogs." He leaned down and petted Smokey's head. "Ready to go, boy? Good boy." He reinforced the scent with the sock and did the same with the lab. "Go."

The dogs galloped off side by side followed by the six human trackers. They stopped about twenty minutes later when they reached a small creek and refilled their canteens and water bottles and took a bathroom break. By that time, the sun had set and the sky, barely visible through the tops of the tall trees, was shedding its light minute by minute, and would be black in thirty minutes. When they were ready to proceed Jack took the lead and began smoothly wending his way through the dense forest. They had flashlights and extra batteries, so they were set.

As night fell the forest was alive with the sounds of the night. Crickets cricked madly, owls hooted and the flying predator wings of barn owls and hawks whipped through the air searching for food and insects for the haphazardly looping bats. The wind was kicking up, rustling the tree leaves like ocean waves hissing against the sand. Somehow, Smokey homed in on a scent and barked twice. Flashlights ablaze the crew searched the area and found one more balled-up tissue.

By nine-thirty the forest was pitch dark and the team decided to bunk down and get a start at dawn. Percy curled up in a ball next to Memphis, hugging Elspeth's sock to his cheek.

10:18 PM
The Cave

Po'Pay watched Elspeth sleep. The girl was tuckered out. He had taken her outside for a couple of hours to hike and enjoy nature. He took her a half mile away where he held her hand tightly and showed her the deep canyon in which a thin but swift river flowed.

He spent most of the rest of the day explaining his artwork. His canvas was now finished and he allowed her to add a few brushstrokes near the center where she filled in the dwarf skull with two neutral colors. When she was done he complimented her and said she had the soul of an artist and should consider becoming one. He squatted down and affixed his signature to the bottom of the canvas. Instead of using the one he put on all of his other canvases, HashNaa, he used a bright red to denote "Po'Pay."

When he was done he turned to her and said, "This is your painting. Cherish it well for it is my last work and you were part of its creation." He waved his arm around the cave. "This is for you now, too, the only one to whom I've revealed my secret place. I have left everything to you."

"Don't you have any family you can leave it to?" she asked.

He shook his head sadly. "Alas, no. I had a sister, but she betrayed me." When he had come home from the dinner at Percy's and found a couple of beetles skittering about the basement, he sensed that someone had been there. He scoured every inch of his house and found other minor, almost unnoticeable evidence of breach. None of the outside locks had been picked, but he smelled and touched the light veneer of WD-40 oil on the key slot of the back door. Someone had entered with a key, and the only person that had a spare key was Aponi. There was a small scuff on the edge of the floor near the inside of that door. He walked past his house into the desert and found two sets of fresh tire tracks. It was then he knew that someone had been there, been inside his home, and of course had found his equipment.

And he knew that the dinner was a ploy to get him away from his house so someone could inspect it. So, Percy was part of the ploy. He didn't know if Tansee had played a part, but that didn't matter. The culprits were no doubt the Warrior Spirit team since they had been involved in searching for missing people. How they had homed in on him he had no idea, but he believed that they did. That clumsy scene at the arts festival was the final proof. He had already put his own plans into action, and he was ready.

He didn't have much time. He wanted to tell his story and show his art to someone worthy, and that was this child. He only hoped she would remember his tale and live her life being a proud member of their race. Tomorrow he would finish his tale of the cave wall, and then he would take her to Questa where she could call her parents.

And then he would fade into eternity, peaceful and fulfilled.

CHAPTER FIFTEEN

Wednesday, October 4, 1978
6:34 AM
Teams 2 & 3

Team 1 Questa	Team 2	Team 3 Red River
Team 4	Team 5 38	Team 6

Dawn was just around the corner and Memphis had been up for a half hour. He found a fir tree that needed watering and when he got back he brought an armful of kindling branches. He built a small circle of rocks around them and lit them on fire. He had a small tin pot in his backpack and filled it with canteen water and held it over the fire until it boiled. Luc groaned and woke up and stumbled off to find his own tree. Memphis noticed that the Chees and Aponi were nowhere around and Percy was coming back from his own morning ablutions.

Memphis pulled out a few Styrofoam cups and poured the boiling water into them then added a packet of instant coffee to each. He glanced over at Percy. "Better than nothing," he said as he handed Percy a cup.

Percy sipped, frowned, then sipped again. "Just barely," he muttered. He glanced up at Luc who was walking towards them pulling his zipper up. Memphis handed his brother another cup.

"Better than the crap we get at the station," Luc said. He looked around. "Where are the cannibals?"

"Huh?" Memphis said.

"Long story. The Chees."

"I have no idea, but—"

His thought was cut off by the three Chees stomping into the clearing, followed by Aponi, their hands full of berries. Chelan dumped her handful into Luc's hands. "Breakfast," she said tartly. She picked up his cup from the ground and drained the coffee. The breakfast was mostly silent although the Chees had their heads together and were mumbling to each other and gesturing. Chelan cast Luc a few glances, usually with a snarl spread across her lips.

When they were done eating Memphis put out the fire and gestured for everyone to gather round.

"Look," he said. "We don't know if there are any more of Elspeth's spore around or how far away they may be. But I think we should let the dogs have the lead and we follow them. Anyone else got a better plan?"

Everyone mumbled no or shook their heads. They gathered their things, gave the dogs the scent again and sent the dogs off. Smokey stopped after a few yards, raised his head, sniffed, and began moving west. They followed. Before they left Memphis checked his topographical map and saw that they were heading towards the edge of where Team 1 had been searching. According to his calculations they were about two miles from Venado Peak in one direction and about eight miles from Questa in another.

7:30 AM
Red River

"They could be in trouble," Tucson said anxiously as he stuffed a muffin into his mouth at his wife's nagging insistence.

"Or they could have found a trail and had to stop and camp out when it got dark," Cameo said reasonably.

"They weren't carrying any camping gear."

"Are you telling me that Hehewuti's sons are incapable of surviving a night in the mountains?" his wife asked archly. Before he could answer she went on. "Besides which they're with three Indians that seem to know their way around nature. Maybe they just decided to keep going until it got too dark and they had brains enough not to try to backtrack."

"What if they got lost?"

"They didn't get lost."

"Who didn't get lost?" Sand asked as he came through the motel room door. Adam was still in their room finishing up a call with Norah. Ata'halne' and Gaagii Chee were off somewhere having breakfast and grumbling about having to endure interrogation by the State Police about the found skeleton. The police had interrogated both teams for a couple of hours after they returned to Red River along with the late Andy Denison. The remains were at the coroner's office being analyzed but it was clear to the police that the teams had nothing to do with his demise.

"Teams 2 and 3," Cameo replied. "Tucson's freaking out about not being able to get ahold of Memphis and Luc."

"Did you call Swan?"

"She's pissed that he didn't come back but I know she's worried. We should go look for them," Tucson said.

"Our charge is to keep scouring our sectors," Sand said.

"All right, guys," Cameo said, sighing. "We have two options. One, continue searching for Elspeth. Two, assume that the other teams found something that has drawn them to spending the night and picking up in the morning. Personally … I vote for number two. I just have a feeling."

"I trust my wife's intuition," Tucson said.

"I don't argue with a woman that can kill a bobcat with a cross bow," Sand said as he sipped his coffee. He winked at Cameo. "However," he said cautiously, "we don't know where exactly they are and we could go looking for them in the wrong direction. Let's take a vote. Does anyone think that heading back out to our sections will be beneficial?" Neither Tucson nor Cameo raised their hand. "Me, too. So, I say we pack up and head back to Questa and link up with Swan and the others and make a plan."

"What about Team 3's room?" Tucson asked.

"We'll take their stuff but leave the room in their name in case they come back."

"I wish to hell we knew what was going on up there," Cameo said as she started packing her bag.

"Hopefully, we'll get some clue. I mean, they're closer to Questa than Red River so it's logical that we head over there," Sand said. "Give Swan a call and I'll go tell Adam and we'll see you in the parking lot in twenty minutes. I'll find the Chee brothers."

8:30 AM
Questa

When Teams 5 and 6 returned to the Questa motel Swan was on the phone with Frack who was giving her updates on the law enforcement search for Naabah. The State Police roadblocks in all four directions and their offshoots had borne no fruit; however, an ad in the *Courant* regarding the sale of a car to Naabah had. A young man in Las Vegas, New Mexico had called in to say that he was pretty sure that the man to whom he had sold his dark green Ford Bronco was Naabah although that wasn't the name used. The man called himself Tony Whirlwind and paid cash. They had the license plate number but there was a good chance Naabah changed it after he took possession of the car. An APB was put out on the Bronco and so far there was an unsubstantiated sighting west of Dalhart, Texas.

Nick's condition had stabilized and he was out of the woods. They planned on keeping him in the hospital for a few more days and then release him to his wife. Yuki's mother had moved into their house to help with the kids while he convalesced. Tansee and Ben were still under the elder Grayhawks' roof and she was doing as well as expected considering her daughter was missing and her husband was off searching for a dangerous man. Her eye was better and thankfully the ophthalmologist said there would be no permanent effects from the pepper spray. Declan had left the brewery in Connor's and Mr. Cho's hands while he tended to Tucson's four kids. Akiro finished the documents necessary for Cameo to formally adopt Braeden and Brianna and become their legal mother and they'd set a court date as soon as the teams returned home and the Naabah matter was resolved.

Frack had a touch of admiration in his voice when he told Swan about how Lancelot was handling the news media that descended on the office when the story broke. "The little fella" (as Frack called him) was deftly holding the press at bay and giving out no information. He had fortified the office with two security men who were necessary when a couple of reporters tried to get inside and break into the various offices. He fielded nonstop phone calls and referred legitimate ones to Skye, who would handle any associated legal matters. Between the two of them no one on the outside was getting any confidential or personal information.

Swan scribbled down notes from the call and relayed them to her colleagues when they were all gathered in the motel dining room eating a mound of food with three tables pushed together in a private area. A few other guests eyed them but kept away.

"Okay," Swan said as the waitress delivered her waffles. She cut a half stick of butter and dumped it on the pile then poured a half cup of syrup over that. "Tucson, I hate to tell you this—shades of Luc—but your twins have been suspended from school for two days for a biology class incident. I won't get into the gruesome details. The principal wants to see you and Cameo when you get back."

"Oh, Lord," Tucson groaned.

"Adam, Norah called about a half hour ago and said that the Gearys are sitting in your office and refuse to leave until they talk to you. No one's said anything about there being the possibility of Taylor being found but they know you're here and they know about the manhunt."

"I'll call them after we finish," Adam said. "I hate to get their hopes up … or dashed."

"Frick, London called just to tell you she misses you. Um, she said something like 'tell Lurch his Morticia is waiting.' Look—I don't even want to know." She nearly rolled her eyes at the lovesick look in Frick's eyes.

"Are we going to talk about the elephant in the room?" Sand said. "What are we going to do about our tardy team members?"

"Nothing," Swan stated flatly, to the surprise of everyone. "We don't know exactly where they are, why they didn't come back, or what their next steps are. It's pointless to go off half-cocked to try to find them in a wilderness where even a seasoned tracker could get lost."

"We should notify the State Police," DeVere said. He saw the deep scowl on Devon's face. "Or not." He suddenly found his scrambled eggs fascinating. Barely a second or two passed before anyone could say anything when he jumped up and dropped to one knee next to Devon, whose jaw had dropped to the floor. He whipped the ring out of his wallet. "Will you marry me?" he gulped.

Everyone around the table held their collective breath.

"Are you out of your ever-lovin' *mind*?" Devon asked in disbelief. "You ask me this *now*?"

"Life's too damn short to wait for the important things," Cameo said quietly. "There's no better time to affirm life."

"Well?" Swan snapped at Devon. "Put the poor guy out of his misery."

Devon stared at the ring then held out her hand and nodded as her eyes filled with tears. DeVere slipped the ring on her finger and they stood at the same time and threw themselves into each other's arms. The entire breakfast room broke out into applause. The newly engaged couple sat back down, grinning shyly.

A blanket of silence fell over the group. Swan said it for all of them.

"So, we wait."

10:30 AM
Teams 2 & 3

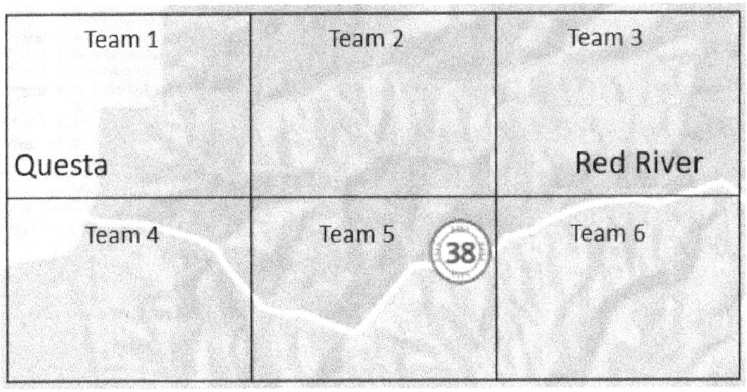

The morning continued cool and refreshing as the six trekkers headed northwest past the area where Smokey found the last spore that Elspeth had left. Jack's eagle eye caught several broken branches that he said had been recently disrupted, and he found two partial footprints belonging to a full-grown person wearing hiking boots; he said they were fairly fresh. About fifty yards after he saw those prints he caught a glimpse of a small footprint that seemed disrupted, as though the person had tripped and obscured the full pattern.

Then they came to a fork on an incline, each leg of which showed some travel activity at some point in the past. Neither of the dogs sensed anything on either leg.

"What do we do?" Luc asked his brother. "Split off or choose one?"

"We've got a better chance splitting off," Chelan answered before Memphis could. "According to your map there are abandoned mines in either direction. The more played out ones are likely to be at a higher elevation because of how difficult it would have been to work them back in the good old days."

"Let's split up, then," Memphis said. Before he could suggest a route Percy spoke up.

"We'll take the higher incline," Percy said.

"Why?" Luc asked.

Percy shrugged. "I don't know. Just a feeling."

Memphis nodded, then dug around in his backpack and pulled out a walkie-talkie. He handed it to Luc. "They don't have much range which is why we didn't think they'd be good enough to talk between teams, but since we're in the same general area maybe we can use them."

"How much of a range?" Luc asked while he examined it.

"Four, five miles maybe at best. Check in every half hour. What time you got?"

Luc checked his watch. "Ten-forty."

"Okay, check in at eleven then eleven-thirty. Get going."

Luc, Chelan, Jack, and their dog headed down the left pathway while Memphis started up the right one with Percy following and Aponi bringing up the rear.

12:00 PM
The Cave

"I like it," Elspeth said, nodding. "The meat's a little tough, though." She was scraping up the last of the squirrel stew that Po'Pay had made for their lunch. He had brought carrots and turnips from his mine store and made a bare-bones stew out of those vegetables and the two squirrels he shot with a bow and arrow at dawn.

"I didn't have enough time to simmer it all day like I normally would," Po'Pay said.

"It still tasted good. Thank you."

"You're welcome." Po'Pay noticed that the girl seemed calmer and didn't seem to be afraid of him. She was still clearly homesick and missing her family, but he was relieved that she didn't seem to think he was going to harm her. That was the last thing on his mind.

He would have to get her home soon he thought as he swallowed a couple of pills and washed them down with milk to settle his stomach. He willed the pain to go away.

But it was there, the cancer that was eating away at him inside and that had been for months. When he was young he thought like all young people that he was immortal and nothing could harm him. He lived well, ate good food, and had few vices, a tequila or beer on occasion but not that often. He had stopped smoking pot by the time he was thirty. During the last ten years he had cut down on red meat and spicy food. And still, still … the cancer had come and fate laughed at him and made it clear that he would never reach his fiftieth birthday. And he wondered—who would eat his sins? No one. He would carry those sins to his grave and beyond. And perhaps that was always to be his ultimate fate as karma collected its own injustice.

The child was pure and would remain so. He had told her the history of their people and demonstrated it with his art. She feared the images at first but then seemed to be entranced. Perhaps someday she would teach her own children.

Today, he thought. He would take her home today.

His work was done.

12:52 PM
Team 2

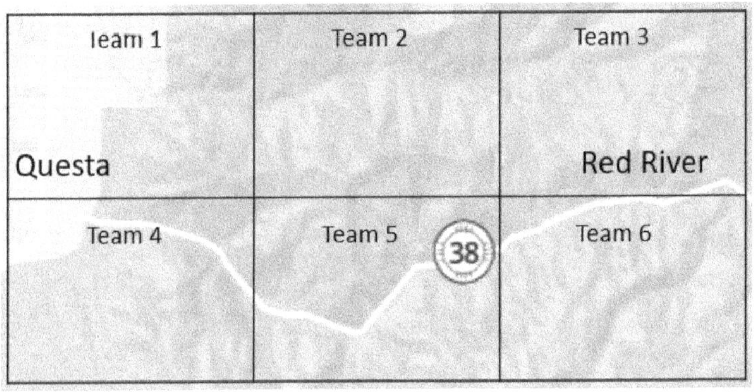

"Up there," Percy said. "See it?" He was pointing to a rock face covered by heavy foliage.

Memphis carefully made his way up a slippery slope with small rocks that rumbled down as his boots disturbed them. He listened and heard nothing, then waved Percy and Aponi to stay still as he carefully started to move the tangled foliage back, revealing a sliver of an opening. "I think it's a cave," he said. He moved a little more of the branches and felt along the opening. "Son of a bitch," he whispered. "I think it's a mine. This is a side plank." Percy started to move towards him. "Stop. Let me check it out first."

Memphis shrugged out of his backpack and left it on the ground. He took out his flashlight, and unholstered his gun. He had pushed enough of the branches away to squeeze sideways into the shaft and a second later he disappeared from view. Percy and Aponi were waiting ten feet away, holding their breath. Percy was trembling.

Memphis reappeared. "I think we've found his hidey-hole," he said quietly and beckoned them in.

Percy and Aponi entered the mine shaft, which was dimly lit but light enough to see everything. Memphis motioned to a small gas generator that was hooked up to a spaghetti-like series of electrical wires. They saw the same shaft contents that Elspeth had when Naabah had brought her there. Smokey stood in the middle of the cluttered area, sniffed and barked twice.

The three of them moved to separate sections of the shaft and began exploring. Aponi was silent as she found several items she knew belonged to her brother. She held one in her hand, a nearly furless rabbit foot that he had made when he was a boy from game he had killed. She clutched it tightly and closed her eyes. Tears edged out as she thought about the young teen that had raised her. How long ago did both of them lose that special human being?

Percy inspected every nook and cranny he could and suddenly he inhaled sharply and dropped down on his knees and dug under the edge of a box. He pulled out a pink sock. He held it up to Memphis.

Memphis nodded and went outside. He tried the walkie-talkie to contact Luc but all he got was static and a half word or two. *Shit*, he thought. He talked again telling Luc where he was and what they'd found although he had no idea if his brother could hear or understand him. He went back into the mine and told Percy and Aponi that the other team was likely unable to join them.

"The good thing is that at least we have a lot of fresh scent for Smokey," he said. Aponi silently handed him a shirt and he made sure Smokey got a good scent once they were outside.

Smokey turned slightly northwest and began to move off.

CHAPTER SIXTEEN

Wednesday, October 4, 1978
1:13 PM
Team 3

Team 1 Questa	Team 2	Team 3 Red River
Team 4	Team 5 38	Team 6

"All I could get was static and something that sounded like 'my,'" Luc said, frowning and shaking his walkie-talkie. "Stupid things. Someday they should make 'em so they have a really long range." He stared at Chelan who had turned around and was headed away. "Hey—where are you going?"

She looked at him balefully and said, "You heard 'my' but I heard 'mine.' I think your brother might have found the trail or the place. We're cutting diagonal and heading up towards where they were going when we split off. Coming, paleface?" Without waiting for an answer, she jumped ahead of Jack and started striding away fast.

Luc looked up at the sky and rolled his eyes and quickly followed. "Paleface my Polish-Indian ass," he muttered.

1:42 PM

Team 2

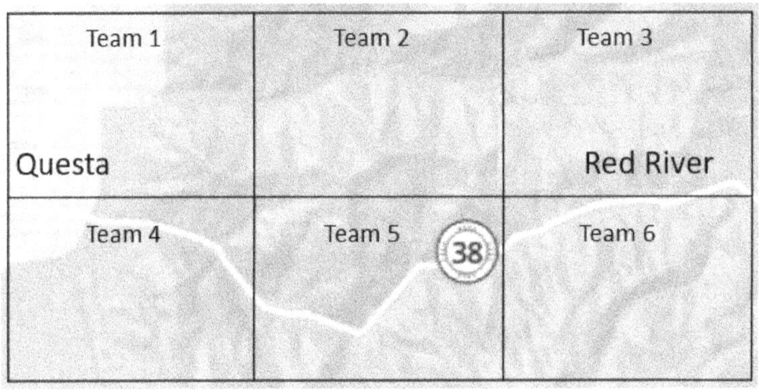

Aponi squatted and pointed out newly broken branches. Memphis nodded. She stood and was very still, her dark eyes surveying the landscape, wondering if her brother were nearby. She sensed him. She didn't know why; they had been too far apart for too long, but they were blood. She glanced at Percy, who was studying her with unfathomable, focused eyes. She nodded just barely.

Close, she thought. They were close.

1:48 PM

The Cave

Po'Pay watched Elspeth sitting on the cave floor examining the wooden kachina he had carved for her the night before. He'd always loved whittling, and the six-inch icon was filled with detailed grooves and cuts that made it appear as realistic as possible. He hoped she kept it always and remembered her time with him and the lessons he had taught her.

But, it was time to return the little girl to her family and her world. And it was time for him to make the exit from his.

He clapped his hands to draw her attention. "Get your jacket and backpack, little one," he said.

Elspeth scrambled off the floor. "Where are we going?"

He leaned down to her eye level. "I'm taking you home." She rewarded him with a huge, happy grin and he felt a pang of guilt over the pain he had caused her and her family. For the first time he thought of her uncle, whom he had shot, and hoped that the young man had survived. Like those two young men, Nick Griffin was simply collateral damage.

While Elspeth was getting herself ready Po'Pay looked over the map he had made to his mine and cave and tucked it into an envelope that he'd put in her backpack. His other personal papers were already stored in a side zipper, including the handwritten will in which he left all of his possessions to Elspeth. He wouldn't be able to come back since his time on the earth was very short, but he wanted the world to see his art. Perhaps not understand it, like he hoped the child had, but to see it. After all, an artist wants some recognition, some appreciation. Narcissistic, perhaps, but human. He wondered how his name would go down in history. He hated to admit to a character flaw of hubris, but he cared.

He knelt in front of Elspeth and checked the straps on her backpack and that her hiking boots were tied tightly. The mid-day temperatures were in the comfortable seventies, but he wanted to make sure that she was warm enough against any winds that might whip against them at the high elevation. He put a bandana over her head and gently tied it under her chin. He winked at her before he stood up and affectionately tugged on a braid.

Po'Pay checked his own backpack and strapped it on, then took one last long look around the cave and at his canvas, wondering where that would end up if it wasn't given to Elspeth as part of her "inheritance." In a police evidence room? A museum? A bonfire? That made him sad. At least he had taken Polaroids of the cave and canvas and put them in Elspeth's belongings. He had also taken a shot of her applying a few brush strokes.

He took her hand and led her out of the cave after he shut down the generator and lights. He urged her down the slight incline to the cave entrance and told her to be careful and watch where she was stepping. He was gratified that she seemed very sure-footed and wondered if that was natural from her mother's side of the family.

He took the lead after about ten yards and moved slowly down back towards the mine.

2:22 PM
Team 3

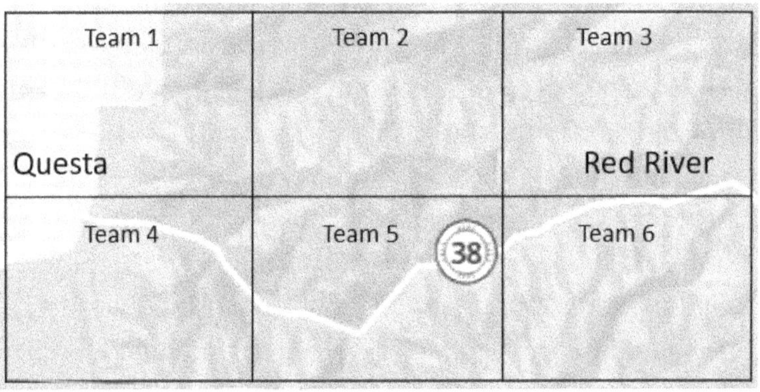

Luc followed Chelan and Jack, not daring to try to take the lead. He wasn't stupid; they were excellent trackers and clearly more at home in the wilderness than he was. No one had spoken since they had begun the trek to intercept Memphis's team. Chelan seemed to be going by the position of the sun and the dog provided no body language or barks to indicate that he sensed any spore from either Elspeth or Naabah, whose shirt they had been using as well.

He watched her move, not a wasted jerk or hesitation. He wondered if a Nazi and an Indian activist could go out on a date without him dying a slow, horrific death … It might be worth the risk.

2:26 PM
Team 2

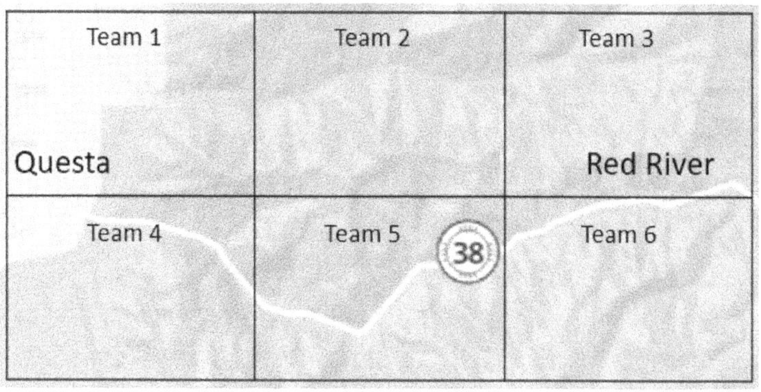

Team 1
Team 2
Team 3
Questa
Red River
Team 4
Team 5
38
Team 6

Smokey had his nose nearly touching the ground as he sniffed and jerked. He lifted his snout and took in the air and moved forward. Memphis was on his heels with Percy behind him and Aponi bringing up the rear. Her alert eyes darted back and forth, trying to see if anything looked remotely familiar. She hadn't told her companions but a savage feeling washed over her shortly before they found the mine, a memory from early childhood that had been tucked away for over thirty years. The memory had exploded into a fireworks' display of nanosecond images once they entered the mine. It took all the strength that she had to not reveal her shock to Memphis and Percy. Not yet, anyway.

She had been on this twisted path before. She had fuzzy snapshots flashing across her mind of a view of a cliff, a view of the mine entrance, a panorama of the valley below, a crackling stream filled with crystal-clear water and brown speckled trout. A coldness washed over her as she remembered now that Antonio had taken her camping up here when she was little. He had begun to teach her about their people and culture and how to survive in the wilderness.

That was the brother she was remembering, the compassionate one that cared, not the monster they were seeking. She cried inside for her lost sibling, but she knew what she had to do.

"Memphis," she said shortly. He and Percy stopped and looked at her. "I remember," she said softly. "I remember Antonio taking me here when I was a child."

Memphis's jaw dropped open and Percy snapped, "You know where he is?"

She nodded. "I think so. Maybe a mile or so that way" —she pointed directly west— "is a big cave. The inside seemed like a palace to me. We camped there one night." She closed her eyes tightly and a tear squeezed down her cheek. "He told me a bedtime story about the creation of the earth."

"Can you find it again?" Memphis asked urgently.

"I don't know. I'll try." With that she took the lead and the recesses of other memory paths clarified and guided her towards the cave.

2:31 PM

Team 3

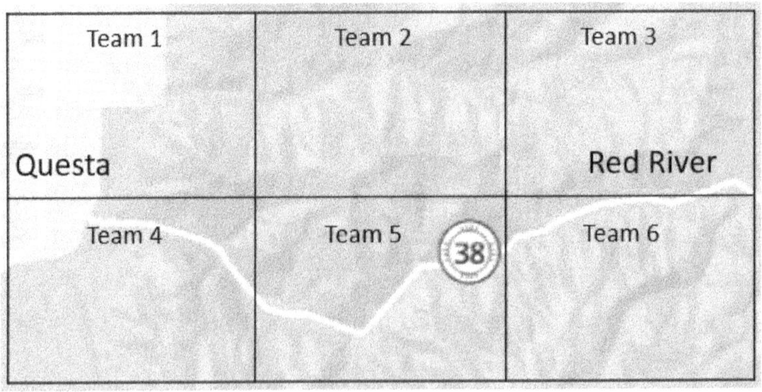

Jack smacked his sister on the shoulder and pointed. Chelan squinted and then nodded, seeing the flashes of color at a higher elevation perhaps a half mile away. She raised the binoculars to her long-lashed eyes and adjusted the sights. She handed them to Luc.

"Your brother's party," she said.

Luc homed in and recognized Memphis, who was behind Aponi with Percy trailing. He dug into his backpack and pulled out the walkie-talkie. He turned it on and tuned it and spoke while still holding the binoculars and after a long minute he saw Memphis stop, look around, and pull out his own walkie-talkie. Luc told him their direction and he jumped up and waved; Memphis caught sight of him and waved back and said they'd wait for them to catch up. He said they were pretty sure they knew where Naabah and Elspeth were.

Luc, Chelan, and Jack tore through the dense trees and shrubbery as they ascended to where Memphis and his team were. The chocolate lab ran with them then passed them as soon as he smelled the other dog. He barked a greeting.

2:42 PM

Naabah stopped dead in his tracks when he heard the bark of a dog. He grabbed Elspeth's arm and made her stop. He told her quietly to be still, then went dead still himself and listened. He listened for less than a minute before his keen hearing picked up the faint sounds of voices and movement against the earth and flora.

They've found us, he thought. His second of acceptance was suddenly tempered with the innate war between any man's heart in such a circumstance, fight or flight. Even though he planned on returning the child the unexpected presence of the hunters between him and the mine prompted an irrational response. He grabbed for Elspeth to flee.

Elspeth heard the voices, too. Somehow she knew—her daddy was coming for her. Her. Daddy. Was. Coming. For. Her.

Elspeth let out an ear-splitting scream with every ounce of power she had in her lungs at the same time that Po'Pay grabbed her arm. She pulled her left hand out of her jacket pocket and slammed the open palm into Po'Pay's hand. He yelled and let go, wide-eyed shocked at the small material sling on the child's hand looping around the thumb and pinkie. Sticking out from the fabric were a dozen sharp, thick cactus spines. Before he could react she screamed again and began barreling down the incline towards the voices. She hadn't gone ten feet before she tripped and began rolling down several yards. At the same time, he could hear more voices and knew the hunters were coming towards the screams. He whispered under his breath, "Goodbye, little rainbow," before he whirled around and headed southwest down the face of the mountain.

Memphis was in the lead as they ran towards the screams and sounds, and despite his long legs he was almost overtaken by Percy who was tearing towards the sound of his daughter as though the hounds of Hell were snapping at his heels. He was literally being hit in the face by the dirt and gravel Memphis's boots were kicking up. He tripped and his face hit the earth but a second later Luc hauled him upright by his collar and belt and they kept going.

Memphis, Percy, and Luc called out for Elspeth and she shrieked in response and a few minutes later they saw her tearing towards them. Memphis slowed and Percy ripped past him and he and his daughter hit one another like brick walls and dropped and rolled for a few feet, their arms around one another. They came to a stop with Elspeth on top of her father who was hugging her with rib-cracking intensity as he cried and kissed her face over and over. After a long minute she pulled away and stood up.

"I'm okay, Daddy, but what took you so long?" she said.

Percy stood up and cupped her cheeks and couldn't speak for a few seconds.

"Sorry, honey," Memphis said. "We had to run a few errands. You're okay? He didn't hurt you?"

Elspeth shook her head. "He pulled me a couple of times when we were walking but he was okay." She gave her uncle a sheepish look. "I tried to run away a couple of times but I couldn't." She held up her left hand where her cactus spike "glove' was dangling from her thumb. "I got free using this. He ran off, I think. But not back to the cave. The other direction, I think."

"Which direction?" Memphis asked. Elspeth pointed southwest. Memphis took the spike weapon off her hand and stared at it, shaking his head. "You'll have to tell your Aunts Swan and Cameo about this."

"I can show them how to make it," Elspeth said brightly. She cocked her head and looked at the three people she didn't recognize. "Hi. Who are you?"

Chelan stuck out her hand. "Chelan Chee. This is my brother, Jack. We came along to help. You're a brave young lady."

"Thank you." She smiled at Aponi. "Who are you?"

"My name is Aponi," Aponi said quietly.

Elspeth's eyebrows shot up. "You're Po'Pay's sister, Butterfly. He told me about you."

"Po'Pay?" Memphis asked.

"That's his Indian soul name," Elspeth said seriously. "I can tell you the story when we're home. Are we going home now? Is Mommy okay?"

"We sure are," Percy said as he took his daughter's hand. "She's fine and wants to see you so badly. Ben, too." He looked up at Memphis. "What about Naabah?"

"We'll keep tracking him," Memphis said. "You, Aponi, and Chelan take Elspeth back down and get to Questa. Call the family and the police in that order."

"I'm going with you," Aponi said firmly.

"I don't think—"

"I'm going with you," Aponi reiterated flatly. She met Memphis's eyes. "When we catch up to him he may surrender if I can talk him down from whatever reality he's in."

"Someone has to go back with Percy and Elspeth. So, it's either Luc or Jack."

"I'm going with you," Luc piped up right away.

"I will take the little man and girl down," Jack said matter-of-factly. "My sister can do anything I can."

"Usually better," Chelan said, winking at her brother. He didn't smile but she knew he was amused. The four big, tall, tough Chee brothers had been under their baby sister's spell since the day she was born.

"Fine," Memphis said. "Get going. Elspeth—is there a cave up there?"

"Yes, Uncle Memphis. Wait'll you see what's inside. It's scary wild."

"Scary wild," he murmured, then leaned down and kissed the top of her head. He straightened and looked at Percy. "Get going."

Percy nodded and took his daughter's hand, then nodded to Jack. Jack handed his sister an immense Bowie knife and another flashlight then turned without a word and began leading the McBeans and the lab down the mountain. Chelan stuck the knife in her belt and nodded at Memphis.

The quartet began moving rapidly up towards where Elspeth had freed herself. When they got to the spot where she broke away Smokey whined, sniffed, and started down the way that Po'Pay had fled.

3:15 PM

Naabah jerked his eyes skyward as a peregrine falcon screeched and continued ascending with a doomed squirrel in its deadly claws. Its large almost four-foot wingspread helped it soar through the sky with the ease and lightness of a single feather. He thought the bird would have a filling meal that day unless it was a mother bringing dinner home to her chicks. He watched as the falcon swooped up nearly parallel to the trunk of a tall, tall fir tree then disappeared within the branches where it probably had its nest. He loved birds. Owls, falcons, hawks, eagles. They had the physicality and inbred instinct to soar through the skies and hunt with stunning ferocity and efficiency and no human-like emotion or malice. They were pure in heart and soul. He envied them.

He stood still for a moment and listened but heard nothing behind him that would indicate that pursuers were close by. Still, he knew that Memphis Grayhawk would be hunting him even though the child had been recovered. He had heard more than two or three voices so he reasoned that one or two of them had already taken the child back down to safety while two or three others pursued.

He didn't know why he was running; it was just on instinct and perhaps a deep fear of being caged for the remaining months of his life. He wanted to die free so he had to elude them. He could spend the remainder of his life in these beautiful mountains, and perhaps in the spring when the winter thawed someone would find his bones and lay them to rest. That, or those bones would remain resting where they had fallen for an untold time.

Po'Pay shook off his disquiet and pushed forward, heading west into a dense area where eluding his hunters would be easier. He knew the forest so well and where he was heading had edible flora and streams that would sustain him. There were squirrels to be stalked and eaten, and birds' nests where he could enjoy small eggs. He could live off the land like his ancestors did.

He froze when he heard a very distant bark and he realized that his pursuers had taken a dog with them. Dogs' sense of smell was superlative, and they would find him. He knew that now and something inside him went dead calm with a mixture of relief and acceptance.

He swerved northeast and scrambled towards a place he had always loved to sit by and contemplate the beauty of nature. He ignored the pain inside his body, willing it away as he whispered an old Puebloan prayer under his ragged breath.

3:35 PM

Chelan squatted then held up a broken branch and said to Memphis, "We are getting closer. His moves indicate that he is slowing down and he is not being as careful in leaving no spore."

"Do you think he's injured?" Aponi asked.

"No blood, hard to tell," Chelan said in a clipped voice. She nodded. "He's changed direction." She pointed then stood and pushed past the others to follow the new trail.

Memphis called after her, "What's in that direction?"

Chelan didn't look back and said, "Cabresto Peak and Creek and several other high peaks."

4:00 PM

Po'Pay had hiked and fished at Cabresto Lake many times. The water was clear and pure and the fishing was spectacular. He had pulled out many fat trout and roasted them over an open campfire. It was a place that many other residents and tourists enjoyed fly fishing and other water sports. Cabresto Creek ran down to Questa and was the confluence for other streams' waters as well. Off-trail there were a few cliffs and small canyons that had taken a few lives of those not smart enough or sure-footed enough to stay on solid ground away from the edge. He would give anything for one more camping night, one more roasted trout.

He swerved past some undergrowth that had run wild over the past monsoon season. He knew he was breaking branches but he didn't care. The chase would end, but on his terms.

4:20 PM

"He's off the beaten path," Chelan said, frowning. "He's not even trying to hide his track."

"It's like he knows we're catching up to him," Luc said as he took a branch from Chelan and studied it.

"He's slowing down," Chelan replied. "Makes me nervous."

Luc suddenly grinned. "Do I make you nervous?"

"No," she said. "You just piss me off." She stood and took the lead again.

4:56 PM

Po'Pay stood at the top of a small, narrow canyon that was virtually hidden by the heavily populated huge fir trees. The edge for an uneven length of around twenty feet was devoid of anything except a few low bushes surrounded by dirt and dozens of sharp rocks. He wasn't close to Cabresto Creek but down at the bottom two hundred feet from the edge was a small, rocky stream. He couldn't hear the fast-moving water rushing but he could see that it was crystal clear. If there were any fish they had to be small, certainly not worth catching and eating. There was no path down to the stream from where he was standing; one would have to go a good distance to find an incline easy enough to traverse. He wished he could drink from the stream; he knew the water would be cold and slake his deep thirst.

He sat down near the edge, cross-legged. He slipped off his backpack and closed his eyes, turning his face to the last remnants of the sun setting down over the tops of the trees. He smiled and waited.

He was ready to meet his fate.

5:22 PM

Smokey barked and scrambled up the incline, his rear paws kicking back dirt and pebbles; he had smelled his prey and his prey was close. Memphis was a few feet away as he struggled to keep up with the dog. Behind him were Chelan, Luc, and Aponi.

Not ten minutes later the dense forest suddenly opened to a small clearing behind which was open space denoting a divide. Antonio Quará, AKA Hashkeh Naabah, AKA HashNaa, AKA Po'Pay was sitting on the ground, his hands loose in his lap, a slight smile on his face. His eyes were focused on his hunters, a crinkle at their edges, a sense of peacefulness radiating from the dark brown orbs. He frowned slightly as his sister came into view but quickly returned to their acceptance. He rose in one smooth movement, not two feet from the edge.

Aponi brushed past Memphis to stand fifteen feet away from her brother. She held out her hand. “Let me take you home, my brother,” she said softly.

“I forgive you,” he said very quietly. “For the key.”

“Antonio,” she said, “come with me. Please. We have such a short time with one another. Let’s not waste it.”

“You know?” he said, surprised.

“We found a doctor’s report when we searched your house the other day,” Memphis said. “Like your sister said—don’t lose the time you have left. And you have a lot to tell us.”

Po’Pay smiled crookedly. “There is a letter in little Rainbow’s backpack. She will also tell you that I harmed her in no way.” He looked at his sister. “I am sorry for the pain I caused you.” He looked at Memphis. “And I regret the pain I have caused your family. You are good people. Perhaps someday you can learn to forgive me.”

Po’Pay sensed that the younger man and the Indian girl wanted to rush him. He took a step back and they all froze.

“Please, Antonio,” Aponi begged. “Come with me.” She held out both her hands and moved a few feet closer to him.

“Adaa’Aháya, adeezhí. Ayóó Ánííníshní,” he said to her then took the last step back, spread his arms wide like the wings he wished they were and fell backwards over the cliff.

Aponi shrieked and rushed to the ledge. Luc dived and caught her legs as the ledge crumbled a little. He felt Chelan grab his legs and haul him and Aponi away from the unstable ledge.

Memphis rushed to the ledge and looked down at the crumpled form over which the bubbling stream rushed as though cleansing his sins. Naabah’s arms were spread wide, his eyes open, a stream of blood issuing from his mouth, his long hair rippling under the rushing water.

Forgive him? Maybe someday.

CHAPTER SEVENTEEN

Saturday, October 7, 1978

Memphis and Sand stood inside the cave where Naabah had rendered his canvas art and the "art" covering the cave walls for thirty feet in on both sides. The FBI forensics team had been processing the cave for two days and were about ready to disassemble the wall art and take it to their lab for analysis and identification. Unless there were any embedded remains in the circular tower that stood near the end of the right wall of the cave, the FBI analysts had counted forty-two skulls.

Elspeth, bless her, had a remarkable memory and told her family in detail about the bones and images decorating the cave walls. Po'Pay, as she called him, had told her the Indian creation myths that he had rendered on the walls using the bones of his victims. He had positioned them on the walls drilling holes into the rock and fastening the bones with metal bindings that held the bones against the rock walls. The skeletons represented aspects of the Puebloan creation myths, heavily articulated with the Hopi mythology; the Hopi were part and parcel of Puebloans.

Memphis scrutinized the wall art starting from the far-left side, which Elspeth had said was the beginning of their people. Naabah had started by imaging the deities under a painted description, Diyin Ayóo Át'éii, the primary gods.

Tawa, the sun spirit, is the creator, and it was he who formed the "First World" out of Tokpella, or endless space, as well as its original inhabitants. In all Tawa created four worlds. He created Sotuknang, whom he called his nephew, and sent him to create the nine universes according to his plan. Sotuknang also created Spider Woman, who served as a messenger for the creator. Some stories say that life was created by Hard Being Woman of the West and Hard Being Woman of the East, while Tawa simply watched the process without intervention. Masauwu, Skeleton Man, was the Spirit of Death, Earth God, door keeper to the Fifth World, and the Keeper of Fire. He was also the Master of the Upper World, or the Fourth World, and was there when the good people escaped the wickedness of the Third World for the promise of the Fourth. Masauwu helped settle the Hopi and gave them stewardship over their land. Other important deities include the twin war gods, the kachinas, and the trickster, Coyote. These deities provided the Hopi with a set of sacred tablets on which were etched symbols and figures associated with their religion.

Each skeleton was maneuvered to represent the specific Puebloan deity. For example, the skeleton presenting as the Spider Woman was clustered in a fetal position resembling a crawling spider as much as possible given the set of available bones. The Coyote was represented by the human skeleton positioned in a hands-and-knees position with the skull elevated backwards to simulate a coyote's baying at the moon.

Memphis walked slowly past the deities to the next section.

The first three worlds were underground, and those creatures living there saw little happiness and longed for a better plane of existence. What would eventually become human beings started out as animals, including wolves and bears. Eventually Tawa created the Fourth World on the earth and under the life-giving sun. The creatures that rose into the Fourth world were finally realized as human beings. It is said that the inhabitants of the Third World had begun to engage in evil and this is when a path to the Fourth World opened up to allow them to migrate to a better life. With the help of Spider Grandmother, or bird spirits, a hollow bamboo reed grew at the opening of the Third World into the Fourth World. This opening, sipapu, is traditionally viewed to be the Grand Canyon. The people with good hearts (kindness) made it to the Fourth World.

Memphis marveled at how Naabah managed to arrange several sets of bones into decent representations of bears and wolves and of fighting men. Two other skeletons were set on an angle, crawling up from the Third World to the Fourth. A final skeleton stood upright with arms stretched to the sun, the skull slightly tilted back.

Several feet separated that skeletal diorama from the next, which represented the expansion of Indian people.

When the Hopis arrived in the Fourth World, they broke into groups and went on a series of great migrations throughout the land. Towns sprang up, but some were abandoned as they continued on with the migration. They always left their spore behind, symbols on the rocks to show that they had been there. The wandering continued on for many, many moons and inevitably they began to form clans with special aspects of tradition and culture. These clans traveled for a long time as a unified community, but almost inevitably a disagreement would occur, the clan would split, and each portion would go its separate way. Sometimes, however, the clans would often join together forming large groups, only to have these associations disband, and then be reformed with other clans. Periods of harmonious living alternated with wickedness, contention, and separation played an important part of the Hopi mythos. This pattern seemingly began in the First World and continues even into recent history. In the course of their migration, each Hopi clan was to go to the farthest extremity of the land in every direction. Far in the north was a land of snow and ice which was called the "Back Door," but this was closed to the Hopi. However, the Hopi say that other peoples came through the Back Door into the Fourth World. Some think this refers to the Bering Strait near Alaska.

This section of the cave wall was the largest expression of the mythology. Naabah had used a dozen skeletons in various "traveling" positions (walking, running) spreading out in different directions. Next to some skeletal hands were weapons and tools etched into the cave wall, along with religious symbols and some animal figures, bears being the most prominent.

There were three more consolidated sections. The first showed typical Indian daily behavior, cooking food, raising children, building pueblos; Naabah had scrunched down smaller skeletons—possibly those of women—to simulate children.

The second section showed the incursion of the white man and the disastrous impact on the native cultures. Clear murder and enslavement and dissipation of native religion and beliefs were splashed across the rock wall with some skeletons wielding weapons and having helmets etched above the skulls; obviously, a representation of the Spanish invaders.

The last section displayed a sense of retribution. Several skeletons representing Indians with raised spears and tomahawks were standing over disarticulated, scattered bones embedded on the walls, clearly showing the destruction of the white man by Indian avengers. Memphis noted right away that one of the skeletons had a metal hip; he remembered that Screamin' Al Demon had had a hip replacement. He shuddered when his eye caught something nailed to the cave wall above the skeleton—a small, tanned, stretched piece of skin with a faded Statue of Liberty tattoo on it. Screamin' Al had found his immortality on an art wall of an injustice collector.

Near the wall was a four-foot-high circular tower of skulls and bones meshed all together in what almost seemed a haphazard fashion. Memphis surmised that the tower was a gruesome trophy showing the results of vengeance.

"Mr. Grayhawk?" came a melodious female voice from behind him.

Memphis and Sand turned to see a woman in her late twenties standing a few feet away. She was wearing a pantsuit and boots, and her red hair was pulled tightly behind her head into a low ponytail. Her face was very fair and a huge spray of freckles washed across her nose and both cheeks. Her eyes were a pale blue. She stuck out her hand.

"Shiloh Frost, Albuquerque FBI office," she said as she gave his hand a strong jerk. She did the same to Sand, who introduced himself. "I'm here assisting in the reclamation of the remains."

"Are you in charge?" Sand asked.

Shiloh broke out into a wide grin. "Of course not. I'm a woman. We may be allowed in the FBI now but it'll take time to prove we can handle any job a man can."

"Hope that time comes soon," Memphis said. "My baby sister plans on joining and she's not the type to be shoved into a closet."

"Neither am I. I just have to play the game while making my own moves. The team leader is SSA Ed Delaney. He's okay but knows he's in charge. He sent me here to study the scene and monitor the forensics. I know you've already been interviewed but I'd appreciate it if you could give me a couple of hours back in Santa Fe for a follow-up."

"No problem," Memphis said. "How long do you think it'll take to match the dental records of the missing people we know about to these skulls?"

"I can't make any promises, but I'll rush the team as much as I can. Also, you should be aware that the dental records may not match many or any of these victims. Your missing kids could have met their fate another way."

"We're betting not," Sand said. "But we appreciate any help you can give."

Shiloh moved a couple of feet to the right and stood in front of the large canvas painting. "He was talented," she said. "Demented, but talented. Your family has a couple of his works, don't you?"

Memphis nodded. "A couple he did of the McBeans. If you need to see them for your records I'll arrange it."

"The little girl is okay?"

"She's fine. The doctors checked her out and there was no sign of physical or sexual abuse. Elspeth confirmed that."

"I talked to the agent that interviewed her and he was impressed by her maturity and eloquence. He said she spoke more like a teenager than a seven-year-old."

"Her parents are particularly bright," Memphis said.

"All the women in the family are," Sand said pointedly.

"I'm not sure how to take that," Memphis replied.

"You just made my point," Sand said, laughing.

"You two have known each other a long time, haven't you?" Shiloh asked.

"Since we were kids," Sand said. "A bumpy road once in a while, but a lifelong commitment."

"Well," Shiloh said with a sigh, "we've still got a lot of work left to do here in the next week or so, so I'll see you gentlemen back in Santa Fe."

Sand looked at Memphis. "Have we been dismissed?"

"I believe so," his best friend replied. Memphis tipped his cowboy hat to Shiloh and said, "Give us a call when you're back in town, ma'am."

"I'll do that. Bye." With that definitive order Shiloh watched as the two men made their way past the FBI team and left the cave. It was a long hike back to their car, the same as it would be for her. She wished she had the clout to order up a helicopter, but even if she could it was too dense and mountainous to land one up here. She didn't envy the chores the forensics team had to do to remove the skeletons from the cave walls and carry them safely down the mountain.

She wanted to get to know the Grayhawks and their teams since she had heard such good things about them from Richard Ballard. She had contacted him in the San Francisco office when she was posted to Albuquerque from a recommendation of a Quantico instructor. Ballard was smart, friendly, and had a good sense of humor, and gave her quite a few pointers not only on fitting in with her new associates, but also with the police and P.I.s up in Santa Fe. That she was pulled into the endgame of this fascinating serial killer case was just icing on the cake. She had read two of the true-crime books written on the "Vampire Killer," Joanna Frid, and was immediately taken with the investigators that were embroiled in the case. Some of the Grayhawks, like Memphis, were intricately linked with the killer. If she could wheedle her way into his good graces perhaps Memphis Grayhawk might give her insight into Frid and her crimes.

The lead forensic tech walked up to her to review a plan of action on dismantling the cave-wall-suspended skeletons. She glanced at it, um-hmm'd a couple of times, and nodded her head. They knew what they were doing. She checked her watch and sighed; it was barely noon. She had a lot of hours to go before she could hike back down to her car.

Memphis dropped Sand off at his house and headed home. When he parked the car and entered the home through the kitchen sliders he groaned in pleasure and relief at the wonderful aromas of the dinner that Swan was making, roasted pork with potatoes and carrots. If she were hellbent on making him happy she'd also have picked up a quart of eggnog.

He had barely gotten through the door when the twins attacked him and began begging him to take them to Disneyland. Chessie wanted to go, too, they said in unison. He looked at his shy niece who smiled, ducked her head, and nodded. Chessie had started calling Memphis and Swan "Daddy" and "Mommy," and he had asked Akiro to start adoption proceedings so that his niece could become their legal daughter. He felt that Troy and Candy would have approved. He imagined that Sage would prefer a slow death in an Iron Maiden than to shepherd her sisters around Mickey's world. That would piss Sage off. He'd have to think about it.

Swan told him to check on Max, whom Memphis found sleeping soundly in his crib. He studied the peaceful, sleeping face of his son and felt a deep satisfaction that the boy had his hair and eyes although he was slightly lighter. He rubbed Max's tummy before returning to the kitchen and the best meal that Swan had ever made. His heart burst with love when she handed him a tumbler of eggnog with a hefty helping of rum in it.

Yuki had taken a leave of absence from her job as a Chemistry teacher at Sangre de Cristo College. She had almost lost her husband and the father of her children to a madman's bullet, and there was no way she'd leave his side until he was as back to normal as possible. She had always worried about him being a private investigator since he came into contact with quite a few unsavory characters, and she had mentioned a career change a few times. Nick, however, had come to love his job and thrive on the adventure and, yes, danger. She was going to bring the subject up again even if he got mad.

She'd give him a couple of weeks of recuperation before she broached the subject. Maybe his brother could talk some sense into him. Percy was visiting with him right now. The two disparate men were cloistered in Nick's den, and Yuki was fairly certain that the imported fine French cognac she had bought for his last birthday was being eagerly consumed.

Nick started to scratch at his wound then pulled away. The doctor said to LEAVE IT ALONE, NICHOLAS. Still, it itched.

Percy was nestled into a soft, well-padded recliner sipping a snifter of cognac. "How's the pain?" he asked.

Nick shrugged. "It's not bad. Itchy, mostly. I have to have physical therapy for a month or so for my arm and shoulder. Damn-ass bullet went in on an angle, just missing my heart and winding up in the shoulder."

Percy sipped. "The doctor said that a quarter inch to your left and we'd be weeping over your grave." Although his tone was light he was still shook up at how close he had come to losing his brother.

"As long as you're not laughing over my grave and telling knock-knock jokes."

"Knock, knock."

"Who's there?"

"Says."

"Says who?"

"Says me."

"That was just ... so bad, brother," Nick said, laughing.

"I'll work on my presentation."

"Vegas is holding its breath." Nick's voice turned serious. "How's Elspeth doing?"

Percy inhaled deeply. "She seems to be doing well. He didn't hurt her physically but there's got to be psychological issues now and in the future. I've asked Tucson to be her therapist."

"Does she have bad dreams? Cry?"

"Not that we've noticed. She seems a little more quiet than usual. I can tell she's thinking deeply. You know, she remembers every minute of her 'adventure,' as she calls it. She remembers the stories Naabah told her word for word. He also wrote a long letter and stuck it in her backpack confessing to abducting and killing a wide variety of people. He said there were even four amongst them that were Indian. They found a hidden box of trophies that revealed identities such as the San Ramon boys and the Frisco couple. Their families will be notified once the dental comparisons are verified."

"Imagine bringing your loved one home as bones that were used in art, to say nothing of how those bones were cleaned," Nick murmured. "There weren't any kids' bones in the cave, were there?"

Percy shook his head. "Memphis said it appeared that all of the bones were of adults. The small skeleton in the photos has to be the missing circus performer."

"Lancelot lucked out," Nick said. "It could just as easily been him instead of Milton." Nick laughed. "I like the little dude. Swan said he's doing a bang-up job."

"Little dude?"

Nick reached over and patted his brother on the arm. "Don't worry—you'll always be my favorite little dude."

"And you'll always be my pain-in-the-ass tall baby brother."

"You know what I'd like to do when I'm all healed?" Nick said.

"What?"

"Have the two of us take our families on a two-week vacation somewhere warm, peaceful, and devoid of excessive criminal activity."

"So, not Chicago or Detroit?"

"I was thinking someplace near a beach. I've heard the coastline of South Carolina has some great beaches and water sports. What is it—Myrtle Beach?"

"I think so. How about something closer, like San Diego?"

"We can discuss it. I just need some family time to hug my kids and kiss my wife and annoy my brother."

"You've got a leg up on the last one. You talk about it with Yuki and I'll discuss it with Tansee. Right now, I've got to get home. I promised I'd play catch with Elspeth. Trust me—it won't be my finest hour."

Snow's binoculars homed in on Elijah, who was helping Sand grill hamburgers on the back patio. He was getting tall, she thought. He seemed to be happy. Through covert channels she learned that her brother had legally adopted Elijah and changed his last name to theirs and his middle name to their father's.

Good. Jackson turned out to be a bastard so she was pleased that the name wouldn't carry forth. She lowered the binoculars and sighed. She was getting hungry.

And after she ate, she had lots of things to do.

CHAPTER EIGHTEEN

November 21, 1978

"It's just unbelievable," Cameo said as she watched the small TV in the kitchen while she prepared scalloped potatoes for Thursday's Thanksgiving dinner. The news on all network channels was still showing the horrific footage from the Jonestown mass murder/ suicide; the death toll was past nine hundred. The first to die were Congressman Leo Ryan and members of his group—NBC newsman Don Harris, NBC cameraman Bob Brown, and *San Francisco Examiner* photographer Greg Robinson. They were shot and killed at the Kaituma Airstrip, as was Temple member Patty Parks. Wounded were Tim Reiterman, Bob Flick, Steve Sung, Jackie Speier, and Monica Bagby.

Ryan had led an exploratory group to find out the truth behind Jim Jones' supposed paradise in Guyana at the prompting of family members who believed their loved ones were in danger and being held against their will. When the truth was outed, especially by cult members who begged Ryan to take them home, Jones sent out a truckload of acolytes who opened fire and shot down as many of the group as they could.

When the killers returned to Jonestown Jones demanded a "revolutionary suicide" so that everyone could die on his terms. His devoted followers batched up barrels of poisoned Flavor Aid (not Kool Aid, as originally reported) of the grape variety, laced with the cyanide and a variety of tranquilizer drugs and forced the cult members to drink. Mothers and fathers gave the poison to their children before taking it themselves. Those that didn't want to die did anyway as Jones' followers shot them to death. A few escaped the compound but were rounded up later. Jones died from a bullet to the head, ostensibly administered by his personal nurse who then took her own life. He had lied again to his followers about the poison which he said would bring about a peaceful death. His followers found out differently; ingestion of cyanide was one of the ugliest ways to die. Jones wasn't going to go that way.

The massacre happened on November 18, 1978, but it took days of examination to discover that the original count of a few hundred dead was masking dead bodies underneath dead bodies until the toll came to nine hundred eighteen men, women, and children. Today, Secretary of State Cyrus Vance suggested that the corpses be buried in a mass grave in Guyana, but the Guyanese government said absolutely not. It would take time to collect the bodies for identification and return them to the United States for burial.

"I know," Tucson said in a disheartened voice. "So many people desperate for a better life put their fate in the hands of a psychotic madman." He mashed the sweet potatoes and mixed in the spices his mother had given him, like cinnamon and nutmeg. Cameo had badgered him into taking a few cooking classes to experiment with foods other than the ones he grew up with. He grumbled but inside he was pleased with his efforts. He had even learned to parboil and season asparagus with olive oil, sea salt, and pepper. He'd prepare that on Thanksgiving morning.

The Grayhawks and Hazelwoods would gather at the McBean Victorian to finish cooking, eat, and watch the Dallas Cowboys battle the Washington Redskins at Texas Stadium; coaches Tom Landry of the Cowboys and Jack Pardee of the Redskins would be battling it out with their remarkable teams. Dallas had won against Washington by a single point in 1974 and was hoping to win again with a greater distance between scores. The McBeans and Griffins had left the previous day for a two-week vacation at Myrtle Beach, South Carolina. They had taken Yuki's parents with them and were nestled in a comfortable seaside rental home. They planned on enjoying the beach (but not swimming—too cold) and traveling by rental car here and there to see the sights. Charleston was only a hundred miles away, and there were plenty of sights to regale both adults and children. The wives wanted to browse the antique stores and historic locations; the husbands wanted to find really good eating places that served real southern foods. Elspeth and Mariko insisted that they take a nightly Ghost Tour. Percy offered his extended family use of the house so they wouldn't be crowded into one of their own.

Devon and DeVere flew back to Portsmouth, New Hampshire, to spend the holiday with his family. Frick, Frack, and London were having a quiet meal at the Smiths' home but promised to stop by in the early evening for a glass of eggnog. Memphis invited Lancelot to join them since he had no family or friends in Santa Fe. Lancelot stuttered when he accepted the invitation and said he knew how to bake pumpkin pie. Memphis assigned him that task. Akiro invited Skye, too, but she had plans to visit a friend in San Francisco. The location made Sand think of Taylor Geary, Stone Powell, Harlan Barrett and Frankie Conway. Taylor and Stone had been positively identified by their dental records and after the investigation was closed their remains were released to their parents. Naabah had written a long letter confessing to the killings and stating that the two San Ramon boys were "simply collateral damage."

Professor Carter's remains were identified, too, and returned to his family in New Jersey. A dozen other missing persons were identified, but more than two dozen were not although the FBI was still trying to identify them. Doomed clown Milton Steinberg was buried in Santa Fe; he had no relatives and out of compassion Memphis claimed the body and ante'd up the funeral costs. The entire team attended the funeral. Memphis gently patted Lancelot's shoulder as the little man mourned.

At least, Tucson thought, the media interest in the case had died down from a roar to an insistent murmur. The family and friends had been subjected to onslaughts of reporters and law enforcement as the denouement and aftermath of the "Indian Injustice Collector" case was resolved. They had been approached by wannebe award-winning writers who proposed true crime books and novels. Each one was turned down politely but firmly. A few didn't take the hint and persisted and received just desserts—one was drenched by the Victorian backyard watering hose wielded by a very irate Dr. Tansee McBean.

Memphis did agree to an interview for Norah Maguire's *Seraphim* magazine and her newspaper, *Voice of Angels*. After all, Adam was a critical participant since the beginning of the case when he engaged Warrior Spirit Investigations to search for the missing Frisco couple, and he played his part in trying to trap and search for Naabah. Norah and Bruce Peterson had flown to Santa Fe the previous weekend and they sat down with Memphis, Sand, and Swan for several hours. They spent the night at Memphis's parents' house and flew back in the morning.

Somehow they all got through October and made it to the third week in November. They were going to relax and enjoy each other's company, fantastic food, and peace and quiet.

Thursday, November 23, 1978 dawned as a beautiful day. The sky was clear, almost cloudless, and the air was brisk and refreshing. The Victorian's dining room was huge and had two tables pushed up against one another to accommodate the people that would be joining the celebration—Memphis, Swan, Sage, Shea, Sara, Chessie, Max, Tucson, Cameo, Brae and Bree, Brett and Beckett, Connor, Declan, Hehewuti, Jakub, Luc, Sand, Akiro, Elijah, and Lancelot. There was an attached alcove set up for the children (except Sage, who was five months away from turning into a teenager; she demanded to be seated at the adults' table), and the round table Jakub brought from his house had plenty of room for the children as long as no one moved.

One long table had been set up on the outside side porch for those who wanted to enjoy the weather.

Hehewuti and Declan both roasted turkeys, and Swan added a pineappled ham to the protein feast. The table was covered with immense pans of stuffing, more stuffing, scalloped potatoes, mashed potatoes, peas, green bean salad (which, as Sage said sardonically, no one in their right mind would ever ask for), asparagus, coleslaw, cranberry sauce, stuffed squash blossoms, freshly baked bread, cornbread, and additional items to pick at if the main meal wasn't enough. There were five pies waiting for consumption on the kitchen counter, including the delectable-looking pumpkin pie that Lancelot had proudly baked. There were pitchers of water, milk, eggnog, and orange juice. Declan brought two quarts of his latest ale concoction, Soaring Hawk Ale.

At noon sharp everyone sat down and Hehewuti stood and offered a Navajo prayer. Jakub reminded everyone that the Dallas-Washington game came on at 1:30 PM and food was not allowed in the McBean living room. Tansee had made it clear that there would be hell to pay if one iota of food or drink got onto her new rug.

The meal was noisy as hell with ravenous people clumsily grabbing over one another to have first dibs on their favorite dishes. Memphis and Sand sliced the turkeys and Swan did her ham. Swan had to stop her oldest daughter from emptying the mashed potato pan and gravy bowl.

The one topic they all stayed away from was the recent denouement of the Naabah case and kept the banter light. Memphis knew Hehewuti and Jakub were sad that their daughter, Raleigh, was back east for the holiday, but they understood it was a long trip. Raleigh promised to come home for Christmas.

Some of the crew were still eating when 1:30 PM rolled around but the men migrated into the living room and turned on the TV to CBS and settled into chairs, couches, and the floor. Lancelot confessed to all-around shock that he had never watched a football game. Memphis told him he was fired unless he made it all the way through this one. Bets were placed and the game began.

Swan cloistered the younger children in the den which was replete with board games, marbles, and jacks. She charged Elijah with taking care of them while Sage helped with the dishes—shockingly, she volunteered. Swan wondered what she was up to. Cameo loaded up the dishwasher and took care of a few plates that couldn't fit. She washed them by hand and Sage dried. Hehewuti occupied herself putting away leftovers and making take-home containers for each family. The quiet, enjoyable camaraderie between the three women and one almost-woman was relaxing. Occasionally their peace and quiet was interrupted by shouts from the living room, happy or pissed-off shouts depending on which team had scored.

Out of the corner of her eye Swan caught a glimpse of movement just to the north of the porch. She tensed, then without a word smoothly retrieved her handgun from the drawer where she had placed it, put a finger to her lips, and slowly moved towards the French doors that opened to the porch. She edged quietly to the door and gently turned the handle, her gun in an upright position but ready for anything.

The door was opened a crack when suddenly it was wrenched from the outside and a loud voice yelled, "Boo!" Swan was startled for a second before she lowered her gun and said, "You asshole." Then she threw her arms around Raleigh and nearly broke her ribs. Hehewuti shrieked and threw herself into her daughter's arms just as the men came running from the living room.

Luc rolled his eyes and said, in exasperation, "God forbid you've make an entrance without making an entrance. I suppose you want us to feed you?"

"I need a hug first," Raleigh said as she disengaged from her oldest brother and held her arms out. Luc and Tucson hugged her at the same time before Jakub pulled her to him and held her closely, his eyes closed.

"We didn't think you could come," Jakub said.

Raleigh laughed. "A classmate had a ticket but decided to stay with her boyfriend for the holiday. She sold the ticket to me for the price plus an extra hundred dollars. I have to fly back on Sunday. Look, it's wonderful to see you all, but seriously—*feed me*."

The women shooed out the men and Hehewuti prepared a huge plate of food for her daughter, who dug into it like she hadn't eaten in a week. Raleigh was mercilessly peppered with questions about her course work, her friends, sightseeing, whether she went to Salem for Halloween, was she dating anyone, and anything else her family could think up. When she licked her plate clean (yes, literally licked it clean) she moseyed off to the living room where she kicked Luc out of his chair and settled in to watch the rest of the football game. She was introduced to Lancelot, whose face showed instant infatuation. She'd had a lot of those looks.

Raleigh gave up pretending to enjoy the football game at the end of the third quarter and went back into the kitchen where the family women were having coffee and pie and gossiping about the men. She told them that Dallas and Washington paled in comparison to the New England Patriots and cut a slice of apple pie.

"Too bad you couldn't be here at the end of the search," Cameo said as they were discussing the contents of the cave.

"I would have liked to have been a part of that," Raleigh said as she shoveled a hearty forkful of pie into her mouth.

"Yes, but what I meant was that Memphis and Sand met a new FBI agent that was helping with the recovery. A woman."

Raleigh perked up. "Really? She's stationed in Albuquerque? What's her name?"

"Shiloh Frost. She interviewed them after the fact and has kept us in the loop about victim identification. I haven't met her but Swan has."

Raleigh looked at her sister-in-law eagerly. Swan sighed and poured herself another cup of coffee.

"She seems very competent and is actually respectful towards the cops and us, unlike most FBI agents, Ballards excepted," Swan said. "I think you'd like her."

"Think she can come here so I can talk to her? I'll even go down there," Raleigh said. "I'd love to have her perspective on women in the FBI."

Swan shook her head. "She called Memphis a couple of days ago for an update and mentioned she'd be back east for the holidays. She said her family lives in Eastham, Massachusetts."

"That's on Cape Cod," Raleigh said. "I wonder how long she'll be there."

"Raleigh," Hehewuti said sternly, "you will not bother that woman on her vacation."

"But—"

"Did you not hear me?"

"Okay, Mom," Raleigh said meekly. No one messed with the warrior woman spirit. She slid off her chair and said, "I think I'll go cuddle my nephews and nieces for a while. Save me a slice of pumpkin pie."

"She's not going to let go of this," Cameo said in amusement.

Hehewuti snorted. "I didn't raise my children to be doormats." She nodded towards the direction that Raleigh had gone. "That one, she's a battering ram."

Swan cracked a walnut. "I was thinking more of a stinger missile."

Cameo laughed. "That's our new nickname for her—Stinger."

CHAPTER NINETEEN

December 30, 1978

The cramps weren't too bad now, Raleigh thought. The pills were helping. She'd be back on her feet by the time classes commenced in early January. She had spent a few days back home for the Christmas holiday and had flown back to Boston on December 28th. Fortunately, her roommate was still in Chicago with her family and wasn't due back until January 2nd.

She wrapped her arms around her stomach which was covered by a pillow. She was lying on the couch watching TV and had been since she threw up her breakfast at 8 AM. She'd had no idea that she'd be vomiting at this point. The doctor said it was possible, but not to worry. She might experience period-type pains, stomach cramps, and vaginal bleeding. This should start to gradually improve after a few days but could last for one to two weeks. This was normal and was usually nothing to worry about. The bleeding was usually similar to normal period bleeding.

These symptoms were the typical but unharmful aftereffects of some abortions.

That wild night celebrating Halloween in Salem had its consequences when she met a guy dressed in a wolf costume and went home with him to finish the night in bed. He was a decent guy and pretty good in the sack, but she realized afterwards that their lust had overtaken their brains and he neglected to put on a condom. And, one time was all it really took to conceive.

She had to make a decision and it was a tough one. Have and keep the baby, give it up for adoption, or end the embryo before it could become a baby. She agonized over the decision before she came home, then made her choice and called the doctor before she flew back to Boston. She had planned a life, a course of action, and a baby didn't fit into that scenario. She wasn't sure if she ever wanted children, but certainly not now.

She told no one in her family, and none of her friends back east. She simply went about the necessary steps to ensure that her commitment to her future didn't waver. She doubted that she would get anyone's approval for that decision, but it was her life, and although she might have regrets, this is what she planned to do.

Besides, in the future she could have a child if she chose that path. Maybe two.

She popped another pill and changed the channel to NBC. *CHiPS* was on, and Erik Estrada was so very easy on the eyes, even when you were nauseous.

Memphis and Swan heard shrieks of joy from their youngest daughters as the offspring were informed that on spring break the family would be traveling to Disneyland. Sage had her arms crossed and rolled her eyes and made a point of sighing heavily. She was not about to admit that she was dying to see the Haunted Mansion and Pirates of the Caribbean. Mom and Dad better not be counting on her to monitor the insects all day.

She rolled her eyes again and groaned as her father told them that Uncle Tucson and his family would be going with them. That meant four more kids. The twins annoyed Sage to no end, even more so than her own twin sisters. They had that strange accent and cheeky attitude that sometimes even frustrated Declan. She did like their red hair, though. When the mid-day sun shone on it they looked like they were wearing helmets of fire.

Sage barely had time to digest the situation when her sisters ran screaming out of the living room, heading to their rooms to pack. She arched her delicate eyebrows at her parents.

"This is not going to go well," she said blandly. "It has disaster written all over it."

"Good news," Memphis said. "We know you don't want to go so you can stay home and live with your grandparents until we get back. We're not going to force you to suffer something clearly anathema to you."

"Oh," Sage said, surprised. "Oh, I … I …" *What the hell is anathema?*

Swan hugged her daughter tightly. "We love you too much to make you endure the unpleasant chore of dealing with your sibs and the thousands of other kids running around the park. It's just not right."

"We'll bring home a pair of Mickey Mouse ears as a souvenir, honey," Memphis said sweetly.

Sage eyed her parents, who were both smiling. *The rats*, she thought, seeing through their ploy. She shrugged her shoulders and sighed deeply.

"No, I should go. It's not fair to you to be saddled watching the swarm. I know my duty as a big sister," Sage said. She almost sounded sincere.

"No, no, it's not fair to *you*," Swan countered and put a hand on her daughter's shoulder.

Sage shrieked and threw her hands up in the air. "All right! All right! Take me to fucking Disneyland."

"Language, young lady," Swan warned.

"Yeah? Tell yourself that when you've endured the place for a day. I double dare you."

"Connor's got a girlfriend," Tucson said to Cameo as he sliced a ham sandwich diagonally in their kitchen. He had two more to make for the twins; for those he'd cut off the crusts and add an extra slice of cheese.

"What?" she exclaimed. "Did he tell you that? Who is she? How long has this been going on?"

Tucson laughed and absently touched the scar on his cheek. "No, he didn't tell me. I deduced it. Look at the facts. He's gotten a haircut, shaves every day, is wearing better clothes, and often acts mysterious. He's either got a girlfriend or he's undercover as a spy."

"I wonder who she is? I should ask him."

"No, honey, please don't. He'll tell us when he's ready."

Ignoring his advice, Cameo said, "I'll bet Declan knows. They work so closely at the brewery. I'll ask Declan."

"Don't ask Declan."

"Don't ask Declan what?" Declan said as he walked into the kitchen. Both Grayhawks froze at the sound of his voice.

Before Tucson could stop her Cameo walked up to him and said, "Tell me about Connor's girlfriend."

"Uh … uh …" Declan stuttered.

"Aha," Cameo declared. "He does have a girlfriend. Spill, Beer Boy."

"Um, you should ask him," Declan said quickly.

"Don't make me hurt you," Cameo warned. "Because I will."

Declan looked at Tucson with pleading eyes. "Help," he said weakly.

Tucson held up his hands. "You're on your own. I know better than to piss off my wife. I don't have a death wish."

Cameo got right up in Declan's face and scowled at him. Declan took a step back and was already sweating. Cameo stood where she was but deepened her scowl.

"Who is my little brother in a romantic relationship with?" she said, enunciating each word.

"Promise you won't get mad?" Declan said.

"I promise. So, who is my brother in love with?" There was a beat of a second or two before Declan replied.

"Me."

Frick was lying on his couch breathing heavily, a wet cloth on his forehead. London was sitting on the edge of the couch moving the washcloth around and dipping it in a bowl of cold water to keep it cool. She wasn't quite sure what she expected when she gave her husband her news, but hyperventilating wasn't high on the list. On the other hand, she could sympathize. She had gone into shock, too.

"It's okay, honey," she said for the dozenth time as she took his hand and kissed it. "We'll get through this. I promise."

Frick sat up suddenly and turned to stare at her, that look of disbelief still on his craggy face. "Are you kidding me?" he exclaimed. "I'm sixty-three. You're forty-six. We can't have a baby at our age. What the hell?"

"The doctor said it was a miracle baby and he's right. We conceived because we were meant to. So, put your big-boy pants on and deal with it."

"What if … what if the baby's not … all right? Can't things happen with a late-life pregnancy?"

"Lots of things. Older mothers have a chance of having a baby with Down's Syndrome. The doctor said we can do an amniocentesis in a month or two and that will tell us if the baby is normal or not. Then, we have to make a choice." She left the implication hanging.

He searched his wife's face. "What would you want to do?"

"I'll know when the times comes. Meanwhile, let's start thinking of names. I like Jessica for a girl and Morgan for a boy." She winked at him; his longtime partner's name was Jesse Morgan.

He took her hand and kissed the palm. "As long as it's not Frick, Junior."

"We could call him Fricassee."

"Oh, hell no."

Sand gently unwrapped the bandage on Elijah's arm and winced at the red punctures and scratches that ran the length of his forearm and the back of his hand. He had been trying to catch a baseball pitch while playing with the neighbors' kids that morning and tripped and fell into a cactus patch. Sand had rushed him to the hospital where he was treated, given a shot of antibiotics, bandaged, and sent home. Akiro was waiting for them, as was a half-gallon of Rocky Road ice cream that his uncle had brought home while he was at the hospital.

All Elijah wanted to do was go back outside and play, but Sand and Akiro nixed that. Elijah grumbled, but an extra helping of ice cream with whipped cream and a cherry on the top mollified him. That, and his dad's suggestion that the three of them take in a movie that evening. Elijah had his choice of *Superman* (Elijah had seen it twice but loved the movie), *Invasion of the Body Snatchers* (which Akiro thought was too dark for a child), and a double-feature of two old Disney movies, *Song of the South* and *Cinderella.* Elijah chose *Superman.*

As they made their way to the theater Elijah gazed at the streets they drove down. He smiled as he saw a car going in the opposite direction; his Aunt Swan was driving. He waved at her and she smiled back.

She'd only caught a glimpse of Elijah, but it was enough to soothe some of Snow's roiling soul. She had given up her children to give them a better life, a life she had abandoned so many years ago. All the wrongheadedness, the terribly bad choices, the uncertainty of who she was and what she wanted, these were all tearing at her heart and mind daily.

She had no concept of what a normal life was, not since she left Santa Fe and Memphis virtually standing at the altar. The three things she had done right since then was to give Sage back to her father, drop off Elijah with her brother, and shoot Ryder Jackson in the head. She was misguided and in some cases stupid; he was evil. His domestic abuse of her was one thing to tolerate to a certain extent, but when he started putting out cigarettes on their son's flesh, that was the breaking point.

She hoped she could see Sage one last time, but that seemed unlikely. She was tired, and played out, and at the end of her rope. The years of stupid and criminal actions were catching up with her, and she knew that the end of the line was coming shortly. She could surrender to law enforcement and take accountability for her actions. She hated the thought of spending her life in a six-foot-by-eight-foot cell. She had been in prison for years, crisscrossing the country, pulling jobs, escaping a few times by the skin of her teeth, living in abandoned buildings and even cars.

It was time to stop running.

CHAPTER TWENTY

January 3, 1979

Twenty-one-year-old Billie Fain stored her jacket and purse in the employees' locker room, which was barely more than a closet with rickety cabinets for such storage. There was a three-year-old Mr. Coffee machine, but the bank manager only bought cheap coffee that was far from robust and tasty. He charged ten cents for a Styrofoam cup. There was no sink in the locker room, so they had to wash the carafe out in the bathroom.

She was thirty minutes early for her shift as a teller, but that was normal. She took great pride in her punctuality and efficiency and had her eye on eventually becoming a bank manager. Her direct supervisor noticed her ambition and gave her opportunities to perform new tasks and move up the ladder. She knew he was infatuated with her, but besides being a married man he was also a homely dork that she wouldn't give the time of day. She had been crafty in fending off his advances without angering him. She'd use him to get what she wanted. Wasn't that the way life was supposed to work? She wasn't going to end up in a cinder heap like her grandmother had in that awful accident. She was never going to wind up a drunk butthole like Granny Robin, roasted in a crushed pile of melted steel.

She smoothed back her dark hair which was wrapped into a meticulous and tasteful chignon at the nape of her neck. She was wearing a crisp white shirt and a tight skirt that ended just above the knee. She slipped on a pair of glasses with clear lenses; she thought they made her look mature and professional even though her eyesight was 20/20. She checked her money drawer and smiled at the co-workers to her left and right, saying brief but pleasant hellos. She eyed the clock behind her and felt the usual thrill just before the Santa Fe Desert Bank opened at nine for business. She cracked her knuckles and shrugged the remaining sleep out of her shoulders, and pasted on a happy, welcoming face.

She could see a few people outside waiting to get in and precisely at 9 AM on the dot the bank manager unlocked the front door and the people came inside. A few went to the counter where they'd fill out their banking requests, but she smiled brightly at the woman that came directly to her window.

"Good morning," she chirped. "How may I assist you?"

The woman smiled back. "You can give me all of your money, sweetheart."

"Wh-what?"

The woman leaned closer and said. "Sweetheart, this is a bank robbery." With that admission the woman whipped out an automatic weapon from underneath her knee-length coat and with no warning shot a volley of bullets into the ceiling. There was a cacophony of shrieks and one fast-thinking man by the door fled into the street.

Snow smiled slightly at the mannequins that weren't moving an inch as she brandished the .45 ACP MAC-10. The automatic weapon could fire 1,145 rounds per minute. It had a magazine in the pistol grip and a fire selector switch. Snow had three extra magazines hidden in her coat.

"Don't anyone make any stupid moves and you'll all live to tell a great story. Make a stupid move, well, I'll leave that to your imagination. You, Barbie Doll—fill this with all the cash you can stuff into it." She tossed the bag to Billie who began stuffing cash into it as fast as she could. A moment later they all heard the distant sound of police sirens coming closer. Snow smiled ever so slightly.

The overweight security guard started to reach for his weapon but when he raised it to shoot, he yelled as the bullet from Snow's second gun tore the gun from his hand and left him with half a thumb.

"What did I say about stupid?" she asked him. "Now, lock the front door and move over there." He shot her a look of hatred but complied.

She snapped her fingers at Billie who scurried over and handed her the bag. "Good girl. Now go stand over there." Billie hustled over to stand by the guard's side.

Snow listened to the approaching sirens. She took out snapshots of Sage and Elijah that she had taken covertly and studied their beautiful faces.

Luc was on a break and on a pay phone. He was trying to convince Chelan to go out with him. He'd asked her six times and was sensing that her resolve not to was crumbling. He thought she admired his persistence; that, or her annoyance meter was running down. He thought that one more old college try, and her barriers would crumble.

He was grinning as he hung up the phone; she'd said, "Maybe" to an offer to hit the movie theatre on Saturday and see *Force 10 From Navarone*, which had been held over for four weeks at the Rivoli. She confessed to loving Harrison Ford; he kept silent about salivating over Barbara Bach. He was walking to his patrol car when his radio crackled, and the dispatcher came on talking excitedly about a possible bank robbery downtown. He was three blocks from the address, so he hopped into the car and tore off. From the west of him he heard another siren.

Luc was the first car to arrive at the bank. There were dozens of people milling about although staying at least twenty feet away from the front door. He jumped out of the car and yelled at everyone to get back. He yelled at the closest guy to come over.

"You see anything?" Luc asked. "Were you in the bank?"

"Uh-uh, no," the man said. "I was about to go in when I saw some broad with a gun threatening people." He pointed across the street to a pay phone. "I ran over there to call the cops."

"You hear any shots?"

"Hell, yeah, a shitload of fire. Sounds to me like an automatic." At Luc's querulous look he added, "I was in the service. I know guns."

"Could you see inside if there was anyone hurt?"

"I couldn't see, sorry."

"You wouldn't happen to know the phone number in there, would you?"

The man grinned widely and pulled out his wallet, then a business card for the bank manager.

"Okay, great. Go over there and give the other officer your name and statement. Thanks, buddy." Luc pointed to the next police car that rolled up. He saw that the driver was Kent Milner, someone he went to the academy with and who was a tough, smart cop. Luc felt that he was the only real competition for detective in their tenure group.

Milner's partner, Martin McCord, ran over to him, gun drawn. Luc told him everything the witness had said then told him to hold people back while he ran over to the pay phone and called the bank. McCord was nervous as hell and Luc could see his hand trembling. *Swell*, he thought. Luc ran over to the phone and pulled the receiver out of the hand of the woman making a call. He apologized and told her to get back.

Luc dialed the business number. The bank phone rang ten times before he hung up, counted to ten, then dialed again. A man came on the line.

"Sir?" Luc said. "I'm a police officer. Can you tell me your name?"

"Um … um … Tom Fisher."

"Are you the bank manager?"

"Yes, yes."

"How many robbers are in there?"

"Just one. A lady."

"Anyone hurt?"

"The guard. He got shot in the hand."

"Let me talk to the … lady."

Luc could hear talking then silence, then "the lady" came on the line. "Hello? Ma'am? Can you tell me exactly what it will take to end this situation?"

Snow laughed. "Well, it's not going to end well in the long run."

"We'll be as honest as we can to accommodate your needs, but you have to do something to show your good faith."

"Such as?"

"Release the women and children hostages. I understand the security guard was injured. Can you release him, too?" There was dead silence. "Ma'am?" Luc tensed and waited, then his eye caught movement at the front of the bank. The door opened and three women and one child rushed out. Several bystanders pulled them to the side for safety. The lady came back on the line.

"Happy?" she asked.

"Very happy. Thank you. Can you tell me your name?"

Snow laughed. "You'll know me when you see me. What's your name, Marshall Dillon?"

"Officer Luc Grayhawk." The words were met with dead silence. "Ma'am?"

Then there was a loud laugh. "Reprobate kid Lucifer Grayhawk a cop. There's a kick in the head. Funny how life turns out."

Luc was thrown for a loop. She knew him, or at least knew of him. Who the hell … He went stock still and inhaled sharply. "Snow?" he whispered.

"Give that man a kewpie doll," she said, laughing.

"Oh, my God," he breathed. "Snow—what the hell are you doing?"

"You ever read poetry in college? I'm assuming you went to college."

"Yeah, I did. Read some. Why?"

"In 1925 T.S. Eliot wrote a poem called *The Hollow Men*. The last line was especially famous and many people have used it to describe many things."

Luc frowned and searched his memory. He had read the poem in his sophomore year and it made an impression on him. "This is the way the world ends, not with a bang but a whimper."

"Very good. But that's not my philosophy. I prefer not with a whimper but a bang." She slammed down the receiver.

Luc dialed again but the phone rang and rang. Snow Hazelwood. *Fuck*, Luc thought. Before he could dial again, he saw an unmarked police car pull up and disgorge Detectives Abbott and Dunbar. Dunbar motioned for him to come over.

"Waddya got?" Dunbar asked.

"One robber, a woman. She's released four hostages, three women and a child," Luc said quickly. Mentally, he took a deep breath. "I know who it is."

"Well, spill, rookie," Abbott snapped.

"Snow Hazelwood," Luc said quietly.

"Holy fucking *shit*," Abbott exclaimed. "You sure?"

"Yeah, I'm sure. Sir—let me go in there. I think I can talk her into surrendering."

"No fucking way," Abbott snapped. "We've got a hostage negotiator on the way and we've called the FBI. They're flying in on a chopper."

"I know her. I mean, I knew her. Please."

"Rookie, do you get the meaning of 'no'? In case you don't—*NO*."

Four more police cars screeched up and two officers pushed back the crowd. A minute after they arrived the front door of the bank opened, and the wounded security guard stumbled out. An officer grabbed him and pulled him away from the glass doors. His partner was in the car and calling for an ambulance.

"Shit," Dunbar said. He nodded towards the intersection where a van from the local CBS station pulled up. The uniformed officer ran over to him breathlessly.

"The guard said she wants to talk to Luc on the pay phone," he gasped.

Abbott scowled menacingly at Luc, then jerked his head. Luc ran across the street and dialed. Snow picked up on the second ring.

"Snow, please. Let's end this without any more violence."

"I'm willing to let go most of the hostages in exchange."

"Exchange for what?"

There was undeniable amusement in her voice. "You."

"They'll never go for that."

"Make it happen, Lucifer." Snow hung up.

Luc stared for a few seconds at the phone then gently put the receiver down. He unstrapped his holster and stuck his gun in his back belt. He walked back across the street. When he got to Abbott and Dunbar, he tossed his holster at Abbott then suddenly bolted towards the bank.

"The fuck?" Dunbar yelled. "Grayhawk, get the hell back here."

Luc reached the glass doors and threw up his hands. A moment later a man nervously opened the door and let him in.

"I am going to have his ass fired," Abbott growled angrily. A minute later the bank doors opened again, and a stream of people came out and scattered. The uniforms rounded them up and moved them to safety. Abbott jogged over to one and asked him how many people were left in the bank. He said three—the robber, the cop, and a female teller.

"What do we do now?" Dunbar asked.

"We wait. We wait for the hostage negotiator, the FBI, and the SWAT team. Give Memphis a call and let him know what's going on."

Inside the bank there was dead quiet except for an occasional sob from Billie Fain. Snow had her arm around Billie's neck and a handgun pointed at her temple.

"Let her go, Snow," Luc said softly, his dark eyes taking in every nuance of his sister-in-law's twin. One could tell that they were sisters but not necessarily twins. Snow's face was thinner and drawn, with creases around her eyes. She looked like she was forty-five instead of thirty-five. She wore jeans, a cable-knit sweater, a knee-length peacoat, and hiking boots. No jewelry. She looked like an urban guerrilla. Her hair was lank, and she was pale. Strangely, her blue eyes were vivid and alert. There was purpose and anticipation in them.

"No can do, Lucifer," Snow replied softly. "She's my insurance to get out of here."

"You're not getting out of here," Luc said flatly. "You know that."

"How are my children?" she asked.

"They're not your children," Luc said, his voice hard. "You gave up that right when you abandoned them."

"I did what was best for them."

"Then do what's best for them again—surrender. I'll guarantee your safety."

Snow smiled. "I don't think so, but thanks for the offer. Sometimes it's just time."

"Time for what?" Luc asked curiously.

"Time to go out with a bang," she said as she shoved Billie away and aimed her gun at Luc.

Time and motion seemed to stop like a film showing its plot in slow-motion. Luc's police instincts kicked in and he reached behind his back for his gun, grabbing the grip and bringing his arm around just as a bullet whizzed past his ear, nicking the lobe. Instinctively he aimed and pulled his trigger twice.

The slow-motion action continued as two bullets burst into Snow's chest and sent her flying backwards as the air was rent with Billie's screams. Snow hit the teller counter hard then slid down into a seated position. Her head rolled to the right. The gun was still clutched in her hand.

Luc dropped to the floor in front of her and felt for a pulse. None. Her eyes were open. There was the slightest smile on her still lips. Luc sat back on his heels, his gun loose in his lap. A second later the front bank doors blew open as a half dozen heavily armed men burst through. Luc couldn't see behind him but one of the cops ushered Billie out of the building.

Luc felt a strong hand on his shoulder and looked up to see Abbott staring down at him.

"You did good, kid," Abbott said softly. "But I'm still thinking of getting you fired. Come on—let's go." He took Luc's gun.

Luc let himself be led out into the bright morning sun. He surveyed the people, the cars, the cops. It all seemed surreal. He sensed rather than felt Abbott put him in the back seat of his unmarked car and drive to the station.

The next few hours were a blur as Luc gave his statement and several detectives asked him question after question. Finally, after three o'clock Captain Carraway told him he was on administrative leave and to go home until he was called back in. Luc nodded mutely and made his way out of the station. His fellow officers patted him on the back and applauded. He nodded numbly. Dunbar was back and ushered him to the station's side entrance where Memphis was leaning on his car waiting for him. Luc got into the car wordlessly and in silence they drove. Luc was surprised that Memphis headed out of town and pulled up in front of the McBean Victorian. There were several cars there.

Memphis put his arm around his brother's shoulders and led him into the house where the family as waiting. Sand and Swan were side by side. Before Luc could say anything the two Hazelwoods rushed to him and engulfed him in their arms. Luc cried. They cried.

It was close to midnight when there was a sharp knocking on Chelan's front door. She opened it to see Luc Grayhawk standing there, bracing himself by a hand on each side of the doorjamb. She knew what had happened that day.

Without a word she beckoned him to enter then shut and locked the door. Wordlessly she took his hand and led him into the bedroom.

EPILOGUE

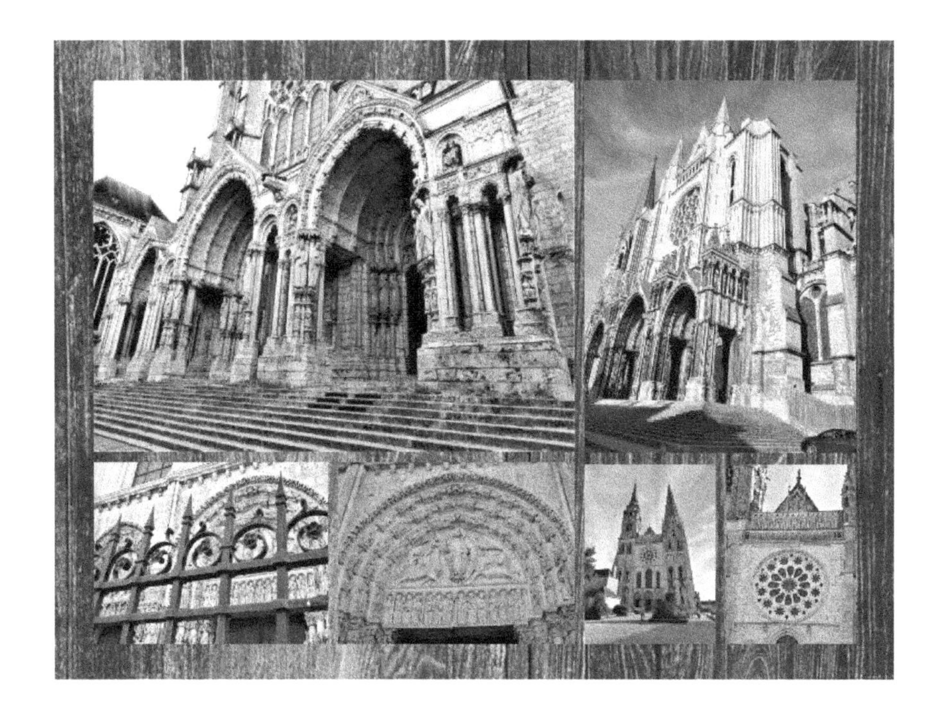

September 16, 1979, Chartres Cathedral, France

Located around fifty-six miles southeast of Paris, Chartres is an administrative division and capital of the Eure-et-Loir department in France. It is world-famous for its magnificent gothic cathedral, which was built between 1130 and 1250 AD. Unfortunately, much of the old town was destroyed by bombs in August 1944 during World War II. The order was given to destroy the cathedral, but Colonel Welborn Barton Griffith Jr. went behind enemy lines to see if it was being used as an observation point by the Germans. Finding none he relayed this information to his superiors and the destruction order was withdrawn.

Sadly, Colonel Griffith was killed in action later on that day in the town of Lèves, 2.2 miles north of Chartres. For his heroic action both at Chartres and Lèves, Colonel Griffith received, posthumously, several decorations awarded by the President of the United States and the U.S. Military, and also from the French government. Chartres was liberated on August 18, 1944, by the U.S. 5th Infantry and 7th Armored Divisions belonging to the XX Corps of the U.S. Third Army commanded by General George S. Patton.

Chartres Cathedral, also known as the Cathedral of Our Lady of Chartres, is a Roman Catholic church and is the seat of the Bishop of Chartres. It stands at the site of at least five cathedrals that have occupied the site since the Diocese of Chartres was formed as an episcopal see in the fourth century. It was designed in the Gothic and Romanesque styles.

France is replete with magnificent churches and cathedrals, but Notre Dame and Chartres stand out. Madame Houdin made it a priority for her granddaughter to visit as many as possible, and although they had visited Chartres years earlier they returned to study the architecture and history in depth.

Madame Houdin walked side by side with Josette, their arms linked as they walked slowly and quietly through the interior.

"Did you know," Madam Houdin said quietly so as not to disturb the people praying in the pews, "that King Henry IV of France was crowned here in 1594? Generally, the kings were crowned at Reims Cathedral, but Paris and Reims were occupied at the time by the Catholic League. Do you know who they were, ma chérie?"

"Mais oui," Josette said. "A major participant in the French Wars of Religion. Henry I, Duke of Guise, formed the league in 1576. The League's charge was the eradication of Protestants—mainly Calvinists or Huguenots—out of Catholic France during the Protestant Reformation, as well as the replacement of King Henry III. Pope Sixtus V, Philip II of Spain, and the Jesuits were all supporters of this Catholic party." Like Houdin Josette spoke in flawless Parisian French.

"Very good," Madame Houdin declared. "You have truly studied your history of religion."

"I like religion, Grand-mère," Josette replied. "I should like someday to visit Turkey and explore their famous mosques."

Madame Houdin gestured to an empty pew and they sat down just three pews from the altar. "What do you like specifically about religion?" she asked.

Josette cocked her head thoughtfully. Most people would have referenced the beauty of the churches and stained glass, the lovely hymns, the message of love and peace, but Josette had other ideas.

"I like the fact that religion can be used to manipulate people and keep them under control," she said. "Once you have people under control you can achieve virtually anything—riches, political power, things like that. You can be a … puppet master. Or, like the Wizard of Oz, the man behind the curtain."

"You have learned well," Madame Houdin said with satisfaction. "I assume you have provided the less controversial explanations in your religion classes."

"Of course," Josette said, nodding. "The less enlightened educators and students wouldn't agree, and I would waste pointless time trying to explain myself. That is a useless effort."

"Oui." Madame Houdin stared up at what was called the "Beautiful Window," a stained-glass masterpiece depicting the Virgin Mary holding baby Jesus on a throne. She pointed at it. "What does that image tell you?"

Josette looked up and contemplated the window for a moment. "She is much larger than the other images of the men, showing that despite being a female she is above them and powerful. To me, it is a vivid depiction that women can be bigger, smarter, and more cunning than men."

"Good," Madame Houdin said. She took Josette's hand. "I believe it is time for you to abandon your Sorbonne studies and branch out into a better university. You have started your sophomore year so it will be less disruptive if we wait until you finish the fall semester and start anew in the spring."

"Why?" Josette asked.

"Because you should have a well-rounded academic and social education than that you have only cultivated in one country. With your superlative grades any university would be glad to get you."

"What did you have in mind?"

"I have done extensive studies on European schools and narrowed the field down to three. I will show you my research when we get home, and you can choose which one to transfer to."

"I'm listening."

"The University of Oxford outside of London. Its history goes back a thousand years and its reputation is stellar. London is a magnificent city that offers the epitome of culture in every way."

"Go on."

"The University of Edinburgh in Scotland. Nearly half of the students are international. They offer free six-week introductory Gaelic classes to get a taste of Scotland's historical language. First-year undergraduate students who are from outside Edinburgh are guaranteed housing."

"And the third?"

"The University of Amsterdam in the Netherlands. Most of the courses are taught in Dutch, so you would have to learn that language quickly. Still, it's in a great location and a short flight from Great Britain."

"How many universities did you research before you whittled them down to three?"

"Ten. You may certainly see all of the analysis for the other seven as well and, in truth, any of them would be an excellent choice. It's strictly up to you."

"What about you? Would you stay in Paris?"

"I would certainly keep the Paris apartment, but if you felt more comfortable I could take a small residence in the city of your choice or visit whenever you need me to. In either case I would arrange a small off-campus apartment for you so that you will have the privacy you need in your academic and personal lives."

Josette smiled slyly. "You'd miss me."

"Of course I would. I've gotten quite used to you, but it's time to open your wings and fly. I would never tether you to a restraint." A further explanation was interrupted when a woman from across the aisle came over and frowned and told them they were being too loud. Josette rose and put her arm around the woman's shoulder and whispered something to her. The woman looked shocked and hurried away to the back of the church where she knelt down and prayed nervously.

"What did you say to her?" Madame Houdin asked curiously as Josette sat back down.

Josette smiled slightly. "I told her if she didn't retreat and not interrupt us again that I'd waylay her in a dark alley and shove a metal pipe up her cunt after I broke all of her arms and legs."

"I do admire a direct approach."

"You taught me that amongst many other things. Shall we tour the outside of the cathedral?"

"We shall."

They rose simultaneously and walked arm in arm back up the aisle. When they passed the quivering woman, who looked at Josette with terror, Josette smiled brightly and moved her finger across her throat in a parting gesture.

Outside of the church one of the priests noticed the two women, one in her mid-seventies and one twenty, if that. They were striking. The old woman was straight and relatively tall, dressed in the height of fashion found only in the finest stores in Paris's Champs-Élysées. She wore a floppy white linen hat that sported a red silk gardenia, and a mid-calf-length silk red dress over red high heels. Her white hair was pulled back into a tight French twist. Unlike many women her age her spine was straight instead of hunched over with curvature.

The young woman was taller by two or three inches and was wearing an ultra-fashionable silver sequin sleeveless wide-leg jumpsuit with a red belt studded with Swarovski crystals. She had an athletic body that was perfectly proportioned. She sported ankle-high white boots with two-inch heels and had a Louis Vuitton bag slung over her shoulder. Her dark brown hair spilled freely down her back. Her face was simply beautiful, oval-shaped with wing-like eyebrows over cerulean blue eyes. She wore but a hint of pink lipstick that matched the paint on her long fingernails.

He watched as they strolled the perimeter of the cathedral. They seemed to keep up a nonstop conversation and the older woman pointed out aspects of the façade. He was pleased that a member of the younger generation was so reverent of religion and churches. She had obviously been brought up right. He wished he could follow them and listen to their conversation, but he had confession to get to. He sighed and entered the church to perform his sacred duties.

Madame Houdin pointed upwards. "Did you know that this cathedral was the first to use flying buttresses to support its structure?"

"I do now," Josette replied, squinting and shielding her eyes from the sun. "But I prefer Notre Dame's if only for the gargoyles. However, this cathedral far outshines Notre Dame with its portals. They are fantastic. Their biblical stories and theologies are well represented by the choice of sculptures. Perhaps I will come back with my easel and paint this portal."

"Your talent exceeds expectations, according to your tutor. You could very well make a living through your art. In fact, that may be the best course. You wouldn't have to worry about bosses or associates that can be annoying at best and dangerous at worst."

Josette smiled slyly. "Like your ex-law student?"

"Just so," Madame Houdin said, nodding.

"You've been keeping tabs on him and his circle of family and friends?"

"Of course. Detailed tabs."

"Are you still of the mind to strike?"

"I waffle about that, my dear. Although it would be nice to strike unexpectedly, we have built an exceptionally good life here and perhaps that is not worth endangering for pointless retribution. I struck quite definitively all those years ago. And, you have the world in front of you and I find myself less and less inclined to drag you into the quagmire of my psychological inclinations."

"I am willing to help. You know that. What kind of life would I have had had you not chosen me and taken me with you when all was said and done? Not much."

Madame Houdin patted Josette on the cheek and smiled affectionately. "You have more than paid me back by being a perfect companion in my golden years. You owe me nothing else. I only want to ensure your future, which is why I have educated you so well and will continue to do so. And when I am gone there will be a great inheritance for you in my Swiss bank account. You will want for nothing. Come. Let's finish our tour and then head back to Paris. I have a dinner reservation for nine o'clock at Le Grand Véfour."

"Their pan-fried scallops are without equal," Josette declared.

"And their Manjari chocolate cube, eh? I know I won't have to entice you to eat that."

"No, Grand-mère. That's my favorite." Josette pouted. "I won't be able to enjoy that if I go to school in another country."

"I'll make sure you don't go without. Come. Let us go home."

They walked arm in arm to the sleek midnight-blue Citroen. Madame Houdin had purchased the car for Josette's eighteenth birthday.

The old woman who had once been known by several other names, including the Santa Fe Vampire Killer and Joanna Frid as well as many aliases derived from historical serial killers, snuggled back into the passenger seat as the girl once known as the hippie child Rainbow started the ignition and flew down the road like a darting hummingbird.

They were women that had many places to go and many things to do.

Excerpt from

Santa Fe Heat,
Volume Three of the New Mexico Trilogy

the upcoming novel by Gloria H. Giroux

Author's Foreword

134.1°F.

That is arguably the highest temperature ever recorded on Earth. It occurred on Thursday, July 10, 1913 at Furnace Creek Ranch in Death Valley, California. Some scientists have challenged this number, stating that it may have been artificially high due to a sandstorm that caused superheated surface materials to register that number. Some historians and meteorologists hold to the veracity of that number, but others believe that the real "highest temperature" occurred at 129.2°F on June 20, 2013 in Death Valley and on July 21, 2016 in Mitribah, Kuwait. In either case, it was hot.

In New Mexico, the hottest temperature ever recorded was 122°F on July 27, 1994 in Lakewood, a tiny community in the southwestern part of the state, sixteen miles from Carlsbad. A short month before that, on June 29, 1994, Lake Havasu City, Arizona recorded its highest temperature at 128°F. In contrast the hottest temperature ever recorded in nearby Colorado was a paltry 114°F on July 1, 1933 at Las Animas.

These temperatures, however, pale in comparison to the heat generated by natural phenomena such as fire, flowing lava, the earth's core, and the stars and suns. Earth's sun is the star at the center of our solar system. Its approximate age is 4.6 billion years. A nearly perfect sphere of hot plasma it is one hundred and nine times the diameter of Earth, its mass 330,000 times of the Earth's mass, and its composition 75% hydrogen. At the sun's core gravitational attraction produces immense pressure and temperature, which can reach more than twenty-seven million degrees Fahrenheit. At its surface, also called the photosphere, the temperature is only a mild six thousand degrees.

In comparison the Earth's core sizzles at 7,952°F to about 10,800°F. The core is comprised of two layers: the outer core, which borders the mantle, and the inner core. The boundary separating these regions is called the Bullen discontinuity. Earth spits out its heat through volcanic lava, which when the fiery molten blob edges out of the volcano reaches temperatures up to 2,200°F. If a person were to fall into that lava he would combust into flames and die. He might survive a fall into "cooler" lava of, say, 1,000°F; there would be significant charring of flesh that even if he survived he'd live with terrible scars forever.

In 79 AD Mount Vesuvius in southern Italy erupted, spewing a high column of hot ash and pumice and then over a period of two days disgorging a rapidly moving, dense lava flow ranging from 570–680°F that eventually destroyed the cities of Pompeii and Herculaneum. Hot ash turned hundreds of citizens into what resembled stone sculptures, some, because of the high heat, who died in a fraction of a second. The contorted postures of bodies as if frozen in suspended action were not the effects of long agony, but of the cadaveric spasm, a consequence of heat shock on corpses. The heat was so intense that organs and blood were vaporized, and at least one victim's brain was vitrified by the temperature; i.e., turned to glass.

Non-star, non-lava, non-lightning-strike fire is another matter entirely. Created by nature or man, the heat depends on the circumstances. The Hiroshima bomb (nicknamed "Little Boy") developed by the Manhattan Project exploded on August 6, 1945 at a height of 1,870 feet above ground for maximum effect. The bomb's explosive force then shot directly down to earth below (ground zero), spread swiftly out to surrounding hills, and then rebounded back into the city. At an energy release of thirteen kilotons of TNT the bomb resulted in a surface temperature of 10,830°F. A fiery holocaust of utter devastation turned a city of 350,000 into an ashen pit of horror with the final death toll settling between 90,000 to 146,000; 80,000 were killed instantly. The radius of total destruction was about one mile with resulting fires across 4.4 square miles.

Three days later a second bomb (nicknamed "Fat Man") was dropped on Nagasaki with a release of a surface temperature of 7,200°F. The bomb itself was more powerful than the one dropped on Hiroshima, but the geography of hills and valleys where the bomb actually hit mitigated the casualties. The final death toll ranged from 39,000 to 80,000 in a similar one-mile radius of the strike.

Nagasaki, August 9, 1945

Famous fires and bombs have ranged in temperature and destructiveness over the decades. The Great Chicago Fire occurred on the same day as the Great Peshtigo Fire in Wisconsin, October 8, 1871. The fire killed more than two hundred fifty people and left 100,000 homeless. Legend says the fire occurred after Mrs. O'Leary's cow kicked over a lamp, setting a barn and the whole city on fire. There's no proof the cow started the fire. The fire caused an estimated $200 million in damages. In 2020 dollars, that's over $5 billion.

The destruction of San Francisco in 1906 was not the direct result of the earthquake itself but rather of the fires started with broken gas lines and other combustible materials.

The Triangle Shirtwaist Factory fire in New York City on March 25, 1911 was an inferno that took the lives of one hundred forty-six people, mostly women workers.

On November 28, 1942 in Boston, Massachusetts the Cocoanut Grove Nightclub Fire, which had its walls and ceilings covered in paper palm tree decorations, caught fire when someone lit a match. The nightclub was filled with more than twice its capacity, killing four hundred ninety-two people. The building didn't have a fire sprinkler system and the primary exit was a revolving door.

On July 6, 1944 Hartford, Connecticut's historical fire took place during a Ringling Brothers' Barnum and Bailey Circus performance. A side wall of a tent caught fire and collapsed; more than one hundred of the one hundred sixty-eight people killed were under the age of fifteen. Overcrowding and an inadequate number of exits made escaping difficult.

The Branch Davidian compound in Waco, Texas went up in flames on April 19, 1993, killing dozens of adults and children. In retaliation the soulless Timothy McVeigh unleashed a bomb of immense power and released heat two years later to the day on the Alfred P. Murrah Federal Building in Oklahoma City.

The fires caused by the deliberate ramming of the Twin Towers by hijacked passenger planes on September 11, 2001 rose to a burn temperature of around 1,800°F. Steel girders can sustain their stability up to 2,800°F. They didn't melt under the temperatures of the burning jet fuel but rather lost enough strength and were softened, eventually bringing down the towers. There was no respite from the sprinkler system whose water pipes had been damaged by the collisions and were unable to function on the floors where the heat burned the hottest. The horror of burning alive caused many people to choose death by throwing themselves out of the building to a quick death as they hit the pavement over a thousand feet below.

The deliberate incineration of corpses, known as cremation, requires 1,400°F-1,800°F to reduce a full-grown body to complete ashes. Lesser temperatures will also reduce flesh and most bones to ashes, but teeth and other human particles may survive.

There are tens of thousands of quotes over the centuries, indeed, the millennia, relating to fire, heat, and anything resplendent with a warmth of a million suns in reality or in the soul.

"The thing with heat is, no matter how cold you are, no matter how much you need warmth, it always, eventually, becomes too much."
Victoria Aveyard, *Glass Sword*

"The month of August had turned into a griddle
where the days just lay there and sizzled."
Sue Monk Kidd, *The Secret Life of Bees*

"A growing heat, like a million blazing suns all focused
on me, lit my insides. It felt like I was being cooked in the
Gabriella Roast Cooker, me spinning around-and-around
to heat my flesh evenly. For some reason I was having
trouble comprehending the sudden change in my revolving
world as I swelled with a horrible, billowing fire."
Laura Kreitzer, *Abyss*

"People change more frequently than the seasons do and
still we blame the sun for bringing in the heat."
Shweta Tale

"Sometimes it is good to fly close to the flame, see
and experience the heat, but then fly away again,
to survive, more wise in the art of heat."
Robert Black

"More murders are committed at ninety-two degrees Fahrenheit
than any other temperature. Over one hundred, it's too hot
to move. Under ninety, cool enough to survive. But right *at*
ninety-two degrees lies the apex of irritability, everything is
itches and hair and sweat and cooked pork. The brain becomes
a rat rushing around a red-hot maze. The least thing - a word, a
look, a sound, the drop of a hair and - irritable murder. *Irritable
murder*, there's a pretty and terrifying phrase for you."
Ray Bradbury, *The October Country*

"Beyond the canopy of my embrace, you shall
feel the blistering heat of the Desert."
Harry Fulgencio

"I believe someone made a grievous mistake when summer was
created; no novitiate or god in their right mind would make a
season akin to hell on purpose. Someone should be fired."
Michelle Franklin

"There may be a great fire in our soul, yet no one ever comes to
warm himself at it, and the passers-by see only a wisp of smoke."
Vincent van Gogh

"Come on baby, light my fire
Come on baby, light my fire
Try to set the night on fire ..."
The Doors, *Light My Fire*

"Love is Fire. But whether it's gonna warm your heart
or burn your house down you can never tell."
Jason Jordan

"The mind is not a vessel to be filled but a fire to be kindled."
Plutarch

Physical heat aside, the concept of "heat" also applies to existential concepts.

Heat of passion.
Dying of the heat.
Catching heat.
Dead Heat.
Packing heat.
Turn up the heat.
Taking heat.
In heat.
The heat (i.e., police).
If you can't stand the heat get out of the kitchen.

And, perhaps the most dangerous of all, heat of anger … that often takes too long to cool down, and sometimes not at all …

Coming in 2021

Lightning Source UK Ltd.
Milton Keynes UK
UKHW042003171220
375465UK00008B/395/J